REBUS: THE EARLY YEARS

'What's extraordinary is how good and assured Rankin was from the start. The hot gossip is that Rebus will fill the gap left by the late lamented Morse. Every bit as meaty, but grittier by far'   Philip Oakes, *Literary Review*

RANKIN AND REBUS

'The Rebus series have been uniformly first rate . . . His is a superbly drawn character; matched by the edgy authenticity of the Scottish locale and dialogue'   Marcel Berlins, *The Times*

'Rankin's ability to create a credible character, delivering convincing dialogue to complement sinister and hard-hitting plots against vividly detailed atmosphere, is simply awesome'   *Time Out*

'His fiction buzzes with energy . . . Essentially he is a romantic storyteller in the tradition of Robert Louis Stevenson . . . His prose is as vivid and terse as the next man's yet its flexibility and rhythm give it a potential for lyrical expression which is distinctively Rankin's own . . . Rankin controls the material with extraordinary authority and even delicacy . . . Rankin ranks alongside P.D. James and Michael Dibdin as Britain's finest detective novelist'   *Scotland on Sunday*

'Rankin has followed one success with another. Sardonic and assured, the novel has a powerful and well paced narrative . . . What is striking is the way Rankin uses his laconic prose as a literary paint stripper, scouring away pretensions to reveal the unwholesome reality beneath'   *Independent*

'Rankin's prose is understated, yet his canvas of Scotland's criminal underclass has a panoramic breadth. His ear for dialogue is as sharp as a switchblade. This is, quite simply, crime writing of the highest order'   *Daily Express*

'Ingeniously, Rankin brings the pieces together to form another complex, many layered mystery. Not to be missed'   *Sunday Telegraph*

Also by Ian Rankin

The Inspector Malcolm Fox Series
The Complaints
The Impossible Dead

The Detective Inspector Rebus Series
Knots & Crosses
Hide & Seek
Tooth & Nail
(previously published as Wolfman)
Strip Jack
The Black Book
Mortal Causes
Let it Bleed
Black & Blue
The Hanging Garden
Death is Not the End (a novella)
Dead Souls
Set in Darkness
The Falls
Resurrection Men
A Question of Blood
Fleshmarket Close
The Naming of the Dead
Exit Music
Standing in Another Man's Grave
Saints of the Shadow Bible

Other Novels
The Flood
Watchman
Westwind
Doors Open

Writing as Jack Harvey
Witch Hunt
Bleeding Hearts
Blood Hunt

Short Stories
A Good Hanging and Other Stories
Beggars Banquet

Non-fiction
Rebus's Scotland

Ian Rankin

Rebus
The Early Years

■

Knots & Crosses
Hide & Seek
Tooth & Nail

An Orion trade paperback

First published in Great Britain in 1999
by Orion Books
an imprint of The Orion Publishing Group Ltd,
Carmelite House, 50 Victoria Embankment,
London EC4Y 0DZ

An Hachette UK company

23 25 27 29 30 28 26 24 22

A CIP catalogue record for this book
is available from the British Library.

ISBN 978-0-7528-3799-4

Typeset by Deltatype Ltd, Birkenhead, Merseyside

Printed in Great Britain by Clays Ltd, St Ives plc

The Orion Publishing Group's policy is to use papers that
are natural, renewable and recyclable products and
made from wood grown in sustainable forests. The logging
and manufacturing processes are expected to conform to
the environmental regulations of the country of origin.

www.orionbooks.co.uk

CONTENTS

Exile on Princes Street

I was a student at Edinburgh University. I'd written a novel called *The Flood*. It was all about a teenage boy living in a Fife mining-town and dreaming of escape to Edinburgh. I wasn't a teenager any more. I'd taken the book home to my dad. The heroine's name was Mary Miller. 'Ohhh,' my dad said, 'she lives just round the corner.' Well, *someone* called Mary Miller lived round the corner, only she wasn't *my* Mary.

My dad saw himself in most of my characters, even if that character was a nun. 'Yes,' he'd say, 'but she speaks just like me.' I don't think my dad really understood *The Flood*. Maybe I didn't understand it either. They taught it for a while at Edinburgh University. Unbeknownst to the students, I sat in on one of the tutorials. Someone had to read out their 'paper' on my book. They saw *Waste Land* imagery, colour symbols, the elements . . . I started taking notes. Could this book really be cleverer than its author?

My dad passed *The Flood* on to his friends, and went back to his bookshelf: James Bond, *Where Eagles Dare*. And I sat in Edinburgh, trying to write another novel, a novel that might be read by a wider audience than students and academics. This was the mid-eighties. No one in Edinburgh was writing novels except me, that's the way it seemed. Over in Glasgow they had McIlvanney and Gray and Kelman. I bought Kelman's first for my dad. His sort of thing, I thought. Working-class working man against the system. Dad couldn't read it. Said it wasn't 'written in English'. Said there wasn't any story. I was shocked. This was *literature*. It was good for you. It was the stuff I was studying. Dad's reaction made me think about the kind of writer I wanted to be.

I wanted to update *Dr Jekyll and Mr Hyde* to 1980s Edinburgh. My idea was: cop as good guy (Jekyll), villain as bad guy (Hyde). So I wrote *Knots & Crosses*. I was living in a room in a ground-floor flat in Arden Street, so my hero, John Rebus, had to live across the road. When the book was published, I found to my astonishment that everyone was saying I'd written a whodunnit, a crime novel. I think I'm still the only crime writer

I know who hadn't a clue about the genre before setting out. There were crime sections in bookshops and libraries – news to me – and a healthy number of practitioners extant. So instead of my literary studies, I turned to the likes of Rendell, James, Hill, Ellroy, Block . . . And the stuff wasn't bad. The form was flexible. I could say everything I wanted to say about the world, and still give readers a pacy, gripping narrative.

But I still wasn't a crime writer. I wrote a Graham Greene-ish spy novel. I wrote a techno-caper thriller. And then I decided to have another bash at *Jekyll and Hyde*, only this time I'd pun Hyde with 'hide'. This became *Hide & Seek*. One reviewer 'got it'. But by then it was too late. I was getting to know and like the character of Rebus. I had more books I wanted to write about Scotland, and this guy would act as my mouthpiece.

I'd moved from Edinburgh and was living in London. *Hide & Seek* had been out for a while, and suddenly police were investigating something similar to the case in my novel. (Lawyers and judges being bribed by rent boys: questions were asked in parliament, and it was decided to get two *lawyers* to investigate the police investigation of the lawyers. To everyone's surprise, this inquiry found that the allegations were false. Police officers involved in the case found themselves demoted . . .) I decided to take Rebus out of Edinburgh for a while.

I didn't much like London: a nice place to visit, but I had a ninety-minute commute each way; three hours of my day spent crossing the city. Why should I be the only one to suffer? I brought Rebus to London so he could suffer, too. The book was called *Wolfman*. Then my American editor came up with an alternative title: *Tooth & Nail*. I liked that better. It kept the sequence going, and suddenly the book didn't sound like a horror novel. Mind you, it *was* a horror novel. A serial killer is stalking London, and Rebus is sent south to assist. I was living in Tottenham at the time, in a flat looking onto some parkland. Other side of the park was a canal, and I decided to site the first corpse there. To get to the canal bank, you use an underpass, a creepy stretch of white tiled wall and graffiti. I moved from the flat in 1990, but in December '98, some friends sent me a recent photo of the underpass. Someone has written the name WOLFMAN in three-foot-high black letters . . .

These three novels represent Rebus's early years. I can't read them without thinking back to my own early years, my apprenticeship as a crime writer. Read and enjoy.

Ian Rankin
June 1999

Knots & Crosses

To Miranda
without whom nothing is worth finishing

Prologue

Prologue

1

The girl screamed once, only the once.

Even that, however, was a minor slip on his part. That might have been the end of everything, almost before it had begun. Neighbours inquisitive, the police called in to investigate. No, that would not do at all. Next time he would tie the gag a little tighter, just a little tighter, just that little bit more secure.

Afterwards, he went to the drawer and took from it a ball of string. He used a pair of sharp nail-scissors, the kind girls always seem to use, to snip off a length of about six inches, then he put the ball of string and the scissors back into the drawer. A car revved up outside, and he went to the window, upsetting a pile of books on the floor as he did so. The car, however, had vanished, and he smiled to himself. He tied a knot in the string, not any special kind of knot, just a knot. There was an envelope lying ready on the sideboard.

2

It was 28th April. Wet, naturally, the grass percolating water as John
Rebus walked to the grave of his father, dead five years to the day. He
placed a wreath so that it lay, yellow and red, the colours of
remembrance, against the still shining marble. He paused for a
moment, trying to think of things to say, but there seemed nothing to
say, nothing to think. He had been a good enough father and that was
that. The old man wouldn't have wanted him to waste his words in any
case. So he stood there, hands respectfully behind his back, crows
laughing on the walls around him, until the water seeping into his
shoes told him that there was a warm car waiting for him at the
cemetery gates.

He drove quietly, hating to be back here in Fife, back where the old
days had never been 'good old days', where ghosts rustled in the shells
of empty houses and the shutters went up every evening on a handful
of desultory shops, those metal shutters that gave the vandals
somewhere to write their names. How Rebus hated it all, this singular
lack of an environment. It stank the way it had always done: of misuse,
of disuse, of the sheer wastage of life.

He drove the eight miles towards the open sea, to where his brother
Michael still lived. The rain eased off as he approached the skull-grey
coast, the car throwing up splashings of water from a thousand
crevasses in the road. Why was it, he wondered, that they never
seemed to fix the roads here, while in Edinburgh they worked on the
surfaces so often that things were made even worse? And why, above
all, had he made the maniacal decision to come all the way through to
Fife, just because it was the anniversary of the old man's death? He
tried to focus his mind on something else, and found himself fantasising
about his next cigarette.

Through the rain, falling as drizzle now, Rebus saw a girl about his
daughter's age walking along the grass verge. He slowed the car,

examined her in his mirror as he passed her, and stopped. He motioned for her to come to his window.

Her short breaths were visible in the cool, still air, and her dark hair fell in rats-tails down her forehead. She looked at him apprehensively.

'Where are you going, love?'

'Kirkcaldy.'

'Do you want a lift?'

She shook her head, drops of water flying from her coiled hair.

'My mum said I should never accept lifts from strangers.'

'Well,' said Rebus, smiling, 'your mum is quite right. I've got a daughter about your age and I tell her the same thing. But it is raining, and I *am* a policeman, so you can trust me. You've still got a fair way to go, you know.'

She looked up and down the silent road, then shook her head again.

'Okay,' said Rebus, 'but take care. Your mum was quite right.'

He wound his window up again and drove off, watching her in his mirror as she watched him. Clever kid. It was good to know that parents still had a little sense of responsibility left. If only the same could be said of his ex-wife. The way she had brought up their daughter was a disgrace. Michael, too, had given his daughter too long a leash. Who was to blame?

Rebus's brother owned a respectable house. He had followed in the old man's footsteps and become a stage hypnotist. He seemed to be quite good at it, too, from all accounts. Rebus had never asked Michael how it was done, just as he had never shown any interest or curiosity in the old man's act. He had observed that this still puzzled Michael, who would drop hints and red herrings as to the authenticity of his own stage act for him to chase up if he so wished.

But then John Rebus had too many things to chase up, and that had been the position during all of his fifteen years on the force. Fifteen years, and all he had to show were an amount of self-pity and a busted marriage with an innocent daughter hanging between them. It was more disgusting than sad. And meantime Michael was happily married with two kids and a larger house than Rebus could ever afford. He headlined at hotels, clubs, and even theatres as far away as Newcastle and Wick. Occasionally he would make six-hundred quid from a single show. Outrageous. He drove an expensive car, wore good clothes, and would never have been caught dead standing in the pissing rain in a graveyard in Fife on the dullest April day for many a year. No, Michael was too clever for that. And too stupid.

*

'John! Christ, what's up? I mean, it's great to see you. Why didn't you phone to warn me you were coming? Come on inside.'

It was the welcome Rebus had expected: embarrassed surprise, as though it were painful to be reminded that one still had some family left alive. And Rebus had noted the use of the word 'warn' where 'tell' would have sufficed. He was a policeman. He noticed such things.

Michael Rebus bounded through to the living-room and turned down the wailing stereo.

'Come on in, John,' he called. 'Do you want a drink? Coffee perhaps? Or something stronger? What brings you here?'

Rebus sat down as though he were in a stranger's house, his back straight and professional. He examined the panelled walls of the room – a new feature – and the framed photographs of his niece and nephew.

'I was just in the neighbourhood,' he said.

Michael, turning from the drinks cabinet with the glasses ready, suddenly remembered, or did a good impersonation of just having remembered.

'Oh, John, I forgot all about it. Why didn't you tell me? Shit, I hate forgetting about Dad.'

'Just as well you're a hypnotist then and not Mickey the Memory Man, isn't it? Give me that drink, or are you two getting engaged?'

Michael, smiling, absolved, handed over the glass of whisky.

'Is that your car outside?' asked Rebus, taking the glass. 'I mean the big BMW?'

Michael, still smiling, nodded.

'Christ,' said Rebus. 'You treat yourself well.'

'As well as I treat Chrissie and the kids. We're building an extension onto the back of the house. Somewhere to put a jacuzzi or a sauna. They're the in thing just now, and Chrissie's desperate to keep ahead of the field.'

Rebus took a swallow of whisky. It turned out to be a malt. Nothing in the room was cheap, but none of it was exactly desirable either. Glass ornaments, a crystal decanter on a silver salver, the TV and video, the inscrutably miniature hi-fi system, the onyx lamp. Rebus felt a little guilty about that lamp. Rhona and he had given it to Michael and Chrissie as a wedding present. Chrissie no longer spoke to him. Who could blame her?

'Where is Chrissie, by the way?'

'Oh, she's out doing some shopping. She has her own car now. The kids will still be at school. She'll pick them up on the way home. Are you staying for something to eat?'

Rebus shrugged his shoulders.

'You'd be welcome to stay,' said Michael, meaning that Rebus wouldn't. 'So how's the cop-shop? Still muddling along?'

'We lose a few, but they don't get the publicity. We catch a few, and they do. It's the same as always, I suppose.'

The room, Rebus was noticing, smelled of toffee-apples, of penny arcades.

Michael was speaking:

'This is a terrible business about those girls being kidnapped.'

Rebus nodded.

'Yes,' he said, 'yes, it is. But we can't strictly call it kidnapping, not yet. There hasn't been a demand note or anything. It's more likely to be a straightforward case of sexual assault.'

Michael started up from his chair.

'Straightforward? What's straightforward about that?'

'It's just the terminology we use, Mickey, that's all.' Rebus shrugged again and finished his drink.

'Well, John,' said Michael, sitting, 'I mean, we've both got daughters, too. You're so casual about the whole thing. I mean, it's frightening to think of it.' He shook his head slowly in the world-wide expression of shared grief, and relief, too, that the horror was someone else's for the moment. 'It's frightening,' he repeated. 'And in Edinburgh of all places. I mean, you never think of that sort of thing happening in Edinburgh, do you?'

'There's more happening in Edinburgh than anyone knows.'

'Yes.' Michael paused. 'I was across there just last week playing at one of the hotels.'

'You didn't tell me.'

It was Michael's turn to shrug his shoulders.

'Would you have been interested?' he said.

'Maybe not,' said Rebus, smiling, 'but I would have come along anyway.'

Michael laughed. It was the laughter of birthdays, of money found in an old pocket.

'Another whisky, sir?' he said.

'I thought you were never going to ask.'

Rebus returned to his study of the room while Michael went to the cabinet.

'How's the act going?' he asked. 'And I really *am* interested.'

'It's going fine,' said Michael. 'In fact, it's going very well indeed. There's talk of a television spot, but I'll believe that when I see it.'

'Great.'

Another drink reached Rebus's willing hand.

'Yes, and I'm working on a new slot. It's a bit scary though.' An inch of gold flashed on Michael's wrist as he tipped the glass to his lips. The watch was expensive: it had no numbers on its face. It seemed to Rebus that the more expensive something was, the less of it there always seemed to be: tiny little hi-fi systems, watches without numbers, the translucent Dior ankle-socks on Michael's feet.

'Tell me about it,' he said, taking his brother's bait.

'Well,' said Michael, sitting forward in his chair, 'I take members of the audience back into their past lives.'

'Past lives?'

Rebus was staring at the floor as if admiring the design of the dark and light green carpet.

'Yes,' Michael continued, 'Reincarnation, born again, that sort of thing. Well, I shouldn't have to spell it out to you, John. After all, *you're* the Christian.'

'Christians don't believe in past lives, Mickey. Only future ones.'

Michael stared at Rebus, demanding silence.

'Sorry,' said Rebus.

'As I was saying, I tried the act out in public for the first time last week, though I've been practising it for a while with my private consultees.'

'Private consultees?'

'Yes. They pay me money for private hypnotherapy. I stop them smoking, or make them more confident, or stop them from wetting the bed. Some are convinced that they have past lives, and they ask me to put them under so that they can prove it. Don't worry though. Financially, it's all above board. The tax-man gets his cut.'

'And do you prove it? Do they have past lives?'

Michael rubbed a finger around the rim of his glass, now empty.

'You'd be surprised,' he said.

'Give me an example.'

Rebus was following the lines of the carpet with his eyes. Past lives, he thought to himself. Now there was a thing. There was plenty of life in *his* past.

'Well,' said Michael, 'remember I told you about my show in

Edinburgh last week? Well,' he leaned further forward in his chair, 'I got this woman up from the audience. She was a small woman, middle-aged. She'd come in with an office-party. She went under pretty easily, probably because she hadn't been drinking as heavily as her friends. Once she was under, I told her that we were going to take a trip into her past, way, way back before she was born. I told her to think back to the earliest memory she had . . .'

Michael's voice had taken on a professional but easy mellifluence. He spread his hands before him as if playing to an audience. Rebus, nursing his glass, felt himself relax a little. He thought back to a childhood episode, a game of football, one brother pitted against the other. The warm mud of a July shower, and their mother, her sleeves rolled up, stripping them both and putting them, giggling knots of arms and legs, into the bath . . .

'. . . well,' Michael was saying, 'she started to speak, and in a voice not quite her own. It was weird, John. I wish you *had* been there to see it. The audience were silent, and I was feeling all cold and then hot and then cold again, and it had nothing to do with the hotel's heating-system by the way. I'd done it, you see. I'd taken that woman into a past life. She was a nun. Do you believe that? A *nun*. And she said that she was alone in her cell. She described the convent and everything, and then she started to recite something in Latin, and some people in the audience actually *crossed* themselves. I was bloody well petrified. My hair was probably standing on end. I brought her out of it as quickly as I could, and there was a long pause before the crowd started to applaud. Then, maybe out of sheer relief, her friends started to cheer and laugh, and that broke the ice. At the end of the show, I found out that this woman was a staunch Protestant, a Rangers supporter no less, and she swore blind that she knew no Latin at all. Well, *somebody* inside her did. I'll tell you that.'

Rebus was smiling.

'It's a nice story, Mickey,' he said.

'It's the truth.' Michael opened his arms wide in supplication. 'Don't you believe me?'

'Maybe.'

Michael shook his head.

'You must make a pretty bad copper, John. I had around a hundred and fifty witnesses. Iron-clad.'

Rebus could not pull his attention away from the design in the carpet.

'Plenty of people believe in past lives, John.'

Past lives ... Yes, he believed in some things ... In God, certainly ... But past lives ... Without warning, a face screamed up at him from the carpet, trapped in its cell.

He dropped his glass.

'John? Is anything wrong? Christ, you look as if you've seen ...'

'No, no, nothing's the matter.' Rebus retrieved the glass and stood up. 'I just ... I'm fine. It's just that,' he checked his watch, a watch with numbers, 'well, I'd better be going. I'm on duty this evening.'

Michael was smiling weakly, glad that his brother was not going to stay, but embarrassed at his relief.

'We'll have to meet again soon,' he said, 'on neutral territory.'

'Yes,' said Rebus, tasting once again the tang of toffee-apples. He felt a little pale, a little shaky, as though he were too far out of his territory. 'Let's do that.'

Once or twice or three times a year, at weddings, funerals, or over the telephone at Christmas, they promised themselves this get-together. The mere promise now was a ritual in itself, and so could be safely proffered and just as safely ignored.

'Let's do that.'

Rebus shook hands with Michael at the door. Escaping past the BMW to his own car, he wondered how alike they were, his brother and him. Uncles and aunts in their funeral-cold rooms occasionally commented, 'Ah, you're both the spitting image of your mother.' That was as far as it went. John Rebus knew that his own hair was a shade of brown lighter than Michael's, and that his eyes were a shade of green darker. He knew also, however, that the differences between them were such that any similarities were made to look unutterably superficial. They were brothers without any sense of brotherhood. Brotherhood belonged to the past.

He waved once from the car and was gone. He would be back in Edinburgh within the hour, and on duty another half-hour after that. He knew that the reason he could never feel comfortable in Michael's house was Chrissie's hatred of him, her unshakeable belief that he alone had been responsible for the break-up of his marriage. Maybe she was right at that. He tried ticking off in his mind the definite chores of the next seven or eight hours. He had to tidy up a case of burglary and serious assault. A nasty one that. The CID was undermanned as it was, and now these abductions would stretch them even more. Those two young girls, girls his own daughter's age. It was best not to think about it. By now they would be dead, or would wish that they were dead. God have mercy on them. In Edinburgh of all places, in his own dear city.

A maniac was on the loose.

People were staying in their homes.

And a screaming in his memory.

Rebus shrugged, feeling a slight sensation of attrition in one of his shoulders. It was not his business after all. Not yet.

Back in his living-room, Michael Rebus poured himself another whisky. He went to the stereo and turned it all the way up, then reached underneath his chair and, after a little fumbling, pulled out an ashtray that was hidden there.

PART ONE

'There Are Clues Everywhere'

1

On the steps of the Great London Road police station in Edinburgh, John Rebus lit his last legitimate cigarette of the day before pushing open the imposing door and stepping inside.

The station was old, its floor dark and marbled. It had about it the fading grandeur of a dead aristocracy. It had character.

Rebus waved to the duty sergeant, who was tearing old pictures from the notice-board and pinning up new ones in their place. He climbed the great curving staircase to his office. Campbell was just leaving.

'Hello, John.'

McGregor Campbell, a Detective Sergeant like Rebus, was donning coat and hat.

'What's the word, Mac? Is it going to be a busy night?' Rebus began checking the messages on his desk.

'I don't know about that, John, but I can tell you that it's been pandemonium in here today. There's a letter there for you from the man himself.'

'Oh yes?' Rebus seemed preoccupied with another letter which he had just opened.

'Yes, John. Brace yourself. I think you're going to be transferred to that abduction case. Good luck to you. Well, I'm off to the pub. I want to catch the boxing on the BBC. I should be in time.' Campbell checked his watch. 'Yes, plenty of time. Is anything wrong, John?'

Rebus waved the now empty envelope at him.

'Who brought this in, Mac?'

'I haven't the faintest, John. What is it?'

'Another crank letter.'

'Oh yes?' Campbell sidled over to Rebus's shoulder. He examined the typed note. 'Looks like the same bloke, doesn't it?'

'Clever of you to notice that, Mac, seeing as it's the exact same message.'

'What about the string?'

'Oh, it's here too.' Rebus lifted a small piece of string from his desk. There was a simple knot tied in its middle.

'Queer bloody business.' Campbell walked to the doorway. 'See you tomorrow, John.'

'Yes, yes, see you, Mac.' Rebus paused until his friend had made his exit. 'Oh, Mac!' Campbell came back into the doorway.

'Yes?'

'Maxwell won the big fight,' said Rebus, smiling.

'God, you're a bastard, Rebus.' Gritting his teeth, Campbell stalked out of the station.

'One of the old school,' Rebus said to himself. 'Now, what possible enemies could I have?'

He studied the letter again, then checked the envelope. It was blank, save for his own name, unevenly typed. The note had been handed in, just like the other one. It was a queer bloody business right enough.

He walked back downstairs and headed for the desk.

'Jimmy?'

'Yes, John.'

'Have you seen this?' He showed the envelope to the desk sergeant.

'That?' The sergeant wrinkled not only his brow but, it seemed to Rebus, his whole face. Only forty years in the force could do that to a man, forty years of questions and puzzles and crosses to bear. 'It must have been put through the door, John. I found it myself on the floor just there.' He pointed vaguely in the direction of the station's front door. 'Is anything up?'

'Oh no, it's nothing really. Thanks, Jimmy.'

But Rebus knew that he would be niggled all night by the arrival of this note, only days after he had received the first anonymous message. He studied the two letters at his desk. The work of an old typewriter, probably portable. The letter S about a millimetre higher than the other letters. The paper cheap, no water-mark. The piece of string, tied in the middle, cut with a sharp knife or scissors. The message. The same typewritten message:

THERE ARE CLUES EVERYWHERE.

Fair enough; perhaps there were. It was the work of a crank, a kind of practical joke. But why him? It made no sense. Then the phone rang.

'Detective Sergeant Rebus?'

'Speaking.'

'Rebus, it's Chief Inspector Anderson here. Have you received my note?'

18

Anderson. Bloody Anderson. That was all he needed. From one crank to another.

'Yes, sir,' said Rebus, holding the receiver under his chin and tearing open the letter on his desk.

'Good. Can you be here in twenty minutes? The briefing will be in the Waverley Road Incident Room.'

'I'll be there, sir.'

The phone went dead on Rebus as he read. It was true then, it was official. He was being transferred to the abduction case. God, what a life. He pushed the messages, envelopes and string into his jacket pocket, looking around the office in frustration. Who was kidding who? It would take an act of God to get him to Waverley Road inside of half an hour. And when was he supposed to get round to finishing all his work? He had three cases coming to court and another dozen or so crying out for some paperwork before his memory of them faded entirely. That would be nice, actually, nice to just erase the lot of them. Wipe-out. He closed his eyes. He opened them again. The paperwork was still there, large as life. Useless. Always incomplete. No sooner had he finished with a case than another two or three appeared in its place. What was the name of that creature? The Hydra, was it? That was what he was fighting. Every time he cut off a head, more popped into his in-tray. Coming back from a holiday was a nightmare.

And now they were giving him rocks to push up hills as well.

He looked to the ceiling.

'With God's grace,' he whispered. Then he headed out to his car.

2

The Sutherland Bar was a popular watering-hole. It contained no jukebox, no video machines, no bandits. The decor was spartan, and the TV usually flickered and jumped. Ladies had not been welcome until well into the 1960s. There had, it seemed, been something to hide: the best pint of draught beer in Edinburgh. McGregor Campbell supped from his heavy glass, his eyes intent on the television set above the bar.

'Who wins?' asked a voice beside him.

'I don't know,' he said, turning to the voice. 'Oh, hello, Jim.'

A stocky man was sitting beside him, money in hand, waiting to be served. His eyes, too, were on the TV.

'Looks like a cracker of a fight,' he said. 'I fancy Mailer to win.'

Mac Campbell had an idea.

'No, I reckon Maxwell will walk it, win by a mile. Fancy a bet?'

The stocky man fished into his pocket for his cigarettes, eyeing the policeman.

'How much?' he asked.

'A fiver?' said Campbell.

'You're on. Tom, give me a pint over here, please. Do you want one yourself, Mac?'

'Same again, thanks.'

They sat in silence for a while, supping the beer and watching the fight. A few muffled roars went up occasionally from behind them as a punch landed or was dodged.

'It's looking good for your man if it goes the distance,' said Campbell, ordering more drinks.

'Aye. But let's wait and see, eh? How's work, by the way?'

'Fine, how's yours?'

'A pure bloody slog at the moment, if you must ask.' Some ash dropped onto his tie as he talked, the cigarette never leaving his mouth, though it wobbled precariously from time to time. 'A pure slog.'

'Are you still chasing up that drugs story?'

'Not really. I've landed on this kidnapping thing.'

'Oh? So has Rebus. You'd better not get into *his* hair.'

'Newspapermen get in *everybody's* hair, Mac. It goes with the etcetera.'

Mac Campbell, though wary of Jim Stevens, was grateful for a friendship, however tenuous and strained it had sometimes been, which had given him some information useful to his career. Stevens kept much of the juiciest tidbits to himself, of course. That's what 'exclusives' were made of. But he was always willing to trade, and it seemed to Campbell that the most innocuous pieces of gossip and information often seemed adequate for Stevens' needs. He was a kind of magpie, collecting everything without prejudice, storing much more of it than, surely, he would ever use. But with reporters you never could tell. Certainly, Campbell was happier with Stevens as a friend than as an enemy.

'So what's happening about your drugs dossier?'

Jim Stevens shrugged his creased shoulders.

'There's nothing in there just now that could be of much use to you boys anyway. I'm not about to let the whole thing drop though, if that's what you mean. No, that's too big a nest of vipers to be allowed to go free. I'll still be keeping my eyes open.'

A bell rang for the last round of the fight. Two sweating, dog-tired bodies converged on one another, becoming a single knot of limbs.

'Still looks good for Mailer,' said Campbell, an uneasy feeling coming over him. It couldn't be true. Rebus wouldn't have done that to him. Suddenly, Maxwell, the heavier and slower-moving of the two fighters, was hit by a blow to the face and staggered back. The bar erupted, sensing blood and victory. Campbell stared into his glass. Maxwell was taking a standing count. It was all over. A sensation in the final seconds of the contest, according to the commentator.

Jim Stevens held out his hand.

I'll kill bloody Rebus, thought Campbell. So help me, I'll kill him.

Later, over drinks bought with Campbell's money, Jim Stevens asked about Rebus.

'So it looks as if I'll be meeting him at last?'

'Maybe, maybe not. He's not exactly friendly with Anderson, so he may well get the shitty end of the stick, sitting at a desk all day. But then John Rebus isn't exactly friendly with anybody.'

'Oh?'

'Ach, he's not that bad, I suppose, but he's not the easiest of men to like.' Campbell, ducking from his friend's interrogative eyes, studied the reporter's tie. The recent layer of cigarette-ash had merely formed a veil over much older stains. Egg, perhaps, fat, alcohol. The scruffiest reporters were always the sharp ones, and Stevens was sharp, as sharp as ten years on the local newspaper could make a man. It was said that he had turned down jobs with London papers, just because he liked to live in Edinburgh. And what he liked best about his job was the opportunity it gave him to uncover the city's murkier depths, the crime, the corruption, the gangs and the drugs. He was a better detective than anyone Campbell knew, and, because of that very fact perhaps, the high-ups in the police both disliked and distrusted him. That seemed proof enough that he was doing his job well. Campbell watched as a little beer escaped from Stevens' glass and dripped onto his trousers.

'This Rebus,' said Stevens, wiping his mouth, 'he's the brother of the hypnotist, isn't he?'

'Must be. I've never asked him, but there can't be too many people about with a name like that, can there?'

'That's what I was thinking.' He nodded to himself as though confirming something of great importance.

'So what?'

'Oh, nothing. Just something. And he's not a popular man, you say?'

'I didn't say that exactly. I feel sorry for him really. The poor bugger has a lot on his plate. He's even started getting crank letters.'

'Crank letters?' Smoke enveloped Stevens for a moment as he puffed on another cigarette. Between the two men lay a thin blue pub-haze.

'I shouldn't have told you that. That was *strictly* off the record.'

Stevens nodded.

'Absolutely. No, it's just that I was interested. That sort of thing does happen though, doesn't it?'

'Not often. And not nearly as queer as the ones he's getting. I mean, they're not abusive or anything. They're just ... queer.'

'Go on. How so?'

'Well, there's a bit of string in each one, tied into a knot, and there's a message that reads something like "clues are everywhere".'

'Bloody hell. That is strange. They're a strange family. One a bloody hypnotist and the other getting anonymous notes. He was in the Army, wasn't he?'

'John was, yes. How did you know?'

'I know everything, Mac. That's the job.'

'Another funny thing is that he won't speak about it.'

The reporter looked interested again. When he was interested in something, his shoulders shivered slightly. He stared at the television.

'Won't speak about the Army?'

'Not a word. I've asked him about it a couple of times.'

'Like I said, Mac, it's a funny family that one. Drink up, I've got lots of your money left to spend.'

'You're a bastard, Jim.'

'Born and bred,' said the reporter, smiling for only the second time that evening.

3

'Gentlemen, and, of course, ladies, thank you for being so quick to gather here. This will remain the centre of operations during the inquiry. Now, as you all know . . .'

Detective Chief Superintendent Wallace froze in mid-speech as the Inquiry Room door pushed itself open abruptly and John Rebus, all eyes turned towards him, entered the room. He looked about in embarrassment, smiled a hopeful but wasted apology towards the senior officer, and sat himself down on a chair nearest to the door.

'As I was saying,' continued the superintendent.

Rebus, rubbing at his forehead, studied the roomful of officers. He knew what the old boy would be saying, and right now the last thing he needed was a pep-talk of the old school. The room was packed. Many of them looked tired, as if they'd been on the case for a while. The fresher, more attentive faces belonged to the new boys, some of them brought in from stations outwith the city. Two or three had notebooks and pencils at the ready, almost as if they were back in the school classroom. And at the front of the group, legs crossed, sat two women, peering up at Wallace, who was in full flight now, parading before the blackboard like some Shakespearean hero in a bad school play.

'Two deaths, then. Yes, deaths I'm afraid.' The room shivered expectantly. 'The body of Sandra Adams, aged eleven, was found on a piece of waste ground adjacent to Haymarket Station at six o'clock this evening, and that of Mary Andrews at six-fifty on an allotment in the Oxgangs district. There are officers at both locations, and at the end of this briefing more of you will be selected to join them.'

Rebus was noticing that the usual pecking-order was in play: inspectors near the front of the room, sergeants and the rest to the back. Even in the midst of murder, there is a pecking-order. The British Disease. And he was at the bottom of the pile, because he had arrived late. Another black mark against him on someone's mental sheet.

He had always been one of the top men while he had been in the

Army. He had been a Para. He had trained for the SAS and come out top of his class. He had been chosen for a crack Special Assignments group. He had his medal and his commendations. It had been a good time, and yet it had been the worst of times, too, a time of stress and deprivation, of deceit and brutality. And when he had left, the police had been reluctant to take him. He understood now that it was something to do with the pressure applied by the Army to get him the job that he wanted. Some people resented that, and they had thrown down banana skins ever since for him to slide on. But he had sidestepped their traps, had performed the job, and had grudgingly been given his commendations here also. But there was precious little promotion, and that had caused him to say a few things out of line, a few things that were always to be held against him. And then he had cuffed an unruly bastard one night in the cells. God forgive him, he had simply lost his head for a minute. There had been more trouble over that. Ah, but it was not a nice world this, not a nice world at all. It was an Old Testament land that he found himself in, a land of barbarity and retribution.

'We will, of course, have more information for you to work on come tomorrow, after the post-mortems. But for the moment I think that will do. I'm going to hand you over to Chief Inspector Anderson, who will assign you to your tasks for the present.'

Rebus noticed that Jack Morton had nodded off in the corner and, if left unattended, would begin snoring soon. Rebus smiled, but the smile was short-lived, killed by a voice at the front of the room, the voice of Anderson. This was all Rebus needed. Anderson, the man at the centre of his out-of-line remarks. It felt for one sickening moment like predestination. Anderson was in charge. Anderson was doling out their tasks. Rebus reminded himself to stop praying. Perhaps if he stopped praying, God would take the hint and stop being such a bastard to one of his few believers on this near-godforsaken planet.

'Gemmill and Hartley will be assigned to door-to-door.'

Well, thank God he'd not been landed with that one. There was only one thing worse than door-to-door . . .

'And for an initial check on the MO files, Detective Sergeants Morton and Rebus.'

. . . and that was it.

Thank you, God, oh, thank you. That's just what I wanted to do with my evening: read through the case histories of all the bloody perverts and sex-

offenders in east central Scotland. You must really hate my guts. Am I Job or something? Is that it?

But there was no ethereal voice to be heard, no voice at all save that of the satanic, leering Anderson, whose fingers slowly turned the pages of the roster, his lips moist and full, his wife a known adulteress and his son – of all things – an itinerant poet. Rebus heaped curse after curse upon the shoulders of that priggish, stick-thin superior officer, then kicked Jack Morton's leg and brought him snorting and chaffing into consciousness.

One of those nights.

4

'One of those nights,' said Jack Morton. He sucked luxuriously on his short, tipped cigarette, coughed loudly, brought his handkerchief from his pocket and deposited something into it from his mouth. He studied the contents of the handkerchief. 'Ah ha, some vital new evidence,' he said. All the same, he looked rather worried.

Rebus smiled. 'Time to stop smoking, Jack,' he said.

They were seated together at a desk upon which were piled about a hundred and fifty files on known sex-offenders in central Scotland. A smart young secretary, doubtless relishing the overtime that came with a murder inquiry, kept bringing more files into the office, and Rebus stared at her in mock outrage every time she entered. He was hoping to scare her away, and if she came back again, the outrage would become real.

'No, John, it's these tipped bastards. I can't take to them, really I can't. Sod that bloody doctor.'

So saying, Morton took the cigarette from his lips, broke off the filter, and replaced the cigarette, now ridiculously short, between thin, bloodless lips.

'That's better. That's more like a fag.'

Rebus had always found two things remarkable. One was that he liked, and in return was liked by, Jack Morton. The other was that Morton could pull so hard on a cigarette and yet release so little smoke. Where did all that smoke go? He could not figure it out.

'I see you're abstaining this evening, John.'

'Limiting myself to ten a day, Jack.'

Morton shook his head.

'Ten, twenty, thirty a day. Take it from me, John, it makes no difference in the end. What it comes down to is this: you either stop or you don't, and if you can't stop, then you're as well smoking as many as you like. That's been proven. I read about it in a magazine.'

'Aye, but we all know the magazines *you* read, Jack.'

Morton chuckled, gave another tremendous cough, and searched for his handkerchief.

'What a bloody job,' said Rebus, picking up the first of the files.

The two men sat in silence for twenty minutes, flicking through the facts and fantasies of rapists, exhibitionists, pederasts, paedophiles, and procurers. Rebus felt his mouth filling with silt. It was as if he saw himself there, time after time after time, the self that lurked behind his everyday consciousness. His Mister Hyde by Robert Louis Stevenson, Edinburgh-born. He felt ashamed of his occasional erection: doubtless Jack Morton had one too. It came with the territory, as did the revulsion, the loathing and the fascination.

Around them, the station whirled in the business of the night. Men in shirtsleeves walked purposefully past their open door, the door of their assigned office, cut off from everyone else so that no one would be contaminated by their thoughts. Rebus paused for a moment to reflect that his own office back in Great London Road was in need of much of this equipment: the modern desk (unwobbly, with drawers that could be opened easily), the filing-cabinets (ditto), the drinks-dispenser just outside. There were carpets even, rather than his own liver-red linoleum with its curled, dangerous edges. It was a very palatable environment this in which to track down the odd pervert or killer.

'What exactly are we looking for, Jack?'

Morton snorted, threw down a slender brown file, looked at Rebus, shrugged his shoulders, and lit a cigarette.

'Garbage,' he said, picking up another folder, and whether or not it was meant as an answer Rebus was never to know.

'Detective Sergeant Rebus?'

A young constable, acne on his throat, cleanly-shaven, stood at the open door.

'Yes.'

'Message from the Chief, sir.'

He handed Rebus a folded piece of blue notepaper.

'Good news?' asked Morton.

'Oh, the best news, Jack, the very best news. Our boss sends us the following fraternal message: "Any leads from the files?" End of message.'

'Will there be any reply, sir?' asked the constable.

Rebus crumpled the note and tossed it into a new aluminium bin.

'Yes, son, there will be,' he said, 'but I very much doubt whether you'd want to deliver it.'

Jack Morton, wiping ash from his tie, laughed.

It was one of those nights. Jim Stevens, walking home at long last, had not found anything interesting since his conversation with Mac Campbell all of four hours ago. He had told Mac then that he was not about to drop his own investigation into Edinburgh's burgeoning drugs racket, and that had been the whole truth. It was becoming a private obsession, and though his boss might move him on to a murder case, still he would follow up his old investigation in his free, spare and private time, time found late at night when the presses were rolling, time spent in lower and lower dives further and further out of town. For he was close, he knew, to a big fish, and yet not close enough to be able to enlist the help of the forces of law and order. He wanted the story to be watertight before he called for the cavalry.

He knew the dangers, too. The ground he walked upon was always likely to fall away beneath his feet, letting him slip into Leith docks of a dark and silent morning, finding him trussed and gagged in some motorway ditch outside Perth. He didn't mind all that. It was no more than a passing thought, brought on by tiredness and a need to lift his emotions out of the rather tawdry, unglamorous world of Edinburgh's dope scene, a scene carried out in the sprawling housing-schemes and after-hours drinking holes more than in the glittery discotheques and chintzy rooms of the New Town.

What he disliked, really disliked, was that the people ultimately behind it all were so silent and so secretive and so alien to it all. He liked his criminals to be involved, to live the life and stick close to the lifestyle. He liked the Glasgow gangsters of the 1950s and '60s, who lived in the Gorbals and operated from the Gorbals and loaned illicit money to neighbours, and who would slash those same neighbours eventually, when the need arose. It was like a family affair. Not like this, not at all like this. This was other, and he hated it for that reason.

His talk with Campbell had been interesting though, interesting for other reasons. Rebus sounded a fishy character. So was his brother. They might be in it together. If the police were involved in all of this, then his task would be all the harder, and all the more satisfying for that.

Now what he needed was a break, a nice break in the investigation. It couldn't be far off. He was supposed to have a nose for that sort of thing.

5

At one-thirty they took a break. There was a small canteen in the building, open even at this ungodly hour. Outside, the majority of the day's petty crime was being committed, but inside it was warm and cosy, and there was hot food to be had and endless cups of coffee for the vigilant policemen.

'This is a complete shambles,' said Morton, pouring coffee back from his saucer into the cup. 'Anderson hasn't a clue what he's up to.'

'Give me a cigarette, will you? I'm out.' Rebus patted his pockets convincingly.

'Christ, John,' said Morton, wheezing an old man's cough and passing across the cigarettes, 'the day you give up smoking is the day I change my underwear.'

Jack Morton was not an old man, despite the excesses that were leading him quickly and inexorably towards that early fate. He was thirty-five, six years younger than Rebus. He, too, had a broken marriage behind him, the four children now resident with their grandmother while their mother was off on a suspiciously long vacation with her present lover. Misery, he had told Rebus, surrounded the whole bloody set-up, and Rebus had agreed with him, having a daughter who troubled his own conscience.

Morton had been a policeman for two decades, and unlike Rebus had started at the extreme bottom of the heap, pulling himself up to his present rank through sheer hard slog alone. He had given Rebus his life story when the two of them had gone off for a day's fly-fishing near Berwick. It had been a glorious day, both of them landing fine catches, and over the course of the day they had become friends. Rebus, however, had not deigned to tell his own life story to Morton. It felt, to Jack Morton, as if the man were in a little prison-cell of his own construction. He seemed especially tight-lipped about his years in the Army. Morton knew that the Army could occasionally do that to a man, and he respected Rebus's silence. Perhaps there were a few skeletons in that particular closet. He knew all about those himself; some of his most noteworthy arrests had not exactly been conducted along 'correct procedural lines'.

Nowadays, Morton did not concern himself with headlines and high-profile arrests. He got on with the job, collected his salary, thought now and then of his pension and the fishing-years to come, and drank his wife and children out of his conscience.

'This is a nice canteen,' said Rebus, smoking, struggling to start a conversation.

'Yes, it is. I'm in here now and again. I know one of the guys who work in the computer room. Comes in handy, you know, having one of those terminal-operators in your pocket. They can track down a car, a name, an address quicker than you can blink. It only costs the occasional drink.'

'Get them to sort out this lot of ours then.'

'Give them time, John. Then *all* the files will be on computer. And a little while after that, they'll find that they don't need the work-horses like us any more. There'll just be a couple of DIs and a desk console.'

'I'll bear that in mind,' said Rebus.

'It's progress, John. Where would we be without it? We'd still be out there with our pipes and our guess-work and our magnifying glasses.'

'I suppose you're right, Jack. But remember what the Super says: "Give me a dozen good men every time, and send your machines back to their makers."'

Rebus looked around him as he spoke. He saw that one of the two women from the briefing room had settled at a table by herself.

'And besides,' said Rebus, 'there'll always be a place for people like us, Jack. Society couldn't do without us. Computers can never have inspired guesses. That's where we've got them beat hands down.'

'Maybe, I don't know. Still, we better be getting back, eh?' Morton looked at his watch, drained his cup, and pushed back his chair.

'You go on ahead, Jack. I'll be with you in a minute. I want to check out an inspired guess.'

'Mind if I join you?'

Rebus, a fresh cup of coffee in his hand, pulled out the chair from opposite the woman officer, who had her head buried in the day's newspaper. He noted the garish headline on the front page. Someone had slipped out a little information to the local media.

'Not at all,' she said, not looking up.

Rebus smiled to himself and sat down. He began to sip the powdery, instant murk.

'Busy?' he asked.

'Yes. Shouldn't you be? Your friend left a few minutes ago.'

Sharp then, very sharp. Very, very sharp indeed. Rebus began to feel a mite uneasy. He disliked ballcrushers, and here were all the outward signs of one.

'Yes, he did, didn't he? But then he's a glutton for punishment. We're working on the Modus Operandi files. I'd do anything to defer that particular pleasure.'

She looked up at last, bitten by the potential insult.

'That's what I am, is it? A delaying tactic?'

Rebus smiled and shrugged.

'What else?' he said.

It was her turn to smile now. She closed the paper and folded it twice, placing it before her on the formica-topped table. She tapped the headline.

'Looks like we're in the news,' she said.

Rebus turned the paper towards him.

EDINBURGH ABDUCTIONS – NOW IT'S MURDER!

'A terrible bloody case,' he offered. 'Just terrible. And the newspapers don't make it any better.'

'Yes, well, we'll have the PM results in a couple of hours, and then we just might have something to go on.'

'I hope so. Just so long as I can put away those bloody files.'

'I thought policemen,' stressing the latter part of the word, 'got their kicks from reading that stuff?'

Rebus spread his hands before him, a gesture he seemed to have picked up from Michael.

'You have us to a T. How long have you been in the force?'

Rebus took her to be thirty, give or take two years. She had thick, short brown hair, and a long, straight ski-slope of a nose. There were no rings on her fingers, but these days that told him nothing.

'Long enough,' she said.

'I think I knew you would say that.'

She was smiling still: no ballcrusher then.

'Then you're cleverer than I took you for,' she said.

'You'd be surprised.'

He was growing tired, realising that the game was going nowhere. It

32

was all midfield, a friendly rather than a cup-tie. He checked his watch conspicuously.

'Time I was getting back,' he said.

She picked up her newspaper.

'Are you doing anything this weekend?' she asked.

John Rebus sat down again.

6

He left the station at four o'clock. The birds were doing their best to persuade everyone that it was dawn, but no one seemed fooled. It was dark still, and the air was chilled.

He decided to leave his car and walk home, a distance of two miles. He needed it, needed to feel the cool, damp air, the expectancy of a morning shower. He breathed deep, trying to relax, to forget, but his mind was too full of those files, and little pieces of recollected fact and figure, pieces of horror no bigger than a paragraph, haunted his walk.

To indecently assault an eight-week old baby girl. The babysitter who had calmly admitted to the assault saying that she had done it 'for a kick'.

To rape a grandmother in front of her two grandchildren, then give the kids some sweets from a jar before leaving. The act premeditated; committed by a bachelor of fifty.

To burn with cigarettes the name of a street gang onto the breasts of a twelve-year old, leaving her for dead in a burning hut. Never caught.

And now the crux: to abduct two girls and then strangle them *without* having sexually abused them. That, Anderson had posited only thirty minutes before, was a perversion in itself, and in a funny way Rebus knew what he meant. It made the deaths even more arbitrary, more pointless – and more shocking.

Well, at least they were not dealing with a sex-offender; not right away. Which only, Rebus was forced to agree, made their task that much more difficult, for now they were confronted with something like a 'serial killer', striking at random and without clues, aiming at the record books rather than at any idea of 'kicks'. The question now was would he stop at two? It seemed unlikely.

Strangulation. It was a fearful way to go, wrestling, kicking your way towards oblivion, panic, the fretful sucking for air, and the killer behind you most likely, so that you faced the fear of something totally anonymous, a death without knowledge of who or why. Rebus had been taught methods of killing in the SAS. He knew what it felt like to have the garotte tighten on your neck, trusting to the opponent's prevailing sanity. A fearful way to go.

Edinburgh slept on, as it had slept on for hundreds of years. There were ghosts in the cobbled alleys and on the twisting stairways of the Old Town tenements, but they were Enlightenment ghosts, articulate and deferential. They were not about to leap from the darkness with a length of twine ready in their hands. Rebus paused and looked around him. Besides, it was morning now and any godfearing spirit would be tucked up in bed, as he, John Rebus, flesh and blood, would be soon.

Near his flat, he passed a little grocery shop outside which were stacked crates of milk and morning rolls. The owner had complained in private to Rebus about petty and occasional thefts, but would not submit a complaint proper. The shop was as dead as the street, the solitude of the moment disturbed only by the distant rumble of a taxi on cobblestones and the persistence of the dawn chorus. Rebus looked around him, examining the many curtained windows. Then, swiftly, he tore six rolls from a layer and stuffed them into his pockets, walking away a little too briskly. A moment later he hesitated, then walked on tiptoe back to the shop, the criminal returning to the scene of the crime, the dog to its vomit. Rebus had never actually seen dogs doing that, but he had it on the authority of Saint Peter.

Looking round again, he lifted a pint of milk out of its crate and made his getaway, whistling silently to himself.

Nothing in the world tasted as good for breakfast as stolen rolls with some butter and jam and a mug of milky coffee. Nothing tasted better than a venial sin.

He sniffed the stairwell of his tenement, catching the faint odour of tom-cats, a persistent menace. He held his breath as he climbed the two flights of stairs, fumbling in his pocket beneath the squashed rolls, trying to liberate his door-key.

The interior of the flat felt damp and smelt damp. He checked the central heating and, sure enough, the pilot-light had gone out again. He cursed as he relit it, turning the heat up all the way, and went through to the living-room.

There were still spaces on the book-case, the wall-unit, the mantel-piece where Rhona's ornaments had once stood, but many of the gaps had already been filled by new mementoes of his own: bills, unanswered letters, old ring-pulls from tins of cheap beer, the occasional unread book. Rebus collected unread books. Once upon a time, he had actually read the books that he bought, but these days he seemed to have so little time. Also, he was more discriminating now than he had been then, back in the old days when he would read a book to its bitter end whether he liked it or not. These days, a book he disliked was unlikely to last ten pages of his concentration.

These were the books that lay around his living-room. His books for reading tended to congregate in the bedroom, lying in co-ordinated rows on the floor like patients in a doctor's waiting-room. One of these days he would take a holiday, would rent a cottage in the Highlands or on the Fife coast, and would take with him all of these waiting-to-be-read-or-reread books, all of that knowledge that could be his for the breaking open of a cover. His favourite book, a book he turned to at least once a year, was *Crime and Punishment*. If only, he thought, modern murderers would exhibit some show of conscience more often. But no, modern killers bragged of their crimes to their friends, then played pool in their local pub, chalking their cues with poise and certainty, knowing which balls would drop in which order . . .

While a police-car slept nearby, its occupants unable to do anything save curse the mountains of rules and regulations and rue the deep chasms of crime. It was everywhere, crime. It was the life-force and the blood and the balls of life: to cheat, to edge; to take that body-swerve at authority, to kill. The higher up you climbed into crime, the more subtly you began to move back towards legitimacy, until a handful of lawyers only could crack open your system, and they were always affordable, always on hand to be bribed. Dostoevsky had known all that, clever old bastard. He had felt the stick burning from both ends.

But poor old Dostoevsky was dead and had not been invited to a party this weekend, while he, John Rebus, had. Often he declined invitations, because to accept meant that he had to dust off his brogues, iron a shirt, brush down his best suit, take a bath, and splash on some cologne. He had also to be affable, to drink and be merry, to talk to strangers with whom he had no inclination to talk and with whom he was not being paid to talk. In other words, he resented having to play the part of a normal human animal. But he had accepted the invitation given to him by Cathy Jackson in the Waverley Road canteen. Of course he had.

And he whistled at the thought of it, wandering through to the kitchen to make some breakfast, which he then took through to his bedroom. This was a ritual after a night duty. He stripped, climbed into bed, balanced the plate of rolls on his chest, and held a book to his nose.

It was not a very good book. It was about a kidnapping. Rhona had taken away the bed proper, but had left him the mattress, so it was easy for him to reach down for his mug of coffee, easy for him to discard one book and find another.

He fell asleep soon enough, the lamp still burning, as cars began to pass by his window.

His alarm did the trick for a change, pulling him off the mattress as a magnet attracts filings. He had kicked off the duvet, and was drenched in sweat. He felt suffocated, and remembered suddenly that the central heating was still boiling away like a steamship. On his way to switching off the thermostat, he stooped at the front door to pick up the day's mail. One of the letters was unstamped and unfranked. It bore only his name in typescript across the front. Rebus's stomach squeezed hard on the paste of rolls and butter. He ripped the envelope open, pulling out the single sheet of paper.

FOR THOSE WHO READ BETWEEN THE TIMES.

So now the lunatic knew where he lived. Checking in the envelope, laconic now and expecting to find the knotted string, he found instead two matchsticks, tied together with thread into the shape of a cross.

PART TWO

'For Those Who Read Between The Times'

7

Organized chaos: that summed up the newspaper office. Organized chaos on the grandest of scales. Stevens rummaged amongst the sheaf of paper in his tray, looking for a needle. Had he perhaps filed it somewhere else? He opened one of the large, heavy drawers of his desk, then shut it quickly, afraid that some of the mess in there might escape. Controlling himself, he took a deep breath and opened it again. He plunged a hand into the jumble of paper inside the drawer, as if something in there would bite. A huge dog-clip, springing loose from one particular file, did bite. It nicked his thumb and he slammed the drawer shut, the cigarette wobbling in his mouth as he cursed the office, the journalistic profession, and trees, begetters of paper. Sod it. He sat back and squeezed his eyes shut as the smoke began to sting. It was eleven in the morning, and already the office was a blue haze, as though everything were happening on the set of a *Brigadoon* marsh-scene. He grabbed a sheet of typescript, turned it over, and began to scribble with a nub of pencil which he had lifted from a betting shop.

'X (Mr Big?) delivers to Rebus, M. How does the policeman fit in? Answer – perhaps everywhere, perhaps nowhere.'

He paused, taking the cigarette from his mouth, replacing it with a fresh one, and using the butt to light its successor.

'Now – anonymous letters. Threats? A code?'

Stevens found it unlikely that John Rebus could not know about his brother's involvement in the Scottish drug-pushing world, and knowing, the chances were that he was involved in it too, perhaps leading the whole investigation the wrong way to protect his flesh and blood. It would make a cracking good story when it broke, but he knew that he would be treading on eggs from here on in. No one would go out of their way to help him nail a policeman, and if anyone found out what he was up to, he would be in very serious trouble indeed. He needed to do two things: check his life insurance policy, and tell nobody about this.

'Jim!'

The editor gestured for him to step into the torture chamber. He rose from his seat, as though tearing himself up from something organic, straightened his mauve and pink striped tie, and headed towards a presumed bawling-out.

'Yes, Tom?'

'Aren't you supposed to be at a press conference?'

'Plenty of time, Tom.'

'Which photographer are you taking?'

'Does it matter? I'd be better off taking my bloody instamatic. These young boys don't know the ropes, Tom. What about Andy Fleming? Can't I have him?'

'No chance, Jim. He's covering the royal tour.'

'What royal tour?'

Tom Jameson seemed about to rise again from his chair, which would have been an unprecedented move. He only straightened his back and shoulders however, and eyed his 'star' crime reporter suspiciously.

'You *are* a journalist, Jim, aren't you? I mean, you've not gone into early retirement, or become a recluse? No history of senile dementia in the family?'

'Listen, Tom, when the Royal Family commits a crime, I'll be the first on the scene. Otherwise, as far as I'm concerned, they don't exist. Not outside of my nightmares, anyway.'

Jameson pointedly examined his wristwatch.

'Okay, okay, I'm going.'

With that, Stevens turned on his heels with amazing speed and left the office, ignoring the cries of his boss at his back, asking which of the available photographers he wanted.

It wouldn't matter. He had yet to meet a policeman who was photogenic. Then, leaving the building, he remembered who was Liaison Officer on this particular case, and he changed his mind, smiling.

' "There are clues everywhere, for those who read between the times." It's pure gobbledygook, isn't it, John?'

Morton was driving the car towards the Haymarket district of the city. It was another afternoon of consistent, wind-driven rain, the rain itself fine and cold, the kind that seeped into bones and marrow. The city had been dull all day, to a point where motorists were using their headlamps at noon. A great day for some outside work.

'I'm not so sure, Jack. The second part leads on from the first as if there was a logical connection.'

'Well, let's hope he sends you some more notes. Maybe that would make things clearer.'

'Maybe. I'd rather he'd just stop this shit altogether. It's not very nice knowing that a crank knows where you work and where you live.'

'Is your phone number in the telephone book?'

'No, unlisted.'

'That rules out that idea then. So how does he know your home address?'

'He *or* she,' said Rebus, tucking the notes back into his pocket. 'How should I know?'

He lit two cigarettes and passed one to Morton, breaking the filter off for him.

'Ta,' said Morton, placing the tiny cigarette in the corner of his mouth. The rain was easing. 'Floods in Glasgow,' he said, expecting no reply.

Both men were bleary-eyed from lack of sleep, but the case had taken possession of them, so they drove, minds numbed, towards the bleak heart of the inquiry. A portakabin had been set up on waste ground next to the spot where the girl's body had been found. From there, a door-to-door operation was being co-ordinated. Friends and family were also to be interviewed. Rebus foresaw much tedium in the day ahead.

'What worries me,' Morton had said, 'is that if the two murders are linked, then we're dealing with someone who probably didn't know either of the girls. *That* makes for a bastard of a job.'

Rebus had nodded. There was still the chance, however, either that both girls had known their murderer, or that the murderer had been someone in a position of trust. Otherwise, the girls being nearly twelve-years old and not daft, they would surely have struggled when abducted. Yet no one had come forward to say that they had witnessed any such thing. It was bloody strange.

The rain had stopped by the time they reached the cramped operations-room. The inspector in charge of outdoor operations was there to hand them lists of names and addresses. Rebus rejoiced to be away from the HQ, away from Anderson and his thirst for paperwork results. *This* was where the work really took place, where the contacts were made, where one slip by a suspect could tip a case one way or the other.

'Do you mind me asking, sir, who it was that suggested my colleague and me for this particular job?'

The DI, his eyes twinkling, studied Rebus for a second.

'Yes, I bloody well do mind, Rebus. It doesn't matter one way or the other, does it? Every single task in this case is as vital and as important as every other. Let's not forget that.'

'Yes, sir,' said Rebus.

'This must be a bit like working inside a shoebox, sir,' said Morton examining the cramped interior.

'Yes, son, I'm in the shoebox, but you lot are the shoes, so get bloody well moving.'

This particular inspector, thought Rebus, pocketing his list, seemed a nice bloke, his tongue just sharp enough for Rebus's taste.

'Don't worry, sir,' he said now, 'this won't take us long.'

He hoped that the inspector noted the irony in his voice.

'Last one back's a fairy,' said Morton.

They were doing this by the rule-book then, yet the case would seem to demand that new rules be drawn up. Anderson was sending them out to look for the usual suspects: family, acquaintances, people with records. Doubtless, back at HQ, groups such as the Paedophile Information Exchange were being investigated. Rebus hoped that there were plenty of crank calls for Anderson to sift through. There usually were: the callers who admitted to the crime, the callers who were psychic and could help by getting in touch with the deceased, the callers who pressed a red-herring to your nose so that you could have a sniff. They were all mastered by past guilt and present fantasies. Perhaps everyone was.

At his first house, Rebus battered on the door and waited. It was opened by a rank old woman, her feet bare, a cardigan comprised of ninety-percent hole to ten-percent wool hanging around her scarp-like shoulders.

'Whit is it?'

'Police, madam. It's about the murder.'

'Eh? Whitever it is, I dinnae want it. Away ye get afore I ca' for the coppers.'

'The murders,' shouted Rebus. 'I'm a policeman. I've come to ask you a few questions.'

'Eh?' She stood back a little to peer at him, and Rebus could swear that he saw the faint glow of a past intelligence in the dulled black of her pupils.

'Whit murders?' she said.

One of those days. To improve matters, the rain began again, heavy dollops of stinging water gripping to his neck and face, seeping into his shoes. Just like that day at the old man's grave . . . Only yesterday? A lot could happen in twenty-four hours, all of it to him.

By seven o'clock, Rebus had covered six of the fourteen individuals on his list. He walked back to the operations-shoebox, his feet sore, his stomach awash with tea and craving something stronger.

At the boggy waste ground, Jack Morton stood and stared out over the acres of clay, strewn with bricks and detritus: a child's heaven.

'What a hellish place to die in.'

'She didn't die here, Jack. Remember what forensic said.'

'Well, you know what I mean.'

Yes, Rebus knew what he meant.

'By the way,' said Morton, 'you're the fairy.'

'I'll drink to that,' said Rebus.

They drank in some of Edinburgh's seedier bars, bars the tourist never sees. They tried to shut the case out of their minds, but could not. It was like that with big murder inquiries; they got to you, physically and mentally, consuming you and making you work all the harder. There was a rush of pure adrenalin behind every murder. It kept them going past the point of no return.

'I'd better be getting back to the flat,' said Rebus.

'No, have another.'

Jack Morton weaved towards the bar, his empty glass in his hand.

Rebus, his mind foggy, thought more about his mysterious correspondent. He suspected Rhona, though it could not be said to be her style. He suspected his daughter Sammy, perhaps taking a delayed-action revenge for her father's dismissal of her from his life. Family and acquaintances were, initially at least, always the chief suspects. But it could be anyone, anyone who knew where he worked and where he lived. Someone in his own force was always a possibility to be feared.

The 10,000 dollar question, as ever, was why?

'Here we go, two lovely pints of beer, *gratis* from the management.'

'I call that very public-spirited,' said Rebus.

'Or publican-spirited, eh, John?' Morton chuckled at his joke, wiping froth from his top lip. He noticed that Rebus wasn't laughing. 'A penny for them,' he said.

'A serial killer,' said Rebus. 'It must be. In which case we've not seen the last of our friend's handiwork.'

Morton put down his glass, suddenly not very thirsty.

'Those girls went to different schools,' continued Rebus, 'lived in different areas of the city, had different tastes, different friends, were of different religions, and were killed by the same murderer in the same way and without noticeable abuse of any kind. We're dealing with a maniac. He could be anywhere.'

A fight was breaking out at the bar, apparently over a game of dominoes, which had gone very badly wrong. A glass fell to the floor, followed by a hush in the bar. Then everyone seemed to calm down a little. One man was led outside by his supporters in the argument. Another remained slumped against the bar, muttering to a woman beside him.

Morton took a gulp of beer.

'Thank God we're off duty,' he said. Then: 'Fancy a curry?'

Morton finished the chicken vindaloo and threw his fork down on to the plate.

'I reckon I ought to have a word with the Health Department boys,' he said, still chewing. 'Either that or the Trading Standards. Whatever that was, it wasn't chicken.'

They were in a small curry-house near Haymarket Station. Purple lighting, red flock wallpaper, a churning wall of sitar-music.

'You looked as if you were enjoying it,' said Rebus, finishing his beer.

'Oh yes, I enjoyed it, but it wasn't chicken.'

'Well, there's nothing to complain about if you enjoyed it.' Rebus sat slant-wise on his chair, his legs straight out before him, an arm along the chair's back while he smoked his umpteenth cigarette that day.

Morton leaned unsteadily towards his partner.

'John, there's *always* something to complain about, especially if you think you can get off with not paying the bill by doing so.'

He winked at Rebus, sat back, burped, and reached into his pocket for a cigarette.

'Garbage,' he said.

Rebus tried to count the number of cigarettes he himself had smoked that day, but his brain told him that such calculations were not to be attempted.

'I wonder what our friend the murderer is up to at this exact moment?' he said.

'Finishing a curry?' suggested Morton. 'Trouble is, John, he could be one of these Joe Normal types, clean on the surface, married with kids, your average suburban hard-working chap, but underneath a nutter, pure and simple.'

'There's nothing simple about our man.'

'True.'

'But you could well be right. You mean that he's a sort of Jekyll and Hyde, right?'

'Exactly.' Morton flicked ash onto the table-top, already splashed with curry sauce and beer. He was peering at his empty plate as though wondering where all the food had gone. 'Jekyll and Hyde. You've got it in a nutshell. I'll tell you, John, I'd lock these bastards up for a million years, a million years of solitary in a cell the size of a shoebox. That's what I'd do.'

Rebus was staring at the flock wallpaper. He thought back to his own days in solitary, days when the SAS were trying to crack him, days of the ultimate testing, of sighs and silence, starvation and filth. No, he wouldn't want that again. And yet they had not beaten him, not really beaten him. The others had not been so lucky.

Trapped in its cell, the face screaming

Let me out Let me out

Let me out . . .

'John? Are you okay there? If you're going to be sick, the toilet's behind the kitchen. Listen, when you're passing, do me a favour and see if you can notice what it is that they're chopping up and throwing into the pot . . .'

Rebus walked smartly to the toilet with the over-cautious gait of the tremendously drunk, yet he did not feel drunk, not *that* drunk. His nostrils filled with the smells of curry, disinfectant, shit. He washed his face. No, he was not going to be sick. It wasn't too much to drink, for he had felt the same shudder at Michael's, the same momentary horror. What was happening to him? It was as if his insides were concretizing, slowing him down, allowing the years to catch up on him. It felt a little like the nervous breakdown which he had been awaiting, yet it was no nervous breakdown. It was nothing. It had passed.

'Can I give you a lift, John?'

'No thanks, I'll walk. Clear my head.'

They parted at the door of the restaurant. An office-party, loosened neckties and strong, sickly perfume, made its way towards Haymarket Station. Haymarket was the last station into Edinburgh before the much grander Waverley. Rebus remembered that the premature withdrawal of the penis during intercourse for contraceptive reasons was often referred to as 'getting off at Haymarket.' Who said the people in Edinburgh were dour? A smile, a song, and a strangulation. Rebus wiped sweat from his forehead. He felt weak still, and leaned against a lamp-post. He knew vaguely what it was. It was a rejection by his whole being of the past, as though his vital organs were rejecting a donor heart. He had pushed the horror of the training so far to the back of his mind that any echo of it at all was now to be violently fought against. And yet it was in that same confinement that he had found friendship, brotherhood, camaraderie, call it what you like. And he had learned more about himself than human beings ever do. He had learned so much.

His spirit had not been broken. He had come out of the training on top. And then had come the nervous breakdown.

Enough. He began to walk, steadying himself with thoughts of his day off tomorrow. He would spend the day reading and sleeping and readying himself for a party, Cathy Jackson's party.

And the day after that, Sunday, he would be spending a rare day with his daughter. Then, perhaps, he would find out who was behind the crank letters.

8

The girl woke up with a dry, salty taste in her mouth. She felt sleepy and numb and wondered where she was. She had fallen asleep in his car. She had not felt sleepy before then, before he had given her a piece of his chocolate-bar. Now she was awake, but not in her bedroom at home. This room had pictures on its walls, pictures cut out of colour magazines. Some were photographs of soldiers with fierce expressions on their faces, others were of girls and women. She looked closely at some self-developing photographs grouped together on one wall. There was a picture of her there, asleep on the bed with her arms spread wide. She opened her mouth in a slight gasp.

Outside, in the living-room, he heard her movements as he prepared the garotte.

That night, Rebus had one of his nightmarish dreams again. A long, lingering kiss was followed by an ejaculation, both in the dream and in reality. He woke up immediately afterwards and wiped himself down. The breath of the kiss was still around him, hanging to him like an aura. He shook his head clear of it. He needed a woman. Remembering the party to come, he relaxed a little. But his lips were dry. He padded into the kitchen and found a bottle of lemonade. It was flat, but served the purpose. Then he remembered that he was still drunk, and would have a hangover if he wasn't careful. He poured himself three glassfuls of water and forced them down.

He was pleased to find that the pilot-light was still on. It was like a good omen. When he slipped back into bed, he even remembered to say his prayers. That would surprise the Big Man upstairs. He would note it in his muckle book: Rebus remembered me tonight. May give him a nice day tomorrow.

Amen.

9

Michael Rebus loved his BMW as dearly as he loved life itself, perhaps more so. As he sped down the motorway, the traffic to his left hardly appearing to move at all, he felt that his car *was* life in a strange, satisfying sort of way. He pointed its nose towards the bright point of the horizon and let it forge towards that future, revving it hard, making no concessions to anyone or anything.

That was the way he liked it; hard, fast luxury, push-button and on-hand. He drummed his fingers on the leather of the steering-wheel, toyed with the radio-cassette, eased his head back onto the padded headrest. He dreamed often of just taking off, leaving wife and children and house, just his car and him. Taking off towards that far point, never stopping except to eat and fill up the car, driving until he died. It seemed like paradise, and so he felt quite safe fantasising about it, knowing that he would never dare put paradise into practice.

When he had first owned a car, he had wakened in the middle of the night, opening his curtains to see if it was still waiting for him outside. Sometimes he would rise at four or five in the morning and take off for a few hours, astonished at the distance he could cover so quickly, glad to be out on the silent roads with only the rabbits and the crows for company, his hand on the horn scaring fluttering clouds of birds into the air. He had never lost that initial love-affair with cars, the manumission of dreams.

People stared at his car now. He would park it in the streets of Kirkcaldy and stand a little distance away, watching people envy that car. The younger men, full of bravado and expectancy, would peer inside, staring at leather and dials as though examining living things at the zoo. The older men, some with their wives in tow, would glance at the machine, sometimes spitting on the road afterwards, knowing that it represented everything they had wanted for themselves and failed to find. Michael Rebus had found his dream, and it was a dream he could watch any time he chose.

In Edinburgh, however, it depended where you parked as to whether your car would attract attention. He had parked on George Street one day, only to find a Rolls-Royce cruising to a stop behind him. He had keyed the ignition again, fuming, near-spitting. He had parked eventually outside a discotheque. He knew that parking an expensive car outside a restaurant or a discotheque would mean that a few people would mistake you for the owner of the particular set-up, and that thought pleased him immensely, erasing the memory of the Rolls-Royce and infusing him with new versions of the dream.

Stopping at traffic-lights, too, could be exciting, except when some half-arsed biker on a big machine roared to a standstill behind him or, even worse, beside him. Some of those bikes were made for initial acceleration. More than once he had been beaten mercilessly in a race from traffic-lights. He tried not to think about those times either.

Today he parked where he had been told to park: in the car park atop Calton Hill. He could see over to Fife from his front window, and from the back he could see Princes Street laid out before him like a toy-set. The hill was quiet; it was not quite the tourist season, and it was cold. He knew that things hotted up at night: car chases, girls and boys hoping for a ride, parties at Queensferry beach. Edinburgh's gay community would mix with those merely curious or lonely, and a couple, hand-in-hand, would now and again enter the graveyard at the bottom of the hill. When darkness fell, the east end of Princes Street became a territory all of its own, to be passed around, to be shared. But he was not about to share his car with anyone. His dream was a fragile entity.

He watched Fife across the Firth of Forth, looking quite splendid from this distance, until the man's car slowed and stopped beside him. Michael slid across to his passenger seat and wound down the window, just as the other man was winding down his.

'Got the stuff?' he said.

'Of course,' said the man. He checked in his mirror. Some people, a family of all things, had just come over the rise. 'We better wait for a minute.'

They paused, staring blankly at the scenery.

'No hassles across in Fife?' asked the man.

'None.'

'The word's going round that your brother was over seeing you. Is that correct?' The man's eyes were hard; his whole being was hard. But the car he drove was a heap. Michael felt safe for the moment.

'Yes, but it was nothing. It was just the anniversary of our dad's death. That was all.'

'He doesn't know anything?'

'Absolutely not. Do you think I'm thick or something?'

The man's glance silenced Michael. It was a mystery to him how this one man could invoke such fear in him. He hated these meetings.

'If anything happens,' the man was saying, 'if *anything* goes wrong, you'll be in for it. I really mean that. Keep well clear of that bastard in future.'

'It wasn't my fault. He just dropped in on me. He didn't even phone first. What could I do?'

His hands were gripping hard to the steering-wheel, cemented there. The man checked in his mirror again.

'All clear,' he said, reaching behind him. A small package slipped through Michael's window. He took a look inside it, brought an envelope out of his pocket, and reached for the ignition.

'Be seeing you around, Mister Rebus,' said the man, opening the envelope.

'Yes,' said Michael, thinking: not if I can help it. This work was getting a bit too hairy for him. These people seemed to know everything about his movements. He knew, however, that the fear always evaporated, to be replaced by euphoria when he had rid himself of another load, pocketing a nice profit on the deal. It was that moment when fear turned to euphoria that kept him in the game. It was like the fastest piece of acceleration from traffic-lights that you could experience – ever.

Jim Stevens, watching from the hill's Victorian folly, a ridiculous, never-completed copy of a Greek temple, saw Michael Rebus leave. That much was old news to him; he was more interested in the Edinburgh connection, a man he could not trace and did not know, a man who had lost him twice before and who could doubtless lose him again. Nobody seemed to know who this mysterious figure was, and nobody particularly wanted to know. He looked like trouble. Stevens, feeling suddenly impotent and old, could do nothing other than jot down the car registration number. He thought that perhaps McGregor Campbell could do something with it, but he was wary of being found out by Rebus. He felt trapped in the middle of something which was proving altogether a knottier problem than he had suspected.

Shivering, he tried to persuade himself that he liked it that way.

10

'Come in, come in, whoever you are.'

Rebus's coat, gloves, and bottle of wine were taken from him by complete strangers, and he was plunged into one of those packed, smoky, loud parties where it is easy to smile at people but near impossible to get to know anyone. He moved from the hall into the kitchen, and from there, through a connecting-door, into the living-room itself.

The chairs, table, settee had been pushed back to the walls, and the floor was filled with writhing, whooping couples, the men tieless, their shirts sticking to them.

The party, it appeared, had started earlier than he had anticipated.

He recognized a few faces around and beneath him, stepping over two inspectors as he waded into the room. He could see that the table at the far end had bottles and plastic cups heaped upon it, and it seemed as good a vantage point as any, and safer than some.

Getting to it was the problem however, and he was reminded of some of the assault courses of his Army days.

'Hi there!'

Cathy Jackson, doing a passable imitation of a rag-doll, reeled into his path for a second before being swept off her feet by the large – the very large – man with whom she was pretending to dance.

'Hello,' managed Rebus, his face twisting into a grimace rather than a smile. He achieved the relative safety of the drinks-table and helped himself to a whisky and a chaser. That would do for starters. Then he watched as Cathy Jackson (for whom he had bathed, polished, scraped, adjusted, and sprayed) pushed her tongue into the cavernous mouth of her dancing-partner. Rebus thought that he was going to be sick. His partner for the evening had done a bunk before the evening had begun! That would teach him to be optimistic. So what did he do now? Leave quietly, or try to pull a few words of introduction out of his hat?

A stocky man, not at all a policeman, came from the kitchen, and, cigarette in mouth, approached the table with a couple of empty glasses in his hand.

'Bloody hell,' he said to nobody in particular, rummaging amongst the bottles, 'this is all a bit fucking grim, isn't it? Excuse my language.'

'Yes, it is a bit.'

Rebus thought to himself, well, there it is, I've done it now, I've spoken to someone. The ice is broken, so I may as well leave while the going's good.

But he did not leave. He watched as the man weaved his way quite expertly back through the dancers, the drinks as safe as tiny animals in his hands. He watched as another record pounded out of the invisible stereo system, the dancers recommenced their war-dance, and a woman, looking every inch as uncomfortable as he did, squeezed her way into the room and was pointed in the direction of Rebus's table.

She was about his own age, a little ragged around the edges. She wore a reasonably fashionable dress, he supposed (who was he to talk about fashion? his suit looked downright funereal in the present company), and her hair had been styled recently, perhaps as recently as this afternoon. She wore a secretary's glasses, but she was no secretary. Rebus could see that much by looking at her, by examining the way she handled herself as she picked her way towards him.

He held a Bloody Mary, newly-prepared, towards her.

'Is this okay for you?' he shouted. 'Have I guessed right or wrong?'

She gulped the drink thankfully, pausing for breath as he refilled the tumbler.

'Thanks,' she said. 'I don't normally drink, but that was much appreciated.'

Great, Rebus thought to himself, the smile never leaving his eyes, Cathy Jackson's out of her head (and her morals) on alcohol, and I'm landed with a TT. Oh, but that thought was unworthy of him, and did no justice to his companion. He breathed a quick prayer of contrition.

'Would you like to dance?' he asked, for his sins.

'You're kidding!'

'I'm not. What's wrong?'

Rebus, guilty of a streak of chauvinism, could not believe it. She was a DI. Moreover, she was Press Liaison Officer on the murder case.

'Oh,' he said, 'it's just that I'm working that case, too.'

'Listen, John, if it keeps on like this, every policeman and police-woman in Scotland is going to be on the case. Believe me.'

'What do you mean?'

'There's been another abduction. The girl's mother reported her missing this evening.'

'Shit. Excuse my language.'

They had danced, drunk, separated, met again, and were now old friends for the evening, it seemed. They stood in the hallway, a little way from the noise and chaos of the dance-floor. A queue for the flat's only toilet was becoming unruly at the end of the corridor.

Rebus found himself staring past Gill Templer's glasses, past all that glass and plastic, to the emerald-green eyes beyond. He wanted to tell her that he had never seen eyes as lovely as hers, but was afraid of being accused of cliché. She was sticking to orange juice now, but he had loosened himself up with a few more whiskies, not expecting anything special from the evening.

'Hello, Gill.'

Rebus recognized the stocky man before them as the person he had spoken with at the drinks-table.

'Long time no see.'

The man attempted to peck Gill Templer's cheek, but succeeded only in falling past her and butting the wall.

'Had a drop too much to drink, Jim?' said Gill, coolly.

The man shrugged his shoulders. He was looking at Rebus.

'We all have our crosses to bear, eh?'

A hand was extended towards Rebus.

'Jim Stevens,' said the man.

'Oh, the reporter?'

Rebus accepted the man's warm, moist hand for a moment.

'This is Detective Sergeant John Rebus,' said Gill.

Rebus noticed the quick flushing in Stevens' face, the startled eyes of a hare. He recovered quickly though, expertly.

'Pleased to meet you,' he said. Then, motioning with his head, 'Gill and I go back a long way, don't we, Gill?'

'Not as far as you seem to think, Jim.'

He laughed then, glancing towards Rebus.

'She's just shy,' he said. 'Another girl murdered, I hear.'

'Jim has spies everywhere.'

Stevens tapped the side of his blood-red nose, grinning towards Rebus.

'Everywhere,' he said, 'and I *get* everywhere, too.'

'Yes, spreads himself a little thin, does our Jim,' said Gill, her voice sharp as a blade's edge, her eyes suddenly shrouded in glass and plastic, inviolable.

'Another press briefing tomorrow, Gill?' said Stevens, searching through his pockets for his cigarettes, lost long before.

'Yes.'

The reporter's hand found Rebus's shoulder.

'A long way, me and Gill.'

Then he was gone, his hand held back towards them as he retreated, waving without the necessity of acknowledgement, searching out his cigarettes, filing away John Rebus's face.

Gill Templer sighed, leaning against the wall where Stevens' failed kiss had landed.

'One of the best reporters in Scotland,' she said, matter-of-factly.

'And your job is dealing with the likes of him?'

'He's not so bad.'

An argument seemed to be starting in the living-room.

'Well,' said Rebus, all smiles, 'shall we phone for the police, or would you rather be taken to a little restaurant I know?'

'Is that a chat-up line?'

'Maybe. You tell me. After all, you're the detective.'

'Well, whatever it is, Detective Sergeant Rebus, you're in luck. I'm starving. I'll get my coat.'

Rebus, feeling pleased with himself, remembered that his own coat was lurking somewhere. He found it in one of the bedrooms, along with his gloves, and – a cracking surprise – his unopened bottle of wine. He pocketed this, seeing it as a divine sign that he would be needing it later.

Gill was in the other bedroom, rummaging through the pile of coats on the bed. Beneath the bedcovers, congress seemed to be taking place, and the whole mess of coats and bedclothes seethed and writhed like some gigantic amoeba. Gill, giggling through it all, found her coat at last and came towards Rebus, who smiled conspiratorially in the doorway.

'Goodbye, Cathy,' she shouted back into the room, 'thanks for the party.'

There was a muffled roar, perhaps an acknowledgement, from beneath the bedclothes. Rebus, his eyes wide, felt his moral fibre crumbling like a dry cheese-biscuit.

In the taxi, they sat a little distance apart.

'So, do you and this Stevens character go back a long way?'

'Only in his memory.' She stared past the driver at the sleek wet road beyond. 'Jim's memory can't be what it was. Seriously, we went out together once, and I do mean once.' She held up a finger. 'A Friday night, I think it was. A big mistake, it certainly was.'

Rebus was satisfied with that. He began to feel hungry again.

By the time they reached the restaurant, however, it was closed – even to Rebus – so they stayed in the taxi and Rebus directed the driver towards his flat.

'I'm a dab hand at bacon sandwiches,' he said.

'What a pity,' she said. 'I'm a vegetarian.'

'Good God, you mean you eat no vegetables at all?'

'Why is it,' acid seeping into her voice, 'that carnivores always have to make a joke out of it? It's the same with men and women's lib. Why is that?'

'It's because we're afraid of them,' said Rebus, quite sober now.

Gill looked at him, but he was watching from his window as the city's late-night drunks rolled their way up and down the obstacle-strewn hazard of Lothian Road, seeking alcohol, women, happiness. It was a never-ending search for some of them, staggering in and out of clubs and pubs and take-aways, gnawing on the packaged bones of existence. Lothian Road was Edinburgh's dustbin. It was also home to the Sheraton Hotel and the Usher Hall. Rebus had visited the Usher Hall once, sitting with Rhona and the other smug souls listening to Mozart's Requiem Mass. It was typical of Edinburgh to have a crumb of culture sited amidst the fast-food shops. A requiem mass and a bag of chips.

'So how is the old Press Liaison these days?'

They were seated in his rapidly tidied living-room. His pride and joy, a Nakamichi tape-deck, was tastefully broadcasting one of his collection of late-night-listening jazz tapes; Stan Getz or Coleman Hawkins.

He had rustled up a round of tuna fish and tomato sandwiches, Gill having admitted that she ate fish occasionally. The bottle of wine was open, and he had prepared a pot of freshly ground coffee (a treat usually reserved for Sunday breakfasts). He now sat across from his guest, watching her eat. He thought with a small start that this was his first female guest since Rhona had left him, but then recalled, very vaguely, a couple of other one-nighters.

'Press Liaison is fine. It's not really a complete waste of time, you know. It serves a useful purpose in this day and age.'

'Oh, I'm not knocking it.'

She looked at him, trying to gauge how serious he was being.

'Well,' she went on, 'it's just that I know a lot of our colleagues who think that a job like mine is a complete waste of time and manpower. Believe me, in a case like this one it's absolutely crucial that we keep the media on *our* side, and that we let them have the information that we want made public *when* it needs to be made public. It saves a lot of hassle.'

'Hear, hear.'

'Be serious, you rat.'

Rebus laughed.

'I'm never anything other than serious. A one-hundred percent policeman's policeman, that's me.'

Gill Templer stared at him again. She had a real inspector's eyes: they worked into your conscience, sniffing out guilt and guile and drive, seeking give.

'And being a Liaison Officer,' said Rebus, 'means that you have to . . . liaise with the press quite closely, right?'

'I know what you're getting at, Sergeant Rebus, and as your superior, I'm telling you to stop it.'

'Ma'am!' Rebus gave her a short salute.

He came back from the kitchen with another pot of coffee.

'Wasn't that a dreadful party?' said Gill.

'It was the finest party I have ever attended,' said Rebus. 'After all, without it, I might never have met you.'

She roared with laughter this time, her mouth filled with a paste of tuna and bread and tomato.

'You're a nutter,' she cried, 'you really are.'

Rebus raised his eyebrows, smiling. Had he lost his touch? He had not. It was miraculous.

Later, she needed to go to the bathroom. Rebus was changing a tape, and realising how limited his musical tastes were. Who were these groups that she kept referring to?

'It's in the hall,' he said. 'On the left.'

When she returned, more jazz was playing, the music at times almost too low to be heard, and Rebus was back in his chair.

'What's that room across from the bathroom, John?'

'Well,' he said, pouring coffee, 'it used to be my daughter's, but now it's just full of junk. I never use it.'

'When did your wife and you split up?'

'Not as long ago as we should have. I mean that seriously.'

'How old is your daughter?' She sounded maternal now, domestic; no longer the acid single woman or the professional.

'Nearly twelve,' he said. 'Nearly twelve.'

'It's a difficult age.'

'Aren't they all.'

When the wine was finished and the coffee was down to its last half-cup, one or the other of them suggested bed. They exchanged sheepish smiles and ritual promises about not promising anything, and, the contract agreed and signed without words, went to the bedroom.

It all started well enough. They were mature, had played this game before too often to let the little fumblings and apologies get to them. Rebus was impressed by her agility and invention, and hoped that she was being impressed by his. She arched her spine to meet him, seeking the ultimate and unobtainable ingress.

'John,' pushing at him now.

'What is it?'

'Nothing. I'm just going to turn over, okay?'

He knelt up, and she turned her back to him, sliding her knees down the bed, clawing at the smooth wall with her fingertips, waiting. Rebus, in the slight pause, looked around at the room, the pale blue light shading his books, the edges of the mattress.

'Oh, a futon,' she had said, pulling her clothes off quickly. He had smiled in the silence.

He was losing it.

'Come on, John. Come on.'

He bent towards her, resting his face on her back. He had talked about books with Gordon Reeve when they had been captured. Talked endlessly, it seemed, reading to him from his memory. In close confinement, torture a closed door away. But they had endured. It was a mark of the training.

'John, oh, John.'

Gill raised herself up and turned her head towards his, seeking a kiss. Gill, Gordon Reeve, seeking something from him, something he couldn't give. Despite the training, despite the years of practice, the years of work and persistence.

'John?'

But he was elsewhere now, back inside the training camp, back trudging across a muddy field, the Boss screaming at him to speed up, back in that cell, watching a cockroach pace the begrimed floor, back in the helicopter, a bag over his head, the spray of the sea salty in his ears ...

'John?'

She turned round now, awkwardly, concerned. She saw the tears about to start from his eyes. She held his head to her.

'Oh, John. It doesn't matter. Really, it doesn't.'

And a little later: 'Don't you like it that way?'

They lay together afterwards, he guiltily, and cursing the facts of his confusion and the fact that he had run out of cigarettes, she drowsily, caring still, whispering bits and pieces of her life-story to him.

After a while, Rebus forgot to feel guilty: there was nothing, after all, to feel guilty about. He felt merely the distinct lack of nicotine. And he remembered that he was seeing Sammy in six hours' time, and that her mother would instinctively know what he, John Rebus, had been up to these past few hours. She was cursed with a witch-like ability to see into the soul, and she had seen his occasional bouts of crying at very close quarters indeed. Partly, he supposed, that had been responsible for their break-up.

'What time is it, John?'

'Four. Maybe a little after.'

He slid his arm from beneath her and rose to leave the room.

'Do you want anything to drink?' he said.

'What did you have in mind?'

'Coffee maybe. It's hardly worth going to sleep now, but if you feel sleepy, don't mind me.'

'No, I'll take a cup of coffee.'

Rebus knew from her voice, from its slurred growliness, that she would be fast asleep by the time he reached the kitchen.

'Okay,' he said.

He made himself a cup of dark, sweet coffee and slumped into a chair with it. He turned on the living-room's small gas fire and began to read one of his books. He was seeing Sammy today, and his mind wandered from the story in front of him, a tale of intrigue which he could not remember having started. Sammy was nearly twelve. She had survived many years of danger, and now, for her, other dangers were imminent. The perverts in watch, the ogling old men, the teenage cockfighters, would be supplemented by the new urges of boys her age, and boys she already knew as friends would become sudden and forceful hunters. How would she cope with it? If her mother had anything to do with it, she would cope admirably, biting in a clinch and ducking on the ropes. Yes, she would survive without her father's advice and protection.

The kids were harder these days. He thought back to his own youth. He had been Mickey's big brother, fighting battles for the two of them, going home to watch his brother coddled by his father. He had pushed himself further into the cushions on the settee, hoping to disappear one day. Then they'd be sorry. Then they'd be sorry . . .

At seven-thirty he went through to the musky bedroom, which smelt two parts sex to one part animal lair, and kissed Gill awake.

'It's time,' he said. 'Get up, I'll run you a bath.'

She smelt good, like a baby on a fireside towel. He admired the shapes of her twisted body as they awoke to the thin, watery sunlight. She had a good body all right. No real stretch-marks. Her legs unscarred. Her hair just tousled enough to be inviting.

'Thanks.'

She had to be at HQ by ten in order to co-ordinate the next press release. There could be no rest. The case was still growing like a cancer. Rebus filled the bath, wincing at the rim of grime around it. He needed a cleaning-lady. Perhaps he could get Gill to do it.

Another unworthy thought, forgive me.

Which brought him to think of church-going. It was another Sunday, after all, and for weeks he had been promising himself that he would try again, would find another church in the city and would try all over again.

He hated congregational religion. He hated the smiles and the manners of the Sunday-dressed Scottish Protestant, the emphasis on a communion not with God but with your neighbours. He had tried seven churches of varying denominations in Edinburgh, and had found none to be to his liking. He had tried sitting for two hours at home of a Sunday, reading the Bible and saying a prayer, but somehow that did not work either. He was caught; a believer outwith his belief. Was a personal faith good enough for God? Perhaps, but not *his* personal faith, which seemed to depend upon guilt and his feelings of hypocrisy whenever he sinned, a guilt assuaged only by public show.

'Is my bath ready, John?'

She re-tousled her hair, naked and confident, her glasses left behind in the bedroom. John Rebus felt his soul to be imperilled. Sod it, he thought, catching her around the hips. Guilt could wait. Guilt could always wait.

*

61

He had to mop up the bathroom floor afterwards, empirical evidence that Archimedes' displacement of water had been proved once again. The bath-water had flowed like milk and honey, and Rebus had nearly drowned.

Still, he felt better now.

'Lord, I am a poor sinner,' he whispered, as Gill dressed. She looked stern and efficient when she opened the front-door, almost as if she had been on a twenty-minute official visit.

'Can we fix a date?' he suggested.

'We can,' she replied, looking through her bag. Rebus was curious to know why women always did that, especially in films and thrillers, after they had been sleeping with a man. Did women suspect their sleeping partners of rifling their purses?

'But it might be difficult,' she continued, 'the case going the way it is. Let's just promise to keep in touch, okay?'

'Okay.'

He hoped that she took note of the dismay in his voice, the disappointment of the small boy at having his request denied.

They pecked a final kiss, mouths brittle by now, and then she was gone. Her scent remained, however, and he breathed it in deeply as he prepared for the day ahead. He found a shirt and a pair of trousers that didn't reek of tobacco, and these he put on slowly, admiring himself in the bathroom mirror, the soles of his feet damp, while he hummed a hymn.

Sometimes it was good to be alive. Sometimes.

11

Jim Stevens poured another three aspirin into his mouth and drank his orange juice. The ignominy of it, being seen in a Leith bar sucking on fruit juice, yet the idea of drinking even a half-pint of the rich, frothing beer made him feel nauseous. He had drunk far too much at that party; too much too quickly, and in too many combinations.

Leith was trying to improve itself. Someone somewhere had decided to give it a bit of a dust and a wash. It boasted French-style cafés and wine bars, studio flats, delicatessen. But it was still Leith, still the old port, an echo of its roaring, bustling past when Bordeaux wines would be unloaded by the gallon and sold on the streets from a horse and cart. If Leith retained nothing else, it would retain a port's mentality, and a port's traditional drinking dens.

'By Christ,' roared a voice behind him, 'the man drinks everything in doubles, even his soft drinks!'

A heavy fist, twice the dimensions of his own, landed on Stevens' back. The swarthy figure landed on a stool beside him. The hand stayed firmly where it was.

'Hello, Podeen,' said Stevens. He was starting to sweat in the heavy atmosphere of the saloon, and his heart was pounding: terminal hangover symptoms; he could smell the alcohol squeezing itself out of his pores.

'Lordy, James me boy, what the hell's that you're supping? Barman, get this man a whisky quick. He's wasting away on kiddies' juice!'

With a roar, Podeen took his hand off the reporter's back just long enough to relieve the pressure, before bringing it back down again in a stinging back-slap. Stevens felt his insides shudder rebelliously.

'Anything I can do for you today?' said Podeen, his voice much lower.

Big Podeen had been a sailor for twenty years, with the scars and nicks of a thousand ports on his body. How he made his money these days, Stevens did not wish to know. He did some bouncing for pubs on

Lothian Road and dubious drinking-dens around Leith, but that would be the tip of his earnings iceberg. Podeen's fingers were so encrusted with dirt that he might have carved out the black economy single-handedly from the rotten, fertile soil beneath him.

'Not really, Big Man. No, I'm just mulling things over.'

'Get me a breakfast, will you? Double helpings of everything.'

The barman, almost saluting, went off to give the order.

'See,' said Podeen, 'you're not the only man who orders everything in doubles, eh, Jimmy?'

The hand was lifted from Stevens' back again. He grimaced, waiting for the slap, but the arm flopped onto the bar beside him instead. He sighed, audibly.

'Rough night last night was it, Jimmy?'

'I wish I could remember.'

He had fallen asleep in one of the bedrooms, very late in the evening. Then a couple had come in, and they had lifted him into the bathroom, depositing him in the bath. There he had slept for two hours, maybe three. He had awakened with a terrific stiffness in his neck, back, and legs. He had drunk some coffee, but not enough, never enough.

And had walked in the chilled morning air, chatting in a newsagent's shop with some taxi-drivers, sitting in the porter's cubby-hole of one of the big hotels on Princes Street, supping sweet tea and talking football with the bleary nightporter. But he had known he would end up down here, for this was his morning off, and he was back on the drugs case, his own little baby.

'Is there much stuff around at the moment, Big?'

'Oh, now, that depends what you're looking for, Jimmy. Word's out that you're getting to be a bit too nosy in every department. Best if you were sticking to the safe drugs. Keep away from the big stuff.'

'Is this a timely warning or a threat or what?' Stevens wasn't in the mood to be threatened, not when he had a Sunday morning hangover to sort out.

'It's a *friendly* warning, a warning from a friend.'

'Who's the friend, Big?'

'Me, you silly sod. Don't be so suspicious all the time. Listen, there's a little cannabis around, but that's about it. Nobody brings the stuff into Leith any more. They land it on the Fife coast, or up by Dundee. Places the Customs men have all but disappeared from. And that's the truth.'

'I know, Big, I know. But there *is* a delivery going on around here.

I've seen it. I don't know what it is. Whether it's big stuff or not. But I've seen a handover. Very recently.'

'How recent?'

'Yesterday.'

'Where?'

'Calton Hill.'

Big Podeen shook his head.

'Then it's nothing at all to do with anyone or anything I know, Jimmy.'

Stevens knew the Big Man, knew him well. He gave out good information, but it was only what was given to him by people who wanted Stevens to get to know about something. So the heroin boys would come across, via Big, with information about cannabis dealing. If Stevens took the story up, chances were the cannabis dealers would be caught. And that left the territory and the demand to the heroin boys. It was clever stuff, ploy and counter-ploy. The stakes were high, too. But Stevens was a clever player himself. He knew that there was a tacit understanding that he was never to aim for the really big players, for that would mean aiming for the city's businessmen and bureaucrats, the titled landowners, the New Town's Mercedes owners.

And that would never be allowed. So he was fed tidbits, enough to keep the presses rolling, the tongues wagging about what a terrible place Edinburgh was becoming. Always a little, never the lot. Stevens understood all that. He had been playing the game so long he hardly knew sometimes what side he was on. In the end, it hardly mattered.

'You don't know about it?'

'Nothing, Jimmy. But I'll nose around. See what's doing. Listen, though, there's a new bar opened up by the Mackay showroom. Know the one I mean?'

Stevens nodded.

'Well,' went on Podeen, 'it's a bar at the front, but it's a brothel at the back. There's a wee cracker of a barmaid does her stuff of an afternoon, if you're interested.'

Stevens smiled. So a new boy was trying to move in, and the old boys, Podeen's ultimate employers, didn't like it. And so he, Jim Stevens, was being given enough information to close down the new boy if he liked. There was a nice headline-catcher in it certainly, but it was a one-day wonder.

Why didn't they just telephone the police anonymously? He thought he knew the answer to that one, though once it had puzzled him: they were playing the game by its old-fashioned rules, which meant no snitching, no grassing to the enemy. He was left to play the part of messenger-boy, but a messenger-boy with power built into the system. Just a little power, but more power than lay in doing things along the straight and narrow.

'Thanks, Big. I'll bear that in mind.'

The food arrived then, great piles of curled, shining bacon, two soft, near-transparent eggs, mushrooms, fried bread, beans. Stevens kept his eyes to the bar, suddenly interested in one of the beer-mats, damp still from Saturday night.

'I'm going across to my table to eat this, okay, Jimmy?'

Stevens could not believe his good luck.

'Oh, fine, Big Man, fine.'

'Cheers, then.'

And with that he was left alone, only the ghost of a smell remaining. He noticed that the barman was standing opposite him. His hand, shiny with grease, was held out.

'Two pounds sixty,' he said.

Stevens sighed. Put that one down to experience, he thought to himself as he paid, or to the hangover. The party had been worth it, however, for he had met John Rebus. And Rebus was friendly with Gill Templer. It was all becoming just a little confusing. But interesting too. Rebus was certainly interesting, though physically he did not resemble his brother in the slightest. The man had looked honest enough, but how did you tell a bent copper from the outside? It was the inside that was rotten. So, Rebus was seeing Gill Templer. He remembered the night they had spent together, and shuddered. That, surely, had been his nadir.

He lit a cigarette, his second of the day. His head was still clotted, but his stomach felt a little more composed. He might even be getting hungry. Rebus looked a tough nut, but not as tough as he would have been ten years ago. At this moment he was probably in bed with Gill Templer. The bastard. The lucky bastard. His stomach turned a tiny somersault of chilled jealousy. The cigarette felt good. It poured life and strength back into him, or seemed to. Yet he knew that it was scooping him out, too, tearing his guts to shreds of darkened meat. The hell with it. He smoked because without cigarettes he couldn't think. And he was thinking now.

'Hey, give me a double here will you?'

The barman came over.

'Orange juice again?'

Stevens looked at him disbelievingly.

'Don't be daft,' he said – 'whisky, Grouse if that's what's in the Grouse bottle.'

'We don't play those sorts of games here.'

'I'm glad to hear it.'

He drank the whisky and felt better. Then he began to feel worse again. He went to the toilet, but the smell in there made him feel even worse. He held himself over the sink and brought up a few bubbles of liquid, retching loudly but emptily. He had to get off the booze. He had to get off the ciggies. They were killing him, yet they were the only things keeping him alive.

He walked over to Big Podeen's table, sweating, feeling older than his years.

'That was a good breakfast, that was,' said the hulk of a man, his eyes gleaming like a child's.

Stevens sat down beside him.

'What's the word on bent coppers?' he asked.

12

'Hello, Daddy.'

She was eleven, but looked and spoke and smiled older: eleven going on twenty-one. That was what living with Rhona had done to his daughter. He pecked her cheek, thinking back to Gill's leavetaking. There was perfume around her, and a hint of make-up on her eyes. He could kill Rhona.

'Hello, Sammy,' he said.

'Mummy says that I'm to be called Samantha now that I'm growing up so quickly, but I suppose it's all right for *you* to call me Sammy.'

'Oh, well, Mummy knows best, Samantha.'

He cast a look towards the retreating figure of his wife, her body pressed, pushed and prodded into a shape attainable only with the aid of some super-strong girdle. She was not, he was relieved to find, wearing as well as their occasional telephone conversations would have had him believe. She stepped into her car now, never looking back. It was a small and expensive model, but had a sizeable dent in one side. Rebus blessed that dent.

He recalled that, making love, he had gloried in her body, in the soft flesh – the padding, as she had called it – of her thighs and her back. Today she had looked at him with cold eyes, filled with a cloud of unknowing, and had seen in his eyes the gleam of sexual satisfaction. Then she had turned on her heels. So it was true: she could still see into his heart. Ah, but she had failed to see into his soul. She had missed that most vital organ completely.

'What do you want to do then?'

They were standing at the entrance to Princes Street Gardens, adjacent to the tourist haunts of Edinburgh. A few people wandered past the closed shops of a Princes Street Sunday, while others sat on benches in the gardens, feeding crumbs to the pigeons and the Canadian squirrels or else reading the heavy-printed Sunday papers. The Castle reared above them, its flag flying briskly in the all-too-typical breeze. The Gothic missile of the Scott Monument pointed religious believers in the right direction, but few of the tourists who snapped it with their expensive Japanese cameras seemed at all interested in the structure's symbolic connotations, never mind its reality, just so long as they had some snaps of it to show off to their friends back home. These tourists spent so much time photographing things that they never actually *saw* anything, unlike the young people milling around, who were too busy enjoying life to be bothered capturing false impressions of it.

'What do you want to do then?'

The tourist side of his capital city. They were never interested in the housing-estates around this central husk. They never ventured into Pilton or Niddrie or Oxgangs to make an arrest in a piss-drenched tenement; they were not moved by Leith's pushers and junkies, the deft-handed corruption of the city gents, the petty thefts of a society pushed so far into materialism that stealing was the only answer to what they thought of as their needs. And they were almost certainly unaware (they were not, after all, here to read local newspapers and watch local TV) of Edinburgh's newest media star, the child murderer the police could not catch, the murderer who was leading the forces of law and order a merry dance without a clue or a lead or a cat in hell's chance of finding him until he slipped up. He pitied Gill her job. He pitied himself. He pitied the city, right down to its crooks and bandits, its whores and gamblers, its perpetual losers and winners.

'So what do you want to do?'

His daughter shrugged her shoulders.

'I don't know. Walk maybe? Go for a pizza? See a film?'

They walked.

John Rebus had met Rhona Phillips just after joining the police. He had suffered a nervous breakdown just prior to his joining the force (*why did you leave the Army, John?*) and had recuperated in a fishing-village on the Fife coast, though he had never told Michael of his presence in Fife during that time.

On his first holiday from police-work, his first proper *holiday* in years, the others having been spent on courses or working towards examinations, Rebus had returned to that fishing-village, and there had met Rhona. She was a school-teacher, already with a brutally short and unhappy marriage behind her. In John Rebus she saw a strong and able husband, someone who would not flinch in a fight; someone she could care for, too, however, since his strength failed to conceal an inner fragility. She saw that he was haunted still by his years in the Army, and especially by his time in 'special services'. He would awake crying some nights, and sometimes would weep as he made love, weeping silently, the tears falling hard and slow on her breasts. He would not speak about it much, and she had never pushed him. She was aware that he had lost a friend during his training days. She understood that much, and he appealed to the child in her and to the mother. He seemed perfect. Too, too perfect.

He was not. He should never have married. They lived happily enough, she teaching English in Edinburgh until Samantha was born. Then, however, niggling fights and power-plays had turned into sourer, unabated periods of resentment and suspicion. Was she seeing another man, a teacher at her school? Was he seeing another woman when he claimed to be involved in his numerous double-shifts? Was she taking drugs without his knowledge? Was he taking bribes without hers? In fact, the answer to all of these suspicions was no, but that did not seem to be what was at stake in any case. Rather, something larger was looming, yet neither could perceive the inevitability of it until too late, and they would cuddle up and make things right between them over and over again, as though in some morality-tale or soap-opera. There was, they agreed, the child to think of.

The child, Samantha, had become the young woman, and Rebus felt his eyes straying appreciatively and guiltily (yet again) over her as they walked through the gardens, around the Castle, and up towards the ABC cinema on Lothian Road. She was not beautiful, for only women could be that, but she was growing towards beauty with a confident inevitability which was breathtaking in itself, and horrifying. He was, after all, her father. There had to be some feelings there. It went with the territory.

'Do you want me to tell you about Mummy's new boy-friend?'

'You know damn well I do.'

She giggled; still something of the girl left in her then, and yet even a giggle seemed different in her now, seemed more controlled, more womanly.

'He's a poet, supposedly, but really he hasn't had a book out or anything yet. His poems are crap, too, but Mummy won't tell him that. She thinks the sun shines out of his you-know-where.'

Was all this 'adult' talk supposed to impress him? He supposed so.

'How old is he?' Rebus asked, flinching at his suddenly revealed vanity.

'I don't know. Twenty maybe.'

He stopped flinching and started to reel. Twenty. She was cradle-snatching now. My God. What effect was all this having on Sammy? On Samantha, the pretend adult? He dreaded to think, but he was no psychoanalyst; that was Rhona's department, or once had been.

'Honest though, Dad, he's an *awful* poet. I've done better stuff than his in my essays at school. I go to the big school after the summer. It'll be funny to go to the school where Mum works.'

'Yes, won't it.' Rebus had found something niggling him. A poet, aged twenty. 'What's this boy's name?' he asked.

'Andrew,' she said, 'Andrew Anderson. Doesn't that sound funny? He's nice really, but he's a bit weird.'

Rebus cursed under his breath: Anderson's son, the dreaded Anderson's itinerant poet son was shacked up with Rebus's wife. What an irony! He didn't know whether to laugh or cry. Laughter seemed marginally more appropriate.

'What are you laughing at, Daddy?'

'Nothing, Samantha. I'm just happy, that's all. What were you saying?'

'I was saying that Mum met him at the library. We go there a lot. Mum likes the literature books, but I like books about romances and adventures. I can never understand the books Mum reads. Did you read the same books as her when you were ... before you ...?'

'Yes, yes we did. But I could never understand them either, so don't worry about it. I'm glad that you read a lot. What's this library like?'

'It's really big, but a lot of tramps go there to sleep and spend a lot of time. They get a book and sit down and just fall asleep. They smell awful!'

'Well, you don't need to go near them, do you? Best to let them keep themselves to themselves.'

'Yes, Daddy.' Her tone was slightly reproachful, warning him that he was giving fatherly advice and that such advice was unnecessary.

'Fancy seeing a film then, do you?'

The cinema, however, was not open, so they went to an ice-cream parlour at Tollcross. Rebus watched Samantha scoop five colours of ice-cream from a Knickerbocker Glory. She was still at the stick-insect stage, eating without putting on an ounce of weight. Rebus was conscious of his sagging waistband, a stomach pampered and allowed to roam as it pleased. He sipped cappuccino (without sugar) and watched from the corner of his eye as a group of boys at another table looked towards his daughter and him, whispering and sniggering. They pushed back their hair and smoked their cigarettes as though sucking on life itself. He would have arrested them for self-afflicted growth-stunting had Sammy not been there.

Also, he envied them their cigarettes. He did not smoke when with Sammy: she did not like him smoking. Her mother also, once upon a time, had screamed at him to stop, and had hidden his cigarettes and lighter, so that he had made secret little nests of cigarettes and matches all around the house. He had smoked on regardless, laughing in victory when he sauntered into the room with another lit cigarette between his lips, Rhona screeching at him to put the bloody thing out, chasing him around the furniture, her hands flapping to knock the incendiary from his mouth.

Those had been happy times, times of loving conflict.

'How's school?'

'It's okay. Are you involved in the murder case?'

'Yes.' God, he could murder for a cigarette, could tear a young male head from its body.

'Will you catch him?'

'Yes.'

'What does he do to the girls, Daddy?' Her eyes, trying to seem casual, examined the near-empty ice-cream glass very scrupulously.

'He doesn't do anything to them.'

'Just murders them?' Her lips were pale. Suddenly she was very much his child, his daughter, very much in need of protection. Rebus wanted to put his arms around her, to comfort her, to tell her that the big bad world was out there, not in here, that she was safe.

'That's right,' he said instead.

'I'm glad that's all he does.'

The boys were whistling now, trying to attract her attention. Rebus felt his face growing red. On another day, any day other than this, he would march up to them and ram the law into their chilled little faces. But he was off-duty. He was enjoying an afternoon out with his daughter, the freakish result of a single grunted climax, that climax which had seen a lucky sperm, crawling through the ooze, make it all the way to the winning-post. Doubtless Rhona would already be reaching over for her book of the day, her literature. She would prise the still, spent body of her lover from her without a word being passed between them. Was her mind on her books all the time? Perhaps. And he, the lover, would feel deflated and empty, a vacant space, but suddenly as if no form of transference had taken place. That was her victory.

And then he would scream at her with a kiss. The scream of longing, of his solitary.

Let me out Let me out . . .

'Come on, let's get out of here.'

'Okay.'

And as they passed the table of hankering boys, their faces full of barely restrained lust, jabbering like monkeys, Samantha smiled at one of them. *She smiled at one of them.*

Rebus, sucking in fresh air, wondered what his world was coming to. He wondered whether his reason for believing in another reality behind this one might not be because the everyday was so frightening and so very sad. If this were all there was, then life was the sorriest invention of all time. He could kill those boys, and he wanted to smother his daughter, to protect her from that which she wanted – and would get. He realised that he had nothing to say to her, and that those boys did; that he had nothing in common with her save blood, while they had everything in common with her. The skies were dark as Wagnerian opera, dark as a murderer's thoughts. Darkening like similes, while John Rebus's world fell apart.

'It's time,' she said, by his side yet so much bigger than him, so much more full of life. 'It's time.'

And indeed it was.

'We better hurry,' said Rebus, 'it's going to rain.'

He felt tired, and recalled that he had not slept, that he had been involved in strenuous labour throughout the short night. He took a taxi back to the flat – sod the expense – and crawled up the winding stairs to his front door. The smell of cats was overpowering. Inside his door, a letter, unstamped, awaited him. He swore out loud. The bastard was everywhere, everywhere and yet invisible. He ripped open the letter and read.

YOU'RE GETTING NOWHERE. NOWHERE. ARE YOU? SIGNED

But there was no signature, not in writing anyway. But inside the envelope, like some child's plaything, lay the piece of knotted twine.

'Why are you doing this, Mister Knot?' said Rebus, fingering the twine. 'And just what are you doing?'
Inside, the flat was like a fridge: the pilot-light had blown out again.

PART THREE
Knot

13

The media, sensing that the 'Edinburgh Strangler' was not about to vanish in the night, took the story by its horns and created a monster. TV crews moved into some of the better hotel rooms in the city, and the city was happy enough to have them, it being not quite the tourist season yet.

Tom Jameson was as astute an editor as any, and he had a team of four reporters working on the story. He could not help noticing, however, that Jim Stevens was not on his best form. He seemed uninterested – never a good sign in a journalist. Jameson was worried. Stevens was the best he had, a household name. He would speak to him about it soon.

As the case grew along with the interest in it, John Rebus and Gill Templer became confined to communicating by telephone and via the occasional chance meeting in or around HQ. Rebus hardly saw his old station now. He was strictly a murder-case victim himself, and was told to think about nothing else during his waking hours. He thought about everything else: about Gill, about the letters, about his car's inability to pass its MOT. And all the time he watched Anderson, father of Rhona's lover, watched him as he grew ever more frantic for a motive, a lead, anything. It was almost a pleasure to watch the man in action.

As to the letters, Rebus had pretty much discounted his wife and daughter. A slight mark on Knot's last missive had been checked by the forensic boys (for the price of a pint) and had turned out to be blood. Had the man nicked his finger while cutting the twine? It was yet another small mystery. Rebus's life was full of mysteries, not the least of which was where his ten legitimate daily cigarettes went. He would open his packet of a late afternoon, count the contents, and find that he was supposed to have smoked all ten of his ration already. It was absurd; he could hardly remember smoking one of the alloted ten, never mind all of them. Yet a count of the butts in his ashtray would

77

produce empirical evidence enough to withstand any denials on his part. Bloody strange though. It was as though he were shutting out a part of his waking life.

He was stationed in the HQ's Incident Room at the moment, while Jack Morton, poor sod, was on door-to-door. From his vantage point he could see how Anderson was running the shambles. It was little wonder the man's son had turned out to be less than bright. Rebus also had to deal with the many phone-calls – from those of the trying-to-be-helpfuls to those of the psychic-cranks-who-want-to-confess – and with the interviews carried out in the building itself at all hours of the day and night. There were hundreds of these, all to be filed and put into some kind of order of importance. It was a huge task, but there was always the chance that a lead would come from it, so he was not allowed to slack.

In the hectic, sweaty canteen he smoked cigarette number eleven, lying to himself that it was from the next day's ration, and read the daily paper. They were straining for new, shocked adjectives now, having exhausted their thesauruses. The appalling, mad, evil crimes of The Strangler. This insane, evil, sex-crazed man. (They did not seem to mind that the killer had never sexually assaulted his victims.) Gymslip Maniac! 'What are our police doing? All the technology in the world cannot replace the reassurance offered by bobbies on the beat. WE NEED THEM NOW.' That was from James Stevens, our crime correspondent. Rebus remembered the stocky drunk man from the party. He recalled the look on Stevens' face when he had been told Rebus's name. That was strange. Everything was bloody strange. Rebus put down the newspaper. Reporters. Again, he wished Gill well in her job. He studied the blurred photograph on the front of the tabloid. It showed a crop-haired, unintelligent child. She was grinning nervously, as though snapped at a moment's notice. There was a slight, endearing gap between her front teeth. Poor Nicola Turner, aged twelve, a pupil at one of the southside's comprehensive schools. She had no attachments to either of the other dead girls. There were no visible links between them, and what was more, the killer had moved up a year, choosing a High School kid this time. So there was to be no regularity about his choice of age-groups. The randomness continued unabated. It was driving Anderson nuts.

But Anderson would never admit that the killer had his beloved police force tied in knots. Tied in absolute knots. Yet there *had* to be clues. There had to be. Rebus drank his coffee and felt his head spin. He was feeling like the detective in a cheap thriller, and wished that he could turn to the last page and stop all his confusion, all the death and the madness and the spinning in his ears.

Back in the Incident Room, he gathered together reports of phone-calls that had come in since he had left for his break. The telephonists were working flat out, and near them a telex-machine was almost constantly printing out some new piece of information thought useful to the case and sent on by other forces throughout the country.

Anderson pushed his way through the noise as if swimming in treacle.

'A car is what we need, Rebus. A car. I want all the sightings of men driving away with children collated and on my desk in an hour. I want that bastard's car.'

'Yes, sir.'

And he was off again, wading through treacle deep enough to drown any normal human being. But not Indestructible Anderson, impervious to any danger. That made him a liability, thought Rebus, sifting through the piles of paper on his desk, which were meant to be in some system of order.

Cars. Anderson wanted cars, and cars he would have. There were swear-on-a-Bible descriptions of a man in a blue Escort, a white Capri, a purple Mini, a yellow BMW, a silver TR7, a converted ambulance, an ice-cream van (the telephone-caller sounding Italian and wishing to remain anonymous), and a great big Rolls-Royce with personalized number plates. Yes, let's put them all into the computer and have it run a check of every blue Escort, white Capri, and Rolls-Royce in Britain. And with all that information at our fingertips . . . then what? More door-to-door, more gathering of telephone-calls and interviews, more paperwork and bullshit. Never mind, Anderson would swim through it all, indomitable amidst all the craziness of his personal world, and at the end of it all he would come out looking clean and shiny and untouchable, like an advertisement for washing powder. Three cheers. Hip hip.

Rebus had not enjoyed bullshit during his Army days either, and there had been plenty of it then. But he had been a good soldier, a very good soldier, when finally they had got down to soldiering. But then, in a fit of madness, he had applied to join the Special Air Service, and there had been very little bullshit there, and an incredible amount of savagery. They had made him run from the railway station to the camp behind a sergeant in his jeep. They had tortured him with twenty-hour marches, brutal instructors, the works. And when Gordon Reeve and he had made the grade, the SAS had tested them just that little bit further, just that inch too far, confining them, interrogating them, starving them, poisoning them, and all for a little piece of worthless information, a few words that would show they had cracked. Two naked, shivering animals with sacks tied over their heads, lying together to keep warm.

'I want that list in an hour, Rebus,' called Anderson, walking past again. He would have his list. He would have his pound of flesh.

Jack Morton arrived back, looking foot-weary and not at all amused with life. He slouched across to Rebus, a sheaf of papers under his arm, a cigarette in the other hand.

'Look at this,' he said, lifting his leg. Rebus saw the foot-long gash in the material.

'What happened to you then?'

'What do you think? I got chased by a great fucking alsatian, that's what happened to me. Will I get a penny for this? Will I hell.'

'You could try claiming for it anyway.'

'What's the point? I'd just be made to look stupid.'

Morton dragged a chair across to the table.

'What are you working on?' he asked, seating himself with visible relief.

'Cars. Lots of them.'

'Fancy a drink later on?'

Rebus looked at his watch, considering.

'Might do, Jack. Thing is, I'm hoping to make a date for tonight.'

'With the ravishing Inspector Templer?'

'How did you know that?' Rebus was genuinely surprised.

'Come on, John. You can't keep that sort of thing a secret – not from policemen. Better watch your step, mind. Rules and regulations, you know.'

'Yes, I know. Does Anderson know about this?'

'Has he said anything?'

'No.'

'Then he can't, can he?'

'You'd make a good policeman, son. You're wasted in this job.'

'You're telling me, dad.'

Rebus busied himself with lighting cigarette number twelve. It was true, you couldn't keep anything secret in a police station, not from the lower ranks anyway. He hoped Anderson and the Chief wouldn't find out about it though.

'Any luck with the door-to-door?' he asked.

'What do you think?'

'Morton, you have an annoying habit of answering a question with another question.'

'Have I? It must be all this work then, spending my days asking questions, mustn't it?'

Rebus examined his cigarettes. He found he was smoking number thirteen. This was becoming ridiculous. Where had number twelve gone?

'I'll tell you, John, there's nothing to be had out there, not a sniff of a lead. No one's seen anything, no one knows anything. It's almost like a conspiracy.'

'Maybe that's what it is then, a conspiracy.'

'And has it been established that all three murders were the work of a single individual?'

'Yes.'

The Chief Inspector did not believe in wasting words, especially with the press. He sat like a rock behind the table, his hands clasped before him, Gill Templer on his right. Her glasses – an affectation really, her vision was near-perfect – were in her bag. She never wore them while on duty, unless the occasion demanded it. Why had she worn them to the party? They were like jewellery to her. She found it interesting, too, to gauge different reactions towards her when she was and was not wearing them. When she explained this to her friends, they looked at her askance as if she were joking. Perhaps it all went back to her first true love, who had told her that girls who wore glasses seemed, in his experience, to be the best fucks. That had been fifteen years ago, but she still saw the look on his face, the smile, the glint. She saw, too, her own reaction – shock at his use of the word 'fuck'. She could smile at that now. These days she swore as much as her male colleagues; again gauging their reaction. Everything was a game to Gill Templer, everything but the job. She had not become an inspector through luck or looks, but through hard, efficient work and the will to climb as high as they would let her go. And now she sat with her Chief Inspector, who was a token presence at these gatherings. It was Gill who made up the handouts, who briefed the Chief Inspector, who handled the media afterwards, and they all knew it. A Chief Inspector might add weight of seniority to the proceedings, but Gill Templer it was who could give the journalists their 'extras', the useful snippets left unsaid.

Nobody knew that better than Jim Stevens. He sat to the back of the room, smoking without removing the cigarette from his mouth once. He took little of the Chief Inspector's words in. He could wait. Still, he jotted down a sentence or two for future use. He was still a newsman after all. Old habits never died. The photographer, a keen teenager, nervously changing lenses every few minutes, had departed with his roll of film. Stevens looked around for someone he might have a drink with later on. They were all here. All the old boys from the Scottish press, and the English correspondents too. Scottish, English, Greek – it didn't matter, pressmen always looked like nothing other than pressmen. Their faces were robust, they smoked, their shirts were a day or two old. They did not look well-paid, yet were extremely well-paid, and with more fringe benefits than most. But they worked for their money, worked hard at building up contacts, squeezing into nooks and crannies, stepping on toes. He watched Gill Templer. What would she know about John Rebus? And would she be willing to tell? They were still friends after all, her and him. Still friends.

Maybe not good friends, certainly not good friends – though he had tried. And now she and Rebus . . . Wait until he nailed that bastard, if there *was* anything there to nail. Of course there was something there to nail. He could sense it. Then her eyes would be opened, truly opened. Then they would see what they would see. He was already preparing the headline. Something to do with 'Brothers in Law – Brothers in Crime!' Yes, that had a nice ring to it. The Rebus brothers put behind bars, and all his own work. He turned his attention back to the murder case. But it was all too easy, too easy to sit down and write about police inefficiency, about the conjectured maniac. Still, it was bread and butter for the moment. And there was always Gill Templer to stare at.

'Gill!'

He caught her as she was getting into her car.

'Hello, Jim.' Cold, businesslike.

'Listen, I just wanted to apologise for my behaviour at the party.' He was out of breath after a brief jog across the car park, and the words came slowly from his burning chest. 'I mean, I was a bit pissed. Anyway, sorry.'

But Gill knew him too well, knew that this was merely a prelude to a question or request. Suddenly she felt a little sorry for him, sorry for his fair thick hair which needed a wash, sorry for his short, stocky – she had once thought it powerful – body, for the way he trembled now and again as though cold. But the pity soon wore off. It had been a hard day.

'Why wait till now to tell me? You could have said something at Sunday's briefing.'

He shook his head.

'I didn't make Sunday's briefing. I was a bit hungover. You must have noticed I wasn't there?'

'Why should I have noticed that? Plenty of other people were there, Jim.'

That cut him, but he let it pass.

'Well, anyway,' he said, 'sorry. Okay?'

'Fine.' She made to step into her car.

'Can I buy you a drink or something? To cement the apology, so to speak.'

'Sorry, Jim, I'm busy.'

'Meeting that man Rebus?'

'Maybe.'

'Look after yourself, Gill. That one might not be what he seems.'

She straightened up again.

'I mean,' said Stevens, 'just take care, all right?'

He wouldn't say any more just yet. Having planted a seed of suspicion, he would give it time to grow. Then he would question her closely, and perhaps then she would be willing to tell. He turned away from her and walked, hands in pockets, towards the Sutherland Bar.

14

At Edinburgh's Main Public Lending Library, a large, unstuffy old building sandwiched between a bookshop and a bank, the tramps were settling down for a day's snoozing. They came here, as though waiting out fate itself, to see through the few days of absolute poverty before their next amount of state benefit was due. This money they would then spend in a day (perhaps, if stretched, two days) of festivity: wine, women, and songs to an unappreciative public.

The attitudes of the library staff towards these down-and-outs ranged from the immensely intolerant (usually voiced by the older members of staff) to the sadly reflective (the youngest librarians). It was, however, a public library, and as long as the worldly-wise travellers picked up a book at the start of the day there was nothing that could be done about them, unless they became rowdy, in which case a security-man was quickly on the scene.

So they slept in the comfortable seats, sometimes frowned upon by those who could not help wondering if this was what Andrew Carnegie had in mind when he put up the finance for the first public libraries all those years ago. The sleepers did not mind these stares, and they dreamed on, though nobody bothered to inquire what it was they dreamed of, and no one thought them important.

They were not, however, allowed into the children's section of the library. Indeed, any browsing adult not dragging a child in tow was looked at askance in the children's section, and especially since the murders of those poor wee girls. The librarians talked about it amongst themselves. Hanging was the answer; they were agreed on that. And indeed, hanging was being discussed again in Parliament, as happens whenever a mass murderer emerges out of the shadows of civilized Britain. The most oft-repeated statement amongst the people of Edinburgh, however, did not concern hanging at all. It was put cogently by one of the librarians: 'But *here*, in Edinburgh! It's unthinkable.' Mass murderers belonged to the smoky back streets of the South and the

Midlands, not to Scotland's picture-postcard city. Listeners nodded, horrified and sad that this was something they all had to face, each and every Morningside lady in her faded hat of gentility, every thug who roamed the streets of the housing-estates, every lawyer, banker, broker, shop-assistant and vendor of evening newspapers. Vigilante groups had been hastily set up and just as hastily disbanded by the swiftly reacting police. This was not, said the Chief Constable, the answer. Be vigilant by all means, but the law was never to be taken into one's own hands. He rubbed together his own gloved hands as he spoke, and some newspapermen wondered if his subconscious were not washing its Freudian hands of the whole affair. Jim Stevens' editor decided to put it thus: LOCK UP YOUR DAUGHTERS!, and left it pretty much at that.

Indeed, the daughters *were* being locked up. Some of them were being kept away from school by their parents, or were under heavy escort all the way there and all the way back home, with an additional check on their welfare at lunch-time. The children's section of the Main Lending Library had grown deathly quiet of late, so that the librarians there had little to do with their days except talk about hanging and read the lurid speculations in the British press.

The British press had cottoned on to the fact that Edinburgh had a rather less than genteel past. They ran reminders of Deacon Brodie (the inspiration, it was said, behind Stevenson's Jekyll & Hyde), Burke and Hare, and anything else that came to light in their researches, right down to the ghosts that haunted a suspicious number of the city's Georgian houses. These tales kept the imaginations of the librarians alive while there was a lull in their duties. They made sure each to buy a different paper, so that they could glean as many pieces of information as possible, but were disillusioned by how often journalists seemed to swap a central story between them, so that an identical piece would appear in two or three different papers. It was as if a conspiracy of writers was at work.

Some children, however, did still come to the library. The vast majority of these were accompanied by mother, father, or minder, but one or two still came alone. This evidence of the foolhardiness of some parents and their offspring further disturbed the faint-hearted librarians, who would ask the children, appalled, where their mothers and fathers were.

Samantha rarely came to the library's children's section, preferring older books, but she did so today to get away from her mother. A male librarian came over to her as she pored over the most childish stuff.

'Are you here on your own, dear?' he said.

Samantha recognised him. He'd been working here ever since she could remember.

'My mum's upstairs,' she said.

'I'm glad to hear it. Stick close to her, that's my advice.'

She nodded, inwardly fuming. Her mother had given her a similar lecture only five minutes before. She wasn't a child, but no one seemed prepared to accept that. When the librarian went over to talk with another girl, Samantha took out the book she wanted and gave her ticket to the old lady librarian with the dyed hair, whom the children called Mrs Slocum. Then she hurried up the steps to the library's reference section, where her mother was busy looking for a critical study of George Eliot. George Eliot, her mother had told her, was a woman who had written books of tremendous realism and psychological depth at a time when men were supposed to be the great realists and psychologists, and women were supposed to be for nothing but the housework. That was why she had been forced to call herself 'George' to get published.

To counter these attempts at indoctrination, Samantha had brought from the children's section an illustrated book about a boy who flies away on a giant cat and has adventures in a fantasy land beyond his dreams. That, she hoped, would piss her mother off. In the reference section, a lot of people sat at desks, coughing, their coughs echoing around the hushed hall. Her mother, glasses perched on her nose, looking very much like a schoolteacher, argued with a librarian about some book she had ordered. Samantha walked between the rows of desks, glancing at what people were reading and writing. She wondered why people spent so much time reading books when there were other things to be doing. She wanted to travel round the world. Perhaps then she would be ready to sit in dull rooms poring over these old books. But not until then.

He watched her as she moved up and down the rows of desks. He stood with his face half to her, looking as if he were studying a shelf of books on angling. She wasn't looking around her though. There was no danger. She was in her own little world, a world of her own design and her own rules. That was fine. All the girls were like that. But this one was with someone. He could see that. He took a book from the shelf and flicked through it. One chapter caught his eye, and turned his thoughts away from Samantha. It was a chapter dealing with fly-knotting. There were lots of designs for knots. Lots of them.

15

Another briefing. Rebus enjoyed the briefings now, for there was always the possibility that Gill would be present, and that afterwards they would be able to go for a cup of coffee together. Last night they had eaten late at a restaurant, but she had been tired and had looked at him strangely, quizzing him a little more even than usual with her eyes, not wearing her spectacles at first, but then slipping them on halfway through the meal.

'I want to see what I'm eating.'

But he knew she could see well enough. The glasses were a psychological strengthener. They protected her. Perhaps he was just being paranoid. Perhaps she had been tired merely. But he suspected something more, though he could not think what. Had he insulted her in some way? Snubbed her without realising? He was tired himself. They went to their separate flats and lay awake, wanting not to be alone. Then he dreamed the dream of the kiss, and awoke to the usual result, the sweat tainting his forehead, his lips moist. Would he awake to another letter? To another murder?

Now he felt lousy from lack of sleep. But still he enjoyed the briefing, and not just because of Gill. There was the inkling of a lead at long last, and Anderson was anxious to have it substantiated.

'A pale blue Ford Escort,' said Anderson. Behind him sat the Chief Superintendent, whose presence seemed to be unnerving the Chief Inspector. 'A pale blue Ford Escort.' Anderson wiped his brow. 'We have reports of such a car being seen in the Haymarket district on the evening when victim number one's body was found, and we have two sightings of a man and a girl, the girl apparently asleep, in such a car on the night that victim number three went missing.' Anderson's eyes came up from the document before him to gaze, it seemed, into the eyes of every officer present. 'I want this made top priority, or better. I want to know the ownership details of every blue Ford Escort in the Lothians, and I want that information *sooner* than possible. Now I know you've been working flat out as it is, but with a little extra push we can nail chummy before he does any more killing. To this end, Inspector Hartley has drawn up a roster. If your name's on it, drop what you're doing and get busy on tracing this car. Any questions?'

Gill Templer was scribbling notes in her tiny note-pad, perhaps concocting a story for the press. Would they want to release this? Probably not, not straight away. They would wait first to see if anything came of the initial search. If nothing did, then the public would be asked to help. Rebus didn't fancy this at all: gathering ownership details, trekking out to the suburbs, and mass-interviewing the suspects, trying to 'nose' whether they were probable or possible suspects, then perhaps a second interview. No, he did not fancy this at all. He fancied accompanying Gill Templer back to his cave and making love to her. Her back was all he could see of her from his present vantage point by the door. He had been last into the room yet again, having stayed at the pub a little longer than anticipated. It had been a prior appointment, lunch (liquid) with Jack Morton. Morton told him about the slow, steady progress of the outdoor inquiry: four-hundred people interviewed, whole families checked and rechecked, the usual cranks and amoral groups examined. And not a jot of actual light had been thrown on the case.

But now they had a car, or at least thought they did. The evidence was tenuous, but it was there, the likeness of a fact, and that was something. Rebus felt a little proud of his own part in the investigation, for it had been his painstaking cross-referencing of sightings which had thrown up this slender link. He wanted to tell Gill all about it, then arrange a rendezvous for later in the week. He wanted to see her again, to see anybody again, for his flat was becoming a prison-cell. He would slouch home of a late evening or early morning, tip onto his bed, and sleep, not bothering these days to tidy or to read or to buy (or even steal) any foodstuffs. He had neither the time nor the energy. Instead, he ate from kebab-houses and chip-shops, early-morning bakeries and chocolate-dispensers. His face was becoming paler than usual, and his stomach groaned as though there were no skin left to distend. He still shaved and put on a tie, as a matter of necessary propriety, but that was about it. Anderson had noticed that his shirts were not as clean as they might have been, but had said nothing so far. For one thing, Rebus was in his good books, begetter of the lead, and for another, anyone could see that in Rebus's present mood he was likely to take a swing at any detractor.

The meeting was breaking up. There were no questions in anyone's mind except the obvious one: when do we start cracking up? Rebus hovered just outside the door, waiting for Gill. She came out in the last group, in quiet conversation with Wallace and Anderson. The Superintendent had his arm around her waist playfully, gently ushering her out of the room. Rebus glared at the group, this motley crew of superior officers. He watched Gill's face, but she did not seem to notice him. Rebus felt himself slide back down the snake on the board, right down to the bottom line again, back into the heap. So this was love. Who was kidding who?

As the group of three walked up the corridor, Rebus stood there like a jilted teenager and cursed and cursed and cursed.

He'd been let down again. Let down.

Don't let me down, John. Please.

Please Please Please

And a screaming in his memory . . .

He felt dizzy, his ears ringing with the sea. Staggering a little, he caught hold of the wall, trying to take comfort in its solidity, but it seemed to be throbbing. He breathed hard, thinking back to his days on the rock-strewn beach, recovering from his breakdown. The sea had been in his ears then, too. The floor adjusted itself slowly. People walked by quizzically, but no one stopped to help. Sod them all. And sod Gill Templer too. He could manage on his own. He could manage on his own, God save him. He would be okay. All he needed was a cigarette and some coffee.

But really he needed their pats on the back, their congratulations on a job well done, their acceptance. He needed someone to assure him that it was all going to be all right.

That *he* would be all right.

That evening, a couple of after-duty drinks under his belt already, he decided to make a night of it. Morton had to go off on some errand, but that was okay, too. Rebus didn't need company. He walked along Princes Street, breathing in the evening's promise. He was a free man after all, just as free as any of the kids hanging about outside the hamburger bar. They preened and joked and waited, waiting for what? He knew that: waiting for the time to come when they could go home and sleep into tomorrow. He too was waiting, in his own way. Killing time.

In the Rutherford Arms he met a couple of drinkers whom he knew from evenings like this just after Rhona had left him. He drank with them for an hour, sucking at the beer as though it were mother's milk. They talked about football, about horse-racing, about their jobs, and the whole scene brought tranquillity to Rebus. It was a normal evening's conversation, and he embraced it greedily, throwing in his own snippets of news. But enough was as good as a feast, and he walked briskly, drunkenly out of the bar, leaving his friends with promises of another time, edging his way down the street towards Leith.

Jim Stevens, sitting at the bar, watched in the mirror as Michael Rebus left his drink on his table and went to the toilet. A few seconds later, the mystery man followed him inside, having been sitting at another table. It looked as though they were meeting to discuss the next swap-over, both seeming too casual actually to be carrying anything incriminating. Stevens smoked his cigarette, waiting. In less than a minute, Rebus reappeared, coming up to the bar for another drink.

John Rebus, pushing through the pub's swing-doors, could not believe his eyes. He slapped his brother on the shoulder.

'Mickey! What are you doing here?'

Michael Rebus nearly died at that moment. His heart leapt high into his throat, causing him to cough.

'Just having a drink, John.' But he looked guilty as hell, he was sure of that. 'You gave me a fright,' he went on, trying to smile, 'hitting me like that.'

'A brotherly slap, that's all it was. What are you drinking?'

While the brothers were in conversation, the man slipped out of the toilet and walked out of the bar, his eyes never glancing to left or right. Stevens watched him go, but had other things on his mind now. He could not let the policeman see him. He turned away from the bar, as if searching for a face amongst the people at the tables. Now he was sure. The policeman had to be in on it. The whole sequence of actions had been very slick indeed, but now he was sure.

'So you're doing a show down here?' John Rebus, cheered by his previous drinks, now felt that things were going right for a change. He was reunited with his brother for that drink they had always been promising themselves. He ordered whiskies with lager chasers. 'This is a quarter-gill pub,' he told Michael. 'That's a decent size of a measure.'

Michael smiled, smiled, smiled, as though his life depended upon it. His mind was racing and jumbled. The last thing he needed was another drink. If word of this got out, it would seem too unlikely to his

Edinburgh connection, too unlikely. He, Michael, would have his legs broken for this if it ever was to get out. He had been warned. And what was John doing here anyway? He seemed complacent enough, drunk even, but what if it were all a set-up? What if his connection had already been arrested outside? He felt as he had when, as a child, he had stolen money from his father's wallet, denying the crime for weeks afterwards, his heart heavy with guilt.

Guilty, guilty, guilty.

John Rebus meantime drank on and chatted, unaware of the sudden change of atmosphere, the sudden interest in him. All he cared about was the whisky in front of him and the fact that Michael was about to go off and do a show at a local bingo hall.

'Mind if I come along?' he asked. 'I might as well see how my brother earns his crust.'

'Sure,' said Michael. He toyed with the whisky glass. 'I'd better not drink this, John. I've got to keep my mind clear.'

'Of course you have. Need to let the mysterious sensations flood over you.' Rebus made an action with his hands as though hypnotising Michael, his eyes wide, smiling.

And Jim Stevens picked up his cigarettes and, his back to them still, left the smoky, noisy public house. If only it had been quieter in there. If only he could have heard what they were saying. Rebus saw him go.

'I think I know him,' he told Michael, gesturing towards the door with his head. 'He's a reporter on the local rag.'

Michael Rebus tried to smile, smile, smile, but it seemed to him that his world was falling apart.

The Rio Grande Bingo Hall had been a cinema. The front twelve rows of seats had been taken out and bingo boards and stools put in their place, but to the back of these were still many rows of dusty, red seats, and the balcony seating was completely intact. John Rebus said that he preferred to sit upstairs, so that he would not distract Michael. He followed an elderly man and his wife upstairs. The seats looked comfortable, but as he eased himself into the second row, Rebus felt springs jar against his buttocks. He moved around a little, trying to get comfortable, and settled finally for a position where one cheek supported most of his weight.

There seemed a good enough crowd downstairs, but up here in the gloom of the neglected balcony there were only the old couple and himself. Then he heard shoes tapping on the aisle. They paused for a second, before a hefty woman slid into the second row. Rebus was forced to look up, and saw her smiling at him.

'Mind if I sit here?' she said. 'Not waiting for anyone, are you?'

Her look was hopeful. Rebus shook his head, smiling politely. 'Thought not,' she said, sitting down beside him. And he smiling. He had never seen Michael smile so much, or so uneasily. Was it so embarrassing for him to meet his elder brother? No, there had to be more to it than that. Michael's had been the smile of the small-time thief, caught yet again. They needed to talk.

'I come here a lot to the bingo. But I thought this might be a good laugh, you know. Ever since my husband died,' meaningful pause, 'well, it's not been the same. I like to get out now and again, you know. Everybody does, don't they? So I thought I'd come along. Don't know what made me come upstairs. Fate, I suppose.' Her smile broadened. Rebus smiled back.

She was in her early forties, a little too much make-up and scent, but quite well-preserved. She talked as if she had not spoken to anyone in days, as if it were important for her to establish that she could still speak and be listened to and understood. Rebus felt sorry for her. He saw a little of himself in her; not much, but almost enough.

'So what are you doing here?' She was forcing him to speak.

'Just here for the show, same as you are.' He didn't dare say that his brother was the hypnotist. That would have left too many avenues for a response.

'You like this sort of thing, do you?'

'I've never been before.'

'Neither have I.' She smiled again, conspiratorially this time. She had found that they had something in common. Thankfully, the lights were going down – what lighting there was – and a spot had come up on the stage. Someone was introducing the show. The woman opened her handbag and produced a noisy bag of boiled sweets. She offered one to Rebus.

Rebus found himself, to his own surprise, enjoying the show, but not half as much as the woman beside him was. She howled with laughter as one willing participant, his trousers left on the stage, pretended to swim up and down the aisles. Another guinea-pig was made to believe that he was ravenously hungry. Another that she was a professional striptease artiste at one of her bookings. Another that he was falling asleep.

Still enjoying the show, Rebus began to nod off himself. It was the effect of too much alcohol, too little sleep, and the warm, broody darkness of the theatre. Only the final applause of the audience awoke him. Michael, sweating in his glittery stage suit, took the applause as though addicted to it, coming back for another bow when most of the people were leaving their seats. He had told his brother that he had to get home quickly, that he would not see him after the show, that he would phone him sometime for his reaction.

And John Rebus had slept through much of it.

He felt refreshed, however, and could hear himself accepting the perfumed woman's offer of a 'one for the road' drink at a local bar. They left the theatre arm-in-arm, smiling at something. Rebus felt relaxed, a child again. This woman was treating him like her son, really, and he was happy enough to be coddled. A final drink, and then he'd go home. Just one drink.

Jim Stevens watched them leave the theatre. It was becoming very strange indeed. Rebus seemed to be ignoring his brother now, and he had a woman with him. What did it all mean? One thing it meant was that Gill should be told about it at some opportune moment. Stevens, smiling, added it to his collection of such moments. It had been a good night's work so far.

So where in the evening had mother-love changed into physical contact? In that pub, perhaps, where her reddened fingers had bitten into his thigh? Outside in the cooling air when he wrapped his arms around her neck in a fumbled attempt at a kiss? Or here in her musty flat, smelling still of her husband, where Rebus and she lie across an old settee and exchange tongues?

No matter. It's too late to regret anything, and too early. So he slouches after her when she retires to her bedroom. He tumbles into the huge double-bed, springy and covered in thick blankets and quilts. He watches her undress in darkness. The bed feels like one he had as a kid, when a hot-water-bottle was all he had to keep the chill off, and mounds of gritty blankets, puffed-out quilts. Heavy and suffocating, tiring in themselves.

No matter.

Rebus did not enjoy the particulars of her heavy body, and was forced to think of everything in the abstract. His hands on her well-suckled breasts reminded him of late nights with Rhona. Her calves were thick, unlike Gill's, and her face was worn with too much living. But she was a woman, and she was with him, so he squeezed her into an abstract and tried to make them both happy. But the heaviness of the bedding oppressed him, caging him, making him feel small and trapped and isolated from the world. He fought against it, fought against the memory of Gordon Reeve and he as they sat in solitary, listening to the screams of those around them, but enduring, always enduring, and reunited finally. Having won. Having lost. Lost everything. His heart was pounding to her grunts, now some distance away it seemed. He felt the first wave of that absolute repulsion hit him in the stomach like a truncheon, and his hands slid around the hanging, yielding throat beneath him. The moans were inhuman now, cat-like, keening. His hands pushed a little, the fingers finding their own purchase against skin and sheet. They locked him up and they threw away the key. They pushed him to his death and they poisoned him. He should not have been alive. He should have died back then, back in the rank, animal cells with their power-hoses and their constant questionings. But he had survived. He had survived. And he was coming.

He alone, all alone
And the screaming
Screaming

Rebus became aware of the gurgling sounds beneath him just before his head started to fry. He fell over onto the gasping figure and lost consciousness. It was like a switch being flipped.

16

He awoke in a white room. It reminded him very much of the hospital room in which he had awoken after his nervous breakdown all those years ago. There were muffled noises from outside. He sat up, his head throbbing. What had happened? Christ, that woman, that poor woman. He had tried to kill her! Drunk, way too drunk. Merciful God, he had tried to strangle her, hadn't he? Why in God's name had he done that? Why?

A doctor pushed open his door.

'Ah, Mister Rebus. Good, you're awake. We're about to move you into one of the wards. How do you feel?'

His pulse was taken.

'Simple exhaustion, we think. Simple nervous exhaustion. Your friend who called for the ambulance—'

'My friend?'

'Yes, she said that you just collapsed. And from what we can gather from your employers, you've been working pretty hard on this dreadful murder hunt. Simple exhaustion. What you need is a break.'

'Where's my . . . my friend?'

'No idea. At home, I expect.'

'And according to her, I just collapsed?'

'That's right.'

Rebus felt immediate relief flooding through him. She had not told them. She had not told them. Then his head began to pulse again. The doctor's wrists were hairy and scrubbed clean. He slipped a thermometer into Rebus's mouth, smiling. Did he know what Rebus had been doing prior to the blackout? Or had his friend dressed him before calling the ambulance? He had to contact the woman. He didn't know where she stayed, not exactly, but the ambulancemen would know, and he could check.

Exhaustion. Rebus did not feel exhausted. He was beginning to feel rested and, though slightly unnerved, quite unworried about life. Had they given him anything while he was asleep?

'Can I see a newspaper?' he muttered past the thermometer.

'I'll get an orderly to fetch you one. Is there anyone you wish us to contact? Any close relative or friend?'

Rebus thought of Michael.

'No,' he said, 'there's nobody to contact. All I want is a newspaper.'

'Fair enough.' The thermometer was removed, the details noted.

'How long do you want to keep me in here?'

'Two or three days. I may want you to see an analyst.'

'Forget the analyst. I'll need some books to read.'

'We'll see what we can do.'

Rebus settled back then, having decided to let things take their course. He would lie here, resting though he needed no rest, and would let the rest of them worry about the murder case. Sod them all. Sod Anderson. Sod Wallace. Sod Gill Templer.

But then he remembered his hands slipping around that ageing throat, and he shivered. It was as though his mind were not his own. Had he been about to kill that woman? Should he see the analyst after all? The questions made his headache worse. He tried not to think about anything at all, but three figures kept coming back to him: his old friend Gordon Reeve, his new lover Gill Templer, and the woman he had betrayed her for, and nearly strangled. They danced in his head until the dance became blurred. Then he fell asleep.

'John!'

She walked quickly to his bed, fruit and vitamin-drink in her hands. She had make-up on her face, and was wearing strictly off-duty clothes. She pecked his cheek, and he could smell her French perfume. He could also see down the front of her silk blouse. He felt a little guilty.

'Hello, D.I. Templer,' he said. 'Here,' lifting one edge of the bedcover, 'get in.'

She laughed, dragging across a stern-looking chair. Other visitors were entering the ward, their smiles and quiet voices redolent of illness, an illness Rebus did not feel.

'How are you, John?'

'Terrible. What have you brought me?'

'Grapes, bananas, diluting orange. Nothing very imaginative, I'm afraid.'

Rebus picked a grape from the bunch and popped it into his mouth, setting aside the trashy novel in which he had been painfully involved.

'I don't know, Inspector, the things I have to do to get a date with you.' Rebus shook his head wearily. Gill was smiling, but nervously.

'We were worried about you, John. What happened?'

'I fainted. In the home of a friend, by all accounts. It's nothing very serious. I have a few weeks to live.'

Gill's smile was warm.

'They say it's overwork.' Then she paused. 'What's all this "Inspector" stuff?'

Rebus shrugged, then looked sulky. His guilt was mixing with the remembrance of that snub he had been given, that snub which had started the whole ball rolling. He turned into a patient again, weakly slumping against his pillow.

'I'm a very ill man, Gill. Too ill to answer questions.'

'Well, in that case I won't bother to slip you the cigarettes sent by Jack Morton.'

Rebus sat up again.

'Bless that man. Where are they?'

She brought two packs from her jacket pocket and slipped them beneath the bedclothes. He gripped her hand.

'I missed you, Gill.' She smiled, and did not withdraw the hand.

Limitless visiting-time being a prerogative of the police, Gill stayed for two hours, talking about her past, asking him about his own. She had been born on an air-force base in Wiltshire, just after the war. She told Rebus that her father had been an engineer in the RAF.

'My dad,' Rebus said, 'was in the Army during the war. I was conceived while he was on one of his last leaves. He was a stage hypnotist by profession.' People usually raised an eyebrow at that, but not Gill Templer. 'He used to work the music-halls and theatres, doing summer stints in Blackpool and Ayr and places like that, so we were always sure of a summer holiday away from Fife.'

She sat with her head cocked to one side, content to be told stories. The ward was quiet once the other visitors had obeyed the leaving-bell. A nurse pushed around a trolley with a huge battered pot of tea on it. Gill was given a cup, the nurse smiling at her in sisterhood.

'She's a nice kid, that nurse,' said Rebus, relaxed. He had been given two pills, one blue and one brown, and they were making him drowsy. 'She reminds me of a girl I knew when I was in the Paras.'

'How long were you in the Paras, John?'

'Six years. No, eight years it was.'

'What made you leave?'

What made him leave? Rhona had asked him the same question over and over, her curiosity piqued by the feeling that he had something to hide, some monstrous skeleton in his closet.

'I don't know really. It's hard to remember that far back. I was picked for special training and I didn't like it.'

And this was the truth. He had no use for memories of his training, the reek of fear and mistrust, the screaming, that screaming in his memory. *Let me out.* The echo of solitary.

'Well,' said Gill, 'if *my* memory serves me right, I've got a case waiting for me back at base-camp.'

'That reminds me,' he said, 'I think I saw your friend last night. The reporter. Stevens, wasn't it? He was in a pub the same time I was. Strange.'

'Not so very strange. That's his kind of hunting-ground. Funny, he's a bit like you in some ways. Not as sexy though.' She smiled and pecked his cheek again, rising from the metal chair. 'I'll try to drop in again before they let you out, but you know what it's like. I can't make any concrete promises, D.S. Rebus.'

Standing, she seemed taller than Rebus had imagined her. Her hair fell forward onto his face for another kiss, full on the lips this time, and he staring at the dark cleft between her breasts. He felt a little tired, so tired. He forced his eyes to remain open while she walked away, her heels clacking on the tiled floor while the nurses floated past like ghosts on their rubber-soled shoes. He pushed himself up so that he could watch her legs retreat. She had nice legs. He had remembered that much. He remembered them gripping his sides, the feet resting on his buttocks. He remembered her hair falling across the pillow like a Turner seascape. He remembered her voice hissing in his ears, that hissing. Oh yes, John, oh, John, yes, yes, yes.

Why did you leave the army?

As she turned over, turning into the woman with the choking cries of his climax.

Why did you?

Oh, oh, oh, oh.

Oh yes, the safety of dreams.

17

The editors loved what the Edinburgh Strangler was doing for the circulations of their newspapers. They loved the way his story grew almost organically, as though carefully nurtured. The *modus operandi* had altered ever so slightly for the killing of Nicola Turner. The Strangler had, it seemed, tied a knot in the cord prior to strangulation. This knot had pressed heavily on the girl's throat, bruising it. The police did not consider this of much significance. They were too busy checking through the records of blue Ford Escorts to be busy with a slight detail of technique. They were out there checking every blue Escort in the area, questioning every owner, every driver.

Gill Templer had released details of the car to the press, hoping for a huge public response. It came: neighbours reported their neighbours, fathers their sons, wives their husbands, and husbands their wives. There were over two-hundred blue Escorts to investigate, and if nothing came of that, they would be re-investigated, before moving on to other colours of Ford Escort, other makes of light-blue saloon car. It might take months; certainly it would take weeks.

Jack Morton, another xeroxed list folded in his hand, had consulted his doctor about swollen feet. The doctor had told him that he walked too much in cheap, unsupportive shoes. This Morton already knew. He had now interviewed so many suspects that it was all becoming a blur to him. They all looked the same and acted the same: nervous, deferential, innocent. If only the Strangler would make a mistake. There were no clues worth going on. Morton suspected the car to be a false trail. No clues worth going on. He remembered John Rebus's anonymous letters. *There are clues everywhere.* Could that be true of this case? Could the clues be too big to notice, or too abstract? Certainly it was a rare – an extraordinarily rare – murder case that did not have some bumper, extravagant clue lying about somewhere just waiting to be picked up. He was damned if he knew where this one was though, and that was why he had visited his doctor – hoping for some sympathy and a few days off. Rebus had landed on *his* feet again, lucky sod. Morton envied him his illness.

He parked his car on a double-yellow line outside the library and sauntered in. The great front hall reminded him of the days when he had used this library himself, clutching picture-books borrowed from the children's section. It used to be situated downstairs. He wondered if it still was. His mother would give him the bus-fare, and he would come into town, ostensibly to change his library books, but really so that he could wander the streets for an hour or two, savouring the taste of what it would be like to be grown up and free. He would trail American tourists, taking note of their swaggering self-confidence and their bulging wallets and waistbands. He would watch them as they photographed Greyfriars Bobby's statue across from the kirkyard. He had stared long and hard at the statue of the small dog, and had felt nothing. He had read of Covenanters, of Deacon Brodie, of public executions on the High Street, wondering what kind of city this was, and what kind of country. He shook his head now, past caring about fantasies, and went to the information desk.

'Hello, Mister Morton.'

He turned to find a girl, more a young lady really, standing before him, a book clasped to her small chest. He frowned.

'It's me, Samantha Rebus.'

His eyes went wide.

'Goodness, so it is. Well, well. You've certainly grown since I last saw you. Mind you, that must have been a year or two back. How are you?'

'I'm fine, thanks. I'm here with my mother. Are you here on police business?'

'Something like that, yes.' Morton could feel her eyes burning into him. God, she had her father's eyes all right. He had left his mark.

'How's Dad keeping?'

To tell or not to tell. Why not tell her? Then again, was it his place to tell her?

'He's fine, so far as I know,' he said, knowing this to be seventy-percent truth.

'I'm just going down to the teenagers' section. Mum's in the Reference Room. It's dead boring in there.'

'I'll go with you. That's just where I was headed.'

She smiled at him, pleased about something that was going on in her adolescent head, and Jack Morton had the thought that she wasn't at all like her father. She was far too nice and polite.

*

A fourth girl was missing. The outcome seemed a foregone conclusion. No bookie would have given odds.

'We need special vigilance,' stressed Anderson. 'More officers are being drafted in tonight. Remember,' the officers present looked hollow-eyed and demoralized, 'if and when he kills this victim, he will attempt to dispose of the body, and if we can spot him doing that, or if any member of the public can spot him doing that, just once, then we've got him.' Anderson slapped a fist into his open hand. Nobody seemed very cheered. So far the Strangler had dumped three corpses, quite successfully, in different areas of the city: Oxgangs, Haymarket, Colinton. The police could not be everywhere (though these days it seemed to the public that they were), no matter how hard they tried.

'Again,' continued the Chief Inspector, consulting a file, 'the recent abduction seems to have little enough in common with the others. The victim's name is Helen Abbot. Eight years of age, a bit younger than the others you'll notice, light-brown shoulder-length hair. Last seen with her mother in a Princes Street store. The mother says that the girl simply disappeared. One minute there, the next minute gone, as was the case with the second victim.'

Gill Templer, thinking this over later, found it curious. The girls could not themselves have been abducted actually in the shops. That would have been impossible without screams, without witnesses. One member of the public had come forward to say that a girl resembling Mary Andrews – the second victim – had been seen by him climbing the steps from the National Gallery up towards The Mound. She had been alone, and had seemed happy enough. In which case, Gill mused, the girl had sneaked away from her mother. But why? For some secret rendezvous with someone she had known, someone who had turned out to be her killer? In that case, it seemed likely that *all* the girls had known their murderer, so they *had* to have something in common. Different schools, different friends, different ages. What was the common denominator?

She admitted defeat when her head started to hurt. Besides, she had reached John's street and had other things to think about. He had sent her here to collect some clean clothes for his release, and to see if there was any mail, as well as to check that the central heating was working still. He had given her his key, and as she climbed the stairs, pinching her nose against the pervasive smell of cats, she felt a bond between John Rebus and herself. She wondered if the relationship were about to turn serious. He was a nice man, but a little hung-up, a little secretive. Maybe that was what she liked.

She opened his door, scooped up the few letters lying on the hall-carpet, and made a quick tour of the flat. Standing by the bedroom door, she recalled the passion of that night, the odour of which seemed to cling in the air still.

The pilot-light was lit. He would be surprised to learn that. What a lot of books he had, but then his wife had been an English teacher. She lifted some of them off the floor and arranged them on the empty shelves of the wall-unit. In the kitchen, she made herself some coffee and sat down to drink it black, looking over the mail. One bill, one circular, and one typed letter, posted in Edinburgh and three days ago at that. She stuffed the letters into her bag and went to inspect the wardrobe. Samantha's room, she noted, was still locked. More memories pushed safely away. Poor John.

Jim Stevens had far too much work to do. The Edinburgh Strangler was proving himself a meaty individual. You couldn't ignore the bastard, even if you felt you had better things to do. Stevens had a staff of three working with him on the newspaper's daily reports and features. Child abuse in Britain today was the flavour of tomorrow's piece. The figures were horrifying enough, but more horrifying yet was the sense of biding time, waiting for the dead girl to turn up. Waiting for the next one to go missing. Edinburgh was a ghost town. Children were kept indoors, those allowed out scuttling through the streets like creatures under chase. Stevens wanted to turn his attentions to the drugs case, the mounting evidence, the police connection. He wanted to, but there simply was not the time. Tom Jameson was on his back every hour of the day, roaming through the office. Where's that copy, Jim? It's about time you earned your keep, Jim. When's the next briefing, Jim? Stevens was burned out by the end of each and every day. He decided that his work on the Rebus case had to stop for the moment. Which was a pity, because with the police at full stretch working on the murders, the field was left wide open for any and all other crimes, including pushing drugs. The Edinburgh Mafia must be having a field-day. He had used the story of the Leith 'bordello', hoping for some information in return, but the big boys appeared not to be playing. Well, sod them. His time would come.

When she arrived in the ward, Rebus was reading through a Bible, courtesy of the hospital. When the Sister had found out about his request, she had asked him if he wished to speak to a priest or a minister, but this offer he had declined strenuously. He was quite content – more than content – to flick through some of the better passages in the Old Testament, refreshing his memory of their power and their moral strength. He read the stories of Moses, Samson, and David, before coming to the Book of Job. Here he found a power he could not remember having encountered before:

> When an innocent man suddenly dies, God laughs.
> God gave the world to the wicked.
> He made all the judges blind,
> And if God didn't do it, who did?
>
> If I smile and try to forget my pain,
> All my suffering comes back to haunt me;
> I know that God does hold me guilty.
> Since I am held guilty, why should I bother?
> No soap can wash away my sins.

Rebus felt his spine shiver, though the ward itself was oppressively warm, and his throat cried out for water. As he poured some of the tepid liquid into a plastic beaker, he saw Gill coming towards him on quieter heels than previously. She was smiling, bringing what joy there was into the ward with her. A few of the men eyed her appreciatively. Rebus felt glad, all of a sudden, to be leaving this place today. He put the Bible aside and greeted her with a kiss on the nape of her neck.

'What have you got there?'

He took the parcel from her and found it to contain his change of clothes.

'Thanks,' he said. 'I didn't think this shirt was clean though.'

'It wasn't.' She laughed and pulled across a chair. 'Nothing was. I'd to wash and iron all your clothes. They constituted a health hazard.'

'You're an angel,' he said, putting the parcel aside.

'Speaking of which, what were you reading in the book?' She tapped the red, fake-leather binding of the Bible.

'Oh, nothing much. Job, actually. I read it once a long time ago. It seems more frightening now though. The man who begins to doubt, who shouts out against his God, looking for a response, and who gets one. "God gave the world to the wicked," he says at one point, and "Why should I bother?" at another.'

'It sounds interesting. But he goes on bothering?'

104

'Yes, that's the incredible thing.'

Tea arrived, the young nurse handing Gill her cup. There was a plate of biscuits for them.

'I've brought you some letters from the flat, and here's your key.' She held the small Yale key towards him, but he shook his head.

'Keep it,' he said, 'please. I've got a spare one.'

They studied one another.

'All right,' Gill said finally. 'I will. Thanks.' With that, she handed him the three letters. He sorted through them in a second.

'He's started sending them by mail, I see.' Rebus tore open the latest bulletin. 'This guy,' he said, 'is haunting me. Mister Knot, I call him. My own personal anonymous crank.'

Gill looked interested, as Rebus read through the letter. It was longer than usual.

YOU STILL HAVEN'T GUESSED, HAVE YOU? YOU'VE NO IDEAS. NOT AN IDEA IN YOUR HEAD. AND IT'S ALMOST OVER NOW, ALMOST OVER. DON'T SAY I'VE NOT GIVEN YOU A CHANCE. YOU CAN NEVER SAY THAT. SIGNED

Rebus pulled a small matchstick cross out of the envelope.

'Ah, Mister Cross today, I see. Well, thank God he's nearly finished. Getting bored, I suppose.'

'What is all this, John?'

'Haven't I told you about my anonymous letters? It's not a very exciting story.'

'How long has this been going on?' Gill, having studied the letter, was now examining the envelope.

'Six weeks. Maybe a little longer. Why?'

'Well, it's just that this letter was posted on the day Helen Abbot went missing.'

'Oh?' Rebus reached for the envelope and looked at its postmark. 'Edinburgh, Lothian, Fife, Borders,' it read. A big enough area. He thought again of Michael.

'I don't suppose you can remember when you received the other letters?'

'What are you getting at, Gill?' He looked up at her, and saw a professional policewoman suddenly staring back at him. 'For Christ's sake, Gill. This case is getting to all of us. We're all beginning to see ghosts.'

'I'm just curious, that's all.' She was reading the letter again. It was not the usual crank's voice, nor a crank's style. That was what worried her. And now that Rebus thought about it, the notes had seemed to appear around the time of each abduction, hadn't they? Had there been a connection of some kind staring him in the face all this time? He had been very myopic indeed, had been wearing a carthorse's blinkers. Either that or it was all a monstrous coincidence.

'It's just a coincidence, Gill.'

'So tell me when the other notes arrived.'

'I can't remember.'

She bent over him, her eyes huge behind her glasses. She said calmly, 'Are you hiding anything from me?'

'No!'

The whole ward turned to his cry, and he felt his cheeks flush.

'No,' he whispered, 'I'm not hiding anything. At least . . .' But how could he be sure? All those years of arrests, of charge-sheets, of forgettings, so many enemies made. But none would torment him like this, surely. Surely.

With pen, paper, and a lot of thought on his part, they went over the arrival of each note: dates, contents, style of delivery. Gill took off her glasses, rubbing between her eyes, sighing.

'It's just too big a coincidence, John.'

And he knew that she was right, way down inside him. He knew that nothing was ever what it seemed, that nothing was arbitrary. 'Gill,' he said at last, pulling at the bedcover, 'I've got to get out of here.'

In the car she goaded him, spurred him on. Who could it be? What was the connection? Why?

'What is this?' he roared at her. 'Am I a suspect now or something?'

She studied his eyes, trying to pierce them, trying to bite right into the truth behind them. Oh, she was a detective at heart, and a good detective trusts nobody. She gazed at him as though he were a scolded schoolboy, with secrets still to spill, with sins to confess. Confess.

Gill knew that all this was only a hunch, insupportable. Yet she could feel something there, something perhaps behind those burning eyes. Stranger things had happened during her time on the force. Stranger things were always happening. Truth was always stranger than fiction, and nobody was ever wholly innocent. Those guilty looks when you questioned somebody, anybody. Everyone had something to hide. Mostly, though, it was small time, and covered by the intervening years. You would need Thought Police to get at those kinds of crime.

But if John . . . If John Rebus proved to be part of this whole caboodle, then that . . . That was too absurd to think about.

'Of course you're not a suspect, John,' she said. 'But it could be important, couldn't it?'

'We'll let Anderson decide,' he said, falling silent, but shaking.

It was then that Gill had the thought: what if he sent the letters to himself?

18

He felt his arms ache and, looking down, saw that the girl had stopped struggling. There came that point, that sudden, blissful point, when it was useless to go on living, and when the mind and body came to accept that such was the case. That was a beautiful, peaceful moment, the most relaxed moment of one's life. He had, many years ago, tried to commit suicide, savouring that very moment. But they had done things to him in hospital and in the clinic afterwards. They had given him back the will to live, and now he was repaying them, repaying all of them. He saw this irony in his life and chuckled, peeling the tape from Helen Abbot's mouth, using the little scissors to snip away her bonds. He brought out a neat little camera from his trouser pocket and took another instant snap of her, a *memento mori* of sorts. If they ever caught him, they'd kick the shit out of him for this, but they would never be able to brand him a sex-killer. Sex had nothing to do with it; these girls were pawns, fated by their christenings. The next and last one was the one that really mattered, and he would do that one today if possible. He chuckled again. This was a better game than noughts and crosses. He was a winner at both.

19

Chief Inspector William Anderson loved the feel of the chase, the battle between instinct and plodding detection. He liked to feel, too, that he had the support of his Division behind him. Dispenser of orders, of wisdom, of strategies, he was in his element.

He would rather have caught the Strangler already – that went without saying. He was no sadist. The law had to be upheld. All the same, the longer an investigation like this went on, the greater became the feel of nearing the kill, and to relish that extended moment was one of the great perks of responsibility.

The Strangler was making an occasional slip, and that was what mattered to Anderson at this stage. The blue Ford Escort, and now the interesting theory that the killer had been or was still an Army man, suggested by the tying of a knot in the garotte. Snippets like that would culminate eventually in a name, an address, an arrest. And at that moment, Anderson would lead his officers physically as well as spiritually. There would be another interview on the television, another rather flattering photograph in the press (he was quite photogenic). Oh yes, victory would be sweet. Unless, of course, the Strangler vanished in the night as so many before him had done. That possibility was not to be considered; it made his legs turn into paper.

He did not dislike Rebus, not exactly. The man was a reasonable enough copper, a bit loud in his methods perhaps. And he understood that Rebus's personal life had experienced an upheaval. Indeed, he had been told that Rebus's ex-wife was the woman with whom his own son was co-habiting. He tried not to think about it. When Andy had slammed the front door on his leaving, he had walked right out of his father's life. How could anyone these days spend their time writing poetry? It was ludicrous. And then moving in with Rebus's wife . . . No, he did not dislike Rebus, but watching Rebus come towards him with that pretty Liaison Officer, Anderson felt his stomach cough, as though his insides suddenly wanted to become his outsides. He leaned back on the edge of a vacant desk. The officer assigned to it had gone off for a break.

'Nice to have you back, John. Feeling fit?'

Anderson had shot out his hand, and Rebus, stunned, was forced to take it and return the grip. 'I'm fine, sir,' he said.

'Sir,' interrupted Gill Templer, 'can we speak to you for a minute? There's been a new development.'

'The mere *hint* of a development, sir,' corrected Rebus, staring at Gill.

Anderson looked from one to the other.

'You'd better come into my office then.'

Gill explained the situation as she saw it to Anderson, and he, wise and safe behind his desk, listened, glancing occasionally towards Rebus, who smiled apologetically at him. Sorry to be wasting your time, Rebus's smile said.

'Well, Rebus?' said Anderson when Gill had finished. 'What do you say to all this? Could someone have a reason for informing you of their plans? I mean, could the Strangler *know* you?'

Rebus shrugged his shoulders, smiling, smiling, smiling.

Jack Morton, sitting in his car, jotted down some remarks on his report-sheet. Saw suspect. Interviewed same. Casual, helpful. Another dead end, he wanted to say. Another dead fucking end. A parking warden was looking at him, trying to scare him as she neared his car. He sighed, putting down the pen and paper and reaching for his ID. One of those days.

Rhona Phillips wore her raincoat, it being the end of May, and the rain slashing through the skyline as though painted upon an artist's canvas. She kissed her curly-headed poet-lover goodbye, as he watched afternoon TV, and left the house, feeling for the car-keys in her handbag. She picked Sammy up from school these days, though the school was only a mile and a quarter away. She also went with her to the library at lunchtimes, not allowing her any escape. With that maniac still on the loose, she was taking no chances. She rushed to her car, got in, and slammed shut the door. Edinburgh rain was like a judgement. It soaked into the bones, into the structures of the buildings, into the memories of the tourists. It lingered for days, splashing up from puddles by the roadside, breaking up marriages, chilling, killing, omnipresent. The typical postcard home from an

110

Edinburgh boarding-house: 'Edinburgh is lovely. The people rather reserved. Saw the Castle yesterday, and the Scott Monument. It's a very small city, almost a town really. You could fit it inside New York and never notice it. Weather could be better.'

Weather could be better. The art of euphemism. Shitty, shitty rain. It was so typical when she had a free day. Typical, too, that Andy and she should have argued. And now he was sulking in his chair, legs tucked beneath him. One of those days. And she had reports to write out this evening. Thank God the exams had started. The kids seemed more subdued at school these days, the older ones gripped by exam-fever or exam-apathy, and the younger ones seeing their ineluctable future mapped out for them in the faces of their doomed superiors. It was an interesting time of year. Soon the fear would be Sammy's, called Samantha to her face now that she was so nearly a woman. There were other fears there, too, for a parent. The fear of adolescence, of experiment.

As she reversed the car out of the driveway, he watched her from his Escort. Perfect. He had about fifteen minutes to wait. When her car had disappeared, he drove his car to the front of the house and stopped. He examined the windows of the house. Her man would be in there alone. He left his car and walked to the front door.

Back in the Incident Room after the inconclusive meeting, Rebus could not know that Anderson was arranging to have him put under surveillance. The Incident Room looked like an incident itself. Paper covered every surface, a small computer was crammed into a spare corner, charts and rotas and the rest covered every available inch of wall-space.

'I've got a briefing,' said Gill. 'I'll see you later. Listen, John, I do think there's a link. Call it female intuition, call it a detective's "nose", call it what you like, but take me seriously. Think it over. Think about possible grudges. Please.'

He nodded, then watched her leave, making for her own office in her own part of the building. Rebus wasn't sure which desk was his any more. He surveyed the room. It all seemed different somehow, as though a few of the desks had been changed around or put together. A telephone rang on the desk next to him. And though there were officers and telephonists nearby, he picked it up himself, making an attempt to get back into the investigation. He prayed that he was not himself the investigation. He prayed, forgetting what prayer was.

'Incident Room,' he said. 'Detective Sergeant Rebus speaking.'

'Rebus? What a curious name that is.' The voice was old but lively, certainly well-educated. 'Rebus,' it said again, as though jotting it down onto a piece of paper. Rebus studied the telephone.

'And your name, sir?'

'Oh, I'm Michael Eiser, that's E-I-S-E-R, Professor of English Literature at the University.'

'Oh, yes, sir?' Rebus grabbed a pencil and jotted down the name. 'And what can I do for you, sir?'

'Well, Mister Rebus, it's more a case of what I *think* I can do for you, though of course I may be mistaken.' Rebus had a picture of the man, if this were not a hoax call: frizzy-haired, bow-tied, wearing crushed tweeds and old shoes, and waving his hands about as he spoke. 'I'm interested in word-play, you see. In fact I'm writing a book on the subject. It's called *Reading Exercises and Directed Exegetic Responses*. Do you see the word-play there? It's an acrostic. The first letter of each word makes up another word – *reader*, in this case. It's a game as old as literature itself. My book, however, concentrates on its manifestation in more recent works. Nabokov and Burgess and the like. Of course, acrostics are a small part of the overall set of ploys used by the author to entertain, direct or persuade his audience.' Rebus tried to interrupt the man, but it was like trying to interrupt a bull. So he was forced to listen, wondering all the time if it were a crank call, if he should – strictly against procedure – simply put down the telephone. He had more important things to think about. The back of his head ached.

'. . . and the point is, Mister Rebus, that I have noticed, quite by chance, a kind of pattern in this murderer's choice of victims.'

Rebus sat down on the edge of the desk. He clasped the pencil as though trying to crush it.

'Oh, yes?' he said.

'Yes. I have the names of the victims here in front of me on a piece of paper. Perhaps one would have noticed it sooner, but it was only today that I saw a report in one newspaper which grouped the poor girls together. I usually take *The Times*, you see, but I quite simply couldn't find one this morning, so I bought another paper, and there it was. It may be nothing at all, mere coincidence, but then again it may not. I'll leave that for you chaps to decide. I merely offer it as a proposition.'

Jack Morton, puffing smoke all around him, entered the office and, noticing Rebus, waved. Rebus jerked his head in response. Jack looked worn out. Everyone looked worn out, and here he was, fresh from a period of rest and relaxation, dealing with a lunatic on the telephone.

'Offer what exactly, Professor Eiser?'

'Well, don't you see? In order, the victims' names were Sandra Adams, Mary Andrews, Nicola Turner, and Helen Abbot.' Jack slouched towards Rebus's table. 'Taken as an acrostic,' continued the voice, 'their names make up another name – Samantha. The murderer's next victim perhaps? Or it may be simple coincidence, a game where no game really exists.'

Rebus slammed down the telephone, was off the desk in a second, and pulled Jack Morton around by his neck-tie. Morton gasped and his cigarette flew from his mouth.

'Got your car outside, Jack?'

Still choking, he nodded a reply.

Jesus Christ, Jesus Christ. It was all true then. It was all to do with *him*. Samantha. All the clues, all the killings had been meant merely as a message to *him*. Jesus Christ. Help me, oh help me.

His daughter was to be the Strangler's next victim.

Rhona Phillips saw the car parked outside her house, but thought nothing of it. All she wanted was to get out of the rain. She ran to the front door, Samantha following desultorily behind, and keyed open the door.

'It's horrible outside!' she shouted into the living-room. She shook off her raincoat and walked through to where the TV still blared. In his chair, she saw Andy. His hands were tied behind him and his mouth was taped shut with a huge piece of sticking-plaster. The length of twine still dangled from his throat.

Rhona was about to let out the most piercing scream of her life, when a heavy object came down on the back of her head and she staggered forward towards her lover, slumping across his legs as she passed out.

'Hello, Samantha,' said a voice she recognised, though his face was masked so that she could not see his smile.

Morton's car tore across town, its blue light flashing, as though it were being followed by all Hell itself. Rebus tried explaining it all as they drove, but he was too edgy to make much sense, and Jack Morton was too busy avoiding traffic to make much attempt at taking it in. They had called for assistance: one car to the school in case she were still there, and two cars to the house, with the warning that the Strangler might be there. Caution was to be exercised.

The car reached eighty-five along Queensferry Road, made an insane right turn across the oncoming traffic, and reached the bright-as-a-pin housing estate where Rhona, Samantha and Rhona's lover now lived. 'Turn right here,' shouted Rebus over the engine's roar, his mind clinging to hope. As they turned into the street they saw the two police cars already motionless in front of the house, and Rhona's car sitting like a potent symbol of futility in the driveway.

20

They wanted to give him sedatives, but he wouldn't take any of their drugs. They wanted him to go home, but he would not take their advice. How could he go home with Rhona lying somewhere above him in the hospital? With his daughter abducted, his whole life ripped apart like a worn garment being transformed into dusters? He paced the hospital waiting-room. He was fine, he told them, fine. He knew that Gill and Anderson were somewhere along the corridor. Poor Anderson. He watched from the grime of the window as nurses walked by outside, laughing in the rain, their capes blowing about them like something out of an old Dracula movie. How could they laugh? Mist was settling over the trees, and the nurses, still laughing, unaware of the world's suffering, faded into that mist as though some Edinburgh of the past had sucked them into its fiction, taking with them all the laughter in the world.

It was nearly dark now, the sun a memory behind the heavy fabric of the clouds. The religious painters of old must have known skies like this, must have lived with them each and every day, accepting the bruised colouring of the clouds as a mark of God's presence, an essence of creation's power. Rebus was no painter. His eyes beheld beauty not in reality but in the printed word. Standing in the waiting-room, he realised that in his life he had accepted secondary experience – the experience of reading someone else's thoughts – over real life. Well, he was face to face with it now all right: he was back in the Paras, he was back in the SAS, his face a sketch-pad of exhaustion, his brain aching, every muscle tensed.

He caught himself beginning to abstract everything again, and slapped the wall with the palms of both hands as though ready to be frisked. Sammy was out there somewhere in the hands of a maniac, and he was composing eulogies, excuses and similes. It wasn't enough.

In the corridor, Gill kept a watch on William Anderson. He, too, had been told to go home. A doctor had examined him for the effects of shock, and had spoken of putting Anderson to bed for the night.

'I'm waiting right here,' Anderson had said with quiet determination. 'If this all has something to do with John Rebus, then I want to stay close to John Rebus. I'm all right, honestly.' But he was not all right. He was dazed and remorseful and a bit confused about everything. 'I can't believe it,' he told Gill. 'I can't believe that this whole thing was merely a prelude to the abduction of Rebus's daughter. It's fantastical. The man must be deranged. Surely John must have an inkling who's responsible?'

Gill Templer was wondering the same thing.

'Why hasn't he told us?' continued Anderson. Then, without warning or any show of ceremony, he became a father again and started to sob very quietly. 'Andy,' he said, 'my Andy.' He put his head in his hands and allowed Gill to put her arm around his crumpled shoulders.

John Rebus, watching darkness descend, thought about his marriage, his daughter. His daughter Sammy.

For those who read between the times

What was it he was blocking out? What was it that had been rejected by him all those years ago as he had walked the Fife shoreline, having his final fit of the breakdown and shutting out the past as securely as if he had been shutting the door on a Jehovah's Witness? It was not that easy. The unwanted caller had waited his time, deciding to break and enter into Rebus's life again. The foot in the door. The door of perception. What good was his reading doing him now? Or his faith, slender thread that it was? Samantha. Sammy, his daughter. Dear God, let her be safe. Dear God, let her live.

John, you must know who it is

But he had shaken his head, shaken his tears onto the folds of his trousers. He did not, he did not. It was Knot. It was Cross. Names meant nothing to him any more. Knots and crosses. He had been sent knots and crosses, string and matches and a load of gobbledygook, as Jack Morton had called it. That was all. Dear God.

He went out into the corridor, and confronted Anderson, who stood before him like a piece of wreckage waiting to be loaded up and shunted away. And the two men came together in a hug, squeezing life into one another; two old enemies realising in a moment that they were on the same side after all. They hugged and they wept, draining themselves of all they had been bottling up, all those years of pounding

116

the beat, having to appear emotionless and unflappable. It was out in the open now: they were human beings, the same as everybody else.

And finally, assured that Rhona had suffered a fractured skull only, allowed into her room for a moment to watch her breathing oxygen, Rebus had let them take him home. Rhona would live. That was something. Andy Anderson, though, was cold on a slab somewhere while doctors examined his leftovers. Poor bloody Anderson. Poor man, poor father, poor copper. It was becoming very personal now, wasn't it? All of a sudden it had become bigger than they had imagined it ever could. It had become a grudge.

They had a description at last, though not a good one. A neighbour had seen the man carry the still form of the girl out to the car. A pale coloured car, she had told them. A normal looking car. A normal looking man. Not too tall, his face hard. He was hurrying. She didn't get a good look at him.

Anderson would be off the case now, and so would Rebus. Oh, it was big now. The Strangler had entered a home, had murdered there. He had gone way too far over the edge. The newspapermen and the cameras outside the hospital wanted to know all about it. Superintendent Wallace would have organised a press conference. The newspaper-readers, the voyeurs, needed to know all about it. It was big news. Edinburgh was the crime capital of Europe. The son of a Chief Inspector murdered and the daughter of a Detective Sergeant abducted, possibly murdered already.

What could he do but sit and wait for another letter? He was better off in his flat, no matter how dark and barren it seemed, no matter how like a cell. Gill promised to visit him later, after the press conference. An unmarked car would be outside his tenement as a matter of course, for who knew how personal the Strangler wanted this to become?

Meantime, unknown to Rebus, his file was being checked back at HQ, his past dusted off and examined. There had to be the Strangler in there somewhere. There had to be.

Of course there had to be. Rebus knew that he alone held the key. But it seemed locked in a drawer to which it itself was the key. He could only rattle that locked away history.

Gill Templer had telephoned Rebus's brother, and though John would hate her for doing so, she had told Michael to come across to Edinburgh at once to be with his brother. He was Rebus's only family after all. He sounded nervous on the phone, nervous but concerned. And now she puzzled over the matter of the acrostic. The Professor had been correct. They were trying to locate him this evening in order to interview him. Again, as a matter of course. But if the Strangler had planned this, then surely he must have been able to get his hands on a list of people whose names would fit the bill, and how would he have done that? A civil servant perhaps? A teacher? Someone working away quietly at a computer-terminal somewhere? There were many possibilities, and they would go through them one by one. First, however, Gill was going to suggest that everyone in Edinburgh called Knott or Cross be interviewed. It was a wild card, but then everything about this case so far had been wild.

And then there was the press conference. Held, since it was convenient, in the hospital's administration building. There was standing room only at the back of the hall. Gill Templer's face, human but unsmiling, was becoming well known to the British public, as well known, certainly, as that of any newscaster or reporter. Tonight, however, the Superintendent would be doing the talking. She hoped he would not take long. She wanted to see Rebus. And more urgently, perhaps, she wanted to talk with his brother. Someone had to know about John's past. He had never, apparently, spoken to any of his friends on the force about his Army years. Did the key lie there? Or in his marriage? Gill listened to the Super saying his piece. Cameras clicked and the large hall grew smoky.

And there was Jim Stevens, smiling from the corner of his mouth, as if he knew something. Gill grew nervous. His eyes were on her, though his pen worked away at its notepad. She recalled that disastrous evening they had spent together, and her much less disastrous evening with John Rebus. Why had none of the men in her life ever been uncomplicated? Perhaps because complications interested her. The case was not becoming more complex. It was becoming simpler.

Jim Stevens, half-listening to the police statement, thought of how complex this story was becoming. Rebus and Rebus, drugs and murder, anonymous messages followed by abduction of daughter. He needed to get behind the police's public face on this one, and knew that the best way forward lay with Gill Templer, with a little trading of knowledge. If the drugs and the abduction were linked, as they probably were, then perhaps one or other of the Rebus brothers had not been playing the game according to the set rules. Maybe Gill Templer would know.

*

He came up behind her as she left the building. She knew it was him, but for once she wanted to speak with him.

'Hello, Jim. Can I give you a lift somewhere?'

He decided that she could. She could drop him off at a bar, unless, of course, he could see Rebus for a moment? He could not. They drove.

'This story is becoming more and more bizarre by the second, don't you think?'

She concentrated her eyes on the road, seeming to mull over his question. Really, she was hoping he would open up a little more and that her silence would lead him to believe that she was holding back on him, that there was something there between them to swop.

'Rebus seems to be the main actor though. Interesting that.'

Gill sensed that he was about to play a card.

'I mean,' he went on, lighting a cigarette, 'don't mind if I smoke, do you?'

'No,' she said slowly, though inside she was jarring with electricity.

'Thanks. I mean, it's interesting because I've got Rebus pencilled into another story I'm working on.'

She pulled the car up at a red light, but her eyes still gazed through the windscreen.

'Would you be interested in hearing about this other story, Gill?'

Would she? Of course she would. But what in return . . .

'Yes, a very interesting man, Mister Rebus. And his brother.'

'His brother?'

'Yes, you know, Michael Rebus, the hypnotist. An interesting pair of brothers.'

'Oh?'

'Listen, Gill, let's cut the crap.'

'I was hoping you would.' She put the car into gear and started off again.

'Are you lot investigating Rebus for anything? That's what I want to know. I mean, do you really know who's behind all this but aren't saying?'

She turned to him now.

'That's not the way it works, Jim.'

He snorted.

'It may not be the way you work, Gill, but don't pretend it doesn't happen. I just wondered if you'd heard anything, any rumbles from higher up. Maybe to the effect that someone had made a botch-up in allowing things to come to this.'

Jim Stevens was watching her face very closely indeed, throwing out ideas and vague theories in the hope that one of them would catch her. But she didn't seem to be taking the bait. Very well. Maybe she didn't know anything. That didn't mean his theories were wrong necessarily. It could just mean that things started at a higher plane than that on which Gill Templer and he operated.

'Jim, what is it you *think* you know about John Rebus? It could be important, you know. We could bring you in if we thought you were withholding . . .'

Stevens began to make tutting sounds, shaking his head.

'We know that's not on, don't we though? I mean, that is just not on.'

She looked at him again.

'I could make a precedent,' she said.

He stared at her. Yes, maybe she could at that.

'This'll do just here,' he said, pointing out of the window. Some ash fell from his cigarette onto his tie. Gill stopped the car and watched him climb out. He leaned back in before shutting the door.

'A swop can be arranged if you'd like one. You know my phone number.'

Yes, she knew his phone number. He had written it down for her a very long time ago, so long ago that they were on different sides of a wall now, so that she could hardly understand him at all. What did he know about John? About Michael? As she drove off towards Rebus's flat, she hoped that she would find out there.

21

John Rebus read a few pages from his *Good News Bible*, but put it down when he realised that he was taking none of it in. He prayed instead, screwing up his eyes into tiny fists. Then he walked around the flat, touching things. This he had done before that first breakdown. He was not afraid now though. Let it come if it would, let everything come. He had no resilience left. He was passive to the will of his malevolent creator.

There was a ring at the door. He did not answer. They would go away, and he would be alone again with his grief, his impotent anger, and his undusted possessions. The bell rang again, more persistently this time. Cursing, he went to the door and pulled it open. Michael was standing there.

'John,' he said, 'I came as soon as I could.'

'Mickey, what are you doing here?' He ushered his brother into the flat.

'Somebody phoned me. She told me all about it. Terrible news, John. Just terrible.' He placed a hand on Rebus's shoulder. Rebus, tingling, realised how long it had been since he had felt the touch of a human being, a sympathetic, brotherly touch. 'I was confronted by two gorillas outside. They seem to have you under close watch here.'

'Procedure,' said Rebus.

Procedure maybe, but Michael knew how guilty he must have looked when they had pounced on him. He had wondered at the phone-call, wondered about the possibility of a trap. So he had listened to the local radio news. There had been an abduction, a killing. It was true. So he had driven over, into this lion's den, knowing that he should stay well away from his brother, knowing that they would kill him if they found out, and wondering whether the abduction could have anything to do with his own situation. Was this a warning to both brothers? He could not say. But when those two gorillas had approached him in the shadows of the tenement stairs, he had thought the game all over.

Firstly, they had been gangsters, out to get him. Then, they had been police officers, about to arrest him. But no, they were 'procedure'.

'You say it was a woman who called you? Did you catch her name? No, never mind, I know who it was anyway.'

They sat in the living-room. Michael, removing his sheepskin jacket, brought a bottle of whisky out of one of the pockets.

'Would this help?' he said.

'It won't do any harm.'

Rebus went to fetch glasses from the kitchen, while Michael inspected the living-room.

'This is a nice place,' he called.

'Well, it's a bit big for my needs,' said Rebus. A choking sound came from the kitchen. Michael walked through to discover his big brother leaning into the sink, weeping grimly but quietly.

'John,' said Michael, hugging Rebus, 'it's okay. It's going to be okay.' He felt guilt well up inside him.

Rebus was fumbling for a handkerchief and, having found it, gave his nose a good blow and wiped his eyes.

'That's easy for you to say,' he sniffed, trying out a smile, 'you're a heathen.'

They drank half of the whisky, sitting back in their chairs, silently contemplating the shadowy ceiling above. Rebus's eyes were red-rimmed, and his eye-lashes stung. He sniffed occasionally, rubbing at his nose with the back of his hand. To Michael, it was like being boys again, but with the roles reversed for a moment. Not that they had been that close, but sentiment would always win over reality. Certainly he remembered John fighting one or two of his playground battles for him. Guilt welled up again. He shivered slightly. He had to get out of this game, but perhaps already he was in too deep, and if he had brought John unknowingly into the game too ... That did not bear thinking about. He had to see the Man, had to explain things to him. But how? He had no telephone number or address. It was always the Man who called him, never the other way round. It was farcical now that he thought about it. Like a nightmare.

'Did you enjoy the show the other night?'

Rebus forced himself to think back to it, to the perfumed and lonely woman, to his fingers around her throat, the scene which had signalled the beginning of his end.

'Yes, it was interesting.' He had fallen asleep had he not? Never mind.

Silence again, the broken sounds of traffic outside, a few shouts from distant drunks.

'They say it's someone with a grudge against me,' he said finally.

'Oh? And is it?'

'I don't know. It looks like it.'

'But surely you would *know*?'

Rebus shook his head.

'That's the trouble, Mickey. I can't remember.'

Michael sat up in his chair.

'You can't remember what exactly?'

'Something. I don't know. Just something. If I knew what, I *would* remember, wouldn't I? But there's a gap. I know there is. I know that there's something I should remember.'

'Something from your past?' Michael was keening now. Perhaps this had nothing at all to do with himself. Perhaps it was all to do with something else, someone else. He grew hopeful.

'From the past, yes. But I can't remember.' Rebus rubbed his forehead as though it were a crystal ball. Michael was fumbling in his pocket.

'I can help you to remember, John.'

'How?'

'Like this.' Michael was holding, between thumb and forefinger, a silver coin. 'You remember what I told you, John. I take my patients back into past lives every day. It should be easy enough to take you back into your *real* past.'

It was John Rebus's turn to sit up. He shook away the whisky fumes.

'Come on then,' he said. 'What do I do?' But inside part of him was saying: *you don't want this, you don't want to know.*

He wanted to know.

Michael came over to his chair.

'Lie back in the chair. Get comfortable. Don't touch any more of that whisky. But remember, not everyone is susceptible to hypnotism. Don't force yourself. Don't try too hard. If it's going to come, it'll come whether you will it or not. Just relax, John, relax.'

The doorbell rang.

'Ignore it,' said Rebus, but Michael had already left the room. There were voices in the hall, and when Michael reappeared he was followed into the room by Gill.

'The telephone caller, it seems,' said Michael.

'How are you, John?' Her face was angled into a portrait of concern.

'Fine, Gill. Listen, this is my brother Michael. The hypnotist. He's going to put me under – that's what you called it, wasn't it, Mickey? – to remove whatever block there might be in my memory. Maybe you should be ready to take some notes or something.'

Gill looked from one brother to the other, feeling a little out of things. An interesting pair of brothers. That's what Jim Stevens had said. She had been working for sixteen hours, and now this. But she smiled and shrugged her shoulders.

'Can a girl get a drink first?'

It was John Rebus's turn to smile. 'Help yourself,' he said. 'There's whisky or whisky and water or water. Come on, Mickey. Let's get on with this. Sammy's out there somewhere. There might still be time.'

Michael spread his legs a little, leaning down over Rebus. He seemed to be about to consume his brother, his eyes close to Rebus's eyes, his mouth working in a mirror-image. That's what it looked like to Gill, pouring whisky into a tumbler. Michael held up the coin, trying to find the angle of the room's single low-wattage bulb. Finally, the glint was reflected in John's retina, the pupils expanding and contracting. Michael felt sure that his brother would be amenable. He certainly hoped so.

'Listen carefully, John. Listen to my voice. Watch the coin, John. Watch it shine and spin. See it spinning. Can you see it spinning, John? Now relax, just listen to me. And watch the spin, watch it glow.'

For a moment it seemed that Rebus would not go under. Perhaps it was the familial tie that was making him immune to the voice, to its suggestive power. But then Michael saw the eyes change a little, imperceptibly to the uninitiated. But he was initiated. His father had taught him well. His brother was in the limbo world now, caught in the coin's light, transported to wherever Michael wanted him to go. Under his power. As ever, Michael felt a little shiver run through him: this was power, power total and irreducible. He could do anything with his patients, anything.

'Michael,' whispered Gill, 'ask him why he left the Army.'

Michael swallowed, lining his throat with saliva. Yes, that was a good question. One he had wanted to ask John himself.

'John?' he said. 'John? Why did you leave the Army, John? What happened, John? Why did you leave the Army? Tell us.'

And slowly, as though learning to use words strange or unknown to him, Rebus began to tell his story. Gill rushed to her bag for a pen and a notepad. Michael sipped his whisky.

They listened.

PART FOUR
The Cross

22

I had been in the Parachute Regiment since the age of eighteen. But then I decided to try for the Special Air Service. Why did I do that? Why will any soldier take a cut in pay to join the SAS? I can't answer that. All I know now is that I found myself in Herefordshire, at the SAS's training camp. I called it The Cross because I'd been told that they would try to crucify me, and there, along with the other volunteers, I went through hell, marching, training, testing, pushing. They took us to the breaking point. They taught us to be lethal.

At that time there were rumours of an imminent civil war in Ulster, of the SAS being used to root out insurrectionists. The day came for us to be badged. We were given new berets and cap-badges. We were in the SAS. But there was more. Gordon Reeve and myself were called into the Boss's office and told that we had been judged the two best trainees of the batch. There was a two-year training period in front of us before we could become regulars, but great things were predicted for us.

Later, Reeve spoke to me as we left the building.

'Listen,' he said, 'I've heard a few of the rumours. I've heard the officers talking. They've got plans for us, Johnny. *Plans.* Mark my words.'

Weeks later, we were put on a survival course, hunted by other regiments, who if they captured us would stop at nothing to prise from us information about our mission. We had to trap and hunt our food, lying low and travelling across bleak moorland by night. We seemed destined to go through these tests together, though on this occasion we were working with two others.

'They've got something special lined up for us,' Reeve kept saying. 'I can feel it in my bones.'

Lying in our bivouac, we had just slipped into our sleeping-bags for a two-hour nap when our guard put his nose into the shelter.

'I don't know how to tell you this,' he said, and then there were

lights and guns everywhere, and we were half-beaten into uncon-
sciousness as the shelter was ripped open. Foreign tongues clacked at
us, their faces masked behind the torches. A rifle-butt to the kidneys
told me that this was for real. *For real.*

The cell into which I was thrown was real enough, too. The cell into
which I was thrown was smeared with blood, faeces, and other things.
It contained a stinking mattress and a cockroach. That was all. I lay
down on the damp mattress and tried to sleep, for I knew that sleep
would be the first thing to be stripped from us all.

The bright lights of the cell came suddenly and stayed on, burning
into my skull. Then the noises started, noises of a beating and a
questioning taking place in the cell next to me.

'Leave him alone, you bastards! I'll tear your fucking heads off!'

I slammed at the wall with fists and boots, and the noises stopped. A
cell door slammed shut, a body was dragged past my metal door, there
was silence. I knew my time would come.

I waited there, waited for hours and days, hungry, thirsty, and every
time I closed my eyes a sound like that of a blaring radio caught
between stations would sound from the walls and the ceiling. I lay with
my hands over my ears.

Fuck you, fuck you, fuck you.

I was supposed to crack now, and if I cracked I would have failed
everything, all the months of training. So I sang tunes loudly to myself.
I scraped my nails across the walls of the cell, walls wet with fungus,
and scratched my name there as an anagram: BRUSE. I played games
in my head, thought up crossword-puzzle clues and little linguistic
tricks. I turned survival into a game. A game, a game, a game. I had to
keep reminding myself that, no matter how bad things seemed to be
getting, this was all a game.

And I thought of Reeve, who had warned me of this. Big plans
indeed. Reeve was the nearest thing I had to a friend in the unit. I
wondered if it had been his body dragged across the floor outside my
cell. I prayed for him.

And one day they sent me food and a mug of brown water. The food
looked as though it had been scooped straight from the mud-crawl and
pushed through the little hole which had suddenly appeared in my
door and just as suddenly vanished. I willed this cold swill into
becoming a steak with two veg, and then placed a spoonful of it in my
mouth. Immediately, I spat it out again. The water tasted of iron. I

made a show of wiping my chin on my sleeve. I felt sure I was being watched.

'My compliments to the chef,' I called.

Next thing I knew, I was falling over into sleep.

I was in the air. There could be no doubt of that. I was in a helicopter, the air blowing into my face. I came round slowly, and opened my eyes on darkness. My head was in some kind of sack, and my arms were tied behind my back. I felt the helicopter swoop and rise and swoop again.

'Awake are you?' A butt prodded me.

'Yes.'

'Good. Now give me the name of your regiment and the details of your mission. We're not going to fuck around with you, sonny. So you better do it now.'

'Get stuffed.'

'I hope you can swim, sonny. I hope you get the *chance* to swim. We're about two-hundred feet above the Irish Sea, and we're about to push you out of this fucking chopper with your hands still tied. You'll hit that water as though it was fucking concrete, do you know that? It may kill you or it may stun you. The fish will eat you alive, sonny. And your corpse will never be found, not out here. Do you understand what I'm saying?'

It was an official and businesslike voice.

'Yes.'

'Good. Now, the name of your regiment, and the details of your mission.'

'Get stuffed.' I tried to sound calm. I'd be another accident statistic, killed on training, no questions asked. I'd hit that sea like a light-bulb hitting a wall.

'Get stuffed,' I said again, intoning to myself: it's only a game, it's only a game.

'This isn't a game, you know. Not anymore. Your friends have already spilled their guts, Rebus. One of them, Reeve I think it was, spilled his guts quite literally. Okay, men, give him the heave.'

'Wait . . .'

'Enjoy your swim, Rebus.'

Hands gripped my legs and torso. In the darkness of the sack, with the wind blowing fiercely against me, I began to feel that it had all been a grave mistake.

'Wait . . .'

I could feel myself hanging in space, two-hundred feet up above the sea, with the gulls shrieking for me to be let go.

'Wait!'

'Yes, Rebus?'

'Take the fucking sack off my head at least!' I was shrieking now, desperate.

'Let the bastard drop.'

And with that they let me go. I hung in the air for a second, then I dropped, dropped like a brick. I was falling through space, trussed up like a Christmas turkey. I screamed for one second, maybe two, and then I hit the ground.

I hit solid ground.

And lay there while the helicopter landed. People were laughing all around me. The foreign voices were back. They lifted me up and dragged me along to the cell. I was glad of the sack over my head. It disguised the fact that I was crying. Inside I was a mass of quivering coils, tiny serpents of fear and adrenaline and relief which bounced through my liver, my lungs, my heart.

The door slammed behind me. Then I heard a shuffling sound at my back. Hands fumbled at the knots of my bonds. With the hood off, it took me a few seconds to regain my sight.

I stared into a face that seemed to be my own. Another twist to the game. Then I recognised Gordon Reeve, at the same time as he recognised me.

'Rebus?' he said. 'They told me you'd . . .'

'They told me the same thing about you. How are you?'

'Fine, fine. Jesus, though, I'm glad to see you.'

We hugged one another, feeling the other's weakened but still human embrace, the smells of suffering and of endurance. There were tears in his eyes.

'It *is* you,' he said. 'I'm not dreaming.'

'Let's sit down,' I said. 'My legs aren't too steady.'

What I meant was that his legs weren't too steady. He was leaning into me as if I were a crutch. He sat down thankfully.

'How has it been?' I asked.

'I kept in shape for a while.' He slapped one of his legs. 'Doing push-ups and stuff. But I soon grew too tired. They've tried feeding me with hallucinogens. I keep seeing things when I'm awake.'

'They've tried me with knockout drops.'

'Those drugs, they're something else. Then there's the power-hose. I get sprayed about once a day I suppose. Freezing cold. Can never seem to get dry.'

'How long do you suppose we've been here?' Did I look as bad to him as he looked to me? I hoped not. He hadn't mentioned the chopper drop. I decided to keep quiet about that one.

'Too long,' he was saying. 'This is fucking ridiculous.'

'You were always saying that they had something special in store for us. I didn't believe you, God forgive me.'

'This wasn't exactly what I had in mind.'

'It *is* us they're interested in though.'

'What do you mean?'

It had been only half a thought until now, but now I was sure.

'Well, when our sentry put his nose into the tent that night, there was no surprise in his eyes, and even less fear. I think they were both in on it from the start.'

'So what's this all about?'

I looked at him, sitting with his chin on his knees. We were frail creatures on the outside. Piles biting like the hungered jaws of vampire bats, mouths aching with sores and ulcers. Hair falling out, teeth loose. But there was strength in numbers. And that was what I could not understand: why had they put us together when, apart, we were both on the edge of breaking?

'So what's this all about?'

Perhaps they were trying to lull us into a false sense of security before really tightening the screws. The worst is not, so long as we can say 'this is the worst'. Shakespeare, *King Lear*. I wouldn't have known that at the time, but I know it now. Let it stand.

'I don't know,' I said. 'They'll tell us when they're good and ready, I suppose.'

'Are you scared?' he said suddenly. His eyes were staring at the raddled door of our cell.

'Maybe.'

'You should be fucking scared, Johnny. I am. I remember once when I was a kid, some of us went along a river near our housing-scheme. It was in spate. It had been pissing down for a week. It was just after the war, and there were a lot of ruined houses about. We headed upriver, and came to a sewage-pipe. I played with older kids. I don't know why. They made me the brunt of all their fucking games, but I stuck with them. I suppose I liked the idea of running about with kids who scared the shit out of all the kids of my own age. So that, though the older kids were treating me like shit, they gave me power over the younger kids. Do you see?'

I nodded, but he wasn't looking.

'This pipe wasn't very thick, but it was long, and it was high above the river. They said I was to cross it first. Christ, I was afraid. I was so fucking scared that my legs wobbled and I froze there, halfway across. And then piss started to run down my legs out of my shorts, and they noticed that and they laughed. They laughed at me, and I couldn't run, couldn't move. So they left me there and went away.'

I thought of the laughter as I had been dragged away from the helicopter.

'Did anything like that ever happen to you when you were a kid, Johnny?'

'I don't think so.'

'Then why the hell did you join up?'

'To get away from home. I didn't get along with my father, you see. He preferred my kid brother. I felt out in the cold.'

'I never had a brother.'

'Neither did I, not in the proper sense. I had an adversary.'

I'm going to bring him out

don't you dare

This isn't telling us anything

keep going

'What did your father do, Johnny?'

'He was a hypnotist. He used to make people come on stage and do stupid things.'

'You're joking!'

'It's true. My brother was going to follow in his footsteps, but I wasn't. So I got out. They weren't exactly sad to see me go.'

Reeve chuckled.

'If you put us into a sale, you'd have to say "slightly soiled" on the ticket, eh, Johnny?'

I laughed at that, laughed longer and louder than necessary, and we put an arm round one another and stayed that way, keeping warm.

We slept side by side, pissed and defecated in the presence of the other, tried to exercise together, played little mind games together, and endured together.

Reeve had a piece of string with him, and would wind it and unwind it, making up the knots we had been taught in training. This led me to explain the meaning of a Gordian knot to him. He waved a miniature reef knot at me.

'Gordian knot, reef knot. Gordian reef. It sounds just like my name, doesn't it?'

Again, there was something to laugh about.

We also played noughts and crosses, scratching the games onto the powdery walls of the cell with our fingernails. Reeve showed me a ploy which meant that the least you could achieve was a draw. We must have played about three-hundred games before then, with Reeve winning two-thirds of them. The trick was simple enough.

'Your first O goes in the top left corner, and your second diagonally across from it. It's an unbeatable position.'

'What if your opponent puts his X diagonally opposite that first O?'

'You can still win by going for the corners.'

Reeve seemed cheered by this. He danced round the cell, then stared at me, a leer on his face.

'You're just like the brother I never had, John.' There and then he took my palm and nicked the flesh open with one of his fingernails, doing the same to his own hand. We touched palms, smearing a spot of blood backwards and forwards.

'Blood brothers,' said Gordon, smiling.

I smiled back at him, knowing that he had become too dependent on me already, and that if we were separated he would not be able to cope.

And then he knelt down in front of me and gave me another hug.

Gordon grew more restless. He did fifty press-ups in any one day which, considering our diet, was phenomenal. And he hummed little tunes to himself. The effects of my company seemed to be wearing off. He was drifting again. So I began to tell him stories.

I talked about my childhood first, and about my father's tricks, but then I started to tell him proper stories, giving him the plots of my favourite books. The time came to tell him the story of Raskolnikov, that most moral of tales, *Crime and Punishment*. He listened enthralled, and I tried to spin it out as long as I could. I made bits up, invented whole dialogues and characters. And when I'd finished it, he said, 'Tell me that one again.'

So I did.

'Was it all inevitable, John?' Reeve was pushing his fingers across the floor of the cell, seated on his haunches. I was lying on the mattress.

'Yes,' I said. 'I think it was. Certainly, it's written that way. The end of the book is there before the beginning's hardly started.'

'Yes, that's the feeling I got.'

There was a long pause, then he cleared his throat.

'What's your idea of God, John? I'd really like to know.'

So I told him, and as I spoke, lacing my erroneous arguments with little stories from the Bible, Gordon Reeve lay down and stared up at me with eyes like the full moons of winter. He was concentrating like mad.

'I can't believe any of that,' he said at last as I swallowed dry saliva. 'I wish I could, but I can't. I think Raskolnikov should have relaxed and enjoyed his freedom. He should have got himself a Browning and blown the lot of them away.'

I thought about that comment. There seemed to me a little justice in it, but a great deal against it also. Reeve was like a man trapped in limbo, believing in a lack of belief, but not necessarily lacking the belief to believe.

What's all this shit?

Sshhhh.

And in between the games and the story-telling, he put his hand on my neck.

'John, we're friends, aren't we? I mean, really close friends? I've never had a close friend before.' His breath was hot, despite the chill in the cell. 'But we're friends, aren't we? I mean, I've taught you how to win at noughts and crosses, haven't I?' His eyes were no longer human. They were the eyes of a wolf. I had seen it coming, but there had been nothing I could do.

Not until now. But now I saw everything with the clear, hallucinogen eyes of one who has seen everything there is to see and more. I could see Gordon bring his face up to mine and slowly – so slowly that it might not have been happening at all – plant a breathy kiss on my cheek, trying to turn my head around so as to connect with the lips.

And I saw myself yield. No, no, this was not to happen! This was intolerable. This wasn't what we'd been building up all these weeks, was it? And if it was, then I'd been a fool throughout.

'Just a kiss,' he was saying, 'just one kiss, John. Hell, come on.' And there were tears in his eyes, because he too could see that everything had gone haywire in an instant. He too could see that something was ending. But that didn't stop him from edging his way behind me, making the two-backed beast. (Shakespeare. Let it go.) And I was trembling, but strangely immobile. I knew that this was beyond my ken, beyond my control. So I forced the tears up into my eyes, and my nose started to run.

'Just a kiss.'

All the training, all the pushing towards that final lethal goal, it had all come to this moment. In the end, love was still behind everything.

'John.'

And I could feel only pity for the two of us, stinking, besmirched, barren in our cell. I could feel only the frustration of the thing, the poor tears of a lifetime's indignation. Gordon, Gordon, Gordon.

'John . . .'

The cell-door burst open, as though it had never been locked.

A man stood there. English, not foreign, and of high rank. He looked in on the spectacle with some distaste; no doubt he had been listening to it all, if not watching it. He pointed to me.

'Rebus,' he said, 'you've passed. You're on our side now.'

I looked at his face. What did he mean? I knew full well what he meant.

'You've passed the test, Rebus. Come on. Come with me. We'll get you kitted up. You're on our side now. The interrogation of your . . . friend . . . continues. You'll be helping us with the interrogation from now on.'

Gordon jumped to his feet. He was directly behind me still. I could feel his breath on the back of my neck.

'What do you mean?' I said. My mouth and stomach were dry. Looking at this crisply starched officer, I became painfully aware of my own filth. But then it was all his fault. 'This is a trick,' I said. 'It must be. I'm not going to tell you. I'm not going *with* you. I've not given away any information. I've not cracked. You can't fail me now!' I was shouting now, delirious. Yet I knew there was truth in what he was saying. He shook his head slowly.

'I can understand your suspicion, Rebus. You've been under a lot of pressure. A hellish lot of pressure. But that's past. You've not failed, you've passed; passed with flying colours. I think we can say that with certainty. You've passed, Rebus. You're on our side now. You'll be helping us now to try to crack Reeve here. Do you understand?'

I shook my head.

'It's a trick,' I said. The officer smiled sympathetically. He'd dealt with the like of me a hundred times before.

'Look,' he said, 'just come with us and everything will be made clear.'

Gordon jumped forward at my side.

'No!' he shouted. 'He's already told you that he's not fucking well going! Now piss off out of here.' Then to me, a hand on my shoulder: 'Don't listen to him, John. It's a trick. It's always a trick with these bastards.' But I could see that he was worried. His eyes moved rapidly, his mouth slightly open. And, feeling his hand on me, I knew that my decision had been made already, and Gordon seemed to sense as much.

'I think that's for Trooper Rebus to decide, don't you?' the officer was saying.

And then the man stared at me, his eyes friendly.

I didn't need to look back at the cell, or at Gordon. I just kept thinking to myself: it's another part of the game, just another part of the game. The decision had been made a long time ago. They were not lying to me, and of course I wanted out of the cell. It was preordained. Nothing was arbitrary. I had been told that at the start of my training. I started forwards, but Gordon held onto the tatters of my shirt.

'John,' he said, his voice full of need, 'don't let me down, John. Please.'

But I pulled away from his weak grip and left the cell.

'No! No! No!' His cries were huge, fiery things. 'Don't let me down, John! Let me out! Let me out!'

And then he screamed, and I almost crumpled on the floor.

It was the scream of the mad.

After I had been cleaned up and seen by a doctor, I was taken to what they euphemistically called the debriefing-room. I'd been through hell – was still going through hell – and they were about to discuss it as though it had been nothing more than a school exercise.

There were four of them there, three captains and a psychiatrist. They told me everything then. They explained that a new, elitist group was about to be set up from within the SAS, and that its role would be the infiltration and destabilization of terrorist groups, starting with the Irish Republican Army, who were becoming more than a mere nuisance as the Irish situation deteriorated into civil war. Because of the nature of the job, only the best – the very best – would be good enough, and Reeve and I had been judged the best in our section. Therefore, we had been trapped, had been taken prisoner, and had been put through tests the like of which had never been tried in the SAS before. None of this really surprised me by now. I was thinking of the other poor bastards who were being put through this whole sick bloody thing. And all so that when we were being kneecapped, we would not let on who we were.

And then they came to Gordon.

'Our attitude towards Trooper Reeve is rather ambivalent.' This was the man in the white coat talking. 'He's a bloody fine soldier, and give him a physical job to do and he'll do it. But he has always worked as a loner in the past, so we put the two of you together to see how you would react to sharing a cell, and, more especially, to see how Reeve would cope once his friend had been taken away from him.'

Did they know of that kiss then, or did they not?

'I'm afraid,' went on the doctor, 'that the result may be negative. He's come to depend upon you, John, hasn't he? We are, of course, aware that you have not been dependent upon him.'

'What about the screams from the other cells?'

'Tape-recordings.'

I nodded, tired suddenly, uninterested.

'The whole thing was another bloody test then?'

'Of course it was.' They had a little smile between them. 'But that needn't bother you now. What matters is that you've passed.'

It did worry me, though. What was it all about? I'd exchanged friendship for this informal debriefing. I'd exchanged love for these smirks. And Gordon's screams were still in my ears. Revenge, he was crying, revenge. I laid my hands on my knees, bent forward, and started to weep.

'You bastards,' I said, 'you bastards.'

And if I'd had a Browning pistol with me at that moment, I'd have put large holes into their grinning skulls.

They had me checked again, more thoroughly this time, in a military hospital. Civil war had indeed broken out in Ulster, but I stared past it towards Gordon Reeve. What had happened to him? Was he still in that stinking cell, alone because of me? Was he falling apart? I took it all on my shoulders and wept again. They had given me a box of tissues. That seemed to be the way of things.

Then I started to weep all day, sometimes uncontrollably, taking it all on, taking everything on my conscience. I suffered from nightmares. I volunteered my resignation. I *demanded* my resignation. It was accepted, reluctantly. I was, after all, a guinea-pig. I went to a small fishing-village in Fife and walked along the pebbled beach, recovering from my nervous breakdown and putting the whole thing out of my mind, stuffing the most painful episode of my life into drawers and attics in my head, locking it all away, learning to forget.

So I forgot.

And they were good to me. They gave me some compensation money and they pulled a lot of strings when I decided that I wanted to join the police force. Oh yes, I could not complain about their attitude towards me, but I wasn't allowed to find out about my friend, and I wasn't ever to get in touch with them again. I was dead, I was strictly off their records.

I was a failure.

And I'm still a failure. Broken marriage. My daughter kidnapped. But it all makes sense now. The whole thing makes sense. So at least I know that Gordon is alive, if not well, and I know that he has my little girl and that he's going to kill her.

And kill me if he can.

And to get her back, I'm going to have to kill him.

And I would do it now. God help me, I would do it now.

Knots & Crosses

PART FIVE

Knots & Crosses

23

When John Rebus awoke from what had seemed a particularly deep and dream-troubled sleep, he found that he was not in bed. He saw that Michael was standing over him, a wary smile on his face, and that Gill was pacing to and fro, sniffing back tears.

'What happened?' said Rebus.

'Nothing,' said Michael.

Then Rebus recalled that Michael had hypnotised him.

'Nothing?' cried Gill. 'You call that nothing?'

'John,' said Michael, 'I didn't realise that you felt that way about the old man and me. I'm sorry we made you feel bad.' Michael rested his hand on his brother's shoulder, *the brother he had never known.*

Gordon, Gordon Reeve. What happened to you? You're all torn and dirty, whirling around me like grit on a wind-swept street. Like a brother. You've got my daughter. Where are you?

'Oh, Jesus.' Rebus let his head fall, screwing his eyes shut. Gill's hand stroked his hair.

It was growing light outside. The birds were back into their untiring routine. Rebus was glad that they were calling him back into the real world. They reminded him that there might be someone out there who was feeling happy. Perhaps lovers awakening in each other's arms, or a man who was realising that today was a holiday, or an elderly woman thanking God that she was alive to see the first hints of reawakening life.

'A real dark night of the soul,' he said, beginning to shake. 'It's cold in here. The pilot-light must have blown out.'

Gill blew her nose and folded her arms.

'No, it's warm enough in here, John. Listen,' she spoke slowly, deferentially, 'we need a physical description of this man. I know that it will have to be a fifteen-year-old description, but it'll be a start. Then we need to check up on what happened to him after you des . . . after you left him.'

'That will be classified, if it exists at all.'

'And we need to tell the Chief about all of this.' Gill went on as if Rebus had said nothing. Her eyes were fixed in front of her. 'We need to find that creep.'

The room seemed very quiet to Rebus, as though a death had occurred, when really it had been a birth of sorts, the birth of his memory. Of Gordon. Of walking out of that cold, merciless cell. Of turning his back . . .

'Can you be sure that this Reeve character is your man?' Michael was pouring more whisky. Rebus shook his head at the proffered glass.

'Not for me thanks. My head feels all fuzzy. Oh yes, I think we can be pretty certain who's behind it. The messages, the knots and the crosses. It all makes sense now. It's been making sense all along. Reeve must think I'm really thick. He's been sending me clear messages for weeks, and I've failed to realise . . . I've let those girls die . . . All because I couldn't face the facts . . . the facts . . .'

Gill bent down behind him and put her hands on his shoulders. John Rebus shot out of his chair and turned to her. *Reeve.* No, Gill, Gill. He shook his head in mute apology. Then burst into tears.

Gill looked towards Michael, but Michael had lowered his eyes. She hugged Rebus hard, not allowing him to break away from her again, all the time whispering that it was she, Gill, beside him, and not any ghost from the past. Michael was wondering what he had got himself into. He had never seen John cry before. Again, the guilt flooded him. He would stop it all. He didn't need it any more. He would lie low and just let his dealer get tired of looking for him, let his clients find new people. He would do it, not for John's sake but for his own.

We treated him like shit, he thought to himself, it's true. The old man and me treated him as though he were an intruder.

Later, over coffee, Rebus seemed calm, though Gill's eyes were still on him, wondering, fearing.

'We can be sure that this Reeve is off his chump,' she said.

'Perhaps,' said Rebus. 'One thing *is* for sure, he'll be armed. He'll be ready for anything. The man was a Seaforths regular and a member of the SAS. He'll be hard as nails.'

'You were too, John.'

'That's why I'm the man to track him down. The Chief must be made to understand that, Gill. I'm back on the case.'

Gill pursed her lips.

'I'm not sure he'll go for that,' she said.

'Well, sod him then. I'll find the bastard anyway.'

'You do that, John,' said Michael. 'You do that. Don't care what any of them say.'

'Mickey,' said Rebus, 'you are absolutely the best brother I could have had. Now, is there any food on the go? I'm starved.'

'And I'm whacked,' said Michael, feeling pleased with himself. 'Do you mind if I lie down for an hour or two here before I drive back?'

'Not at all, go through to my room, Mickey.'

'Goodnight, Michael,' said Gill.

He was smiling as he left them.

Knots and crosses. Noughts and crosses. It was so blatant, really. Reeve must have taken him for a fool, and in a way he had been right. Those endless games they had played, all those tricks and manoeuvres, and their talk about Christianity, those reef knots and Gordian knots. And The Cross. God, how stupid he had been, allowing his memory into tricking him that the past was a cracked and useless vessel, emptying its spirit. How stupid.

'John, you're spilling your coffee.'

Gill was bringing in a plateful of cheese on toast from the kitchen. Rebus roused himself awake.

'Eat this. I've been on to HQ. We've to be there in two hours' time. They've already started running a check on Reeve's name. We should find him.'

'I hope so, Gill. Oh God, I hope so.'

They hugged. She suggested that they lie on the couch. They did so, tight in a warming embrace. Rebus couldn't help wondering whether his dark night had been an exorcism of sorts, whether the past would still haunt him sexually. He hoped not. Certainly, it was neither the time nor the place to try it out.

Gordon, my friend, what did I do to you?

24

Stevens was a patient man. The two policemen had been firm with him. No one could see Detective Sergeant Rebus for the moment. Stevens had returned to the newspaper office, worked on a report for the paper's three-a.m. print-run, and then had driven back to Rebus's flat. There were still lights on up there, but also there were two new gorillas by the door of the tenement. Stevens parked across the street and lit another cigarette. It was tying together nicely. The two threads were becoming one. The murders and the drug-pushing were involved in some way, and Rebus was the key by the look of things. What were his brother and he talking about at this hour? A contingency plan perhaps. God, he would have given anything to be a fly on the living-room wall just now. Anything. He knew reporters in Fleet Street who went in for sophisticated surveillance techniques – bugs, high-powered micro-phones, telephone-taps – and he wondered if it might not be worthwhile to invest in some of that equipment himself.

He formulated new theories in his head, theories with hundreds of perm-utations. If Edinburgh's drug-racketeers had gone into the abduction-and-murder business to put the frights on some poor bastards, then things were taking a very grim turn indeed, and he, Jim Stevens, would have to be even more careful in future. Yet Big Podeen had known nothing. Say, then, that a new gang had broken into the game, bringing with it new rules. That would make for a gang-war, Glasgow-style. But things, surely, were not done that way today. Maybe.

In this way, Stevens kept himself awake and alert, scribbling his thoughts into a notebook. His radio was on, and he listened to the half-hourly news reports. A policeman's daughter was the new victim of Edinburgh's child-murderer. In the most recent abduction, a man was killed, strangled in the house of the child's mother. And so on. Stevens went on formulating, went on speculating.

It had not yet been revealed that *all* the murders were linked to

Rebus. The police were not about to make that public, not even to Jim Stevens.

At seven-thirty, Stevens managed to bribe a passing newspaper-boy into bringing him rolls and milk from a nearby shop. He washed the dry, powdery rolls down with the icy milk. The heating was on in his car, but he felt chilled to the marrow. He needed a shower, a shave, and some sleep. Not necessarily in that order. But he was too close to let this go now. He had the tenacity – some would call it madness, fanaticism – of every good reporter. He had watched other hacks arriving in the night and being sent away again. One or two had seen him sitting in his car and had come across for a chat and to sniff out any leads. He had hidden away his notebook then, feigning disinterest, telling them that he would be going home shortly. Lies, damned lies.

That was part of the business.

And now, finally, they were emerging from the building. A few cameras and microphones were there, of course, but nothing too tasteless, no pushing and shoving and harassing. For one thing, this was a grieving father; for another, he was a policeman. Nobody was about to harass him.

Stevens watched as Gill and Rebus were allowed to disappear into the back of an idling Rover police-car. He studied their faces. Rebus looked washed-out. That was only to be expected. But, behind that, lay a grimness of look, something about the way his mouth made a straight line. That bothered Stevens a little. It was as if the man were about to enter a war. Bloody hell. And then there was Gill Templer. She looked rough, rougher even than Rebus. Her eyes were red, but here too there was something a little out of the ordinary. Something was not quite as it should be. Any self-respecting reporter could see that, if he knew what he was looking for. Stevens gnawed at himself. He needed to know more. It was like a drug, his story. He needed bigger and bigger injections of it. He was a bit startled, too, to find himself admitting that the reason he needed these injections was not for the sake of his job, but for his own curiosity. Rebus intrigued him. Gill Templer, of course, interested him.

And Michael Rebus . . .

Michael Rebus had not appeared from the flat. The circus was leaving now, the Rover turning right out of the quiet Marchmont street, but the gorillas remained. New gorillas. Stevens lit a cigarette. It might be worth a try at that. He walked back to his car and locked it. Then, taking a walk round the block, formed another plan.

*

'Excuse me, sir. Do you live here?'

'Of course I live here! What's all this about, eh? I need to get to my bed.'

'Had a heavy night, sir?'

The bleary-eyed man shook three brown paper-bags at the policeman. The bags each contained six rolls.

'I'm a baker. Shift-work. Now if you'll . . .'

'And your name, sir?'

Making to pass the man, Stevens had just had time enough to make out a few of the names on the door-buzzer.

'Laidlaw,' he said. 'Jim Laidlaw.'

The policeman checked this against a list of names in his hand.

'All right, sir. Sorry to have bothered you.'

'What's all this about?'

'You'll find out soon enough, sir. Good night now.'

There was one more obstacle, and Stevens knew that for all his cunning, if the door was locked then the door was locked, and his game was up. He made a plausible push at the heavy door and felt it give. They had not locked it. His patron saint was smiling on him today.

In the tenement hallway, he ditched the rolls and thought of another ploy. He climbed the two flights of stairs to Rebus's door. The tenement seemed to smell exclusively of cats'-piss. At Rebus's door he paused, catching his breath. Partly, he was out of condition, but partly, also, he was excited. He had not felt anything like this on a story for years. It felt good. He decided that he could get away with anything on a day like this. He pushed the doorbell relentlessly.

The door was opened at last by a yawning, puffy-faced Michael Rebus. So at last they were face to face. Stevens flashed a card at Michael. The card identified James Stevens as a member of an Edinburgh snooker club.

'Detective Inspector Stevens, sir. Sorry to get you out of bed.' He put the card away. 'Your brother told us that you'd probably still be asleep, but I thought I'd come up anyway. May I come in? Just a few questions, sir. Won't keep you too long.'

The two policemen, their feet numb despite thermal socks and the fact that it was the beginning of summer, shuffled one foot and then the other, hoping for a reprieve. The talk was all of the abduction and the fact that a Chief Inspector's son had been murdered. The main door opened behind them.

'You lot still here? The wife told me there was bobbies at the door, but I didnae believe her. Yon wis last night though. What's the matter?'

This was an old man, still in his slippers but with a thick, winter overcoat on. He was half-shaven only, and his bottom false-teeth had been lost or forgotten about. He was attaching a cap to his bald head as he sidled out of the door.

'Nothing for you to worry about, sir. You'll be told soon enough, I'm sure.'

'Oh aye, well then. I'm just away to fetch the paper and the milk. We usually have toast for breakfast, but some bugger's gone and left about twa dozen new rolls in the lobby. Well, if they're no' wanted, they're aye welcome in my house.'

He chuckled, showing the raw red of his bottom gum.

'Can I get you twa anything at the shop?'

But the two policemen were staring at one another, alarmed, speechless.

'Get up there,' one said, finally, to the other. Then: 'And your name, sir?'

The old man preened himself; an old trooper.

'Jock Laidlaw,' he said, 'at your service.'

Stevens was drinking, thankfully, the black coffee. The first hot thing he'd had in ages. He was seated in the living-room, his eyes everywhere.

'I'm glad you woke me,' Michael Rebus was saying. 'I've got to get back home.'

I'll bet you have, thought Stevens. I'll bet you have. Rebus looked altogether more relaxed than he had foreseen. Relaxed, rested, easy with his conscience. Curiouser and curiouser.

'Just a few questions, Mister Rebus, as I said.'

Michael Rebus sat down, crossing his legs, sipping his own coffee. 'Yes?'

Stevens produced his notebook.

'Your brother has had a very great shock.'

'Yes.'

'But he'll be all right you think?'

'Yes.'

Stevens pretended to write in his book.

'Did he have a good night, by the way? Did he sleep all right?'

'Well, none of us got much sleep. I'm not sure John slept at all.' Michael's eyebrows were gathering. 'Look, what is all this?'

'Just routine, Mister Rebus. You understand. We need all the details from everyone involved if we're going to crack this case.'

'But it's cracked, isn't it?'

Stevens' heart jumped.

'Is it?' he heard himself say.

'Well, don't you know?'

'Yes, of course, but we have to get *all* the details –'

'From everyone concerned. Yes, so you said. Look, can I see your identification again? Just to be on the safe side.'

There was the sound of a key prodding at the front door.

Christ, thought Stevens, they're back already.

'Listen,' he said through his teeth, 'we know all about your little drugs-racket. Now tell us who's behind it or else we'll put you behind bars for a hundred years, sonny!'

Michael's face went light-blue, then grey. His mouth seemed ready to drop open with a word, the one word Stevens needed.

But then one of the gorillas was in the room, propelling Stevens out of his chair.

'I've not finished my coffee yet!' he protested.

'You're lucky I don't break your flaming neck, pal,' replied the policeman.

Michael Rebus stood up, too, but he was saying nothing.

'A name!' cried Stevens. 'Just give me the name! This'll be spread right across the front pages, my friend, if you don't co-operate! Give me the name!'

He kept up his cries all the way down the stairwell. Right down to the last step.

'All right, I'm going,' he said eventually, breaking free of the heavy grip on his arm. 'I'm going. You were a bit slack there, boys, weren't you? I'll keep it quiet this time, but next time you better be ready. Okay?'

'Get to fuck out of here,' said one gorilla.

Stevens got to fuck. He slid into his car, feeling more frustrated and more curious than ever. God, he'd been close. But what did the hypnotist mean by that? The case was cracked. Was it? If so, he wanted to be there with the first details. He was not used to being so far behind in the game. Usually, games were played by his rules. No, he was not used to this, and he did not like it at all.

He loved it.

But, if the case was cracked, then time was tight. And if you could not get what you wanted from one brother, then go to the other. He thought he knew where John Rebus would be. His intuition ran high today. He felt inspired.

25

'Well, John, this all seems quite fantastical, but I'm sure it's a possibility. Certainly, it's the best lead we've got, though I find it hard to conceive of a man with so much hate that he would murder four innocent girls just to give you the clues as to his ultimate victim.'

Chief Superintendent Wallace looked from Rebus to Gill Templer and back again. To Rebus's left sat Anderson. Wallace's hands lay like dead fish on his desk, a pen in front of him. The room was large and uncluttered, a self-assured oasis. Here, problems were always solved, decisions were made – always correctly.

'The problem now is finding him. If we make this thing public, then that might scare him off, endangering your daughter's life in the process. On the other hand, a public appeal would be by far the quickest way of finding him.'

'You can't possibly . . .!' It was Gill Templer who, in that quiet room, was on the verge of exploding, but Wallace silenced her with a wave of his hand.

'I am merely thinking aloud at this stage, Inspector Templer, merely casting stones into a pond.'

Anderson sat like a corpse, his eyes to the floor. He was on leave now officially and in mourning, but he had insisted on keeping in touch with the case and Superintendent Wallace had acquiesced.

'Of course, John,' Wallace was saying, 'it's impossible for you to remain on the case.'

Rebus rose to his feet.

'Sit down, John, please.' The Super's eyes were hard and honest, the eyes of a real copper, one of the old school. Rebus sat down again. 'Now I know how you must feel, believe it or believe it not. But there's too much at stake here. Too much for all of us. You're far too involved to be of any objective use, and the public would cry out about vigilante tactics. You must see that.'

'All I see is that without me Reeve will stop at nothing. It's me he wants.'

'Exactly. And wouldn't we be stupid to hand you over to him on a plate? We'll do everything we can, as much as you could do. Leave it to us.'

'The Army won't tell you anything, you know.'

'They'll have to.' Wallace began to toy with his pen, as though it were there for that very purpose. 'Ultimately, they've got the same boss we have. They'll be made to tell.'

Rebus shook his head.

'They're a law unto themselves. The SAS is hardly even a part of the Army. If they don't want to tell you, then believe me, they won't tell you a bloody thing.' Rebus's hand came down onto the desk. 'Not a bloody thing.'

'John.' Gill's hand squeezed his shoulder, asking him to be calm. She herself looked like a fury, but she knew when to keep quiet and let looks alone transmit her anger and her displeasure. For Rebus, however, it was actions that counted. He'd been sitting outside reality for way too long.

He rose from his small chair like a pure force, no longer human, and left the room in silence. The Superintendent looked at Gill.

'He's off the case, Gill. He must be made to realise that. I believe that you,' he paused while opening and shutting a drawer, 'that you and he have an understanding. That, at least, is how we used to phrase it in my day. Perhaps you should make him aware of his position. We'll get this man, but not with Rebus hanging around intent on revenge.' Wallace looked towards Anderson, who stared drily at him. 'We don't want vigilante tactics,' he went on. 'Not in Edinburgh. What would the tourists say?' Then his face broke into a cold smile. He looked from Anderson to Gill, then rose from his chair. 'This is all becoming extremely . . .'

'Internecine?' suggested Gill.

'I was going to say incestuous. What with Chief Inspector Anderson here, his son and Rebus's wife, yourself and Rebus, Rebus and this man Reeve, Reeve and Rebus's daughter. I hope the press don't get wind of this. You'll be responsible for seeing that they don't, and for punishing any that do. Am I making myself clear?'

Gill Templer nodded, stifling a sudden yawn.

'Good.' The Super nodded across to Anderson. 'Now see that Chief Inspector Anderson gets home safely will you?'

*

William Anderson, seated in the back of the car, went through his mental list of informants and friends. He knew a couple of people who might know about the Special Air Service. Certainly, something like the Rebus-Reeve case could not have been hushed up totally, though it might well have been struck from the records. The soldiers would have known about it though. Grapevines existed everywhere, and especially where you would least expect them. He might need to twist a few arms and lay out a few tenners, but he would find the bastard if it was his last action on God's earth.

Or he would be there when Rebus did.

Rebus had left the HQ by a back entrance, as Stevens had hoped. He followed Rebus as the policeman, looking the worse for wear, stalked away. What was it all about? No matter. As long as he stuck to Rebus, he could be sure of getting his story, and what a story it promised to be. Stevens kept checking behind him, but there seemed to be no tail on Rebus. No police tail, that was. It seemed strange to him that they would allow Rebus to go off on his own when there was no telling what a man would do whose daughter had been abducted. Stevens was hoping for the ultimate plot: he was hoping that Rebus would lead him straight to the big boys behind this new drugs ring. If not one brother, then the other.

Like a brother to me, and I to him. What happened? He knew what was to blame at heart. The method, that was the cause of all of this. The caging and the breaking and then the patching up. The patching up had not been a success, had it? They were both broken men in their own ways. That knowledge wouldn't stop him from shearing Reeve's head from its shoulders though. Nothing would stop that. But he had to find the bastard yet, and he had no idea where to start. He could feel the city closing in on him, bringing to bear all of its historical weight, smothering him. Dissent, rationalism, enlightenment: Edinburgh had specialized in all three, and now he too would need these charms. He needed to work on his own, quickly, yet methodically, using ingenuity and every tool at his disposal. Most of all he needed instinct.

After five minutes, he knew he was being followed, and the hair stood up at the back of his neck. It was not the usual police tail. That would not have been so easy to spot. But was it . . . Could he be so close . . . At a bus-stop, he stopped and turned suddenly, as though checking to see if a bus was coming. He saw the man dodge into a doorway. It wasn't Gordon Reeve. It was that bloody reporter.

Rebus listened to his heart slow again, but the adrenaline was already pumping through him, filling him with a desire to run, to take off along this long straight road and run into the strongest head-wind imaginable. But then a bus came trundling round the corner, and he boarded that instead.

From the back window, he saw the reporter jump out of the doorway and desperately flag down a taxi-cab. Rebus had no time to be bothered with the man. He had some thinking to do, thinking about how in the world he could find Reeve. The possibility haunted him: he'll find *me*. I don't need to chase. But somehow that scared him most of all.

Gill Templer could not find Rebus. He had disappeared as though he had been a shadow merely and not a man at all. She telephoned and hunted and asked and did all the things a good copper should do, but she was confronted by the fact of a man who was not only a good copper himself, but had been one of the best in the SAS to boot. He might have been hiding under her feet, under her desk, in her clothes, and she would never have found him. So he stayed hidden.

He stayed hidden, she surmised, because he was on the move, swiftly and methodically moving through the streets and bars of Edinburgh in search of his prey, knowing that when found, the prey would turn hunter once more.

But Gill went on trying, shivering now and then when she thought of her lover's grim and horrific past, and of the mentality of those who decided that such things were necessary. Poor John. What would she have done? She would have walked right out of that cell and kept on walking, just as he had done. And yet she would have felt guilty, too, just as he had felt guilt, and she would have put it all behind her, scarred invisibly.

Why did the men in her life have to be such complicated, fraught, screwed-up bastards? Did she attract the soiled goods only? It might have been humorous, but then there was Samantha to think about, and that wasn't funny at all. Where did you start looking if you wanted to find a needle? She remembered Superintendent Wallace's words: *they've got the same boss we have.* That was a truth well worth contemplating in all its complexity. For if they had the same boss, then perhaps a cover-up could be arranged at this end, now that the ancient and terrible truth had surfaced again. If this got into the papers, all hell would be let loose at every level of the service. Perhaps they would want to co-operate in hushing it up. Perhaps they would want Rebus silenced. My God, what if they should want John Rebus silenced? That would mean silencing Anderson, too, and herself. It would mean bribes or a total wipe-out. She would have to be very careful indeed. One false move now might mean her dismissal from the force, and that would not do at all. Justice had to be seen to be done. There could be no cover-ups. The Boss, whoever or whatever that anonymous term was meant to imply, would not have his or its day. There had to be truth, or the whole thing was a sham, and so were its actors.

And what of her feelings towards John Rebus himself, spotlit on the reddened stage? She hardly knew what to think. The notion still niggled at her that, no matter how absurd it might appear, John was somehow behind this whole thing: no Reeve, the notes sent to himself, jealousy leading him to kill his wife's lover, his daughter now hidden somewhere – somewhere like that locked room.

It was hardly to be contemplated, which, considering the way the whole thing had gone thus far, was why Gill contemplated it very hard indeed. And rejected it, rejected it for no other reason than that John Rebus had once made love to her, once bared his soul to her, once clasped her hand beneath a hospital blanket. Would a man with something to hide have become involved with a policewoman? No, it seemed wholly unlikely.

So, again, it became a possibility, joining the others. Gill's head began to pulse. Where the hell was John? And what if Reeve found him before they found Reeve? If John Rebus was a walking beacon to his enemy, then wasn't it crazy for him to be out there on his own, wherever he was? Of course it was stupid. It had been stupid to let him walk out of the room, out of the building, vanishing like a whisper. Shit. She picked up the telephone again and dialled his flat.

26

John Rebus was moving through the jungle of the city, that jungle the tourists never saw, being too busy snapping away at the ancient golden temples, temples long since gone but still evident as shadows. This jungle closed in on the tourists relentlessly but unseen, a natural force, the force of dissipation and destruction.

Edinburgh's an easy beat, his colleagues from the west coast would say. Try Partick for a night and tell me that it's not. But Rebus knew different. He knew that Edinburgh was all appearances, which made the crime less easy to spot, but no less evident. Edinburgh was a schizophrenic city, the place of Jekyll & Hyde sure enough, the city of Deacon Brodie, of fur coats and no knickers (as they said in the west). But it was a small city, too, and that would be to Rebus's advantage.

He hunted in the hard-man's drinking dens, in the housing estates where heroin and unemployment were the totem kings, for he knew that somewhere in this anonymity a hard man could hide and could plan and could survive. He was trying to get inside Gordon Reeve's skin. It was a skin sloughed many times, and Rebus had to admit, finally, that he was further away from his insane, murderous blood-brother than ever before. If he had turned his back on Gordon Reeve, then Reeve was refusing to show himself anyway. Perhaps there would be another note, another teasing clue. Oh, Sammy, Sammy, Sammy. Please God let her live, let her live.

Gordon Reeve had levitated right out of Rebus's world. He was floating overhead, floating and gloating in his new-found power. It had taken him fifteen years to accomplish his trick, but my God what a trick. Fifteen years within which time he had probably changed his name and appearance, taken on a menial job, researched Rebus's life. How long had this man been watching him? Watching and hating and scheming? All those times that he had felt his flesh creep for no reason, that the telephone had rung without a voice behind it, that small, easily forgotten accidents had occurred. And Reeve, grinning above him, a little god over Rebus's destiny. Rebus, shivering, entered a pub for the hell of it and ordered a triple whisky.

'It's quarter-gills in here, pal. Are you sure you want a treble?'

'Sure.'

What the hell. It was all one. If God swirled in his heaven, leaning down to touch his creatures, then it was a curious touch indeed that he gave them. Looking around, Rebus stared into a heart of desperation. Old men sat with their half-pint glasses, staring emptily towards the front door. Were they wondering what was outside? Or were they just scared that whatever was out there would one day force its way in, pushing into their dark corners and cowered glances with the wrath of some Old Testament monster, some behemoth, some flood of destruction? Rebus could not see behind their eyes, just as they could not see behind his. That ability not to share the sufferings of others was all that kept the mass of humanity rolling on, concentrating on the 'me', shunning the beggars and their folded arms. Rebus, behind his eyes, was begging now, begging to that strange God of his to allow him to find Reeve, to explain himself to the madman. God did not answer. The TV blared out some banal quiz show.

'Fight Imperialism, fight Racism.'

A young girl wearing a mock-leather coat and little round glasses stood behind Rebus. He turned to her. She had a collecting tin in one hand and a pile of newspapers in the other.

'Fight Imperialism, fight Racism.'

'So you said.' Even now he could feel the alcohol working on his jaw muscles, freeing them of stiffness. 'Who are you from?'

'Workers Revolutionary Party. The only way to smash the Imperialist system is for the workers to unite and smash racism. Racism is the backbone of repression.'

'Oh? Aren't you confusing two entirely different arguments there, love?'

She bristled, but was ready to argue. They always were.

'The two are inextricable. Capitalism was built on slave labour and is maintained by slave labour.'

'You don't sound much like a slave, dear. Where did you get that accent? Cheltenham?'

'My father was a slave to capitalist ideology. He didn't know what he was doing.'

'You mean you went to an expensive school?'

She was bristling now all right. Rebus lit a cigarette. He offered her one, but she shook her head. A capitalist product, he supposed, the leaves picked by slaves in South America. She was quite pretty though. Eighteen, nineteen. Funny Victorian shoes on, tight pointed little things. A long, straight black skirt. Black, the colour of dissent. He was all for dissent.

'You're a student, I suppose?'

'That's right,' she said, shuffling uncomfortably. She knew a buyer when she saw one. This was not a buyer.

'Edinburgh University?'

'Yes.'

'Studying what?'

'English and politics.'

'English? Have you heard of a guy called Eiser? He teaches there.' She nodded.

'He's an old fascist,' she said. 'His theory of reading is a piece of right-wing propaganda to pull the wool over the eyes of the proletariat.'

Rebus nodded.

'What was your party again?'

'Workers Revolutionary.'

'But you're a student, eh? Not a worker, not one of the proletariat either by the sound of you.' Her face was red, her eyes burning fire. Come the revolution, Rebus would be first against the wall. But he had not yet played his trump card. 'So really, you're contravening the Trades Description Act, aren't you? And what about that tin? Do you have a licence from the proper authority to collect money in that tin?'

The tin was old, its old job-description torn from it. It was a plain, red cylinder, the kind used on poppy-day. But this was no poppy-day.

'Are you a cop?'

'Got it in one, love. *Have* you got a licence? I may have to pull you in otherwise.'

'Fucking pig!'

Feeling this a fitting exit line, she turned from Rebus and walked to the door. Rebus, chuckling, finished his whisky. Poor girl. She would change. The idealism would vanish once she saw how hypocritical the whole game was, and what luxuries lay outside university. When she left, she'd want it all: the executive job in London, the flat, car, salary, wine-bar. She would chuck it all in for a slice of pie. But she wouldn't understand that just now. Now was for the reaction against upbringing. That was what university was about. They all thought they could change the world once they got away from their parents. Rebus had thought that too. He had thought to return home from the Army with a row of medals and a list of commendations, just to show them. It had not been that way, though. Chastened, he was about to go when a voice called to him from three or four bar-stools away.

'It disnae cure anything, dis it, son?'

An aged crone offered him these few pearls of wisdom from her carious mouth. Rebus watched her tongue slopping around in that black cavern.

'Aye,' he said, paying the barman, who thanked him with green teeth. Rebus could hear the television, the jingle of the cash-register, the shouted conversations of the old men, but behind it all, behind the cacophony, lay another sound, low and pure but more real to him than any of the others.

It was the sound of Gordon Reeve screaming.

Let me out Let me out

But Rebus did not go dizzy this time, nor did he panic and run for it. He stood up to the sound and allowed it to make its point, let it wash over him until it had had its say. He would never run away from that memory again.

'Drink never cured anything, son,' continued his personal witch. 'Look at me. I wis as guid as anybody once upon a time, but when my husband died I just went tae pieces. D'ye ken whit I mean, son? The drink wis a great comfort tae me then, or so I thocht. But it tricks ye. It plays games wi ye. Ye jist sit aw day daein' nothing but drinking. And life passes ye by.'

She was right. How could he take the time to sit here guzzling whisky and sentiment when his daughter's life was balanced so finely? He must be mad; he was losing reality again. He had to hang onto that at the very least. He could pray again, but that only seemed to take him further away from the brute facts, and it was facts that he was chasing now, not dreams. He was chasing the fact that a lunatic from his cupboard of bad dreams had sneaked into this world and carried off his daughter. Did it resemble a fairy tale? All the better: there was bound to be a happy ending.

'You're right, love,' he said. Then, ready to leave, he pointed to her empty glass. 'Want another of those?'

She stared at him through rheumy eyes, then wagged her chin in a parody of compliance.

'Another of what the lady's drinking,' Rebus said to the green-toothed barman. He handed over some coins. 'And give her the change.' Then he left the bar.

'I need to talk. I think you do, too.'

Stevens was lighting a cigarette, rather melodramatically to Rebus's mind, directly outside the bar. Beneath the glare of the street-lighting, his skin seemed almost yellow, seemed hardly thick enough to cover his skull.

'Well, can we talk?' The reporter put his lighter back in his pocket. His fair hair looked greasy. He had not shaved for a day or so. He looked hungry and cold.

But inside, he felt electric.

'You've led me a merry dance, Mister Rebus. Can I call you John?'

'Look, Stevens, you know the score here. I've got enough on my plate without all this.'

Rebus made to move past the reporter, but Stevens caught his arm.

'No,' he said, 'I *don't* know the score, not the final score. I seem to have been ejected from the park at half-time.'

'What do you mean?'

'You know exactly who's behind all this, don't you? Of course you do, and so do your superiors. Or do they? Have you told them the whole truth and nothing but the truth, John? Have you told them about Michael?'

'What about him?'

'Oh, come on.' Stevens started to shuffle his feet, looking around him at the high blocks of flats, the late-afternoon sky behind them. He chuckled, shivering. Rebus recalled seeing him make that curious shivery motion at the party. 'Where can we talk?' said the reporter now. 'What about in the pub? Or is there someone in there you'd rather I didn't see?'

'Stevens, you're off your bloody head. I'm serious. Go home, get some sleep, eat, have a bath, just get to hell away from me. Okay?'

'Or you'll do what exactly? Get your brother's heavy friend to rough me up a little? Listen, Rebus, the game's over. I *know*. But I don't know all of it. You'd be wise to have me as a friend rather than as an enemy. Don't take me for a monkey. I credit you with more sense than to do that. Don't let me down.'

Don't let me down

'After all, they've got your daughter. You need my help. I've got friends everywhere. We've got to fight this together.'

Rebus, confused, shook his head.

'I don't have a bloody clue what you're talking about, Stevens. Go home, will you?'

Jim Stevens sighed, shaking his own head ruefully. He threw his cigarette onto the pavement and stubbed it out heavily, sending little flares of burning tobacco across the concrete.

'Well, I'm sorry, John. I really am. Michael's going to be put behind bars for a very long time on the evidence I have against him.'

'Evidence? Of what?'

'His drug-pushing, of course.'

Stevens didn't see the blow coming. It wouldn't have helped if he had. It was a vicious, curving swipe, sweeping up from Rebus's side and catching him very low in the stomach. The reporter coughed out a little puff of wind, then fell to his knees.

'Liar!'

Stevens coughed and coughed. It was as if he had run a marathon. He gulped in air, staying on his knees, his arms folded in front of his belly.

'If you say so, John, but it's the truth anyway.' He looked up at Rebus. 'You mean you honestly don't know anything about it? Nothing at all?'

'You better have some good proof, Stevens, or I'm going to see you swing.'

Stevens hadn't expected this, he hadn't expected this at all.

'Well,' he said, 'this puts a different complexion on everything. Christ, I need a drink. Will you join me? I think we should talk a little now, don't you? I won't keep you long, but I think you should know.'

And, of course, thinking back, Rebus realised that he had known, but not consciously. That day, the day of the old man's death, of visiting the rain-soaked graveyard, of visiting Mickey, he had smelled that toffee-apple smell in the living-room. He knew now what it had been. He had thought of it then, but had been distracted. Jesus Christ. Rebus felt his whole world sinking into the morass of a personal madness. He hoped the breakdown was not far off; he couldn't keep going on like this for much longer.

Toffee-apples, fairy-tales, Sammy, Sammy, Sammy. Sometimes it was hard to hold onto reality when that reality was overpowering. The shield came to protect you. The shield of the breakdown, of forgetting. Laughter and forgetting.

'This round's on me,' said Rebus, feeling calm again.

*

162

Gill Templer knew what she had always known: there was method in the killer's choice of girls, so he must have had access to their names prior to the abductions. That meant that the four girls had to have something in common, some way that Reeve could have picked them all out. But what? They had checked up on everything. Certain hobbies the girls did have in common; netball, pop music, books.

Netball. Pop music. Books.

Netball. Pop music. Books.

That meant checking through netball-coaches (all women, so scratch that), record-shop workers and DJs, and bookshop-workers and librarians. Libraries.

Libraries.

Rebus had told stories to Reeve. Samantha used the city's main lending library. So, occasionally, had the other girls. One of the girls had been seen heading up The Mound towards the library on the day she disappeared.

But Jack Morton had checked the library already. One of the men there had owned a blue Ford Escort. The suspect had been passed over. But had that initial interview been enough? She had to speak to Morton. Then she would conduct a second interview herself. She was about to look for Morton when her telephone rang.

'Inspector Templer,' she said to the beige mouthpiece.

'The kid dies tonight,' hissed a voice on the other end.

She sat bolt upright in her chair, almost causing it to topple.

'Listen,' she said, 'if you're a crank . . .'

'Shut up, bitch. I'm no crank and you know it. I'm the real thing. Listen.' There was a muffled cry from somewhere, the sob of a young girl. Then the hiss returned. 'Tell Rebus tough luck. He can't say I never gave him a chance.'

'Listen, Reeve, I . . .'

She had not meant to say that, had not meant to let him know. But she had panicked on hearing Samantha's cry. Now she heard another cry, the banshee cry of the madman who has been discovered. It sent the hairs on her neck climbing up each other. It froze the air around her. It was the cry of Death itself in one of its many guises. It was a lost soul's final triumphant scream.

'You know,' he gasped, his voice a mixture of joy and terror, 'you know, you know, you know. Aren't you clever? And you've got a very sexy voice, too. Maybe I'll come for you sometime. Was Rebus a good lay? Was he? Tell him that I've got his baby, and she dies tonight. Got that? Tonight.'

'Listen, I . . .'

'No, no, no. No more from me, Miss Templer. You've had nearly long enough to trace this. Bye.'

Click. Brrrr.

Time to trace it. She had been stupid. She should have thought of that first; indeed, she had not thought of it at all. Perhaps Superintendent Wallace had been right. Perhaps it was not only John who was too emotionally involved in the whole affair. She felt tired and old and spent. She felt as if all the case-work was suddenly an impossible burden, all the criminals invincible. Her eyes were irritating her. She thought of putting on her glasses, her personal shield from the world.

She had to find Rebus. Or should she seek out Jack Morton first? John would have to be told of this. They had a little time, but not much. The first guess had to be the right one. Who first? Rebus or Morton? She made the decision: John Rebus.

Unnerved by Stevens' revelations, Rebus made his way back to his flat. He needed to find out about some things. Mickey could wait. He had drawn too many bad cards in the course of his afternoon's foot-slogging. He had to get in touch with his old employers, the Army. He had to make them see that a life was at stake, they who prized life so strangely. A lot of phone-calls might be necessary. So be it.

But the first call he made was to the hospital. Rhona was fine. That was a relief. Still, however, she had not been told of Sammy's abduction. Rebus swallowed hard. Had she been told of her lover's death? She had not. Of course not. He arranged for some flowers to be sent to her. He was about to pluck up the courage to telephone the first of a long list of numbers when his own telephone rang. He let it ring for a while, but the caller was not about to let him go.

'Hello?'

'John! Thank God. I've been looking for you everywhere.' It was Gill, sounding excited and nervous and yet trying to sound sympathetic, too. Her voice modulated wildly, and Rebus felt his heart – what was left of it for public consumption – go out to her.

'What is it, Gill? Has anything happened?'

'I've had a call from Reeve.'

Rebus's heart pounded against the walls of its cell. 'Tell me,' he said.

'Well, he just phoned up and said that he's got Samantha.'

'And?'

Gill swallowed hard. 'And that he's going to kill her tonight.' There was a pause at Rebus's end, strange distant sounds of movement. 'John? Hello, John?'

Rebus stopped punching the telephone-stool. 'Yes, I'm here. Jesus Christ. Did he say anything else?'

'John, you really shouldn't be on your own you know. I could –'

'Did he say anything else?' He was shouting now, his breath short like a runner's.

'Well, I . . .'

'Yes?'

'I let slip that we know who he is.'

Rebus sucked in his breath, examining his knuckles, noting that he had torn one of them open. He sucked blood, staring from his window. 'What was his reaction to that?' he said at last.

'He went wild.'

'I'll bet he did. Jesus, I hope he doesn't take it out on . . . Oh, Jesus. Why do you suppose he phoned you specifically?' He had stopped licking his wound, and now turned his attention on his dark fingernails, tearing at them with his teeth, spitting them out across the room.

'Well, I am Liaison Officer on the case. He may have seen me on the television or read my name in the newspapers.'

'Or maybe he's seen us together. He may have been following me during this whole thing.' He looked from his window as a shabbily-dressed man shuffled his way up the street, stopping to pick up a cigarette-end. Christ, he needed a cigarette. He looked around for an ashtray, source of a few reusable butts.

'I never thought of that.'

'How the hell could you? We didn't know that any of this was to do with me until . . . it was yesterday, wasn't it? It seems like days ago. But remember, Gill, his notes were delivered by hand in the beginning.' He lit the remnants of a cigarette, sucking in the stinging smoke. 'He's been so close to me, and I didn't feel a thing, not a tingle. So much for a policeman's sixth sense.'

'Speaking of sixth senses, John, I've had a hunch.' Gill was relieved to hear how his voice had become calmer. She felt a little calmer, too, as though they were helping each other to hang on to a crowded lifeboat in a storm-torn sea.

'What's that?' Rebus slumped himself into his chair, looking around his barren room, dusty and chaotic. He saw the glass used by Michael, a plate of toast crumbs, two empty cigarette packets, and two coffee cups. He would sell this place soon, no matter how low the price. He would move well away from here. He would.

'Libraries,' Gill was saying, staring at her own office, the files and mounds of paperwork, the clutter of months and years, the electric buzz in the air. 'The one thing that all the girls, Samantha included, have in common is that they used, if irregularly, the same library, the Central Library. Reeve might have worked there once and been able to find the names he needed to fit his puzzle.'

'That's certainly a thought,' said Rebus, suddenly interested. It was too much of a coincidence, surely – or was it? How better to find out about John Rebus than to get a quiet job for a few months or a few years? How better to trap young girls than by posing as a librarian? Reeve had gone undercover all right, so well-camouflaged as to be invisible.

'It just so happens,' Gill continued, 'that your friend Jack Morton has been to the Central Library already. He checked up on a suspect there who owned a blue Escort. He gave the man a clean bill of health.'

'Yes, and they gave the Yorkshire Ripper a clean bill of health on more than one occasion, didn't they? It's worth rechecking. What was the suspect's name?'

'I've no idea. I've been trying to find Jack Morton, but he's off somewhere. John, I've been worried about you. Where have you been? I've been trying to find you.'

'I call that a waste of police time and effort, Inspector Templer. Get your nose back to the *real* grindstone. Find Jack. Find that name.'

'Yes, sir.'

'I'll be here for a while if you need me. I've got a few phone calls of my own to make.'

'I hear that Rhona is stable . . .' But Rebus had already put down his receiver. Gill sighed, rubbing at her face, desperate for some rest. She decided to arrange for someone to be sent over to John Rebus's flat. He could not be left to fester and, perhaps, explode. Then she had to find that name. She had to find Jack Morton.

Rebus made himself some coffee, thought about going out for milk, but decided in the end to have the coffee bitter and black, the taste and the colour of his thoughts. He thought over Gill's idea. Reeve as a librarian? It seemed improbable, unthinkable, but then everything that had happened to him of late had been unthinkable. Rationality could be a powerful enemy when you were faced with the irrational. Fight fire with fire. Accept that Gordon Reeve might have secured a job in the library; something innocuous yet essential to his plan. And suddenly, for John Rebus as for Gill, it all seemed to fit. 'For those who read between the times.' For those who are involved with books between one time (The Cross) and another (the present). My God, was nothing arbitrary in this life? No, nothing at all. Behind the seemingly irrational lay the clear golden path of the design. Behind this world there was another. Reeve was in the library: Rebus felt sure of that. It was five o'clock. He could reach the library just as it was closing. But would Gordon Reeve still be there, or would he have moved on now that he had his final victim?

But Rebus knew that Sammy was not Reeve's final victim. She was not a 'victim' at all. She was merely another device. There could be only one victim: Rebus himself. And for that reason Reeve would still be nearby, still within Rebus's reach. For Reeve wanted to be found, but slowly, a sort of cat-and-mouse game in reverse. Rebus thought back to the game of cat-and-mouse as played in his schooldays. Sometimes the boy being chased by a girl, or the girl being chased by a boy, would want to be caught, because he or she felt something for the chaser. And so the whole thing became something other than it seemed. That was Reeve's game. Cat and mouse, and he the mouse with the sting in his tail, the bite in his teeth, and Rebus as soft as milk, as pliant as fur and contentment. There had been no contentment for Gordon Reeve, not for many years, not since he had been betrayed by one whom he had come to call brother.

Just a kiss

The mouse caught.

The brother I never had

Poor Gordon Reeve, balancing on that slender pipe, the piss trickling down his legs, and everybody laughing at him.

And poor John Rebus, shunned by his father and his brother, a brother who had turned to crime now and who must be punished eventually.

And poor Sammy. She was the one he should be thinking of. Think only of her, John, and everything will turn out all right.

But if this was a serious game, a game of life and death, then he had to remember that it was still a game. Rebus knew now that he had Reeve. But having caught him, what would happen? The roles would switch in some way. He did not yet know all the rules. There was one way and only the one way to learn them. He left the coffee to go cold on his coffee-table, beside all the other waste. There was bitterness enough in his mouth as it was.

And out there, out in the iron-grey drizzle, there was a game to be finished.

27

From his flat in Marchmont to the library could be a delightful walk, showing the strengths of Edinburgh as a city. He passed through a verdant open area called The Meadows, and on the skyline before him stood the great grey Castle, a flag blowing in the fine rain over its ramparts. He passed the Royal Infirmary, home of discoveries and famous names, part of the University, Greyfriars Kirkyard and the tiny statue of Greyfriars Bobby. How many years had that little dog lain beside its master's grave? How many years had Gordon Reeve gone to sleep at night with burning thoughts of John Rebus on his mind? He shuddered. Sammy, Sammy, Sammy. He hoped that he would get to know his daughter better. He hoped that he would be able to tell her that she was beautiful, and that she would find great love in her life. Dear God, he hoped she was alive.

Walking along George IV Bridge, which took tourists and others over the city's Grassmarket, safely away from that area's tramps and derelicts, latter-day paupers with nowhere to turn, John Rebus's mind churned a few facts. For one, Reeve would be armed. For another, he might be in disguise. He remembered Sammy talking about the down-and-outs who sat around all day in the library. He could be one of them. He wondered what he would do if and when he met Reeve face to face. What would he say? Questions and theories began to disturb him, frightened him almost as much as did the recognition that Sammy's fate at the hands of Reeve would be painful and protracted. But she was more important to him than memory: she was the future. And so he stalked towards the Gothic façade of the library with determination, not fear, on his face.

A news vendor outside, his coat wrapped around him like damp tissue-paper, cried out the latest news, not of the Strangler today but of some disaster at sea. News did not last for long. Rebus swerved past the man, eyeing his face carefully. He noticed that his own shoes were letting in water as usual, then he entered the oak swing-doors.

*

At the main desk a security man flicked through a newspaper. He did not resemble Gordon Reeve, not in any way at all. Rebus breathed deeply, trying to stop himself from shaking.

'We're closing, sir,' said the guard from behind his newspaper.

'Yes, I'm sure you are.' The guard did not appear to like the sound of Rebus's voice; it was a hard, icy voice, used like a weapon. 'My name's Rebus. Detective Sergeant Rebus. I'm looking for a man called Reeve who works here. Is he around?'

Rebus hoped that he sounded calm. He did not feel calm. The guard left his newspaper on the chair and came up to face him. He studied Rebus, as though wary of him. Good: Rebus wanted it that way.

'Can I see your identification?'

Clumsily, his fingers not ready to be delicate, Rebus fished out his ID card. The guard looked at it for some time, glancing up at him.

'Reeve did you say?' He handed Rebus's card back and brought out a list of names attached to a yellow plastic clip-board. 'Reeve, Reeve, Reeve, Reeve. No, there's nobody called Reeve works here.'

'Are you sure? He may not be a librarian. He could be a cleaner or something, anything.'

'No, everybody's on my list, from the Director down to the porter. Look, that's my name there. Simpson. Everybody's on this list. He'd be on this list if he worked here. You must have made a mistake.'

Staff were beginning to leave the building, calling out their 'good-night's' and their 'see you's'. He might lose Reeve if he didn't hurry. Always supposing that Reeve still worked here. It was such a slender straw, such a tenuous hope, that Rebus began to panic again.

'Can I see that list?' He put out his hand, making his eyes burn with authority. The guard hesitated, then handed over the clip-board. Rebus searched it furiously, looking for anagrams, clues, anything.

He didn't have to look far.

'Ian Knott,' he whispered to himself. Ian Knott. *Gordian knot.* Reef knot. Gordian reef. *It's just like my name.* He wondered if Gordon Reeve could smell him. He could smell Reeve. He was as close as a short walk, perhaps a flight of stairs. That was all.

'Where does Ian Knott work?'

'Mister Knott? He works part-time in the children's section. Nicest man you could hope to meet. Why? What's he done?'

'Is he in today?'

'I think so. I think he comes in for two hours at the end of the afternoon. Look, what's this all about?'

'The children's section, you said? That's downstairs, isn't it?'

'That's right.' The guard was really flustered now. He knew trouble when he saw it. 'I'll just phone down and let him . . .'

Rebus leaned across the desk so that his nose touched that of the guard. 'You'll do nothing, understand? If you buzz down to him, I'll come back up and kick that telephone so far up your arse that you really will be able to make internal calls. Do you get my drift?'

The guard started to nod slowly and carefully, but Rebus had already turned his back on him and was heading for the gleaming stairwell.

The library smelled of used books, of damp, of brass and polish. In Rebus's nostrils it was the smell of confrontation, a smell that would remain with him. Walking down the stairs, down into the heart of the library, it became the smell of a hosing down in the middle of the night, of wrenching a gun away from its owner, of lonely marches overland, of wash-houses, of that whole nightmare. He could smell colours and sounds and sensations. There was a word for that feeling, but he could not remember it for the moment.

He counted the steps down, using the exercise to calm himself. Twelve stairs, then around a corner, then twelve more. And he found himself at a glass door with a small painting on it: a teddy bear and a skipping-rope. The bear was laughing at something. To Rebus, it was smiling at him. Not a pleasant smile, but a gloating one. Come in, come in, whoever you are. He studied the room's interior. There was nobody about, not a soul. Quietly, he pushed open the door. No children, no librarians. But he could hear someone placing books on a shelf. The sound came from a partition behind the lending-desk. Rebus tiptoed over to the desk and pressed a little bell there.

From behind the partition, humming, brushing invisible dust from his hands, came an older, chubbier, smiling Gordon Reeve. He looked a bit like a teddy bear himself. Rebus's hands were gripping the edge of the desk.

Gordon Reeve stopped humming when he saw Rebus, but the smile still played games with his face, making him seem innocent, normal, safe.

'Good to see you, John,' he said. 'So you've tracked me down at last, you old devil. How are you?' He was holding out a hand for Rebus to shake. But John Rebus knew that if he lifted his fingers from the edge of the desk, he would crumple to the floor.

He remembered Gordon Reeve now, recalled every detail of their time together. He remembered the man's gestures and his jibes and his thoughts. Blood brothers they had been, enduring together, able to read the other's mind almost. Blood brothers they would be again. Rebus could see it in the mad, clear eyes of his smiling tormentor. He felt the sea rushing through him, stinging his ears. This was it then. This was what had been expected of him.

'I want Samantha,' he enunciated. 'I want her alive and I want her now. Then we can settle this any way you like. Where is she, Gordon?'

'Do you know how long it is since anyone called me that? I've been Ian Knott for so long I can hardly bring myself to think of me as a "Gordon Reeve".' He smiled, looking behind Rebus's back. 'Where's the cavalry, John? Don't tell me you've come along here on your own? That's against procedure, isn't it?'

Rebus knew better than to tell him the truth. 'They're outside, don't worry. I've come in here to talk, but I've got plenty of friends outside. You're finished, Gordon. Now tell me where she is.'

But Gordon Reeve only shook his head, chuckling. 'Come on, John. It wouldn't be your style to bring anyone with you. You forget that I *know* you.' He looked tired suddenly. 'I know you so well.' His disguise was slipping away, piece by careful piece. 'No, you're alone all right. All alone. Just like I was, remember?'

'Where is she?'

'Not telling.'

There could be no doubt that the man was insane; perhaps he always had been. He looked the way he had looked on the days just before the bad days in their cell, on the edge of an abyss, an abyss created in his own mind. But fearful all the same, for the very reason that it was outwith any physical control. He was, smiling, surrounded by colourful posters, glossy drawings and picture-books, the most dangerous-looking man Rebus had met in his entire life.

'Why?'

Reeve looked at him as though he could not have asked a more infantile question. He shook his head, smiling still, the whore's smile, the cool, professional smile of the killer.

'You know why,' he said. 'Because of everything. Because you left me in the lurch, just as surely as if we *had* been in the hands of the enemy. You deserted, John. You deserted *me*. You know what the sentence is for that, don't you? You know what the sentence is for desertion?'

Reeve's voice had become hysterical. He chuckled again, trying to calm himself. Rebus steadied himself for violence, pumping adrenaline through his body, knotting his fists and his muscles.

'I know your brother.'

'What?'

'Your brother Michael, I know him. Did you know that he's a drugs pusher? Well, more of a middle-man really. Anyway, he's up to his neck in trouble, John. I've been his supplier for a while. Long enough to find out about you. Michael was very keen to reassure me that he wasn't a plant, a police informer. He was keen to spill the beans about you, John, so that we'd believe him. He always thought of the set-up as a "we", but it was just little me. Wasn't that clever of me? I've already fixed your brother. His head's in a noose, isn't it? You could call it a contingency plan.'

He had John Rebus's brother, and he had his daughter. There was only one more person he wanted, and Rebus had walked straight into this trap. He needed time to think.

'How long have you been planning all this?'

'I'm not sure.' He laughed, growing in confidence. 'Ever since you deserted, I suppose. Michael was the easiest part, really. He wanted easy money. It was simple enough to persuade him that drugs were the answer. He's in it up to his neck, your brother.' The last word was spat out at Rebus as though it were venom. 'Through him I found out a little more about you, John. And that made everything easier in its turn.' Reeve shrugged his shoulders. 'So you see, if you turn me in, I'll turn him in.'

'It won't work. I want you too badly.'

'So you'll let your brother rot in jail? Fair enough. Either way, I win. Can't you see that?'

Yes, Rebus could see it, but dimly, as though it were a difficult equation in a hot classroom.

'What happened to you anyway?' he asked now, unsure why he was playing for time. He had come charging in here without a self-protective thought or a plan in his head. And now he was stuck, awaiting Reeve's move, which must surely come. 'I mean, what happened after I . . . deserted?'

'Oh, they cracked me quite quickly after that.' Reeve was nonchalant. He could afford to be. 'I was out on my ear. They put me into a hospital for a while, then let me go. I heard that you'd gone ga-ga. That cheered me up a little. But then I heard a rumour that you'd joined the police force. Well, I couldn't stand the thought of you having a cosy life of it.

Not after what we'd been through and what you'd done.' His face began to jerk a little. His hands rested on the desk, and Rebus could smell the vinegary sweat coming from him. He spoke as though drifting off to sleep, but with each word Rebus knew that he was becoming more dangerous still, and yet he could not make himself move, not yet.

'It took you long enough to get to me.'

'It was worth the wait.' Reeve rubbed at his cheek. 'Sometimes I thought I might die before it was all finished, but I think I always knew that I wouldn't.' He smiled. 'Come on, John, I've got something to show you.'

'Sammy?'

'Don't be fucking stupid.' The smile disappeared again, only for a second. 'Do you think I'd keep her here? No, but I've got something else that will interest you. Come on.'

He led Rebus behind the partition. Rebus, his nerves jangling, studied Reeve's back, the muscles covered in a layer of easy living. A librarian. A *children's* librarian. And Edinburgh's own mass murderer.

Behind the partition were shelves and shelves of books, some piled haphazardly, others in neat rows, their spines matching.

'These are all waiting to be reshelved,' said Reeve, waving a custodial hand around him. 'It was you that got me interested in books, John. Do you remember?'

'Yes, I told you stories.' Rebus had started to think about Michael. Without him, Reeve might never have been found, might never have been suspected even. And now he would go to jail. Poor Mickey.

'Now where did I put it? I know it's here somewhere. I put it aside to show you, if you ever found me. God knows, it's taken you long enough. You've not been very bright, have you, John?'

It was easy to forget that the man was insane, that he had killed four girls in a game and had another at his mercy. It was so easy.

'No,' said Rebus, 'I've not been very bright.'

He could feel himself tightening. The very air around him seemed to be getting thinner. Something was about to happen. He could feel it. And to stop it from happening, all he had to do was punch Reeve in the kidneys, chop him behind the neck, restrain him and bundle him out of here.

So why didn't he do just that? He did not know himself. All he knew was that whatever would happen would happen, and that it had been set out like the plan of a building or a game of noughts and crosses many years before. Reeve had started the game. That left Rebus in a no-win situation. But he could not leave it unfinished. There had to be this rummaging in the shelves, this find.

'Ah, here it is. It's a book I've been reading . . .'

But, John Rebus realised, if Reeve had been reading it, then why was it so well hidden?

'*Crime and Punishment*. You told me the story, do you remember?'

'Yes, I remember. I told it to you more than once.'

'That's right, John, you did.'

The book was a quality leather edition, quite old. It did not seem like a library copy. Reeve handled it as though he were handling money or diamonds. It was as though he had owned nothing so precious in all his life.

'There's one illustration in here that I want you to see, John. Do you recall what I said about old Raskolnikov?'

'You said he should have shot the lot of them ...'

Rebus caught the under-meaning a second too late. He had misread this clue as he had misread so many of Reeve's clues. Meantime, Gordon Reeve, his eyes shining, had opened the book and brought out a small snub-nosed revolver from its hollowed-out interior. The gun was being raised to meet Rebus's chest when he sprang forward and butted Reeve on the nose. Planning was one thing, but sometimes dirty inspiration was needed. Blood and mucus came crashing from the suddenly broken bones. Reeve gasped, and Rebus's hand pushed the gun-arm away from him. Reeve was screaming now, a scream from the past, from so many living nightmares. It set Rebus off balance, plunging him back into his act of betrayal. He could see the guards, the open door, and he with his back to the screams of the trapped man. The scene before him blurred, and was replaced by an explosion.

The soft thump in his shoulder turned quickly to a spreading numbness and then to an intense pain, seeming to fill his entire body. He clutched at his jacket, feeling blood soak through the padding, through the lightweight material. Jesus Christ, so that was what it was like to be shot. He felt as though he would be sick, would faint clean away, but then he felt an onrush of something, coming up from his soul. It was the blinding force of anger. He was not about to lose this one. He saw Reeve wiping the mess from his face, trying to stop his eyes from watering, the gun still wavering before him. Rebus picked up a heavy-looking book and swiped at Reeve's hand, sending the gun flying into a pile of books.

And then Reeve was gone, staggering through the shelves, pulling them down after him. Rebus ran back to the desk and telephoned for help, his eyes wary for Gordon Reeve's return. There was silence in the room. He sat down on the floor.

Suddenly the door opened and William Anderson came through it, dressed in black like some clichéd avenging angel. Rebus smiled.

'How the hell did you find me?'

'I've been following you for quite a while.' Anderson bent down to examine Rebus's arm. 'I heard the shot. I take it you've found our man?'

'He's still in here somewhere, unarmed. The gun's back there.'

Anderson tied a handkerchief around Rebus's shoulder.

'You need an ambulance, John.' But Rebus was already rising to his feet.

'Not yet. Let's get this finished. How come I didn't spot you trailing me?'

Anderson allowed himself a smile. 'It takes a very good copper to know when *I'm* trailing them, and you're not very good, John. You're just good.'

They went behind the partition and began to move carefully further and further into the shelves. Rebus had picked up the gun. He pushed it deep into his pocket. There was no sign of Gordon Reeve.

'Look.' Anderson was pointing to a half open door at the very back of the stacks. They moved towards it, slowly still, and Rebus pushed it open. He confronted a steep iron stairwell, badly lit. It seemed to twist down into the foundations of the library. There was nowhere to go but down.

'I've heard about this, I think,' whispered Anderson, his whispers echoing around the deep shaft as they descended. 'The library was built on the site of the old Sheriff Court, and the cells which used to be beneath the courthouse are still there. The library stores old books in them. A whole maze of cells and passageways, leading right under the city.'

Smooth plaster walls gave way to ancient brickwork as they descended. Rebus could smell fungus, an old bitter smell left over from a previous age.

'He could be anywhere then.'

Anderson shrugged his shoulders. They had reached the bottom of the stairs, and found themselves in a wide passageway, clear of books. But off this passageway were alcoves – the old cells presumably – in which were stacked rows of books. There seemed no order, no pattern. They were just old books.

'He could probably get out of here,' whispered Anderson. 'I think there are exits to places like the present-day court-house and Saint Giles Cathedral.'

Rebus was in awe. Here was a piece of old Edinburgh, intact and undefiled. 'It's incredible,' he said. 'I never knew about this.'

'There's more. Underneath the City Chambers there are supposed to be whole streets of the old city which the builders just built right on top of. Whole streets, shops, houses, roads. Hundreds of years old.' Anderson shook his head, realising, as was Rebus, that you could not trust your own knowledge: you could walk right over a reality without necessarily encroaching on it.

They worked their way along the passage, thankful for the dim electric lighting on the ceiling, checking each and every cell with no success.

'Who is he then?' Anderson whispered.

'He's an old friend of mine,' said Rebus, feeling a little dizzy. It seemed to him that there was very little oxygen down here. He was sweating profusely. He knew that it had to do with the loss of blood, and that he shouldn't be here at all, yet he needed to be here. He remembered that there were things he should have done. He should have found out Reeve's address from the guard and sent a police car round in case Sammy were there. Too late now.

'There he is!'

Anderson had spotted him, way ahead of them in such shadow that Rebus could not make out a shape until Reeve started to run. Anderson ran after him, with Rebus, swallowing hard, trying to keep up.

'Watch him, he's dangerous.' Rebus felt his words fall away from him. He had not the strength to shout. Suddenly everything was going wrong. Ahead, he saw Anderson catch up with Reeve, and saw Reeve lash out with a near-perfect roundhouse kick, learned all those years ago and not forgotten. Anderson's head swivelled to one side as the kick landed, and he fell against the wall. Rebus had slumped to his knees, panting hard, his eyes hardly able to focus. Sleep, he needed sleep. The cold, uneven ground felt comfortable to him, as comfortable as the best bed he could want. He wavered, ready to fall. Reeve seemed to be walking towards him, while Anderson slid down the wall. Reeve seemed massive now, still in shadow, growing larger with each step until he consumed Rebus, and Rebus could see him grinning from ear to ear.

'Now you,' Reeve roared. 'Now for you.' Rebus knew that somewhere above them traffic was probably moving effortlessly across George IV Bridge, people were probably walking smartly home to an evening of television and family comfort, while he knelt at the feet of this nightmare, a poor forked animal at the end of the chase. It would do him no good to scream, no good to fight against it. He saw a blur of Gordon Reeve bend down in front of him, its face pushed awkwardly to one side. Rebus remembered that he had broken Reeve's nose quite successfully.

So did Reeve. He stood back and swung a heaving kick at John Rebus's chin. Rebus managed to move slightly, something still working away inside him, and the blow caught him on the cheek, sending him sideways. Lying in a half-protective foetal position he heard Reeve laugh, and watched the hands as they closed around his throat. He thought of the woman and his own hands around her neck. This was justice then. So be it. And then he thought of Sammy, of Gill, of Anderson and Anderson's murdered son, of those little girls, all dead. No, he could not let Gordon Reeve win. It wouldn't be right. It wouldn't be fair. He felt his tongue and eyes bulging, straining. He slipped his hand into his pocket, as Gordon Reeve whispered to him: 'You're glad it's all over, aren't you, John? You're actually relieved.'

And then another explosion filled the passage, hurting Rebus's ears. The recoil from the gunshot tingled through his hand and his arm, and he caught the sweet smell again, something like the smell of toffee-apples. Reeve, startled, froze for a second, then folded like paper, falling across Rebus, smothering him. Rebus, unable to move, decided it was safe to go to sleep now . . .

Epilogue

Epilogue

They kicked down the door of Ian Knott's small bungalow, a tiny, quiet suburban house, in full view of his curious neighbours, and found Samantha Rebus there, petrified, tied to a bed, her mouth taped shut, and with pictures of the dead girls for company. Everything became very professional after that, as Samantha was led weeping from the house. The driveway was hidden from the neighbouring bungalow by a tall hedge, and so nobody had seen anything of Reeve's comings and goings. He was a quiet man, the neighbours said. He had moved into the house seven years ago, at the time when he had started work as a librarian.

Jim Stevens was happy enough with the conclusion of the case. It made for a full week's stories. But how could he have been so wrong about John Rebus? He couldn't work that one out at all. Still, his drugs story had been completed too, and Michael Rebus would go to jail. There was no doubt about that.

The London press came in search of their own versions of the truth. Stevens met one journalist in the bar of the Caledonian Hotel. The man was trying to buy Samantha Rebus's story. He patted his pocket, assuring Jim Stevens that he had his editor's cheque-book with him. This seemed to Stevens to be part of some larger malaise. It wasn't just that the media could create reality and then tamper with that creation whenever they liked. There was something beneath the surface of it all, something different to the usual dirt and squalor and mess, something much more ambiguous. He didn't like it at all, and he didn't like what it had done to him. He talked with the London journalist about vague concepts such as justice and trust and balance. They talked for hours, drinking whisky and beer, but still the same questions remained. Edinburgh had shown itself to Jim Stevens as never before, cowering beneath the shadow of the Castle Rock in hiding from something. All the tourists saw were shadows from history, while the city itself was something else entirely. He didn't like it, he didn't like the job he was doing, and he didn't like the hours. The London offers were still there. He clutched at the biggest straw and drifted south.

Acknowledgements

The writing of this novel was aided hugely by the help given to me by the Leith CID in Edinburgh, who were patient about my many questions and my ignorance of police procedures. And although this is a work of fiction, with all the faults of such, I was aided in my research into the Special Air Service by Tony Geraghty's excellent book *Who Dares Wins* (Fontana, 1983).

Acknowledgements

The writing of this novel was aided hugely by the help given to me by the Leith CID in Edinburgh, who were patient about my many questions and my ignorance of police procedures. And although this is a work of fiction, with all the faults of such, I was aided in my research into the Special Air Service by Tony Geraghty's excellent book Who Dares Wins (Fontana, 1983).

Hide & Seek

To Michael Shaw,
not before time

'My devil had long been caged, he came out roaring.'
– *The Strange Case of Dr Jekyll and Mr Hyde*

'Hide!'

He was shrieking now, frantic, his face drained of all colour. She was at the top of the stairs, and he stumbled towards her, grabbing her by the arms, propelling her downstairs with unfocussed force, so that she feared they would both fall. She cried out.

'Ronnie! Hide from who?'

'Hide!' he shrieked again. 'Hide! They're coming! They're coming!'

He had pushed her all the way to the front door now. She'd seen him pretty strung out before, but never this bad. A fix would help him, she knew it would. And she knew, too, that he had the makings upstairs in his bedroom. The sweat trickled from his chilled rat's-tails of hair. Only two minutes ago, the most important decision in her life had been whether or not to dare a trip to the squat's seething lavatory. But now. . . .

'They're coming,' he repeated, his voice a whisper now. 'Hide.'

'Ronnie,' she said, 'you're scaring me.'

He stared at her, his eyes seeming almost to recognise her. Then he looked away again, into a distance all of his own. The word was a snakelike hiss.

'Hide.' And with that he yanked open the door. It was raining outside, and she hesitated. But then fear took her, and she made to cross the threshold. But his hand grabbed at her arm, pulling her back inside. He embraced her, his sweat sea-salty, his body throbbing. His mouth was close to her ear, his breath hot.

'They've murdered me,' he said. Then with sudden ferocity he pushed her again, and this time she was outside, and the door was slamming shut, leaving him alone in the house. Alone with himself. She stood on the garden path, staring at the door, trying to decide whether to knock or not.

It wouldn't make any difference. She knew that. So instead she started to cry. Her head slipped forward in a rare show of self-pity and she wept for a full minute, before, breathing hard three times, she turned and walked quickly down the garden path (such as it was). Someone would take her in. Someone would comfort her and take away the fear and dry her clothes.

Someone always did.

John Rebus stared hard at the dish in front of him, oblivious to the conversation around the table, the background music, the flickering candles. He didn't really care about house prices in Barnton, or the latest delicatessen to be opened in the Grassmarket. He didn't much want to speak to the other guests – a female lecturer to his right, a male bookseller to his left – about . . . well, whatever they'd just been discussing. Yes, it was the perfect dinner party, the conversation as tangy as the starter course, and he was glad Rian had invited him. Of course he was. But the more he stared at the half lobster on his plate, the more an unfocussed despair grew within him. What had he in common with these people? Would they laugh if he told the story of the police alsatian and the severed head? No, they would not. They would smile politely, then bow their heads towards their plates, acknowledging that he was . . . well, *different* from them.

'Vegetables, John?'

It was Rian's voice, warning him that he was not 'taking part', was not 'conversing' or even looking interested. He accepted the large oval dish with a smile, but avoided her eyes.

She was a nice girl. Quite a stunner in an individual sort of way. Bright red hair, cut short and pageboyish. Eyes deep, striking green. Lips thin but promising. Oh yes, he liked her. He wouldn't have accepted her invitation otherwise. He fished about in the dish for a piece of broccoli that wouldn't break into a thousand pieces as he tried to manoeuvre it onto his plate.

'Gorgeous food, Rian,' said the bookseller, and Rian smiled, accepting the remark, her face reddening slightly. That was all it took, John. That was all you had to say to make this girl happy. But in his mouth he knew it would come out sounding sarcastic. His tone of voice was not something he could suddenly throw off like a piece of clothing. It was a part of him, nurtured over a course of years. So when the lecturer agreed with the bookseller, all John Rebus did was smile and nod, the smile too fixed, the nod going on a second or two too long, so that they were all looking at him again. The piece of broccoli snapped into two neat halves above his plate and splattered onto the tablecloth.

'Shite!' he said, knowing as the word escaped his lips that it was not quite appropriate, not quite the *right* word for the occasion. Well, what was he, a man or a thesaurus?

'Sorry,' he said.

'Couldn't be helped,' said Rian. My God, her voice was cold.

It was the perfect end to a perfect weekend. He'd gone shopping on Saturday, ostensibly for a suit to wear tonight. But had baulked at the prices, and bought some books instead, one of which was intended as a gift to Rian: *Doctor Zhivago*. But then he'd decided he'd like to read it himself first, and so had brought flowers and chocolates instead, forgetting her aversion to lilies (*had he known in the first place?*) and the diet she was in the throes of starting. Damn. And to cap it all, he'd tried a new church this morning, another Church of Scotland offering, not too far from his flat. The last one he'd tried had seemed unbearably cold, promising nothing but sin and repentance, but this latest church had been the oppressive opposite: all love and joy and what was there to forgive anyway? So he'd sung the hymns, then buggered off, leaving the minister with a handshake at the door and a promise of future attendance.

'More wine, John?'

This was the bookseller, proffering the bottle he'd brought himself. It wasn't a bad little wine, actually, but the bookseller had talked about it with such unremitting pride that Rebus felt obliged to decline. The man frowned, but then was cheered to find this refusal left all the more for himself. He replenished his glass with vigour.

'Cheers,' he said.

The conversation returned to how busy Edinburgh seemed these days. Here was something with which Rebus could agree. This being the end of May, the tourists were almost in season. But there was more to it than that. If anyone had told him five years ago that in 1989 people would be emigrating north from the south of England to the Lothians, he'd have laughed out loud. Now it was fact, and a fit topic for the dinner table.

Later, much later, the couple having departed, Rebus helped Rian with the dishes.

'What was wrong with you?' she said, but all he could think about was the minister's handshake, that confident grip which bespoke assurances of an afterlife.

'Nothing,' he said. 'Let's leave these till morning.'

Rian stared at the kitchen, counting the used pots, the half-eaten lobster carcasses, the wine glasses smudged with grease.

'Okay,' she said. 'What did you have in mind instead?'

He raised his eyebrows slowly, then brought them down low over his eyes. His lips broadened into a smile which had about it a touch of the leer. She became coy.

'Why, Inspector,' she said. 'Is that supposed to be some kind of a clue?'

'Here's another,' he said, lunging at her, hugging her to him, his face buried in her neck. She squealed, clenched fists beating against his back.

'Police brutality!' she gasped. 'Help! Police, help!'

'Yes, madam?' he inquired, carrying her by the waist out of the kitchen, towards where the bedroom and the end of the weekend waited in shadow.

Late evening at a building site on the outskirts of Edinburgh. The contract was for the construction of an office development. A fifteen-foot-high fence separated the works from the main road. The road, too, was of recent vintage, built to help ease traffic congestion around the city. Built so that commuters could travel easily from their countryside dwellings to jobs in the city centre.

There were no cars on the road tonight. The only sound came from the slow chug-chugging of a cement mixer on the site. A man was feeding it spadefuls of grey sand and remembering the far distant days when he had laboured on a building site. Hard graft it had been, but honest.

Two other men stood above a deep pit, staring down into it.

'Should do it,' one said.

'Yes,' the other agreed. They began walking back to the car, an ageing purple Mercedes.

'He must have some clout. I mean, to get us the keys to this place, to set all this up. Some clout.'

'Ours is not to ask questions, you know that.' The man who spoke was the oldest of the three, and the only Calvinist. He opened the car boot. Inside, the body of a frail teenager lay crumpled, obviously dead. His skin was the colour of pencil shading, darkest where the bruises lay.

'What a waste,' said the Calvinist.

'Aye,' the other agreed. Together they lifted the body from the boot, and carried it gently towards the hole. It dropped softly to the bottom, one leg wedging up against the sticky clay sides, a trouser leg slipping to show a naked ankle.

'All right,' the Calvinist said to the cement man. 'Cover it, and let's get out of here. I'm starving.'

Monday

For close on a generation, no one had appeared
to drive away these random visitors or to repair
their ravages

What a start to the working week.

The housing estate, what he could see of it through the rain-lashed windscreen, was slowly turning back into the wilderness that had existed here before the builders had moved in many years ago. He had no doubt that in the 1960s it, like its brethren clustered around Edinburgh, had seemed the perfect solution to future housing needs. And he wondered if the planners ever learned through anything other than hindsight. If not, then perhaps today's 'ideal' solutions were going to turn out the same way.

The landscaped areas comprised long grass and an abundance of weeds, while children's tarmacadamed playgrounds had become bomb-sites, shrapnel glass awaiting a tripped knee or stumbling hand. Most of the terraces boasted boarded-up windows, ruptured drainpipes pouring out teeming rainwater onto the ground, marshy front gardens with broken fences and missing gates. He had the idea that on a sunny day the place would seem even more depressing.

Yet nearby, a matter of a few hundred yards or so, some developer had started building private apartments. The hoarding above the site proclaimed this a LUXURY DEVELOPMENT, and gave its address as MUIR VILLAGE. Rebus wasn't fooled, but wondered how many young buyers would be. This was Pilmuir, and always would be. This was the dumping ground.

There was no mistaking the house he wanted. Two police cars and an ambulance were already there, parked next to a burnt-out Ford Cortina. But even if there hadn't been this sideshow, Rebus would have known the house. Yes, it had its boarded-up windows, like its neighbours on either side, but it also had an open door, opening into the darkness of its interior. And on a day like this, would any house have its door flung wide open were it not for the corpse inside, and the superstitious dread of the living who were incarcerated with it?

Unable to park as close to this door as he would have liked, Rebus cursed under his breath and pushed open the car door, throwing his raincoat over his head as he made to dash through the stiletto shower. Something fell from his pocket onto the verge. Scrap paper, but he picked it up anyway, screwing it into his pocket as he ran. The path to the open door was cracked and slick with weeds, and he almost slipped and fell, but reached the threshold intact, shaking the water from him, awaiting the welcoming committee.

A constable put his head around a doorway, frowning.

'Detective Inspector Rebus,' said Rebus by way of introduction.

'In here, sir.'

'I'll be there in a minute.'

The head disappeared again, and Rebus looked around the hall. Tatters of wallpaper were the only mementoes of what had once been a home. There was an overpowering fragrance of damp plaster, rotting wood. And behind all that, a sense of this being more of a cave than a house, a crude form of shelter, temporary, unloved.

As he moved further into the house, passing the bare stairwell, darkness embraced him. Boards had been hammered into all the window-frames, shutting out light. The intention, he supposed, had been to shut out squatters, but Edinburgh's army of homeless was too great and too wise. They had crept in through the fabric of the place. They had made it their den. And one of their number had died here.

The room he entered was surprisingly large, but with a low ceiling. Two constables held thick rubber torches out to illuminate the scene, casting moving shadows over the plasterboard walls. The effect was of a Caravaggio painting, a centre of light surrounded by degrees of murkiness. Two large candles had burnt down to the shapes of fried eggs against the bare floorboards, and between them lay the body, legs together, arms outstretched. A cross without the nails, naked from the waist up. Near the body stood a glass jar, which had once contained something as innocent as instant coffee, but now held a selection of disposable syringes. Putting the fix into crucifixion, Rebus thought with a guilty smile.

The police doctor, a gaunt and unhappy creature, was kneeling next to the body as though about to offer the last rites. A photographer stood by the far wall, trying to find a reading on his light meter. Rebus moved in towards the corpse, standing over the doctor.

'Give us a torch,' he said, his hand commanding one from the nearest constable. He shone this down across the body, starting at the bare feet, the bedenimed legs, a skinny torso, ribcage showing through the pallid skin. Then up to the neck and face. Mouth open, eyes closed. Sweat looked to have dried on the forehead and in the hair. But wait. . . . Wasn't that moisture around the mouth, on the lips? A drop of water suddenly fell from nowhere into the open mouth. Rebus, startled, expected the man to swallow, to lick his parched lips and return to life. He did not.

'Leak in the roof,' the doctor explained, without looking up from his work. Rebus shone the torch against the ceiling, and saw the damp patch which was the source of the drip. Unnerving all the same.

'Sorry I took so long to get here,' he said, trying to keep his voice level. 'So what's the verdict?'

'Overdose,' the doctor said blandly. 'Heroin.' He shook a tiny polythene envelope at Rebus. 'The contents of this sachet, if I'm not mistaken. There's another full one in his right hand.' Rebus shone his torch towards where a lifeless hand was half clutching a small packet of white powder.

'Fair enough,' he said. 'I thought everyone chased the dragon these days instead of injecting.'

The doctor looked up at him at last.

'That's a very naive view, Inspector. Go talk to the Royal Infirmary. They'll tell you how many intravenous abusers there are in Edinburgh. It probably runs into hundreds. That's why we're the AIDS capital of Britain.'

'Aye, we take pride in our records, don't we? Heart disease, false teeth, and now AIDS.'

The doctor smiled. 'Something you might be interested in,' he said. 'There's bruising on the body. Not very distinct in this light, but it's there.'

Rebus squatted down and shone the torch over the torso again. Yes, there was bruising all right. A lot of bruising.

'Mainly to the ribs,' the doctor continued. 'But also some to the face.'

'Maybe he fell,' Rebus suggested.

'Maybe,' said the doctor.

'Sir?' This from one of the constables, his eyes and voice keen. Rebus turned to him.

'Yes, son?'

'Come and look at this.'

Rebus was only too glad of the excuse to move away from the doctor and his patient. The constable was leading him to the far wall, shining his torch against it as he went. Suddenly, Rebus saw why.

On the wall was a drawing. A five-pointed star, encompassed by two concentric circles, the largest of them some five feet in diameter. The whole had been well drawn, the lines of the star straight, the circles almost exact. The rest of the wall was bare.

'What do you think, sir?' asked the constable.

'Well, it's not just your usual graffiti, that's for sure.'

'Witchcraft?'

'Or astrology. A lot of druggies go in for all sorts of mysticism and hoodoo. It goes with the territory.'

'The candles. . . .'

'Let's not jump to conclusions, son. You'll never make CID that way. Tell me, why are we all carrying torches?'

'Because the electric's been cut off.'

'Right. Ergo, the need for candles.'

'If you say so, sir.'

'I do say so, son. Who found the body?'

'I did, sir. There was a telephone call, female, anonymous, probably one of the other squatters. They seem to have cleared out in a hurry.'

'So there was nobody else here when you arrived?'

'No, sir.'

'Any idea yet who he is?' Rebus nodded the torch towards the corpse.

'No, sir. And the other houses are all squats, too, so I doubt we'll get anything out of them.'

'On the contrary. If anyone knows the identity of the deceased, they're the very people. Take your friend and knock on a few doors. But be casual, make sure they don't think you're about to evict them or anything.'

'Yes, sir.' The constable seemed dubious about the whole venture. For one thing, he was sure to get an amount of hassle. For another, it was still raining hard.

'On you go,' Rebus chided, but gently. The constable shuffled off, collecting his companion on the way.

Rebus approached the photographer.

'You're taking a lot of snaps,' he said.

'I need to in this light, to make sure at least a few come out.'

'Bit quick off the mark in getting here, weren't you?'

'Superintendent Watson's orders. He wants pictures of any drugs-related incidents. Part of his campaign.'

'That's a bit gruesome, isn't it?' Rebus knew the new Chief Superintendent, had met him. Full of social awareness and community involvement. Full of good ideas, and lacking only the manpower to implement them. Rebus had an idea.

'Listen, while you're here, take one or two of that far wall, will you?'

'No problem.'

'Thanks.' Rebus turned to the doctor. 'How soon will we know what's in that full packet?'

'Later on today, maybe tomorrow morning at the latest.'

Rebus nodded to himself. What was his interest? Maybe it was the dreariness of the day, or the atmosphere in this house, or the positioning of the body. All he knew was that he felt something. And if it turned out to be just a damp ache in his bones, well, fair enough. He left the room and made a tour of the rest of the house.

The real horror was in the bathroom.

The toilet must have blocked up weeks before. A plunger lay on the floor, so some cursory attempt had been made to unblock it, but to no avail. Instead, the small, splattered sink had become a urinal, while the bath had become a dumping ground for solids, upon which crawled a dozen large and jet-black flies. The bath had also become a skip, filled with bags of refuse, bits of wood. . . . Rebus didn't stick around, pulling the door tight shut behind him. He didn't envy the council workmen who would eventually have to come and fight the good fight against all this decay.

One bedroom was completely empty, but the other boasted a sleeping bag, damp from the drips coming through the roof. Some kind of identity had been imposed upon the room by the pinning of pictures to its walls. Up close, he noticed that these were original photographs, and that they comprised a sort of portfolio. Certainly they were well taken, even to Rebus's untrained eye. A few were of Edinburgh Castle on damp, misty days. It looked particularly bleak. Others showed it in bright sunshine. It still looked bleak. One or two were of a girl, age indeterminate. She was posing, but grinning broadly, not taking the event seriously.

Next to the sleeping bag was a bin-liner half filled with clothes, and next to this a small pile of dog-eared paperbacks: Harlan Ellison, Clive Barker, Ramsey Campbell. Science fiction and horror. Rebus left the books where they were and went back downstairs.

'All finished,' the photographer said. 'I'll get those photos to you tomorrow.'

'Thanks.'

'I also do portrait work, by the way. A nice family group for the grandparents? Sons and daughters? Here, I'll give you my card.'

Rebus accepted the card and pulled his raincoat back on, heading out to the car. He didn't like photographs, especially of himself. It wasn't just that he photographed badly. No, there was more to it than that.

The sneaking suspicion that photographs really could steal your soul.

On his way back to the station, travelling through the slow midday traffic, Rebus thought about how a group photograph of his wife, his daughter and him might look. But no, he couldn't visualise it. They had grown so far apart, ever since Rhona had taken Samantha to live in London. Sammy still wrote, but Rebus himself was slow at responding, and she seemed to take umbrage at this, writing less and less herself. In her last letter she had hoped Gill and he were happy.

He hadn't the courage to tell her that Gill Templer had left him several months ago. Telling Samantha would have been fine: it was the idea of Rhona's getting to hear of it that he couldn't stand. Another notch in his bow of failed relationships. Gill had taken up with a disc jockey on a local radio station, a man whose enthusing voice Rebus seemed to hear whenever he entered a shop or a filling station, or passed the open window of a tenement block.

He still saw Gill once or twice a week of course, at meetings and in the station-house, as well as at scenes of crimes. Especially now that he had been elevated to her rank.

Detective Inspector John Rebus.

Well, it had taken long enough, hadn't it? And it was a long, hard case, full of personal suffering, which had brought the promotion. He was sure of that.

He was sure, too, that he wouldn't be seeing Rian again. Not after last night's dinner party, not after the fairly unsuccessful bout of love-making. *Yet another* unsuccessful bout. It had struck him, lying next to Rian, that her eyes were almost identical to Inspector Gill Templer's. A surrogate? Surely he was too old for that.

'Getting old, John,' he said to himself.

Certainly he was getting hungry, and there was a pub just past the next set of traffic lights. What the hell, he was entitled to a lunch break.

The Sutherland Bar was quiet, Monday lunchtime being one of the lowest points of the week. All money spent, and nothing to look forward to. And of course, as Rebus was quickly reminded by the barman, the Sutherland did not exactly cater for a lunchtime clientele.

'No hot meals,' he said, 'and no sandwiches.'

'A pie then,' begged Rebus, *anything*. Just to wash down the beer.'

'If it's food you want, there's plenty of cafes around here. This particular pub happens to sell beers, lagers and spirits. We're not a chippie.'

'What about crisps?'

The barman eyed him for a moment. 'What flavour?'

'Cheese and onion.'

'We've run out.'

'Well, ready salted then.'

'No, they're out too.' The barman had cheered up again.

'Well,' said Rebus in growing frustration, 'what in the name of God *have* you got?'

'Two flavours. Curry, or egg, bacon and tomato.'

'*Egg?*' Rebus sighed. 'All right, give me a packet of each.'

The barman stooped beneath the counter to find the smallest possible bags, past their sell-by dates if possible.

'Any nuts?' It was a last desperate hope. The barman looked up.

'Dry roasted, salt and vinegar, chilli flavour,' he said.

'One of each then,' said Rebus, resigned to an early death. 'And another half of eighty-shillings.'

He was finishing this second drink when the bar door shuddered open and an instantly recognisable figure entered, his hand signalling for refreshment before he was even halfway through the door. He saw Rebus, smiled, and came to join him on one of the high stools.

'Hello, John.'

'Afternoon, Tony.'

Inspector Anthony McCall tried to balance his prodigious bulk on the tiny circumference of the bar stool, thought better of it, and stood instead, one shoe on the foot-rail, and both elbows on the freshly wiped surface of the bar. He stared hungrily at Rebus.

'Give us one of your crisps.'

When the packet was offered, he pulled out a handful and stuffed them into his mouth.

'Where were you this morning then?' said Rebus. 'I'd to take one of your calls.'

'The one at Pilmuir? Ach, sorry about that, John. Heavy night last night. I had a bit of a hangover this morning.' A pint of murky beer was placed in front of him. 'Hair of the dog,' he said, and took four slow gulps, reducing it to a quarter of its former size.

'Well, I'd nothing better to do anyway,' said Rebus, sipping at his own beer. 'Christ, those houses down there are a mess though.'

McCall nodded thoughtfully. 'It wasn't always like that, John. I was born there.'

'Really?'

'Well, to be exact, I was born on the estate that was there before this one. It was so bad, so they said, that they levelled it and built Pilmuir instead. Bloody hell on earth it is now.'

'Funny you should say that,' said Rebus. 'One of the young uniformed kids thought there might be some kind of occult tie-in.' McCall looked up from his drink. 'There was a black-magic painting on the wall,' Rebus explained. 'And candles on the floor.'

'Like a sacrifice?' McCall offered, chuckling. 'My wife's dead keen on all those horror films. Gets them out of the video library. I think she sits watching them all day when I'm out.'

'I suppose it must go on, devil worship, witchcraft. It can't *all* be in the imagination of the Sunday newspaper editors.'

'I know how you might find out.'

'How?'

'The university,' said McCall. Rebus frowned, disbelieving. 'I'm serious. They've got some kind of department that studies ghosts and all that sort of thing. Set up with money from some dead writer.' McCall shook his head. 'Incredible what people will do.'

Rebus was nodding. 'I *did* read about that, now you mention it. Arthur Koestler's money, wasn't it?'

McCall shrugged.

'Arthur Daley's more my style,' he said, emptying his glass.

Rebus was studying the pile of paperwork on his desk when the telephone rang.

'DI Rebus.'

'They said you were the man to talk to.' The voice was young, female, full of unfocused suspicion.

'They were probably right. What can I do for you, miss . . .?'

'Tracy. . . .' The voice fell to a whisper on the last syllable of the name. She had already been tricked into revealing herself. 'Never mind who I am!' She had become immediately hysterical, but calmed just as quickly. 'I'm phoning about that squat in Pilmuir, the one where they found. . . .' The voice trailed off again.

'Oh yes.' Rebus sat up and began to take notice. 'Was it you who phoned the first time?'

'What?'

'To tell us that someone had died there.'

'Yes, it was me. Poor Ronnie. . . .'

'Ronnie being the deceased?' Rebus scribbled the name onto the back of one of the files from his in-tray. Beside it he wrote 'Tracy – caller'.

'Yes.' Her voice had broken again, near to tears this time.

'Can you give me a surname for Ronnie?'

'No.' She paused. 'I never knew it. I'm not sure Ronnie was even his real name. Hardly anyone uses their real name.'

'Tracy, I'd like to talk to you about Ronnie. We can do it over the telephone, but I'd rather it was face to face. Don't worry, you're not in any trouble –'

'But I *am*. That's why I called. Ronnie told me, you see.'

'Told you what, Tracy?'

'Told me he'd been murdered.'

The room around Rebus seemed suddenly to vanish. There was only this disconnected voice, the telephone, and him.

'He said that to you, Tracy?'

'Yes.' She was crying now, sniffing back the unseen tears. Rebus visualised a frightened little girl, just out of school, standing in a distant callbox. 'I've got to hide,' she said at last. 'Ronnie said over and over that I should hide.'

'Shall I bring my car and fetch you? Just tell me where you are.'

'No!'

'Then tell me how Ronnie was killed. You know how we found him?'

'Lying on the floor by the window. That's where he was.'

'Not quite.'

'Oh yes, that's where he was. By the window. Lying wrapped up into a little ball. I thought he was just sleeping. But when I touched his arm he was cold. . . . I went to find Charlie, but he'd gone. So I just panicked.'

'You say Ronnie was lying in a ball?' Rebus had begun to draw pencilled circles on the back of the file.

'Yes.'

'And this was in the living room?'

She seemed confused. 'What? No, not in the living room. He was upstairs, in his bedroom.'

'I see.' Rebus kept on drawing effortless circles. He was trying to imagine Ronnie dying, but not really dead, crawling downstairs after Tracy had fled, ending up in the living room. That might explain those bruises. But the candles. . . . He had been so perfectly positioned between them. . . . 'And when was this?'

'Late last night, I don't know exactly when. I panicked. When I calmed down, I phoned for the police.'

'What time was it when you phoned?'

She paused, thinking. 'About seven this morning.'

'Tracy, would you mind telling this to some other people?'

'Why?'

'I'll tell you when I pick you up. Just tell me where you are.'

There was another pause while she considered this. 'I'm back in Pilmuir,' she said finally. 'I've moved into another squat.'

'Well,' said Rebus, 'you don't want me to come down there, do you? But you must be quite close to Shore Road. What about us meeting there?'

'Well. . . .'

'There's a pub called the Dock Leaf,' continued Rebus, giving her no time to debate. 'Do you know it?'

'I've been kicked out of it a few times.'

'Me too. Okay, I'll meet you outside it in an hour. All right?'

'All right.' She didn't sound over-enthusiastic, and Rebus wondered if she would keep the appointment. Well, what of it? She sounded straight enough, but she might just be another casualty, making it up to draw attention to herself, to make her life seem more interesting than it was.

But then he'd had a feeling, hadn't he?

'All right,' she said, and the connection was severed.

Shore Road was a fast road around the north coast of the city. Factories, warehouses, and vast DIY and home furnishing stores were its landmarks, and beyond them lay the Firth of Forth, calm and grey. On most days, the coast of Fife was visible in the distance, but not today, with a cold mist hanging low on the water. On the other side of the road from the warehouses were the tenements, four-storey predecessors of the concrete high-rise. There was a smattering of corner shops, where neighbour met neighbour, and information was passed on, and a few small unmodernised pubs, where strangers did not go unnoticed for long.

The Dock Leaf had shed one generation of low-life drinkers, and discovered another. Its denizens now were young, unemployed, and living six to a three-bedroom rented flat along Shore Road. Petty crime though was not a problem: you didn't mess your own nest. The old community values still held.

Rebus, early for the meeting, just had time for a half in the saloon bar. The beer was cheap but bland, and everyone seemed to know if not who he was then certainly *what* he was, their voices turned down to murmurs, their eyes averted. When, at three thirty, he stepped outside, the sudden daylight made him squint.

'Are you the policeman?'

'That's right, Tracy.'

She had been standing against the pub's exterior wall. He shaded his eyes, trying to make out her face, and was surprised to find himself looking at a woman of between twenty and twenty-five. Her age was transparent in her face, though her style marked her out as the perennial rebel: cropped peroxide hair, two stud earrings in her left ear (but none in the right), tie-dye T-shirt, tight, faded denims, and red basketball boots. She was tall, as tall as Rebus. As his eyes adjusted to the light, he saw the tear-tracks on either cheek, the old acne scars. But there were also crow's-feet around her eyes, evidence of a life used to laughter. There was no laughter in those olive-green eyes though. Somewhere in Tracy's life a wrong turning had been made, and Rebus had the idea that she was still trying to reverse back to that fork in the road.

The last time he had seen her she had been laughing. Laughing as her semblance curled from the wall of Ronnie's bedroom. She was the girl in the photographs.

'Is Tracy your real name?'

'Sort of.' They had begun to walk. She crossed the road at a zebra crossing, not bothering to check whether any cars were approaching, and Rebus followed her to a wall, where she stopped, staring out across the Forth. She wrapped her arms around herself, examining the lifting mist.

'It's my middle name,' she said.

Rebus leaned his forearms against the wall. 'How long have you known Ronnie?'

'Three months. That's how long I've been in Pilmuir.'

'Who else lived in that house?'

She shrugged. 'They came and went. We'd only been in there a few weeks. Sometimes I'd go downstairs in the morning, and there'd be half a dozen strangers sleeping on the floor. Nobody minded. It was like a big family.'

'What makes you think somebody killed Ronnie?'

She turned towards him angrily, but her eyes were liquid. 'I told you on the phone! He *told* me. He'd been off somewhere and come back with some stuff. He didn't look right though. Usually, when he's got a little smack, he's like a kid at Christmas. But he wasn't. He was scared, acting like a robot or something. He kept telling me to hide, telling me they were coming for him.'

'Who were?'

'I don't know.'

'Was this after he'd taken the stuff?'

'No, that's what's really crazy. This was *before*. He had the packet in his hand. He pushed me out of the door.'

'You weren't there while he was fixing?'

'God no. I hated that.' Her eyes drilled into his. 'I'm not a junkie, you know. I mean, I smoke a little, but never. . . . You know. . . .'

'Was there anything else you noticed about Ronnie?'

'Like what?'

'Well, the state he was in.'

'You mean the bruises?'

'Yes.'

'He often came back looking like that. Never talked about it.'

'Got in a lot of fights, I suppose. Was he short-tempered?'

'Not with me.'

Rebus sunk his hands into his pockets. A chill wind was whipping up off the water, and he wondered whether she was warm enough. He couldn't help noticing that her nipples were very prominent through the cotton of her T-shirt.

'Would you like my jacket?' he asked.

'Only if your wallet's in it,' she said with a quick smile.

He smiled back, and offered a cigarette instead, which she accepted. He didn't take one for himself. There were only three left out of the day's ration, and the evening stretched ahead of him.

'Do you know who Ronnie's dealer was?' he asked casually, helping her to light the cigarette. With her head tucked into his open jacket, the lighter shaking in her hand, she shook her head. Eventually, the windbreak worked, and she sucked hard at the filter.

'I was never really sure,' she said. 'It was something else he didn't talk about.'

'What did he talk about?'

She thought about this, and smiled again. 'Not much, now you mention it. That was what I liked about him. You always felt there was more to him than he was letting on.'

'Such as?'

She shrugged. 'Might have been anything, might have been nothing.'

This was harder work than Rebus had anticipated, and he really was getting cold. It was time to speed things up.

'He was in the bedroom when you found him?'

'Yes.'

'And the squat was empty at the time?'

'Yes. Earlier on, there'd been a few people there, but they'd all gone. One of them was up in Ronnie's room, but I didn't know him. Then there was Charlie.'

'You mentioned him on the telephone.'

'Yes, well, when I found Ronnie, I went looking for him. He's usually around somewhere, in one of the other squats or in town doing a bit of begging. Christ, he's strange.'

'In what way?'

'Didn't you see what was on the living-room wall?'

'You mean the star?'

'Yes, that was Charlie. He painted it.'

'He's keen on the occult then?'

'Mad keen.'

'What about Ronnie?'

'Ronnie? Jesus, no. He couldn't even stand to watch horror films. They scared him.'

'But he had all those horror books in his bedroom.'

'That was Charlie, trying to get Ronnie interested. All they did was give him more nightmares. And all those did was push him into taking more smack.'

'How did he finance his habit?' Rebus watched a small boat come gliding through the mist. Something fell from it into the water, but he couldn't tell what.

'I wasn't his accountant.'

'Who was?' The boat was turning in an arc, slipping further west towards Queensferry.

'Nobody wants to know where the money comes from, that's the truth. It makes you an accessory, doesn't it?'

'That depends.' Rebus shivered.

'Well, *I* didn't want to know. If he tried to tell me, I put my hands over my ears.'

'He's never had a job then?'

'I don't know. He used to talk about being a photographer. That's what he'd set his heart on when he left school. It was the only thing he wouldn't pawn, even to pay for his habit.'

Rebus was lost. 'What was?'

'His camera. It cost him a small fortune, every penny saved out of his social security.'

Social security: now there was a phrase. But Rebus was sure there had been no camera in Ronnie's bedroom. So add robbery to the list.

'Tracy, I'll need a statement.'

She was immediately suspicious. 'What for?'

'Just so I've got it on record, so we can do something about Ronnie's death. Will you help me do that?'

It was a long time before she nodded. The boat had disappeared. There was nothing floating in the water, nothing left in its wake. Rebus put a hand on Tracy's shoulder, but gently.

'Thanks,' he said. 'The car's this way.'

After she had made her statement, Rebus insisted on driving her home, dropping her several streets from her destination but knowing her address now.

'Not that I can swear to be there for the next ten years,' she had said. It didn't matter. He had given her his work and home telephone numbers. He was sure she would keep in touch.

'One last thing,' he said, as she was about to close the car door. She leaned in from the pavement. 'Ronnie kept shouting "They're coming." Who do you think he meant?'

She shrugged. Then froze, remembering the scene. 'He was strung out, Inspector. Maybe he meant the snakes and spiders.'

Yes, thought Rebus, as she closed the door and he started the car. And then maybe he meant the snakes and spiders who'd supplied him.

Back at Greater London Road station, there was a message that Chief

Superintendent Watson wanted to see him. Rebus called his superior's office.

'I'll come along now, if I may.'

The secretary checked, and confirmed that this would be okay.

Rebus had come across Watson on many occasions since the superintendent's posting had brought him from the far north to Edinburgh. He seemed a reasonable man, if just a little, well, agricultural for some tastes. There were a lot of jokes around the station already about his Aberdonian background, and he had earned the whispered nickname of 'Farmer' Watson.

'Come in, John, come in.'

The Superintendent had risen from behind his desk long enough to point Rebus in the vague direction of a chair. Rebus noticed that the desk itself was meticulously arranged, files neatly piled in two trays, nothing in front of Watson but a thick, newish folder and two sharp pencils. There was a photograph of two young children to one side of the folder.

'My two,' Watson explained. 'They're a bit older than that now, but still a handful.'

Watson was a large man, his girth giving truth to the phrase 'barrel-chested'. His face was ruddy, hair thin and silvered at the temples. Yes, Rebus could picture him in galoshes and a trout-fishing hat, stomping his way across a moor, his collie obedient beside him. But what did he want with Rebus? Was he seeking a human collie?

'You were at the scene of a drugs overdose this morning.' It was a statement of fact, so Rebus didn't bother to answer. 'It should have been Inspector McCall's call, but he was ... well, wherever he was.'

'He's a good copper, sir.'

Watson stared up at him, then smiled. 'Inspector McCall's qualities are not in question. That's not why you're here. But your being on the scene gave me an idea. You probably know that I'm interested in this city's drugs problem. Frankly, the statistics appal me. It's not something I'd encountered in Aberdeen, with the exception of some of the oil workers. But then it was mostly the executives, the ones they flew in from the United States. They brought their habits, if you'll pardon the pun, with them. But here –' He flicked open the folder and began to pick over some of the sheets. 'Here, Inspector, it's Hades. Plain and simple.'

'Yes, sir.'

'Are you a churchgoer?'

'Sir?' Rebus was shifting uncomfortably in his chair.

'It's a simple enough question, isn't it? Do you go to church?'

'Not regularly, sir. But sometimes I do, yes.' Like yesterday, Rebus thought. And here again he felt like fleeing.

'Someone said you did. Then you should know what I'm talking about when I say that this city is turning into Hades.' Watson's face was ruddier than ever. 'The Infirmary has treated addicts as young as eleven and twelve. Your own brother is serving a prison sentence for dealing in drugs.' Watson looked up again, perhaps expecting Rebus to look shamed. But Rebus's eyes were a fiery glare, his cheeks red not with embarrassment.

'With respect, sir,' he said, voice level but as taut as a wire, 'what has this got to do with me?'

'Simply this.' Watson closed the folder and settled back in his chair. 'I'm putting into operation a new anti-drugs campaign. Public awareness and that sort of thing, coupled with funding for discreet information. I've got the backing, and what's more I've got the *money*. A group of the city's businessmen are prepared to put fifty thousand pounds into the campaign.'

'Very public-spirited of them, sir.'

Watson's face became darker. He leaned forward in his chair, filling Rebus's vision. 'You better bloody believe it,' he said.

'But I still don't see where I —'

'John.' The voice was anodyne now. 'You've had . . . experience. Personal experience. I'd like you to help me front our side of the campaign.'

'No, sir, really —'

'Good. That's agreed then.' Watson had already risen. Rebus tried to stand, too, but his legs had lost all power. He pushed against the armrests with his hands and managed to heave himself upright. Was this the price they were demanding? Public atonement for having a rotten brother? Watson was opening the door. 'We'll talk again, go through the details. But for now, try to tie up whatever you're working on, casenotes up to date, that sort of thing. Tell me what you can't finish, and we'll find someone to take it off your hands.'

'Yes, sir.' Rebus clutched at the proffered hand. It was like steel, cool, dry and crushing.

'Goodbye, sir,' Rebus said, standing in the corridor now, to a door that had already closed on him.

*

That evening, still numb, he grew bored with television and left his flat, planning to drive around a bit, no real destination in mind. Marchmont was quiet, but then it always was. His car sat undisturbed on the cobbles outside his tenement. He started it up and drove, entering the centre of town, crossing to the New Town. At Canonmills he stopped in the forecourt of a petrol station and filled the car, adding a torch, some batteries, and several bars of chocolate to his purchases, paying by credit card.

He ate the chocolate as he drove, trying not to think of the next day's cigarette ration, and listened to the car radio. Gill Templer's lover, Calum McCallum, began his broadcast at eight thirty, and he listened for a few minutes. It was enough. The mock-cheery voice, the jokes so lame they needed wheelchairs, the predictable mix of old records and telephone-linked chatter. . . . Rebus turned the tuning knob until he found Radio Three. Recognising the music of Mozart, he turned up the volume.

He had always known that it would end here of course. He drove through the ill-lit and winding streets, threading his way further into the maze. A new padlock had been fitted to the door of the house, but Rebus had in his pocket a copy of the key. Switching on his torch, he walked quietly into the living room. The floor was bare. There was no sign that a corpse had lain there only ten hours before. The jar of syringes had gone, too, as had the candlesticks. Ignoring the far wall, Rebus left the room and headed upstairs. He pushed open the door of Ronnie's bedroom and walked in, crossing to the window. This was where Tracy said she had found the body. Rebus squatted, resting on his toes, and shone the torch carefully over the floor. No sign of a camera. Nothing. It wasn't going to be made easy for him, this case. Always supposing there *was* a case.

He only had Tracy's word for it, after all.

He retraced his steps, out of the room and towards the stairwell. Something glinted against the top step, right in at the corner of the stairs. Rebus picked it up and examined it. It was a small piece of metal, like the clasp from a cheap brooch. He pushed it into his pocket anyway and took another look at the staircase, trying to imagine Ronnie regaining consciousness and making his way to the ground floor.

Possible. Just possible. But to end up positioned like that . . .? Much less feasible.

And why bring the jar of syringes downstairs with him? Rebus nodded to himself, sure that he was wandering the maze in something like the right direction. He went downstairs again and into the living room. It had a smell like the mould on an old jar of jam, earthy and sweet at the same time. The earth sterile, the sweetness sickly. He went over to the far wall and shone his torchlight against it.

Then came up short, blood pounding. The circles were still there, and the five-pointed star within them. But there were fresh additions, zodiac signs and other symbols between the two circles, painted in red. He touched the paint. It was tacky. Bringing his fingers away, he shone the torch further up the wall, and read the dripping message:

HELLO RONNIE

Superstitious to his core, Rebus turned on his heels and fled, not bothering to relock the door behind him. Walking briskly towards his car, his eyes turned back in the direction of the house, he fell into someone, and stumbled. The other figure fell awkwardly, and was slow to rise. Rebus switched on his torch, and confronted a teenager, eyes sparkling, face bruised and cut.

'Jesus, son,' he whispered, 'what happened to you?'

'I got beat up,' the boy said, shuffling away on a painful leg.

Rebus made the car somehow, his nerves as thin as old shoelaces. Inside, he locked the door and sat back, closing his eyes, breathing hard. Relax, John, he told himself. Relax. Soon, he was even able to smile at his momentary lapse of courage. Tomorrow he'd come back. In daylight.

He'd seen enough for now.

Tuesday

I have since had reason to believe the cause
to lie much deeper in the nature of man, and to
turn on some nobler hinge than the principle
of hatred.

Sleep did not come easy, but eventually, slumped in his favourite chair, a book propped open on his lap, he must have dozed off, because it took a nine o'clock call to bring him to life.

His back, legs and arms were stiff and aching as he scrabbled on the floor for his new cordless telephone.

'Yes?'

'Lab here, Inspector Rebus. You wanted to know first thing.'

'What have you got?' Rebus slumped back into the warm chair, pulling at his eyes with his free hand, trying to engage their cooperation in this fresh and waking world. He glanced at his watch and realised just how late he'd slept.

'Well, it's not the purest heroin on the street.'

He nodded to himself, confident that his next question hardly needed asking. 'Would it kill whoever injected it?'

The reply jolted him upright.

'Not at all. In fact, it's very clean, all things considered. A bit watered down from its pure form, but that's not uncommon. In fact, it's mandatory.'

'But it would be okay to use?'

'I imagine it would be very good to use.'

'I see. Well, thank you.' Rebus pressed the disconnect button. He had been so sure. So sure. . . . He reached into his pocket, found the number he needed, and pushed the seven digits quickly, before the thought of morning coffee could overwhelm him.

'Inspector Rebus for Doctor Enfield.' He waited. 'Doctor? Fine thanks. How about you? Good, good. Listen, that body yesterday, the druggie on the Pilmuir Estate, any news?' He listened. 'Yes, I'll hold.'

Pilmuir. What had Tony McCall said? It had been lovely once, a place of innocence, something like that. The old days always were though, weren't they? Memory smoothed the corners, as Rebus himself knew well.

'Hello?' he said to the telephone. 'Yes, that's right.' Paper was rustling in the background, Enfield's voice dispassionate.

'Bruising on the body. Fairly extensive. Result of a heavy fall or some kind of physical confrontation. The stomach was almost completely empty. HIV negative, which is something. As for the cause of death, well. . . .'

'The heroin?' Rebus prompted.

'Mmm. Ninety-five percent impure.'

'Really?' Rebus perked up. 'What had it been diluted with?'

'Still working on that, Inspector. But an educated guess would be anything from ground-up aspirin to rat poison, with the emphasis strictly on rodent control.'

'You're saying it was lethal?'

'Oh, absolutely. Whoever sold the stuff was selling euthanasia. If there's more of it about . . . well, I dread to think.'

More of it about? The thought made Rebus's scalp tingle. What if someone were going around poisoning junkies? But why the one perfect packet? One perfect, one as rotten as could be. It didn't make sense.

'Thanks, Doctor Enfield.'

He rested the telephone on the arm of the chair. Tracy had been right in one respect at least. They *had* murdered Ronnie. Whoever 'they' were. And Ronnie had known, known as soon as he'd used the stuff. . . . No, wait. . . . Known *before* he'd used the stuff? Could that be possible? Rebus had to find the dealer. Had to find out why Ronnie had been chosen to die. Been, indeed, sacrificed. . . .

It was Tony McCall's backyard. All right, so he had moved out of Pilmuir, had eventually bought a crippling mortgage which some people called a house. It was a nice house, too. He knew this because his wife told him it was. Told him continually. She couldn't understand why he spent so little time there. After all, as she told him, it was his home too.

Home. To McCall's wife, it was a palace. 'Home' didn't quite cover it. And the two children, son and daughter, had been brought up to tiptoe through the interior, not leaving crumbs or fingerprints, no mess, no breakages. McCall, who had lived a bruising childhood with his brother Tommy, thought it unnatural. His children had grown up in fear and in a swaddling of love – a bad combination. Now Craig was fourteen, Isabel eleven. Both were shy, introspective, maybe even a bit strange.

Bang had gone McCall's dream of a professional footballer for a son, an actress for a daughter. Craig played chess a lot, but no physical sports. (He had won a small plaque at school after one tournament. McCall had tried to learn to play after that, but had failed.) Isabel liked knitting. They sat in the too-perfect living room created by their mother, and were almost silent. The clack-clack of needles; the soft movement of chess pieces.

Christ, was it any wonder he kept away?

So here he was in Pilmuir, not checking on anything exactly, just walking. Taking some air. From his own ultra-modern estate, all detached shoeboxes and Volvos, he had to cross some waste ground, avoid the traffic on a busy arterial road, pass a school playing-field and manoeuvre between some factory units to find himself in Pilmuir. But it was worth the effort. He knew this place; knew the minds that festered here.

He was one of them, after all.

'Hello, Tony.'

He swirled, not recognising the voice, expecting hassle. John Rebus stood there, smiling at him, hands in pockets.

'John! Christ, you made me jump.'

'Sorry. Stroke of luck bumping into you though.' Rebus checked around them, as though looking for someone. 'I tried phoning, but they said it was your day off.'

'Aye, that's right.'

'So what are you doing here?'

'Just walking. We live over that way.' He jerked his head towards the south-west. 'It's not far. Besides, this is my patch, don't forget. Got to keep an eye on the boys and girls.'

'That's why I wanted to speak to you actually.'

'Oh?'

Rebus had begun to walk along the pavement, and McCall, still rattled by his sudden appearance, followed.

'Yes,' Rebus was saying. 'I wanted to ask if you know someone, a friend of the deceased's. The name is Charlie.'

'That's all? Charlie?' Rebus shrugged. 'What does he look like?'

Rebus shrugged again. 'I've no idea, Tony. It was Ronnie's girlfriend Tracy who told me about him.'

'Ronnie? Tracy?' McCall's eyebrows met. 'Who the hell are they?'

'Ronnie is the deceased. That junkie we found on the estate.'

Everything was suddenly clear in McCall's mind. He nodded slowly. 'You work quickly,' he said.

'The quicker the better. Ronnie's girlfriend told me an interesting story.'

'Oh?'

'She said Ronnie was murdered.' Rebus kept on walking, but McCall had stopped.

'Wait a minute!' He caught Rebus up. 'Murdered? Come on, John, you saw the guy.'

'True. With a needle's worth of rat poison scuppering his veins.'

McCall whistled softly. 'Jesus.'

'Quite,' said Rebus. 'And now I need to talk to Charlie. He's young, could be a bit scared, and interested in the occult.'

McCall sorted through a few mental files. 'I suppose there are one or two places we could try looking,' he said at last. 'But it'd be a slog. The concept of neighbourhood policing hasn't quite stretched this far yet.'

'You're saying we won't be made very welcome?'

'Something like that.'

'Well, just give me the addresses and point me in the right direction. It's your day off after all.'

McCall looked slighted. 'You're forgetting, John. This is my patch. By rights, this should be my case, if there is a case.'

'It would've been your case if you hadn't had that hangover.' They smiled at this, but Rebus was wondering whether, in Tony McCall's hands, there *would* have been anything to investigate. Wouldn't Tony just have let it slip? Should he, Rebus, let it slip, too?

'Anyway,' McCall was saying on cue, 'surely you must have better things to do?'

Rebus shook his head. 'Nothing. All my work's been farmed out, with the emphasis on "farmed".'

'You mean Superintendent Watson?'

'He wants me working on his anti-drugs campaign. Me, for Christ's sake.'

'That could be a bit embarrassing.'

'I know. But the idiot thinks I've got "personal experience".'

'He's got a point, I suppose.' Rebus was about to argue, but McCall got in first. 'So you've nothing to do?'

'Not until summoned by Farmer Watson, no.'

'You jammy bugger. Well, that does change things a bit, but not enough, I'm sorry to say. You're my guest here, and you're going to have to put up with me. Until I get bored, that is.'

Rebus smiled. 'I appreciate it, Tony.' He looked around them. 'So, where to first?'

McCall inclined his head back the way they had just come. They turned around and walked.

'So tell me,' said Rebus, 'what's so awful at home that you'd think of coming here on your day off?'

McCall laughed. 'Is it so obvious then?'

'Only to someone who's been there himself.'

'Ach, I don't know, John. I seem to have everything I've never wanted.'

'And it's still not enough.' It was a simple statement of belief.

'I mean, Sheila's a wonderful mother and all that, and the kids never get into trouble, but. . . .'

'The grass is always greener,' said Rebus, thinking of his own failed marriage, of the way his flat was cold when he came home, the way the door would close with a hollow sound behind him.

'Now Tommy, my brother, I used to think he had it made. Plenty of money, house with a jacuzzi, automatic-opening garage. . . .' McCall saw that Rebus was smiling, and smiled himself.

'Electric blinds,' Rebus continued, 'personalised number plate, car phone. . .'

'Time share in Malaga,' said McCall, close to laughter, 'marble-topped kitchen units.'

It was too ridiculous. They laughed out loud as they walked, adding to the catalogue. But then Rebus saw where they were, and stopped laughing, stopped walking. This was where he'd been heading all along. He touched the torch in his jacket pocket.

'Come on, Tony,' he said soberly. 'There's something I want to show you.'

'He was found here,' Rebus said, shining the torch over the bare floorboards. 'Legs together, lying on his back, arms outstretched. I don't think he got into that position by accident, do you?'

McCall studied the scene. They were both professionals now, and acting almost like strangers. 'And the girlfriend says she found him upstairs?'

'That's right.'

'You believe her?'

'Why would she lie?'

'There could be a hundred reasons, John. Would I know the girl?'

'She hasn't been in Pilmuir long. Bit older than you'd imagine, midtwenties, maybe more.'

'So this Ronnie's already dead, and he's brought downstairs and laid out with the candles and everything.'

'That's right.'

'I'm beginning to see why you need to find the friend who's into the occult.'

'Right. Now come and look at this.' Rebus led McCall to the far wall and shone the torch onto the pentagram, then further up the wall.

'"Hello Ronnie",' McCall read aloud.

'And this wasn't here yesterday.'

'Really?' McCall sounded surprised. 'Kids, John, that's all.'

'Kids didn't draw that pentagram.'

'No, agreed.'

'Charlie drew that pentagram.'

'Right.' McCall slipped his hands into his pockets and drew himself upright. 'Point taken, Inspector. Let's go squat hunting.'

But the few people they found seemed to know nothing, and to care even less. As McCall pointed out, it was the wrong time of day. Everyone from the squats was in the city centre, stealing purses from handbags, begging, shoplifting, doing deals. Reluctantly, Rebus agreed that they were wasting their time.

Since McCall wanted to listen to the tape Rebus had made of his interview with Tracy, they headed back to Great London Road. McCall had the idea that there might be some clue on the tape that would lead them to Charlie, something that would help him place the guy, something Rebus had missed.

Rebus was a weary step or two ahead of McCall as they climbed the front steps to the station's heavy wooden door. A fresh duty officer was beginning his shift at the desk, still fussing with his shirt collar and his clip-on tie. Simple but clever, Rebus thought to himself. Simple but clever. All uniformed officers wore clip-on ties, so that in a clinch, if the attacker tried to yank the officer's head forwards, the tie would simply come away in his hands. Likewise, the desk sergeant's glasses had special lenses which, if hit, would slip out of their frame without shattering. Simple but clever. Rebus hoped that the case of the crucified junkie would be simple.

He didn't feel very clever.

'Hello, Arthur,' he said, passing the desk, making towards the staircase. 'Any messages for me?'

'Give me a break, John. I've only been on two minutes.'

'Fair enough.' Rebus pushed his hands deep into his pockets, where the fingers of his right hand touched something alien, metal. He brought the brooch-clip out and studied it. Then froze.

McCall looked at him, puzzled.

'Go on up,' Rebus told him. 'I'll just be a second.'

'Right you are, John.'

Back at the desk, Rebus held his left hand out to the sergeant. 'Do me a favour, Arthur. Give me your tie.'

'What?'

'You heard me.'

Knowing that he would have a story to tell tonight in the canteen, the desk sergeant pulled at his tie. As it came away from his shirt, the clip made a single snapping sound. Simple but clever, thought Rebus, holding the tie between finger and thumb.

'Thanks, Arthur,' he said.

'Anytime, John,' the sergeant called, watching carefully as Rebus walked back towards the stairs. 'Anytime.'

'Know what this is, Tony?'

McCall had seated himself in Rebus's chair, behind Rebus's desk. He had one fist in a drawer, and looked up, startled. Rebus was holding the necktie out in front of him. McCall nodded, then brought his hand out of the drawer. It was curved around a bottle of whisky.

'It's a tie,' he said. 'Got any cups?'

Rebus placed the tie on the desk. He went to a filing cabinet and searched amongst the many cups which sat unloved and uncleaned on top of it. Finally, one seemed to satisfy him, and he brought it to the desk. McCall was studying the cover of a file lying on the desk.

' "Ronnie," ' he read out, ' "Tracy – caller". I see your casenotes are as precise as ever.'

Rebus handed the cup to McCall.

'Where's yours?' asked McCall, pointing to the cup.

'I don't feel like drinking. To tell you the truth, I hardly touch the stuff now.' Rebus nodded at the bottle. 'That's for visitors.' McCall pursed his lips, his eyes opening wide. 'Besides,' Rebus went on, 'I've got the mother and father of a headache. In-laws, too. Kids, neighbours, town and country.' He noticed a large envelope on the desk: PHOTOGRAPHS – DO NOT BEND.

'You know, Tony, when I was a sergeant, this sort of thing would take days to arrive. It's like royalty being an inspector.' He opened the envelope and took out the set of prints, ten by eights, black and white. He handed one to McCall.

'Look,' Rebus said, 'no writing on the wall. And the pentagram's unfinished. Today it was complete.' McCall nodded, and Rebus took back the picture, handing over another in its place. 'The deceased.'

'Poor little sod,' said McCall. 'It could be one of our kids, eh, John?'

'No,' said Rebus firmly. He rolled the envelope into the shape of a tube, and put it in his jacket pocket.

McCall had picked up the tie. He waved it towards Rebus, demanding an explanation.

'Have you ever worn one of those?' Rebus asked.

'Sure, at my wedding, maybe a funeral or a christening. . . .'

'I mean like this. A clip-on. When I was a kid, I remember my dad decided I'd look good in a kilt. He bought me the whole get-up, including a little tartan bow tie. It was a clip-on.'

'I've worn one,' said McCall. 'Everybody has. We all came through the ranks, didn't we?'

'No,' said Rebus. 'Now get out of my bloody chair.'

McCall found another chair, dragging it over from the wall to the desk. Rebus meantime sat down, picking up the tie.

'Police issue.'

'What is?'

'Clip-on ties,' said Rebus. 'Who else wears them?'

'Christ, I don't know, John.'

Rebus threw the clip across to McCall, who was slow to react. It fell to the floor, from where he retrieved it.

'It's a clip-on,' he said.

'I found it in Ronnie's house,' said Rebus. 'At the top of the stairs.'

'So?'

'So someone's tie broke. Maybe when they were dragging Ronnie downstairs. Maybe a police constable someone.'

'You think one of our lot . . .?'

'Just an idea,' said Rebus. 'Of course, it could belong to one of the lads who found the body.' He held out his hand, and McCall gave him back the clip. 'Maybe I'll talk to them.'

'John, what the hell. . . .' McCall ended with a sort of choking sound, unable to find words for the question he wanted to ask.

'Drink your whisky,' said Rebus solicitously. 'Then you can listen to that tape, see if you think Tracy's telling the truth.'

'What are you going to do?'

'I don't know.' He put the desk sergeant's tie in his pocket. 'Maybe I'll tie up a few loose ends.' McCall was pouring out a measure of whisky as Rebus left, but the parting shot, called from the staircase, was loud enough for him to hear.

'Maybe I'll just go to the devil!'

'Yes, a simple pentangle.'

The psychologist, Dr Poole, who wasn't really a psychologist, but rather, he had explained, a lecturer in psychology, quite a different thing, studied the photographs carefully, bottom lip curling up to cover his top lip in a sign of confident recognition. Rebus played with the empty envelope and stared out of the office window. The day was bright, and some students were lying in George Square Gardens, sharing bottles of wine, their text books forgotten.

Rebus felt uncomfortable. Institutes of higher education, from the simplest college up to the present confines of the University of Edinburgh, made him feel stupid. He felt that his every movement, every utterance, was being judged and interpreted, marking him down as a clever man who could have been cleverer, given the breaks.

'When I returned to the house,' he said, 'someone had drawn some symbols between the two circles. Signs of the zodiac, that sort of thing.'

Rebus watched as the psychologist went over to the bookshelves and began to browse. It had been easy to find this man. Making use of him might be more difficult.

'Probably the usual arcana,' Dr Poole was saying, finding the page he wanted and bringing it back to the desk to show Rebus. 'This sort of thing?'

'Yes, that's it.' Rebus studied the illustration. The pentagram was not identical to the one he had seen, but the differences were slight. 'Tell me, are many people interested in the occult?'

'You mean in Edinburgh?' Poole sat down again, pushing his glasses back up his nose. 'Oh yes. Plenty. Look at how well films about the devil do at the box office.'

Rebus smiled. 'Yes, I used to like horror films myself. But I mean an *active* interest.'

The lecturer smiled. 'I know you do. I was being facetious. So many people think that's what the occult is about – bringing Old Nick back to life. There's much more to it, believe me, Inspector. Or much less to it, depending on your point of view.'

Rebus tried to work out what this meant. 'You know occultists?' he said meantime.

'I know *of* occultists, practising covens of white and black witches.'

'Here? In Edinburgh?'

Poole smiled again. 'Oh yes. Right here. There are six working covens in and around Edinburgh.' He paused, and Rebus could almost see him doing a recount. 'Seven, perhaps. Fortunately, most of these practise white magic.'

'That's using the occult as a supposed force for good, right?'

'Quite correct.'

'And black magic . . .?'

The lecturer sighed. He suddenly became interested in the scene from his window. A summer's day. Rebus was remembering something. A long time ago, he'd bought a book of paintings by H.R. Giger, paintings of Satan flanked by vestal whores. . . . He couldn't say why he'd done it, but it must still be somewhere in the flat. He remembered hiding it from Rhona. . . .

'There is one coven in Edinburgh,' Poole was saying. 'A black coven.'

'Tell me, do they . . . do they make sacrifices?'

Dr Poole shrugged. 'We all make sacrifices.' But, seeing that Rebus was not laughing at his little joke, he straightened in his chair, his face becoming more serious. 'Probably they do, some token. A rat, a mouse, a chicken. It may not even go that far. They could use something symbolic, I really don't know.'

Rebus tapped one of the photographs which were spread across the desk. 'In the house where we found this pentagram, we also found a body. A dead body, in case you were wondering.' He brought these photographs out now. Dr Poole frowned as he glanced at them. 'Dead from a heroin overdose. Laid out with legs together, arms apart. The body was lying between two candles, which had burned down to nothing. Mean anything to you?'

Poole looked horror-struck. 'No,' he said. 'But you think that Satanists. . . .'

'I don't think anything, sir. I'm just trying to piece things together, going through all the possibilities.'

Poole thought for a moment. 'One of our students *might* be of more use to you than I can. I'd no idea we were talking about a death. . . .'

'A student?'

'Yes. I only know him vaguely. He seems very interested in the occult, wrote rather a long and knowledgeable essay this term. Wants to do some project on demonism. He's a second-year student. They have to do a project over the summer. Yes, maybe he can give you more help than I'm able to.'

'And his name is . . .?'

'Well, his surname escapes me for the moment. He usually just calls himself by his first name. Charles.'

'Charles?'

'Or maybe Charlie. Yes, Charlie, that's it.'

Ronnie's friend's name. The hair on Rebus's neck began to prickle.

'That's right, Charlie,' Poole confirmed to himself, nodding. 'Bit of an eccentric. You can probably find him in one of the student union buildings. I believe he's addicted to these video machines. . . .'

No, not video machines. Pinball machines. The ones with all the extras, all the little tricks and treats that made a game a game. Charlie loved them with a vengeance. It was the kind of love which was all the more fervent for having come to him late in life. He was nineteen after all, life was streaming past, and he wanted to hang on to any piece of driftwood he could. Pinball had played no part in his adolescence. That had belonged to books and music. Besides, there had been no pinball machines at his boarding school.

Now, released into university, he wanted to live. And to play pinball. And do all the other things he had missed out on during the years of prep, sensitive essay-writing, and introspection. Charlie wanted to run faster than anyone had ever run, to live not one life, but two or three or four. As the silver ball made contact with the left flipper, he threw it back up the table with real ferocity. There was a pause while the ball sat in one of the bonus craters, collecting another thousand points. He picked up his lager, took a gulp of it, and then returned his fingers to the buttons. In another ten minutes, he'd have the day's high score.

'Charlie?'

He turned at the sound of his name. A bad mistake, a naive mistake. He turned back to the game again, but too late. The man was striding towards him. The serious man. The unsmiling man.

'I'd like a word, Charlie.'

'Okay, how about carbohydrate. That was always one of my favourites.'

John Rebus's smile lasted less than a second.

'Very clever,' he said. 'Yes, that's what we call a smart answer.'

'We?'

'Lothian CID. My name's Inspector Rebus.'

'Pleased to meet you.'

'Likewise, Charlie.'

'No, you're mistaken. My name's not Charlie. He comes in here sometimes though. I'll tell him you called.'

Charlie was just about to hit the high score, five minutes ahead of schedule, when Rebus gripped his shoulder and spun him around. There were no other students in the games room, so he kept squeezing the shoulder while he spoke.

'You're about as funny as a maggot sandwich, Charlie, and patience isn't my favourite card game. So you'll excuse me if I become irritable, short-tempered, that sort of thing.'

'Hands off.' Charlie's face had taken on a new sheen, but not of fear.

'Ronnie,' Rebus said, calmly now, releasing his grip on the young man's shoulder.

The colour drained from Charlie's face. 'What about him?'

'He's dead.'

'Yes.' Charlie's voice was quiet, his eyes unfocussed. 'I heard.'

Rebus nodded. 'Tracy tried to find you.'

'Tracy.' There was venom in the word. 'She's no idea, no idea at all. Have you seen her?' Rebus nodded. 'Yeah, what a loser that woman is. She never understood Ronnie. Never even tried.'

As Charlie spoke, Rebus was learning more about him. His accent was Scottish private school, which was the first surprise. Rebus didn't know what he had expected. He knew he hadn't expected this. Charlie was well built, too, a product of the rugby-playing classes. He had curly dark brown hair, cut not too long, and was dressed in traditional student summer wear: training shoes, denims, and a T-shirt. The T-shirt was black, torn loose at the arms.

'So,' Charlie was saying, 'Ronnie did the big one, eh? Well, it's a good age to die. Live fast, die young.'

'Do you want to die young, Charlie?'

'Me?' Charlie laughed, a high-pitched squeal like a small animal. 'Hell, I want to live to be a hundred. I never want to die.' He looked at Rebus, something sparkling in his eyes. 'Do you?'

226

Rebus considered the question, but wasn't about to answer. He was here on business, not to discuss the death instinct. The lecturer, Dr Poole, had told him about the death instinct.

'I want to know what you know about Ronnie.'

'Does that mean you're going to take me away for questioning?'

'If you like. We can do it here if you'd prefer. . . .'

'No, no. I *want* to go to the police station. Come on, take me there.' There was a sudden eagerness about Charlie which made him seem much younger than his years. Who the hell wanted to *go* to a police station for questioning?

On the route to the car park and Rebus's car, Charlie insisted on walking a few paces ahead of Rebus, and with his hands behind his back, head slumped. Rebus saw that Charlie was pretending to be handcuffed. He was doing a good impersonation too, drawing attention to Rebus and himself. Someone even called out 'bastard' in Rebus's direction. But the word had lost all meaning over the years. They would have disturbed him more by wishing him a pleasant trip.

'Can I buy a couple of these?' Charlie asked, examining the photographs of his work, his pentagram.

The interview room was bleak. It was its purpose to be bleak. But Charlie had settled in like he was planning to rent it.

'No,' Rebus said, lighting a cigarette. He didn't offer one to Charlie. 'So, why did you paint it?'

'Because it's beautiful.' He still studied the photographs. 'Don't you think? So full of meaning.'

'How long had you known Ronnie?'

Charlie shrugged. For the first time, he looked in the direction of the cassette recorder. Rebus had asked if he minded having the dialogue recorded. He had shrugged. Now he seemed a little pensive. 'Maybe a year,' he said. 'Yes, a year. I met him around the time of my first-year exams. That was when I started to get interested in the *real* Edinburgh.'

'The real Edinburgh?'

'Yes. Not just the piper on the ramparts, or the Royal Mile, or the Scott Monument.' Rebus recalled Ronnie's photographs of the Castle.

'I saw some photos on Ronnie's wall.' Charlie screwed up his face.

'God, those. He had the idea he was going to be a professional photographer. Taking bloody tourist snaps for postcards. That didn't last long. Like most of Ronnie's schemes.'

'Nice camera he had though.'

'What? Oh, yes, his camera. Yes, it was his pride and joy.' Charlie crossed his legs. Rebus continued to stare into the young man's eyes, but Charlie was busily studying the photographs of the pentagram.

'So what was that you were telling me about the "real" Edinburgh?'

'Deacon Brodie,' said Charlie, suddenly interested again, 'Burke and Hare, justified sinners, the lot. But it's all been cleaned up for the tourists, you see. And I thought, hang on, all this Lowland low-life still exists. That was when I started touring the housing estates, Wester Hailes, Oxgangs, Craigmillar, Pilmuir. And sure enough, it's all still here, the past replaying itself in the present.'

'So you started hanging around Pilmuir?'

'Yes.'

'In other words, you became a tourist yourself?' Rebus had seen Charlie's kind before, though usually the older model, the prosperous businessman debasing himself for kicks, visiting sleazy rooms for a dry cough of pleasure. He didn't like the species.

'I wasn't a tourist!' Charlie's anger rose, a trout snapping a hooked worm. 'I was there because I wanted to be there, and they wanted me there.' His voice began to sound sulky. 'I belong there.'

'No you don't, son, you belong in a big house somewhere with parents interested in your university career.'

'Crap.' Charlie pushed back his chair and walked to the wall, resting his head against it. Rebus thought for a moment that he might be about to beat himself senseless, then claim police brutality. But he seemed merely to need something cool against his face.

The interview room was stifling. Rebus had removed his jacket. Now he rolled up his sleeves before stubbing out the cigarette.

'Okay, Charlie.' The young man was soft now, pliable. It was time to ask some questions. 'The night of the overdose, you were in the house with Ronnie, right?'

'That's right. For a little while.'

'Who else was there?'

'Tracy was there. She was there when I left.'

'Anyone else?'

'Some guy visited earlier in the evening. He didn't stay long. I'd seen him with Ronnie before a couple of times. When they were together, they kept to themselves.'

'Was this person his dealer, do you think?'

'No. Ronnie could always get stuff. Well, up until recently. Past couple of weeks, he found it tough. They seemed pretty close, though. Really close, if you get my meaning.'

'Go on.'

'Close as in loving. As in gay.'

'But Tracy . . .?'

'Yeah, yeah, but what's that supposed to prove, huh? You know how most addicts make their money.'

'How? Theft?'

'Yeah, theft, muggings, whatever. And doing a bit of business over by Calton Hill.'

Calton Hill, large, sprawling, lying to the east of Princes Street. Yes, Rebus knew all about Calton Hill, and about the cars which sat much of the night at the foot of it, along Regent Road. He knew about Calton Cemetery, too, about what went on there. . . .

'You're saying Ronnie was a rent boy?' The phrase sounded ridiculous out loud. It was tabloid talk.

'I'm saying he used to hang around there with a load of other guys, and I'm saying he always had money at the end of the night.' Charlie swallowed. 'Money and maybe a few bruises.'

'Jesus.' Rebus added this information to what was becoming a very grubby little dossier in his head. How far would you sink for a fix? The answer was: all the way. And then a little lower. He lit another cigarette.

'Do you know this for a fact?' he asked.

'No.'

'Was Ronnie from Edinburgh, by the way?'

'Stirling.'

'And his surname was –'

'McGrath, I think.'

'What about this guy he was so chummy with? Have you a name for him?'

'He called himself Neil. Ronnie called him Neilly.'

'Neilly? Did you get the impression they'd known one another for a while?'

'Yeah, a goodish while. A nickname like that's a sign of affection, right?' Rebus studied Charlie with new admiration. 'I don't do psychology for nothing, Inspector.'

'Right.' Rebus checked that the small cassette recorder still had some tape left to run. 'Give me a physical description of this Neil character, will you?'

'Tall, skinny, short brown hair. Kind of spotty face, but always clean. Usually wore jeans and a denim jacket. Carried a big black holdall with him.'

'Any idea what was in it?'

'I got the feeling it was just clothes.'

'Okay.'

'Anything else?'

'Let's talk about the pentagram. Someone has been back to the house and added to it since these photographs were taken.'

Charlie said nothing, but did not look surprised.

'It was you, wasn't it?'

Charlie nodded.

'How did you get in?'

'Through the downstairs window. Those wooden slats couldn't keep out an elephant. It's like an extra door. Lots of people used to come into the house that way.'

'Why did you go back?'

'It wasn't finished, was it? I wanted to add the symbols.'

'And the message.'

Charlie smiled to himself. 'Yes, the message.'

'"Hello Ronnie",' Rebus quoted. 'What's that all about?'

'Just what it says. His spirit's still in the house, his soul's still there. I was just saying hello. I had some paint left. Besides, I thought it might give somebody a fright.'

Rebus remembered his own shock at seeing the scrawl. He felt his cheeks redden slightly, but covered the fact with a question.

'Do you remember the candles?'

Charlie nodded, but was becoming restless. Helping police with their inquiries was not as much fun as he had hoped.

'What about your project?' said Rebus, changing tack.

'What about it?'

'It's on demonism, isn't it?'

'Maybe. I haven't decided yet.'

'What aspect of demonism?'

'I don't know. Maybe the popular mythology. How old fears become new fears, that sort of thing.'

'Do you know any of the covens in Edinburgh?'

'I know people who claim to be in some of them.'

'But you've never been along to one?'

'No, worse luck.' Charlie seemed suddenly to come to life. 'Look, what is all this? Ronnie OD'd. He's history. Why all the questions?'

'What can you tell me about the candles?'

Charlie exploded. 'What *about* the candles?'

Rebus was all calmness. He exhaled smoke before responding. 'There were candles in the living room.' He was getting close to telling Charlie something Charlie didn't seem to know. All during the interview, he had been spiralling inwards towards this moment.

'That's right. Big candles. Ronnie got them from some shop that specialises in candles. He *liked* candles. They gave the place *ambience*.'

'Tracy found Ronnie in his bedroom. She thinks he was already dead.' Rebus's voice became lower still, and as flat as the desktop. 'But by the time she'd phoned us, and an officer had turned up at the house, Ronnie's body had been moved downstairs. It was laid out between two candles, which had been burnt down to nothing.'

'There wasn't much left of those candles anyway, not when I left.'

'You left when?'

'Just before midnight. There was supposed to be a party somewhere on the estate. I thought I might get invited in.'

'How long would the candles have burned for?'

'An hour, two hours. God knows.'

'How much smack did Ronnie have?'

'Christ, I don't know.'

'Well, how much would he normally use at any one time?'

'I really don't know. I'm not a user, you know. I hate all that stuff. I've got two friends who were in my sixth form. They're both in private clinics.'

'That's nice for them.'

'Like I said, Ronnie hadn't been able to find any stuff for days. He was a bit whacked out, just about to fall right over the edge. Then he came back with some. End of story.'

'Isn't there much about then?'

'So far as I know, there's plenty, but don't bother asking for names.'

'So if there's plenty, how come Ronnie was finding it so hard?'

'God knows. He didn't know himself. It was like he'd suddenly become bad news. Then he was good news again, and he got that packet.'

It was time. Rebus picked an invisible thread from his shirt.

'He was murdered,' he said. 'Or as good as.'

Charlie's mouth opened. The blood drained from his face, as though a tap had been opened somewhere. 'What?'

'He was murdered. His body was full of rat poison. Self-inflicted, but supplied by someone who probably knew it was lethal. A lot of work was then done to manoeuvre his body into some kind of ritualistic position in the living room. Where your pentagram is.'

'Now wait —'

'How many covens are there in Edinburgh, Charlie?'

'What? Six, seven, I don't know. Look —'

'Do you know them? Any of them? I mean know them personally?'

'Christ, man, you're not going to pin this on me!'

'Why not?' Rebus stubbed out his cigarette.

'Because it's crazy.'

'Seems to me it all fits, Charlie.' String him out, Rebus was thinking. He's already stretched to snapping point. 'Unless you can convince me otherwise.'

Charlie walked to the door purposefully, then paused.

'Go on,' Rebus called, 'it's not locked. Walk out of here if you like. Then I'll *know* you had something to do with it.'

Charlie turned. His eyes seemed moist in the hazy light. A sunbeam from the barred window, penetrating the frosted glass, caught motes of dust and turned them into slow-motion dancers. Charlie moved through them as he returned to the desk.

'I didn't have anything to do with it, honest.'

'Sit down,' said Rebus, a kindly uncle now. 'Let's talk some more.'

But Charlie didn't like uncles. Never had. He placed his hands on the desk and leaned down, looming over Rebus. Something had hardened somewhere within him. His teeth when he spoke glistened with venom.

'Go to hell, Rebus. I see what you're up to, and I'm damned if I'm going to play along. Arrest me if you like, but don't insult me with cheap tricks. I did those in my first term.'

Then he walked, and this time opened the door, and left it open behind him. Rebus got up from the desk, switched off the recorder, took out the tape and, pushing it into his pocket, followed. By the time he reached the entrance hall, Charlie had gone. He approached the desk. The duty sergeant looked up from his paperwork.

'You just missed him,' he said.

Rebus nodded. 'It doesn't matter.'

'He didn't look too happy.'

'Would I be doing my job if they all left here laughing and holding their sides?'

The sergeant smiled. 'I suppose not. So what can I do for you?'

'The Pilmuir overdose. I've got a name for the corpse. Ronnie McGrath. Originally from Stirling. Let's see if we can find his parents, eh?'

The sergeant scribbled the name onto a pad. 'I'm sure they'll be delighted to hear how their son is doing in the big city.'

'Yes,' said Rebus, staring towards the front door of the police station. 'I'm sure they will.'

John Rebus's flat was his castle. Once through the door, he would pull up the drawbridge and let his mind go blank, emptying himself of the world for as long as he could. He would pour himself a drink, put some tenor sax music on the cassette machine, and pick up a book. Many weeks ago, in a crazed state of righteousness, he had put up shelves along one wall of the living room, intending his sprawling collection of books to rest there. But somehow they managed to crawl across the floor, getting under his feet, so that he used them like stepping-stones into the hallway and the bedroom.

He walked across them now, on his way to the bay window where he pulled down the dusty venetian blinds. The slats he left open, so that strawberry slants of evening light came pouring through, reminding him of the interview room. . . .

No, no, no, that wouldn't do. He was being sucked back into work again. He had to clear his mind, find some book which would pull him into its little universe, far away from the sights and smells of Edinburgh. He stepped firmly on the likes of Chekhov, Heller, Rimbaud and Kerouac as he made his way to the kitchen, seeking out a bottle of wine.

There were two cardboard boxes beneath the kitchen worktop, taking up the space where the washing machine had once been. Rhona had taken the washing machine, which was fair enough. He called the resultant space his wine cellar, and now and then would order a mixed case from a good little shop around the corner from his flat. He put a hand into one of the boxes and brought out something called Château Potensac. Yes, he'd had a bottle of this before. It would do.

He poured a third of the bottle into a large glass and returned to the living room, plucking one of the books from the floor as he went. He was seated in his armchair before he looked at its cover: *The Naked*

Lunch. No, bad choice. He threw the book down again and groped for another. *Dr Jekyll and Mr Hyde*. Fair enough, he'd been meaning to reread it for ages, and it was blissfully short. He took a mouthful of wine, sloshed it around before swallowing, and opened the book.

With the timing of a stage-play, there was a rapping at the front door. The noise Rebus made was somewhere between a sigh and a roar. He balanced the book, its covers open, on the arm of the chair, and rose to his feet. Probably it was Mrs Cochrane from downstairs, telling him that it was his turn to wash the communal stairwell. She would have the large, imperative card with her: IT IS YOUR TURN TO WASH THE STAIRS. Why she couldn't just hang it on his door like everyone else seemed to do . . .?

He tried to arrange a neighbourly smile on his face as he opened the door, but the actor in him had left for the evening. So there was something not unlike pain rippling his lips as he stared at the visitor on his doormat.

It was Tracy.

Her face was red, and there were tears in her eyes, but the redness was not from crying. She looked exhausted, her hair cloying with sweat.

'Can I come in?' There was an all too visible effort in her voice. Rebus hadn't the heart to say no. He pushed the door open wide and she stumbled in past him, walking straight through to the living room as though she'd been here a hundred times. Rebus checked that the stairwell was empty of inquisitive neighbours, then closed the door. He was tingling, not a pleasant feeling: he didn't like people visiting him here.

Especially, he didn't like work following him home.

By the time he reached the living room, Tracy had drained the wine and was exhaling with relief, her thirst quenched. Rebus felt the discomfort in him increase until it was almost unbearable.

'How the hell did you find this place?' he asked, standing in the doorway as though waiting for her to leave.

'Not easy,' she said, her voice a little more calm. 'You told me you lived in Marchmont, so I just wandered around looking for your car. Then I found your name on the bell downstairs.'

He had to admit it, she'd have made a good detective. Footwork was what it was all about.

'Somebody's been following me,' she said now. 'I got scared.'

'Following you?' He stepped into the room now, curious, his sense of encroachment easing.

'Yes, two men. I think there were two. They've been following me all afternoon. I was up Princes Street, just walking, and they were always there, a little way behind me. They must've known I could see them.'

'What happened?'

'I lost them. Went into Marks and Spencer, ran like hell for the Rose Street exit, then dived into the ladies' in a pub. Stayed in there for an hour. That seemed to do the trick. Then I headed here.'

'Why didn't you telephone me?'

'No money. That's why I was up Princes Street in the first place.'

She had settled in his chair, her arms hanging over its sides. He nodded towards the empty glass.

'Do you want another?'

'No thanks. I don't really like plonk, but I was thirsty as hell. I could manage a cup of tea though.'

'Tea, right.' Plonk, she had called it! He turned and walked through to the kitchen, his mind half on the idea of tea, half on her story. In one of his sparsely populated cupboards he found an unopened box of teabags. There was no fresh milk in the flat, but an old tin yielded a spoonful or two of powdered substitute. Now, sugar. . . . Music came suddenly from the living room, a loud rendering of *The White Album*. God, he'd forgotten he still had that old tape. He opened the cutlery drawer, looking for nothing more than a teaspoon, and found several sachets of sugar, stolen from the canteen at some point in his past. Serendipity. The kettle was beginning to boil.

'This flat's huge!'

She startled him, he was so unused to other voices in this place. He turned and watched her lean against the door-jamb, her head angled sideways.

'Is it?' he said, rinsing a mug.

'Christ, yes. Look how high your ceilings are! I could just about touch the ceiling in Ronnie's squat.' She stood on tiptoe and stretched an arm upwards, waving her hand. Rebus feared that she had taken something, some pills or powders, while he'd been on the trail of the furtive teabag. She seemed to sense his thoughts, and smiled.

'I'm just relieved,' she said. 'I feel light-headed from the running. And from being scared, I suppose. But now I feel safe.'

'What did the men look like?'

'I don't know. I think they looked a bit like you.' She smiled again.

'One had a moustache. He was sort of fat, going thin on top, but not old. I can't remember the other one. He wasn't very memorable, I suppose.'

Rebus poured water into the mug and added the teabag. 'Milk?'

'No, just sugar if you've got it.'

He waved one of the sachets at her.

'Great.'

Back in the living room, he went to the stereo and turned it down.

'Sorry,' she said, back in the chair now, sipping tea, her legs tucked under her.

'I keep meaning to find out whether my neighbours can hear the stereo or not,' Rebus said, as if to excuse his action. 'The walls are pretty thick, but the ceiling isn't.'

She nodded, blew onto the surface of the drink, steam covering her face in a veil.

'So,' said Rebus, pulling his director's foldaway chair out from beneath a table and sitting down. 'What can we do about these men who've been following you?'

'I don't know. You're the policeman.'

'It all sounds like something out of a film to me. I mean, *why* should anyone want to follow you?'

'To scare me?' she offered.

'And why should they want to scare you?'

She thought about this, then shrugged her shoulders.

'By the way, I saw Charlie today,' he said.

'Oh?'

'Do you like him?'

'Charlie?' Her laughter was shrill. 'He's horrible. Always hanging around, even when it's obvious nobody wants him anywhere near. Everybody hates him.'

'Everybody?'

'Yes.'

'Did Ronnie hate him?'

She paused. 'No,' she said at last. 'But then Ronnie didn't have much sense that way.'

'What about this other friend of Ronnie's? Neil, or Neilly. What can you tell me about him?'

'Is that the guy who was there last night?'

'Yes.'

She shrugged her shoulders. 'I never saw him before.' She seemed interested in the book on the arm of the chair, picked it up and flipped its pages, pretending to read.

'And Ronnie never mentioned a Neil or a Neilly to you?'

'No.' She waved the book at Rebus. 'But he did talk about someone called Edward. Seemed angry with him about something. Used to shout the name out when he was alone in his room, after a fix.'

Rebus nodded slowly. 'Edward. His dealer maybe?'

'I don't know. Maybe. Ronnie got pretty crazy sometimes after he fixed. He was like a different person. But he was so sweet at times, so gentle....' Her voice died away, eyes glistening.

Rebus checked his watch. 'Okay, what about if I drive you back to the squat now? We can check that there's no one watching.'

'I don't know....' The fear had returned to her face, erasing years from her, turning her into a child again, afraid of shadows and ghosts.

'I'll be there,' Rebus added.

'Well.... Can I do something first?'

'What?'

She pulled at her damp clothes. 'Take a bath,' she said. Then she smiled. 'I know it's a bit brassnecked, but I really could use one, and there's no water at all in the squat.'

Rebus smiled too, nodding slowly. 'My bathtub is at your disposal,' he said.

While she was in the bath, he hung her clothes over the radiator in the hall. Turning the central heating on made a sauna of the flat, and Rebus struggled with the sash windows in the living room, trying without success to open them. He made more tea, in a pot this time, and had just carried it into the living room when he heard her call from the bathroom. When he came out into the hall, she had her head around the bathroom door, steam billowing out around her. Her hair, face and neck were gleaming.

'No towels,' she explained.

'Sorry,' said Rebus. He found some in the cupboard in his room, and brought them to her, pushing them through the gap in the door, feeling awkward despite himself.

'Thanks,' she called.

He had swopped *The White Album* for some jazz – barely audible – and was sitting with his tea when she came in. One large red towel was expertly tied around her body, another around her head. He had often wondered how women could be so good at wearing towels. . . . Her arms and legs were pale and thin, but there was no doubting that her shape was pleasing, and the glow from the bath gave her a kind of nimbus. He remembered the photographs of her in Ronnie's room. Then he recalled the missing camera.

'Was Ronnie still keen on photography? I mean, of late.' The choice of words was accidentally unsubtle, and he winced a little, but Tracy appeared not to notice.

'I suppose so. He was quite good, you know. He had a good eye. But he didn't get the breaks.'

'How hard did he try?'

'Bloody hard.' There was resentment in her voice. Perhaps Rebus had allowed too much professional scepticism to creep into his tone.

'Yes, I'm sure. Not an easy profession to get into, I'd imagine.'

'Too true. And there were some who knew how good Ronnie was. They didn't want the competition. Put obstacles in his way whenever and wherever they could.'

'You mean other photographers?'

'That's right. Well, when Ronnie was going through his really keen spell, before disillusionment set in, he didn't know quite how to get the breaks. So he went to a couple of studios, showed some of his work to the guys who worked there. He had some really inspired shots. You know, everyday things seen from weird angles. The Castle, Waverley Monument, Calton Hill.'

'Calton Hill?'

'Yes, the whatsit.'

'The folly?'

'That's it.' The towel was slipping a little from around her body, and as Tracy sat with her legs tucked beneath her, sipping tea, it also fell away to reveal more than enough thigh. Rebus tried to concentrate his eyes on her face. It wasn't easy. 'Well,' she was saying, 'a couple of his ideas got ripped off. He'd see a photo in one of the local rags, and it'd be exactly the angle he'd used, the same time of day, same filters. Those bastards had copied his ideas. He'd see their names beneath the pictures, the same guys he'd shown his portfolio to.'

'What were their names?'

'I don't remember now.' She readjusted the towel. There seemed something defensive in the action. Was it so hard to remember a name? She giggled. 'He tried to get me to pose for him.'

'I saw the results.'

'No, not those ones. You know, nude shots. He said he could sell them for a fortune to some of the magazines. But I wasn't having it. I mean, the money would've been all well and good, but these mags get passed around, don't they? I mean, they never get thrown away. I'd always be wondering if anybody could recognise me on the street.' She waited for Rebus's reaction, and when it was one of thoughtful bemusement, laughed throatily. 'So, it's not true what they say. You *can* embarrass a copper.'

'Sometimes.' Rebus's cheeks were tingling. He put a hand self-consciously to one of them. He had to do something about this. 'So,' he said, 'was Ronnie's camera worth much then?'

She seemed nonplussed by this turn in the conversation, and pulled the towel even tighter around her. 'Depends. I mean, worth and value, they're not the same thing, are they?'

'Aren't they?'

'Well, he might have paid only a tenner for the camera, but that doesn't mean it was only *worth* a tenner to him. Do you see?'

'So he paid a tenner for the camera?'

'No, no, no.' She shook her head, dislodging the towel. 'I thought you had to be brainy to get in the CID? What I mean is . . .' She raised her eyes to the ceiling, and the towel slipped from her head, so that bedraggled rat's-tails of hair strung themselves out across her forehead. 'No, never mind. The camera cost about a hundred and fifty quid. Okay?'

'Fine.'

'Interested in photography are you?'

'Only since recently. More tea?'

He poured from the teapot, then added a sachet of sugar. She liked lots of sugar.

'Thanks,' she said, cradling the mug. 'Listen.' She was bathing her face in the steam from the surface of the tea. 'Can I ask you a favour?'

Here it comes, thought Rebus: money. He had already made a mental note to check whether anything in the flat was missing before letting her leave. 'What?'

Her eyes were on his now. 'Can I stay the night?' Her words came out in a torrent. 'I'll sleep on the couch, on the floor. I don't mind. I just don't want to go back to the squat, not tonight. It's been getting pretty crazy lately, and those men following me. . . .' She shivered, and Rebus had to admit that if this were all an act, she was a top-of-the-form drama student. He shrugged, was about to speak, but rose and went to the window instead, deferring a decision.

The orange street lamps were on, casting a Hollywood film-set glow over the pavement. There was a car outside, directly opposite the flat. Being two floors up, Rebus couldn't quite see into the car, but the driver's side window had been rolled down, and smoke oozed from it.

'Well?' the voice said behind him. It had lost all confidence now.

'What?' Rebus said distractedly.

'Can I?' He turned towards her. 'Can I stay?' she repeated.

'Sure,' Rebus said, making for the door. 'Stay as long as you like.'

He was halfway down the curving stairwell before he realised that he was not wearing any shoes. He paused, considering. No, to hell with it. His mother had always warned him about catching chilblains, and he never had. Now was as good a time as any to find out whether his medical luck was holding.

He was passing a door on the first floor when it rattled open and Mrs Cochrane thrust her whole frame out, blocking Rebus's path.

'Mrs Cochrane,' he said after the initial shock had passed.

'Here.' She shoved something towards him, and he could do nothing but take it from her. It was a piece of card, about ten inches by six. Rebus read it: IT IS YOUR TURN TO WASH THE STAIRS. By the time he looked up again, Mrs Cochrane's door was already closing. He could hear her carpet slippers shuffling back towards her TV and her cat. Smelly old thing.

Rebus carried the card downstairs with him, the cold steps penetrating his stockinged soles. The cat didn't smell too good either, he thought maliciously.

The front door was on the latch. He eased it open, trying to keep the aged mechanism as silent as possible. The car was still there. Directly opposite him as he stepped outside. But the driver had already seen him. The cigarette stub was flicked onto the road, and the engine started. Rebus moved forward on his toes. The car's headlamps came on suddenly, their beam as full as a Stalag searchlight. Rebus paused, screwing his eyes, and the car started forward, then swerved to the left, racing downhill to the end of the street. Rebus stared after it, trying to make out the number plate, but his eyes were full of white fuzziness. It had been a Ford Escort. Of that much he was sure.

Looking down the road, he realised that the car had stopped at the junction with the main road, waiting for a space in the traffic. It was less than a hundred yards away. Rebus made up his mind. He had been a handy sprinter in his youth, good enough for the school team when they had been a man short. He ran now with a kind of drunken euphoria, and remembered the wine he had opened. His stomach turned sour at the mere thought, and he slowed. Just then he slipped, skidding on something on the pavement, and, brought up short, he saw the car slip across the junction and roar away.

Never mind. That first glimpse as he'd opened the door had been enough. He'd seen the constabulary uniform. Not the driver's face, but the uniform for sure. A policeman, a constable, driving an Escort. Two young girls were approaching along the pavement. They giggled as they passed Rebus, and he realised that he was standing panting on the pavement, without any shoes but holding a sign telling him it was his turn to WASH THE STAIRS. When he looked down, he saw what it was he had skidded on.

Cursing silently, he removed his socks, tossed them into the gutter, and walked back on bare feet towards the flat.

Dectective Constable Brian Holmes was drinking tea. He had turned this into something of a ritual, holding the cup to his face and blowing on it, then sipping. Blowing then sipping. Swallowing. Then releasing a steamy breath of air. He was chilled tonight, as cold as any tramp on any park bench bed. He didn't even have a newspaper, and the tea tasted revolting. It had come out of one or other of the thermos flasks, piping hot and smelling of plastic. The milk wasn't of the freshest, but at least the brew was warming. Not warming enough to touch his toes, supposing he still had toes.

'Anything happening?' he hissed towards the SSPCA officer, who held binoculars to his eyes as though to hide his embarrassment.

'Nothing,' the officer whispered. It had been an anonymous tip-off. The third this month and, to be fair, the first non-starter. Dog fighting was back in vogue. Several 'arenas' had been found in the past three months, small dirt pits enclosed by lengths of sheet tin. Scrap yards seemed the main source of these arenas, which gave an added meaning to the term 'scrap yard'. But tonight they were watching a piece of waste ground. Goods trains clattered past nearby, heading towards the centre of the city, but apart from that and the low hum of distant traffic, the place was dead. Yes, there was a makeshift pit all right. They'd taken a look at it in daylight, pretending to walk their own alsatian dogs, which were in fact police dogs. Pit bull terriers: that was what they used in the arenas. Brian Holmes had seen a couple of ex-combatants, their eyes maddened with pain and fear. He hadn't stuck around for the vet with his lethal injection.

'Hold on.'

Two men were walking, hands in pockets, across the wilderness, picking their way carefully over the uneven surface, wary of sudden craters. They seemed to know where they were headed: straight towards the shallow pit. Once there, they took a final look around. Brian Holmes stared directly back at them, knowing he could not be seen. Like the SSPCA officer, he was crouching behind thick bracken, behind him one remaining wall of what had been a building of sorts. Though there was some light over towards the pit itself, there was precious little here, and so, as with a two-way mirror, he could see without being seen.

'Got you,' said the SSPCA man as the two men jumped down into the pit.

'Wait . . .' said Holmes, suddenly getting a funny feeling about all of this. The two men had begun to embrace, and their faces merged in a slow, lingering kiss as they sank down towards the ground.

'Christ!' exclaimed the SSPCA man.

Holmes sighed, staring down at the damp, rock-hard earth beneath his knees.

'I don't think pit bulls enter the equation,' he said. 'Or if they do, bestiality rather than brutality might be the charge.'

The SSPCA officer still held his binoculars to his eyes, horror-struck and riveted.

'You hear stories,' he said, 'but you never . . . well . . . you know.'

'Get to watch?' Holmes suggested, getting slowly, painfully to his feet.

He was talking with the night duty officer when the message came through. Inspector Rebus wanted a word.

'Rebus? What does he want?' Brian Holmes checked his watch. It was two fifteen a.m. Rebus was at home, and he had been told to phone him there. He used the duty officer's telephone.

'Hello?' He knew John Rebus of course, had worked with him on several cases. Still, middle-of-the-night calls were something else entirely.

'Is that you, Brian?'

'Yes, sir.'

'Have you a sheet of paper? Write this down.' Fumbling with pad and biro, Holmes thought he could hear music playing on the line. Something he recognised. The Beatles' *White Album*. 'Ready?'

'Yes, sir.'

'Right. There was a junkie found dead in Pilmuir yesterday, or a couple of days ago now, strictly speaking. Overdose. Find out who the constables who found him were. Get them to come into my office at ten o'clock. Got that?'

'Yes, sir.'

'Good. Now, when you've got the address where the body was found, I want you to pick up the keys from whoever's got them and go to the house. Upstairs in one of the bedrooms there's a wall covered in photographs. Some are of Edinburgh Castle. Take them with you and go to the local newspaper's office. They'll have files full of photographs. If you're lucky they might even have a little old man on duty with a memory like an elephant. I want you to look for any photographs that have been published in the newspaper recently and look to have been taken from the same angle as the ones on the bedroom wall. Got that?'

'Yes, sir,' said Holmes, scribbling furiously.

'Good. I want to know who took the newspaper photographs. There'll be a sticker or something on the back of each print giving a name and address.'

'Anything else, sir?' It came out as sarcasm, meant or not.

'Yes.' Rebus seemed to drop his voice a decibel. 'On the bedroom wall you'll also find some photos of a young lady. I'd like to know more about her. She says her middle name is Tracy. That's what she calls herself. Ask around, show the picture to anyone you think might have an inkling.'

'Right, sir. One question.'

'Go ahead.'

'Why me? Why now? What's all this in aid of?'

'That's three questions. I'll answer as many of them as I can when I see you tomorrow afternoon. Be in my office at three.'

And with that, the line went dead on Brian Holmes. He stared at the drunken rows of writing on his pad, his own shorthand of a week's worth of work, delivered to him in a matter of minutes. The duty officer was reading it over his shoulder.

'Rather you than me,' he said with sincerity.

John Rebus had chosen Holmes for a whole bundle of reasons, but mostly because Holmes didn't know much about him. He wanted someone who would work efficiently, methodically, without raising too much fuss. Someone who didn't know Rebus well enough to complain about being kept in the dark, about being used as a shunting engine. A message boy and a bloodhound and a dogsbody. Rebus knew that Holmes was gaining a reputation for efficiency and for not being a complaining sod. That was enough to be going on with.

He carried the telephone back from the hall into the living room, placed it on the bookshelves, and went across to the hi-fi, where he switched off the tape machine, then the amplifier. He went to the window and looked out on an empty street whose lamplight was the colour of Red Leicester cheese. The image reminded him of the midnight snack he had promised himself a couple of hours ago, and he decided to make himself something in the kitchen. Tracy wouldn't be wanting anything. He was sure of that. He stared at her as she lay along the settee, her head at an angle towards the floor, one hand across her stomach, the other hanging down to touch the wool carpet. Her eyes were unseeing slits, her mouth open in a pout, revealing a slight gap between her two front teeth. She had slept soundly as he had thrown a blanket over her, and was sleeping still, her breathing regular. Something niggled him, but he couldn't think what it was. Hunger perhaps. He hoped the freezer would yield a pleasant surprise. But first he went to the window and looked out again. The street was absolutely dead, which was just how Rebus himself was feeling: dead but active. He picked *Dr Jekyll and Mr Hyde* from the floor and carried it through to the kitchen.

Wednesday

The more it looks like Queer Street, the less I ask.

Police Constables Harry Todd and Francis O'Rourke were standing outside Rebus's office when he arrived next morning. They had been leaning against the wall, enjoying a lazy conversation, seemingly unconcerned that Rebus was twenty minutes late. He was damned if he was going to apologise. He noted with satisfaction that as he reached the top of the stairs they pulled themselves up straight and shut their mouths.

That was a good start.

He opened the door, walked into the room, and closed the door again. Let them stew for another minute. Now they'd have something really to talk about. He had checked with the desk sergeant, and Brian Holmes wasn't in the station. He took a slip of paper from his pocket and rang Holmes's house. The telephone rang and rang. Holmes must be out working.

The good run was continuing.

There was mail on his desk. He flipped through it, stopping only to extract a note from Superintendent Watson. It was an invitation to lunch. Today. At twelve thirty. Hell. He was meeting Holmes at three. The lunch was with some of the businessmen who were putting up the hard cash for the drugs campaign. Hell. And it was in The Eyrie, which meant wearing a tie and a clean shirt. Rebus looked down at his shirt. It would do. But the tie would not. Hell.

The smile left his soul.

It had been too good to last. Tracy had woken him with breakfast on a tray. Orange juice, toast and honey, strong coffee. She'd gone out early, she explained, taking with her a little money she found on the shelves in the living room. She hoped he didn't mind. She had found a corner shop open, made the purchases, come back to the flat, and made him breakfast.

'I'm surprised the smell of burning toast didn't wake you,' she had said.

'You're looking at the man who slept through *Towering Inferno*,' he had replied. And she had laughed, sitting on the bed taking dainty bites of toast with her exposed teeth, while Rebus chewed his slices slowly, thoughtfully. Luxuriously. How long had it been since he'd been brought breakfast in bed? It frightened him to think. . . .

'Come in!' he roared now, though no one had knocked.

Tracy had left without complaint, too. She felt all right, she said. She couldn't stay cooped up forever, could she? He had driven her back towards Pilmuir, then had done something stupid. Given her ten pounds. It wasn't just money, as he realised a second after handing it over. It was a bond between them, a bond he shouldn't be making. It lay there in her hand, and he felt the temptation to snatch it back. But then she was out of the car and walking away, her body fragile as bone china, her gait determined, full of strength. Sometimes she reminded him of his daughter Sammy, other times. . . .

Other times of Gill Templer, his ex-lover.

'Come in!' he roared again. This time the door opened an inch, then another ten or eleven. A head looked into the room.

'Nobody's been knocking, sir,' the head said nervously.

'Is that so?' said Rebus in his best stage voice. 'Well, in that case I'd better just speak to you two instead. So why don't you *come in*!'

A moment later, they shuffled through the doorway, a bit less cocky now. Rebus pointed to the two chairs on the other side of his desk. One of them sat immediately, the other stood to attention.

'I'd rather stand, sir,' he said. The other one looked suddenly fearful, terrified that he had broken some rule of protocol.

'This isn't the bloody army,' Rebus said to the standing one, just as the sitting one was rising. 'So sit down!'

They both sat. Rebus rubbed his forehead, pretending a headache. Truth be told, he had almost forgotten who these constables were and why they were here.

'Right,' he said. 'Why do you think I've called you here this morning?' Corny but effective.

'Is it to do with the witches, sir?'

'Witches?' Rebus looked at the constable who had said this, and remembered the keen young man who had shown him the original pentagram. 'That's right, witches. And overdoses.'

They blinked at him. He sought frantically for a route into the interrogation, if interrogation this was to be. He should have thought more about it before coming in.

He should have at least remembered that it had been arranged. He saw a ten-pound note, a smile, could smell burning toast. . . . He looked at the pentagram constable's tie.

'What's your name, son?'

'Todd, sir.'

'Todd? That's German for dead, did you know that, Todd?'

'Yes, sir. I did German at school up to Highers.'

Rebus nodded, pretending to be impressed. Damn, he *was* impressed. They all had Highers these days, it seemed, all these extraordinarily young-looking constables. Some had gone further: college, university. He had the feeling Holmes had been to university. He hoped he hadn't enlisted the aid of a smart arse. . . .

Rebus pointed to the tie.

'That looks a bit squint, Todd.'

Todd immediately looked down towards his tie, his head angled so sharply Rebus feared the neck would snap.

'Sir?'

'That tie. Is it your usual one?'

'Yes, sir.'

'So you haven't broken a tie recently?'

'Broken a tie, sir?'

'Broken the clip,' explained Rebus.

'No, sir.'

'And what's your name, son?' Rebus said quickly, turning to the other constable, who looked completely stunned by proceedings so far.

'O'Rourke, sir.'

'Irish name,' Rebus commented.

'Yes, sir.'

'What about your tie, O'Rourke? Is that a new tie?'

'Not really, sir. I mean, I've got about half a dozen of these things kicking around.'

Rebus nodded. He picked up a pencil, examined it, set it down again. He was wasting his time.

'I'd like to see the reports you made of finding the deceased.'

'Yes, sir,' they said.

'Nothing unusual in the house, was there? I mean, when you first arrived? Nothing out of the ordinary?'

'Only the dead man, sir,' said O'Rourke.

'And the painting on the wall,' said Todd.

'Did either of you bother to check upstairs?'

249

'No, sir.'

'The body was where, when you arrived?'

'In the downstairs room, sir.'

'And you didn't go upstairs?'

Todd looked towards O'Rourke. 'I think we shouted to see if anyone was up there. But no, we didn't go up.'

So how could the tie clip have got upstairs? Rebus exhaled, then cleared his throat. 'What kind of car do you drive, Todd?'

'Do you mean police car, sir?'

'No I bloody well don't!' Rebus slapped the pencil down against the desk. 'I mean for private use.'

Todd seemed more confused now than ever. 'A Metro, sir.'

'Colour?'

'White.'

Rebus turned his gaze to O'Rourke.

'I don't have a car,' O'Rourke admitted. 'I like motorbikes. Just now I've got a Honda seven-fifty.'

Rebus nodded. No Ford Escorts then. Nobody hurtling away from his road at midnight.

'Well, that's all right then, isn't it?' And with a smile he dismissed them, picked up the pencil again, examined its point, and very deliberately broke it against the edge of his desk.

Rebus was thinking of Charlie as he stopped his car in front of the tiny old-fashioned men's-wear shop off George Street. He was thinking of Charlie as he grabbed the tie and paid for it. Back in the car, he thought of Charlie as he knotted the tie, started the ignition, and drove off. Heading towards lunch with some of the wealthiest businessmen in the city, all he could think of was Charlie, and how Charlie could probably still choose to be like those businessmen one day. He'd leave university, use his family connections to land a good job, and progress smoothly through to upper management in the space of a year or two. He would forget all about his infatuation with decadence, and would become decadent himself, the way only the rich and successful ever can. . . . True decadence, not the second-hand stuff of witchcraft and demonism, drugs and violence. That bruising on Ronnie's body: could it really have been rough trade? A sadomasochistic game gone wrong? A game played, perhaps, with the mysterious Edward, whose name Ronnie had screamed?

Or a ritual carried too far?

Had he dismissed the Satanism angle too readily? Wasn't a policeman supposed to keep an open mind? Perhaps, but Satanism found him with his mind well and truly closed. He was a Christian, after all. He might not attend church often, detesting all the hymn-singing and the bald sermonising, but that didn't mean he didn't believe in that small, dark personal God of his. Everyone had a God tagging along with them. And the God of the Scots was as ominous as He came.

Midday Edinburgh seemed darker than ever, reflecting his mood perhaps. The Castle appeared to be casting a shadow across the expanse of the New Town, but that shadow did not, could not reach as high as The Eyrie. The Eyrie was the city's most expensive restaurant, and also the most exclusive. Rumour had it that lunchtime was solidly booked twelve months in advance, while dinner entailed the small wait of eight to ten weeks. The restaurant itself was situated on the entire top floor of a Georgian hotel in the heart of the New Town, away from the city centre's human bustle.

Not that the streets here were exactly quiet, a steady amount of through traffic pausing long enough to make parking a problem. But not to a detective. Rebus stopped his car on a double yellow line directly outside the hotel's main door, and, despite the doorman's warnings about wardens and fines, left it there and entered the hotel. He squeezed his stomach as the lift carried him four floors high, and was satisfied that he felt hungry. These businessmen might well bore the pants off him, and the thought of spending two hours with Farmer Watson was almost too much to bear, but he would eat well. Yes, he would eat exceedingly well.

And, given his way with the wine list, he'd bankrupt the buggers to boot.

Brian Holmes left the snack bar carrying a polystyrene cup of grey tea, and studied it, trying to remember when he had last had a cup of good tea, of real tea, of tea he had brewed himself. His life seemed to revolve around polystyrene cups and thermos flasks, unexciting sandwiches and chocolate biscuits. Blow, sip. Blow, sip. Swallow.

For this he had given up an academic career.

Which was to say that he had careered around academia for some eight months, studying History at the University of London. The first month he had spent in awe of the city itself, trying to come to terms with its size, the complexities of actually trying to live and travel and survive with dignity. The second and third months he had spent trying to come to terms with university life, with new friends, the persistent openings for discussion, argument, for inclusion in this or that group. He tested the water each time before joining in, all of them nervous as children learning to swim. By months four and five, he had become a Londoner, commuting to the University every day from his digs in Battersea. Suddenly his life had come to be ruled by numbers, by the times of trains and buses and tube connections, the times, too, of late buses and tubes which would whisk him away from coffee-bar politics towards his noisy single room again. Missing a train connection began to be agony, suffering the rush-hour tube, a season spent in hell. Months six and seven he spent isolated in Battersea, studying from his room, hardly attending lectures at all. And in month eight, May, with the sun warming his back, he left London and returned north, back to old friends and a sudden emptiness in his life that had to be filled by work.

But why in the name of God had he chosen the police?

He screwed up the now empty polystyrene cup and threw it towards a nearby bin. It missed. So what, he thought. Then caught himself, went to the cup, stooped, picked it up, and deposited it in the bin. You're not in London now, Brian, he told himself. An elderly woman smiled at him.

So shines a good deed in a naughty world.

A naughty world all right. Rebus had landed him in a soup of melted humanity. Pilmuir, Hiroshima of the soul; he couldn't escape quickly enough. Fear of radiation. He had a little list with him, copied down neatly from last night's scrawled telephone conversation, and he took this from his pocket now to examine it. The constables had been easy to locate. Rebus would have seen them by now. Then he had gone to the house in Pilmuir. In his inside pocket he had the photographs. Edinburgh Castle. Good shots, too. Unusual angles. And the girl. She looked quite pretty, he supposed. Hard to tell her age, and her face seemed tempered by hard living, but she was bonny enough in a rough and ready way. He had no idea how he would find out anything about her. All he had to go on was that name, Tracy. True, there were people he could ask. Edinburgh was his home turf, an enormous advantage in this particular line of work. He had contacts all right, old friends, friends of friends. He'd re-established contact after the London fiasco. They'd all told him not to go. They'd all been pleased to see him again so soon after their warnings, pleased because they could boast of their foresight. That had only been five years ago. . . . It seemed longer somehow.

Why had he joined the force? His first choice had been journalism. That went way back, back to his schooldays. Well, childhood dreams could come true, if only momentarily. His next stop would be the offices of the local daily. See if he could find some more unusual angles on the Castle. With any luck, he'd get a decent cup of tea, too.

He was about to walk on when he saw an estate agent's window across the street. He had always assumed that this particular agency would, because of its name, be expensive. But what the hell: he was a desperate man. He manoeuvred his way through the queue of unmoving traffic and stopped in front of the window of Bowyer Carew. After a minute, his shoulders slightly more hunched than before, he turned away again and stalked towards the Bridges.

'And this is James Carew, of Bowyer Carew.'

James Carew lifted his well-upholstered bottom a millimetre off his well-upholstered chair, shook Rebus's hand, then sat again. Throughout the introduction, his eyes had not left Rebus's tie.

'Finlay Andrews,' continued Superintendent Watson, and Rebus shook another firm masonic hand. He didn't need to know the secret pressure spots to be able to place a freemason. The grip itself told you everything, lasting as it did a little longer than normal, the extra time it took the shaker to work out whether you were of the brotherhood or not.

'You might know Mr Andrews. He has a gaming establishment in Duke Terrace. What's it called again?' Watson was trying too hard: too hard to be the host, too hard to get along with these men, too hard for everyone's comfort.

'It's just called Finlay's,' Finlay Andrews supplied, releasing his grip on Rebus.

'Tommy McCall,' said the final luncheon guest, making his own introduction, and giving Rebus's hand a quick, cool shake. Rebus smiled, and sat down, joining them at the table, thankful to be sitting down at last.

'Not Tony McCall's brother?' he asked conversationally.

'That's right.' McCall smiled. 'You know Tony then?'

'Pretty well,' said Rebus. Watson was looking bemused. 'Inspector McCall,' Rebus explained. Watson nodded vigorously.

'So,' said Carew, shifting in his seat, 'what will you have to drink, Inspector Rebus?'

'Not while on duty, sir,' said Rebus, unfolding his prettily arranged napkin. He saw the look on Carew's face and smiled. 'Just a joke. I'll have a gin and tonic, please.'

They all smiled. A policeman with a sense of humour: it usually surprised people. It would have surprised them even more had they known how seldom Rebus made jokes. But he felt the need to conform here, to 'mix', in that unhappy phrase.

There was a waiter at his shoulder.

'Another gin and tonic, Ronald,' Carew told the waiter, who bowed and moved off. Another waiter replaced him, and started handing out huge leather-bound menus. The thick cloth napkin was heavy on Rebus's lap.

'Where do you live, Inspector?' The question was Carew's. His smile seemed more than a smile, and Rebus was cautious.

'Marchmont,' he said.

'Oh,' Carew enthused, 'that's always been a very good area. Used to be a farming estate back in the old days, you know.'

'Really?'

'Mmm. Lovely neighbourhood.'

'What James means,' interrupted Tommy McCall, 'is that the houses are worth a few bob.'

'So they are,' Carew answered indignantly. 'Handy for the centre of town, close to The Meadows and the University. . . .'

'James,' Finlay Andrews warned, 'you're talking shop.'

'Am I?' Carew seemed genuinely surprised. He gave Rebus that smile again. 'Sorry.'

'I recommend the sirloin,' said Andrews. When the waiter returned to take their order, Rebus made a point of ordering sole.

He tried to be casual, not to stare at the other diners, not to examine the minutiae of the tablecloth, the implements unknown to him, the finger bowls, the hallmarked cutlery. But then this was one of those once-in-a-lifetime things, wasn't it? So why not stare? He did, and saw fifty or so well-fed, happy faces, mostly male, with the occasional decorative female for the sake of decency, of elegance. Prime fillet. That's what everyone else seemed to be having. And wine.

'Who wants to choose the wine?' said McCall, flourishing the list. Carew looked eager to snatch, and Rebus held back. It wouldn't do, would it? To grab the list, to say me, me, me. To look with hungry eyes at the prices, wishing. . . .

'If I may,' said Finlay Andrews, lifting the wine list from McCall's hand. Rebus studied the hallmark on his fork.

'So,' said McCall, looking at Rebus, 'Superintendent Watson has roped you in on our little mission, eh?'

'I don't know that any rope was needed,' said Rebus. 'I'm glad to help if I can.'

'I'm sure your experience will be invaluable,' Watson said to Rebus, beaming at him. Rebus stared back evenly, but said nothing.

As luck would have it, Andrews seemed to know a bit about wine himself, and ordered a decent '82 claret and a crisp Chablis. Rebus perked up a bit as Andrews did the ordering. What was the name of the gaming club again? Andrews? Finlay's? Yes, that was it. Finlay's. He'd heard of it, a small casino, quiet. There had never been any cause for Rebus to go there, either on business or for pleasure. What pleasure was there in losing money?

'Is your Chinaman still haunting the place, Finlay?' asked McCall now, while two waiters ladled a thin covering of soup into wide-circumferenced Victorian soup plates.

'He won't get in again. Management reserves the right to refuse entry, et cetera.'

McCall chuckled, turned to Rebus.

'Finlay had a bad run back there. The Chinese are terrible for gambling, you know. Well, this one Chinaman was taking Finlay for a ride.'

'I had an inexperienced croupier,' Andrews explained. 'The experienced eye, and I do mean *experienced*, could tell pretty much where the ball was going to land on the roulette wheel, just by watching carefully how this youngster was flicking the ball.'

'Remarkable,' said Watson, before blowing on a spoonful of soup.

'Not really,' said Andrews. 'I've seen it before. It's simply a matter of spotting the type before they manage to lay on a really heavy bet. But then, you have to take the rough with the smooth. This has been a good year so far, a lot of money moving north, finding there's not so much to do up here, so why not simply gamble it away?'

'Money moving north?' Rebus was interested.

'People, jobs. London executives with London salaries and London habits. Haven't you noticed?'

'I can't say I have,' Rebus confessed. 'Not around Pilmuir at any rate.'

There were smiles at this.

'My estate agency has certainly noticed it,' said Carew. 'Larger properties are in great demand. Corporate buyers in some cases. Businesses moving north, opening offices. They know a good thing

255

when they see it, and Edinburgh is a good thing. House prices have gone through the roof. I see no reason for them to stop.' He caught Rebus's eye. 'They're even building new homes in Pilmuir.'

'Finlay,' McCall interrupted, 'tell Inspector Rebus where the Chinese players keep their money.'

'Not while we're eating, please,' said Watson, and when McCall, chuckling to himself, looked down at his soup plate, Rebus saw Andrews flash the man a hateful look.

The wine had arrived, chilled and the colour of honey. Rebus sipped. Carew was asking Andrews about some planning permission to do with an extension to the casino.

'It seems to be all right.' Andrews tried not to sound smug. Tommy McCall laughed.

'I'll bet it does,' he said. 'Would your neighbours find the going as smooth if they tried to stick a big bloody extension on the back of *their* premises?'

Andrews gave a smile as cold as the Chablis. 'Each case is considered individually and scrupulously, Tommy, so far as I know. Maybe you know better?'

'No, no.' McCall had finished his first glass of wine, and was reaching for a second. 'I'm sure it's all totally above board, Finlay.' He looked conspiratorially at Rebus. 'I hope you're not going to tell tales, John.'

'No.' Rebus glanced towards Andrews, who was finishing his soup. 'Over lunch, my ears are closed.'

Watson nodded agreement.

'Hello there, Finlay.' A large man, heavily built but with the accent on muscularity, was standing by the table. He was wearing the most expensive-looking suit Rebus had ever seen. A silken sheen of blue with threads of silver running through it. The man's hair was silvered, too, though his face looked to be fortyish, no more. Beside him, leaning in towards him, stood a delicate Oriental woman, more girl than woman. She was exquisite, and everyone at the table rose in a kind of awe. The man waved an elegant hand, demanding they be seated. The woman hid her pleasure beneath her eyelashes.

'Hello, Malcolm.' Finlay Andrews gestured towards the man. 'This is Malcolm Lanyon, the advocate.' The last two words were unnecessary. Everyone knew Malcolm Lanyon, the gossip column's friend. His very public lifestyle provoked either hatred or envy. He was at the same time all that was most despised about the law profession, and a walking TV mini-series. If his lifestyle occasionally scandalised the prurient, it also satisfied a deep need in the readers of Sunday tabloids. He was also, to Rebus's sure knowledge, an extraordinarily good lawyer. He had to be, otherwise the rest of his image would have been wallpaper, nothing more. It wasn't wallpaper. It was bricks and mortar.

'These,' Andrews said, gesturing now to the occupants of the table, 'are the working members of that committee I was telling you about.'

'Ah.' Lanyon nodded. 'The campaign against drugs. An excellent idea, Superintendent.'

Watson almost blushed at the compliment: the compliment was that Lanyon knew who Watson was.

'Finlay,' Lanyon continued, 'you've not forgotten tomorrow night?'

'Firmly etched in my diary, Malcolm.'

'Excellent.' Lanyon glanced over the table. 'In fact, I'd like you all to come. Just a little gathering at my house. No real reason for it, I just felt like having a party. Eight o'clock. Very casual.' He was already moving off, an arm around the porcelain waist of his companion. Rebus caught his final words: his address. Heriot Row. One of the most exclusive streets in the New Town. This was a new world. Although he couldn't be sure that the invitation was serious, Rebus was tempted to take it up. Once in a lifetime, and all that.

A little later, conversation moved to the anti-drugs campaign itself and the waiter brought more bread.

'Bread,' the nervous young man said, carrying another bound file of newspapers over to the counter where Holmes stood. 'That's what worries me. Everybody's turning into a bread head. You know, nothing matters to them except getting more than anyone else. Guys I went to school with, knew by the age of fourteen that they wanted to be bankers or accountants or economists. Lives were over before they'd begun. These are May.'

'What?' Holmes was shifting his weight from one leg to another. Why couldn't they have chairs in this place? He had been here over an hour, his fingers blackened by old newsprint as he flicked through each day's editions, one daytime, one evening. Now and then, a headline or some football story he'd missed first time around would attract his attention. But soon enough he had tired, and now it was merely routine. What's more, his arms were aching from all that page turning.

'May,' the youth explained. 'These are the May editions.'

'Right, thanks.'

'Finished with June?'

'Yes, thanks.'

The youth nodded, buckled shut two leather straps on the open end of the bound file, and heaved the whole up into his arms, shuffling out of the room. Here we go again, thought Holmes, unbuckling this latest batch of old news and space fillers.

Rebus had been wrong. There had been no old retainer to act as a computer memory, and no computer either. So it was down to hard graft and page turning, looking for photographs of familiar places, made fresh through the use of odd camera angles. Why? He didn't know even that yet, and the thought frustrated him. He'd find out later this afternoon hopefully, when he met with Rebus. There was a shuffling sound again as the youth re-entered, arms dangling now, jaw hanging.

'So why didn't you do the same as your friends?' Holmes said conversationally.

'You mean go in for banking?' The youth wrinkled his nose. 'Wanted something different. I'm learning journalism. Got to start somewhere, haven't you?'

Indeed you have, thought Holmes, turning another page. Indeed you have.

'Well, it's a start,' said McCall, rising. They were crumpling their used napkins, tossing them onto the dishevelled tablecloth. What had once been pristine was now covered with breadcrumbs and splashes of wine, a dark patch of butter, a single dripped coffee stain. Rebus felt woozy as he pulled himself out of the chair. And full. His tongue was furred from too much wine and coffee, and that cognac – Christ! Now these men were about to go back to work, or so they claimed. Rebus, too. He had a meeting at three with Holmes, didn't he? But it was already gone three. Oh well, Holmes wouldn't complain. Couldn't complain, thought Rebus smugly.

'Not a bad spread that,' said Carew, patting his girth. Rebus couldn't be sure whether this, or the food itself, was the spread he meant.

'And we covered a lot of ground,' said Watson, 'let's not forget that.'

'Indeed not,' said McCall. 'A very useful meeting.'

Andrews had insisted on paying the bill. A good three figures' worth by Rebus's hasty calculation. Andrews was studying the bill now, lingering over each item as though checking it against his own mental price list. Not only a businessman, thought Rebus unkindly, but a bloody good Scot. Then Andrews called over the brisk maitre d' and told him quietly about one item for which they had been overcharged.

The maitre d' took Andrews' word for it, and altered the bill there and then with his own ballpoint pen, apologising unreservedly.

The restaurant was just beginning to empty. A nice lunch hour over for all the diners. Rebus felt sudden guilt overwhelm him. He had just eaten and drunk his share of about two hundred pounds. Forty quid's worth, in other words. Some had dined better, and were noisily, laughingly making their way out of the dining room. Old stories, cigars, red faces. McCall put an unwelcome arm around Rebus's back, nodding towards the leavetaking.

'If there were only fifty Tory voters left in Scotland, John, they'd all be in this room.'

'I believe it,' said Rebus.

Andrews, turning from the maitre d', had heard them. 'I thought there *were* only fifty Tories left up here,' he said.

There, Rebus noted, were those quiet, confident smiles again. I have eaten ashes for bread, he thought. Ashes for bread. Cigar ash burned red all around him, and for a moment he thought he might be sick. But then McCall stumbled, and Rebus had to hold him up until he found his balance.

'Bit too much to drink, Tommy?' said Carew.

'Just need a breath of air,' said McCall. 'John'll help me, won't you, John?'

'Of course,' said Rebus, glad of this excuse for the very thing he needed.

McCall turned back towards Carew. 'Got your new car with you?'

Carew shook his head. 'I left it in the garage.'

McCall, nodding, turned to Rebus. 'The flash bugger's just bought himself a V-Twelve Jag,' he explained. 'Nearly forty thousand, and I'm not talking about miles on the clock.'

One of the waiters was standing by the lift.

'Nice to have seen you gentlemen again,' he said, his voice as automatic as the lift doors which closed when Rebus and McCall stepped inside.

'I must have arrested him some time,' Rebus said, 'because I've never been here before, so he can't have seen me here before.'

'This place is nothing,' said McCall, screwing up his face. 'Nothing. You want some fun, you should come to the club one night. Just say you're a friend of Finlay's. That'll get you in. Great place it is.'

'I might do that,' said Rebus as the lift doors opened. 'Just as soon as my cummerbund comes back from the dry cleaners.'

McCall laughed all the way out of the building.

Holmes was stiff as he left the building by its staff entrance. The youth, having shown him through the maze of corridors, had already turned back inside, hands in pockets, whistling. Holmes wondered if he really would end up with a career in journalism. Stranger things had happened.

He had found the photographs he wanted, one in each of three consecutive Wednesday daytime's editions. From these, the photographic library had traced the originals, and on the backs of the originals was the same golden rectangular sticker, denoting that the photos were the property of Jimmy Hutton Photographic Studios. The stickers, bless them, even mentioned an address and phone number. So Holmes allowed himself the luxury of a stretch, cracking his spine back into some semblance of shape. He thought about treating himself to a pint, but after leaning over the study table for the best part of two hours the last thing he wanted to do was lean against a bar as he drank. Besides, it was three fifteen. He was already, thanks to a quick-witted but slow-moving photo library, late for his meeting – his *first* – with Inspector Rebus. He didn't know how Rebus stood on the issue of punctuality; he feared the stand would be hard. Well, if the day's work so far didn't cheer him up, he wasn't human.

But then that was the rumour anyway.

Not that Holmes believed rumours. Well, not always.

As it turned out, Rebus was the later of the two for the meeting, though he had phoned ahead to apologise, which was something. Holmes was seated in front of Rebus's desk when Rebus finally arrived, pulling off rather a gaudy tie and dumping it into a drawer. Only then did he turn to Holmes, stare at him, smile, and stretch out a hand, which Holmes accepted.

Well that's something, thought Rebus: he's not a mason either.

'Your first name is Brian, isn't it?' said Rebus sitting down.

'That's right, sir.'

'Good. I'll call you Brian, and you can keep on calling me sir. That seem fair enough?'

Holmes smiled. 'Very fair, sir.'

'Right, any progress?'

So Holmes started at the beginning. As he spoke, he noticed that Rebus, though trying his damnedest to be attentive, was drowsy. His breath across the table was strong-smelling. Whatever he'd had for lunch had agreed with him too well. Finishing his report, he waited for Rebus to speak.

Rebus merely nodded, and was silent for some time. Collecting his thoughts? Holmes felt the need to fill the vacuum.

'What's the problem, sir, if you don't mind my asking?'

'You've every right to ask,' said Rebus at last. But he stopped at that.

'Well, sir?'

'I'm not sure, Brian. That's the truth. Okay, here's what I know – and I stress *know*, because there's plenty I *think*, which isn't quite the same thing in this case.'

'There is a case then?'

'You tell me, as soon as you've listened.' And it was Rebus's turn to make his 'report' of sorts, fixing it again in his mind as he told the story. But it was too fragmented, too speculative. He could see Holmes struggling with the pieces, trying to see the whole picture. Was there a picture there to see?

'So you see,' Rebus ended, 'we've got a junkie full of poison, self-inflicted. Someone who supplied the poison. Bruising on the body, and the hint of a witchcraft connection. We've got a missing camera, a tie clip, some photographs, and a girlfriend being followed. You see my problem?'

'Too much to go on.'

'Exactly.'

'So what do we do now?'

That 'we' caught Rebus's attention. For the first time, he realised that he was no longer in this alone, whatever 'this' was. The thought cheered him a little, though the hangover was starting now, the sleepy slow thumping either side of his forehead.

'I'm going to see a man about a coven,' he said, sure now of the next steps. 'And you're going to visit Hutton's Photographic Studios.'

'That sounds reasonable,' said Holmes.

'So it bloody well should,' said Rebus. 'I'm the one with the brains, Brian. You're the one with the shoeleather. Call me later on to let me know how you get on. Meantime, bugger off.'

Rebus didn't mean to be unkind. But there had been something just too cosy and conspiratorial in the younger man's tone towards the end, and he'd felt the need to re-establish boundaries. His own mistake, he realised as the door closed behind Holmes. His own mistake, for coming on so chattily, for telling all, for confiding, and for using Holmes's first name. That bloody lunch had been to blame. Call me Finlay, call me James, call me Tommy. . . . Never mind, it would all work out. They had begun well, then less well. Things could only get worse, which was fine by Rebus. He enjoyed a measure of antagonism, of competition. They were distinct bonuses in this line of work.

So Rebus was a bastard after all.

Brian Holmes stalked out of the station with hands in pockets tightened to fists. Knuckles red. *You're the one with the shoeleather.* That had really brought him down with a thump, just when he'd thought they were getting on so well. Almost like human beings rather than coppers. Should've known better, Brian. And as for the reason behind all this work. . . . Well, it hardly bore thinking about. It was so flimsy, so personal to Rebus. It wasn't police work at all. It was an inspector with nothing to do for a while, trying to fill the time by playing at being Philip Marlowe. Jesus, they both had better things they could be doing. Well, Holmes did anyway. He wasn't about to head some cushy anti-drugs campaign. And what a choice Rebus was for that! Brother inside Peterhead, doing time for pushing. Biggest dealer in Fife, he'd been. That should have screwed up Rebus's career forever and anon, but instead they'd given him promotion. A naughty world, all right.

He had to visit a photographer. Maybe he could get some passport shots done at the same time. Pack his bags and fly off to Canada, Australia, the States. Sod his flat hunting. Sod the police force. And sod Detective Inspector John Rebus and his witch hunt.

There, it was done.

Rebus found some aspirin in one of his chaotic drawers, and crunched them to a bitter powder as he made his way downstairs. Bad mistake. They removed every fleck of saliva from his mouth, and he couldn't even swallow, couldn't speak. The desk sergeant was sipping a polystyrene beaker of tea. Rebus grabbed it from him and gulped at the tepid liquid. Then squirmed.

'How much sugar did you put in that, Jack?'

'If I'd known you were coming to tea, John, I'd have made it just the way you like it.'

The desk sergeant always had a smart answer, and Rebus could never think of a smarter rejoinder. He handed back the cup and walked away, feeling the sugar cloy inside him.

I'll never touch another drop, he was thinking as he started his car.

Honest to God, only the occasional glass of wine. Allow me that. But no more indulgence, and no more mixing wine and spirits. Okay? So give me a break, God, and lift this hangover. I only drank the one glass of cognac, maybe two glasses of claret, one of Chablis. One gin and tonic. It was hardly the stuff of legend, hardly a case for the detox ward.

The roads were quiet though, which was a break. Not enough of a break, but a break. So he made good time to Pilmuir, and then remembered that he didn't know where Charlie boy lived. Charlie, the person he needed to talk to if he was going to find an address for a coven. A white coven. He wanted to double-check the witchcraft story. He wanted to double-check Charlie, too, come to that. But he didn't want Charlie to know he was being checked.

The witchcraft thing niggled. Rebus believed in good and evil, and believed stupid people could be attracted towards the latter. He understood pagan religions well enough, had read about them in books too thick and intense for their own good. He didn't mind people worshipping the Earth, or whatever. It all came down to the same thing in the end. What he did mind was people worshipping Evil as a force, and as *more* than a force: as an entity. Especially, he disliked the idea of people doing it for 'kicks' without knowing or caring what it was they were involved in.

People like Charlie. He remembered that book of Giger prints again. Satan, poised at the centre of a pair of scales, flanked by a naked woman left and right. The women were being penetrated by huge drills. Satan was a goat's head in a mask. . . .

But where would Charlie be now? He'd find out. Stop and ask. Knock on doors. Hint at retribution should information be withheld. He'd act the big bad policeman if that was what it took.

He didn't need to do anything, as it happened. He just had to find the police constables who were loitering outside one of the boarded-up houses, not too far from where Ronnie had died. One of the constables held a radio to his mouth. The other was writing in a notebook. Rebus stopped his car, stepped out. Then remembered something, leaned back into the car and drew his keys from out of the ignition. You couldn't be too careful around here. A second later, he actually locked his driver's side door, too.

He knew one of the constables. It was Harry Todd, one of the men who had found Ronnie. Todd straightened when he saw Rebus, but Rebus waved this acknowledgment aside, so Todd continued with his radio conversation. Rebus concentrated on the other officer instead.

'What's the score here?' The constable turned from his writing to give Rebus that suspicious, near-hostile look almost unique to the constabulary. 'Inspector Rebus,' Rebus explained. He was wondering where Todd's Irish sidekick O'Rourke was.

'Oh,' said the constable. 'Well . . .' He started to put away his pen. 'We were called to a domestic, sir. In this house. A real screaming match. But by the time we got here, the man had fled. The woman is still inside. She's got herself a black eye, nothing more. Not really your territory, sir.'

'Is that right?' said Rebus. 'Well, thank you for telling me, sonny. It's nice to be told what is and isn't my "territory". Thank you so much. Now, may I have your permission to enter the premises?'

The constable was blushing furiously, his cheeks an almighty red against his bloodless face and neck. No: even his *neck* was blushing now. Rebus enjoyed that. He didn't even mind that behind the constable, but in full view of Rebus himself, Todd was smirking at this encounter.

'Well?' Rebus prompted.

'Sorry, sir,' said the constable.

'Right,' said Rebus, walking towards the door. But before he reached it, it was opened from the inside, and there stood Tracy, both eyes reddened from crying, one eye bruised a deep blue. She didn't seem surprised to see Rebus standing in front of her; she seemed relieved, and threw herself at him, hugging him, her head against his chest, the tears beginning all over again.

Rebus, startled and embarrassed, returned the embrace only lightly, with a patting of his hands on her back: a father's 'there, there' to a frightened child. He turned his head to look at the constables, who were pretending to have noticed nothing. Then a car drew up beside his own, and he saw Tony McCall put on his handbrake before pushing open the driver's door, stepping out and seeing Rebus there, and the girl.

Rebus laid his hands on Tracy's arms and pushed her away from him a little, but still retaining that contact between them. His hands, her arms. She looked at him, and began to fight against the tears. Finally, she pulled one arm away so that she could wipe her eyes. Then the other arm relaxed and Rebus's hand fell from it, the contact broken. For now.

'John?' It was McCall, close behind him.

'Yes, Tony?'

'Why is it my patch has suddenly become your patch?'

'Just passing,' said Rebus.

*

The interior of the house was surprisingly neat and tidy. There were numerous, if uncoordinated, sticks of furniture – two well-worn settees, a couple of dining chairs, trellis table, half a dozen pouffes, burst at the seams and oozing stuffing – and, most surprising of all, the electricity was connected.

'Wonder if the electric board know about that,' said McCall as Rebus switched on the downstairs lights.

For all its trappings, the place had an air of impermanence. There were sleeping bags laid out on the living-room floor, as though ready for any stray waifs and passers by. Tracy went to one of the settees and sat down, wrapping her hands around her knees.

'Is this your place, Tracy?' said Rebus, knowing the answer.

'No. It's Charlie's.'

'How long have you known?'

'I only found out today. He moves around all the time. It wasn't easy tracking him down.'

'It didn't take you long.' She shrugged her shoulders. 'What happened?'

'I just wanted to talk to him.'

'About Ronnie?' McCall watched Rebus as he said this. McCall was concentrating now, aware that Rebus was trying to fill him in on the situation while at the same time questioning Tracy. Tracy nodded.

'Stupid, maybe, but I needed to talk to someone.'

'And?'

'And we got into an argument. He started it. Told me I was the cause of Ronnie's death.' She looked up at them; not pleadingly, but just to show that she was sincere. 'It's not true. But Charlie said I should have looked after Ronnie, stopped him taking the stuff, got him away from Pilmuir. How could I have done that? He wouldn't have listened to me. I thought he knew what he was doing. Nobody could tell him otherwise.'

'Is that what you told Charlie?'

She smiled. 'No. I only thought of it just now. That's what always happens, isn't it? You only think of the clever comeback after the argument's finished.'

'I know what you mean, love,' said McCall.

'So you started a slanging match –'

'I never started the slanging match!' she roared at Rebus.

'Okay,' he said quietly, 'Charlie started shouting at you, and you shouted back, then he hit you. Yes?'

'Yes.' She seemed subdued.

'And maybe,' Rebus prompted, 'you hit him back?'

'I gave as good as I got.'

'That's my girl,' said McCall. He was touring the room, turning up cushions on the settees, opening old magazines, crouching to pat each sleeping bag.

'Don't patronise me, you bastard,' said Tracy.

McCall paused, looked up, surprised. Then smiled, and patted the next sleeping bag along. 'Ah-ha,' he said, lifting the sleeping bag and shaking it. A small polythene bag fell out onto the floor. He picked it up, satisfied. 'A little bit of blaw,' he said. 'Makes a house into a home, eh?'

'I don't know anything about that,' said Tracy, looking at the bag.

'We believe you,' said Rebus. 'Charlie did a runner then?'

'Yes. The neighbours must've phoned for the pigs . . . I mean, the police.' She averted her eyes from them.

'We've been called worse,' said McCall, 'haven't we, John?'

'That's for sure. So the constables arrived at one door, and Charlie left by another, right?'

'Out of the back door, yes.'

'Well,' said Rebus, 'while we're here we might as well have a look at his room, if such a thing exists.'

'Good idea,' said McCall, pocketing the polythene bag. 'There's no smoke without fire.'

Charlie had a room all right. It consisted of a single sleeping bag, a desk, anglepoise lamp, and more books than Rebus had ever seen in such an enclosed space. They were piled against the walls, reaching in precarious pillars from floor to ceiling. Many were library books, well overdue.

'Must owe the City Fathers a small fortune,' said McCall.

There were books on economics, politics and history, as well as learned and not so learned tomes on demonism, devil worship and witchcraft. There was little fiction, and most of the books had been read thoroughly, with much underlining and pencilled marginalia. On the desk sat a half-completed essay, part of Charlie's university course work no doubt. It seemed to be trying to link 'magick' to modern society, but was mostly, to Rebus's eye, rambling nonsense.

'Hello!'

This was shouted from downstairs, as the two constables started to climb the staircase.

'Hello yourselves,' McCall called back. Then he shook the contents of a large supermarket carrier bag onto the floor, so that pens, toy cars, cigarette papers, a wooden egg, a spool of cotton, a personal cassette player, a Swiss army knife, and a camera fell out. McCall stooped to pick up the camera between thumb and middle finger. Nice model, thirty-five-millimetre SLR. Good make. He gestured with it towards Rebus, who took it from him, having first produced a handkerchief from his pocket, with which he held it. Rebus turned towards Tracy who was standing against the door with her arms folded. She nodded back at him.

'Yes,' she said. 'That's Ronnie's camera.'

The constables were at the top of the stairs now. Rebus accepted McCall's offer of the supermarket carrier and dropped the camera into it, careful not to mess up any prints.

'Todd,' he said to the constable he knew, 'take this young lady down to Great London Road station.' Tracy's mouth opened. 'It's for your own protection,' Rebus said. 'Go on with them. I'll see you later, soon as I can.'

She still seemed ready to voice a complaint, but thought better of it, nodded and turned, leaving the room. Rebus listened as she went downstairs, accompanied by the officers. McCall was still searching, though without real concern. Two finds were quite enough to be going on with.

'No smoke without fire,' he said.

'I had lunch with Tommy today,' said Rebus.

'My brother Tommy?' McCall looked up. Rebus nodded. 'Then that's one up to you. He's never taken me to lunch these past fifteen years.'

'We were at The Eyrie.' Now McCall whistled. 'To do with Watson's anti-drugs campaign.'

'Yes, Tommy's shelling out for it, isn't he? Ach, I shouldn't be hard on him. He's done me a few favours in his time.'

'He had a few too many.'

McCall laughed gently. 'He hasn't changed then. Still, he can afford it. That transport company of his, it runs itself. He used to be there twenty-four hours a day, fifty-two weeks of the year. Nowadays, he can take off as long as he likes. His accountant once told him to take a *year* off. Can you imagine that? For tax purposes. If only we had those kinds of problem, eh, John?'

'You're right there, Tony.' Rebus was still holding the supermarket bag. McCall nodded towards it.

'Does this tie it up?'

'It makes things a bit clearer,' said Rebus. 'I might get it checked for prints.'

'I can tell you what you'll find,' said McCall. 'The deceased's and this guy Charlie's.'

'You're forgetting someone.'

'Who?'

'You, Tony. You picked the camera up with your fingers, remember?'

'Ah, sorry. I didn't think.'

'Never mind.'

'Anyway, it's something, isn't it? Something to celebrate, I mean. I don't know about you, but I'm starved.'

As they left the room, one pillar of books finally gave way, slewing down across the floor like dominoes waiting to be shuffled. Rebus opened the door again to look in.

'Ghosts,' said McCall. 'That's all. Just ghosts.'

It wasn't much to look at. Not what he'd been expecting. Okay, so there was a potted plant in one corner, and black roller blinds over the windows, and even a word processor gathering dust on a newish plastic desk. But it was still the second floor of a tenement, still designed as somebody's home and never meant to be used as office, studio, workplace. Holmes gave the room – the so-called 'front office' – a tour as the cute little school-leaver went off to fetch 'His Highness'. That was what she'd called him. If your staff didn't hold you in esteem, or at the very least in frightened awe, there was something wrong with you. Certainly, as the door opened and 'His Highness' walked in, it was evident to Holmes that there was something wrong with Jimmy Hutton.

For a start, he was the other side of fifty, yet what hair he still had was long, thin strands covering his forehead almost down to his eyes. He was also wearing denims: a mistake easily made by those aspiring to youth from the wrong side. And he was short. Five foot two or three. Now Holmes began to see the relevance of the secretary's pun. His highness, indeed.

He had a harassed look on his face, but had left the camera through in the back bedroom or box room or whichever room of the smallish flat served as his studio. He stuck out a hand, and Holmes shook it.

'Detective Constable Holmes,' he announced. Hutton nodded, took a cigarette from the packet on his secretary's desk and lit it. She frowned openly at this as she sat down again, smoothing her tight skirt beneath her. Hutton had not yet looked at Holmes. His eyes seemed to be mirroring some distraction in his mind. He went to the window, looked out, arched his neck to blow a plume of smoke towards the high, dark ceiling, then let his head go limp, leaning against the wall.

'Get me a coffee, Christine.' His eyes met Holmes's momentarily. 'Do you want one?' Holmes shook his head.

'Sure?' said Christine kindly, rising out of her seat again.

'Okay then. Thanks.'

With a smile she left the room, off to the kitchen or darkroom to fill a kettle.

'So,' said Hutton. 'What can I do for you?'

That was another thing about the man. His voice was high, not shrill or girlish, just high. And slightly rasping, as though he had damaged his vocal cords at some point in his youth and they had never recovered.

'Mr Hutton?' Holmes needed to be sure. Hutton nodded.

'Jimmy Hutton, professional photographer, at your service. You're getting married and you want me to do you a discount?'

'No, nothing like that.'

'A portrait then. Girlfriend perhaps? Mum and dad?'

'No, this is business, I'm afraid. *My* business, that is.'

'But no new business for me, right?' Hutton smiled, chanced another glance towards Holmes, drew on his cigarette again. 'I *could* do a portrait of you, you know. Nice strong chin, decent cheekbones. With the proper lighting. . . .'

'No, thanks. I hate having my picture taken.'

'I'm not talking about pictures.' Hutton was moving now, circling the desk. 'I'm talking about art.'

'That's why I came here actually.'

'What?'

'Art. I was impressed by some of your photos I saw in a newspaper. I was wondering whether you might be able to help me.'

'Oh?'

'It's a missing person.' Holmes was not a great liar. His ears tingled when he told a real whopper. Not a great liar, but a good one. 'A young man called Ronnie McGrath.'

'Name doesn't mean anything.'

'He wanted to be a photographer, that's why I was wondering.'

'Wondering what?'

'If he'd ever come to you. You know, asking advice, that sort of thing.

269

You're an established name, after all.' It was almost too blatant. Holmes could sense it: could sense Hutton just about realising what the game was. But vanity won in the end.

'Well,' the photographer said, leaning against the desk, folding his arms, crossing his legs, sure of himself. 'What did he look like, this Ronnie?'

'Tallish, short brown hair. Liked to do studies. You know the sort of thing, the Castle, Calton Hill. . . .'

'Are you a photographer yourself, Inspector?'

'I'm only a constable.' Holmes smiled, pleased by the error. Then caught himself: what if Hutton were trying to play the vanity game with *him*? 'And no, I've never really done much photography. Holiday snaps, that sort of thing.'

'Sugar?' Christine put her head around the door, smiling at Holmes again.

'No thanks,' he said. 'Just milk.'

'Put a drop of whisky in mine,' said Hutton. 'There's a love.' He winked towards the door as it closed again. 'Sounds familiar, I have to admit. Ronnie. . . . Studies of the Castle. Yes, yes. I *do* remember some young guy coming in, bloody pest he was. I was doing a portfolio, some long-term stuff. Mind had to be one hundred percent on the job. He was always coming round, asking to see me, wanting to show me his work.' Hutton raised his hands apologetically. 'I mean, we were all young once. I wish I could have helped him. But I didn't have the time, not right then.'

'You didn't look at his work?'

'No. No time, as I say. He stopped coming by after a few weeks.'

'How long ago was this?'

'Few months. Three or four.'

The secretary appeared with their coffees. Holmes could smell the whisky wafting out of Hutton's mug, and was jealous and repelled in equal measure. Still, the interview was going well enough. Time for a side road.

'Thanks, Christine,' he said, seeming to please her with the familiarity. She sat down, not drinking herself, and lit a cigarette. He thought for a moment of reaching out to light it for her, but held back.

'Look,' said Hutton. 'I'd like to be of assistance, but. . . .'

'You're a busy man.' Holmes nodded agreement. 'I really do appreciate your giving me any time at all. Anyway, that just about wraps it up.' He took a scalding mouthful of coffee, but dared not spit it back into the mug, so swallowed hard instead.

'Right,' said Hutton, rising from the edge of the desk.

'Oh,' said Holmes. 'Just one thing. Curiosity really, but is there any chance I could have a peek at your studio? I've never been in a proper studio before.'

Hutton looked at Christine, who muffled a smile behind her fingers as she pretended to puff on her cigarette.

'Sure,' he said, smiling himself. 'Why not? Come on.'

The room was large, but otherwise pretty much as Holmes had expected, excepting one significant detail. Half a dozen different types of camera stood on half a dozen tripods. There were photographs covering three of the walls, and against the fourth was a large white backcloth, looking suspiciously like a bedsheet. This was all obvious enough. However, in front of the backcloth had been arranged the set for Hutton's present 'portfolio': two large, freestanding sections, painted pink. And in front of these was a chair, against which, arms folded, stood a young, blonde and bored-looking man.

A man who was naked.

'Detective Holmes, this is Arnold,' said Hutton by way of introduction. 'Arnold is a male model. Nothing wrong, is there?'

Holmes, who had been staring, now tried not to. The blood was rising to his face. He turned to Hutton.

'No, no, nothing.'

Hutton went to one camera and bent down to squint through the viewfinder, aiming in Arnold's general direction. Not at head height.

'The male nude can be quite exquisite,' Hutton was saying. 'Nothing photographs quite as well as the human body.' He clicked the shutter, ran the film on, clicked again, then looked up at Holmes, smiling at the policeman's discomfort.

'What will you do with the . . .' Holmes searched for some decorous word. 'I mean, what are they for?'

'My portfolio, I told you. To show to possible future clients.'

'Right.' Holmes nodded, to show he understood.

'I am an artist, you see, as well as a portrait snapper.'

'Right,' Holmes said, nodding again.

'Not against the law, is it?'

'I don't think so.' He went to the heavily draped window and peeked out through a slight opening. 'Not unless it disturbs the neighbours.'

271

Hutton laughed. Even the sober face of the model opened in a momentary grin.

'They queue up,' said Hutton, coming to the window and peering out. 'That's why I had to put up the curtains. Dirty buggers that they were. Women *and* men, crammed into the width of a window.' He pointed to a top-storey window in the tenement across the way. 'There. I caught them one day, took a couple of quick shots of them with the motor-drive. They didn't like that.' He turned away from the window. Holmes was browsing along the walls, picking out this and that photograph and nodding praise towards Hutton, who lapped it up and began to walk with him, pointing out this or that angle or trick.

'That's good,' said Holmes, gesturing towards one shot of Edinburgh Castle bathed in mist. It was almost identical to the one he had seen in the newspaper, which made it a very near relative to the one in Ronnie's bedroom. Hutton shrugged.

'That's nothing,' he said, resting a hand on Holmes's shoulder. 'Here, have a look at some of my nude work.'

There was a cluster of a dozen black and white ten-by-eights, pinned to the wall in one corner of the room. Men and women, not all of them young or pretty. But well enough taken, artistic even, Holmes supposed.

'These are just the best,' said Hutton.

'The best, or the most tasteful?' Holmes tried not to make the remark sound judgmental, but even so Hutton's good humour vanished. He went to a large chest of drawers and pulled open the bottom one, scooping up an armful of photographs which he threw to the floor.

'Have a look,' he said. 'There's no porn. Nothing sleazy or disgusting or obscene. They're just bodies. Posed bodies.'

Holmes stood over the photographs, not seeming to pay them any attention.

'I'm sorry,' he said, 'if I seemed –'

'Forget it.' Hutton turned away, so that his face was towards the male model. He rubbed at his eyes, shoulders slumped. 'I'm just tired. I didn't mean to snap like that. Just tired.'

Holmes stared at Arnold over Hutton's shoulder, then, because there was no way it could be done stealthily, bent down, picked out a photograph from the selection on the floor, and, coming upright again, stuffed the photo into his jacket. Arnold saw, of course, and Holmes just had time to wink at him conspiratorially before Hutton turned back towards him.

'People imagine it's easy, just taking photos all day,' Hutton said. Holmes risked a look over the man's shoulder and saw Arnold wag an admonitory finger. But he was smiling archly. He wasn't about to tell. 'You're thinking all the time,' Hutton went on. 'Every waking minute of every day, every time you look at something, every time you use your eyes. Everything's material, you see.'

Holmes was at the door now, not about to linger.

'Yes, well, I'd better let you get on,' he said.

'Oh,' said Hutton, as though coming out of a dream. 'Right.'

'Thanks for all your help.'

'Not at all.'

'Bye, Arnold,' Holmes called, then pulled the door shut behind him and was gone.

'Back to work,' said Hutton. He stared at the photographs on the floor. 'Give me a hand with these, Arnold.'

'You're the boss.'

As they began to scoop the photos back into the drawer, Hutton commented, 'Nice enough bloke for a copper.'

'Yes,' said Arnold, standing naked with his hands full of paper. 'He didn't look like one of the dirty raincoat brigade, did he?'

And though Hutton asked him what he meant, Arnold just shrugged. It wasn't his business after all. It was a shame though, the policeman being interested in women. A waste of a good-looking man.

Holmes stood outside for a minute. For some reason, he was trembling, as though a small motor had stuck somewhere inside him. He touched a hand to his chest. Slight heart murmur, nothing more. Everybody got them, didn't they? He felt as though he had just committed some petty crime, which he supposed, really, he had. He had taken someone's property away without their knowledge or consent. Wasn't that theft? As a child, he had stolen from shops, always throwing away whatever he stole. Ach, all kids did it, didn't they? . . . Didn't they?

He brought from his pocket the gains from this latest pilfering. The photograph was curled now, but he straightened it between his hands. A woman, pushing a pram past him, glanced at the photograph then hurried on, throwing back a disgusted look towards him. It's all right, madam, I'm a police officer. He smiled at the thought, then studied the nude shot again. It was mildly salacious, nothing more. A young woman, stretched out on what appeared to be silk or satin. Photographed from above, as she lay spreadeagled on this sheet. Her mouth open in an amateur's pout, eyes narrowed to slits of fake ecstasy. All this was common enough. More interesting though was the model's identity.

For Holmes was sure it was the girl Tracy, the one whose photograph he already had from the squat. The one whose background he was trying to ascertain. The girlfriend of the deceased. Posed for the camera, uncovered, not at all shy, and enjoying herself.

What was it that kept bringing him back to this house? Rebus wasn't sure. He turned his torch onto Charlie's wall painting again, trying to make sense of the mind that had created it. But why did he want to try to understand a piece of jetsam like Charlie anyway? Perhaps because of the nagging feeling that he was absolutely integral to the case.

'What case?'

There, he had actually, finally said it aloud. What case? There was no 'case', not in the sense in which any criminal court would understand the term. There were personalities, misdeeds, questions without answers. Illegalities, even. But there was no case. That was the frustrating thing. If there were only a case, only something structured enough, tangible enough for him to hold on to, some casenotes which he could *physically* hold up and say, look, here it is. But there was nothing like that. It was all as insubstantial as candle wax. But candle wax left its mark, didn't it? And nothing ever vanished, not totally. Instead, things altered shape, substance, meaning. A five-pointed star within two concentric circles was nothing in itself. To Rebus it looked like nothing so much as a tin sheriff's badge he'd had as a boy. Lawman of the Texas tin badge state, cap-firing six-gun in his plastic holster.

To others it was evil itself.

He turned his back on it, remembering how proudly he had worn that badge, and went upstairs. Here was where the tie clip had lain. Past it, he entered Ronnie's bedroom and walked over to the window, peering out through a chink in the boards covering the glass. The car had drawn up now, not too far from his own. The car that had followed him from the station. The car he had recognised at once as the Ford Escort which had waited outside his flat, the one which had roared away. Now it was here, parked next to the burnt-out Cortina. It was here. Its driver was here. The car itself was empty.

He heard the floorboard creak just the once, and knew that the man was behind him.

'You must know this place pretty well,' he said. 'You managed to miss most of the noisy ones.'

He turned from the window and shone his torch onto the face of a young man with short dark hair. The man shielded his eyes from the beam, and Rebus angled the light down onto the man's body.

It was dressed in a police constable's uniform.

'You must be Neil,' said Rebus calmly. 'Or do you prefer Neilly?'

He levelled the torch at the floor. There was enough light for him to see and be seen by. The young man nodded.

'Neil's fine. Only my friends call me Neilly.'

'And I'm not your friend,' Rebus said, nodding acquiescence. 'Ronnie was though, wasn't he?'

'He was more than that, Inspector Rebus,' said the constable, moving into the room. 'He was my brother.'

There was nowhere in Ronnie's bedroom for them to sit, but that didn't matter, since neither could have sat still for more than a second or two anyway. They were filled with energy: Neil needing to tell his story, Rebus needing to be told. Rebus chose in front of the window as his territory, and paced backwards and forwards without seeming to, his head down, stopping from time to time to lend more concentration to Neil's words. Neil stayed by the door, swinging the handle to and fro, listening for that moment before the whole door creaked, and then pulling or pushing the door through that slow, rending sound. The torch served the scene well, casting unruly shadows over the walls, making silhouettes of each man's profile, the talker and the listener.

'Sure, I knew what he was up to,' Neil said. 'He may have been older than me, but I always knew him better than he knew me. I mean, I knew how his mind worked.'

'So you knew he was a junkie?'

'I knew he took drugs. He started when we were at school. He was caught once, almost expelled. They let him back in after three months, so he could do his exams. He passed the lot of them. That's more than I did.'

Yes, Rebus thought, admiration could make you turn a blind eye. . . .

'He ran away after the exams. We didn't hear anything from him for months. My mum and dad almost went crazy. Then they just shut him out completely, switched off. It was like he didn't exist. I wasn't supposed to mention him in the house.'

'But he got in touch with you?'

'Yes. Wrote a letter to me care of a pal of mine. Clever move that. So I got the letter without Mum and Dad knowing. He told me he had come to Edinburgh. That he liked it better than Stirling. That he had a job and a girlfriend. That was it, no address or phone number.'

'Did he write often?'

'Now and then. He lied a lot, made things seem better than they were. Said he couldn't come back to Stirling until he had a Porsche and a flat, so he could prove something to Mum and Dad. Then he stopped writing. I left school and joined the police.'

'And came to Edinburgh.'

'Not straight away, but yes, eventually.'

'Specifically to find him?'

Neil smiled.

'Not a bit of it. I was forgetting him, too. I had my own life to think about.'

'So what happened?'

'I caught him one night, out on my regular beat.'

'What beat is that exactly?'

'I'm based out at Musselburgh.'

'Musselburgh? Not exactly walking distance of here, is it? So what do you mean "caught him"?'

'Well, not caught, since he wasn't really doing anything. But he was high as a kite, and he'd been bashed up a bit.'

'Did he tell you what he'd been doing?'

'No. I could guess though.'

'What?'

'Acting as a punchbag for some of the rough traders around Calton Hill.'

'Funny, someone else mentioned that.'

'It happens. Quick money for people who don't give a shit.'

'And Ronnie didn't give a shit?'

'Sometimes he did. Other times. . . . I don't know, maybe I didn't know his mind as well as I thought.'

'So you started to visit him?'

'I had to help him home that first night. I came back the next day. He was surprised to see me, didn't even remember that I'd helped him home the previous night.'

'Did you try to get him off drugs?'

Neil was silent. The door creaked on its hinges.

'At the beginning I did,' he said at last. 'But he seemed to be in control. That sounds stupid, I know, after what I've said about finding him in such a state that first night, but it was *his* choice, after all, as he kept reminding me.'

'What did he think of having a brother in the force?'

'He thought it was funny. Mind you, I never came round here with my uniform on.'

'Not till tonight.'

'That's right. Anyway, yes, I visited a few times. We stayed up here mostly. He didn't want the others to see me. He was afraid they'd smell pork.'

It was Rebus's turn to smile. 'You didn't happen to follow Tracy, did you?'

'Who's Tracy?'

'Ronnie's girlfriend. She turned up at my flat last night. Some men had been following her.'

Neil shook his head. 'Wasn't me.'

'But you *were* at my flat last night?'

'Yes.'

'And you were here the night Ronnie died.' It was blunt, but necessarily so. Neil stopped playing with the door handle, was silent this time for twenty or thirty seconds, then took a deep breath.

'For a while I was, yes.'

'You left this behind.' Rebus held out the shiny clip, but Neil couldn't quite make it out in the torchlight. Not that he needed to see it to know what it was.

'My tie clip? I wondered about that. My tie had broken that day, it was in my pocket.'

Rebus made no attempt to hand over the clip. Instead, he put it back in his pocket. Neil just nodded, understanding.

'Why did you start following me?'

'I wanted to talk to you. I just couldn't pluck up the courage.'

'You didn't want news of Ronnie's death getting back to your parents?'

'Yes. I thought maybe you wouldn't be able to trace his identity, but you did. I don't know what it'll do to my mum and dad. I think at worst it'll make them happy, because they'll know they were right all along, right not to give him a second's thought.'

'And at best?'

'Best?' Neil stared through the gloom, searching out Rebus's eyes. 'There's no best.'

'I suppose not,' said Rebus. 'But they've still got to be told.'

'I know. I've always known.'

'Then why follow me?'

'Because now you're closer to Ronnie than I am. I don't know why you're so interested in him, but you are. And that interests me. I want you to find whoever sold him that poison.'

'I intend to, son, don't worry.'

'And I want to help.'

'That's the first stupid thing you've said, which isn't bad going for a PC. Truth is, Neil, you'd be the biggest bloody nuisance I could ask for. I've got all the help I need for now.'

'Too many cooks, eh?'

'Something like that.' Rebus decided that the confession was ending, that there was little left to be said. He came away from the window and walked to the door, stopping in front of Neil. 'You've already been a bigger nuisance than I needed. It's not pork I can smell off you, it's fish. Herrings, to be precise. And guess what colour they are.'

'What?'

'Red, son, red.'

There was a noise from downstairs, pressure on floorboards, better than an infra-red alarm anyday. Rebus turned off the torch.

'Stay here,' he whispered. Then he went to the top of the stairs. 'Who's there?' A shadow appeared below him. He switched on the torch, and shone it into Tony McCall's squinting face.

'Christ, Tony.' Rebus started downstairs. 'What a fright.'

'I knew I'd find you here,' said McCall. 'I just knew it.' His voice was nasal, and Rebus reckoned that since the time they'd parted some three hours before, McCall had kept on drinking. He stopped on the staircase, then turned and headed back up.

'Where are you going now?' called McCall.

'Just shutting the door,' said Rebus, closing the bedroom door, leaving Neil inside. 'Don't want the ghosts to catch cold, do we?'

McCall was chuckling as Rebus headed downstairs again.

'Thought we might have a wee snifter,' he said. 'And none of that bloody alcohol-free stuff you were quaffing before.'

'Fair enough,' said Rebus, expertly manoeuvring McCall out of the front door. 'Let's do that.' And he locked the door behind him, figuring that Ronnie's brother would know of the many easy ways in and out of the house. Everybody else seemed to know them, after all.

Everybody.

'Where'll it be?' said Rebus. 'I hope you didn't drive here, Tony.'

'Got a patrol car to drop me off.'

'Fine. We'll take my car then.'

'We could drive down to Leith.'

'No, I fancy something more central. There are a few good pubs in Regent Road.'

'By Calton Hill?' McCall was amazed. 'Christ, John, I can think of better places to go for a drink.'

'I can't,' said Rebus. 'Come on.'

Nell Stapleton was Holmes's girlfriend. Holmes had always preferred tall women, tracing the fixation back to his mother who had been five foot ten. Nell was nearly three quarters of an inch taller than Holmes's mother, but he still loved her.

Nell was more intelligent than Holmes. Or, as he liked to think, they were more intelligent than one another in different ways. Nell could crack the *Guardian* cryptic crossword in under quarter of an hour on a good day. But she had trouble with arithmetic and remembering names: both strengths possessed by Holmes. People said they looked good together in public, looked comfortable with one another, which was probably true. They felt good together, too, living as they did by several simple rules: no talk of marriage, no thoughts of children, no hinting at living together, and definitely no cheating.

Nell worked as a librarian at Edinburgh University, a vocation Holmes found handy. Today, for example, he had asked her to find him some books on the occult. She had done even better, locating a thesis or two which he could read on the premises if he wished. She also had a printed bibliography of relevant materials, which she handed to him in the pub when they met that evening.

The Bridge of Sighs was at a mid-week and mid-evening cusp, as were most of the city centre bars. The just-one-after-work brigade had slung their jackets over their arms and headed off, while the revitalised night-time crowd had yet to catch their buses from the housing estates into the middle of town. Nell and Holmes sat at a corner table, away from the video games, but a bit too close to one of the hi-fi system's loudspeakers. Holmes, at the bar to buy another half for himself, an orange juice and Perrier for Nell, asked if the volume could be turned down.

'Sorry, can't. The customers like it.'

'We *are* the customers,' Holmes persisted.

'You'll have to speak to the manager.'

'Fine.'

'He's not in yet.'

Holmes shot the young barmaid a filthy look before turning towards his table. What he saw made him pause. Nell had opened his briefcase and was examining the photograph of Tracy.

'Who is she?' Nell said, closing the case as he placed her drink on the table.

'Part of a case I'm working on,' he said frostily, sitting down. 'Who said you could open my briefcase?'

'Rule seven, Brian. No secrets.'

'All the same –'

'Pretty, isn't she?'

'What? I haven't really –'

'I've seen her around the university.'

He was interested now. 'You have?'

'Mmm. In the library cafeteria. I remember her because she always seemed a little bit older than the other students she was with.'

'She's a student then?'

'Not necessarily. Anybody can go into the cafe. It's students only in the library itself, but I can't recall having seen her there. Only in the cafe. So what's she done?'

'Nothing, so far as I know.'

'So why is there a nude photo of her in your briefcase?'

'It's part of this thing I'm doing for Inspector Rebus.'

'You're collecting dirty pictures for him.'

She was smiling now, and he smiled too. The smile vanished as Rebus and McCall walked into the pub, laughing at some shared joke as they made for the bar. Holmes didn't want Rebus and Nell to meet. He tried very hard to leave his police life behind him when he was spending the evening with her – favours such as the occult booklist notwithstanding. He was also planning to keep Nell very much up his sleeve, so that he could have a booklist ready to hand should Rebus ever need such a thing.

Now it looked as though Rebus was going to spoil everything. And there was something else, another reason he didn't want Rebus to come sauntering across to their table. He was afraid Rebus would call him 'Shoeleather'.

He kept his eyes to the table as Rebus took in the bar with a single sweep of his head, and was relieved when the two senior officers, drinks purchased, wandered off towards the distant pool table, where they started another argument about who shouldn't and should provide the two twenty-pence pieces for the game.

'What's wrong?'

Nell was staring at him. To do so, she had brought herself to his level, her head resting against the table.

'Nothing.' He turned towards her, offering the rest of the room a hard profile. 'Are you hungry?'

'I suppose so, yes.'

'Good, me too.'

'I thought you said you'd eaten.'

'Not enough. Come on, I'll treat you to an Indian.'

'Let me finish my drink first.' She did so in three swallows, and they left together, the door swinging shut silently behind them.

'Heads or tails?' Rebus asked McCall, flipping a coin.

'Tails.'

Rebus examined the coin. 'Tails it is. You break.'

As McCall angled his cue down onto the table, closing one eye as he concentrated on the distant triangle of balls, Rebus stared at the door of the bar. Fair enough, he supposed. Holmes was off duty, and had a girl with him, too. He supposed that gave him grounds for ignoring his senior officer. Perhaps there had been no progress, nothing to report. Fair enough again. But Rebus couldn't help thinking that the whole thing was meant to be taken as a snub. He had given Holmes a mouthful earlier on, and now Holmes was sulking.

'You to play, John,' said McCall, who had broken without potting.

'Right you are, Tony,' said Rebus, chalking the tip of his cue. 'Right you are.'

McCall came to Rebus's side as he was making ready to play.

'This must be just about the only straight pub in the whole street,' he said quietly.

'Do you know what homophobia means, Tony?'

'Don't get me wrong, John,' said McCall, straightening up and watching Rebus's chosen ball miss the pocket. 'I mean, each to his own and all that. But some of those pubs and clubs. . . .'

'You seem to know a lot.'

'No, not really. It's just what I hear.'

'Who from?'

McCall potted one striped ball, then another. 'Come on, John. You know Edinburgh as well as I do. Everybody knows the gay scene here.'

'Like you said, Tony, each to his own.' A voice suddenly sounded in Rebus's mind: *you're the brother I never had*. No, no, shut that out. He'd been there too often before. McCall missed on his next shot and Rebus approached the table.

'How come,' he said, completely miscuing, 'you can drink so much and play so well?'

McCall chuckled. 'Alcohol cures the shakes,' he said. 'So finish that pint and I'll buy you another. My treat.'

James Carew felt that he deserved his treat. He had sold a substantial property on the outskirts of Edinburgh to the financial director of a company new to Scotland, and a husband and wife architects' partnership – Scottish in origin, but now relocating from Sevenoaks in Kent – had just made a rather better offer than expected for an estate of seven acres in the Borders. A good day. By no means the best, but nevertheless worthy of celebration.

Carew himself owned a *pied à terre* in one of the loveliest of the New Town's Georgian streets, and a farmhouse with some acreage on the Isle of Skye. These were good days for him. London was shifting north, it seemed, the incomers brimming with cash from properties sold in the south-east, wanting bigger and better and prepared to pay.

He left his George Street offices at six thirty, and returned to his split-level flat. Flat? It seemed an insult to term it such: five bedrooms, living room, dining room, two bathrooms, adequate kitchen, walk-in cupboards the size of a decent Hammersmith bedsit. . . . Carew was in the right place, the only place, and the time was right, too. This was a year to be clutched, embraced, a year unlike any other. He removed his suit in the master bedroom, showered, and changed into something more casual, but without shrugging off the mark of wealth. Though he had walked home, he would need the car for tonight. It was garaged in a mews to the rear of his street. The keys were hanging on their appointed hook in the kitchen. Was the Jaguar an indulgence? He smiled, locking the flat as he left. Perhaps it was. But then his list of indulgences was long, and about to grow longer.

Rebus waited with McCall until the taxi arrived. He gave the driver McCall's address, and watched the cab pull away. Damn, he felt a little groggy himself. He went back into the pub and headed for the toilets. The bar was busier now, the jukebox louder. The bar staff had grown in strength from one to three, and they were working hard to cope. The toilets were a cool tiled haven, free from much of the bar's cigarette smoke. Pine disinfectant caught in Rebus's nostrils as he leaned over into one of the sinks. Two fingers sought out his tonsils, pausing there at the back of his throat until he retched, bringing up half a pint of beer, then another half. He breathed deeply, feeling a little better already, then washed his face thoroughly with cold water, drying himself off with a fistful of paper towels.

'You all right?' The voice lacked real sympathy. Its owner had just pushed open the door to the gents' and was already seeking the closest urinal.

'Never felt better,' said Rebus.

'That's good.'

Good? He didn't know about that, but at least his head was clearer, the world more in focus. He doubted if he'd fail a breathalyser, which was just as well, since his next port of call was his car, parked on a darkened side road. He was still wondering how Tony McCall, shaky on his pins after half a dozen pints, had managed to play pool with such a steady eye and steady hand. The man was miraculous. He'd beaten Rebus six straight games. And Rebus had been trying. By the end he'd *really* been trying. After all, it didn't look good when a man barely able to stand upright could pot ball after ball, cleaning up and roaring to yet another victory. It didn't look good. It hadn't felt good.

It was eleven o'clock, perhaps a little early yet. He allowed himself one cigarette in the stationary car, window open, picking up the sounds from the world around him. The honest sounds of the late evening: traffic, heightened voices, laughter, the clatter of shoes on cobblestones. One cigarette, that was all. Then he started the car, and slowly drove the half mile or so to his destination. There was still some light in the sky, typical of the Edinburgh summer. Further north he knew it never got truly dark at this time of year.

But the night could be dark in other ways.

He spotted the first one on the pavement outside the Scottish Assembly building. There was no reason for the teenager to be standing there. It was an unlikely time of night to have arranged to meet friends, and the nearest bus stop was a hundred yards further up Waterloo Place. The lad stood there, smoking, one foot up behind him resting against the stone wall. He watched Rebus as the car slowly went past, and even lowered his head forward a little so that he could peer in, as though inspecting the driver. Rebus thought there was a smile there, but couldn't be sure. Further along the road, he turned the car and came back. Another car had stopped beside the boy, and a conversation was taking place. Rebus kept driving. Two young men were talking together outside the Scottish Office building on this side of the road. A little way past them, a line of three cars stood outside Calton Cemetery. Rebus cruised one more circuit, then parked near these cars, and walked.

The night was fresh. No cloud cover. There was a slight breeze, nothing more. The lad outside the Assembly building had gone off in the car. No one stood there now. Rebus crossed the road, stopped by the wall, and waited, biding his time. He watched. One or two cars drove past him slowly, the drivers turning to stare at him. But nobody stopped. He tried memorising the number plates, unsure why.

'Got a light, mister?'

He was young, no more than eighteen or nineteen. Dressed in jeans, training shoes, a shapeless T-shirt and denim jacket. His hair had been razored short, face clean-shaven but scarred with acne. There were two gold studs in his left ear.

'Thanks,' he said as Rebus held out a box of matches. Then: 'What's happening then?', with an amused glance towards Rebus before lighting the cigarette.

'Not much,' Rebus said, taking back the matchbox. The young man blew smoke out through his nostrils. He didn't seem about to go. Rebus wondered if there were any codes he should be using. He felt clammy beneath his thin shirt, despite the gooseflesh.

'Nah, there's never much happens around here. Fancy a drink?'

'At this time? Whereabouts?'

The young man nodded a vague direction. 'Calton Cemetery. You can always get a drink there.'

'No, thanks anyway.' Rebus was appalled to find himself blushing. He hoped the street lighting would disguise it.

'Fair enough. See you around then.' The young man was moving off.

'Yes,' Rebus said, relieved. 'See you.'

'And thanks for the light.'

Rebus watched him go, walking slowly, purposefully, turning from time to time at the sign of an approaching car. A hundred yards or so on, he crossed the road and began walking back, paying Rebus no attention, his mind on other things. It struck Rebus that the boy was sad, lonely, certainly no hustler. But no victim either.

Rebus stared at the wall of Calton Cemetery, broken only by its metal gates. He'd taken his daughter in there once to show her the graves of the famous – David Hume, the publisher Constable, the painter David Allan – and the statue of Abraham Lincoln. She'd asked him about the men who walked briskly from the cemetery, their heads bowed down. One older man, two teenagers. Rebus had wondered about them, too. But not too much.

No, he couldn't do it. Couldn't go in there. It wasn't that he was afraid. Jesus, no, not that, not for one minute. He was just . . . he didn't know what. But he was feeling giddy again, unsteady on his pins. I'll go back to the car, he thought.

He went back to the car.

He had been sitting in the driver's seat, smoking another cigarette thoughtfully for about a minute before he caught sight of the figure out of the corner of his eye. He turned and looked towards where the boy was seated; no, not seated, crouching against a low wall. Rebus turned away and resumed smoking. Only then did the boy rise to his feet and walk towards the car. He tapped on the passenger side window. Rebus took a deep breath before unlocking the door. The boy got in without a word, closing the door solidly behind him. He sat there, staring out through the windscreen, silent. Rebus, unable to think of a single sensible thing to say, stayed silent, too. The boy cracked first.

'Hiya.'

It was a man's voice. Rebus turned to examine the boy. He was maybe sixteen. Dressed in leather jacket, open-necked shirt. Torn jeans.

'Hello,' he said in reply.

'Got a cigarette?'

Rebus handed over the packet. The boy took one and swopped the packet for a box of matches. He inhaled the cigarette smoke deeply, holding it for a long time, then exhaling almost nothing of it back into the atmosphere. Take without give, thought Rebus. The creed of the street.

'So what are you up to tonight then?' The question had been on Rebus's own lips, but the boy had given voice to it.

'Just killing time,' said Rebus. 'I couldn't sleep.'

The boy laughed harshly. 'Yeah, couldn't sleep, so you came for a drive. Got tired driving so you just happened to stop here. This particular street. This time of night. Then you went for a walk, a stretch of the legs, and came back to the car. Right?'

'You've been watching me,' Rebus admitted.

'I didn't *need* to watch you. I've seen it all before.'

'How often?'

'Often enough, James.'

The words were tough, the voice was tough. Rebus had no cause to doubt the teenager. Certainly he was as dissimilar to the first boy as chalk to cheese.

'The name's not James,' he said.

'Of course it is. Everybody's called James. Makes it easier to remember a name, even if you can't recall the face.'

'I see.'

The boy finished the cigarette in silence, then flicked it out of the window.

'So what's it to be?'

'I don't know,' said Rebus sincerely. 'A drive maybe?'

'Fuck that.' He paused, seeming to change his mind. 'Okay, let's drive to the top of Calton Hill. Take a look out over the water, eh?'

'Fine,' said Rebus, starting the car.

They drove up the steep and winding road to the top of the hill, where the observatory and the folly – a copy of one side of Greece's Parthenon – sat silhouetted against the sky. They were not alone at the top. Other darkened cars had parked, facing across the Firth of Forth towards the dimly lit coast of Fife. Rebus, trying not to look too closely at the other cars, decided to park at a discreet distance from them, but the boy had other ideas.

'Stop next to that Jag,' he ordered. 'What a great-looking car.'

Rebus felt his own car take the insult with as much pride as it could muster. The brakes squealed in protest as he pulled to a halt. He turned off the ignition.

'What now?' he asked.

'Whatever you want,' said the boy. 'Cash on delivery, of course.'

'Of course. What if we just talk?'

'Depends on the kind of talk you want. The dirtier it is, the more it'll cost.'

'I was just thinking about a guy I met here once. Not so long ago. Haven't seen him around. I was wondering what happened to him.'

The boy suddenly placed his hand on Rebus's crotch, rubbing hard and fast against the material. Rebus stared at the hand for a full second before calmly, but with a deliberate grip, removing it. The boy grinned, leaning back in his seat.

'What's his name, James?'

Rebus tried to stop himself trembling. His stomach was filling with bile. 'Ronnie,' he said at last, clearing his throat. 'Not too tall. Dark hair, quite short. Used to take a few pictures. You know, keen on photography.'

The boy's eyebrows rose. 'You're a photographer, are you? Like to take a few snaps? I see.' He nodded slowly. Rebus doubted that he did see, but wasn't about to say more than was necessary. And yes, that Jag was nice. New-looking. Paintwork brightly reflective. Someone with a bit of money. And dear God why did he have an erection?

'I think I know which Ronnie you mean now,' said the boy. 'I haven't seen him around much myself.'

'So what can you tell me about him?'

The boy was staring out of the windscreen again. 'Great view from here, isn't it?' he said. 'Even at night. *Especially* at night. Amazing. I hardly ever come here in the daytime. It all looks so ordinary. You're a copper, aren't you?'

Rebus looked towards him, but the boy was still staring out of the windscreen, smiling, unconcerned.

'Thought you were,' he went on. 'Right from the start.'

'So why did you get in the car?'

'Curious, I suppose. Besides,' and now he looked towards Rebus, 'some of my best customers are officers of the law.'

'Well, that's none of my concern.'

'No? It should be. I'm underage, you know.'

'I guessed.'

'Yeah, well. . . .' The boy slumped in his seat, putting his feet up on the dashboard. For a moment, Rebus thought he was about to do something, and jerked himself upright. But the boy just laughed.

'What did you think? Think I was going to *touch* you again? Eh? No such luck, James.'

'So what about Ronnie?' Rebus wasn't sure whether he wanted to punch this rather ugly little kid in the gut, or take him to a good and a caring home. But he knew, above all, that he wanted answers.

'Give me another ciggie.' Rebus obliged. 'Ta. Why are you so interested in him?'

'Because he's dead.'

'Happens all the time.'

'He overdosed.'

'Ditto.'

'The stuff was lethal.'

The boy was silent for a moment.

'Now that *is* bad news.'

'Has there been any poisoned stuff going around recently?'

'No.' He smiled again. 'Only good stuff. Got any on you?' Rebus shook his head, thinking: *I do want to punch him in the gut.* 'Pity,' said the boy.

'What's your name, by the way?'

'No names, James, and no pack drill.' He put out his hand, palm up. 'I need some money.'

'I need some answers first.'

'So give me the questions. But first, a little goodwill, eh?' The hand was still there, expectant as any father-to-be. Rebus found a crumpled tenner in his jacket and handed it over. The boy seemed satisfied. 'This gets you the answers to two questions.'

Rebus's anger ignited. 'It gets me as many answers as I want, or so help me –'

'Rough trade? That your game?' The boy seemed unconcerned. Maybe he'd heard it all before. Rebus wondered.

'Is there much rough stuff goes on?' he asked.

'Not much.' the boy paused. 'But still too much.'

'Ronnie was into it, wasn't he?'

'That's your second question,' stated the boy. 'And the answer is, I don't know.'

'Don't knows don't count,' said Rebus. 'And I've got plenty of questions left.'

'Okay, if that's the way –' The boy was reaching for the door handle, ready to walk away from it all. Rebus grabbed him by the neck and brought his head down against the dashboard, right between where both feet were still resting.

'Jesus Christ!' The boy checked for blood on his forehead. There was none. Rebus was pleased with himself: maximum shock, minimum visible damage. 'You can't –'

'I can do anything I like, son, and that includes tipping you over the edge of the highest point in the city. Now tell me about Ronnie.'

'I can't tell you about Ronnie.' There were tears in his eyes now. He rubbed at his forehead, trying to erase the hurt. 'I didn't know him well enough.'

'So tell me what you *do* know.'

'Okay, okay.' He sniffed, wiping his nose on the sleeve of his jacket. 'All I know is that a few friends of mine have gotten into a scene.'

'What scene?'

'I don't know. Something heavy. They don't talk about it, but the marks are there. Bruises, cuts. One of them ended up in the Infirmary for a week. Said he fell down the stairs. Christ, he looked like he fell down a whole high-rise.'

'But nobody's talking?'

'There must be good money in it somewhere.'

'Anything else?'

'It may not be important. . . .' The kid had broken. Rebus could hear it in his voice. He'd talk from now till judgment day. Good: Rebus didn't have too many ears in this part of the city. A fresh pair might make all the difference.

'What?' he barked, enjoying his role now.

'Photographs. Somebody's putting a whisper around that there's interest in photographs. Not faked ones, either. The real McCoy.'

'Porn shots?'

'I suppose so. The rumours have been a bit vague. Rumours get that way when they've gone past being second-hand.'

'Chinese whispers,' said Rebus. He was thinking: this whole thing is like a game of Chinese whispers, everything at second and third remove, nothing absolutely proof positive.

'What?'

'Never mind. Anything else?'

The boy shook his head. Rebus reached into his pocket and, to his own surprise, found yet another tenner. Then he remembered that he'd visited a cashpoint machine somewhere during the drinking session with McCall. He handed the money over.

'Here. And I'll give you my name and phone number. I'm always open to bits of information, no matter how small. Sorry about your head, by the way.'

The boy took the money. 'That's all right. I've seen worse pay.' Then he smiled.

'Can I give you a lift?'

'The Bridges maybe?'

'No problem. What's your name?'

'James.'

'Really?' Rebus was smiling.

'Yes, really.' The boy was smiling, too. 'Listen, there *is* one other thing.'

'Go ahead, James.'

'It's just a name I've been hearing. Maybe it doesn't mean anything.'

'Yes?'

'Hyde.'

Rebus frowned. 'Hide? Hide what?'

'No, *Hyde*. H-y-d-e.'

'What about Hyde?'

'I don't know. Like I said, it's just a name.'

Rebus gripped the steering wheel. Hyde? *Hyde?* Was that what Ronnie had been telling Tracy? Not just to hide, but to hide from some man called Hyde? Trying to think, he found himself staring at the Jag again. Or rather, staring at the profile of the man in the driver's seat. The man with his hand up around the neck of the much younger occupant of the passenger seat. Stroking, and all the time talking in a low voice. Stroking, talking. All very innocent.

A wonder then that James Carew of Bowyer Carew Estate Agents should look so startled when, being stared at, he returned the stare and found himself eye to eye with Dectective Inspector John Rebus.

Rebus was taking all this in as Carew fumbled with his ignition key, revved up the new V12 engine and reversed out of the car park as though Cutty Sark herself were after him.

'He's in a hurry,' said James.

'Have you seen him before?'

'Didn't really catch his face. Haven't seen the car before though.'

'No, well, it's a new car, isn't it?' said Rebus, lazily starting his own.

The flat was still redolent of Tracy. She lingered in the living room and the bathroom. He saw her with a towel falling down around her head, legs tucked beneath her. . . . Bringing him breakfast: the dirty dishes were still lying beside his unmade bed. She had laughed to find that he slept on a mattress on the floor. 'Just like in a squat,' she had said. The flat seemed emptier now, emptier than it had felt for a while. And Rebus could do with a bath. He returned to the bathroom and turned the hot tap on. He could still feel James's hand on his leg. . . . In the living room, he looked at a bottle of whisky for a full minute, but turned his back on it and fetched a low-alcohol lager from the fridge instead.

The bath was filling slowly. An Archimedean screw would have been more efficient. Still, it gave him time to make another telephone call to the station, to check on how they were treating Tracy. The news was not good. She was becoming irritable, refusing to eat, complaining of pains in her side. Appendicitis? More likely cold turkey. He felt a fair amount of guilt at not having gone to see her before now. Another layer of guilt wouldn't do any harm, so he decided to put off the visit until morning. Just for a few hours he wanted to be away from it all, all the sordid tinkering with other people's lives. His flat didn't feel so secure any more, didn't feel like the castle it had been only a day or two ago. And there was internal damage as well as the structural kind: he was feeling soiled in the pit of his gut, as though the city had scraped away a layer of its surface grime and force-fed him the lot.

To hell with it.

He was caught all right. He was living in the most beautiful, most civilised city in northern Europe, yet every day had to deal with its flipside, with the minor matter of its animus. *Animus?* Now there was a word he hadn't used in a while. He wasn't even sure now what it meant exactly; but it sounded right. He sucked from the beer bottle, holding the foam in his mouth like a child playing with toothpaste. This stuff was all foam. No substance.

All foam. Now there was another idea. He would put some foaming bath oil in the water. Bubblebath. Who the hell had given him this stuff? Oh. Yes. Gill Templer. He remembered now. Remembered the occasion, too. She had been gently chiding him about how he never cleaned the bath. Then had presented him with this bath oil.

'It cleans you *and* your bath,' she had said, reading from the bottle. 'And puts the fun back into bathtime.'

He had suggested that they test this claim together, and they had. . . . Jesus, John, you're getting morbid again. Just because she's gone off with some vacuum-headed disc jockey with the unlikely name of Calum McCallum. It wasn't the end of anybody's world. The bombs weren't falling. There were no sirens in the sky.

Nothing but . . . Ronnie, Tracy, Charlie, James and the rest. And now Hyde. Rebus was beginning to know now the meaning of the term 'dead beat'. He rested his naked limbs in the near-scalding water and closed his eyes.

Thursday

That house of voluntary bondage . . .
with its inscrutable recluse.

Dead beat: Holmes yawned again, dead on his feet. For once, he had actually beaten the alarm, so that he was returning to bed with instant coffee when the radio blared into action. What a way to wake up every day. When he had a spare half hour, he'd retune the bloody thing to Radio Three or something. Except he knew Radio Three would send him straight back to sleep, whereas the voice of Calum McCallum and the grating records he played in between hoots and jingles and enthusiastic bad jokes brought him awake with a jolt, ready, teeth gritted, to face another day.

This morning, he had beaten the smug little voice. He switched the radio off.

'Here,' he said. 'Coffee, and time to get up.'

Nell turned her head from the pillow, squinting up at him.

'Has it gone nine?'

'Not quite.'

She turned back into the pillow again, moaning softly.

'Good. Wake me up again when it does.'

'Drink your coffee,' he chided, touching her shoulder. Her shoulder was warm, tempting. He allowed himself a wistful smile, then turned and left the bedroom. He had gone ten paces before he paused, turned, and went back. Nell's arms were long, tanned, and open in welcome.

Despite the breakfast he had brought her in the cell, Tracy was furious with Rebus, and especially when he explained to her that she could leave whenever she wanted, that she wasn't under arrest.

'This is called *protection*,' he told her. 'Protection from the men who were chasing you. Protection from Charlie.'

'Charlie. . . .' She calmed a little at the sound of his name, and touched her bruised eye. 'But why didn't you come to see me sooner?' she complained. Rebus shrugged.

'Things to do,' he said.

*

He stared at her photograph now, while Brian Holmes sat on the other side of the desk, warily sipping coffee from a chipped mug. Rebus wasn't sure whether he hated Holmes or loved him for bringing this into the office, for laying it flat on the desktop in front of him. Not saying a word. No good morning, no hail fellow well met. Just this. This photograph, this nude shot. Of Tracy.

Rebus had stared at it while Holmes made his report. Holmes had worked hard yesterday, and had achieved a result. *So why had he snubbed Rebus in the bar?* If he'd seen this picture last night, it would not now be ruining his morning, not now be eroding the memory of a good night's sleep. Rebus cleared his throat.

'Did you find out anything about her?'

'No, sir,' said Holmes. 'All I got was that.' He nodded towards the photograph, his eyes unblinking: *I've given you that. What more do you want from me?*

'I see,' said Rebus, his voice level. He turned the photo over and read the small label on the back. Hutton Studios. A business telephone number. 'Right. Well, leave this with me, Brian. I'll have to give it some thought.'

'Okay,' said Holmes, thinking: *he called me Brian! He's not thinking straight this morning.*

Rebus sat back, sipping from his own mug. Coffee, milk no sugar. He had been disappointed when Holmes had asked for his coffee the same way. It gave them something in common. A taste in coffee.

'How's the househunting going?' he said conversationally.

'Grim. How did you . . .?' Holmes remembered the *Houses for Sale* list, folded in his jacket pocket like a tabloid newspaper. He touched it now. Rebus smiled, nodded.

'I remember buying my flat,' he said. 'I scoured those freesheets for weeks before I found a place I liked.'

'Liked?' Holmes snorted. 'That would be a bonus. The problem for me is just finding somewhere I can afford.'

'That bad, is it?'

'Haven't you noticed?' Holmes was slightly incredulous. So involved was he in the game, it was hard to believe that anyone wasn't. 'Prices are going through the roof. In fact, a roof's about all I can afford near the centre of the city.'

'Yes, I remember someone telling me about it.' Rebus was thoughtful. 'At lunch yesterday. You know I was with the people putting up the money for Farmer Watson's drugs campaign? One of them was James Carew.'

'He wouldn't be anything to do with Carew Bowyers?'

'The head honcho. Do you want me to have a word? See about a discount on your house?'

Holmes smiled. Some of the glacier between them had been chipped away. 'That would be great,' he said. 'Maybe he could arrange for a summertime sale, bargains in all departments.' Holmes started this sentence with a grin, but it trailed away with his words. Rebus wasn't listening, was lost somewhere in thought.

'Yes,' Rebus said quietly. 'I've got to have a word with Mr Carew anyway.'

'Oh?'

'To do with some soliciting.'

'Thinking of moving houses yourself?'

Rebus looked at Holmes, not comprehending. 'Anyway,' he said, 'I suppose we need a plan of attack for today.'

'Ah.' Holmes looked uncomfortable. 'I wanted to ask you about that, sir. I had a phone call this morning. I've been working for some months on a dog-fighting ring, and they're about to arrest the gang.'

'Dog fighting?'

'Yes, you know. Put two dogs in a ring. Let them tear each other to shreds. Place bets on the result.'

'I thought that died with the depression.'

'There's been a revival of late. Vicious it is, too. I could show you some photos –'

'Why the revival?'

'Who knows? People looking for kicks, something less tame than a bet at the bookie's.'

Rebus was nodding now, almost lost to his own thoughts again.

'Would you say it was a yuppie pursuit, Holmes?'

Holmes shrugged: *he's getting better. Stopped calling me by my first name.* 'Well, never mind. So you want to be in on the arrest?'

Holmes nodded. 'If possible, sir.'

'Entirely possible,' said Rebus. 'So where's it all happening?'

'I still have to check that out. Somewhere in Fife though.'

'Fife? Home territory for me.'

'Is it? I didn't know. What's that saying again . . .?'

' "Ye need a lang spoon tae sup wi' a Fifer." '

Holmes smiled. 'Yes, that's it. There's a similar saying about the devil, isn't there?'

'All it means is that we're close, Holmes, tightly knit. We don't suffer fools and strangers gladly. Now off you go to Fife and see what I'm on about.'

'Yes, sir. What about you? I mean, what will you do about . . .?' His eyes were on the photograph again. Rebus picked it up and placed it carefully in the inside pocket of his jacket.

'Don't worry about me, son. I've plenty to keep me busy. Just keeping out of range of Farmer Watson is work enough for a day. Maybe I'll take the car out. Nice day for a drive.'

'Nice day for a drive.'

Tracy was doing her best to ignore him. She stared from her passenger side window, seemingly interested in the passing parade of shops and shoppers, tourists, kids with nothing to do now the schools had broken up for summer.

She'd been keen enough to get out of the station though. He'd held the car door open for her, dissuading her from just walking away. And she'd complied, but silently, sullenly. Okay, she was in the huff with him. He'd get over it. So would she.

'Point taken,' he said. 'You're pissed off. But how many times do I have to tell you? It was for your own safety, while I was doing some checking up.'

'Where are we going?'

'Do you know this part of town?'

She was silent. There was to be no conversation. Only questions and answers: *her* questions.

'We're just driving,' he said. 'You must know this side of town. A lot of dealing used to go on around here.'

'I'm not into that!'

It was Rebus's turn to be silent. He wasn't too old to play a game or two himself. He took a left, then another, then a right.

'We've been here already,' she commented. She'd noticed then, clever girl. Still, that didn't matter. All that mattered was that slowly, by degrees, by left and right then left and right again, he was guiding them towards the destination.

He pulled into the kerb abruptly and yanked on the handbrake.

'Right,' he said. 'We're here.'

'Here?' She looked out of the side window, up at the tenement building. The red stone had been cleaned in the past year, giving it the look of a child's plasticine, pinky ochre and malleable. 'Here?' she repeated, the word choking off as she recognised the exact address, and then tried not to let that recognition show.

The photograph was on her lap when she turned from the window. She flicked it from her with a squeal, as though it were an insect. Rebus plucked the photo from the floor of the car and held it out to her.

'Yours, I believe.'

'Where the hell did you get that?'

'Do you want to tell me about it?'

Her face was as red as the stonework now, her eyes flitting in panic like a bird's. She fumbled with the seatbelt, desperate to be out of the car, but Rebus's hand on the catch was rock hard.

'Let me go!' she yelled, thumping down on his fist. Then she pushed open the door, but the camber of the road pulled it shut again. There was not enough give in the seatbelt anyway. She was securely bound.

'I thought we'd pay Mr Hutton a call,' Rebus was saying, his voice like a blade. 'Ask him about this photo. About how he paid you a few quid to model for him. About how you brought him Ronnie's pictures. Looking for a few bob more maybe, or just to spite Ronnie. Is that how it was, Tracy? I'll bet Ronnie was pissed off when he saw Hutton had stolen his ideas. Couldn't prove it though, could he? And how was he to know how the hell Hutton got them in the first place? I suppose you put the blame on Charlie, and that's why the two of you aren't exactly on speaking terms. Some friend to Ronnie you were, sweetheart. Some friend.'

She broke down at that, and gave up trying to free herself from the seatbelt. Her head angled forward into her hands, and she wept, loudly and at length. While Rebus caught his breath. He wasn't proud of himself, but it had needed saying. She had to stop hiding from the truth. It was all conjecture, of course, but Rebus was sure Hutton could confirm the details if pressed. She had modelled for money, maybe happened to mention that her boyfriend was a photographer. Had taken the photos to Hutton, giving away Ronnie's glimmer of a chance, his creativity, for a few more pound notes. If you couldn't trust your friends, who could you trust?

He had left her overnight in the cells to see if she would crack. She hadn't, so he supposed she must be clean. But that didn't mean she didn't have some kind of habit. If not needles, then something else.

Everybody needed a little something, didn't they? And the money was needed, too. So she had ripped off her boyfriend. . . .

'Did you plant that camera in Charlie's squat?'

'No!' It was as though, after all that had gone before, the accusation still hurt. Rebus nodded. So Charlie had taken the camera, or someone else had planted it there. For him to find. No . . . not quite, because *he* hadn't found it: McCall had. And very easily at that, the way he had blithely found the dope in the sleeping bag. A true copper's nose? Or something else? A little information perhaps, *inside* information? If you can't trust your friends. . . .

'Did you see the camera the night Ronnie died?'

'It was in his room, I'm sure it was.' She blinked back the tears and wiped her nose on the handkerchief Rebus gave her. Her voice was cracked still, her throat a little clogged, but she was recovering from the shock of the photo, and the greater shock that Rebus knew now of her betrayal.

'That guy who came to see Ronnie, he was in Ronnie's room after me.'

'You mean Neil?'

'I think that was his name, yes.'

Too many cooks, Rebus was thinking. He was going to have to revise his definition of 'circumstantial'. He had very little so far that *wasn't* circumstantial. It felt like the spiral was widening, taking him further and further away from the central, crucial point, the point where Ronnie lay dead on a damp, bare floor, flanked by candles and dubious friends.

'Neil was Ronnie's brother.'

'Really?' Her voice was disinterested. The safety curtain between her and the world was coming down again. The matinee was over.

'Yes, really.' Rebus felt a sudden chill. If nobody, *nobody* cares what happened to Ronnie except Neil and me, why am I bothering?

'Charlie always thought they had some kind of gay thing going. I never asked Ronnie. I don't suppose he would have told me.' She rested her head against the back of the seat, seeming to relax again. 'Oh God.' She released a whistle of breath from her lungs. 'Do we have to stick around here?'

Her hands were rising slowly, ready to clasp her head, and Rebus was beginning to answer in the negative, when he saw those same hands come swiftly down, curling into tiny fists. There was no room to escape them, and so they hit him full in the groin. A flashgun exploded somewhere behind his eyes, the world turning into nothing but sound and blinding pain. He was roaring, doubled up in agony, head coming to rest on the steering wheel, which was also the car's horn. It was blaring lazily as Tracy undid her seatbelt, opened the door, and swivelled out of the car. She left the door wide open as she ran. Rebus watched through eyes brimming with tears, as if he were in a swimming pool, watching her running along the edge of the pool away from him, chlorine stinging his pupils.

'Jesus Almighty Christ,' he gasped, still hunched over the wheel, and not about to move for some considerable time.

Think like Tarzan, his father had told him once: one of the old man's few pieces of advice. He was talking about fights. About one-to-one scrapes with the lads at school. Four o'clock behind the bike shed, and all that. *Think like Tarzan. You're strong, king of the jungle, and above all else you're going to protect your nuts.* And the old boy had raised a bent knee towards young John's crotch. . . .

'Thanks, Dad,' Rebus hissed now. 'Thanks for reminding me.' Then the reaction hit his stomach.

By lunchtime he could just about walk, so long as he kept his feet close to the ground, moving as though he had wet himself. People stared, of course, and he tried to improvise a limp specially for them. Ever the crowd pleaser.

The thought of the stairs to his office was too much, and driving the car had been excruciating, the foot pedals impossible to operate. So he had taken a taxi to the Sutherland Bar. Three quarter-gill measures of whisky later, he felt the pain replaced by a drowsy numbness.

'"As though of hemlock . . .",' he muttered to himself.

He wasn't worried about Tracy. Anyone with a punch like that could look after herself. There were probably kids on the street harder than half the bloody police force. Not that Tracy was a kid. He still hadn't found out anything about her. That was supposed to be Holmes's department, but Holmes was off on a wild dog chase in Fife. No, Tracy would be all right. Probably there had been no men chasing her. But then why come to him that night? There could be a hundred reasons. After all, she'd conned a bed, the best part of a bottle of wine, a hot bath and breakfast out of him. Not bad going that, and him supposed to be a hardened old copper. Too old maybe. Too much the 'copper', not enough the police officer. Maybe.

Where to next? He already had the answer to that, legs permitting and pray God he could drive.

He parked at a distance from the house, not wanting to scare off anyone who might be there. Then he simply walked up to the door and knocked. Standing there, awaiting a response, he remembered Tracy opening that door and running into his arms, her face bruised, her eyes welling with tears. He didn't think Charlie would be here. He didn't think Tracy would be here. He didn't *want* Tracy to be here.

The door opened. A bleary teenage boy squinted up at Rebus. His hair was lank, lifeless, falling into his eyes.

'What is it?'

'Is Charlie in? I've got a bit of business with him.'

'Naw. Havenae seen him the day.'

'All right if I wait a while?'

'Aye.' The boy was already closing the door on Rebus's face. Rebus stuck a hand up against the door and peered round it.

'I meant, wait indoors.'

The boy shrugged, and slouched back inside, leaving the door ajar. He slipped back into his sleeping bag and pulled it over his head. Just passing through, and catching up on lost sleep. Rebus supposed the boy had nothing to lose by letting a stranger into this way station. He left him to his sleep, and, after a cursory check that there was no one else in the downstairs rooms, climbed the steep staircase.

The books were still slewed like so many felled dominoes, the contents of the bag McCall had emptied still lying in a clutter on the floor. Rebus ignored these and went to the desk, where he sat, studying the pieces of paper in front of him. He had flicked on the light switch beside the door of Charlie's room, and now switched on the desk lamp, too. The walls were miraculously free from posters, postcards and the like. It wasn't like a student's room. Its identity had been left suspended, which was probably exactly the way Charlie wanted it. He didn't want to look like a student to his drop-out friends; he didn't want to look like a drop-out to his student friends. He wanted to be all things to all people. Chameleon, then, as well as tourist.

The essay on Magick was Rebus's main interest, but he gave the rest of the desk a good examination while he was here. Nothing out of the ordinary. Nothing to suggest that Charlie was pushing bad drugs around the city streets. So Rebus picked up the essay, opened it, and began to read.

*

302

Nell liked the library when it was quiet like this. During term time, a lot of the students used it as a meeting place, a sort of glorified youth club. Then, the first-floor reading room was filled with noise. Books tended to be left lying everywhere, or to go missing, to be shifted out of their proper sections. All very frustrating. But during the summer months, only the most determined of the students came in: the ones with a thesis to write, or work to catch up on, or those precious few who were passionate about their chosen fields, and who were giving up sunshine and freedom to be here, indoors, in studied silence.

She got to know their faces, and then their names. Conversations could be struck up in the deserted coffee shop, authors' names swopped. And at lunchtime, one could sit in the gardens, or walk behind the library building onto The Meadows, where more books were being read, more faces rapt in thought.

Of course, summer was also the time for the library's most tedious jobs. The check on stock, the rebinding of misused volumes. Reclassification, computer updating, and so on. The atmosphere more than made up for all this. All traces of hurry and haste were gone. No more complaints about there being too few copies of this or that title, desperately needed by a class of two hundred for some overdue essay. But after the summer there would be a new intake, and with every year's fresh intake, she felt that whole year older, and more distanced from the students. They already seemed hopelessly young to her, a glow surrounding them, reminding her of something she could never have.

She was sorting through request forms when the commotion began. The guard on the library entrance had stopped someone who was trying to get in without any identification. Normally, Nell knew, the guard wouldn't have worried, but the girl was so obviously distraught, so obviously not a reader, not even a student. She was loudly argumentative, where a real student would have quietly explained that they had forgotten to bring their matriculation card with them. There was something else, too ... Nell frowned, trying to place the girl. Catching her profile, she remembered the photograph in Brian's briefcase. Yes, it was the same girl. No girl, really, but a fully grown, if youthful, woman. The lines around the eyes were the giveaway, no matter how slender the body, how fashionably young the clothes. But why was she making this fuss? She'd always gone to the coffee shop, had never, to Nell's knowledge, tried to get into the library proper before now. Nell's curiosity was aroused.

The guard was holding Tracy by the arm, and she was shrieking abuse at him, her eyes frantic. Nell tried to be authoritarian in her walk as she approached the pair of them.

'Is there some problem, Mr Clarke?'

'I can handle it, miss.' His eyes betrayed his words. He was sweating, past retirement age, neither used to this sort of physical struggle nor knowing what to do about it. Nell turned to the girl.

'You can't just barge in here, you know. But if you want a message passed on to one of the students inside, I'll see what I can do.'

The girl struggled again. 'I just want to come in!' All reasoning had gone now. She knew only that if someone was stopping her getting in, then she *had* to get in somehow.

'Well you can't,' Nell said angrily. She should not have interfered. She was used to dealing with quiet, sane, rational people. Okay, some of them might lose their tempers momentarily when frustrated in their search for a book. But they would always remember their place. The girl stared at her, and the stare seemed absolutely malevolent. There was no trace of human kindness in it at all. Nell felt the hairs on her neck bristle. Then the girl gave a banshee wail, throwing herself forward, loosing the guard's grip. Her forehead smashed into Nell's face, sending the librarian flying, feet rooted to the spot, so that she fell like so much timber. Tracy stood there for a moment, seeming to come to herself. The guard made to grab her, but she gave another yell, and he backed off. Then she pushed past him out of the library doors and started running again, head down, arms and legs uncoordinated. The guard watched her, fearful still, then turned his attention to the bloody and unconscious face of Nell Stapleton.

The man who answered the door was blind.

'Yes?' he asked, holding the door, sightless eyes discernible behind the dark green lenses of his glasses. The hallway behind him was in deep shadow. What need had it of light?

'Mr Vanderhyde?'

The man smiled. 'Yes?' he repeated. Rebus couldn't take his own eyes off those of the elderly man. Those green lenses reminded him of claret bottles. Vanderhyde would be sixty-five, maybe seventy. His hair was silvery yellow, thick, well groomed. He was wearing an open-necked shirt, brown waistcoat, a watch chain hanging from one pocket. And he was leaning ever so slightly on a silver-topped stick. For some reason, Rebus had the idea that Vanderhyde would be able to handle that cane swiftly and effectively as a weapon, should anyone unpleasant ever come calling.

'Mr Vanderhyde, I'm a police officer.' Rebus was reaching for his wallet.

'Don't bother with identification, unless it's in Braille.' Vanderhyde's words stopped Rebus short, his hand frozen in his inside jacket pocket.

'Of course,' he mumbled, feeling ever so slightly ridiculous. Funny how people with disabilities had that special gift of making you seem so much less able than them.

'You'd better come in, Inspector.'

'Thank you.' Rebus was in the hall before it hit him. 'How did you –?'

Vanderhyde shook his head. 'A lucky guess,' he said, leading the way. 'A shot in the dark, you might say.' His laughter was abrasive. Rebus, studying what he could see of the hall, was wondering how even a blind man could make such a botched job of interior decoration. A stuffed owl stared down from its dusty pedestal, next to an umbrella stand which seemed to consist of a hollowed elephant's foot. An ornately carved occasional table boasted a pile of unread mail and a cordless telephone. Rebus gave this latter item most attention.

'Technology has made such progress, don't you agree?' Vanderhyde was saying. 'Invaluable for those of us who have lost one of the senses.'

'Yes,' Rebus replied, as Vanderhyde opened the door to another room, almost as dark to Rebus's eyes as the hall.

'In here, Inspector.'

'Thank you.' The room was musty, and smelled of old people's medicaments. It was comfortably furnished, with a deep sofa and two robust armchairs. Books lay behind glass along one wall. Some uninspired watercolours stopped the other walls from seeming bare. There were ornaments everywhere. Those on the mantelpiece caught Rebus's eye. There wasn't a spare centimetre of space on the deep wooden mantelpiece, and the ornaments were exotic. Rebus could identify African, Caribbean, Asian and Oriental influences, without being able to pinpoint any one country for any one piece.

Vanderhyde flopped into a chair. It struck Rebus that there were no occasional tables scattered through the room, no extraneous furniture into which the blind man might bump.

'Nick-nacks, Inspector. Gewgaws collected on my travels as a younger man.'

'Evidence of a lot of travel.'

'Evidence of a magpie mind,' Vanderhyde corrected. 'Would you care for some tea?'

'No, thank you, sir.'

'Something a little stronger perhaps?'

'Thank you, but no.' Rebus smiled. 'I'd a bit too much last night.'

'Your smile comes over in your voice.'

'You don't seem curious as to why I'm here, Mr Vanderhyde.'

'Perhaps that's because I *know*, Inspector. Or, perhaps it's because my patience is limitless. Time doesn't mean as much to me as to most people. I'm in no hurry for your explanations. I'm not a clock watcher, you see.' He was smiling again, eyes fixed somewhere just right of Rebus and above him. Rebus stayed silent, inviting further speculation. 'Then again,' Vanderhyde continued, 'since I no longer go out, and have few visitors, and since I have never to my knowledge broken the laws of the land, that certainly narrows the possible reasons for your visit. You're sure you won't have some tea?'

'Don't let me stop you making some for yourself.' Rebus had spotted the near-empty mug sitting on the floor beside the old man's chair. He looked down around his own chair. Another mug sat on the muted pattern of the carpet. He reached a silent arm down towards it. There was a slight warmth on the base of the mug, a warmth on the carpet beneath.

'No,' Vanderhyde said. 'I had one just recently. As did my visitor.'

'Visitor?' Rebus sounded surprised. The old man smiled, giving a slight and indulgent shake of his head. Rebus, feeling caught, decided to push on anyway. 'I thought you said you didn't get many visitors?'

'No, I don't recall *quite* saying that. Still, it happens to be true. Today is the exception that proves the rule. Two visitors.'

'Might I ask who the other visitor was?'

'Might *I* ask, Inspector, why you're here?'

It was Rebus's turn to smile, nodding to himself. The blood was rising in the old man's cheeks. Rebus had succeeded in riling him.

'Well?' There was impatience in Vanderhyde's voice.

'Well, sir.' Rebus deliberately pulled himself out of the chair and began to circuit the room. 'I came across your name in an under-graduate essay on the occult. Does that surprise you?'

The old man considered this. 'It pleases me slightly. I do have an ego that needs feeding, after all.'

'But it doesn't surprise you?' Vanderhyde shrugged. 'This essay mentioned you in connection with the workings of an Edinburgh-based group, a sort of coven, working in the nineteen sixties.'

' "Coven" is an inexact term, but never mind.'

'You were involved in it?'

'I don't deny the fact.'

'Well, while we're dealing in fact, you were, more correctly, its guiding light. "Light" may be an inexact term.'

Vanderhyde laughed, a piping, discomfiting sound. 'Touché, Inspector. Indeed, touché. Do continue.'

'Finding your address wasn't difficult. Not too many Vanderhydes in the phone book.'

'My kin are based in London.'

'The reason for my visit, Mr Vanderhyde, is a murder, or at the very least a case of tampering with evidence at the scene of a death.'

'Intriguing.' Vanderhyde put his hands together, fingertips to his lips. It was hard to believe the man was sightless. Rebus's movements around the room were failing to have any effect on Vanderhyde at all.

'The body was discovered lying with arms stretched wide, legs together –'

'Naked?'

'No, not quite. Shirtless. Candles had been burning either side of the body, and a pentagram had been painted on one wall.'

'Anything else?'

'No. There were some syringes in a jar by the body.'

'The death was caused by an overdose of drugs?'

'Yes.'

'Hmm.' Vanderhyde rose from his chair and walked unerringly to the bookcase. He did not open it, but stood as though staring at the titles. 'If we're dealing with a sacrifice, Inspector – I take it that's your theory?'

'One of many, sir.'

'Well, *if* we are dealing with a sacrifice, then the means of death are quite unusual. No, more than that, are unheard of. To begin with, very few Satanists would ever contemplate a human sacrifice. Plenty of psychopaths have carried out murder and then excused it as ritual, but that's something else again. But in any case, a human sacrifice – a sacrifice of any kind – requires blood. Symbolic in some rites, as in the blood and body of Christ. Real in others. A sacrifice *without* blood? That would be original. And to administer an overdose. . . . No, Inspector, surely the more plausible explanation is that, as you say, someone muddied the water as it were, after the life had expired.'

Vanderhyde turned into the room again, picking out Rebus's position. He raised his arms high, to signal that this was all he had to offer.

Rebus sat down again. The mug when he touched it was no longer warm. The evidence had cooled, dissipated, vanished.

He picked up the mug and looked at it. It was an innocent thing, patterned with flowers. There was a single crack running downwards from its rim. Rebus felt a sudden surge of confidence in his own abilities. He got to his feet again and walked to the door.

'Are you leaving?'

He did not reply to Vanderhyde's question, but walked smartly to the bottom of the dark oak staircase. Halfway up, it twisted in a ninety-degree angle. From the bottom, Rebus's view was of this halfway point, this small landing. A second before, there had been someone there, someone crouching, listening. He hadn't seen the figure so much as *sensed* it. He cleared his throat, a nervous rather than necessary action.

'Come down here, Charlie.' He paused. Silence. But he could still sense the young man, just beyond that turning on the stairs. 'Unless you want me to come up. I don't think you want that, do you? Just the two of us, up there in the dark?' More silence, broken by the shuffling of Vanderhyde's carpet-slippered feet, the walking cane tapping against the floor. When Rebus looked round, the old man's jaw was set defiantly. He still had his pride. Rebus wondered if he felt any shame.

Then the single creak of a floorboard signalled Charlie's presence on the stair landing.

Rebus broke into a smile: of conquest, of relief. He had trusted himself, and had proved worthy of that trust.

'Hello, Charlie,' he said.

'I didn't mean to hit her. She had a go at me first.'

The voice was recognisable, but Charlie seemed rooted to the landing. His body was slightly hunched, his face in silhouette, his arms hanging by his side. The educated voice seemed discorporate, somehow not part of this shadow-puppet.

'Why don't you join us?'

'Are you going to arrest me?'

'What's the charge?' The question was Rebus's, his voice tinged with amusement.

'That should be *your* question, Charles,' Vanderhyde called out, making it sound like an instruction.

Rebus was suddenly bored with these games. 'Come on down,' he commanded. 'Let's have another mug of Earl Grey.'

Rebus had pulled open the crimson velvet curtains in the living room. The interior seemed less cramped in what was left of the daylight, less overpowering, and certainly a lot less gothic. The ornaments on the mantelpiece were revealed as just that: ornaments. The books in the bookcase were revealed as by and large works of popular fiction: Dickens, Hardy, Trollope. Rebus wondered if Trollope *was* still popular.

Charlie had made tea in the narrow kitchen, while Vanderhyde and Rebus sat in silence in the living room, listening to the distant sounds of cups chinking and spoons ringing.

'You have good hearing,' Vanderhyde stated at last. Rebus shrugged. He was still assessing the room. No, he couldn't live here, but he could at least imagine visiting some aged relative in such a place.

'Ah, tea,' said Vanderhyde as Charlie brought in the unsteady tray. Placing it on the floor between chairs and sofa, his eyes sought Rebus's. They had an imploring look. Rebus ignored it, accepting his cup with a curt nod of the head. He was just about to say something about how well Charlie seemed to know his way around his chosen bolthole, when Charlie himself spoke. He was handing a mug to Vanderhyde. The mug itself was only half filled – a wise precaution – and Charlie sought out the old man's hand, guiding it to the large handle.

'There you go, Uncle Matthew,' he said.

'Thank you, Charles,' said Vanderhyde, and if he had been sighted, his slight smile would have been directed straight at Rebus, rather than a few inches over the detective's shoulder.

'Cosy,' Rebus commented, sipping the dry perfume of Earl Grey.

Charlie sat on the sofa, crossing his legs, almost relaxed. Yes, he knew this room well, was slipping into it the way one slipped into an old, comfortable pair of trousers. He might have spoken, but Vanderhyde seemed to want to put his points forward first.

'Charles has told me all about it, Inspector Rebus. Well, when I say that, I mean he has told me as much as he deems it necessary for me to know.' Charlie glared at his uncle, who merely smiled, knowing the frown was there. 'I've already told Charles that he should talk to you again. He seems unwilling. *Seemed* unwilling. Now the choice has been taken away from him.'

'How did you know?' asked Charlie, so much more at home here, Rebus was thinking, than in some ugly squat in Pilmuir.

'Know?' said Rebus.

'Know where to find me? Know about Uncle Matthew?'

'Oh, that.' Rebus picked at invisible threads on his trousers. 'Your essay. It was sitting on your desk. Handy that.'

'What?'

'Doing an essay on the occult, and having a warlock in the family.'

Vanderhyde chuckled. 'Not a warlock, Inspector. Never that. I think I've only ever met one warlock, one *true* warlock, in my whole life. Local he is, mind.'

'Uncle Matthew,' Charlie interrupted, 'I don't think the Inspector wants to hear –'

'On the contrary,' said Rebus. 'It's the reason I'm here.'

'Oh.' Charlie sounded disappointed. 'Not to arrest me then?'

'No, though you deserve a good slap for that bruise you gave Tracy.'

'She deserved it!' Charlie's voice betrayed petulance, his lower lip filling out like a child's.

'You struck a woman?' Vanderhyde sounded aghast. Charlie looked towards him, then away, as if unable to hold a stare that didn't – couldn't – exist.

'Yes,' Charlie hissed. 'But look.' He pulled the polo-necked jumper down from around his neck. There were two huge weals there, the result of prising fingernails.

'Nice scratches,' Rebus commented for the blind man's benefit. 'You got the scratches, she got a bruise on her eye. I suppose that makes it neck and neck in the eye-for-an-eye stakes.'

Vanderhyde chuckled again, leaning forward slightly on his cane.

'Very good, Inspector,' he said. 'Yes, very good. Now –' he lifted the mug to his lips and blew. 'What can we do for you?'

'I saw your name in Charlie's essay. There was a footnote quoting you as an interview source. I reckoned that made you local and reasonably extant, and there aren't too many –'

'– Vanderhydes in the phone book,' finished the old man. 'Yes, you said.'

'But you've already answered most of my questions. Concerning the black magic connection, that is. However, I would just like to clear up a few points with your nephew.'

'Would you like me to –?' Vanderhyde was already rising to his feet. Rebus waved for him to stay, then realised the gesture was in vain. However, Vanderhyde had already paused, as though anticipating the action.

310

'No, sir,' Rebus said now, as Vanderhyde seated himself again. 'This'll only take a couple of minutes.' He turned to Charlie, who was almost sinking into the deep padded cushions of the sofa. 'So, Charlie,' Rebus began. 'I've got you down this far as thief, and as accessory to murder. Any comments to make?'

Rebus watched with pleasure as the young man's face lost its tea-like colour and became more like uncooked pastry. Vanderhyde twitched, but with pleasure, too, rather than discomfort. Charlie looked from one man to the other, seeking friendly eyes. The eyes he saw were blind to his pleas.

'I – I –'

'Yes?' Rebus prompted.

'I'll just fill my cup,' Charlie said, as though only these five meagre words were left in his vocabulary. Rebus sat back patiently. Let the bugger fill and refill and boil another brew. But he'd have his answers. He'd make Charlie sweat tannin, and he'd have his answers.

'Is Fife always this bleak?'

'Only the more picturesque bits. The rest's no' bad at a'.'

The SSPCA officer was guiding Brian Holmes across a twilit field, the area around almost completely flat, a dead tree breaking the monotony. A fierce wind was blowing, and it was a cold wind, too. The SSPCA man had called it an 'aist wind'. Holmes assumed that 'aist' translated as 'east', and that the man's sense of geography was somewhat askew, since the wind was clearly blowing from the west.

The landscape proved deceptive. Seeming flat, the land was actually slanting. They were climbing a slope, not steep but perceptible. Holmes was reminded of some hill somewhere in Scotland, the 'electric brae', where a trick of natural perspective made you think you were going uphill when in fact you were travelling *down*. Or was it vice versa? Somehow, he didn't think his companion was the man to ask.

Soon, over the rise, Holmes could see the black, grainy landscape of a disused mineworking, shielded from the field by a line of trees. The mines around here were all worked out, had been since the 1960s. Now, money had appeared from somewhere, and the long-smouldering bings were being levelled, their mass used to fill the chasms left by surface mining. The mine buildings themselves were being dismantled, the landscape reseeded, as though the history of mining in Fife had never existed.

This much Brian Holmes knew. His uncles had been miners. Not here perhaps, but nevertheless they had been great deep workings of information and anecdote. The child Brian had stored away every detail.

'Grim,' he said to himself as he followed the SSPCA officer down a slight slope towards the trees, where a cluster of half a dozen men stood, shuffling, turning at the sound of approach. Holmes introduced himself to the most senior-looking of the plain-clothes men.

'DC Brian Holmes, sir.'

The man smiled, nodded, then jerked his head in the direction of a much younger man. Everyone, uniformeds, plain-clothes, even the SSPCA Judas, was smiling, enjoying Holmes's mistake. He felt a rush of blood to his face, and was rooted to the spot. The young man saw his discomfort and stuck out a hand.

'I'm DS Hendry, Brian. Sometimes I'm in charge here.' There were more smiles. Holmes joined in this time.

'Sorry, sir.'

'I'm flattered actually. Nice to think I'm so young-looking, and Harry here's so old.' He nodded towards the man Holmes had mistaken for the senior officer. 'Right, Brian. I'll just tell you what I've been telling the lads. We have a good tip that there's going to be a dog fight here tonight. It's secluded, half a mile from the main road, a mile from the nearest house. Perfect, really. There's a track the lorries take from the main road up to the site here. That's the way they'll come in, probably three or four vans carrying the dogs, and then who knows how many cars with the punters. If it gets to Ibrox proportions, we'll call in reinforcements. As it is, we're not bothered so much about nabbing punters as about catching the handlers themselves. The word is that Davy Brightman's the main man. Owns a couple of scrap yards in Kirkcaldy and Methil. We know he keeps a few pit bulls, and we think he fights them.'

There was a blast of static from one of the radios, then a call sign. DS Hendry responded.

'Do you have a Detective Constable Holmes with you?' came the message. Hendry stared at Holmes as he handed him the radio. Holmes could only look apologetic.

'DC Holmes speaking.'

'DC Holmes, we've a message for you.'

'Go ahead,' said Holmes.

'It's to do with a Miss Nell Stapleton.'

*

Sitting in the hospital waiting room, eating chocolate from a vending machine, Rebus went over the day's events in his mind. Remembering the incident with Tracy in the car, his scrotum began to rise up into his body in an act of self-protection. Painful still. Like a double hernia, not that he'd ever had one.

But the afternoon had been very interesting indeed. Vanderhyde had been interesting. And Charlie, well, Charlie had sung like a bird.

'What is it you want to ask me?' he had said, bringing more tea into the living room.

'I'm interested in time, Charlie. Your uncle has already told me that *he's* not interested in time. He isn't ruled by it, but policemen are. Especially in a case like this. You see, the chronology of events isn't quite right in my mind. That's what I want to clear up, if possible.'

'All right,' Charlie said. 'How can I help?'

'You were at Ronnie's that night?'

'Yes, for a while.'

'And you left to look for some party or other?'

'That's right.'

'Leaving Neil in the house with Ronnie?'

'No, he'd left by then.'

'You didn't know, of course, that Neil was Ronnie's brother?'

The look of surprise on Charlie's face seemed authentic, but then Rebus knew him for an accomplished actor, and was taking nothing for granted, not any more.

'No, I didn't know that. Shit, his brother. Why didn't he want any of us to meet him?'

'Neil and I are in the same profession,' Rebus explained. Charlie just smiled and shook his head. Vanderhyde was leaning back thoughtfully in his chair, like a meticulous juror at some trial.

'Now,' Rebus continued, 'Neil says he left quite early. Ronnie was being uncommunicative.'

'I can guess why.'

'Why?'

'Easy. He'd just scored, hadn't he? He hadn't seen any stuff for ages, and suddenly he'd scored.' Charlie suddenly remembered that his aged uncle was listening, and stopped short, looking towards the old man. Vanderhyde, shrewd as ever, seemed to sense this, and waved his hand regally before him, as if to say, I've been too long on this planet and can't be shocked any more.

'I think you're right,' Rebus said to Charlie. 'One hundred per cent.

313

So, in an empty house, Ronnie shoots up. The stuff's lethal. When Tracy comes in, she finds him in his room –'

'So *she* says,' interrupted Charlie. Rebus nodded, acknowledging his scepticism.

'Let's accept for the moment that's what happened. He's dead, or seems so to her. She panics, and runs off. Right. So far so good. Now it begins to get hazy, and this is where I need your help, Charlie. Thereafter, someone moves Ronnie's body downstairs. I don't know why. Maybe they were just playing silly buggers, or, as Mr Vanderhyde put it so succinctly, trying to muddy the water. Anyway, around this stage in the chronology, a second packet of white powder appears. Tracy only saw one –' Rebus saw that Charlie was about to interrupt again '– so she says. So, Ronnie had one packet and shot up with it. When he died, his body came downstairs and another packet magically appeared. This new packet contains good stuff, not the poison Ronnie used on himself. And, to add a little more to the concoction, Ronnie's camera disappears, to turn up later in your squat, Charlie, in your room, and in your black polythene bag.'

Charlie had stopped looking at Rebus. He was looking at the floor, at his mug, at the teapot. His eyes still weren't on Rebus when he spoke.

'Yes, I took it.'

'You took the camera?'

'I just said I did, didn't I?'

'Okay.' Rebus's voice was neutral. Charlie's smouldering shame might at any moment catch light and ignite into anger. 'When did you take it?'

'Well, I didn't exactly stop to look at my watch.'

'Charles!' Vanderhyde's voice was loud, the word coming from his mouth like a bite. Charlie took notice. He straightened in his chair, reduced to some childhood fear of this imposing creature, his uncle the magician.

Rebus cleared his throat. The taste of Earl Grey was thick on his tongue. 'Was there anyone in the house when you got back?'

'No. Well, yes, if you're counting Ronnie.'

'Was he upstairs or down?'

'He was at the top of the stairs, if you must know. Just lying there, like he'd been trying to come down them. I thought he was crashed out. But he didn't look right. I mean, when someone's sleeping, there's *some* kind of movement. But Ronnie was . . . rigid. His skin was cold, damp.'

'And he was at the top of the stairs?'

'Yes.'

'What did you do then?'

'Well, I knew he was dead. And it was like I was dreaming. That sounds stupid, but it was like that. I know now that I was just trying to shut it out. I went into Ronnie's room.'

'Was the syringe jar there?'

'I can't remember.'

'Never mind. Go on.'

'Well, I knew that when Tracy got back –'

'Yes?'

'God, this is going to make me sound like a monster.'

'What is it?'

'Well, I knew that when she came back, she'd see Ronnie was dead and grab what she could of his. I *knew* she would, I just felt it. So I took something I thought he'd have wanted me to have.'

'For sentimental reasons then?' asked Rebus archly.

'Not totally,' Charlie admitted. Rebus had a sudden cooling thought: *this is going too easily.* 'It was the only thing Ronnie had that was worth any money.'

Rebus nodded. Yes, that was more like it. Not that Charlie was short of a few bob; he could always rely on Uncle Matthew. But it was the illicit nature of the act that appealed. Something Ronnie would have wanted him to have. Some chance.

'So you lifted the camera?' Rebus said. Charlie nodded. 'Then you left?'

'Went straight back to my squat. Somebody said Tracy had come looking for me. Said she'd been in a right state. So I assumed she already knew about Ronnie.'

'And she hadn't made off with the camera. She'd come looking for you instead.'

'Yes.' Charlie seemed almost contrite. Almost. Rebus wondered what Vanderhyde was making of all this.

'What about the name Hyde, does it mean anything to you?'

'A character in Robert Louis Stevenson.'

'Apart from that.'

Charlie shrugged.

'What about someone called Edward?'

'A character in Robert Louis Stevenson.'

'I don't understand.'

'Sorry, I'm being facetious. Edward is Hyde's first name in *Jekyll and Hyde*. No, I don't know anyone called Edward.'

'Fair enough. Do you want to know something, Charlie?'

'What?'

Rebus looked to Vanderhyde, who sat impassively. 'Actually, I think your uncle already knows what I'm going to say.'

Vanderhyde smiled. 'Indeed. Correct me if I'm wrong, Inspector Rebus, but you were about to say that, the young man's corpse having moved from the bedroom to the stairs, you can only assume that the person who moved the body was actually in the house when Charles arrived.'

Charlie's jaw dropped open. Rebus had never witnessed the effect in real life before.

'Quite right,' he said. 'I'd say you were lucky, Charlie. I'd say that someone was moving the body downstairs and heard you arrive. Then they hid in one of the other rooms, maybe even that stinking bathroom, until you'd left. They were in the house all the time you were.'

Charlie swallowed. Then closed his mouth. Then let his head fall forward and began to weep. Not quite silently, so that his uncle caught the action, and smiled, nodding towards Rebus with satisfaction.

Rebus finished the chocolate. It had tasted of antiseptic, the same strong flavour of the corridor outside, the wards themselves, and this waiting room, where anxious faces buried themselves in old colour supplements and tried to look interested for more than a second or two. The door opened and Holmes came in, looking anxious and exhausted. He'd had the distance of a forty-minute car journey in which to mentally live his worst fears, and the result was carved into his face. Rebus knew that swift treatment was needed.

'She's fine. You can see her whenever you like. They're keeping her in overnight for no good reason at all, and she's got a broken nose.'

'A broken nose?'

'That's all. No concussion, no blurred vision. A good old broken nose, curse of the bare-knuckle fighter.'

Rebus thought for one moment that Holmes was about to take offence at his levity. But then relief flooded the younger man and he smiled, his shoulders relaxing, head dropping a little as though from a sense of anticlimax, albeit a welcome one.

'So,' Rebus said, 'do you want to see her?'

'Yes.'

'Come on, I'll take you.' He placed a hand on Holmes's shoulder and guided him out of the door again.

'But how did you know?' Holmes asked as they walked up the corridor.

'Know what?'

'Know it was Nell? Know about Nell and me?'

'Well now, you're a detective, Brian. Think about it.'

Rebus could see Holmes's mind take on the puzzle. He hoped the process was therapeutic. Finally, Holmes spoke.

'Nell's got no family, so she asked for me.'

'Well, she *wrote* asking for you. The broken nose makes it hard to understand what she's saying.'

Holmes nodded dully. 'But I couldn't be located, and you were asked if you knew where I was.'

'That's close enough. Well done. How was Fife anyway? I only get back there once a year.' *April 28th*, he thought to himself.

'Fife? It was okay. I'd to leave before the bust. That was a shame. And I don't think I exactly impressed the team I was supposed to be part of.'

'Who was in charge?'

'A young DS called Hendry.'

Rebus nodded. 'I know him. I'm surprised you don't, at least by reputation.'

Holmes shrugged. 'I just hope they nab those bastards.'

Rebus had stopped outside the door of a ward.

'This it?' Holmes asked. Rebus nodded.

'Want me to come in with you?'

Holmes stared at his superior with something approaching gratitude, then shook his head.

'No, it's all right. I won't stay if she's asleep. One last thing though.'

'Yes?'

'Who did it?'

Who did it. That was the hardest part to understand. Walking back along the corridor, Rebus saw Nell's puffy face, saw her distress as she tried to talk, and couldn't. She had signalled for some paper. He had taken a notebook from his pocket, and handed her his pen. Then she had written furiously for a full minute. He stopped now and took out the notebook, reading it through for the fourth or fifth time that evening.

'I was working at the library. A woman tried to push her way into the building, past the guard. Talk to him if you want to check. This woman then butted me on the face. I was trying to help, to calm her down. She must have thought I was interfering. But I wasn't. I was trying to help. She was the girl in that photograph, the nude photograph Brian had in his briefcase last night in the pub. You were there, weren't you, in the same pub as us? Not easy not to notice – the place was empty, after all. Where's Brian? Out chasing more salacious pictures for you, Inspector?'

Rebus smiled now, as he had smiled then. She had guts, that one. He rather liked her, her face taped, eyes blackened. She reminded him a lot of Gill.

So, Tracy was leaving a silvery snail's trail of chaos by which to follow her. Little bitch. Had she simply flipped, or was there a real motive for her trip to the University Library? Rebus leaned against the wall of the corridor. God, what a day. He was supposed to be between cases. Supposed to be 'tidying things up' before starting full time on the drugs campaign. He was supposed, for the sake of Christ, to be having things *easy*. That'd be the day.

The ward doors swung shut, alerting him to the figure of Brian Holmes in the corridor. Holmes seemed lacking direction, then spotted his superior and came walking briskly up the hall. Rebus wasn't sure yet whether Holmes was invaluable, or a liability. Could you be both things at once?

'Is she all right?' he asked solicitously.

'Yes. I suppose so. She's awake. Face looks a bit of a mess though.'

'Just bruises. They say the nose will heal. You'll never know it was broken.'

'Yes, that's what Nell said.'

'She talking? That's good.'

'She also told me who did it.' Holmes looked at Rebus, who looked away. 'What's this all about? What's Nell got to do with it?'

'Nothing, so far as I know. She just happened to be in the wrong place, et cetera. Chalk it down to coincidence.'

'Coincidence? That's a nice easy word to say. Put it down to "coincidence" and then we can forget all about it, is that it? I don't know what your game is, Rebus, but I'm not going to play it any longer.'

Holmes turned and stalked off along the hall. Rebus almost warned him that there was no exit at that end of the building, but favours weren't what Holmes wanted. He needed a bit of time, a break. So did

Rebus, but he had some thinking to do, and the station was the best place for that.

By taking them slowly, Rebus managed the stairs to his office. He had been at his desk fully ten minutes before a craving for tea had him reaching for the telephone. Then he sat back, holding in front of him a piece of paper on which he had attempted to set out the 'facts' of the 'case'. He was chilled by the thought that he might be wasting time and effort. A jury would have to work hard to see any crime there at all. There was no suggestion that Ronnie had not injected himself. However, he *had* been starved of his supply, despite there being no shortage of dope in the city, and someone *had* moved his body, and left behind a packet of good heroin, hoping, perhaps, that this would be tested, found clean, and therefore death by misadventure would be recorded: a simple overdose. But the rat poison had been found.

Rebus looked at the paper. Already 'perhapses' and conjecture had entered the picture. Maybe the frame wasn't right. So, turn the picture another way round, John, and start again.

Why had someone gone to the trouble of killing Ronnie? After all, the poor bugger would have topped himself given time. Ronnie had been starved of a fix, then given some, but had known this stuff to be less than pure. So doubtless he had known that the person who supplied it wanted him dead. But he had taken it anyway. . . . No, viewed this way round it was making even less sense. Start again.

Why would someone want Ronnie dead? There were several obvious answers. Because he knew something he shouldn't. Because he possessed something he shouldn't. Because he didn't possess something he should. Which was correct? Rebus didn't know. Nobody seemed to know. The picture still lacked meaning.

There was a knock on the door, and the door itself was pushed open by a constable carrying a mug of tea. The constable was Harry Todd. Rebus recognised him.

'You get around a bit, son.'

'Yes, sir,' said Todd, placing the tea on a corner of the desk, the only three square inches of wood visible from beneath a surface covering of paperwork.

'Is it quiet tonight?'

'The usual, sir. A few drunks. Couple of break-ins. Nasty car crash down near the docks.'

Rebus nodded, reaching for the tea. 'Do you know another constable, name of Neil McGrath?' Raising the mug to his lips, Rebus stared up at Todd, who had begun to blush.

'Yes, sir,' he said. 'I know him.'

'Mm-hm.' Rebus tested the tea, seeming to relish the bland flavour of milk and hot water. 'Told you to keep an eye on me, did he?'

'Sir?'

'If you happen to see him, Todd, tell him everything's fine.'

'Yes, sir.' Todd was turning to leave.

'Oh, and Todd?'

'Yes, sir?'

'Don't let me see you near me again, understood?'

'Yes, sir.' Todd was clearly downhearted. At the door, he paused, seeming to have a sudden plan that would ingratiate himself with his superior. Smiling, he turned back to Rebus.

'Did you hear about the action across in Fife, sir?'

'What action?' Rebus sounded uninterested.

'The dog fight, sir.' Rebus tried hard to still look unmoved. 'They broke up some dog fight. Guess who got arrested?'

'Malcolm Rifkind?' guessed Rebus. This deflated Todd totally. The smile left his face.

'No, sir,' he said, turning again to leave. Rebus's patience was short.

'Well who then?' he snapped.

'That disc jockey, Calum McCallum,' Todd said, closing the door after him. Rebus stared at the door for a count of five before it struck home: Calum McCallum . . . Gill Templer's lover!

Rebus raised his head and let out a roar which mixed laughter with a kind of twisted victory cry. And when he had stopped laughing, and was wiping his eyes with a handkerchief, he looked towards the door again and saw that it was open. There was someone standing in the doorway, watching his performance with a look of puzzlement on their face.

It was Gill Templer.

Rebus checked his watch. It was nearly one in the morning.

'Working the late shift, Gill?' he said to cover his confusion.

'I suppose you've heard,' she said, ignoring him.

'Heard what?'

She walked into the room, pushed some papers off the chair onto the floor, and sat down, looking exhausted. Rebus looked at all that paper slewed across the floor.

'The cleaners come in in the morning anyway,' he said. Then: 'I've heard.'

'Is that what all the screaming was about?'

'Oh, that.' Rebus tried to shrug it off, but could feel the blood tingling in his cheeks. 'No,' he said, 'that was just something ... well, something else. . . .'

'Not very convincing, Rebus, you bastard.' Her words were tired. He wanted to buoy her up, tell her she was looking well or something. But it wouldn't have been true and she would just scowl at him again. So he left it. She *was* looking drawn, not enough sleep and no fun left any more. She'd just had her world locked up in a cell somewhere in Fife. They would be photographing and fingerprinting it perhaps, ready to file it away. Her life, Calum McCallum.

Life was full of surprises.

'So what can I do for you?'

She looked up at him, studying his face as though she wasn't sure who he was or why she was here. Then she shook herself awake with a twitch of the shoulders.

'It sounds corny, but I really was just passing. I dropped into the canteen for a coffee before going home, and then I heard –' She shivered again; the twitch which wasn't quite a twitch. Rebus could see how fragile she was. He hoped she wasn't going to shake apart. 'I heard about Calum. How could he do that to me, John? Keep a secret like that? I mean, where's the fun in watching dogs ripping each other –'

'That's something you'll have to ask him yourself, Gill. Can I get you some more coffee?'

'Christ no, I'm going to find it hard enough getting to sleep as it is. Tell you what I would like though, if it's not too much trouble.'

'Name it.'

'A lift home.' Rebus was already nodding agreement. 'And a hug.'

Rebus got up slowly, donned his jacket, put the pen and piece of paper in his pocket, and met her in the middle of the room. She had already risen from her chair, and, standing on reports to be read, paperwork to be signed, arrest statistics and the rest, they hugged, their arms strong. She buried her head in his shoulder. He rested his chin on her neck, staring at the closed door, rubbing her back with one hand, patting with the other. Eventually, she pulled away, head first, then chest, but still holding him with her arms. Her eyes were moist, but it was over now. She was looking a little better.

'Thanks,' she said.

'I needed it as much as you did,' said Rebus. 'Come on, let's get you home.'

Friday

The inhabitants were all doing well, it seemed, and all
emulously hoping to do better still, and
laying out the surplus of their grains in coquetry.

Someone was knocking on his door. An authoritarian knock, using the old brass knocker that he never cleaned. Rebus opened his eyes. The sun was streaming into his living room, a record's run-out track crackling. Another night spent in the chair, fully clothed. He'd be as well selling the mattress in the bedroom. Would anyone buy a mattress without a bed-frame?

Knockity knock knock again. Still patient. Still waiting for him to answer. His eyes were gummy, and he pushed his shirt back into his trousers as he walked from the living room to the door. He felt not too bad, considering. Not stiff, no tightness in the neck. A wash and a shave, and he might even feel human.

He opened the door, just as Holmes was about to knock again.

'Brian.' Rebus sounded genuinely pleased.

'Morning. Mind if I come in?'

'Not at all. Is Nell okay?'

'I phoned this morning. They say she had a good night.'

They were walking in the direction of the kitchen, Rebus leading. Holmes had imagined the flat would smell of beer and cigarettes, a typical bachelor pad. In fact, it was tidier than he'd expected, furnished with a modicum of taste. There were a lot of books. Rebus had never struck him as a reader. Mind you, not all the books looked as though they'd been read: bought with a rainy, dead weekend in mind. The weekend that never came.

Rebus pointed vaguely in the direction of kettle and cupboards.

'Make us some coffee, will you? I'll just take a quick shower.'

'Right.' Holmes thought that his news could probably wait. At least until Rebus was fully awake. He sought in vain for instant coffee, but found, in one cupboard, a vacuum pack of ground coffee, several months past its sell-by date. He opened it and spooned some into the teapot while the kettle was boiling. Sounds of running water came from the bathroom, and above these the tinny sound of a transistor radio. Voices. Some talk show, Holmes supposed.

While Rebus was in the bathroom, he took the opportunity to wander through the flat. The living room was huge, with a high corniced ceiling. Holmes felt a pang of jealousy. He'd never be able to buy a place like this. He was looking around Easter Road and Gorgie, near the football grounds of Hibs and Hearts respectively. He could afford a flat in both these parts of the city, a decent-sized flat, too, three bedrooms. But the rooms were small, the areas mean. He was no snob. Hell, yes he was. He wanted to live in the New Town, in Dean Village, here in Marchmont, where students philosophised in pretty coffee shops.

He wasn't overcareful with the stylus when he lifted the arm off the record. The record itself was by some jazz combo. It looked old, and he sought in vain for its sleeve. The noises from the bathroom had stopped. He walked stealthily back to the kitchen and found a tea strainer in the cutlery drawer. So he was able to keep the grounds out of the coffee he now poured into two mugs. Rebus came in, wrapped in a bath-towel, rubbing at his head with another, smaller towel. He needed to lose weight, or to exercise what weight he had. His chest was beginning to hang, pale like a carcass.

He picked up a mug and sipped.

'Mmm. The real McCoy.'

'I found it in the cupboard. No milk though.'

'Never mind. This is fine. You say you found it in the cupboard? We might make a detective of you yet. I'll just put on some togs.' And he was off again, for only two minutes this time. The clothes he came back wearing were clean, but unironed. Holmes noticed that though there was plumbing in the kitchen for a washing machine, there was no machine. Rebus seemed to read his mind.

'My wife took it when she moved out. Took a lot of stuff. That's why the place looks so bare.'

'It doesn't look bare. It looks planned.'

Rebus smiled. 'Let's go into the living room.'

Rebus motioned for Holmes to sit, then sat down himself. The chair was still warm from his night's sleep. 'I see you've already been in here.'

Holmes looked surprised. Caught. He remembered that he'd lifted the stylus off the record.

'Yes,' he said.

'That's what I like to see,' Rebus said. 'Yes, we'll make a detective of you yet, Brian.'

Holmes wasn't sure whether Rebus was being flattering or condescending. He let it go.

'Something I thought you might like to know,' he began.

'I already know,' said Rebus. 'Sorry to spoil the surprise, but I was at the station late last night, and somebody told me.'

'Last night?' Holmes was confused. 'But they only found the body this morning.'

'The body? You mean he's dead?'

'Yes. Suicide.'

'Jesus, poor Gill.'

'Gill?'

'Gill Templer. She was going out with him.'

'Inspector Templer?' Holmes was shocked. 'I thought she was living with that disc jockey?'

Now Rebus was confused. 'Isn't that who we're talking about?'

'No,' said Holmes. The surprise was still intact. He felt real relief.

'So who *are* we talking about?' asked Rebus with a growing sense of dread. 'Who's committed suicide?'

'James Carew.'

'Carew?'

'Yes. Found him in his flat this morning. Overdose apparently.'

'Overdose of what?'

'I don't know. Some kind of pills.'

Rebus was stunned. He recalled the look on Carew's face that night atop Calton Hill.

'Damn,' he said. 'I wanted a word with him.'

'I was wondering . . .' said Holmes.

'What?'

'I don't suppose you ever got round to asking him about getting me a flat?'

'No,' said Rebus. 'I never got the chance.'

'I was only joking,' Holmes said, realising that Rebus had taken his comment literally. 'Was he a friend? I mean, I know you met him for lunch, but I didn't realise –'

'Did he leave a note?'

'I don't know.'

'Well who *would* know?'

Holmes thought for a second. 'I think Inspector McCall was at the scene.'

'Right, come on.' Rebus was up on his feet.

'What about your coffee?'

'Sod the coffee. I want to see Tony McCall.'

'What was all that about Calum McCallum?' said Holmes, rising now.

'You mean you haven't heard?' Holmes shook his head. 'I'll tell you on the way.'

And then Rebus was on the move, grabbing jacket, getting out his keys to lock the front door. Holmes wondered what the secret was. What had Calum McCallum done? God, he hated people who hung on to secrets.

Rebus read the note as he stood in Carew's bedroom. It was elegantly written with a proper nib pen, but in one or two of the words fear could be clearly read, the letters trembling uncontrollably, scribbled out to be tried again. Good-quality writing paper too, thick and watermarked. The V12 was in a garage behind the flat. The flat itself was stunning, a museum for art deco pieces, modern art prints, and valuable first editions, locked behind glass.

This is the flipside of Vanderhyde's home, Rebus had thought as he moved through the flat. Then McCall had handed him the suicide note.

'If I am the chief of sinners, I am the chief of sufferers also.' Was that a quote from somewhere? Certainly, it was a bit prolix for a suicide note. But then Carew would have gone through draft upon draft until satisfied. It had to be exact, had to stand as his monument. 'Some day you may perhaps come to learn the right and wrong of this.' Not that Rebus needed to seek too hard. He had the queasy feeling, reading the note, that Carew's words were directed straight at him, that he was saying things only Rebus could fully understand.

'Funny sort of note to leave behind,' said McCall.

'Yes,' said Rebus.

'You met him recently, didn't you?' said McCall. 'I remember you saying. Did he seem okay then? I mean, he wasn't depressed or anything?'

'I've seen him since then.'

'Oh?'

'I was sniffing around Calton Hill a couple of nights back. He was there in his car.'

'Ah-ha.' McCall nodded. Everything was starting to make a little bit of sense.

Rebus handed back the note and went over to the bed. The sheets were rumpled. Three empty pill bottles stood in a neat line on the bedside table. On the floor lay an empty cognac bottle.

'The man went out in style,' McCall said, pocketing the note. 'He'd gone through a couple of bottles of wine before that.'

'Yes, I saw them in the living room. Lafite sixty-one. The stuff of a very special occasion.'

'They don't come more special, John.'

Both men turned as a third presence became evident in the room. It was Farmer Watson, breathing heavily from the effort of the stairs.

'This is bloody awkward,' he said. 'One of the linchpins of our campaign tops himself, and by taking a bloody overdose. How's that going to look, eh?'

'Awkward, sir,' replied Rebus, 'just as you say.'

'I do say. I do say.' Watson thrust a finger out towards Rebus. 'It's up to you, John, to make sure the media don't make a meal of this, or of us.'

'Yes, sir.'

Watson looked over towards the bed. 'Waste of a bloody decent man. What makes someone do it? I mean, look at this place. And there's an estate somewhere on one of the islands. Own business. Expensive car. Things we can only dream about. Makes you wonder, doesn't it?'

'Yes, sir.'

'Right.' Watson took a last glance towards the bed, then slapped a hand on Rebus's shoulder. 'I'm depending on you, John.'

'Yes, sir.'

McCall and Rebus watched their superior go.

'Bloody hell!' whispered McCall. 'He didn't look at me, not once. I might as well have not been there.'

'You should thank your lucky stars, Tony. I wish I had your gift of invisibility.'

Both men smiled. 'Seen enough?' McCall asked.

'Just one more circuit,' said Rebus. 'Then I'll get out of your hair.'

'Whatever you say, John. Just one thing.'

'What's that?'

'What the hell were you doing up Calton Hill in the middle of the night?'

'Don't ask,' said Rebus, blowing a kiss as he headed for the living area.

It *would* be big news locally, of course. There was no getting away from the fact. The radio stations and newspapers would have trouble deciding which headline deserved most prominence: Disc Jockey Arrested at Illegal Dog Fight or Suicide Shock of Estate Agent Giant. Well, something along those lines. Jim Stevens would have loved it, but then Jim Stevens was in London and married, by all accounts, to some girl half his age.

Rebus admired that kind of dangerous move. He had no admiration for James Carew: none. Watson was right in at least one respect: Carew had everything going for him, and Rebus was finding it difficult to believe that he would commit suicide solely because he had been spotted by a police officer on Calton Hill. No, that might have been the trigger, but there *had* to be something more. Something, perhaps, in the flat, or in the offices of Bowyer Carew on George Street.

James Carew owned a lot of books. A quick examination showed that they were for the most part expensive, impressive titles, but unread, their spines crackling as they were opened by Rebus for the first time. The top right hand section of the bookcase held several titles which interested him more than the others. Books by Genet and Alexander Trocchi, copies of Forster's *Maurice* and even *Last Exit to Brooklyn*. Poems by Walt Whitman, the text of *Torchlight Trilogy*. A mixed bag of predominantly gay reading. Nothing wrong in that. But their positioning in the bookshelves – right at the top and separated from the other titles – suggested to Rebus that here was a man ashamed of himself. There was no reason for this, not these days. . . .

Who was he kidding? AIDS had squeezed homosexuality back into the darker corners of society, and by keeping the truth a secret Carew had laid himself open to feelings of shame, and, therefore, to blackmail of all kinds.

Yes, blackmail. Suicides were occasionally victims of blackmail who could see no way out of their dilemma. Just maybe there would be some evidence, a letter or a note or something. *Anything*. Just so Rebus could prove to himself he wasn't completely paranoid.

Then he found it.

In a drawer. A locked drawer, to be sure, but the keys were in Carew's trousers. He had died in his pyjamas, and his other clothes had not been taken away with the corpse. Rebus got the keys from the bedroom and headed back to the desk in the living room. A gorgeous writing desk, antique for sure: its surface was barely large enough to accommodate a sheet of A4 paper and an elbow. What had been once a useful piece of furniture now found itself an ornament in a rich man's apartment. Rebus opened the drawer carefully and drew out a leather-bound desk diary. A page a day, the pages large. Not a diary for appointments, not locked away in darkness like that. A personal diary then. Eagerly, Rebus flipped it open. His disappointment was immediate. The pages were blank for the most part. A line or two of pencil per page was as much as there was.

Rebus cursed.

All right, John. It's better than nothing. He rested at one of the pages with some writing on it. The pencil marking was faint, neatly written. 'Jerry, 4pm'. A simple appointment. Rebus flipped to the day on which they had all met for lunch at The Eyrie. The page was blank. Good. That meant the appointments weren't of the business lunch variety. There weren't many of them. Rebus felt sure that Carew's diary at his office would be crammed. This was a much more private affair.

'Lindsay, 6.30.'

'Marks, 11am.' An early start that day, and what about that name: two individuals, each named Mark? Or one individual whose surname was Marks? Maybe even the department store . . .? The other names – Jerry, Lindsay – were androgynous, anonymous. He needed a telephone number, a location.

He turned another page. And had to look twice at what was written there. His finger ran along the letters.

'Hyde, 10pm.'

Hyde. What had Ronnie said to Tracy the night he'd died? *Hide, he's after me?* Yes, and James had given him the name, too: not hide but H-y-d-e.

Hyde!

Rebus whooped. Here was a connection, no matter how tenuous. A connection between Ronnie and James Carew. Something more than a fleeting business transaction on Calton Hill. A name. He hurried through the other pages. There were three more mentions of Hyde, always in the late evening (when Calton Hill was starting its trade), always on a Friday. Sometimes the second Friday of the month, sometimes the third. Four mentions in the course of six months.

'Anything?' It was McCall, leaning over Rebus's shoulder for a peek.

'Yes,' Rebus said. Then he changed his mind. 'No, not really, Tony. Just an old diary, but the bugger wasn't much of a writer.'

McCall nodded and moved away. He was more interested in the hi-fi system.

'The old guy had taste,' McCall said, scrutinising it. 'Linn turntable. Know how much one of those costs, John? Hundreds. They're not showy. They're just bloody good at what they do.'

'A bit like us then,' said Rebus. He was thinking of pushing the diary into his trousers. It wasn't allowed, he knew. And what good would it do him? But with Tony McCall's back turned so conveniently. . . . No, no, he couldn't. He threw it noisily back into its drawer, shut the drawer again and locked it. He handed the key to McCall, who was still squatting in front of the hi-fi.

'Thanks, John. Nice piece of equipment this, you know.'

'I didn't know you were interested in all that stuff.'

'Since I was a kid. Had to get rid of my system when we got married. Too noisy.' He straightened. 'Are we going to find any answers here, do you think?'

Rebus shook his head. 'I think he kept all his secrets in his head. He was a very private man, after all. No, I think he's taken the answers with him to the grave.'

'Oh, well. Makes it nice and clear-cut then, doesn't it?'

'Clear as crystal, Tony,' said Rebus.

What was it the old man, Vanderhyde, had said? Something about muddying the water. Rebus had the gnawing feeling that the solution to these many conundrums was a simple one, as crystal clear as one could wish. The problem was that extraneous stories were being woven into the whole. *Do I mix my metaphors? Very well then, I mix my metaphors.* All that counted was getting to the bottom of the pool, muddied or no, and bringing up that tiny cache of treasure called the truth.

He knew, too, that the problem was one of classification. He had to break the interlinked stories into separate threads, and work from those. At the moment, he was guilty of trying to weave them all into a pattern, a pattern that might not be there. By separating them all, maybe he'd be in with a chance of solving each.

Ronnie committed suicide. So did Carew. That gave them a second thing in common to add to the name of Hyde. Some client of Carew's perhaps? Buying a substantial piece of property with money made through the dealing of hard drugs? That would be a link, for sure. Hyde.

The name couldn't be real. How many Hydes were there in the Edinburgh directory? It could always be an assumed name. Male prostitutes seldom used their own names, after all. Hyde. Jekyll and Hyde. Another coincidence: Rebus had been reading Stevenson's book the night Tracy had visited. Maybe he should be looking for someone called Jekyll? Jekyll, the respectable doctor, admired by society; Hyde, his alter ego, small and brutish, a creature of the night. He remembered the shadowy forms he'd encountered by Calton Hill. . . . Could the answer be so obvious?

He parked in the only vacant bay left outside Great London Road station and climbed the familiar steps. They seemed to grow larger with the passing years, and he could swear there were more of them now than there had been when he'd first come to this place, all of – what was it? – six years ago? That wasn't so long in the span of a man's life, was it? So why did it feel so bloody Sisyphean?

'Hello, Jack,' he said to the desk sergeant, who watched him walk past without the usual nod of the head. Strange, Rebus thought. Jack had never been a cheery bugger, but he'd usually had the use of his neck muscles. He was famous for his slight bow of the head, which he could make mean anything from approbation to insult.

But today, for Rebus, nothing.

Rebus decided to ignore the slight, and went upstairs. Two constables, in the act of coming down, fell quiet as they passed him. Rebus began to redden, but kept walking, sure now that he had forgotten to zip his fly, or had somehow contrived to get a smudge on his nose. Something like that. He'd check in the privacy of his office.

Holmes was waiting for him, seated in Rebus's chair, at Rebus's desk, some property details spread across the tabletop. He began to rise as Rebus entered, gathering together the sheets of paper like a kid caught with a dirty book.

'Hello, Brian.' Rebus took off his jacket, hanging it on the back of the door. 'Listen, I want you to get me the names and addresses of all Edinburgh inhabitants whose names are Jekyll or Hyde. I know that may sound daft, but just do it. Then –'

'I think you should sit down, sir,' said Holmes tremulously. Rebus stared at him, saw the fear in the young man's eyes, and knew that the worst had happened.

Rebus pushed open the door of the interview room. His face was the colour of pickled beetroot, and Holmes, following, feared that his superior was about to suffer a coronary. There were two CID men in the room, both in their shirtsleeves as though after a hard session. They turned at Rebus's entrance, and the one who was seated rose as if for combat. On the other side of the table, the weasel-faced teenager known to Rebus as 'James' actually squealed, and flew to his feet, knocking the chair with a clatter onto the stone floor.

'Don't let him near me!' he yelled.

'Now, John –' started one detective, a Sergeant Dick. Rebus held up a hand to show that he was not here to cause violence. The detectives eyed one another, not sure whether to believe him. Then Rebus spoke, his eyes on the teenager.

'You're going to get what's coming to you, so help me.' There was calm, lucid anger in Rebus's voice. 'I'm going to have you by your balls for this, son. You better believe that. Really, you better.'

The teenager saw now that the others would restrain Rebus, that the man himself presented an empty physical threat. He sneered.

'Yeah, sure,' he said dismissively. Rebus lurched forward, but Holmes's hand was rigid against his shoulder, pulling him back.

'Leave it be, John,' the other detective, DC Cooper, cautioned. 'Just let the wheels grind round. It won't take long.'

'Too long though,' Rebus hissed, as Holmes pulled him out of the room, closing the door after them. Rebus stood in the shadowy corridor, all rage spent, head bowed. It was so very hard to believe. . . .

'Inspector Rebus!'

Rebus and Holmes both jerked their heads towards the voice. It belonged to a WPC. She looked scared, too.

'Yes?' Rebus managed, swallowing.

'The Super wants to see you in his office. I think it's urgent.'

'I'm sure it is,' said Rebus, walking towards her with such menace that she retreated hurriedly, back towards the reception area and daylight.

'It's a bloody set-up, with all due respect, sir.'

Remember the golden rule, John, Rebus thought to himself: never swear at a superior without adding that 'with all due respect'. It was something he'd learned in the Army. As long as you added that coda, the brass couldn't have you for insubordination.

'John.' Watson interlaced his fingers, studying them as if they were the latest craze. 'John, we've got to investigate it. That's our duty. *I* know it's daft, and everyone else knows it's daft, but we've got to *show* that it's daft. That's our duty.'

'All the same, sir –'

Watson cut him off with a wave of his hand. Then started twining fingers again.

'God knows, you're already "suspended" from duty as it is, until our little campaign gets into full swing.'

'Yes, sir, but this is just what he wants.'

'He?'

'Some man called Hyde. He wants me to stop poking about in the Ronnie McGrath case. That's what this is all about. That's why it's a set-up job.'

'That's as maybe. The fact remains, a complaint has been made against you –'

'By that little bastard downstairs.'

'He says you gave him money, twenty pounds, I believe.'

'I *did* give him twenty quid, but not for a shag, for Chrissake!'

'For what then?'

Rebus made to answer, but was defeated. Why *had* he handed the teenager called James that money? He'd set himself up, all right. Hyde couldn't have done it better himself. And now James was downstairs, spilling his carefully rehearsed story to CID. And say what you liked, mud stuck. By Christ, it didn't half. No amount of soap and water would clean it off. The little toerag.

'This is playing right into Hyde's hands, sir,' Rebus tried: one last shot. 'If his story's true, why didn't he come in yesterday? Why wait till today?'

But Watson was decided.

'No, John. I want you out of here for a day or two. A week even. Take a break. Do whatever you like, but leave well alone. We'll clear it up, don't worry. We'll break his story down into pieces so small he won't be able to see them any more. One of those pieces will snap, and with it, his whole story. Don't you worry.'

Rebus stared at Watson. What he said made sense; more than that, it was actually fairly subtle and shrewd. Maybe the Farmer wasn't so agricultural in his ways after all. He sighed.

'Whatever you say, sir.'

Watson nodded, smiling.

'By the way,' he said. 'Remember that fellow Andrews, ran a club called Finlay's?'

'We had lunch with him, sir.'

'That's right. He's invited me to apply for membership.'

'Good for you, sir.'

'Apparently the waiting list's about a year long – all these rich Sassenachs coming north – but he said he could do a bit of pruning in my case. I told him not to bother. I seldom drink, and I certainly don't gamble. Still, a nice gesture all the same. Maybe I should ask him to consider you in my place. That'd give you something to do with your time off, eh?'

'Yes, sir.' Rebus seemed to consider the suggestion. Booze and gambling: not a bad combination. His face brightened. 'Yes, sir,' he said. 'That would be very kind of you.'

'I'll see what I can do then. One last thing.'

'Yes, sir?'

'Are you intending to go to Malcolm Lanyon's party tonight? Remember, he invited us at The Eyrie?'

'I'd forgotten all about it, sir. Would it be more . . . proper for me to stay away?'

'Not at all. I may not manage along myself, but I see no reason why you shouldn't attend. But not a word about. . . .' Watson nodded towards the door, and by implication to the interview room beyond.

'Understood, sir. Thank you.'

'Oh, and John?'

'Yes, sir?'

'Don't swear at me. Ever. With respect or otherwise. Okay?'

Rebus felt his cheeks reddening, not in anger but in shame. 'Yes, sir,' he said, making his exit.

Holmes was waiting impatiently in Rebus's office.

'What did he want then?'

'Who?' Rebus was supremely nonchalant. 'Oh, Watson you mean? He wanted to tell me that he's put my name forward for Finlay's.'

'Finlay's Club?' Holmes' face was quizzical; this wasn't what he'd been expecting at all.

'That's right. At my age, I think I deserve a club in town, don't you?'

'I don't know.'

'Oh, and he also wanted to remind me about a party tonight at Malcolm Lanyon's place.'

'The lawyer?'

'That's him.' Rebus had Holmes at a disadvantage, and knew it. 'I hope you've been busy while I've been having a chinwag.'

'Eh?'

'Hydes and Jekylls, Brian. I asked you for addresses.'

'I've got the list here. Not too long, thank the Lord. I suppose I'm going to be Shoeleather on this one?'

Rebus looked flabbergasted. 'Not at all. You've got better things to be doing with your time. No, I think this time the shoeleather ought to be mine.'

'But . . . with respect, shouldn't you be keeping out of things?'

'With respect, Brian, that's none of your bloody business.'

From home, Rebus tried phoning Gill, but she couldn't be reached. Keeping out of things, no doubt. She had been quiet during the drive home last night, and hadn't invited him in. Fair enough, he supposed. He wasn't about to take advantage. . . . So why was he trying to telephone her? Of course he was trying to take advantage! He wanted her back.

He tidied the living room, did some washing up, and took a binbag's-worth of dirty washing to the local laundrette for a service wash. The attendant, Mrs Mackay, was full of outrage about Calum McCallum.

'Yon's a celebrity and a'. They should ken better.'

Rebus smiled and nodded agreement.

Back in the flat, he sat down and picked up a book, knowing he wouldn't be able to keep his mind on it. He didn't want Hyde to win, and, kept away from the case, that's exactly what would happen. He took the slip of paper from his pocket. There were no people with the surname Jekyll in the Lothians, and a scant dozen with the surname Hyde. At least, those were the ones he could be sure about. What if Hyde possessed an unlisted number? He'd get Brian Holmes to check the possibility.

He reached for the telephone and was halfway through the number before he realised he was calling Gill's office. He punched in the rest of the number. What the hell, she wouldn't be there anyway.

'Hello?'

It was Gill Templer's voice, sounding as unflappable as ever. Yes, but that sort of trick was easy by phone. All the oldest tricks were.

'It's John.'

'Hello there. Thanks for the lift home.'

'How are you?'

'I'm fine, honestly. I just feel a bit . . . I don't know, confused doesn't seem to cover it. I feel as though I've been conned. That's as near as I can get to an explanation.'

'Are you going to see him?'

'What? In Fife? No, I don't think so. It's not that I couldn't face *him*. I *want* to see *him*. It's the thought of walking into the station with everyone knowing who I was, why I was there.'

'I'd go with you, Gill, if you wanted.'

'Thanks, John. Maybe in a day or two. But not yet.'

'Understood.' He became aware that he was gripping the receiver too hard, that his fingers were hurting. God, this was hurting him all over. Did she have any inkling of his feelings right this minute? He was sure he couldn't put them into words. The words hadn't been coined. He felt so close to her, and yet so far away, like a schoolkid who'd lost his first girlfriend.

'Thanks for phoning, John. I appreciate it. But I'd better be getting –'

'Oh, right, right you are. Well, you've got my number, Gill. Take care.'

'Bye, J –'

He broke the connection. Don't crowd her, John, he was thinking. That's how you lost her the first time. Don't go making any assumptions. She doesn't like that. Give her space. Maybe he had made a mistake phoning in the first place. Hell and damn.

With respect.

That little weasel called James. That little toerag. He'd rip his head from his shoulders when he got him. He wondered how much Hyde had paid the kid. Considerably more than two ten-pound notes, that was for sure.

The telephone rang.

'Rebus here.'

'John? It's Gill again. I've just heard the news. Why didn't you tell me?'

'Tell you what?' He affected indifference, knowing she'd see through it immediately.

'About this complaint against you.'

'Oh, that. Come on, Gill, you know this sort of thing happens from time to time.'

'Yes, but why didn't you *say*? Why did you let me prattle on like that?'

'You weren't prattling.'

'Dammit!' She was almost in tears now. 'Why do you always have to try and hide things from me like that? What's the matter with you?'

He was about to explain, when the line went dead. He stared at the receiver dumbly, wondering just *why* he hadn't told her in the first place. Because she had worries of her own? Because he was embarrassed? Because he hadn't wanted the pity of a vulnerable woman? There were reasons enough.

Weren't there?

Of course there were. It was just that none of them seemed to make him feel any better. *Why do you always have to try and hide things from me?* There was that word again: hide. A verb, an action, and a noun, a place. And a person. Faceless, but Rebus was beginning to know him so well. The adversary was cunning, there was no doubting that. But he couldn't hope to tie up all the loose threads the way he'd tied up Ronnie and Carew, the way he was trying to tie up John Rebus.

The telephone rang again.

'Rebus here.'

'It's Superintendent Watson. I'm glad I caught you at home.'

Because, Rebus added silently, it means I'm not out on the street causing trouble for you.

'Yes, sir. Any problem?'

'Quite the reverse. They're still questioning this male prostitute. Shouldn't be too long now. But meantime, the reason I called is because I've been on to the casino.'

'Casino, sir?'

'You know, Finlay's.'

'Oh, yes.'

'And they say that you'll be welcome there anytime, should you wish to pop in. You've just to mention Finlay Andrews' name, and that's your ticket.'

'Right, sir. Well, thanks for that.'

'My pleasure, John. Shame you're having to take it easy, what with this suicide business and all. The press are all over it, sniffing around for any little piece of dirt they can find. What a job, eh?'

'Yes, sir.'

'McCall's fielding their questions. I just hope he doesn't appear on the box. Not exactly photogenic, is he?'

Watson made this sound like Rebus's fault, and Rebus was on the point of apologising when the Superintendent placed a hand over the mouthpiece at his end, while he had a few words with someone. And when he came on again it was to say a hasty goodbye.

'Press conference apparently,' he said. And that was that.

Rebus stared at the receiver for a full minute. If there were to be any more calls, let them come now. They didn't. He threw the instrument onto the floor, where it landed heavily. Secretly, he was hoping to break it one of these days, so he could go back to an old-style handset. But the blasted thing seemed tougher than it looked.

He was opening the book when the door-knocker sounded. Tappity tap tap. A business call then, and not Mrs Cochrane wondering why he hadn't washed the communal stairwell yet.

It was Brian Holmes.

'Can I come in?'

'I suppose so.' Rebus felt no real enthusiasm, but left the door open for the young detective to follow him through to the living room if he so desired. He so desired, following Rebus with mock heartiness.

'I was just looking at a flat near Tollcross, and thought I'd –'

'Skip the excuses, Brian. You're checking up on me. Sit down and tell me what's been happening in my absence.' Rebus checked his watch while Holmes seated himself. 'An absence, for the record, of just under two hours.'

'Ach, I was concerned, that's all.'

Rebus stared at him. Simple, direct, and to the point. Maybe Rebus could learn something from Holmes after all.

'It's not Farmer's orders then?'

'Not at all. And as it happens, I *did* have a flat to look at.'

'What was it like?'

'Ghastly beyond speech. Cooker in the living room, shower in a wee cupboard. No bath, no kitchen.'

'How much did they want for it? No, on second thoughts don't tell me. It would just depress me.'

'It certainly depressed me.'

'You can always make an offer on this place when they throw me inside for corrupting a minor.'

Holmes looked up, saw that Rebus was smiling, and gave a relieved grin.

'The guy's story's already coming apart at the seams.'

'Did you ever doubt it?'

'Of course not. Anyway, I thought these might cheer you up.' Holmes brandished a large manilla envelope, which had been discreetly tucked inside his cord jacket. Rebus hadn't seen this cord jacket before, and supposed it to be the Detective Constable's flat-buying uniform.

'What are they?' said Rebus, accepting the packet.

'Pics. Last night's raid. Thought you might be interested.'

Rebus opened the envelope and withdrew a set of ten-by-eight black and whites. They showed the more or less blurred shapes of men scrambling across waste ground. What light there was had about it a halogen starkness, sending up huge black shadows and capturing some faces in chalky states of shock and surprise.

'Where did you get these?'

'That DS Hendry sent them across with a note sympathising over Nell. He thought these might cheer me up.'

'I told you he was a good bloke. Any idea which one of these goons is the DJ?'

Holmes leapt from his seat and crouched beside Rebus, who was holding a photograph at the ready.

'No,' Holmes said, 'there's a better shot of him.' He thumbed through the set until he found the picture he was looking for. 'Here we are. That one there. That's McCallum.'

Rebus studied the fuzzy semblance before him. The look of fear, so distinct against the blurred face, could have been drawn by a child. Wide eyes and a mouth puckered into an 'O', arms suspended as though between rapid flight and final surrender.

Rebus smiled a smile that reached all the way up to his eyes.

'You're sure this is him?'

'One of the PCs at the station recognised him. He said he once got McCallum to sign an autograph for him.'

'I'm impressed. Shouldn't think he'll be signing too many more though. Where are they holding him?'

'Everybody they arrested has gone to Dunfermline nick'.

'That's nice for them. By the by, did they nab the ringleaders?'

'Each and every one. Including Brightman. He was the boss.'

'Davy Brightman? The scrappie?'

'That's him.'

'I played against that bugger at football a couple of times when I was at school. He played left back for his team when I was on the wing for ours. He gave me a good studding one match.'

'Revenge is sweet,' said Holmes.

'It is that, Brian.' Rebus was studying the photograph again. 'It is that.'

'Actually, a couple of the punters did scarper apparently, but they're all on film. The camera never lies, eh, sir?'

Rebus began to sift through the other pictures. 'A powerful tool, the camera,' he said. His face suddenly changed.

'Sir? Are you all right?'

Rebus's voice was reduced to a whisper. 'I've just had a revelation, Brian. A whatsit . . .? epiphany, is it?'

'No idea, sir.' Holmes was sure now that something inside his superior had snapped.

'Epiphany, yes. I *know* where this has all been leading, Brian. I'm sure of it. That bastard on Calton Hill said something about pictures, some pictures everybody was interested in. They're *Ronnie's* pictures.'

'What? The ones in his bedroom?'

'No, not those.'

'The ones at Hutton's studio then?'

'Not quite. No, I don't know exactly *where* these particular pictures are, but I've got a bloody good idea. "Hide" can be a noun, Brian. Come on.'

'Where?' Holmes watched as Rebus sprang from his chair, heading for the door. He started to collect the photographs, which Rebus had let fall from his hands.

'Never mind those,' Rebus ordered, slipping on a jacket.

'But where the hell are we going?'

'You just answered your own question,' Rebus said, turning back to grin at Holmes. 'That's exactly where we're going.'

'But *where?*'

'To hell, of course. Come on.'

It was turning cold. The sun had just about tired itself out, and was retiring from the contest. The clouds were sticking-plaster pink. Two great final sunbeams shone down like torchlight upon Pilmuir, and picked out just the one building, leaving the other houses in the street untouched. Rebus sucked in breath. He had to admit, it was quite a sight.

'Like the stable at Bethlehem,' said Holmes.

'A damned queer stable,' Rebus retorted. 'God's got a funny sense of humour if this is His idea of a joke.'

'You did say we were going to hell.'

'I wasn't expecting Cecil B. DeMille to be in on it though. What's going on there?'

Almost hidden by the day's last gasp of sunlight, a van and a hire skip were parked directly in front of Ronnie's house.

'The council?' Holmes suggested. 'Probably cleaning the place up.'

'Why, in God's name?'

'There's plenty that need housing,' Holmes replied. Rebus wasn't listening. As the car pulled to a stop, he was out and walking briskly towards the skip. It was filling up with the detritus of the squat's interior. There were sounds of hammering from within. In the back of the van, a workman supped from a plastic cup, his thermos clutched in his other hand.

'Who's in charge here?' Rebus demanded.

The workman blew on the contents of his cup, then took another swig before replying. 'Me, I suppose.' His eyes were wary. He could smell authority a mile off. 'This is a legitimate tea-break.'

'Never mind that. What's going on?'

'Who wants to know.'

'CID wants to know.'

He looked hard at Rebus's harder face, and made up his mind instantly. 'Well, we got word to come and clean this place up. Make it habitable.'

'On whose orders?'

'I don't know. Somebody's. We just take the chitty and go do the job.'

'Right.' Rebus had turned from the man and was walking up the path to the front door. Holmes, having smiled apologetically at the foreman, followed. In the living room, two workmen in overalls and thick red rubber gloves were whitewashing the walls. Charlie's pentagram had already been covered, its outline barely visible through the drying layer of paint. The men looked towards Rebus, then to the wall.

'We'll cover it up next coat,' said one. 'Don't worry yourself about that.'

Rebus stared at the man, then marched past Holmes out of the room. He started to climb the stairs, and turned into Ronnie's bedroom. Another workman, much younger than the two downstairs, was gathering Ronnie's few belongings together into a large black plastic bag. As Rebus entered the room, the boy was caught, frozen, stuffing one of the paperbacks into the pocket of his overalls.

Rebus pointed to the book.

'There's a next of kin, son. Put it in the bag with the rest.'

Something about his tone persuaded the teenager to obey.

'Come across anything else interesting?' Rebus asked now, hands in pockets, approaching the teenager.

'Nothing,' the boy said, guiltily.

'In particular,' Rebus went on, as though the teenager had not spoken, 'photographs. Maybe just a few, maybe a whole packet. Hmm?'

'No. Nothing like that.'

'You're sure?'

'Sure.'

'Right. Get down to the van and bring up a crowbar or something. I want these floorboards up.'

'Eh?'

'You heard me, son. Do it.'

Holmes just stood and watched in silent appreciation. Rebus seemed to have grown in physical stature, becoming broader, taller. Holmes couldn't quite fathom the trick: maybe it had something to do with the hands in the pockets, the way the elbows jarred outwards, lending apparent substance to the frame. Whatever it was, it worked. The young workman stumbled out of the door and down the stairs.

'You're sure they'll be here?' said Holmes quietly. He tried to keep his tone level, not wishing to sound too sceptical. But Rebus was way past that stage. In Rebus's mind, the photographs were already in his hand.

'I'm certain, Brian. I can *smell* them.'

'You're sure that's not just the bathroom?'

Rebus turned and looked at him, as though seeing him for the very first time. 'You might have a point, Brian. You just might.'

Holmes followed Rebus to the bathroom. As Rebus kicked open the door, the stench embraced both men, arching them forward in a convulsive fit of gagging. Rebus brought a handkerchief from his pocket, pushed it to his face, and leaned towards the door handle, pulling the door shut again.

'I'd forgotten about that place,' he said. Then: 'Wait here.'

He returned with the foreman, a plastic dustbin, a shovel, and three small white face-masks, one of which he handed to Holmes. An elasticated band held the cardboard snout in place, and Holmes breathed deeply, testing the apparatus. He was just about to say something about the smell still being noticeable, when Rebus toed open the door again, and, as the foreman angled an industrial lamp into the bathroom, walked over the threshold.

Rebus pulled the dustbin to the rim of the bath and left it there, gesturing for the lamp to be shone into the bath itself. Holmes nearly fell backwards out of the room. A fat rat, caught in the act of feasting upon the rotten contents of the bath, squealed, red eyes burning directly into the light. Rebus swung the shovel down and cut the animal in two neat halves. Holmes spun from the room and, lifting the mask, retched against the damp wall. He tried taking gulps of air, but the smell was overpowering, the nausea returning in quickening floods.

Back inside the room, the foreman and Rebus exchanged a smile which wrinkled their eyes above the face-masks. They had seen worse than this – much worse – in their time. Then, neither man naive enough to want to linger, they set to work, the foreman holding the lamp while Rebus shovelled the contents of the bath slowly into the dustbin. The mess of raw sewage ran slickly from the shovel, spattering Rebus's shirt and trousers. He ignored it, ignored everything but the task at hand. He had done dirtier jobs in the Army, dirtier jobs by far during his failed training in the SAS. This was routine. And at least here there was some purpose to the task, some end in view.

Or so he hoped.

Holmes meantime was wiping his moist eyes with the back of his hand. Through the open door he could see the progress being made, eerie shadows cast across the wall and ceiling by the lamp, as one silhouette shovelled shit into a bin, filling it noisily. It was like a scene from some latter-day *Inferno*, lacking only the devils to goad the damned workers on. But these men looked, if not happy in their work, then at least ... well, *professional* sprang to mind. Dear God, all he wanted was a flat to call his own, and the occasional holiday, and a decent car. And Nell, of course. This would make a funny story for her one day.

But the last thing he felt like doing was smiling.

Then he heard the cackle of laughter, and, looking around him, it took several moments to realise that it was coming from the bathroom, that it was John Rebus's laugh, and that Rebus was dipping his hand into the mess, drawing it out again with something clinging to it. Holmes didn't even notice the thick rubberised gloves which protected Rebus up to his elbows. He simply turned and walked downstairs on brittle legs.

'Got you!' Rebus cried.

'There's a hose outside,' the foreman said.

'Lead on,' said Rebus, shaking the packet free of some of its clots. 'Lead on, Macduff.'

'The name's MacBeth,' the foreman called back, heading for the stairway.

In the cool, fresh air, they hosed down the package, standing it up against the front wall of the house as they did so. Rebus peered at it closely. A red plastic bag, like the carrier from a record shop, had been wrapped around some cloth, a shirt or the like. The whole had been stuck down with a roll's worth of sellotape, then tied with string, knotted resolutely in the middle.

'Clever little tyke, weren't you, Ronnie?' Rebus said to himself as he picked up the package. 'Cleverer than they could ever have thought.'

At the van, he threw down the rubber gloves, shook the foreman's hand, and exchanged the names of local watering holes with him, making promises of a drink, a nippy sweetie some night in the future. Then he headed for the car, Holmes following sheepishly. All the way back to Rebus's flat, Holmes didn't once dare to suggest that they open a window and let in some fresh air.

Rebus was like a child on a birthday morning who has just found his surprise. He clutched the parcel to him, staining his shirt even more, yet seemed loath to open it. Now that he possessed it, he could forestall the revelation. It would happen; that was all that mattered.

When they arrived at the flat, however, Rebus's mood changed again, and he dashed to the kitchen for some scissors. Holmes meantime made his excuses and went to the bathroom, scrubbing his hands, bared arms, and face thoroughly. His scalp itched, and he wished he could throw himself into the shower and stand beneath it for an hour or two.

As he was coming out of the bathroom, he heard the sound from the kitchen. It was the antithesis of the laughter he had heard earlier, a kind of exasperated wail. He walked quickly to the kitchen, and saw Rebus standing there, head bowed, hands held out against the worktop as though supporting himself. The packet was open in front of him.

'John? What's wrong?'

Rebus's voice was soft, suddenly tired. 'They're just pictures of a bloody boxing match. That's all they are. Just bloody sports photos.'

Holmes came forward slowly, fearing noise and movement might crack Rebus completely.

'Maybe,' he suggested, peering over Rebus's slumped shoulder, 'maybe there's somebody in the crowd. In the audience. This Hyde could be one of the spectators.'

'The spectators are just a blur. Take a look.'

Holmes did. There were twelve or so photographs. Two feather-weights, no love lost, were slugging it out. There was nothing subtle about the contest, but nothing unusual about it either.

'Maybe it's Hyde's boxing club.'

'Maybe,' said Rebus, not really caring any more. He had been so sure that he would find the pictures, and so sure that they would prove the final, clinching piece of the puzzle. Why were they hidden away so carefully, so cunningly? And so well protected. There had to be a reason.

'Maybe,' said Holmes, who was becoming irritating again, 'maybe there's something we're missing. The cloth they're wrapped in, the envelope . . .?'

'Don't be so bloody thick, Holmes!' Rebus slammed a hand against the worktop, and immediately calmed. 'Sorry. Jesus, sorry.'

'That's all right,' Holmes said coldly. 'I'll make some coffee or something. Then why don't we take a *good* look at those snaps? Eh?'

'Yes,' Rebus said, pushing himself upright. 'Good idea.' He headed towards the door. 'I'm going to take a shower.' He turned and smiled at Holmes. 'I must stink to high heaven.'

'A very agricultural smell, sir,' Holmes said, smiling also. They laughed at the shared reference to Farmer Watson. Then Rebus went to have his shower, and Holmes made the coffee, jealous of the sounds from the bathroom. He took another look at the photographs, a close look, hoping for something, something he could use to impress Rebus with, to cheer Rebus up just a little.

The boxers were young, photographed from ringside or near as dammit. But the photographer – Ronnie McGrath presumably – hadn't used a flash, depending instead upon the smoky lights above the ring. Consequently, neither boxers nor audience were recognisable as distinct individuals. Their faces were grainy, the outlines of the combatants themselves blurred with sluggish movement. Why hadn't the photographer used a flash?

In one photo, the right-hand side of the frame was dark, cut off at an angle by something getting in the way of the lens. What? A passing spectator? Somebody's jacket?

It struck Holmes with sudden clarity: the *photographer's* jacket had got in the way, and it had done so because the photos were being taken surreptitiously, from beneath a jacket. This would explain the poor quality of the photos, and the uneven angles of most of them. So there *had* to be a reason for them, and they had to be the clue Rebus was seeking. All they had to do now was discover just *what* kind of clue.

The shower became a drip, then died altogether. A few moments later, Rebus appeared clad only in a towel, holding it around his gut as he went to the bedroom to change. He was balancing with one foot poised above a trouser leg when Holmes burst in, waving the photographs.

'I think I've got it!' he exclaimed. Rebus looked up, surprised, then slipped on the trousers.

'Yes,' he said. 'I think I've worked it out, too. It came to me just now in the shower.'

'Oh.'

'So fetch us a coffee,' said Rebus, 'and let's go into the living room and see if we've worked out the same thing. Okay?'

'Right,' said Holmes, wondering again why it was that he'd joined the police when there were so many more rewarding careers out there to be had.

When he arrived in the living room, carrying the two mugs of coffee, Rebus was pacing up and down, his telephone handset wedged against his ear.

'Right,' he was saying. 'I'll wait. No, no, I won't call back. I said I'll *wait*. Thank you.'

Taking the coffee from Holmes, he rolled his eyes, exhibiting disbelief at the stupidity of the person on the other end of the telephone.

'Who is it?' Holmes mouthed silently.

'The council,' said Rebus aloud. 'I got a name and an extension number from Andrew.'

'Who's Andrew?'

'Andrew MacBeth, the foreman. I want to find out who authorised the cleaning out of the house. A bit of a coincidence that, don't you think? Cleaning it out just as we were about to do a bit of poking around.' He turned his attention to the handset. 'Yes? That's right. Oh, I see.' He looked at Holmes, his eyes betraying nothing. 'How might that have happened?' He listened again. 'Yes, I see. Oh yes, I agree, it does seem a bit curious. Still, these things happen, eh? Roll on computerisation. Thanks for your help anyway.'

He pressed a button, killing the connection. 'You probably caught the gist of that.'

'They've no record of who authorised the clear-out?'

'Quite so, Brian. The documentation is all in order, but for the little matter of a signature. They can't understand it.'

'Any handwriting to go on?'

'The chitty Andrew showed me was typed.'

'So, what are you saying?'

'That Mr Hyde seems to have friends everywhere. In the council, for starters, but probably in the police, too. Not to mention several less savoury institutions.'

'What now?'

'Those pictures. What else is there to go on?'

They studied each frame closely, taking their time, pointing out this or that blur or detail, trying ideas out on one another. It was a painstaking business. And throughout Rebus was muttering to himself about Ronnie McGrath's final words to Tracy, about how they had been the key throughout. The triple meaning: make yourself scarce, beware a man called Hyde, and I've hidden something away. So clever. So compact. Almost *too* clever for Ronnie. Maybe the meanings had been there without his realising it himself. . . .

At the end of ninety minutes, Rebus threw the final photograph down onto the floor. Holmes was half lying along the settee, rubbing his forehead with one hand as he held up one of the pictures in the other, his eyes refusing to focus any longer.

'It's no use, Brian. No use at all. I can't make sense out of any of them, can you?'

'Not a lot,' Holmes admitted. 'But I take it Hyde wanted – wants – these pictures badly.'

'Meaning?'

'Meaning he knows they exist, but he doesn't know how crude they are. He thinks they show something they don't.'

'Yes, but what? I'll tell you something, Ronnie McGrath had bruises on his body the night he died.'

'Not surprising when you remember that someone dragged his body down the stairs.'

'No, he was already dead then. This was before. His brother noticed, Tracy noticed, but nobody ever asked. Somebody said something to me about rough trade.' He pointed towards the scattering of snapshots. 'Maybe this is what they meant.'

'A boxing match?'

'An illegal bout. Two unmatched kids knocking blue hell out of one another.'

'For what?'

Rebus stared at the wall, looking for the word he lacked. Then he turned to Holmes.

'The same reason men set up dog fights. For kicks.'

'It all sounds incredible.'

'Maybe it *is* incredible. The way my mind is just now, I could believe bombers have been found on the moon.' He stretched. 'What time is it?'

'Nearly eight. Aren't you supposed to be going to Malcolm Lanyon's party?'

'Jesus!' Rebus sprang to his feet. 'I'm late. I forgot all about it.'

'Well, I'll leave you to get ready. There's not much we can do about this.' Holmes gestured towards the photographs. 'I should visit Nell anyway.'

'Yes, yes, off you go, Brian.' Rebus paused. 'And thanks.'

Holmes smiled and shrugged his shoulders.

'One thing,' Rebus began.

'Yes?'

'I don't have a clean jacket. Can I borrow yours?'

It wasn't a great fit, the sleeves being slightly too long, the chest too small, but it wasn't bad either. Rebus tried to seem casual about it all as he stood on Malcolm Lanyon's doorstep. The door was opened by the same stunning Oriental who had been by Lanyon's side at The Eyrie. She was dressed in a low-cut black dress which barely reached down to her upper thighs. She smiled at Rebus, recognising him, or at least pretending to do so.

'Come in.'

'I hope I'm not late.'

'Not at all. Malcolm's parties aren't run by the clock. People come and go as they please.' Her voice had a cool but not unpleasant edge to it. Looking past her, Rebus was relieved to see several male guests wearing lounge suits, and some wearing sports jackets. Lanyon's personal (Rebus wondered just *how* personal) assistant led him into the dining room, where a barman stood behind a table laden with bottles and glasses.

The doorbell rang again. Fingers touched Rebus's shoulder. 'If you'll excuse me,' she said.

'Of course,' said Rebus. He turned towards the barman. 'Gin and tonic,' he said. Then he turned again to watch her pass through the large hallway towards the main door.

'Hello, John.' A much firmer hand slapped Rebus's shoulder. It belonged to Tommy McCall.

'Hello, Tommy.' Rebus accepted a drink from the barman, and McCall handed over his own empty glass for a refill.

'Glad you could make it. Of course, it's not quite as lively as usual tonight. Everyone's a bit subdued.'

'Subdued?' It was true, the conversations around them were muted. Then Rebus noticed a few black ties.

'I only came along because I thought James would have wanted it that way.'

'Of course,' Rebus said, nodding. He'd forgotten all about James Carew's suicide. Christ, it had only happened this morning! It seemed like a lifetime ago. And all these people had been Carew's friends or acquaintances. Rebus's nostrils twitched.

'Had he seemed depressed lately?' he asked.

'Not especially. He'd just bought himself that car, remember. Hardly the act of a depressed man!'

'I suppose not. Did you know him well?'

'I don't think any of us knew him well. He kept himself pretty much to himself. And of course he spent a lot of time away from town, sometimes on business, sometimes staying on his estate.'

'He wasn't married, was he?'

Tommy McCall stared at him, then took a large mouthful of whisky. 'No,' he said. 'I don't believe he ever was. It's a blessing in a way.'

'Yes, I see what you mean,' said Rebus, feeling the gin easing itself into his system. 'But I still don't understand why he would do it.'

'It's always the quiet ones though, isn't it? Malcolm was just saying that a few minutes ago.'

Rebus looked around them. 'I haven't seen our host yet.'

'I think he's in the lounge. Shall I give you the tour?'

'Yes, why not?'

'It's quite a place.' McCall turned to Rebus. 'Shall we start upstairs in the billiards room, or downstairs at the swimming pool?'

Rebus laughed and shook his empty glass. 'I think the first place to visit is the bar, don't you?'

The house was stunning, there was no other word for it. Rebus thought briefly of poor Brian Holmes, and smiled. You and me both, kid. The guests were nice, too. He recognised some of them by face, some by name, a few by reputation, and many by the titles of the companies they headed. But of the host there was no sign, though everyone claimed to have spoken with him 'earlier in the evening'.

Later, as Tommy McCall was becoming noisy and inebriated, Rebus, by no means on his steadiest legs himself, decided on another tour of the house. But alone this time. There was a library on the first floor, which had received cursory attention on the first circuit. But there was a working desk in there, and Rebus was keen to take a closer look. On the landing, he glanced around him, but everyone seemed to be downstairs. A few guests had even donned swimsuits, and were lounging by (or in) the twenty-foot-long heated pool in the basement.

He turned the heavy brass handle and slipped into the dimly lit library. In here there was a smell of old leather, a smell which took Rebus back to past decades – the 'twenties, say, or perhaps the 'thirties. There was a lamp on the desktop, illuminating some papers there. Rebus was at the desk before he realised something: the lamp had not been lit on his first visit here. He turned and saw Lanyon, standing against the far wall with his arms folded, grinning.

'Inspector,' he said, his voice as rich as his tailoring. 'What an interesting jacket that is. Saiko told me you'd arrived.'

Lanyon walked forward slowly and extended a hand, which Rebus took. He returned the firm grip.

'I hope I'm not . . .' he began. 'I mean, it was kind of you. . . .'

'Good lord, not at all. Is the Superintendent coming?'

Rebus shrugged his shoulders, feeling the jacket tight across his back.

'No, well, never mind. I see that like me you are a studious man.' Lanyon surveyed the shelves of books. 'This is my favourite room in the whole house. I don't know why I bother holding parties. It is expected, I suppose, and that's why I do it. Also of course it is interesting to note the various permutations, who's talking with whom, whose hand just happened to squeeze whose arm a touch too tenderly. That sort of thing.'

'You won't see much from here,' Rebus said.

'But Saiko tells me. She's marvellous at catching that sort of thing, no matter how subtle people think they are being. For example, she told me about your jacket. Beige, she said, cord, neither matching the rest of your wardrobe nor quite fitting your figure. Therefore borrowed, am I right?'

Rebus applauded silently. 'Bravo,' he said. 'I suppose that's what makes you such a good lawyer.'

'No, years and years of study are what have made me a good lawyer. But to be a *known* lawyer, well, that demands a few simple party tricks, such as the one I've just shown you.'

Lanyon walked past Rebus and stopped at the writing desk. He sifted through the papers.

'Was there anything special you were interested in?'

'No,' said Rebus. 'Just this room.'

Lanyon glanced towards him, smiling, not quite believing. 'There are more interesting rooms in the house, but I keep those locked.'

'Oh?'

'One doesn't want *everyone* to know just what paintings one has collected for example.'

'Yes, I see.'

Lanyon sat at the desk now, and slipped on a pair of half-moon glasses. He seemed interested in the papers before him.

'I'm James Carew's executor,' he said. 'That's what I've been trying to sort out, who will benefit from his will.'

'A terrible business.'

Lanyon seemed not to understand. Then he nodded. 'Yes, yes, tragic.'

'I take it you were close to him?'

Lanyon smiled again, as though he knew this same question had been asked of several people at the party already. 'I knew him fairly well,' he said at last.

'Did you know he was homosexual?'

Rebus had been hoping for a response. There was none, and he cursed having played his trump card so soon in the game.

'Of course,' Lanyon said in the same level voice. He turned towards Rebus. 'I don't believe it's a crime.'

'That all depends, sir, as you should know.'

'What do you mean?'

'As a lawyer, you must know that there are still certain laws. . . .'

'Yes, yes, of course. But I hope you're not suggesting that James was involved in anything sordid.'

'Why do *you* think he killed himself, Mr Lanyon? I'd appreciate your professional opinion.'

'He was a friend. Professional opinions don't count.' Lanyon stared at the heavy curtains in front of his desk. 'I don't know why he committed suicide. I'm not sure we'll ever know.'

'I wouldn't bet on that, sir,' said Rebus, going to the door. He stopped, hand on the handle. 'I'd be interested to know who *will* benefit from the estate, when you've worked it all out of course.'

Lanyon was silent. Rebus opened the door, closed it behind him, and paused on the landing, breathing deeply. Not a bad performance, he thought to himself. At the very least it was worthy of a drink. And this time he would toast – in silence – the memory of James Carew.

Nursemaid was not his favourite occupation, but he'd known all along that it would come to this.

Tommy McCall was singing a rugby song in the back of the car, while Rebus waved a hasty goodbye to Saiko, who was standing on the doorstep. She even managed a smile. Well, after all he was doing her a favour in quietly removing the loud drunkard from the premises.

'Am I under arrest, John?' McCall yelled, interrupting his song.

'No, now shut up, for Christ's sake!'

Rebus got into the car and started the engine. He glanced back one last time and saw Lanyon join Saiko on the doorstep. She seemed to be filling him in on events, and he was nodding. It was the first Rebus had seen of him since their confrontation in the library. He released the handbrake, pulled out of the parking space, and drove off.

'Left here, then next right.'

Tommy McCall had had too much to drink, but his sense of direction seemed unimpaired. Yet Rebus had a strange feeling. . . .

'Along to the end of this road, and it's the last house on the corner.'

'But this isn't where you live,' Rebus protested.

'Quite correct, Inspector. This is where my brother lives. I thought we'd drop in for a nightcap.'

'Jesus, Tommy, you can't just –'

'Rubbish. He'll be delighted to see us.'

As Rebus pulled up in front of the house, he looked out of his side window and was relieved to see that Tony McCall's living room was still illuminated. Suddenly, Tommy's hand thrust past him and pushed down on the horn, sending a loud blare into the silent night. Rebus pushed the hand away, and Tommy fell back into his seat, but he'd done enough. The curtains twitched in the McCall living room, and a moment later a door to the side of the house opened and Tony McCall came out, glancing back nervously. Rebus wound down the window.

'John?' Tony McCall seemed anxious. 'What's the matter?'

But before Rebus could explain, Tommy was out of the car and hugging his brother.

'It's my fault, Tony. All mine. I just wanted to see you, that's all. Sorry though, sorry.'

Tony McCall took the situation in, glanced towards Rebus as if to say *I don't blame you*, then turned to his brother.

'Well, this is very thoughtful of you, Tommy. Long time no see. You'd better come in.'

Tommy McCall turned to Rebus. 'See? I told you there'd be a welcome waiting for us at Tony's house. Always a welcome at Tony's.'

'You'd better come in, too, John,' said Tony.

Rebus nodded unhappily.

Tony directed them through the hall and into the living room. The carpet was thick and yielding underfoot, the furnishings looking like a showroom display. Rebus was afraid to sit, for fear of denting one of the puffed-up cushions. Tommy, however, collapsed immediately into a chair.

'Where's the wee ones?' he said.

'In bed,' Tony answered, keeping his voice low.

'Ach, wake them up then. Tell them their Uncle Tommy's here.'

Tony ignored this. 'I'll put the kettle on,' he said.

Tommy's eyes were already closing, his arms slumped either side of him on the arms of the chair. While Tony was in the kitchen, Rebus studied the room. There were ornaments everywhere: along the length of the mantelpiece, covering the available surfaces of the large wall-unit, arranged on the surface of the coffee table. Small plaster figurines, shimmering glass creations, holiday souvenirs. The arms and backs of chairs and sofa were protected by antimacassars. The whole room was busy and ill at ease. Relaxation would be almost impossible. He began to understand now why Tony McCall had been out walking in Pilmuir on his day off.

A woman's head peered round the door. Its lips were thin and straight, eyes alert but dark. She was staring at the slumbering figure of Tommy McCall, but caught sight of Rebus and prepared a kind of smile. The door opened a little wider, showing that she was wearing a dressing gown. A hand clutched this tight around her throat as she began to speak.

'I'm Sheila, Tony's wife.'

'Yes, hello, John Rebus.' Rebus made to stand, but a nervous hand fluttered him back down.

'Oh yes,' she said, 'Tony's talked about you. You work together, don't you?'

'That's right.'

'Yes.' Her attention was wandering, and she turned her gaze back to Tommy McCall. Her voice became like damp wallpaper. 'Would you look at him. The successful brother. His own business, big house. Just look at him.' She seemed about to launch into a speech on social injustice, but was interrupted by her husband, who was now squeezing past her carrying a tray.

'No need for you to get up, love,' he said.

'I could hardly sleep through that horn blaring, could I?' Her eyes now were on the tray. 'You've forgotten the sugar,' she said critically.

'I don't take sugar,' Rebus said. Tony was pouring tea from the pot into two cups.

'Milk first, Tony, then tea,' she said, ignoring Rebus's remark.

'It doesn't make a blind bit of difference, Sheila,' said Tony. He handed a cup to Rebus.

'Thanks.'

She stood for a second or two watching the two men, then ran a hand down the front of her dressing gown.

'Right then,' she said. 'Good night.'

'Good night,' concurred Rebus.

'Try not to be too long, Tony.'

'Right, Sheila.'

They listened, sipping tea, as she climbed the stairs to her bedroom. Then Tony McCall exhaled.

'Sorry about that,' he said.

'What for?' said Rebus. 'If a couple of drunks had walked into *my* home at this time of night, you wouldn't *want* to hear the reception I'd give them! I thought she stayed remarkably calm.'

'Sheila's always remarkably calm. On the outside.'

Rebus nodded towards Tommy. 'What about him?'

'He'll be all right where he is. Let him sleep it off.'

'Are you sure? I can take him home if you –'

'No, no. Christ, he's my brother. I think a chair for the night is called for.' Tony looked across towards Tommy. 'Look at him. You wouldn't believe the tricks we got up to when we were kids. We had the neighbourhood terrified of what we'd do next. Chap-Door-Run, setting bonfires, putting the football through somebody's window. We were wild, I can tell you. Now I never see him unless he's like this.'

'You mean he's pulled this stunt before?'

'Once or twice. Turns up in a taxi, crashes out in the chair. When he wakes up the next morning, he can't believe where he is. Has breakfast, slips the kids a few quid, and he's off. Never phones or visits. Then one night we hear the taxi chugging outside, and there he is.'

'I didn't realise.'

'Ach, I don't know why I'm telling you, John. It's not your problem, after all.'

'I don't mind listening.'

But Tony McCall seemed reluctant to go further. 'How do you like this room?' he asked instead.

'It's nice,' Rebus lied. 'A lot of thought's gone into it.'

'Yes.' McCall sounded unconvinced. 'A lot of money, too. See those little glass bauble things? You wouldn't believe how much one of those can cost.'

'Really?'

McCall was examining the room as though he were the visitor. 'Welcome to my life,' he said at last. 'I think I'd rather have one of the cells down the station.' He got up suddenly and walked across to Tommy's chair, then crouched down in front of his brother, one of whose eyes was open but glazed with sleep. 'You bugger,' Tony McCall whispered. 'You bugger, you bugger.' And he bowed his head so as not to show the tears.

It was growing light as Rebus drove the four miles back to Marchmont. He stopped at an all night bakery and bought warm rolls and refrigerated milk. This was the time when he liked the city best, the peaceful camaraderie of early morning. He wondered why people couldn't be happy with their lot. *I've got everything I've never wanted and it isn't enough.* All he wanted now was sleep, and in his bed for a change rather than on the chair. He kept playing the scene over and over: Tommy McCall dead to the world, saliva on his chin, and Tony McCall crouched in front of him, body shaking with emotion. A brother was a terrible thing. He was a lifelong competitor, yet you couldn't hate him without hating yourself. And there were other pictures too: Malcolm Lanyon in his study, Saiko standing at the door, James Carew dead in his bed, Nell Stapleton's bruised face, Ronnie McGrath's battered torso, old Vanderhyde with his unseeing eyes, the fear in Calum McCallum's eyes, Tracy with her tiny fists. . . .

If I am the chief of sinners, I am the chief of sufferers also.

Carew had stolen that line from somewhere . . . but where? Who cares, John, who cares? It would just be another bloody thread, and there were far too many of those already, knotted into an impenetrable tangle. Get home, sleep, forget.

One thing was for sure: he'd have some wild dreams.

Saturday

Or, if you shall so prefer to choose, a new province of knowledge and new avenues to fame and power shall be laid open to you, here, in this room, upon the instant.

In fact, he didn't dream at all. And when he woke up, it was the weekend, the sun was shining, and his telephone was ringing.

'Hello?'

'John? It's Gill.'

'Oh, hello, Gill. How are you?'

'I'm fine. What about you?'

'Great.' This was not a lie. He hadn't slept so well in weeks, and there was not a trace of hangover within him.

'Sorry to ring so early. Any progress on the smear?'

'Smear?'

'The things that kid was saying about you.'

'Oh, that. No, I haven't heard anything yet.' He was thinking about lunch, about a picnic, about a drive in the country. 'Are you in Edinburgh?' he asked.

'No, Fife.'

'Fife? What are you doing there?'

'Calum's here, remember.'

'Of course I remember, but I thought you were steering clear of him?'

'He wanted to see me. Actually, that's why I'm calling.'

'Oh?' Rebus wrinkled his brow, curious.

'Calum wants to talk to you.'

'To *me*? Why?'

'He'll tell you that himself, I suppose. He just asked me to tell you.'

Rebus thought for a moment. 'Do you want me to talk to him?'

'Can't say I'm much bothered either way. I told him I'd pass on the message, and I told him it was the last favour he could expect from me.' Her voice was as slick and cool as a slate roof in the rain. Rebus felt himself sliding down that roof, wanting to please her, wanting to help. 'Oh yes,' she said, 'and he said that if you sounded dubious, I was to tell you it's to do with Hyde's.'

'Hydes?' Rebus stood up sharply.

'H-y-d-e-apostrophe-s.'

'Hyde's what?'

She laughed. 'I don't know, John. But it sounds as if it means *some*thing to you.'

'It does, Gill. Are you in Dunfermline?'

'Calling from the station's front desk.'

'Okay. I'll see you there in an hour.'

'Fine, John.' She sounded unconcerned. 'Bye.'

He cut the connection, put his jacket on, and left the flat. The traffic was busy towards Tollcross, busy all the way down Lothian Road and winding across Princes Street towards Queensferry Road. Since the deregulation of public transport, the centre of the city had become a black farce of buses: double deckers, single deckers, even mini-buses, all vying for custom. Locked behind two claret-coloured LRT double deckers and two green single deckers, Rebus began to lose his tiny cache of patience. He slammed his hand down hard on the horn and pulled out, revving past the line of stalled traffic. A motorcycle messenger, squeezing through between the two directions of slower traffic, had to swerve to avoid the imminent accident, and slewed against a Saab. Rebus knew he should stop. He kept on going.

If only he'd had one of those magnetic flashing sirens, the kind CID used on the roofs of their cars whenever they were late for dinner or an engagement. But all he had were his headlights – full-beam – and the horn. Having cleared the tailback, he eased his hand off the horn, switched off the lamps, and cruised into the outside lane of the widening road.

Despite a pause at the dreaded Barnton roundabout, he made good time to the Forth Road Bridge, paid the toll, and drove across, not too fast, wanting, as ever, to take in the view. Rosyth Naval Dockyard was below him on the left. A lot of his schoolfriends ('lot' being relative: he'd never made that many friends) had slipped easily into jobs at Rosyth, and were probably still there. It seemed to be about the only place in Fife where work was still available. The mines were closing with enforced regularity. Somewhere along the coast in the other direction, men were burrowing beneath the Forth, scooping out coal in a decreasingly profitable curve. . . .

Hyde! Calum McCallum knew something about Hyde! Knew, too, that Rebus was interested, so word must have got around. His foot pressed down further on the accelerator. McCallum would want a trade, of course: charges dropped, or somehow jigged into a shape less damning. Fine, fine, he'd promise him the sun and the moon and the stars.

Just so long as he knew. Knew who Hyde was; knew where Hyde was. Just so long as he knew. . . .

The main police station in Dunfermline was easy to find, situated just off a roundabout on the outskirts of the town. Gill was easy to find, too. She was sitting in her car in the spacious car park outside the station. Rebus parked next to her, got out of his car and into the passenger side of hers.

'Morning,' he said.

'Hello, John.'

'Are you okay?' This was, on reflection, perhaps the most unnecessary question he had ever posed. Her face had lost colour and substance, and her head seemed to be shrinking into her shoulders, while her hands gripped the steering wheel, fingernails rapping softly against the top of the dashboard.

'I'm fine,' she said, and they both smiled at the lie. 'I told them at the desk that you were coming.'

'Anything you want me to tell our friend?'

Her voice was resonant. 'Nothing.'

'Okay.'

Rebus pushed open the car door and closed it again, but softly, then he headed towards the station entrance.

She had wandered the hospital corridors for over an hour. It was visiting time, so no one much minded as she walked into this and that ward, passing the beds, smiling down occasionally on the sick old men and women who stared up at her with lonely eyes. She watched families decide who should and should not take turns at grandpa's bedside, there being two only at a time allowed. She was looking for one woman in particular, though she wasn't sure she would recognise her. All she had to go on was the fact that the librarian would have a broken nose.

Maybe she hadn't been kept in. Maybe she'd already gone home to her husband or boyfriend or whatever. Maybe Tracy would be better off waiting and going to the library again. Except that they'd be watching and waiting for her. The guard would know her. The librarian would know her.

But would *she* know the librarian?

A bell rang out, drilling into her the fact that visiting hours were coming to an end. She hurried to the next ward, wondering: what if the librarian's in a private room? Or in another hospital? Or. . . .

No! There she was! Tracy stopped dead, turned in a half-circle, and walked to the far end of the ward. Visitors were saying their goodbyes and take cares to the patients. Everybody looked relieved, both visitors and visited. She mingled with them as they put chairs back into stacks and donned coats, scarves, gloves. Then she paused and looked back towards the librarian's bed. There were flowers all around it, and the single visitor, a man, was leaning over the librarian to kiss her lingeringly on the forehead. The librarian squeezed the man's hand and. . . . And the man looked familiar to Tracy. She'd seen him before. . . . At the police station! He was some friend of Rebus's, and he was a policeman! She remembered him checking on her while she was being held in the cells.

Oh Jesus, she'd attacked a policeman's wife!

She wasn't sure now, wasn't sure at all. Why had she come? Could she go through with it now? She walked with one family out of the ward, then rested against the wall in the corridor outside. Could she? Yes, if her nerve held. Yes, she could.

She was pretending to examine a drinks vending machine when Holmes sauntered through the swinging ward doors and walked slowly down the corridor away from her. She waited a full two minutes, counting up to one hundred and twenty. He wasn't coming back. He hadn't forgotten anything. Tracy turned from the vending machine and made for the swing doors.

For her, visiting time was just beginning.

She hadn't even reached the bed when a young nurse stopped her. 'Visiting hour's finished now,' the nurse said.

Tracy tried to smile, tried to look normal; it wasn't easy for her, but lying was.

'I just lost my watch. I think I left it at my sister's bed.' She nodded in Nell's direction. Nell, hearing the conversation, had turned towards her. Her eyes opened wide as she recognised Tracy.

'Well, be as quick as you can, eh?' said the nurse, moving away. Tracy smiled at the nurse, and watched her push through the swing doors. Now there were only the patients in their beds, a sudden silence, and her. She approached Nell's bed.

'Hello,' she said. She looked at the chart attached to the end of the iron bedstead. 'Nell Stapleton,' she read.

'What do you want?' Nell's eyes showed no fear. Her voice was thin, coming from the back of her throat, her nose having no part in the process.

'I want to tell you something,' Tracy said. She came close to Nell, and crouched on the floor, so that she would be barely visible from the doors of the ward. She thought this made her look as though she were searching for a lost watch.

'Yes?'

Tracy smiled, finding Nell's imperfect voice amusing. She sounded like a puppet on a children's programme. The smile vanished quickly, and she blushed, remembering that the reason she was here was because *she* was responsible for this woman being here at all. The plasters across the nose, the bruising under the eyes: all her doing.

'I came to say I'm sorry. That's all, really. Just, I'm sorry.'

Nell's eyes were unblinking.

'And,' Tracy continued, 'well . . . nothing.'

'Tell me,' said Nell, but it was too much for her. She'd done most of the talking while Brian Holmes had been in, and her mouth was dry. She turned and reached for the jug of water on the small cupboard beside the bed.

'Here, I'll do that.' Tracy poured water into a plastic beaker, and handed it to Nell, who sipped, coating the inside of her mouth. 'Nice flowers,' said Tracy.

'From my boyfriend,' said Nell, between sips.

'Yes, I saw him leaving. He's a policeman, isn't he? I know he is, because I'm a friend of Inspector Rebus's.'

'Yes, I know.'

'You do?' Tracy seemed shocked. 'So you know who I am?'

'I know your name's Tracy, if that's what you mean.'

Tracy bit her bottom lip. Her face reddened again.

'It doesn't matter, does it?' Nell said.

'Oh no.' Tracy tried to sound nonchalant. 'It doesn't matter.'

'I was going to ask . . .'

'Yes?' Tracy seemed keen for a change of subject.

'What were you going to do in the library?'

This wasn't quite to Tracy's liking. She thought about it, shrugged, and said: 'I was going to find Ronnie's photographs.'

'Ronnie's photographs?' Nell perked up. What little Brian had said during visiting hour had been limited to the progress of Ronnie McGrath's case, and especially the discovery of some pictures at the dead boy's house. What was Tracy talking about?

'Yes,' she said. 'Ronnie hid them in the library.'

'What were they exactly? I mean, why did he need to hide them?'

Tracy shrugged. 'All he told me was that they were his life insurance policy. That's exactly what he said, "life insurance policy".'

'And where exactly did he hide them?'

'On the fifth floor, he said. Inside a bound volume of something called the *Edinburgh Review*. I think it's a magazine.'

'That's right,' said Nell, smiling, 'it is.'

Brian Holmes was made light-headed by Nell's telephone call. His first reaction, however, was pure shock, and he chastised her for being out of bed.

'I'm still in bed,' she said, her voice becoming indistinct in her excitement. 'They brought the payphone to my bedside. Now listen. . . .'

Thirty minutes later, he was being shown down an aisle on the fifth floor of Edinburgh University Library. The member of staff checked complicated decimal numbers exhibited at each stack, until, satisfied, she led him down one darkened row of large bound titles. At the end of the aisle, seated at a study desk by a large window, a student stared disinterestedly towards Holmes, a pencil crunching in his mouth. Holmes smiled sympathetically towards the student, who stared right through him.

'Here we are,' said the librarian. '*Edinburgh Review* and *New Edinburgh Review*. It becomes "New" in 1969, as you can see. Of course, we keep the earlier editions in a closed environment. If you want those years specifically, it will take a little time –'

'No, these are fine, really. These are just what I need. Thank you.'

The librarian bowed slightly, accepting his thanks. 'You *will* remember us all to Nell, won't you?' she said.

'I'll be talking to her later today. I won't forget.'

With another bow, the librarian turned and walked back to the end of the stack. She paused there, and pressed a switch. Strip lighting flickered above Holmes, and stayed on. He smiled his thanks, but she was gone, her rubber heels squeaking briskly towards the lift.

Holmes looked at the spines of the bound volumes. The collection was not complete, which meant that someone had borrowed some of the years. A stupid place to hide something. He picked up 1971–72, held its spine by the forefingers of both his right and left hands, and rocked it. No scraps of paper, no photographs were shaken free. He put the volume back on the shelf and selected its neighbour, shook it, then replaced it.

The student at the study desk was no longer looking through him. He was looking *at* him, and doing so as if Holmes were mad. Another volume yielded nothing, then another. Holmes began to fear the worst. He'd been hoping for something with which to surprise Rebus, something to tie up all the loose ends. He'd tried contacting the Inspector, but Rebus wasn't to be found, wasn't anywhere. He had vanished.

The photos made more noise than he'd expected as they slid from the sheaves and hit the polished floor, hit it with their glossy edges, producing a sharp crack. He bent and began to gather them up, while the student looked on in fascination. From what he could see of the images strewn across the floor, Holmes already felt disappointment curdling his elation. They were copies of the boxing match pictures, nothing more. There were no new prints, no revelations, no surprises.

Damn Ronnie McGrath for giving him hope. All they were was life insurance. On a life already forfeit.

He waited for the lift, but it was busy elsewhere, so he took the stairs, winding downwards steeply, and found himself on the ground floor, but in a part of the library he didn't know, a sort of antiquarian bookshop corridor, narrow, with mouldering books stacked up against both walls. He squeezed through, feeling a sudden chill he couldn't place, and found himself opening a door onto the main concourse. The librarian who had shown him around was back behind her desk. She saw him, and waved frantically. He obeyed the command and hurried forward. She picked up a telephone and pressed a button.

'Call for you,' she said, stretching across the desktop to hand him the receiver.

'Hello?' He was quizzical: who the hell knew he was here?

'Brian, where in God's name have you been?' It was Rebus, of course. 'I've been trying to find you everywhere. I'm at the hospital.'

Holmes's heart deflated within his chest. 'Nell?' he said, so dramatically that even the librarian's head shot up.

'What?' growled Rebus. 'No, no, Nell's fine. It's just that she told me where to find you. I'm phoning from the hospital, and it's costing me a fortune.' In confirmation, the pips came, and were followed by the chankling of coins in a slot. The connection was re-established.

'Nell's okay,' Brian told the librarian. She nodded, relieved, and turned back to her work.

'Of course she is,' said Rebus, having caught the words. 'Now listen, there are a few things I want you to do. Have you got a pen and paper?'

Brian found them on the desk. He smiled, remembering the first telephone conversation he'd ever had with John Rebus, so similar to this, a few things to be done. Christ, so much had been done since. . . .

'Got that?'

Holmes started. 'Sorry, sir,' he said. 'My mind was elsewhere. Could you repeat that?'

There was an audible sound of mixed anger and excitement from the receiver. Then Rebus started again, and this time Brian Holmes heard every word.

Tracy couldn't say why it was that she'd visited Nell Stapleton, or why she'd told Nell what she had. She felt some kind of bond, not merely because of what she'd done. There was something about Nell Stapleton, something wise and kind, something Tracy had lacked in her life until now. Maybe that's why she was finding it so hard to leave the hospital. She had walked the corridors, drunk two cups of coffee in a cafe across the road from the main building, wandered in and out of Casualty, X-Ray, even some clinic for diabetics. She'd tried to leave, had walked as far as the city's art college before turning round and retreading the two hundred paces to the hospital.

And she was entering the side gates when the men grabbed her.

'Hey!'

'If you'll just come with us, miss.'

They sounded like security men, policemen even, so she didn't resist. Maybe Nell Stapleton's boyfriend wanted to see her, to give her a good kicking. She didn't care. They were taking her towards the hospital entrance, so she didn't resist. Not until it was too late.

At the last moment, they stopped short, turned her, and pushed her into the back of an ambulance.

'What's –! Hey, come on!' The doors were closing, locking, leaving her alone in the hot, dim interior. She thumped on the doors, but the vehicle was already moving off. As it pulled away, she was thrown against the doors, then back onto the floor. When she had recovered herself, she saw that the ambulance was an old one, no longer used for its original purpose. Its insides had been gutted, making it merely a van. The windows had been boarded over, and a metal panel separated her from the driver. She clawed her way to this panel and began hitting it with her fists, teeth gritted, yelling from time to time as she

368

remembered that the two men who had grabbed her at the gates were the same two men who'd been following her that day on Princes Street, that day she'd run to John Rebus.

'Oh God,' she murmured, 'oh God, oh God.'

They'd found her at last.

The evening was sticky with heat, the streets quiet for a Saturday.

Rebus rang the doorbell and waited. While he waited, he looked to left and right. An immaculate double row of Georgian houses, stone frontages dulled black through time and car fumes. Some of the houses had been turned into offices for Writers to the Signet, chartered accountants, and small, anonymous finance businesses. But a few – a precious few – were still very comfortable and well-appointed homes for the wealthy and the industrious. Rebus had been to this street before, a long time ago now in his earliest CID days, investigating the death of a young girl. He didn't remember much about the case now. He was too busy getting ready for the evening's pleasures.

He tugged at the black bow tie around his throat. The whole outfit, dinner jacket, shirt, bow tie and patent shoes, had been hired earlier in the day from a shop on George Street. He felt like an idiot, but had to admit that, examining himself in his bathroom mirror, he looked pretty sharp. He wouldn't be too out of place in an establishment like Finlay's of Duke Terrace.

The door was opened by a beaming woman, young, dressed exquisitely, and greeting him as though wondering why he didn't come more often.

'Good evening,' she said. 'Will you come in?'

He would, he did. The entrance hall was subtle. Cream paint, deep pile carpeting, a scattering of chairs which might have been designed by Charles Rennie Mackintosh, high backs and looking extraordinarily uncomfortable to sit in.

'I see you're admiring our chairs,' the woman said.

'Yes,' Rebus answered, returning her smile. 'The name's Rebus, by the way. John Rebus.'

'Ah yes. Finlay told me you were expected. Well, as this is your first visit, would you like me to show you around?'

'Thank you.'

'But first, a drink, and the first drink is always on the house.'

Rebus tried not to be nosey, but he was a policeman after all, and not being nosey would have gone against all that he held most dear. So he asked a few questions of his hostess, whose name was Paulette, and pointed to this and that part of the gaming club, being shown the direction of the cellars ('Finlay has their contents insured for quarter of a million'), kitchen ('our chef is worth his weight in Beluga'), and guest bedrooms ('the judges are the worst, there are one or two who always end up sleeping here, too drunk to go home'). The lower ground floor housed the cellars and kitchen, while the ground floor comprised a quiet bar area, and the small restaurant, with cloakrooms and an office. On the first floor, up the carpeted staircase and past the collection of eighteenth- and nineteenth-century Scottish paintings by the likes of Jacob More and David Allan, was the main gaming area: roulette, blackjack, a few other tables for card games, and one table given over to dice. The players were businessmen, their bets discreet, nobody losing big or winning big. They held their chips close to them.

Paulette pointed out two closed rooms.

'Private rooms, for private games.'

'Of what?'

'Poker mainly. The serious players book them once a month or so. The games can go on all night.'

'Just like in the movies.'

'Yes,' she laughed. 'Just like the movies.'

The second floor consisted of the three guest bedrooms, again locked, and Finlay Andrews' own private suite.

'Off limits, of course,' Paulette said.

'Of course,' Rebus concurred, as they started downstairs again.

So this was it: Finlay's Club. Tonight was quiet. He had seen only two or three faces he recognised: an advocate, who did not acknowledge him, though they'd clashed before in court, a television presenter, whose dark tan looked fake, and Farmer Watson.

'Hello there, John.' Watson, stuffed into suit and dress shirt, looked like nothing more than a copper out of uniform. He was in the bar when Paulette and Rebus went back in, his hand closed around a glass of orange juice, trying to look comfortable but instead looking distinctly out of place.

'Sir.' Rebus had not for one moment imagined that Watson, despite the threat he had made earlier, would turn up here. He introduced Paulette, who apologised for not being around to greet him at the door.

Watson waved aside her apology, revolving his glass. 'I was well enough taken care of,' he said. They sat at a vacant table. The chairs here were comfortable and well padded, and Rebus felt himself relax. Watson, however, was looking around keenly.

'Finlay not here?' he asked.

'He's somewhere around,' said Paulette. 'Finlay's always around.'

Funny, thought Rebus, that they hadn't bumped into him on their tour.

'What's the place like then, John?' Watson asked.

'Impressive,' Rebus answered, accepting Paulette's smile like praise from a teacher to a doting pupil. 'Very impressive. It's much bigger than you'd think. Wait till you see upstairs.'

'And there's the extension, too,' said Watson.

'Oh yes, I'd forgotten.' Rebus turned to Paulette.

'That's right,' she said. 'We're building out from the back of the premises.'

'Building?' said Watson. 'I thought it was a fait accompli?'

'Oh no.' She smiled again. 'Finlay is very particular. The flooring wasn't quite right, so he had the workmen rip it all up and start again. Now we're waiting on some marble arriving from Italy.'

'That must be costing a few bob,' Watson said, nodding to himself.

Rebus wondered about the extension. Towards the back of the ground floor, past toilets, cloakroom, offices, walk-in cupboards, there must be another door, ostensibly the door to the back garden. But now the door to the extension, perhaps.

'Another drink, John?' Watson was already on his feet, pointing at Rebus's empty glass.

'Gin and fresh orange, please,' he said, handing over the glass.

'And for you, Paulette?'

'No, really.' She was rising from the chair. 'Work to do. Now that you've seen a bit of the club, I'd better get back to door duties. If you want to play upstairs, the office can supply chips. A few of the games accept cash, but not the most interesting ones.'

Another smile, and she was gone in a flurry of silk and a glimpse of black nylon. Watson saw Rebus watching her leave.

'At ease, Inspector,' he said, laughing to himself as he headed for the bar where the barman explained that if he wanted drinks, he only had to signal, and an order would be taken at the gentlemen's table and brought to them directly. Watson slumped back into his chair again.

'This is the life, eh, John?'

'Yes, sir. What's happening back at base?'

'You mean the little sodomite who made the complaint? He's buggered off. Disappeared. Gave us a false address, the works.'

'So I'm off the butcher's hook?'

'Just about.' Rebus was about to remonstrate. 'Give it a few more days, John, that's all I'm asking. Time for it to die a natural death.'

'You mean people are talking?'

'A few of the lads have had a laugh about it. I don't suppose you can blame them. In a day or so, there'll be something else for them to joke about, and it'll all be forgotten.'

'There's nothing *to* forget!'

'I know, I know. It's all some plot to keep you out of action, and this mysterious Mr Hyde's behind it all.'

Rebus stared at Watson, his lips clamped shut. He could yell, could scream and shout. He breathed hard instead, and snatched at the drink when the waiter placed the tray on the table. He'd taken two gulps before the waiter informed him that he was drinking the other gentleman's orange juice. His own gin and orange was the one still on the tray. Rebus reddened as Watson, laughing again, placed a five-pound note on the tray. The waiter coughed in embarrassment.

'Your drinks come to six pounds fifty, sir,' he told Watson.

'Ye gods!' Watson searched in his pocket for some change, found a crumpled pound note and some coins, and placed them on the tray.

'Thank you, sir.' The waiter lifted the tray and turned away before Watson had the chance to ask about any change that might be owing. He looked at Rebus, who was smiling now.

'Well,' Watson said, 'I mean, six pounds fifty! That would feed some families for a week.'

'This is the life,' Rebus said, throwing the Superintendent's words back at him.

'Yes, well said, John. I was in danger of forgetting there can be more to life than personal comfort. Tell me, which church do you attend?'

'Well, well. Come to take us all in, have you?' Both men turned at this new voice. It was Tommy McCall. Rebus checked his watch. Eight thirty. Tommy looked as though he'd been to a few pubs en route to the club. He sat down heavily in what had been Paulette's chair.

'What're you drinking?' He snapped his fingers, and the waiter, a frown on his face, came slowly towards the table.

'Sirs?'

Tommy McCall looked up at him. 'Hello, Simon. Same again for the constabulary, and I'll have the usual.'

Rebus watched the waiter as McCall's words sank in. That's right, son, Rebus thought to himself, we're the police. Now why should that fact frighten you so much? The waiter turned, seeming to read Rebus's mind, and headed stiffly back to the bar.

'So what brings you two here?' McCall was lighting a cigarette, glad to have found some company and ready to make a night of it.

'It was John's idea,' Watson said. 'He wanted to come, so I fixed it with Finlay, then reckoned I might as well come along, too.'

'Quite right.' McCall looked around him. 'Nobody much in tonight though, not yet leastways. The place is usually packed to the gunnels with faces you'd recognise, names you'd know like you know your own. This is tame tonight.'

He had offered round his pack of cigarettes, and Rebus had taken one, which he now lit, inhaling gratefully, regretting it immediately as the smoke mixed with the alcohol fumes in his chest. He needed to think fast and hard. Watson and now McCall: he had planned on dealing with neither.

'By the way, John,' Tommy McCall said, 'thanks for the lift last night.' His tone made the subtext clear to Rebus. 'Sorry if it was any trouble.'

'No trouble, Tommy. Did you sleep well?'

'I never have trouble sleeping.'

'Me neither,' interrupted Farmer Watson. 'The benefits of a clear conscience, eh?'

Tommy turned to Watson. 'Shame you couldn't get to Malcolm Lanyon's party. We had a pretty good time, didn't we, John?'

Tommy smiled across at Rebus, who smiled back. A group at the next table were laughing at some joke, the men drawing on thick cigars, the women playing with their wrist jewellery. McCall leaned across towards them, hoping perhaps to share in the joke, but his shining eyes and uneven smile kept him apart from them.

'Had many tonight, Tommy?' Rebus asked. McCall, hearing his name, turned back to Rebus and Watson.

'One or two,' he said. 'A couple of my trucks didn't deliver on time, drivers on the piss or something. Lost me two big contracts. Drowning my sorrows.'

'I'm sorry to hear that,' Watson said with sincerity. Rebus nodded agreement, but McCall shook his head theatrically.

'It's nothing,' he said. 'I'm thinking of selling the business anyway, retiring while I'm still young. Barbados, Spain, who knows. Buy a little villa.' His eyes narrowed, his voice dropping to a whisper. 'And guess who's interested in buying me out? You'll never guess in a million years. Finlay.'

'Finlay Andrews?'

'The same.' McCall sat back, drew on his cigarette, blinking into the smoke. 'Finlay Andrews.' He leaned forward again confidentially. 'He's got a finger in quite a few pies, you know. It's not just this place. He's got this and that directorship, shares here there and everywhere, you name it.'

'Your drinks.' The waiter's voice had more than a note of disapproval in it. He seemed to want to linger, even after McCall had pitched a ten-pound note onto the tray and waved him away.

'Aye,' McCall continued after the waiter had retreated. 'Fingers in plenty of pies. All strictly above board, mind. You'd have a hellish job proving otherwise.'

'And he wants to buy you out?' Rebus asked.

McCall shrugged. 'He's made a good price. Not a great price, but I won't starve.'

'Your change, sir.' It was the waiter again, his voice cold as a chisel. He held the salver out towards McCall, who stared up at him.

'I didn't want any change,' he explained. 'It was a tip. Still,' he winked at Rebus and Watson, scooping the coins from the tray, 'if you don't want it, son, I suppose I might as well have it back.'

'Thank you, sir.'

Rebus loved this. The waiter was giving McCall every kind of danger signal there was, but McCall was too drunk or too naive to notice. At the same time, Rebus was aware of complications which might be about to result from the presence of Superintendent Watson and Tommy McCall at Finlay's, on the night Finlay's erupted.

There was a sudden commotion from the entrance hall, raised voices, boisterous rather than angry. And Paulette's voice, too, pleading, then remonstrative. Rebus glanced at his watch again. Eight fifty. Right on time.

'What's going on?' Everybody in the bar was interested, and a few had risen from their seats to investigate. The barman pushed a button on the wall beside the optics, then made for the hall. Rebus followed. Just inside the front door Paulette was arguing with several men, dressed in business suits but far the worse for wear. One was telling her that she couldn't refuse him, because he was wearing a tie. Another explained that they were in town for the evening and had heard about the club from someone in a bar.

'Philip, his name was. He told us to say Philip had said it was okay and we could come in.'

'I'm sorry, gentlemen, but this is a *private* club.' The barman was joining in now, but his presence was unwanted.

'Talking to the lady here, pal, okay? All we want is a drink and maybe a wee flutter, isn't that right?'

Rebus watched as two more 'waiters', hard young men with angular faces, came quickly down the stairs from the first floor.

'Now look –'

'Just a wee flutter –'

'In town for the night –'

'I'm sorry –'

'Watch the jacket, pal –'

'Hey! –'

Neil McGrath struck the first blow, catching one of the heavies with a solid right to the gut, doubling the man over. People were gathering in the hallway now, leaving the bar and the restaurant untended. Rebus, still watching the fight, began to move backwards through the crowd, past the door to the bar, past the restaurant, towards the cloakroom, the toilets, the office door, and the door behind that.

'Tony! Is that you?' It had to happen. Tommy McCall had noticed his brother Tony as one of the apparent out-of-town drunks. Tony, his attention diverted, received a blow to the face which sent him flying back against the wall. 'That's my brother you're punching!' Tommy was in there now too, mixing it with the best of them. Constables Neil McGrath and Harry Todd were fit and healthy young men, and they were holding their own. But when they saw Superintendent Watson, they automatically froze, even though he could have no idea who they were. Each was caught with a sickening blow, which woke them to the fact that this was for real. They forgot about Watson and struck out for all they were worth.

Rebus noticed that one of the fighters was hanging back just a little, not really throwing himself into it. He stayed near the door, too, ready to flee when necessary, and he kept glancing towards the back of the hallway, where Rebus stood. Rebus waved an acknowledgment. Detective Constable Brian Holmes did not wave back. Then Rebus turned and faced the door at the end of the hallway, the door to the club's extension. He closed his eyes, screwed up his courage, made a fist of his right hand, and brought it flying up into his own face. Not full strength, some self-protection circuit wouldn't let him do that, but hard. He wondered how people managed to slit their wrists, then opened his watering eyes and checked his nose. There was blood smeared over his top lip, dripping from both nostrils. He let it drip, and hammered on the door.

Nothing. He hammered again. The noise of the fight was at its height now. *Come on, come on.* He pulled a handkerchief from his pocket and held it below his nostrils, catching droplets of brightest crimson. The door was unlocked from within. It opened a couple of inches and eyes peered out at Rebus.

'Yeah?'

Rebus pulled back a little so the man could see the commotion at the front door. The eyes opened wide with surprise, and the man glanced back at Rebus's bloody face before opening the door wider. The man was hefty, not old, but with hair unnaturally thin for his age. As if to compensate for this, he had a copious moustache. Rebus remembered Tracy's description of the man who had followed her the night she'd come to his flat. This man would fit that description.

'We need you out here,' Rebus said. 'Come on.'

The man paused, thinking it over. Rebus thought he was about to close the door again, and was getting ready to kick out with all his might, but the man pulled open the door and stepped out, passing Rebus. Rebus slapped the man's muscular back as he went.

The door was open. Rebus stepped through, sought the key, and locked it behind him. There were bolts top and bottom. He slid the top one across. Let nobody in, he was thinking, and nobody out. Then, and only then, did he look around him. He was at the top of a narrow flight of stairs, concrete, uncarpeted. Maybe Paulette had been right. Maybe the extension wasn't finished after all. It didn't look like it was meant to be part of Finlay's Club though, this staircase. It was too narrow, almost furtive. Slowly, Rebus moved downwards, the heels of his hired shoes making all-too-audible sounds against the steps.

Rebus counted twenty steps, and figured that he was now below the level of the building's lower ground floor, somewhere around cellar level or a bit below that even. Maybe planning restrictions *had* got Finlay Andrews after all. Unable to build up, he had built *down*. The door at the bottom of the stairs looked fairly solid. Again, a utilitarian-looking construction, rather than decorative. It would take a good twenty-pound hammer to break through this door. Rebus tried the handle instead. It turned, and the door opened.

Utter darkness. Rebus shuffled through the door, using what light there was from the top of the stairs to make out what he could. Which was to say, nothing. It looked like he was in some kind of storage area. Some big empty space. Then the lights came on, four rows of strip lights on the ceiling high above him. Their wattage low, they still gave enough illumination to the scene. A small boxing ring stood in the centre of the floor, surrounded by a few dozen stiff-backed chairs. This *was* the place then. The disc jockey had been right.

Calum McCallum had needed all the friends he could get. He had told Rebus all about the rumours he'd heard, rumours of a little club within a club, where the city's increasingly jaded begetters of wealth could place some 'interesting bets'. A bit out of the ordinary, McCallum had said. Yes, like betting on two rent boys, junkies paid handsomely to knock the daylights out of one another and keep quiet about it afterwards. Paid with money and drugs. There was no shortage of either now that the high rollers had spun north.

Hyde's Club. Named after Robert Louis Stevenson's villain, Edward Hyde, the dark side of the human soul. Hyde himself was based on the city's Deacon Brodie, businessman by day, robber by night. Rebus could smell guilt and fear and rank expectation in this large room. Stale cigars and spilt whisky, splashes of sweat. And amongst it all moved Ronnie, and the question which still needed to be answered. Had Ronnie been paid to photograph the influential and the rich – without their knowing they were being snapped, of course? Or had he been freelancing, summoned here only as a punchbag, but stealthy enough to bring a hidden camera with him? The answer was perhaps unimportant. What mattered was that the owner of this place, the puppet-master of all these base desires, had killed Ronnie, had starved him of his fix and then given him some rat poison. Had sent one of his minions along to the squat to make sure it looked like a simple case of an overdose. So they had left the quality powder beside Ronnie. And to muddy the water, they had moved the body downstairs, leaving it in candlelight. Thinking the tableau shockingly effective. But by candlelight they hadn't seen the pentagram on the wall, and they hadn't meant anything by placing the body the way they had.

Rebus had made the mistake of reading too much into the situation, all along. He had blurred the picture himself, seeing connections where there were none, seeing plot and conspiracy where none existed. The real plot was so much bigger, the size of a haystack to his needle.

'Finlay Andrews!' The shout echoed around the room, hanging emptily in air. Rebus hauled himself up into the boxing ring and looked around at the chairs. He could almost see the gleaming, gloating faces of the spectators. The canvas floor of the ring was pockmarked with brown stains, dried blood. It didn't end here, of course. There were also the 'guest bedrooms', the locked doors behind which 'private games' were played. Yes, he could visualise the whole Sodom, held on the third Friday of the month, judging by James Carew's diary. Boys brought back from Calton Hill to service the clients. On a table, in bed, wherever. And Ronnie had perhaps photographed it all. But Andrews had found out that Ronnie had some insurance, some photos stashed away. He couldn't know, of course, that they were next to useless as weapons of blackmail or evidence. All he knew was that they existed.

So Ronnie had died.

Rebus climbed out of the ring and walked past one row of chairs. At the back of the hall, lurking in shadow, were two doors. He listened outside one, then outside the other. No sounds, yet he was sure. . . . He was about to open the door on the left, but something, some instinct, made him choose the right-hand door instead. He paused, turned the handle, pushed.

There was a light switch just inside the door. Rebus found it, and two delicate lamps either side of the bed came on. The bed was against the side wall. There wasn't much else in the room, apart from two large mirrors, one against the wall opposite the bed, and one above the bed. The door clicked shut behind Rebus as he walked over to the bed. Sometimes he had been accused by his superiors of having a vivid imagination. Right now, he shut his imagination out altogether. Stick to the facts, John. The fact of the bed, the fact of the mirrors. The door clicked again. He leapt forwards and yanked at the handle, but it was fast, the door locked tight.

'Shit!' He stood back and kicked out, hitting the belly of the door with the heel of his shoe. The door trembled, but held. His shoe did not, the heel flapping off. Great, bang went his deposit on the dress hire. Hold on though, think it through. Someone had locked the door, therefore someone was down here with him, and the only other place they could have been hiding was the other room, the room next to this. He turned again and studied the mirror opposite the bed.

'Andrews!' he yelled to the mirror. 'Andrews!'

The voice was muffled by the wall, sounding distant, but still lucid.

'Hello, Inspector Rebus. Nice to see you.'

Rebus almost smiled, but managed to hide it.

'I wish I could say the same.' He stared into the mirror, visualising Andrews standing directly behind it, watching him. 'A nice idea,' he said, making conversation, needing time to gather his strength and his thoughts. 'People screwing in one room, while everyone else is free to watch through a two-way mirror.'

'Free to watch?' The voice seemed closer. 'No, not free, Inspector. Everything costs.'

'I suppose you set the camera up in there too, did you?'

'Photographed and framed. Framed being quite apt under the circumstances, don't you think?'

'Blackmail.' It was an observation, nothing more.

'Favours merely. Often given without question. But a photograph can be a useful tool when favours are being withheld.'

'That's why James Carew committed suicide?'

'Oh no. That was your doing really, Inspector. James told me you'd recognised him. He thought you might be able to follow your nose from him back to Hyde's.'

'You killed him?'

'*We* killed him, John. Which is a pity. I liked James. He was a good friend.'

'Well, you have lots of friends, don't you?'

There was laughter now, but the voice was level, elegiac almost. 'Yes, I suppose they'd have a job finding a judge to try me, an advocate to prosecute me, fifteen good men and true to stand as jury. They've all been to Hyde's. All of them. Looking for a game with just a little more edge than those played upstairs. I got the idea from a friend in London. He runs a similar establishment, though perhaps with a less sharp edge than Hyde's. There's a lot of new money in Edinburgh, John. Money for all. Would you like money? Would you like a sharper edge to your life? Don't tell me you're happy in your little flat, with your music and your books and your bottles of wine.' Rebus's face showed surprise. 'Yes, I know quite a bit about you, John. Information is *my* edge.' Andrews' voice fell. 'There's a membership available here if you want it, John. I think maybe you *do* want it. After all, membership has its privileges.'

Rebus leaned his head against the mirror. His voice was a near whisper.

'Your fees are too high.'

'What's that?' Andrews' voice seemed closer than ever, his breathing almost audible. Rebus's voice was still a whisper.

'I said your fees are too high.'

Suddenly, he pulled back an arm, made a fist, and pushed straight through the mirror, shattering it. Another trick from his SAS training. Don't punch *at* something; always punch *through*, even if it's a brick wall you're attacking. Glass splintered around him, digging into the sleeve of his jacket, seeking flesh. His fist uncurled, became a claw. Just through the mirror, he found Andrews' throat, clamped it, and hauled the man forward. Andrews was shrieking. Glass was in his face, flakes of it in his hair, his mouth, prickling his eyes. Rebus held him close, teeth gritted.

'I said,' he hissed, 'your fees are too high.' Then he brought his other hand into a fresh new fist and placed a blow on Andrews' chin, releasing him so that the unconscious figure fell back into the room.

Rebus pulled off the useless shoe and tapped away the shards of glass which still clung around the edges of the frame. Then, carefully, he hauled himself through into the room, went to the door, and opened it.

He saw Tracy immediately. She was standing hesitantly in the middle of the boxing ring, arms hanging by her sides.

'Tracy?' he said.

'She may not hear you, Inspector Rebus. Heroin can do that, you know.'

Rebus watched as Malcolm Lanyon stepped out from the shadows. Behind him were two men. One was tall, well built for a man of his mature years. He had thick black eyebrows and a thick moustache tinged with silver. His eyes were deep-set, his whole face louring. He was the most Calvinist-looking thing Rebus had ever seen. The other man was stouter, less justified in his sinning. His hair was curly but thinning, his face scarred like a knuckle, a labourer's face. He was leering.

Rebus stared at Tracy again. Her eyes were like pinpoints. He went to the ring and climbed in, hugging her to him. Her body was totally compliant, her hair damp with sweat. She might have been a life-sized rag doll for all the impetus in her limbs. But when Rebus held her face so that she had to look back at him, her eyes glimmered, and he felt her body twitch.

'*My* edge,' Lanyon was saying. 'It seems I needed it.' He glanced towards the room where Andrews was lying unconscious. 'Finlay said he could handle you himself. Having seen you last night, I doubted that.' He beckoned to one of the men. 'See if Finlay's going to be all right.' The man headed off. Rebus liked the way the odds were going.

'Would you care to step into my office and talk?' he said.

Lanyon considered this, saw that Rebus was a strong man, but that he had his hands full with the girl. Also, of course, Lanyon had his men, while Rebus was alone. He walked to the ring, grabbed onto a rope, and hauled himself up and in. Now, face to face with Rebus, he saw the cuts on Rebus's arm and hand.

'Nasty,' he said. 'If you don't get those seen to. . . .'

'I might bleed to death?'

'Exactly.'

Rebus looked down at the canvas, where his own blood was making fresh stains beside those of nameless others. 'How many of them died in the ring?' he asked.

'I really don't know. Not many. We're not animals, Inspector Rebus. There may have been the occasional . . . accident. I seldom came to Hyde's. I merely introduced new members into it.'

'So when do they make you a judge?'

Lanyon smiled. 'Not for a considerable time yet. But it *will* happen. I once attended a club similar to Hyde's in London. Actually, that's where I met Saiko.' Rebus's eyes widened. 'Oh yes,' Lanyon said, 'she's a very versatile young woman.'

'I suppose Hyde's has given you and Andrews carte blanche throughout Edinburgh?'

'It has helped with the odd planning application, the odd court case just happening to go the right way, that sort of thing.'

'So what happens now that I know all about it?'

'Ah, well, you needn't worry there. Finlay and I see a long-term future for you in the development of Edinburgh as a great city of commerce and industry.' The guard below chuckled.

'What do you mean?' asked Rebus. He could feel Tracy's body tensing, growing strong again. How long it would last he couldn't know.

'I mean,' Lanyon was saying, 'that you could be preserved in concrete, supporting one of the new orbital roads.'

'You've done that before, have you?' The question was rhetorical; the goon's chuckle had already answered it.

'Once or twice, yes. When there was something that needed clearing away.'

Rebus saw that Tracy's hands were slowly closing into fists. Then the goon who had gone to see Andrews came back.

'Mr Lanyon!' he called. 'I think Mr Andrews is pretty bad!'

Just then, as Lanyon turned from them, Tracy flew from Rebus with a terrifying shriek and swung her fists in a low arc, catching Lanyon with a sickening thump between his legs. He didn't so much fall as deflate, gagging as he went, while Tracy stumbled, the effort having been too great, and fell to the canvas.

Rebus was quick, too. He grabbed Lanyon and pulled him upright, locking his arm behind his back with one hand while the other hand went to his throat. The two heavies made a move towards the ring, but Rebus dug his fingers into Lanyon's flesh just a little deeper, and they hesitated. There was a moment's stalemate before one of them made a dash for the stairs, closely followed by his partner. Rebus was breathing heavily. He released his grip on Lanyon and watched him crumple to the floor. Then, standing in the centre of the ring, he counted softly to ten – referee style – before raising one arm high into the air.

Upstairs, things had quietened down. The staff were tidying themselves up, but held their heads high, having acquitted themselves well. The drunks – Holmes, McCall, McGrath and Todd – had been seen off, and Paulette was smoothing the rumpled atmosphere with offers of free drinks all round. She saw Rebus coming through the door of Hyde's, and froze momentarily, then turned back into the perfect hostess, but with her voice slightly less warm than before, and her smile counterfeit.

'Ah, John.' It was Superintendent Watson, glass still in hand. 'Wasn't that a tussle? Where did you disappear to?'

'Is Tommy McCall around, sir?'

'Somewhere around, yes. Heard the offer of a free drink and headed in the direction of the bar. What have you done to your hand?'

Rebus looked down and saw that his hand was still bleeding in several places.

'Seven years bad luck,' he said. 'Do you have a minute, sir? There's something I'd like to show you. But first I need to phone for an ambulance.'

'But why, for God's sake? The rumpus is over, surely?'

Rebus looked at his superior. 'I wouldn't bet on that, sir,' he said. 'Not even if the chips were on the house.'

Rebus made his way home wearily, not from any real physical

tiredness, but because his mind felt abused. The stairwell almost defeated him. He paused on the first floor, outside Mrs Cochrane's door, for what seemed minutes. He tried not to think about Hyde's, about what it meant, what it had been, what emotions it had serviced. But, not consciously thinking of it, bits of it flew around inside his head anyway, little jagged pieces of horror.

Mrs Cochrane's cats wanted out. He could hear them on the other side of the door. A cat-flap would have been the answer, but Mrs Cochrane didn't believe in them. Like leaving your door open to strangers, she had said. Any old moggie could just waltz in.

How true. Somehow, Rebus found that little unwrapped parcel of strength which was necessary to climb the extra flight. He unlocked his door and closed it again behind him. Sanctuary. In the kitchen, he munched on a dry roll while he waited for the kettle to boil.

Watson had listened to his story with mounting unease and disbelief. He had wondered aloud just how many important people were implicated. But then only Andrews and Lanyon could answer that. They'd found some video film as well as an impressive selection of still photographs. Watson's lips had been bloodless, though many of the faces meant nothing to Rebus. Still, a few of them did. Andrews had been right about the judges and the lawyers. Thankfully, there were no policemen on display. Except one.

Rebus had wanted to clear up a murder, and instead had stumbled into a nest of vipers. He wasn't sure any of it would come to light. Too many reputations would fall. The public's faith in the beliefs and institutions of the city, of the country itself would be shattered. How long would it take to pick up the pieces of *that* broken mirror? Rebus examined his bandaged wrist. How long for the wounds to heal?

He went into the living room, carrying his tea. Tony McCall was seated in a chair, waiting.

'Hello, Tony,' Rebus said.

'Hello, John.'

'Thanks for your help back there.'

'What are friends for?'

Earlier in the day, when Rebus had asked for Tony McCall's help, McCall had broken down.

'I know all about it, John,' he had confessed. 'Tommy took me along there once. It was hideous, and I didn't stick around. But maybe there are pictures of me ... I don't know ... Maybe there are.'

Rebus hadn't needed to ask any more. It had come spilling out like beer from a tap: things bad at home, bit of fun, couldn't tell anyone about it because he didn't know who already knew. Even now he thought it best to keep quiet about it. Rebus had accepted the warning.

'I'm still going ahead,' he had said. 'With you or without. Your choice.'

Tony McCall had agreed to help.

Rebus sat down, placed the tea on the floor, and reached into his pocket for the photograph he had lifted from the files at Hyde's. He threw it in McCall's direction. McCall lifted it, stared at it with fearful eyes.

'You know,' Rebus said, 'Andrews was after Tommy's haulage company. He'd have had it, too, and at a bargain-basement price.'

'Rotten bastard,' McCall said, tearing the photograph methodically into smaller and smaller pieces.

'Why did you do it, Tony?'

'I told you, John. Tommy took me along. Just a bit of fun –'

'No, I mean why did you break into the squat and plant that powder on Ronnie?'

'Me?' McCall's eyes were wider than ever now, but the look in them was still fear rather than surprise. It was all guesswork, but Rebus knew he was guessing right.

'Come on, Tony. Do you think Finlay Andrews is going to let any names stay secret? He's going down, and he's got no reason to let anyone's head stay above water.'

McCall thought about this. He let the bits of the photograph flutter into the ashtray, then set light to them with a match. They dissolved to blackened ash, and he seemed satisfied.

'Andrews needed a favour. It was always "favours" with him. I think he'd seen *The Godfather* too many times. Pilmuir was my beat, my territory. We'd met through Tommy, so he thought to ask me.'

'And you were happy to oblige.'

'Well, he had the picture, didn't he?'

'There must've been more.'

'Well . . .' McCall paused again, crushed the ash in the ashtray with his forefinger. A fine dust was all that was left. 'Yes, hell, I was happy enough to do it. The guy was a junkie after all, a piece of rubbish. And he was already dead. All I had to do was place a little packet beside him, that's all.'

'You never questioned why?'

'Ask no questions and all that.' He smiled. 'Finlay was offering me membership, you see. Membership of Hyde's. Well, I knew what that meant. I'd be on nodding terms with the big boys, wouldn't I? I even started to dream about career advancement, something I hadn't done in quite some time. Let's face it, John, we're tiny fish in a small pool.'

'And Hyde was offering you the chance to play with the sharks?'

McCall smiled sadly. 'I suppose that was it, yes.'

Rebus sighed. 'Tony, Tony, Tony. Where would it have ended, eh?'

'Probably with you having to call me "sir",' McCall answered, his voice firming up. 'Instead of which, I suppose the trial will see me on the front of the scum sheets. Not quite the kind of fame I was looking for.'

He rose from the chair.

'See you in court,' he said, leaving John Rebus to his flavourless tea and his thoughts.

Rebus slept fitfully, and was awake early. He showered, but without any of his usual vocal accompaniment. He telephoned the hospital, and ascertained that Tracy was fine, and that Finlay Andrews had been patched up with the loss of very little blood. Then he drove to Great London Road, where Malcolm Lanyon was being held for questioning.

Rebus was still officially a non-person, and DS Dick and DC Cooper had been assigned to the interrogation. But Rebus wanted to be close by. He knew the answers to all their questions, knew the sorts of trick Lanyon was capable of pulling. He didn't want the bastard getting away with it because of some technicality.

He went to the canteen first, bought a bacon roll, and, seeing Dick and Cooper seated at a table, went to join them.

'Hello, John,' Dick said, staring into the bottom of a stained coffee mug.

'You lot are early birds,' Rebus noted. 'You must be keen.'

'Farmer Watson wants it out of the way as soon as poss, sooner even.'

'I'll bet he does. Look, I'm going to be around today, if you need me to back up anything.'

'We appreciate that, John,' said Dick, in a voice which told Rebus his offer was as welcome as a dunce's cap.

'Well . . .' Rebus began, but bit off the sentence, and ate his breakfast instead. Dick and Cooper seemed dulled by the enforced early rise. Certainly, they were not the most vivacious of table companions. Rebus finished quickly and rose to his feet.

'Mind if I take a quick look at him?'

'Not at all,' said Dick. 'We'll be there in five minutes.'

Passing through the ground-floor reception area, Rebus almost bumped into Brian Holmes.

'Everyone's after the worm today,' Rebus said. Holmes gave him a puzzled, sleepy look. 'Never mind. I'm off to take a peek at Lanyon-alias-Hyde. Fancy a bit of voyeurism?'

Holmes didn't answer, but fell in stride with Rebus.

'Actually,' Rebus said, 'Lanyon might appreciate that image.' Holmes gave him a more puzzled look yet. Rebus sighed. 'Never mind.'

'Sorry, sir, bit of a late night yesterday.'

'Oh, yes. Thanks for that, by the way.'

'I nearly died when I saw the bloody Farmer staring at the lot of us, him in his undertaker's suit and us pretending to be pissed Dundonians.'

They shared a smile. Okay, the plan had been lame, conceived by Rebus during the course of his fifty-minute drive back from Calum McCallum's cell in Fife. But it had worked. They'd got a result.

'Yes,' Rebus said. 'I thought you looked a bit nervy last night.'

'What do you mean?'

'Well, you were doing your Italian army impression, weren't you? Advancing backwards, and all that.'

Holmes stopped dead, his jaw dropping. 'Is that the thanks I get? We put our careers on the line for you last night, all four of us. You've used me as your gofer – go find this, go check that – as a bit of bloody shoeleather, half the time for jobs that weren't even official, you've had my girlfriend half killed –'

'Now wait just one second –'

'– and all to satisfy your own curiosity. Okay, so there are bad guys behind bars, that's good, but look at the scales. You've got them, the rest of us have got sod all except a few bruises and no bloody soles on our shoes!'

Rebus stared at the floor, almost contrite. The air flew from his nostrils as from a Spanish bull's.

'I forgot,' he said at last. 'I meant to take that bloody suit back this morning. The shoes are ruined. It was you talking about shoeleather that reminded me.'

Then he set off again, along the corridor, towards the cells, leaving Holmes speechless in his wake.

Outside the cell, Lanyon's name had been printed in chalk on a board. Rebus went up to the steel door and pulled aside the shutter, thinking how it reminded him of the shutter on the door of some prohibition club. Give the secret knock and the shutter opened. He peered into the cell, started, and groped for the alarm bell situated beside the door. Holmes, hearing the siren, forgot to be angry and hurt and hurried forward. Rebus was pulling at the edge of the locked door with his fingernails.

'We've got to get in!'

'It's locked, sir.' Holmes was afraid: his superior looked absolutely manic. 'Here they come.'

A uniformed sergeant came at an undignified trot, keys jangling from his chain.

'Quick!'

The lock gave, and Rebus yanked open the door. Inside, Malcolm Lanyon lay slumped on the floor, head resting against the bed. His feet were splayed like a doll's. One hand lay on the floor, some thin nylon wire, like a fishing-line, wrapped around the knuckles, which were blackened. The line was attached to Lanyon's neck in a loop which had embedded itself so far into the flesh that it could hardly be seen. Lanyon's eyes bulged horribly, his swollen tongue obscene against the blood-darkened face. It was like a last macabre gesture, and Rebus watched the tongue protruding towards him, seeming to take it as a personal insult.

He knew it was way too late, but the sergeant loosened the wire anyway and laid the corpse flat on the floor. Holmes was resting his head against the cold metal door, screwing shut his eyes against the parody inside the cell.

'He must've had it hidden on him,' the sergeant said, seeking excuses for the monumental blunder, referring to the wire which he now held in his hands. 'Jesus, what a way to go.'

Rebus was thinking: he's cheated me, he's cheated me. I wouldn't have had the guts to do that, not slowly choke myself. . . . I could never do it, something inside would have stopped me. . . .

'Who's been in here since he was brought in?'

The sergeant stared at Rebus, uncomprehending.

'The usual lot, I suppose. He had a few questions to answer last night when you brought him in.'

'Yes, but *after* that?'

'Well, he had a meal when you lot went. That's about it.'

'Sonofabitch,' growled Rebus, stalking out of the cell and back along the corridor. Holmes, his face white and slick, was a few steps behind, and gaining.

'They're going to bury it, Brian,' Rebus said, his voice an angry vibrato. 'They're going to bury it, I know they are, and there'll be no cross marking the spot, nothing. A junkie died of his own volition. An estate agent committed suicide. Now a lawyer tops himself in a police cell. No connection, no crime committed.'

'But what about Andrews?'

'Where do you think we're headed?'

They arrived at the hospital ward in time to witness the efficiency of the staff in a case of emergency. Rebus hurried forward, pushing his way through. Finlay Andrews, lying on his bed, chest exposed, was being given oxygen while the cardiac apparatus was installed. A doctor held the pads in front of them, then pushed them slowly against Andrews' chest. A moment later, a jolt went through the body. There was no reading from the machine. More oxygen, more electricity. . . . Rebus turned away. He'd seen the script; he knew how the film would end.

'Well?' said Holmes.

'Heart attack.' Rebus's voice was bland. He began to walk away. 'Let's call it that anyway, because that's what the record will say.'

'So what next?' Holmes kept pace with him. He, too, was feeling cheated. Rebus considered the question.

'Probably the photos will disappear. The ones that matter at any rate. And who's left to testify? Testify to what?'

'They've thought of everything.'

'Except one thing, Brian. *I* know who they are.'

Holmes stopped. 'Will that matter?' he called to his superior's retreating figure. But Rebus just kept walking.

There was a scandal, but it was a small one, soon forgotten. Shuttered rooms in elegant Georgian terraces soon became light again, in a great resurrection of spirit. The deaths of Finlay Andrews and Malcolm Lanyon were reported, and journalists sought what muck and brass they could. Yes, Finlay Andrews had been running a club which was not strictly legitimate in all of its dealings, and yes, Malcolm Lanyon had committed suicide when the authorities had begun to close in on this little empire. No, there were no details of what these 'activities' might have been.

The suicide of local estate agent James Carew was in no way

connected to Mr Lanyon's suicide, though it was true the two men were friends. As for Mr Lanyon's connection with Finlay Andrews and his club, well, perhaps we would never know. It was no more than a sad coincidence that Mr Lanyon had been appointed Mr Carew's executor. Still, there were other lawyers, weren't there?

And so it ended, the story petering out, the rumours dying a little less slowly. Rebus was pleased when Tracy announced that Nell Stapleton had found her a job in a cafe/deli near the University Library. One evening, however, having spent some time in the Rutherford Bar, Rebus decided to opt for a takeaway Indian meal before home. In the restaurant, he saw Tracy, Holmes and Nell Stapleton at a corner table, sharing a joke with their meal. He turned and left without ordering.

Back in his flat, he sat at the kitchen table for the umpteenth time, writing a rough draft of his letter of resignation. Somehow, the words failed to put across any of his emotions adequately. He crumpled the paper and tossed it towards the bin. He had been reminded in the restaurant of just how much Hyde's had cost in human terms, and of how little justice there had been. There was a knock at the door. He had hope in his heart as he opened it. Gill Templer stood there, smiling.

In the night, he crept through to the living room, and switched on the desk lamp. It threw light guiltily, like a constable's torch, onto the small filing cabinet beside the stereo. The key was hidden under a corner of the carpet, as secure a hiding place as a granny's mattress. He opened the cabinet and lifted out a slim file, which he carried to his chair, the chair which had for so many months been his bed. There he sat, composed, remembering the day at James Carew's flat. Back then he had been tempted to lift Carew's private diary and keep it for himself. But he had resisted temptation. Not the night at Hyde's though. There, alone in Andrews' office for a moment, he had filched the photograph of Tony McCall. Tony McCall, a friend and colleague with whom, these days, he had nothing in common. Except perhaps a sense of guilt.

He opened the file and took out the photographs. He had taken them along with the one of McCall. Four photographs, lifted at random. He studied the faces again, as he did most nights when he found sleep hard to come by. Faces he recognised. Faces attached to names, and names to handshakes and voices. Important people. Influential people. He'd thought about this a lot. Indeed, he had thought about little else since that night in Hyde's club. He brought out a metal wastepaper bin from beneath the desk, dropped the photographs into it, and lit a match, holding it over the bin, as he had done so many times before.

Tooth & Nail

For Miranda, again,
but this time for Mugwump too ...

'How many wolves do we feel on our heels,
while our real enemies go in sheepskin'
Malcom Lowry, *Under the Volcano*

Prologue

She drives home the knife.

The moment, she knows from past experience, is a very intimate one. Her hand is gripped around the knife's cool handle and the thrust takes the blade into the throat up to the hilt until her hand meets the throat itself. Flesh upon flesh. Jacket first, or woollen jersey, cotton shirt or T-shirt, then flesh. Now rent. The knife is writhing, like an animal sniffing. Warm blood covering hilt and hand. (The other hand covers the mouth, stifling screams.) The moment is complete. A meeting. Touching. The body is hot, gaping, warm with blood. Seething inside, as insides become outsides. Boiling. The moment is coming to an end all too soon.

And still she feels hungry. It isn't right, isn't usual, but she does. She removes some of the clothing; in fact, removes quite a lot of it, removes more, perhaps, than is necessary. And she does what she must do, the knife squirming again. She keeps her eyes screwed tightly shut. She does not like this part. She has never liked this part, not then, not now. But especially not *then*.

Finally, she brings out her teeth and sinks them into the white stomach, until they grind together in a satisfying bite, and whispers, as she always does, the same four words.

'It's only a game.'

* * *

It is evening when George Flight gets the call. Sunday evening. Sunday should be his blessed relief, beef and Yorkshires, feet up in front of the television, papers falling from his lap. But he's had a feeling all day. In the pub at lunchtime he'd felt it, a wriggling in his gut like there were worms in there, tiny blind white worms, hungry worms, worms he could not hope to satisfy. He knew what they were and they knew what they were. And then he'd won third prize in the pub raffle: a three-foot high orange and white teddy bear. Even the worms had laughed at him then and he'd known the day would end badly.

As it was doing now, the phone as insistent as last orders. Ringing with whatever bad news couldn't wait until the morning shift. He knew what it meant of course. Hadn't he been expecting it these past weeks? But still he was reluctant to pick up the receiver. At last he did.

'Flight speaking.'

'There's been another one, sir. The Wolfman. He's done another.'

Flight stared at the silent television. Highlights of the previous day's rugby match. Grown men running after a funny-shaped ball as though their lives depended on it. It was only a bloody game after all. And propped up against the side of the TV that smirking prize, the teddy bear. What the hell could he do with a teddy bear?

'Okay,' he said, 'just tell me where . . .'

'After all, it *is* only a game.'

Rebus smiled and nodded at the Englishman across the table. Then he stared out of the window, pretending once more to be interested in the blur of dark scenery. If the Englishman had said it once, he had said it a dozen times. And during the trip, he had said little else. He also kept stealing precious legroom from Rebus, while his collection of empty beer cans was creeping across the table, invading Rebus's space, pushing against the neatly folded stack of newspapers and magazines.

'Tickets, please!' yelled the guard from the other end of the carriage.

So, with a sigh, and for the third time since leaving Edinburgh, Rebus sought out his ticket. It was never where he thought it was. At Berwick, he'd thought it was in his shirt pocket. It was in the outer top pocket of his Harris tweed jacket. Then at Durham he'd looked for it in his jacket, only to find it beneath one of the magazines on the table. Now, ten minutes out of Peterborough, it had moved to the back pocket of his trousers. He retrieved it, and waited for the guard to make his way forward.

The Englishman's ticket was where it had always been: half-hidden beneath a beer can. Rebus, although he knew every word almost by heart, glanced again at the back page of one of his Sunday papers. He had kept it to the top of the pile for no reason other than a sense of devilment, enjoying the thick black letters of the headline – SCOTS WHA HAE! – beneath which was printed the story of the previous day's Calcutta Cup clash at Murrayfield. And a clash it had been: no day for weak stomachs, but a day for stout hearts and determination. The Scots had triumphed by thirteen points to ten, and now here Rebus was on a late evening Sunday train packed with disappointed English rugby supporters, heading towards London.

London. Never one of Rebus's favourite places. Not that he was a frequent visitor. But this was not pleasure. This was strictly business, and as a representative of the Lothian and Borders Police, he was to be on best behaviour. Or, as his boss had put it so succinctly, 'No fuck-ups, John.'

Well, he would do his best. Not that he reckoned there was much he *could* do, right or wrong. But he would do what he could. And if that meant wearing a clean shirt and tie, polished shoes and a respectable jacket, then so be it.

'All tickets, please.'

Rebus handed over his ticket. Somewhere in the corridor up ahead, in the no-man's-land of the buffet car between first and second class, a few voices were raised in a verse of Blake's *Jerusalem*. The Englishman across from Rebus smiled.

'Only a game,' he said to the tins in front of him. 'Only a game.'

The train pulled in to King's Cross five minutes late. It was a quarter past eleven. Rebus was in no hurry. A hotel room had been booked for him in central London, courtesy of the Metropolitan Police. He carried a typed list of notes and directions in his jacket pocket, again sent up from London. He had not brought much luggage with him, feeling that the courtesy of the Met would extend only so far. He expected the trip to last two or three days at most, after which time even they would realise, surely, that he was not going to be of much help to them in their investigations. So: one small suitcase, one sports bag and one briefcase. The suitcase contained two suits, a change of shoes, several pairs of socks and underpants and two shirts (with matching ties). In the sports bag were a small washbag, towel, two paperback novels (one partly read), a travel alarm clock, a thirty-five millimetre camera with flashgun and film, a T-shirt, retractable umbrella, sunglasses, transistor radio, diary, Bible, a bottle containing ninety-seven paracetamol tablets and another bottle (protected by the T-shirt) containing best Islay malt whisky.

The bare essentials, in other words. The briefcase contained notepad, pens, a personal tape recorder, some blank tapes and prerecorded tapes and a thick manila file filled with photocopied sheets of Metropolitan Police paper, ten-by-eight inch colour photographs held together in a small ring-binder affair and newspaper clippings. On the front of this file was a white sticky label with one word typed upon it. The word was WOLFMAN.

Rebus was in no hurry. The night – what was left of it – was his. He had to attend a meeting at ten on Monday morning, but his first night in the capital city could be spent however he chose. He thought he would probably choose to spend it in his hotel room. He waited in his seat until the other passengers had left the train, then slid his bag and briefcase from the luggage rack and made for the sliding door to the carriage, beside which, in another luggage rack, sat his suitcase. Manoeuvring these out of the train door and onto the platform, he paused for a moment and breathed in. The smell was not quite like any other railway station. Certainly it was not like Waverley Station in Edinburgh. The air wasn't quite foetid, but it did seem to Rebus somehow overused and tired. He felt suddenly fatigued. And there was something else in his nostrils, something sweet and revolting at the same time. He couldn't quite think what it reminded him of.

On the concourse, instead of making directly for the Underground, he wandered over to a bookstall. There he purchased an A-Z of London, slipping it into his briefcase. The next morning's editions were just arriving, but he ignored them. This was Sunday, not Monday. Sunday was the Lord's day, which was perhaps why he had packed a Bible along with his other possessions. He hadn't been to a church service in weeks . . . maybe even months. Not since he'd tried the Cathedral on Palmerston Place in fact. It had been a nice place, light and bright, but too far from his home to make for a viable proposition. And besides, it was still organised religion and he had not lost his mistrust of organised religion. If anything, he was warier these days than ever before. He was also hungry. Perhaps he would grab a bite on the way to the hotel . . .

He passed two women having an animated discussion.

'I heard it on the radio just twenty minutes ago.'

'Done another, has he?'

'That's what they're saying.'

The woman shivered. 'Don't bear thinking about. Did they say it was definitely him?'

'Not definitely, but you just know, don't you?'

There was a truth in that. So, Rebus had arrived in time for another small piece of the drama to unfold around him. Another murder, making four in all. Four in the space of three months. He was a busy little man, this killer they had named the Wolfman. They had named him the Wolfman and then they had sent word to Rebus's boss. Lend us your man, they had said. Let's see what he can do. Rebus's boss, Chief Superintendent Watson, had handed the letter over to him.

'Better take some silver bullets with you, John,' he had said. 'It looks like you're their only hope.' And then he had chuckled, knowing as well as Rebus knew himself that he could be of little help in the case. But Rebus had gnawed on his bottom lip, silent in front of his desk-bound superior. He would do what he could. He would do *everything* he could. Until they saw through him and sent him back home.

Besides, perhaps he needed the break. Watson seemed glad to be rid of him, too.

'If nothing else, it'll keep us out of one another's hair for a while.'

The Chief Superintendent, an Aberdonian, had earned the nickname 'Farmer Watson', a nickname every police officer beneath him in Edinburgh understood. But then one day Rebus, a nip of malt too many beneath his belt, had blurted out the nickname in front of Watson himself, since when he had found himself assigned to more than his fair share of tedious details, desk jobs, lookouts and training courses.

Training courses! At least Watson had a sense of humour. The most recent had been termed 'Management for Senior Officers' and had been a minor disaster – all psychology and how to be nice to junior officers. How to *involve* them, how to *motivate* them, how to *relate* to them. Rebus had returned to his station and tried it for one day, a day of involving, of motivating, of relating. At the end of the day, a DC had slapped a hand onto Rebus's back, smiling.

'Bloody hard work today, John. But I've enjoyed it.'

'Take your hand off my fucking back,' Rebus had snarled. 'And don't call me John.'

The DC's mouth fell open. 'But you said . . .' he began, but didn't bother finishing. The brief holiday was over. Rebus had tried being a manager. Tried it and loathed it.

He was halfway down the steps to the Underground when he stopped, put down his suitcase and briefcase, pulled open the zip on his sports bag and found the transistor radio. Switching it on, he held it to his ear with one hand while the other turned the tuning dial. Eventually, he found a news bulletin, listening as the other travellers passed him, a few of them staring, but mostly ignoring him. At last he heard what he had been waiting for, then switched off the radio and threw it back into the sports bag. Now, he released the two catches on his briefcase and brought out the A-Z. Flipping through the pages of street names at the back, he remembered just how large London really was. Large and populous. Something like ten million, was it? Wasn't that twice the population of Scotland? It didn't bear thinking about. Ten million souls.

'Ten million and one,' Rebus whispered to himself, finding the name he had been looking for.

The Chamber of Horrors

'Not a pretty sight.'

Looking around him, Detective Inspector George Flight wondered whether the sergeant had been referring to the body or to the surrounding area. You could say what you liked about the Wolfman, he wasn't choosy about his turf. This time it was a riverside path. Not that Flight had ever really thought of the Lea as a 'river'. It was a place where supermarket trolleys came to die, a dank stretch of water bordered on one side by marshland and on the other by industrial sites and lo-rise housing. Apparently you could walk the course of the Lea from the Thames to up past Edmonton. The narrow river ran like a mottled black vein from east central London to the most northerly reaches of the capital and beyond. The vast majority of Londoners didn't even know it existed.

George Flight knew about it though. He had been brought up in Tottenham Hale, not far from the Lea. His father had fished on the Navigation section, between Stonebridge and Tottenham Locks. When he was young he had played football on the marshes, smoked illicit cigarettes in the long grass with his gang, fumbled with a blouse or a brassiere on the wasteland just across the river from where he now stood.

He had walked along this path. It was popular on warm Sunday afternoons. There were riverside pubs where you could stand outside supping a pint and watching the Sunday sailors plying their crafts, but at night, only the drunk, the reckless and the brave would use the quiet and ill-lit path. The drunk, the reckless, the brave . . . and the locals. Jean Cooper was a local. Ever since the separation from her husband, she had lived with her sister in a small, recently-built estate just off the towpath. She worked in an off-licence on Lea Bridge Road, and finished work at seven. The riverside path was a quick route home.

Her body had been found at nine forty-five by a couple of young lads on their way to one of the pubs. They had run back to Lea Bridge Road and flagged down a passing police car. The operation thereafter had about it a fluid, easy movement. The police doctor arrived, to be met by detectives from Stoke Newington police station, who, recognising the *modus operandi*, contacted Flight.

By the time he arrived, the scene was organised but busy. The body had been identified, questions asked of nearby residents, the sister found. Scene of Crime Officers were in discussion with a couple of people from Forensics. The area around the body had been cordoned off and nobody crossed the tape without first of all donning polythene cover-alls for their feet and hair. Two photographers were busy taking flash photographs under portable lighting powered by a nearby generator. And next to the generator stood an operations van, where another photographer was trying to fix his jammed video camera.

'It's these cheap tapes,' he complained. 'They look like a bargain when you buy them, but then halfway through you find there's a twist or a snag in them.'

'So don't buy cheap tapes,' Flight had advised.

'Thank you, Sherlock,' had been the cameraman's ill-meant response, before once again cursing the tapes, the seller of the tapes and the seller's market stall in Brick Lane. He'd only bought the tapes that day.

Meantime, having discussed their plan of attack, the forensic scientists moved in towards the body armed with sticky tape, scissors and a pile of large polythene bags. Then, with extraordinary care, they began to 'tape' the body in the hope of lifting hairs and fibres from the clothing. Flight watched them from a distance. The portable lights cast a garish white glow over the scene, so that, standing further back in unlit gloom, Flight felt a bit like someone in a theatre, watching a distant play unfold. By God, you had to have patience for a job like this. Everything had to be done by the book and had to be done in meticulous detail. He hadn't gone near the body yet himself. His chance would come later. Perhaps much later.

The wailing started again. It was coming from a police Ford Sierra parked on Lea Bridge Road. Jean Cooper's sister, being comforted in the back of the car by a WPC, being told to drink the hot sweet tea, knowing she would never see her sister alive again. But this was not the worst. Flight knew the worst was still to come, when the sister would formally identify Jean's body in the mortuary.

Jean Cooper had been easy enough to identify. Her handbag lay beside her on the path apparently untouched. In it were letters and house keys with an address tag attached. Flight couldn't help thinking about those house keys. It wasn't very clever to put your address on your keys, was it? A bit late for that now though. A bit late for crime prevention. The crying started again, a long plaintive howl, reaching into the orange glow of the sky above the River Lea and its marshes.

Flight looked towards the body, then retraced the route Jean had taken from Lea Bridge Road. She had walked less than fifty yards before being attacked. Fifty yards from a well-lit and busy main thoroughfare, less than twenty from the back of a row of flats. But this section of path depended for light upon a street lamp which was broken (the council would probably get round to fixing it now) and from whatever illumination was given from the windows of the flats. It was dark enough for the purpose all right. Dark enough for murder most foul.

He couldn't be sure that the Wolfman was responsible, not completely and utterly sure at this early stage. But he could feel it, like a numbing injection in his bones. The terrain was right. The stab wounds reported to him seemed right. And the Wolfman had been quiet for just under three weeks. Three weeks during which the trail had gone stone cold, as cold as a canal path. The Wolfman had taken a risk this time however, striking in late evening instead of at the dead of night. Someone might have seen him. The need for a rapid escape might have led him to leave a clue. Please, God, let him have left a clue. Flight rubbed at his stomach. The worms were gone, consumed by acid. He felt calm, utterly calm, for the first time in days.

'Excuse me.' The voice was muffled, and Flight half-turned to let the diver past him. This diver was followed by another, both of them holding powerful torches. Flight did not envy the police frogmen their job. The river was dark and poisonous, chilled and most probably the consistency of soup. But it had to be searched now. If the killer had dropped something into the Lea by mistake, or had thrown his knife into the river, it had to be recovered as soon as possible. Silt or shifting rubbish might cover it before daybreak. Simply, they couldn't afford the time. And so he had ordered a search just after hearing the news, before he had even left his warm and comfortable home to hurry to the scene. His wife had patted him on the arm. 'Try not to be late.' Both knew the words were meaningless.

He watched the first frogman slip into the water and stared entranced as the water began to glow from the torchlight. The second diver followed the first into the water and disappeared from view. Flight checked the sky. A thick layer of cloud lay still and silent above him.

The weather report was for early morning rain. It would dissolve footprints and wash fibres, bloodstains and hair into the hard-packed soil of the path. With any luck, they would complete the initial scene of crime work without the need for plastic tents.

'George!'

Flight turned to greet the newcomer. The man was in his mid-fifties, tall with cadaverous features lit up by a wide grin, or as wide as the long and narrow face would allow. He carried a large black bag in his left hand, and stretched out his right for Flight to shake. By his side walked a handsome woman of Flight's own age. In fact, as far as he could recall she was exactly one month and a day younger than him. Her name was Isobel Penny, and she was, in a euphemistic phrase, the cadaverous man's 'assistant' and 'secretary'. That they had been sleeping together these past eight or nine years was something nobody really discussed, though Isobel had told Flight all about it, for no other reason than that they had been in the same class together at school and had kept in touch with one another ever since.

'Hello, Philip,' said Flight, shaking the pathologist's hand.

Philip Cousins was not just a Home Office pathologist: he was by far the *best* Home Office pathologist, with a reputation resulting from twenty-five years' worth of work, twenty-five years during which, to Flight's knowledge, the man had never once 'got it wrong'. Cousins's eye for detail and his sheer bloody doggedness had seen him crack, or help crack, several dozen murder investigations, ranging from stranglings in Streatham to the poisoning of a government official in the West Indies. People who did not know him said that he looked the part, with his dark blue suits and cold grey features. They could not know about his quick and ready humour, his kindness, or the way he thrilled student doctors at his packed lectures. Flight had attended one of those lectures, something to do with arterial sclerosis and hadn't laughed so much in years.

'I thought you two were in Africa,' he said now, pecking Isobel on the cheek by way of greeting.

Cousins sighed. 'We were, but Penny got homesick.' He always called her by her surname. She gave him a playful thump on his forearm.

'You liar!' Then she turned her pale blue eyes to Flight. 'It was Philip,' she said. 'He couldn't bear to be away from his corpses. The first decent holiday we've had in years and he says he's *bored*. Can you believe that, George?'

Flight smiled and shook his head. 'Well, I'm glad you were able to make it. Looks like another victim of the Wolfman.'

Cousins looked over Flight's shoulder towards where the photographers were still photographing, the crouched scientists still sticky-taping, like so many flies about to settle on the corpse. He had examined the first three Wolfman victims, and that sort of continuity helped in a case. It wasn't just that he would know what to look for, what marks were indicative of the Wolfman; he would also spot anything not in keeping with the other killings, anything that might hint at a change of *modus operandi*: a different weapon, say, or a new angle of attack. Flight's mental picture of the Wolfman was coming together piece by tiny piece, but Cousins was the man who could show him where those pieces fitted.

'Inspector Flight?'

'Yes?' A man in a tweed jacket was approaching, carrying several cases and trailing a uniformed constable behind him. He placed the bags on the ground and introduced himself.

'John Rebus.' Flight's face remained blank. 'Inspector John Rebus.' The hand shot out, and Flight accepted it, feeling his grip strongly returned.

'Ah yes,' he said. 'Just arrived, have you?' He glanced meaningfully towards the bags. 'We weren't expecting you until tomorrow, Inspector.'

'Well, I got into King's Cross and heard about . . .' Rebus nodded towards the illuminated towpath. 'So I thought I'd come straight over.'

Flight nodded, trying to appear preoccupied. In fact, he was playing for time while he tried to come to grips with the Scotsman's thick accent. One of the forensic scientists had risen from his squatting position and was coming towards the group.

'Hello, Dr Cousins,' he said, before turning to Flight. 'We're pretty much finished if Dr Cousins wants to take a look.' Flight turned to Philip Cousins, who nodded gravely.

'Come on, Penny.'

Flight was about to follow them, when he remembered the new arrival. He turned back to John Rebus, his eyes immediately drifting down from Rebus's face to his loud and rustic jacket. He looked like something out of *Dr Finlay's Casebook*. Certainly, he looked out of place on this urban towpath at the dead of night.

'Do you want to take a look?' Flight asked generously. He watched as

Rebus nodded without enthusiasm. 'Okay, leave your bags where they are then.'

The two men started forward together, Cousins and Isobel a couple of yards in front. Flight pointed towards them. 'Dr Philip Cousins,' he said. 'You've probably heard of him.' But Rebus shook his head slowly. Flight stared at him as though Rebus had just failed to pick out the Queen from a row of postage stamps. 'Oh,' he said coldly. Then, pointing again: 'And that's Isobel Penny, Dr Cousins's assistant.'

Hearing her name, Isobel turned her head back and smiled. She had an attractive face, round and girl-like with a shiny glow to her cheeks. Physically, she was the antithesis of her companion. Though tall, she was well-built – what Rebus's father might have called big boned – and she boasted a healthy complexion to balance Cousins's sickly colour. Rebus couldn't recall ever having seen a really healthy looking pathologist. He put it down to all the time they spent standing under artificial light.

They had reached the body. The first thing Rebus saw was someone aiming a video camera towards him. But the camera moved away again to focus on the corpse. Flight was in conversation with one of the forensics team. Neither looked at the other's face, but concentrated instead on the strips of tape which had been carefully lifted from the corpse and which the scientist now held.

'Yes,' said Flight, 'no need to send them to the lab yet. We'll do another taping at the mortuary.' The man nodded and moved away. There was a noise from the river and Rebus turned to watch as a frogman broke the surface, looked around him, and then dived again. He knew a place like this in Edinburgh, a canal running through the west of the city, between parks and breweries and stretches of nothingness. He'd had to investigate a murder there once, the battered body of a tramp found beneath a road bridge, one foot in the canal. The killer had been easy to find: another tramp, an argument over a can of cider. The court had settled for manslaughter, but it hadn't been manslaughter. It had been murder. Rebus would never forget that.

'I think we should wrap those hands up right away,' Dr Cousins was saying in a rich Home Counties voice. 'I'll have a good look at them at the mortuary.'

'Right you are,' said Flight, going off to fetch some more polythene bags. Rebus watched the pathologist at work. He held a small tape recorder in one hand and talked into it from time to time. Isobel Penny meantime had produced a sketch-pad, and was drawing a picture of the body.

'Poor woman was probably dead before she hit the ground,' Cousins was saying. 'Little signs of bruising. Hypostasis seems consistent with the terrain. I'd say she certainly died on this spot.'

By the time Flight returned with some bags, Cousins, watched intermittently by Rebus, had taken readings of the air temperature and of internal temperature. The path on which they all stood was long and reasonably straight. The killer would have had ample visual warning of any approach. At the same time, there were homes and a main road nearby, so any screams would surely have been heard. Tomorrow there would be house-to-house enquiries. The path near the body was littered with rubbish: rusting drinks cans, crisp packets, sweet wrappers, torn and faded sheets of newsprint. In the river itself floated more rubbish and the red handle of a supermarket shopping-trolley broke the surface. Another diver had appeared, head and shoulders bobbing above the water. Where the main road crossed over the river, a crowd had gathered on the bridge, looking down towards the murder scene. Uniformed officers were doing their best to move the sightseers on, cordoning off as much of the area as they could.

'From the marks on the legs, dirt, some grazing and bruising,' continued the voice, 'I would say the victim fell to the ground or was pushed or lowered to the ground on her front. Only later was she turned over.' Dr Cousins's voice was level, disinterested. Rebus took in a few deep breaths and decided he had postponed the inevitable long enough. He had only come here to show willing, to show that he wasn't in London on a joyride. But now that he was here he supposed he should take a good close look at the body for himself. He turned away from the canal, the frogmen, the sightseers, and all the police officers standing behind the cordon. He turned away from the sight of his baggage standing all alone at the end of the path and gazed down on the corpse.

She was lying on her back, arms by her sides, legs together. Her tights and knickers had been pulled down to knee level, but her skirt was covering her, though he could see it was rucked up at the back. Her bright ski-style jacket was unzipped and her blouse had been ripped open, though her bra was intact. She had long straight black hair and wore large circlet earrings. Her face might have been pretty a few years ago, but life had ravaged it, leaving its marks. The killer had left marks, too. There was blood smeared across the face and matting the hair. The source of the blood was a gaping hole in the woman's throat. But there was also blood lying beneath her, spreading out from under the skirt.

'Turning her over,' said Dr Cousins to his tape recorder. He did so, with Flight's help, and then lifted the woman's hair away from the nape of her neck. 'Puncture wound,' he said into his tape recorder, 'consistent with larger wound to the throat. An exit wound, I'd say.'

But Rebus wasn't really listening to the doctor any longer. He was staring in horror at where the woman's skirt was rucked up. There was blood on the body, a lot of blood, staining the small of the back, the buttocks, the tops of the thighs. From the reports in his briefcase, he knew the cause of all this blood, but that didn't make it any easier to face the reality of it, the cold clear horror of it all. He took in more deep breaths. He had never yet vomited at a murder scene and he wasn't about to start now.

'No fuck-ups,' his boss had told him. It was a matter of pride. But Rebus knew now that the purpose of his trip to London was very serious indeed. It wasn't to do with 'pride' or 'putting up a good show' or 'doing his best'. It was to do with catching a pervert, a horrifically brutal sadist, and doing so before he could strike again. And if it took silver bullets, by God silver bullets there would be.

* * *

Rebus was still shaking when, at the operations van, someone handed him a plastic beaker of tea.

'Thanks.'

He could always blame his gooseflesh on the cold. Not that it was cold, not really. The cloud cover helped and there was no wind. Of course, London was usually a few degrees warmer than Edinburgh at any time of year and there wasn't the same wind, that bitter and biting wind which whipped across the streets of Edinburgh in summer as well as winter. In fact, if Rebus were asked to describe the weather on this night, the word he would use would be balmy.

He closed his eyes for a moment, not tired, just trying to shut out the sight of Jean Cooper's cooling body. But she seemed etched onto his eyelids in all her grim glory. Rebus had been relieved to note that even Inspector George Flight was not unmoved. His actions, movements and speech had become somehow damped or more muted, as though he were consciously holding back some emotion, the urge to scream or kick out. The divers were coming up from the river, having found nothing. They would look again in the morning, but their voices betrayed a lack of hope. Flight listened to their report and nodded, all the time watched, from behind his beaker of tea, by Rebus.

George Flight was in his late forties, a few years older than Rebus. He wasn't short, yet he had an appearance best described as stocky. There was the hint of a paunch, but a much greater hint of muscle. Rebus didn't rate his own chances against him in a clinch. Flight's wiry brown hair was thin at the crown, but thick elsewhere. He was dressed in a leather bomber jacket and denims. Most men in their forties looked stupid in denims, but not Flight. They fitted his attitude and his brisk, businesslike walk.

A long time before, Rebus had graded CID men into three sartorial groups: the leather-and-denim brigade, who wanted to look as tough as they felt; the suit-and-tie dapper merchants, who were looking for promotion and respect (not necessarily in that order); and the nondescripts, men who wore anything that came to hand of a morning, their year's fashions usually the result of an hour's shopping in a big-name department store.

Most CID men were nondescripts. Rebus reckoned he himself fell into that group. Yet catching a glimpse of himself in a wing-mirror, he noticed that he had a dapper look. Suit-and-ties never got on with leather-and-denims.

Now Flight was shaking hands with an important looking man, who other than for the handshake, kept his hands in his pockets and listened to Flight with head angled downwards, nodding occasionally as though deep in thought. He wore a suit and a black woollen coat. He couldn't have been more crisply dressed if it had been the middle of the day. Most people were beginning to look fatigued, their clothes and faces crumpled. There were only two exceptions: this man and Philip Cousins.

The man was shaking hands with Dr Cousins now and even extended a greeting to Dr Cousins's assistant. And then Flight gestured towards the van . . . no, towards *Rebus*! They were coming towards him. Rebus brought the beaker away from his face, and swapped it from his right to his left hand, just in case a handshake was in the offing.

'This is Inspector Rebus,' Flight said.

'Ah, our man from north of the border,' said the important looking man with a wry, rather superior smile. Rebus returned the smile but looked to Flight.

'Inspector Rebus, this is Chief Inspector Howard Laine.'

'How do you do.' The handshake. Howard Laine: it sounded like a street-name.

'So,' said Chief Inspector Laine, 'you're here to help us with our little problem?'

'Well,' said Rebus, 'I'm not sure what I can do, sir, but rest assured I'll do what I can.'

There was a pause, then Laine smiled but said nothing. The truth hit Rebus like lightning splitting a tree: *they couldn't understand him!* They were standing there smiling at him, but they couldn't understand his accent. Rebus cleared his throat and tried again.

'Whatever I can do to help, sir.'

Laine smiled again. 'Excellent, Inspector, excellent. Well, I'm sure Inspector Flight here will show you the ropes. Settled in all right, have you?'

'Well, actually –'

Flight himself interrupted. 'Inspector Rebus came straight here, sir, as soon as he heard about the murder. He's only just arrived in London.'

'Is that so?' Laine sounded impressed, but Rebus could see that the man was growing restless. This was smalltalk, and he did not like to think he had time for smalltalk. His eyes sought some escape. 'Well, Inspector,' he said, 'I'm sure we'll meet again.' And turning to Flight: 'I'd better be off, George. Everything under control?' Flight merely nodded. 'Good, fine, well . . .' And with that the Chief Inspector started back towards his car, accompanied by Flight. Rebus exhaled noisily. He felt completely out of his territory here. He knew when he was not wanted and wondered just whose idea it had been to second him to the Wolfman case. Someone with a warped sense of humour, that was for sure. His boss had passed the letter over to him.

'It seems,' he had said, 'you've become an expert on serial killers, John, and they're a bit short on those in the Met just now. They'd like you to go down to London for a few days, see if you can come up with anything, maybe give them a few ideas.'

Rebus had read the letter through in growing disbelief. It referred to a case from a few years before, the case of a child murderer, a case Rebus had cracked. But that had been personal, not really a serial killer at all.

'I don't know anything about serial killers,' Rebus had protested to his boss.

'Well then, it seems like you'll be in good company, doesn't it?'

And now look at him, standing on a stretch of ground in north-east London, a cup of unspeakably bad tea nursed in both hands, his stomach churning, nerves buzzing, his bags looking as lonely and out of place as he felt. Here to help solve the insoluble, *our man from north of the border*. Whose idea had it been to bring him here? No police force in the country liked to admit failure; yet by lugging Rebus down here the Met was doing precisely that.

Laine had gone and Flight seemed a little more relaxed. He even found time to smile reassuringly across to Rebus before giving orders to two men who, Rebus knew, would be from a funeral parlour. The men went back to their vehicle and returned with a large folded piece of plastic. They crossed the cordon and stopped at the body, laying the plastic out beside it. It was a translucent bag, over six feet long with a zip running from head to toe. Dr Cousins was in close attendance as the two men opened the bag and lifted the body into it, closing the zipper. One photographer had decided to shoot off a few more flash photographs of the spot where the body had lain, while the attendants carried the corpse back through the cordon and up to their vehicle.

Rebus noticed that the crowd of onlookers had disappeared, and only a few curious souls remained. One of them, a young man, was carrying a crash helmet and wore a shiny black leather jacket with shinier silver zips. A very tired constable was trying to move him on.

Rebus felt like an onlooker himself and thought of all the TV dramas and films he'd seen, with detectives swarming over the murder site in minute one (destroying any forensic evidence in the process) and solving the murder by minute fifty-nine or eighty-nine. Laughable, really. Police work was just that: work. Relentless, routine, dull, frustrating, and above all time-consuming. He checked his watch. It was exactly 2 am. His hotel was back in central London, tucked somewhere behind Piccadilly Circus. It would take another thirty to forty minutes to get back there, always supposing a spare patrol car was available.

'Coming?'

It was Flight, standing a few yards in front of him.

'Might as well,' said Rebus, knowing exactly what Flight was talking about, or more accurately *where* he was talking about.

Flight smiled. 'I'll give you this, Inspector Rebus, you don't give up.'

'The famous tenacity of the Scots,' said Rebus, quoting from one of Sunday's newspaper rugby reports. Flight actually laughed. It didn't last long, but it made Rebus feel glad that he'd come here tonight. The ice hadn't been broken completely perhaps, but an important chunk had been chipped away from one corner of the berg.

'Come on then. I've got my car. I'll get one of the drivers to put your bags in his boot. The lock's stuck on mine. Somebody tried to crowbar it open a few weeks back.' He glanced towards Rebus, a rare moment of eye contact. 'Nowhere is safe these days,' he said. 'Nowhere.'

There was already a lot of commotion up at road level. Voices and the slamming shut of car doors. Some officers would stay behind, of course, guarding the site. And a few might be going back to the warmth of the station or – luxury hardly to be imagined! – their own beds. But a few of the cars would be following the funeral van, following it all the way to the mortuary.

Rebus travelled in the front of Flight's own car. Both men spent the journey in desperate pursuit of a conversational opening and as a result said very little until they were near their destination.

'Do we know who she was?' asked Rebus.

'Jean Cooper,' said Flight. 'We found ID in her handbag.'

'Any reason for her to be on that path?'

'She was going home from work. She worked in an off-licence nearby. Her sister tells us she finished work at seven.'

'When was the body found?'

'Quarter to ten.'

'That's a fair gap.'

'We've got witnesses who saw her in the Dog and Duck. That's a pub near where she works. She used to go in there for a drink some evenings. The barmaid reckons she left at nine or thereabouts.'

Rebus stared out of the windscreen. The roads were still fairly busy considering the time of night and they passed groups of youthful and raucous pedestrians.

'There's a club in Stokie,' Flight explained. 'Very popular, but the buses have stopped by the time it comes out so everyone walks home.'

Rebus nodded, then asked: 'Stokie?'

Flight smiled. 'Stoke Newington. You probably passed through it on your way from King's Cross.'

'God knows,' said Rebus. 'It all looked the same to me. I think my taxi driver had me down as a tourist. We took so long from King's Cross I think we might have come via the M25.' Rebus waited for Flight to laugh, but all he raised was a sliver of a smile. There was another pause. 'Was this Jean Cooper single?' Rebus asked at last.

'Married.'

'She wasn't wearing a wedding ring.'

Flight nodded. 'Separated. She lived with her sister. No kids.'

'And she went drinking by herself.'

Flight glanced towards Rebus. 'What are you saying?'

Rebus shrugged. 'Nothing. It's just that if she liked a good time, maybe that's how she met her killer.'

'It's possible.'

'At any rate, whether she knew him or not, the killer could have followed her from the pub.'

'We'll be talking to everybody who was there, don't worry.'

'Either that,' said Rebus, thinking aloud, 'or the killer was waiting by the river for anyone who happened along. Somebody might have seen him.'

'We'll be asking around,' said Flight. His voice had taken on a much harder edge.

'Sorry,' said Rebus. 'A severe case of teaching my granny to suck eggs.'

Flight turned to him again. They were about to take a left through some hospital gates. 'I am not your granny,' he said. 'And any comments you have to make are welcome. Maybe eventually you'll come up with something I haven't already thought of.'

'Of course,' said Rebus, 'this couldn't have happened in Scotland.'

'Oh?' Flight had a half-sneer on his face. 'Why's that then? Too civilised up there in the frozen north? I remember when you had the worst football hooligans in the world. Maybe you still do, only these days they look like butter wouldn't melt in their underpants.'

But Rebus was shaking his head. 'No, it wouldn't have happened to Jean Cooper, that's all I meant. Our off-licences don't open on Sunday.'

Rebus fell silent and stared fixedly at the windscreen, keeping his thoughts to himself, thoughts which ran along a very simple plane: fuck you, too, pal. Over the years, those four words had become his mantra. Fuck you, too, pal. FYTP. It had taken the Londoner only the length of a twenty-minute car ride to show what he really thought of the Scots.

As Rebus got out of the car, he glanced in through the rear window and saw, for the first time, the contents of the back seat. He opened his mouth to speak, but Flight raised a knowing hand.

'Don't even ask,' he growled, slamming shut the driver's-side door. 'And listen, I'm sorry about what I said . . .'

Rebus merely shrugged, but his eyebrows descended in a private and thoughtful frown. After all, there had to be *some* logical explanation as to why a Detective Inspector would have a huge stuffed teddy bear in the back of his car at the scene of a murder. It was just that Rebus was damned if he could think of one right this second . . .

*

Mortuaries were places where the dead stopped being people and turned instead into bags of meat, offal, blood and bone. Rebus had never been sick at the scene of a crime, but the first few times he had visited a mortuary the contents of his stomach had fairly quickly been rendered up for examination.

The mortuary technician was a gleeful little man with a livid birthmark covering a full quarter of his face. He seemed to know Dr Cousins well enough and had prepared everything for the arrival of the deceased and the usual retinue of police officers. Cousins checked the post-mortem room, while Jean Cooper's sister was taken quietly into an ante-room, there to make the formal identification. It took only a tearful few seconds, after which she was escorted well away from the scene by consoling officers. They would take her home, but Rebus doubted if she would get any sleep. In fact, knowing how long a scrupulous pathologist could take, he was beginning to doubt that any of them would get to bed before morning.

Eventually, the body bag was brought into the post-mortem room and the corpse of Jean Cooper placed on a slab, beneath the hum and glare of powerful strip lighting. The room was antiseptic but antique. Its tiled walls were cracking and there was a stinging aroma of chemicals. Voices were kept muffled, not so much out of respect but from a strange kind of fear. The mortuary, after all, was one vast memento mori, and what was about to happen to Jean Cooper's body would serve to remind each and every one of them that if the body were a temple, then it was possible to loot that temple, scattering its treasures, revealing its precious secrets.

A hand landed gently on Rebus's shoulder, and he turned, startled, towards the man who was standing there. 'Man' was by way of simplification. This tall and unsmiling individual had cropped fair hair and the acne-ridden face of an adolescent. He looked about fourteen, but Rebus placed him in his mid-twenties.

'You're the Jock, aren't you?' There was interest in the voice, but little emotion. Rebus said nothing. FYTP. 'Yeah, thought so. Cracked the case yet, have you?' The grin accompanying this question was three-quarters sneer and one-quarter scowl. 'We don't *need* any help.'

'Ah,' said George Flight, 'I see you've already met DC Lamb. I was just about to introduce you.'

'Delighted,' said Rebus, gazing stonily at the join-the-dots pattern of spots on Lamb's forehead. Lamb! No surname in history, Rebus felt, had ever been less deserved, less accurate. Over by the slab, Dr Cousins cleared his throat noisily.

'Gentlemen,' he said to the room at large. It was little more than an indication that he was about to start work. The room fell quiet again. A microphone hung down from the ceiling to within a few feet of the slab. Cousins turned to the technician. 'Is this thing on now?' The technician nodded keenly from between arranging a row of clanging metallic instruments along a tray.

Rebus knew all the instruments, had seen them all in action. The cutters and the saws and the drills. Some of them were electrical, some needed a human force to drive them home. The sounds the electrical ones made were horrible, but at least the job was over quickly; the manual tools made similarly revolting sounds that seemed to last forever. Still, there would be an interval before that particular shop of horrors. First of all there was the slow and careful business of removing the clothing and bagging it up for Forensics.

As Rebus and the others watched, the two photographers clicked away, one taking black and white shots and the other colour, recording for posterity each stage of the process. The video cameraman had given up, however, his equipment having jammed irreparably on one of the bargain tapes. Or at least that was the story which kept him away from the mortuary.

Finally, when the corpse was naked, Cousins pointed to a few areas meriting particular close-up shots. Then the Forensics men moved in again, armed with more lengths of sticky tape. Now that the body was unclothed, the same process as was carried out on the tow-path had to be gone through again. Not for nothing were these people known as Sellotape Men.

Cousins wandered over towards the group where Rebus, Flight and Lamb stood.

'I'd kill for a cup of tea, George.'

'I'll see what I can do, Philip. What about Isobel?'

Cousins looked back towards where Isobel Penny stood, making another drawing of the corpse despite the welter of camera shots. 'Penny,' he called, 'care for a cuppa?' Her eyes opened a little and she nodded enthusiastically.

'Right,' said Flight, moving towards the door. Rebus thought the man seemed more than a little relieved to be leaving, albeit temporarily.

'Nasty little chap,' Cousins commented. Rebus wondered for a moment if he were talking about George Flight, but Cousins waved a hand towards the corpse. 'To do this sort of thing time after time, without motive, out of some need for . . . well, pleasure, I suppose.'

'There's always a motive, sir,' said Rebus. 'You just said so yourself. Pleasure, that's his motive. But the way he kills. What he does. There's some other motive there. It's just that we can't see it yet.'

Cousins stared at him. Rebus could see a warm light in his deep eyes. 'Well, Inspector, let us hope *somebody* spots whatever it is before too long. Four deaths in as many months. The man's as constant as the moon.'

Rebus smiled. 'But we all know that werewolves are affected by the moon, don't we?'

Cousins laughed. It was deep and resonant and sounded extraordinarily out of place in this environment. Lamb wasn't laughing, wasn't even smiling. He was following little of this conversation, and the realisation pleased Rebus. But Lamb wasn't going to be left out.

'I reckon he's barking mad. Hee, get it?'

'Well,' said Cousins, as though this joke was too well-worn even to merit acknowledgment, 'must press on.' He turned towards the slab. 'If you've finished, gentlemen?' The Forensics men nodded in unison. 'Jewellery removed?' They nodded again. 'Good. Then if you are ready, I suggest we begin.'

The beginning was never too awful. Measurements, a physical description – five feet and seven inches tall, brown hair, that sort of thing. Fingernail scrapings and clippings were deposited in yet more polythene bags. Rebus made a note to buy shares in whichever company manufactured these bags. He'd seen murder investigations go through hundreds of them.

Slowly but determinedly, things got worse. Swabs were taken from Jean Cooper's vagina, then Cousins got down to some serious work.

'Large puncture wound to the throat. From size of wound, I'd say the knife itself had been twisted in the wound. A small knife. From the extent of the exit wound I would say the blade was about five inches long, perhaps a little less, and about an inch deep, ending in a very fine point. The skin surrounding the entry wound shows some bruising, perhaps caused by the hilt-guard or handle. This would seem to indicate that the knife was driven in with a certain amount of force.

'The hands and arms show no signs of defence wounding, so the victim had no time in which to defend herself. The possibility exists that she was approached from behind. There is some colouring around the mouth and the victim's lipstick had been slightly smeared across her right cheek. If she was approached from behind, a possible scenario would be that the attacker's left hand closed over her mouth to stop her from screaming, thus smearing the lipstick while the attacker stabbed with the right hand. The wound to the throat shows a slight downward angle, which would indicate someone taller than the victim.'

Cousins cleared his throat again. Well, thought Rebus, so far they could strike the mortuary attendant and one of the photographers off the possible list of suspects: everyone else in the room was five feet eight or over.

The pause in proceedings gave the onlookers a chance to shuffle their feet, clear their own throats, and glance at each other, taking note of how pale this or that face was. Rebus was surprised at the pathologist's 'scenarios': that was supposed to be *their* job, not his. All the pathologists Rebus had ever worked with had given the bare facts, leaving the deductions to Rebus himself. But Cousins obviously did not work that way. Perhaps he was a frustrated detective. Rebus still found it hard to believe that people came to pathology through choice.

Tea appeared, carried in three beakers on a plastic tray by Inspector Flight. Cousins and Isobel Penny took a cup each, and Flight himself took the other. There were jealous stares from a few dry-mouthed officers. Rebus was among them.

'Now,' said Cousins between sips, 'I'm going to examine the anal wound.'

It just kept on getting worse. Rebus tried to concentrate on what Cousins was saying, but it wasn't easy. The same knife had been used to make several stabs to the anus. There were friction marks on the thighs from where the tights had been roughly pulled down. Rebus looked over to Isobel Penny, but, apart from some slight heightening of the colour in her cheeks, she seemed dispassionate. A cool customer and no mistake. But then she'd probably seen worse in her time. No, no, she couldn't possibly have seen worse than *this*. Could she?

'The stomach is interesting,' Cousins was saying. 'The blouse has been torn away to expose the stomach, and there are two lines of curved indentations in the skin, enough to have bruised and broken the skin, but there is little actual marking of the skin and no blood, from which I would say that this act was perpetrated only *after* the stabbings. After, in fact, the victim was dead. There are a few dried stains on the stomach near these bite marks. Without prejudging, past evidence from three very similar cases showed these stains to be saline in nature –

teardrops or perhaps beads of sweat. I'm now going to take a deep body temperature.'

Rebus felt parched. He was hot, and the tiredness was seeping into his bones, lack of sleep giving everything a hallucinatory quality. There were halos around the pathologist, his assistant, and the technician. The walls seemed to be moving, and Rebus dared not concentrate on them for fear that he would lose his balance. He happened to catch Lamb's eye and the Detective Constable gave him an ugly grin and an uglier wink.

The body was washed now, washed for the first time, freed from a staining of light brown and black, from the pale matt covering of blood. Cousins examined it again, finding nothing new, after which another set of fingerprints was taken. Then came the internal examination.

A deep incision was made down the front of the body. Blood samples were taken and handed to the forensics team, as were samples of urine, stomach contents, liver, body hair (eyebrows included) and tissue. The process used to make Rebus impatient. It was obvious how the victim had died, so why bother with everything else? But he had learned over the years that what you could *see*, the external injuries, often wasn't as important as what you couldn't see, the tiny secrets only a microscope or a chemical test could reveal. So he had learned patience and exercised it now, stifling a yawn every half minute or so.

'Not boring you am I?' Cousins's voice was a polite murmur. He looked up from his work and caught Rebus's eyes, then smiled.

'Not a bit,' said Rebus.

'That's all right then. I'm sure we'd all rather be at home tucked up in bed than in this place.' Only the birthmarked technician seemed doubtful as to the truth of this statement. Cousins was reaching a hand into the corpse's chest. 'I'll be out of here as soon as I can.'

It wasn't the sight of this examination, Rebus decided, that turned men pale. It was the accompanying sound effects. The tearing of flesh, as though a butcher were yanking meat from a flank. The bubbling of liquids and the soft rasping of the cutting tools. If he could somehow block up his ears, maybe everything would be bearable. But on the contrary, his ears seemed extraordinarily sensitive in this room. Next time, he'd bring plugs of cotton wool with him. Next time . . .

The chest and abdominal organs were removed and taken to a clean slab, where a hose was used to wash them clean before Cousins dissected them. The attendant meantime was called into action, removing the brain with the help of a tiny powered circular-saw. Rebus had his eyes shut now, but the room seemed to swirl all the same. Not long to go now though. Not long, thank God. But it wasn't just the sounds now, was it? It was the smell too, that unmistakable aroma of raw meat. It clung to the nostrils like perfume, filling the lungs, catching the back of the throat and clinging there, so that eventually it became a tang in the mouth and he found himself actually tasting it. His stomach moved momentarily, but he rubbed it gently, surreptitiously with a hand. Not surreptitiously enough.

'If you're going to throw up,' it was Lamb again, like a succubus over his shoulder, hissing, 'go outside.' And then the chuckle, throaty and slow like a stalled engine. Rebus half-turned his head and gave a dangerous smile.

Soon enough, the whole mess of matter was being put together again, and Rebus knew that by the time any grieving relatives viewed the mortal remains of Jean Cooper, the body would look quite natural.

As ever, by the end of the autopsy the room had been reduced to silent introspection. Each man and woman present was made of the same stuff as Jean Cooper, and now they stood, momentarily stripped of their individual personalities. They were all bodies, all animals, all collections of viscera. The only difference between them and Jean Cooper was that their hearts still pumped blood. But one day soon enough each heart would stop, and that would be an end of it, save for the possibility of a visit to this butcher's shop, this abattoir.

Cousins removed his rubber gloves and washed his hands thoroughly, accepted from the attendant a proffered sheaf of paper towels. 'That's about it then, gentlemen, until Penny can type up the notes. Murdered between nine o'clock and nine-thirty I'd guess. Same *modus operandi* as our so-called Wolfman. I think I've just examined his fourth victim. I'll get in Anthony Morrison tomorrow, let him have a look at the teeth marks. See what he says.'

Since everyone seemed to know except Rebus, Rebus asked, 'Who's Anthony Morrison?'

Flight was first to answer. 'A dentist.'

'A dental pathologist,' corrected Cousins. 'And quite a good one. He's got details of the other three murders. His analyses of the bite marks have been quite useful.' Cousins turned to Flight for confirmation of this, but Flight's eyes were directed towards his shoes, as if to say *I wouldn't go that far.*

'Well,' said Cousins, seeming to take the silent hint, 'at any rate, you know my findings. It's down to your lab chaps now. There's precious little there . . .' Cousins nodded back towards the scooped-out husk of the corpse, 'to help with your investigation. That being so, I think I'll go home to bed.'

Flight seemed to realise that Cousins was displeased with him. 'Thank you, Philip.' And the detective lifted a hand to rest it against the pathologist's arm. Cousins looked at the hand, then at Flight, and smiled.

The performance at an end, the audience began to shuffle out into the cold, still darkness of an emerging day. By Rebus's watch, it was four thirty. He felt completely exhausted, could happily have lain down on the lawn in front of the main building and taken a nap, but Flight was walking towards him, carrying his bags.

'Come on,' he said. 'I'll give you a lift.'

In his fragile state, Rebus felt this to be the nicest, kindest thing anyone had said to him in weeks. 'Are you sure you have room?' he said. 'I mean, with the teddy bear and all.'

Flight paused. 'Or if you'd prefer to walk, Inspector?'

Rebus threw up his hands in surrender, then, when the door was unlocked, slipped into the passenger seat of Flight's red Sierra. The seat seemed to wrap itself around him.

'Here,' said Flight, handing a hip flask to Rebus. Rebus unscrewed the top of the flask and sniffed. 'It won't kill you,' Flight called. This was probably true. The aroma was of whisky. Not great whisky, not a smoky island malt, but a decent enough proprietary brand. Well, it would help keep him awake perhaps until they reached the hotel. Rebus toasted the windscreen and let the liquid trickle into his mouth.

Flight got behind the steering-wheel and started the car, then, as the car idled, accepted the flask from Rebus and drank from it greedily.

'How far to the hotel from here?' Rebus asked.

'About twenty minutes at this time of night,' said Flight, screwing tight the stopper and replacing the flask in his pocket. 'That's if we stop for red lights.'

'You have my permission to run every red light you see.'

Flight laughed tiredly. Both men were wondering how to turn the conversation around to the autopsy.

'Best leave it until morning, eh?' said Rebus, speaking for them both. Flight merely nodded and moved off, waving to Cousins and Isobel Penny, who were about to get into their car. Rebus stared out of his side window to where DC Lamb stood beside his own car, a flash little sports model. Typical, thought Rebus. Just typical. Lamb stared back at him, and then gave that three-quarters sneer again.

FYTP, Rebus mentally intoned. FYTP. Then he turned in his seat to examine the teddy bear behind him. Flight was resolutely refusing to take the hint, and Rebus, though curious, wasn't about to jeopardise whatever relationship he might be able to strike up with this man by asking the obvious question. Some things were always best left until morning.

The whisky had cleared his nostrils, lungs and throat. He breathed deeply, seeing in his mind the little mortuary attendant, that livid birthmark, and Isobel Penny, sketching like any amateur artist. She might have been in front of a museum exhibit for all the emotion she had shown. He wondered what her secret was, the secret of her absolute calmness, but thought he probably knew in any case. Her job had become merely that: a job. Maybe one day Rebus would feel the same way. But he hoped not.

If anything, Flight and Rebus said less during the drive to the hotel than they had done on the way to the mortuary. The whisky was working on Rebus's empty stomach and the interior of the car was oppressively hot. He tried opening his window a quarter of an inch, but the blast of chill air only made things worse.

The autopsy was being played out again before him. The cutting tools, the lifting of organs out of the body, the incisions and inspections, Cousins's face peering at spongy tissue from no more than an inch away. One twitch and his face would have been smothered in . . . Isobel Penny watching all, recording all, the slice from throat to pubis . . . London sped past him. Flight, true to his word, was cruising through some red lights and slowing merely for others. There were still cars on the streets. The city never slept. Nightclubs, parties, drifters, the homeless. Sleepless dog-walkers, all night bakeries and beigel shops. Some spelt 'beigel' and some spelt 'bagel'. What the hell was a beigel? Wasn't that what they were always eating in Woody Allen films?

Samples from her eyebrows, for Christ's sake. What use were samples from her eyebrows? They should be concentrating on the attacker, not the victim. Those teeth marks. What was the dentist's name again? Not a dentist, a dental *pathologist*. Morrison. Yes, that was it. Morrison, like the street in Edinburgh, Morrison Street, not too far from the brewery canal, where the swans lived, a single pair of swans. What happened when they died? Did the brewery replace them? So damned hot in this shiny red car. Rebus could feel his insides wanting to become his outsides. The knife twisted in the throat. A small knife. He could almost visualise it. Something like a kitchen knife. Sharp, sour taste in his mouth.

'Nearly there,' said Flight. 'Just along Shaftesbury Avenue. That's Soho on the right. By God, we've cleaned that den up this past few years. You wouldn't believe it. You know, I've been thinking, where the body was found, it's not so far from where the Krays used to live. Somewhere on Lea Bridge Road. I was just a young copper when they were on the go.'

'Please . . .' said Rebus.

'They did somebody in Stokie. Jack McVitie, I think it was. Jack the Hat, they called him.'

'Can you stop here?' Rebus blurted out. Flight looked at him.

'What's up?'

'I need some air. I'll walk the rest of the way. Just stop the car, please.'

Flight began to protest, but pulled over to the kerb. Stepping out of the car, Rebus immediately felt better. There was cold sweat on his forehead, neck and back. He breathed deeply. Flight deposited his bags on the pavement.

'Thanks again,' said Rebus. 'Sorry about this. Just point me in the general direction.'

'Just off the Circus,' Flight said.

Rebus nodded. 'I hope there's a night porter.' Yes, he was feeling much better.

'It's a quarter to five,' said Flight. 'You'll probably catch the day shift coming on.' He laughed, but the laugh died quickly and he gave Rebus a serious nod of his head. 'You made your point tonight, John. Okay?'

Rebus nodded back. *John*. Another chip from the iceberg, or just good management?

'Thanks,' he said. They shook hands. 'Are we still on for a meeting at ten?'

'Let's make it eleven, eh? I'll have someone pick you up from your hotel.'

Rebus nodded and picked up his bags. Then bent down again towards the car's back window. 'Good night, teddy,' he said.

'Watch you don't get lost!' Flight called to him from the car. Then the car moved off, making a screeching u-turn before roaring back the way they had come. Rebus looked around him. Shaftesbury Avenue. The buildings seemed about to swamp him. Theatres. Shops. Litter: the debris from a Sunday night out. A dull roar preceded the arrival, from one of the misty side streets, of a dustcart. The men were dressed in orange overalls. They paid no attention to Rebus as he trudged past them. How long was this street? It seemed to follow a vast curve, longer than he had expected.

Bloody London. Then he spotted Eros atop his fountain, but there was something wrong. The Circus was no longer a Circus. Eros had been paved in, so that traffic had to sweep past it rather than around it. Why the hell had anyone decided to do that? A car was slowing behind him, coming parallel with him. White car with an orange stripe: a police car. The officer in the passenger seat had wound down his window and now called out to him.

'Excuse me, sir, do you mind telling me where you're going?'

'What?' The question stunned Rebus, stopped him in his tracks. The car had stopped too and both driver and passenger were emerging.

'Are those your bags, sir?'

Rebus felt it rise within him, a shining hard steel pole of anger. Then he happened to catch sight of himself in the window of the patrol car. A quarter to five on the streets of London. A dishevelled, unshaven man, a man obviously without sleep, carrying a suitcase, a bag and a briefcase. A *briefcase*? Who the hell would be carrying a briefcase around at this time of the morning? Rebus put down his luggage and rubbed at the bridge of his nose with one hand. And before he knew what was happening, his shoulders began moving, his body convulsing with laughter. The two uniformed officers were looking at one another. Rebus sniffed back the laughter and reached into his inside pocket. One of the officers stepped back a pace.

'Take it easy, son,' Rebus said. He produced his ID. 'I'm on your side.' The less cagey officer, the passenger, took the ID from Rebus, examined it, then handed it back.

'You're a long way off your patch, sir.'

'You don't have to tell me that,' said Rebus. 'What's your name, son?'

The constable was wary now. 'Bennett, sir. Joey Bennett. I mean, Joseph Bennett.'

'All right, Joey. Would you like to do me a favour?' The constable nodded. 'Do you know the Prince Royal Hotel?'

'Yes, sir.' Bennett began to point with his left hand. 'It's about fifty yards —'

'All right,' Rebus interrupted. 'Just show me, will you?' The young man said nothing. 'Will you do that, Constable Bennett?'

'Yes, sir.'

Rebus nodded. Yes, he could handle London. He could take it on and win. 'Right,' he said, moving off towards the Prince Royal. 'Oh,' he said, turning back and taking in both men with his glance, 'and bring my bags, will you?' Rebus had his back to them again, but he could almost hear the sound of two jaws dropping open. 'Or,' he called back, 'shall I just inform Chief Inspector Laine that two of his officers harassed me on my first night as his guest in this fine city?'

Rebus kept on walking, hearing the two officers pick up his luggage and hurry after him. They were arguing as to whether or not they should leave the patrol car unlocked. He was smiling, despite everything. A small victory, a bit of a cheat, but what the hell. This was London, after all. This was Shaftesbury Avenue. And that was showbiz.

* * *

Home at last, she had a good wash, and after that she felt a little better. She had brought in a black bin-liner from the boot of her car. It contained the clothes she had been wearing, cheap flimsy things. Tomorrow evening she would tidy the back garden and light a bonfire.

She wasn't crying any more. She had calmed down. She always calmed down afterwards. From a polythene shopping bag she removed another polythene bag, from which she removed the bloodied knife. The kitchen sink was full of boiling, soapy water. The polythene bags went into the bin-liner with the clothes, the knife went into the sink. She washed it carefully, emptying and refilling the washing bowl, all the time humming to herself. It wasn't a recognisable song, nor even really a tune. But it calmed her, it soothed her, the way her mother's hummed lullabies always had.

There, all done. It was hard work, and she was pleased to be finished with it. Concentration was the key. A lapse in concentration, and you could make a slip, then fail to spot that slip. She rinsed the sink three times, sluicing away every last speckle of blood, and left the knife to dry on the draining-board. Then she walked out into the hallway and paused at one of the doors while she found the key.

This was her secret room, her picture gallery. Inside, one wall was all but covered by oil and watercolour paintings. Three of these paintings were damaged beyond repair. A pity, since all three had been favourites. Her favourite now was a small countryside stream. Simple, pale colours and a naive style. The stream was in the foreground and beside it sat a man and a boy, or it could have been a man and a girl. It was hard to tell, that was the problem with the naive style. It was not as though she could even ask the artist, for the artist had been dead for years.

She tried not to look at the other wall, the wall directly opposite. It was a horrid wall. She didn't like what she could see there from the corner of one eye. She decided that what she liked about her favourite painting was its size. It was about ten inches by eight, excluding the rather Baroque gilt frame (which did not suit it at all – her mother had never had much taste in frames). These petite dimensions, added to the washed colours, gave the whole a subtlety and a lack of vision, a humility, a gentleness, which pleased her. Of course, it depicted no great truth, this painting. In fact, it was a monstrous lie, the absolute opposite of the facts. There had been no stream, no touching scene of father and child. There had been only horror. That was why Velasquez was her favourite painter: shadowplay, rich shades of black, skulls and suspicion . . . the dark heart exposed.

'The dark heart.' She nodded to herself. She had seen things, felt things, which few were ever privileged to witness. This was her life. This was her existence. And the painting began to mock her, the stream turning into a cruel turquoise grin.

Calmly, humming to herself again she picked up a pair of scissors from a nearby chair and began to slash at the painting with regular vertical strokes, then horizontal strokes, then vertical again, tearing and tearing its heart out until the scene disappeared forever.

Underground

'And this,' said George Flight, 'is where the Wolfman was born.'

Rebus looked. It was a depressing location for a birth. A cobblestoned alley, a cul-de-sac, the buildings three storeys high, every window either boarded up or barred and grilled. The black bags of rubbish looked to have been languishing by the side of the road for weeks. A few had been impaled on the steel spiked fencing in front of the shut-up windows, and these bags leaked their rank contents the way a cracked sewage pipe would.

'Nice,' he said.

'The buildings are mainly disused. Local bands use the basement of one of them as a practice room, and make quite a racket while they're about it.' Flight pointed to a barred and grilled window. 'And I think that's a clothing manufacturer or distributor. Anyway, he hasn't been back since we started taking an interest in the street.'

'Oh?' Rebus sounded interested, but Flight shook his head.

'Nothing suspicious in that, believe me. These guys use slave labour, Bangladeshis, mostly illegal immigrants. The last thing they want is policemen sniffing around. They'll move the machines and set up again somewhere else.'

Rebus nodded. He was looking around the cul-de-sac, trying to remember, from the photographs he had been sent, just where the body had been found.

'It was there.' Flight was pointing to a gate in the iron railings. Ah yes, Rebus remembered now. Not at street level, but down some stone steps leading to a basement. The victim had been found at the bottom of the steps, same *modus operandi* as last night, down to the bite marks on the stomach. Rebus opened his briefcase and brought out the manila folder, opening it at the sheet he needed.

'Maria Watkiss, age thirty-eight. Occupation: prostitute. Body found on Tuesday 16th January by council workmen. Estimated that victim had been murdered two to three days prior to being discovered. Rudimentary attempt had been made to conceal body.'

Flight nodded towards one of the impaled bin-liners. 'He emptied a bag of rubbish out over her. It pretty well covered the body. The rats alerted the workmen.'

'Rats?'

'Dozens of them, from all accounts. They'd had a bloody good feed, had those rats.'

Rebus was standing at the top of the steps. 'We reckon,' said Flight, 'the Wolfman must have paid her for a knee-trembler and brought her down here. Or maybe she brought him. She worked out of a pub on Old Street. It's a five minute walk. We interviewed the regulars, but nobody saw her leave with anyone.'

'Maybe he was in a car?'

'It's more than possible. Judging by the physical distance between the murder sites, he must be pretty mobile.'

'It says in the report that she was married.'

'That's right. Her old man, Tommy, he knew she was on the game. It didn't bother him, so long as she handed over the cash.'

'And he didn't report her missing?'

Flight wrinkled his nose. 'Not Tommy. He was on a bender at the time, practically comatose with drink when we went to see him. He said later that Maria often disappeared for a few days, told us she used to go off to the seaside with one or two of her regular johns.'

'I don't suppose you've been able to find these . . . clients?'

'Leave it out.' Flight laughed as though this were the best joke he'd heard all week. 'For the record, Tommy thought one of them might be called Bill or Will. Docs that help?'

'It narrows things down,' Rebus said with a smile.

'In any event,' said Flight, 'I doubt Tommy would have come to us for help if she hadn't come back. He's got form as long as your inside leg. To tell you the truth, he was our first suspect.'

'It follows.' Every policeman knew it as a universal truth: most murders happen in the family.

'A couple of years back,' Flight was saying, 'Maria was beaten up pretty badly. A hospital case, in fact. Tommy's doing. She'd been seeing another man and he hadn't been paying for it, if you understand my meaning. And a couple of years before that, Tommy served time for aggravated assault. It would have been rape if we could have got the woman into the witness box, but she was scared seven colours shitless.

There were witnesses, but we were never going to pin rape on him. So aggravated assault it was. He got eight months.'

'A violent man then.'

'You could say that.'

'With a record of particular violence against women.'

Flight nodded. 'It looked good at first. We thought we could pin Maria's murder on him and make it stick. But nothing added up. He had an alibi for openers. Then there were the bite marks: not his size, according to the dentist.'

'You mean Dr Morrison?'

'Yes, that's right. I call him the dentist to annoy Philip.' Flight scratched at his chin. The elbow of his leather jacket gave a creak. 'Anyway, nothing added up. And then when the second murder came along, well, we knew we were working in a different league from Tommy.'

'You're absolutely sure of that?'

'John, I'm not *absolutely* sure what colour of socks I've put on in the morning, I'm sometimes not even sure that I've put socks on at all. But I'm *fairly* sure this isn't Tommy Watkiss's work. He gets his kicks from watching Arsenal, not mutilating dead women.'

Rebus's eyes had not left Flight's. 'Your socks are blue,' he said. Flight looked down, saw that this was indeed the case, and smiled broadly.

'They're also different shades,' Rebus added.

'Bloody hell, so they are.'

'I'd still like to talk to Mr Watkiss,' Rebus continued. 'No hurry, and if it's all right with you.'

Flight shrugged. 'Whatever you say, Sherlock. Now, shall we get out of this shit-hole, or is there anything else you want to see?'

'No,' said Rebus. 'Let's get out of here.' They started back towards the mouth of the cul-de-sac, where Flight's car waited. 'What's this part of town called again?'

'Shoreditch. Remember your nursery rhymes? "When I am rich, say the bells of Shoreditch".'

Yes, Rebus had a vague memory. A memory of his mother, holding him on her knee, or maybe it was his father, singing him songs and bouncing the knee in time. It had never happened that way, but he had a memory of it all the same. They were at the end of the cul-de-sac now. A larger road flowed past, busy with daytime traffic. The buildings were black with grime, windows thick with the stuff. Offices of some kind, warehouses. No shops, save one selling professional kitchenware.

No houses or even flats in the upper storeys by the look of it. No one to hear a muffled scream at the dead of night. No one to see, from an unwashed window, the killer slinking away, dappled with blood.

Rebus stared back into the cul-de-sac, then up at the corner of the first building, where a barely legible plaque bore the cul-de-sac's name: Wolf Street E1.

This was the reason why the police had come to call the killer Wolfman. Nothing to do with the savagery of his attacks, or the teeth marks he left at the scene, but simply because, as Flight had said, this was so far as they could know his place of birth, the place where he had defined himself for the very first time. He was the Wolfman. He could be anywhere, but that was relatively unimportant. What was more important was that he could be *anyone*, anyone at all in this city of ten million faces, ten million secret lairs.

'Where next?' he said, opening the passenger door.

'Kilmore Road,' said Flight. He exchanged a glance with Rebus, acknowledging the irony.

'Kilmore Road it is,' said Rebus, getting into the car.

The day had started early. Rebus, waking after three hours' sleep and unable to drop off again, switched on the radio in his room and listened to the morning news programme as he dressed. Not knowing exactly what the day would bring, he dressed casually: caramel cord trousers, light jacket, shirt. No tweeds or tie today. He wanted a bath, but the facilities on his floor of the hotel were locked. He would have to ask in reception. Near the stairs there stood an automatic shoeshine machine. He polished the toes of both well-worn black shoes before starting down to breakfast.

The restaurant area was busy, most of the customers looking like businessmen or tourists. The day's newspapers had been arranged across one vacant table and Rebus lifted a *Guardian* before being directed to a table laid for one by the harassed waitress.

Breakfast was mainly help-yourself, with juices, cereals and fruit crammed onto a large central display. A pot of coffee appeared, unasked for, on his table, as did a toastrack filled with cool half-slices of lightly tanned bread. Not so much toasted as wafted in front of a lightbulb, Rebus thought to himself as he smeared a portion of butter across one pitiful triangle.

The Full English Breakfast consisted of one slice of bacon, one warm tomato (from a tin), three small mushrooms, a sickly egg and a curious little sausage. Rebus wolfed down the lot. The coffee wasn't quite strong enough, but he finished the pot anyway and asked for a refill. All the time he was flicking through the paper, but only on a second examination did he find anything about the previous night's murder: a short, bare-bones paragraph near the foot of page four.

Bare bones. He looked around him. An embarrassed looking couple were trying to hush their two vociferous children. Don't, thought Rebus, don't stifle them, let them live. Who could know what might happen tomorrow? They might be killed. The parents might be killed. His own daughter was here in London somewhere, living in a flat with his ex-wife. He should get in touch. He *would* get in touch. A businessman at a corner table rustled his tabloid noisily, drawing Rebus's attention towards the front cover.

WOLFMAN BITES AGAIN.

Ah, that was more like it. Rebus reached for a final half-slice of toast, only to find that he'd run out of butter. A hand landed heavily on his shoulder from behind, causing him to drop the toast. Startled, he turned to see George Flight standing there.

'Morning, John.'

'Hello, George. Sleep okay?'

Flight pulled out the chair across from Rebus and sat down heavily, hands in his lap.

'Not really. What about you?'

'I managed a few hours.' Rebus was about to turn his near-arrest on Shaftesbury Avenue into a morning anecdote, but decided to save it. There might come a time when they would need a funny story. 'Do you want some coffee?'

Flight shook his head. He examined the food on display. 'Some orange juice wouldn't go amiss though.' Rebus was about to rise, but Flight waved him down and rose himself to fetch a glassful, which he promptly downed. He squeezed his eyelids together. 'Tastes like powdered,' he said. 'Better give me some of that coffee after all.'

Rebus poured another cup. 'Seen that?' he said, nodding towards the corner table. Flight glanced at the tabloid and smiled.

'Well, it's their story now as much as ours. Only difference is, *we'll* keep things in perspective.'

'I'm not sure just what that perspective is.'

Flight stared at Rebus, but said nothing. He sipped at the coffee. 'There's a conference in the Murder Room at eleven o'clock. I didn't think we'd be able to make it, so I left Laine in charge. He likes being in charge.'

'And what are *we* going to be doing?'

'Well, we could go up to the Lea and check on the house-to-house. Or we could visit Mrs Cooper's place of employment.' Rebus didn't look enthusiastic. 'Or I could give you a tour of the other three murder scenes.' Rebus perked up. 'Okay,' said Flight, 'the scenic route it is. Drink up, Inspector. There's a long day ahead.'

'Just one thing,' said Rebus, lifting the cup halfway to his mouth. 'Why the nursemaid treatment? I'd have thought you'd have better things to do with your time than act as my chauffeur?'

Flight examined Rebus closely. Should he tell Rebus the real reason, or invent some story? He opted for invention and shrugged. 'Just easing you into the case, that's all.' Rebus nodded slowly, but Flight knew he didn't wholly believe him.

Out at the car, Rebus glanced in through the back window, seeking the teddy bear.

'I killed it,' Flight said, unlocking the driver's door. 'The perfect murder.'

'So what's Edinburgh like?'

Rebus knew Flight wasn't talking about the tourist Edinburgh, home to the Festival and the Castle. He was talking about criminal Edinburgh, which was another city altogether.

'Well,' he replied, 'we've still got a drug problem, and loan sharks seem to be making a comeback, but other than that things are fairly quiet at the moment.'

'But,' Flight reminded him, 'you did have that child killer a few years back.'

Rebus nodded.

'And you solved it.' Rebus made no reply to this. They'd managed to keep out of the media the fact that it had been personal, had not exactly been 'serial'.

'Thousands of man hours solved it,' he said casually.

'That's not what the chiefs think,' said Flight. 'They think you're some kind of serial killer guru.'

'They're wrong,' said Rebus. 'I'm just a copper, the same as you are. So who exactly *are* the chiefs? Whose idea was it?'

But Flight shook his head. 'I'm not exactly sure. I mean, I know who the chiefs are – Laine, Chief Superintendent Pearson – but not which one of them is responsible for your being here.'

'It was Laine's name on the letter,' said Rebus, knowing this didn't really mean anything.

Then he watched the midday pedestrians scurrying along the pavements. The traffic was at a standstill. He and Flight had come just over three miles in the best part of half an hour. Roadworks, double (and triple) parking, a succession of traffic lights and pedestrian crossings and some maddening tactics from selfish drivers had reduced their progress to a crawl. Flight seemed to read his mind.

'We'll be out of this in a couple of minutes,' he said. He was thinking over what Rebus had said, *just a copper, the same as you are.* But Rebus *had* caught the child killer, hadn't he? The files on the case credited him with the collar, a collar which had earned him the rank of Inspector. No, Rebus was just being modest, that was it. And you had to admire him for that.

A couple of minutes later, they had moved a further fifteen yards and were about to pass a narrow junction with a No Entry sign at its mouth. Flight glanced up this side-street. 'Time to take a few liberties,' he said, turning the steering-wheel hard. One side of the street was lined with market stalls. Rebus could hear the stall-holders sharpening their patter against the whetstone of passing trade. Nobody paid the slightest attention to a car travelling the wrong way down a one-way street, until a boy pulling a mobile stall from one side of the road to the other halted their progress. A meaty fist banged on the driver's side window. Flight rolled down the window, and a head appeared, extraordinarily pink and round and totally hairless.

'Oi, what's your fucking game then?' The words died in his throat. 'Oh, it's you Mister Flight. Didn't recognise the motor.'

'Hello, Arnold,' Flight said quietly, his eyes on the ponderous movement of the stall ahead. 'How's tricks?'

The man laughed nervously. 'Keeping me nose clean, Mister Flight.'

Only now did Flight deign to turn his head towards the man. 'That's good,' he said. Rebus had never heard those two words sound so threatening. Their road ahead was now clear. 'Keep it that way,' Flight said, moving off.

Rebus stared at him, waiting for an explanation.

'Sex offender,' Flight said. 'Two previous. Children. The psychiatrists say he's okay now, but I don't know. With that sort of thing, one hundred percent sure isn't quite sure enough. He's been working the market now for a few weeks, loading and unloading. Sometimes he gives me good gen. You know how it is.'

Rebus could imagine. Flight had this huge, strong-looking man in the palm of his hand. If Flight told the market-traders what he knew about Arnold, not only would Arnold lose his job, but he'd be in for a good kicking as well. Maybe the man *was* all right now, maybe he was, in psychiatric parlance, 'a fully integrated member of society'. He had paid for his crimes, and now was trying to go straight. And what happened? Policemen, men like Flight and like Rebus himself (if he was being honest), used his past against him to turn him into an informant.

'I've got a couple of dozen snitches,' Flight went on. 'Not all like Arnold. Some are in it for the cash, some simply because they can't keep their gobs shut. Telling what they know to somebody like me makes them feel important, makes them feel like they're in the know. A place this size, you'd be lost without a decent network of snitches.'

Rebus merely nodded, but Flight was warming to his subject.

'In some ways London is too big to take in. But in other ways it's tiny. Everyone knows everyone else. There's north and south of the river, of course, those are like two different countries. But the way the place divides, the loyalties, the same old faces, sometimes I feel like a village bobby on his bicycle.' Because Flight had turned towards him, Rebus nodded again. Inside he was thinking: here we go, the same old story, London is bigger, better, rougher, tougher and more important than anywhere else. He had come across this attitude before, attending courses with Yard men or hearing about it from visitors to London. Flight hadn't seemed the type, but really everybody was the type. Rebus, too, in his time had exaggerated the problems the police faced in Edinburgh, so that he could look tougher and more important in somebody's eyes.

The facts still had to be faced. Police work was all about paperwork and computers and somebody stepping forward with the truth.

'Nearly there,' said Flight. 'Kilmore Road's the third on the left.'

Kilmore Road was part of an industrial estate and therefore would be deserted at night. It nestled in a maze of back streets about two hundred yards from a tube station. Rebus had always looked on tube stations as busy places, sited in populous areas, but this one stood on a narrow back street, well away from high road, bus route or railway station.

'I don't get it,' he said. Flight merely shrugged and shook his head.

Anyone coming out of the tube station at night found themselves with a lonely walk through the streets, past net-curtained windows where televisions blared. Flight showed him that a popular route was to cut into the industrial estate and across the parkland behind it. The park was flat and lifeless, boasting a single set of goalposts, two orange traffic cones substituting for the missing set. On the other side of the park three hi-rise blocks and some lo-rise housing sprang up. May Jessop had been making for one of those houses, where her parents lived. She was nineteen and had a good job, but it kept her late at her office, so it wasn't until ten o'clock that her parents started to worry. An hour later, there was a knock at the door. Her father rushed to answer, relieved, only to find a detective there, bearing the news that May's body had been found.

And so it went. There seemed no connection between the victims, no real geographical link other than that, as Flight pointed out, all the killings had been committed north of the river, by which he meant north of the Thames. What did a prostitute, an office manageress and the assistant in an off-licence have in common? Rebus was damned if he knew.

The third murder had taken place much further west in North Kensington. The body had been found beside a railway line and Transport Police had handled the investigation initially. The body was that of Shelley Richards, forty-one years old, unmarried and unem-ployed. She was the only coloured victim so far. As they drove through Notting Hill, Ladbroke Grove and North 'Ken' (as Flight termed it) Rebus was intrigued by the scheme of things. A street of extraordinarily grand houses would suddenly give way to a squalid, rubbish-strewn road with boarded-up windows and bench-bound tramps, the wealthy and the poor living almost cheek by jowl. It would never happen in Edinburgh; in Edinburgh, certain boundaries were observed. But this, this was incredible. As Flight put it, 'race riots one side, diplomats the other'.

The spot where Shelley Richards had died was the loneliest, the most pathetic so far. Rebus clambered down from the railway line, down the embankment, lowered himself over the brick wall and dropped to the ground. His trousers were smeared with green moss. He brushed them with his hands, but to little effect. To get to the car where Flight was waiting he had to walk under a railway bridge. His footsteps echoed as he tried to avoid the pools of water and the rubbish, and then he stopped, listening. There was a noise all around him, a sort of wheezing, as if the bridge itself were drawing its dying breath. He looked up and saw the dark outlines of pigeons, still against the supporting girders. Cooing softly. That was what he could hear, not wheezing at all. There was a sudden rumble of thunder as a train passed overhead and the pigeons took to the wing, flapping around his head. He shivered and walked back out into sunlight.

Then, finally, it was back to the Murder Room. This was, in fact, a series of rooms covering most of the top floor of the building. Rebus reckoned there to be about twenty men and women working flat out when Flight and he entered the largest of the rooms. There was little to differentiate the scene from that of any murder investigation anywhere in the country. Officers were busy on telephones or working at computer terminals. Clerical staff moved from desk to desk with seemingly endless sheafs of paper. A photocopier was spewing out more paper in a corner of the room and two delivery-men were wheeling a new five-drawer filing cabinet into position beside the three which already stood against one wall. On another wall was a detailed street map of London, with the murder sites pinpointed. Coloured tapes ran from these sites to spaces on the wall where pictures, details and notes had been pinned. A duty roster and progress chart took up what space was left. All very efficient, but the faces told Rebus their own story: everyone here, working hard as they were, was waiting for the Lucky Break.

Flight was immediately in tune with the glaze of efficiency in the office, firing off questions. How did the meeting go? Any word from Lambeth? (He explained to Rebus that the police lab was based there.) Any news on last night? What about house-to-house? Well, does anyone know *anything*?

There were shrugs and shakes of the head. They were simply going through the motions, waiting for that Lucky Break. But what if it didn't come? Rebus had an answer to that: you made your own luck.

A smaller room off this main office was being used as a communications centre, keeping the Murder Room in touch with the investigation, and off this room were two smaller offices yet, each crammed with three desks. This was where the senior detectives worked. Both were empty.

'Sit down,' Flight said. He picked up the telephone on his desk, and dialled. While he waited for an answer, he surveyed with a frown the four-inch high pile of paper which had appeared in his in-tray during the morning. 'Hello, Gino?' he said into the mouthpiece. 'George Flight here. Can I order some sandwiches? Salami salad.' He looked to Rebus for confirmation that this would be acceptable. 'On brown bread, please, Gino. Better make it four rounds. Thanks.' He cut the connection and dialled again. Only two numbers this time: an internal call. 'Gino has a cafe round the corner,' he explained to Rebus. 'He makes great sandwiches, and he delivers.' Then: 'Oh, hello. Inspector Flight here. Can we have some tea? A decent-sized pot should do it. We're in the office. Is it wet milk today or that powdered crap? Great, thanks.' He dropped the receiver back into its cradle and spread his hands, as if some feat of magic had just been performed. 'This is your lucky day, John. We've got real milk for a change.'

'So what now?'

Flight shrugged, then slapped a hand on the bulging in-tray. 'You could always read through this little lot, keep yourself up-to-date with the investigation.'

'Reading about it isn't going to do any good.'

'On the contrary,' said Flight, 'it helps you answer any awkward questions that may be asked by those on high. How tall was the victim? What colour was her hair? Who found her? It's all in there.'

'She was five feet seven and her hair was brown. As to who found her, I don't give a tinker's cuss.'

Flight laughed, but Rebus was being serious. 'Murderers don't just appear,' he continued. 'They're created. To create a serial killer takes time. It's taken this guy years to make himself what he is. What's he been doing during that time? He may well be a loner, but he's probably got a job, maybe even a wife and kids. *Somebody* must know something. Maybe his wife wonders where he goes at night, or how blood got onto the tips of his shoes, or where her kitchen knife disappeared to.'

'All right, John.' Flight spread his hands again, this time in a gesture of peace-making. Rebus realised that his voice had been getting louder. 'Calm down a little. For a start, when you go on like that I can hardly make out a word you're saying, but I get your point. So what are we supposed to do?'

'Publicity. We need the public's help. We need anything they've got.'

'We already get dozens of calls a day. Anonymous tip-offs, nutters who want to confess, people snitching on their next door neighbour, people with grudges, maybe even a few with genuine suspicions. We check them all out. And we've got the media on our side. The Chief Super will be interviewed a dozen times today. Newspapers, magazines, radio, TV. We give them what we can, and we tell them to spread the word. We've got the best bloody Liaison Officer in the country working round the clock to make sure the public knows what we're dealing with here.'

There was a knock on the already open door and a WPC carried a tray into the room and left it on Flight's desk. 'I'll be mother, shall I?' he said, already starting to pour the tea into two plain white mugs.

'What's the Liaison Officer's name?' Rebus asked. He knew a Liaison Officer himself. She, too, was the best there was. But she wasn't in London; she was back in Edinburgh . . .

'Cath Farraday,' said Flight. 'Detective Inspector Cath Farraday.' He sniffed the milk carton, before pouring a dollop into his tea. 'If you stick around long enough, you'll get to meet her. She's a bit of a cracker is our Cath. Mind you, if she heard me talking about her like that, she'd have my head on a plate.' Flight chuckled.

'And salad on the side,' came a voice from just outside the door. Flight, flinching, spilt tea down his shirt and jumped to his feet. The door was swinging open now, to reveal a platinum blonde woman leaning against the jamb, her arms folded, one leg casually crossed over the other. Rebus's gaze was drawn to her eyes, which were slanted like a cat's. They made her whole face seem narrower than it was. Her lips were thin, lined with a thin coat of bright red lipstick. Her hair had a hard, metallic look to it, reflecting the look of the woman herself. She was older than either of the men in the room by several years and if age hadn't withered her, the frequent use of cosmetics had. Her face was lined and puffy. Rebus didn't like a lot of make-up on a woman, but plenty of men did.

'Hello, Cath,' said Flight, trying to regain at least an outer shell of composure. 'We were just . . .'

'. . . talking about me. I know.' She unfolded her arms and took a couple of steps into the room, extending a hand to Rebus. 'You must be Inspector Rebus,' she said. 'I've heard all about you.'

'Oh?' Rebus looked to Flight, whose attention, however, was fixed on Cath Farraday.

'I hope George here is giving you an easy ride.'

Rebus shrugged. 'I've had worse.'

Her eyes became more feline still. 'I'll bet,' she said. She lowered her voice. 'But watch your back, Inspector. Not everyone's as nice as George. How would you feel if someone from London suddenly started to poke his nose into one of your cases, hmm?'

'Cath,' said Flight, 'there's no need for . . .'

She raised a hand, silencing him. 'Just a friendly warning, George,

one Inspector to another. We've got to look after our own, haven't we?'
She glanced at her watch. 'Must be going. I've a meeting with Pearson
in five minutes. Nice to have met you, Inspector. Bye, George.'

And then she was gone, the door left wide open, a strong perfume
lingering in the room. Both men were silent for a moment. Rebus was
the first to speak.

'I believe your description was "a cracker", George. Remind me never
to let you arrange a blind date for me.'

It was late afternoon and Rebus sat in Flight's office alone, a pad of
paper in front of him on the desk. He tapped his pen like a drumstick
against the edge of the table and stared at the two names he had written
so far.

Dr Anthony Morrison. Tommy Watkiss.

These were people he wanted to see. He drew a thick line beneath
them and wrote two more names: Rhona. Samantha. These, too, were
people he wanted to see, though for personal reasons.

Flight had gone off to see Chief Inspector Laine on another floor of
the building. The invitation did not extend to Rebus. He picked up the
last remaining quarter of his salami sandwich, but thought better of it
and tossed it into the office's metal bin. Too salty. And what kind of
meat was salami anyway? He now had a craving for more tea. He
thought Flight had dialled 18 to order up the first pot, but decided
against trying it. He didn't want to make a fool of himself, did he? It
would be just his luck to get through to Chief Superintendent Pearson.

Just a friendly warning. The point was not lost on Rebus. He crumpled
up his list and threw that in the bin too, then got up out of his chair and
made for the main office. He knew he should be doing something, or
should at least *seem* to be doing something. They had brought him four
hundred miles to help them. But he couldn't for the life of him see any
gaps in their investigation. They were doing everything they could, but
to no avail. He was just another straw to be clutched at. Just another
chance for that elusive Lucky Break.

He was studying the wall-map when the voice sounded behind him.
'Sir?'

He turned to see one of the Murder Room team standing there. 'Yes?'
'Someone to see you, sir.'
'Me?'
'Well, you're the most senior detective around at the moment, sir.'
Rebus considered this. 'Who is it?'

The officer checked the scrap of paper in his hand. 'A Dr Frazer, sir.'

Rebus considered a moment longer. 'All right,' he said, turning back towards the tiny office. 'Give me a minute and then send him in.' He stopped. 'Oh, and bring some tea, will you?'

'Yes, sir,' said the officer. He waited until Rebus had left the room, then turned to the others, seated at their desks and smiling at him. 'The cheek of these fucking jocks,' he said, loud enough for everyone to hear. 'Remind me to piss in the teapot before I take it in.'

Dr Frazer turned out to be a woman. What was more, as she entered the office, she was attractive enough to have Rebus half-rise from his desk in welcome.

'Inspector Rebus?'

'That's right. Dr Frazer, I presume?'

'Yes.' She showed a row of perfect teeth as Rebus invited her to take a seat. 'Though I'd better explain.' Rebus fixed his eyes on her own and nodded. He kept his eyes fixed on hers for fear that otherwise they would be drawn down to her slim tanned legs, to that point where, an inch above the knee, her cream skirt began, hugging her thighs. He had taken her body in with a single sweeping glance. She was tall, almost as tall as him. Her legs were bare and long, her body supple. She was wearing a jacket to match the skirt and a plain white blouse, set off by a single string of pearls. There was a slight, exquisite scar on her throat just above the pearls and her face was tanned and without make-up, her jaw square, her hair straight and black, tied back with a black band, so that a shock of it fell onto one shoulder. She had brought a soft black leather briefcase into the room, which she now held up in her lap, running her fingers around the handles as she spoke.

'I'm not a medical doctor.' Rebus registered slight surprise. 'I'm a doctor courtesy of my Ph.D. I teach psychology at University College.'

'And you're American,' said Rebus.

'Canadian actually.'

Yes, he should have known. There was a soft lilt to her accent, something few Americans possessed. And she wasn't quite as nasal as the tourists who stopped in Princes Street to get a picture of the Scott Monument.

'I'm sorry,' he said, 'so, what can I do for you, Dr Frazer?'

'Well, I did talk to someone on the telephone this morning and I told them of my interest in the Wolfman case.'

Rebus could see it all now. Another nutter with some crazy idea about the Wolfman, that's probably what the Murder Room had thought. So they'd decided to play a joke on him, arranged a meeting without letting him know, and then Flight, forewarned, had made himself scarce. Well, the joke was on them. Rebus could always find time for an attractive woman, crazy or not. After all, he had nothing better to do, had he?

'Go on,' he said.

'I'd like to try to put together a profile of the Wolfman.'

'A profile?'

'A psychological profile. Like an identikit, but building up a picture of the mind rather than the face. I've been doing some research on criminal profiling and I think I can use similar criteria to help you come to a clearer understanding of the killer.' She paused. 'What do you think?'

'I'm wondering what's in it for you, Dr Frazer.'

'Perhaps I'm just being public spirited.' She looked down into her lap and smiled. 'But really, what I'm looking for is validation of my methods. So far I've been experimenting with old police cases. Now I want to tackle something real.'

Rebus sat back in his chair and picked up the pen again, pretending to study it. When he looked up, he saw that she was studying him. She was a psychologist after all. He put down the pen. 'It isn't a game,' he said, 'and this isn't a lecture theatre. Four women are dead, a maniac is loose somewhere and right now we're quite busy enough following up all the leads and the false trails we've got. Why should we make time for you, Dr Frazer?'

She coloured, her cheekbones blushed a deep red. But she seemed to have no ready answer. Rebus hadn't much to add, so he too sat in silence. His mouth was sour and dry, his throat coated in a layer of resin. Where was the tea?

Eventually she spoke. 'All I want to do is read through the material on the case.'

Rebus found some spare sarcasm. 'That's *all*?' He tapped the mound of paperwork in the in-tray. 'No problem then, it'll only take you a couple of months.' She was ignoring him, fumbling with the briefcase. She produced a slim orange folder.

'Here,' she said stonily. 'Just read this. It'll only take you twenty minutes. It's one of the profiles I did of an American serial killer. If you think it has no validity in helping to identify the killer or target where he might have struck next, fair enough, I'll leave.'

Rebus took the file. Oh God, he thought, not more psychology! *Relating . . . involving . . . motivating.* He'd had his fill of psychology on the management training course. But then again, he didn't want her to leave. He didn't want to be left sitting here on his own with everyone in the Murder Room smirking at their little trick. He opened the folder, drew out a typed and bound thesis about twenty-five pages long and began to read. She sat watching him, waiting for a question perhaps. Rebus read with his chin held up, so that she wouldn't see the sagging folds of flesh on his neck, and with his shoulders back, making the best of his admittedly not very muscular chest. He cursed his parents for not feeding him up as a child. He had grown skinny, and when eventually he had started to put weight on, it had been to his gut and his backside, not his chest and arms.

Backside. Chest. Arms. He gazed hard at the words in front of him, but aware of her body resting in his line of peripheral vision, just above the top edge of the paper. He didn't even know her first name. Perhaps he never would. He frowned as though deep in thought and read through the opening page.

By page five he was interested and by page ten he felt there might be something in it after all. A lot of it was speculative. Be honest, John, it was almost all conjecture, but there were a few points where she made a telling deduction. He saw what it was: her mind worked in a different orbit from a detective's. They circled the same sun, however, and now and then the satellites touched. And what harm could come from letting her do a profile for the Wolfman? At worst, it would lead them up another dead end. At best, he might enjoy some female company during his stay in London. Yes, some pleasant female company. Which reminded him: he wanted to telephone his ex-wife and arrange a visit. He read through the final pages quickly.

'All right,' he said, closing the thesis, 'very interesting.'

She seemed pleased. 'And useful?'

He hesitated before replying. 'Perhaps.'

She wanted more from him than that. 'But worth letting me have a go on the Wolfman?'

He nodded slowly, ruminatively, and her face lit up. Rebus couldn't help returning her smile. There was a knock at the door. 'Come in,' he called.

It was Flight. He was carrying a tray, swimming with spilt tea. 'I believe you asked for some refreshment,' he said. Then he caught sight of Dr Frazer, and Rebus delighted in the stunned look on his face.

'Christ,' said Flight, looking from woman to Rebus to woman, before realising that he had somehow to justify his outburst. 'They told me you were with someone, John, but they didn't, I mean, I didn't know . . .' He tumbled to a halt, mouth still open, and placed the tray on the desk before turning towards her. 'I'm Inspector George Flight,' he said, reaching out a hand.

'Dr Frazer,' she replied, 'Lisa Frazer.'

As their hands met, Flight looked towards Rebus from the corner of his eye. Rebus, beginning to feel a little more at home in the metropolis, gave him a slow, cheerful wink.

'Christ.'

She left him a couple of books to read. One, *The Serial Mind*, was a series of essays by various academics. It included 'Sealing the Bargain: Modes of Motivation in the Serial Killer' by Lisa Frazer, University of London. Lisa: nice name. No mention of her doctorate though. The other book was an altogether heavier affair, dense prose linked by charts and graphs and diagrams: *Patterns of Mass Murder* by Gerald Q MacNaughtie.

MacNaughtie? That had to be a joke of some kind. But on the dustjacket Rebus read that Professor MacNaughtie was Canadian by birth and taught at the University of Columbia. Nowhere could he find out what the Q stood for. He spent what was left of the office day working through the books, paying most attention to Lisa Frazer's essay (which he read twice) and to the chapter in MacNaughtie's book concentrating on 'Patterns of Mutilation'. He drank tea and coffee and two cans of fizzy orange, but the taste in his mouth was sour and as he read on he began to feel physically dirty, made grubby by tale after tale of casual horror. When he got up to visit the bathroom at a quarter to five, everyone in the outer office had already quit for the day, but Rebus hardly registered the fact. His mind was elsewhere.

Flight, who had left him to his own devices for most of the afternoon, came into the office at six. 'Fancy a jar?' Rebus shook his head. Flight sat down on the edge of the chair. 'What's the matter?'

Rebus waved a hand over the books. Flight examined the cover of one. 'Oh,' he said, 'not exactly bedtime reading, I take it?'

'Not exactly. It's just . . . evil.'

Flight nodded. 'Got to keep a perspective though, John, eh? Otherwise they'd go on getting away with it. If it's so horrible, we all shy away from the truth, then everybody gets away with murder. And worse than murder.'

Rebus looked up. 'What's worse than murder?'

'Lots of things. What about someone who tortures and rapes a six-month old child and films the whole thing so he can show it to similarly minded individuals?'

Rebus's words were barely audible. 'You're kidding.' But he knew Flight was not.

'Happened three months ago,' Flight said. 'We haven't caught the bastard, but Scotland Yard have got the video – and a few more besides. Ever seen a thalidomide porn film?' Rebus shook his head wearily. Flight leaned down so that their heads were nearly touching. 'Don't go soft on me, John,' he said quietly, 'that's not going to solve anything. You're in London now, not the Highlands. The top deck of a midday bus isn't safe here, never mind a tow-path after dark. Nobody sees any of it. London gives you a thick skin and temporary blindness. You and I can't afford to be blind. But we can afford the occasional drink. Coming?'

He was on his feet now, rubbing his hands, lecture over. Rebus nodded and rose slowly to his feet. 'Only a quick one though,' he said. 'I've got an appointment this evening.'

An appointment reached by way of a packed tube train. He checked his watch: 7.30 pm. Did the rush hour never stop? The compartment smelt of vinegar and stale air, and three not-so-personal stereos battled it out above the roar of speeding and juddering. The faces around Rebus were blank. Temporary blindness: Flight was right. They shut it all out because to acknowledge what they were going through was to realise the monotony, the claustrophobia and the sheer agony of it all. Rebus was depressed. And tired. But he was also a tourist, so it had to be savoured. Thus the tube journey instead of a closeted taxi ride. Besides, he'd been warned about how expensive the black cabs were and he had checked in his A-Z, and found that his destination was only a quarter of an inch from an Underground station.

So Rebus travelled through the Underground and tried hard not to look out of place, not to gawp at the buskers and the beggars, not to pause in a busy conduit the better to read this or that advertising poster. A tramp actually entered his carriage at one stop and as the doors closed and the train pulled away again he began to rave, but his audience were deaf and dumb as well as blind and they successfully ignored his existence until the next stop where, daunted, he slouched from the carriage onto the platform. As the engine pulled away, Rebus could hear his voice again, coming from the next carriage along. It had been an astonishing performance, not by the tramp but by the passengers. They had closed off their minds, refusing involvement. Would they do the same if they saw a fight taking place? Saw a thick-set man stealing a tourist's wallet? Yes, they probably would. This wasn't an environment of good and evil: it was a moral vacuum and that frightened Rebus more than anything else.

But there were compensations of a sort. Every beautiful woman he saw reminded him of Lisa Frazer. Squeezed into one compartment on the Central Line, he found himself pressed against a young blonde girl. Her blouse was undone to the cleft of her breasts, giving the taller Rebus an occasionally breathtaking view of slopes and swells. She glanced up from her paperback and caught him staring. He looked away quickly, but felt her cold gaze focussing on the side of his head.

Every man is a rapist: hadn't someone said that once? *Traces of salt . . . Bite marks on the . . .* The train slowed into another station: Mile End, his stop. The girl was getting out, too. He lingered on the platform until she was gone, without really knowing why, then headed up towards ground level and a taste of fresh air.

Taste of monoxide, more like. Three lanes of traffic were jammed in either direction, the result of an articulated lorry failing to reverse through the narrow gates of some building. Two exasperated constables were trying to untie this Gordian Knot and for the first time it struck Rebus how silly their tall rounded hats looked. The Scottish-issue flat caps were more sensible. They also made less of a target at football matches.

Rebus wished the constables a silent 'Good luck' and made for Gideon Park – not a park but a road – and for number 78, a three-storey house which, according to the front door's entry system, had been split somehow into four flats. He pressed the second-from-bottom buzzer and waited. The door was opened by a tall skinny teenage girl, her long straight hair dyed black, three earrings in each ear. She smiled and gave him an unexpected hug.

'Hello, Dad,' she said.

Samantha Rebus led her father up a narrow staircase to the first-floor flat she shared with her mother. If the change in his daughter was striking, then the change in Rebus's ex-wife was doubly so. He had never seen her looking so good. There were strands of grey in her hair, but it had been cut fashionably short and there was a healthy suntanned look to her face, a gleam to her eyes. They studied one another without words, then embraced quickly.

'John.'

'Rhona.'

She had been reading a book. He looked at its cover: *To the Lighthouse*, Virginia Woolf. 'Tom Wolfe's more my style,' he said. The living-room was small, cramped even, but a lot of clever work with shelves and wall-mirrors gave the impression of space. It was a strange sensation, seeing things he recognised, that chair, a cushion-cover, a lamp, things from his life with Rhona, now transported to this pokey flat. But he praised the interior decoration, the snug feel of the place and then they sat down to drink tea. Rebus had brought gifts: record tokens for Samantha, chocolates for Rhona – received with a knowing, coded look between the two women.

Two women. Samantha was no longer a child. Her figure might retain a child's suppleness, but her way of moving, her actions, her face were all fully formed and adult.

'You look good, Rhona.'

She paused, accepting the compliment. 'Thank you, John,' she said at last. He noted her inability to say the same of him. Mother and daughter shared another of their secret looks. It was as though their time together had led to a kind of telepathy between them, so that during the course of the evening Rebus was to do most of the talking, nervously filling the many silent gaps in the conversation.

None of it was very important anyway. He spoke of Edinburgh, without going into detail about his work. This wasn't easy, since work apart he did very little. Rhona asked about mutual friends and he had to admit that he saw none of the old crowd. She talked about her teaching, of property prices in London. (Rebus heard nothing in her tone to suggest that he should pay something towards a bigger place for his kin. After all, it had been her idea to leave him. No real grounds, except, as she'd put it, that she'd loved a man but married a job.) Then Samantha told him about her secretarial course.

'Secretarial?' said Rebus, trying to sound enthusiastic. Samantha's reply was cool.

'I told you about it in one of my letters.'

'Oh.' There was another break in the conversation. Rebus wanted to burst out: I read your letters, Sammy! I devour your letters! And I'm sorry I so seldom write back, but you know what a lousy letter-writer I am, how much effort it takes, how little time and energy I have. So many cases to solve, so many people depending on me.

But he said nothing. Of course he said nothing. Instead, they played out this little sham scenario. Polite chit-chat in a tiny living-room off Bow Road. Everything to say. Saying nothing. It was unbearable. Truly unbearable. Rebus moved his hands to his knees, spreading the fingers, ready to rise to his feet in the expected manner of one about to leave. Well, it's been nice seeing you, but there's a starched hotel bed waiting for me, and a machine to dispense ice, and another to shine shoes. He started to rise.

And the buzzer sounded. Two short, two long. Samantha fairly flew to the stairs. Rhona smiled.

'Kenny,' she explained.

'Oh?'

'Samantha's current gentleman.'

Rebus nodded slowly, the understanding father. Sammy was sixteen. She'd left school. A secretarial course at college. Not a boyfriend, a gentleman. 'What about you, Rhona?' he said.

She opened her mouth, forming a reply, when the thump of feet climbing the stairs closed it for her. Samantha's face was flushed as she led her gentleman by his hand into the room. Instinctively, Rebus stood up.

'Dad, this is Kenny.'

Kenny was clad in black leather zip-up jacket and black leather trousers, with boots reaching almost to his knees. He squeaked as he moved and in his free hand he carried an upturned crash-helmet, from which poked the fingers of a pair of black leather gloves. Two fingers were prominent, and appeared to be pointing directly at Rebus. Kenny removed his hand from Samantha's grip and held it out towards her father.

'Wotcher.'

The voice was abrupt, the tone deep and confident. He had lank black hair, almost parted at centre, some residual acne on cheeks and neck, a day's growth of stubble. Rebus shook the hot hand with little enthusiasm.

'Hello, Kenny,' Rhona said. Then, for Rebus's benefit: 'Kenny's a motorcycle messenger.'

'Oh,' said Rebus, taking his seat again.

'Yeah, that's right,' Kenny enthused, 'down the City.' He turned to Rhona. 'Made a fair old packet today, Rhona,' he said, winking. Rhona smiled warmly. This young gentleman, this lad of eighteen or so (so much older, so much more worldly than Samantha) had obviously charmed his way into mother's heart as well as daughter's. He turned now to Rebus with that same winning way. 'I make a hundred quid on a good day. Course, it used to be better, back at Big Bang. There were a lot of new companies then, all of them trying to show off how much dosh they had. Still, there's a killing to be made if you're fast and reliable. A lot of the customers ask for me by name now. That shows I'm getting somewhere.' He sat down on the sofa beside Samantha and waited, as did they all, for Rebus to say something.

He knew what was expected of him. Kenny had thrown down a gauntlet, and the message was, Just you dare disapprove of me now. What did the kid want? A pat on the ego? Rebus's permission to deflower his daughter? A few tips on how to avoid speed-traps? Whatever, Rebus wasn't about to knuckle under.

'Can't be good for your lungs,' he said instead. 'All those exhaust fumes.'

Kenny seemed perplexed by this turn in the conversation. 'I keep myself fit,' he said, sounding slightly piqued. Good, thought Rebus, I can nettle this little bastard. He knew Rhona was warning him to lay off, warning him with her piercing eyes, but Rebus kept his attention on Kenny.

'Must be a lot of prospects for a lad like you.'

Kenny cheered up immediately. 'Yeah,' he said, 'I might even set up my own fleet. All you need's –' He fell silent as he belatedly noticed that use of 'lad', as though he were dressed in shorts and school-cap. But it was too late to go back and correct it, way too late. He had to push on, but now it all sounded like pipe-dreams and playground fantasies. This rozzer might be from Jockland, but he was every bit as oily as an East End old-timer. He'd have to watch his step. And what was happening now? This Jock, this rough-looking tosser in the ill-fitting gear, the completely uncoordinated gear, this 'man at C&A' type, was reminiscing about a grocery shop from his youth. For a time, Rebus had been the grocer's 'message boy'. (He explained that in Scotland 'messages' meant 'groceries'.) He'd run about on a heavy-framed black bicycle, with a metal rectangle in front of the handlebars. The box of groceries would be held in this rectangle and off he would pedal to do his deliveries.

'I thought I was rich,' Rebus said, obviously coming to a punch line. 'But when I wanted more money, there wasn't any to be had. I had to wait till I was old enough to get a proper job, but I loved running around on that bike, doing errands and delivering messages to the old folk. Sometimes they'd even give me a tip, a piece of fruit or a jar of jam.'

There was silence in the room. A police siren sped past outside. Rebus sat back and folded his arms, a sentimental smile spread across his face. And then it dawned on Kenny: *Rebus was comparing the two of them!* His eyes widened. Everyone knew it. Rhona knew it. Sam knew it. For tuppence, he'd get up and stick the nut on the copper, Sam's dad or not. But he held back and the moment passed. Rhona got up to make more tea, and the big bastard got up and said he had to be going.

It had all happened so fast. Kenny was still trying to unravel Rebus's story and Rebus could see it. The poor half-educated runt was trying to work out just how far Rebus had put him down. Rebus could answer that: as far as was necessary. Rhona hated him for it, of course, and Samantha looked embarrassed. Well to hell with them. He'd done his duty, he'd paid his respects. He wouldn't bother them any more. Let them live in their cramped flat, visited by this . . . gentleman, this mock adult. Rebus had more important things to do. Books to read. Notes to make. And another busy day ahead. It was ten o'clock. He could be back at his hotel by eleven. An early night, that's what was needed. Eight hours' sleep in the last two days. No wonder he was ratty, looking for a fight.

He began to feel a little bit ashamed. Kenny was too easy a target. He'd crushed a tiny fly beneath a tower-block of resentment. Resentment, John, or plain jealousy? That was not a question for a tired man. Not a question for a man like John Rebus. Tomorrow. Tomorrow, he might start getting some answers. He was determined to pay for his keep now that he had been brought to London. Tomorrow, the task began in earnest.

He shook Kenny's hand again and gave him a man-to-man half-wink before leaving the flat. Rhona offered to see him to the door. They went into the hall, leaving Samantha and Kenny in the living-room, behind a closed door.

'It's okay,' Rebus said quickly. 'I'll see myself out.' He started downstairs, aware that to linger was to invite an argument with Rhona. What was the point? 'Better go keep an eye on Lothario,' he called, unable to resist the parting shot.

Outside, he remembered that Rhona liked her lovers young, too. Perhaps she . . . but no, that thought was unworthy of him. 'Sorry,

God,' he said, turning with a steady stride back towards the Underground.

* * *

Something is going wrong.

After the first killing, she had felt horror, remorse, guilt. She had
begged forgiveness; she would not kill again.

After a month, a month of not being found, she grew more
optimistic, and grew hungry too. So she killed again. This had satisfied
for another month, and so it had gone on. But now, only twenty-four
hours after the fourth time, she had felt the urge again. An urge more
powerful and focussed than ever. She would get away with it, too. But
it would be dangerous. The police were still hunting. Time had not
elapsed. The public was wary. If she killed now, she would break her
patternless pattern, and perhaps that would give the police some clue
that she could not predict.

There was only one solution. It was wrong; she knew it was wrong.
This wasn't her flat, not really. But she did it anyway. She unlocked the
door and entered the gallery. There, tied up on the floor, lay the latest
body. She would store this one. Keep it out of sight of the police.
Examining it, she realised that now she would have more time with it,
more time in which to play. Yes, storage was the answer. This lair was
the answer. No fear of being found. After all, this was a private place,
not a public place. No fear. She walked around the body, enjoying its
silence. Then she raised the camera to her eye.

'Smile please,' she says, snapping her way through the film. Then she
has an idea. She loads another film cartridge and photographs one of
the paintings, a landscape. This is the one she will carve, just as soon as
she has finished playing with her new toy. But now she has a record of
it, too. A permanent record. She watches the photograph develop but
then starts to scratch across the plate, smearing the colours and the
focus until the picture becomes a chemical swirl, seemingly without
form. God, her mother would have hated that.

'Bitch,' she says, turning from the wall filled with paintings. Her face
is creased with anger and resentment. She picks up a pair of scissors and
goes to her plaything again, kneels in front of it, takes a firm hold of the
head and brings the scissors down towards the face until they hover a
centimetre away from the nose. 'Bitch,' she says again, then carefully

snips at the nostrils, her hand shaking. 'Long nosehairs,' she wails, 'are so unbecoming. So unbecoming.'

At last she rises again and crosses to the opposite wall, lifts an aerosol and shakes it noisily. This wall – she calls it her Dionysian wall – is covered in spray-painted black slogans: DEATH TO ART, KILLING IS AN ART, THE LAW IS AN ARSE, FUCK THE RICH, FEEL THE POOR. She thinks of something else to say, something worth the diminishing space. She sprays with a flourish.

'This is art,' she says, glancing over her shoulder towards the Apollonian wall with its framed paintings. 'This is fucking art. This is fuck art.' She sees that the doll's eyes are open and throws herself down to within an inch of those eyes, which suddenly screw themselves shut. Carefully, she uses both hands to prise apart the eyelids. Faces are close now, *so* intimate. The moment is always *so* intimate. Her breath is fast. So is the doll's. The doll's mouth struggles against the tape holding it shut. The nostrils flare.

'Fuck art,' she hisses to the doll. 'This is fuck art.' She has the scissors in her hand again now, and slides one blade into the doll's left nostril. 'Long nosehairs, Johnny, are so unbecoming in a man. So unbecoming in a man.' She pauses, as though listening to something, as though considering this statement. Then she nods. 'Good point,' she says, smiling now.

'Good point.'

Catching a Bite

The telephone woke Rebus. He could not locate it for a moment, then realised that it was mounted on the wall just to the right of his headboard. He sat up, fumbling with the receiver.

'Hello?'

'Inspector Rebus?' The voice was full of zest. He didn't recognise it. Took his Longines (his father's Longines actually) from the bedside table and peered through the badly scratched face to find that it was seven fifteen. 'Did I wake you up? Sorry. It's Lisa Frazer.'

Rebus came to life. Or rather his voice did. He still sat slumped and jangling on the edge of the bed, but heard himself say a bright, 'Hello, Dr Frazer. What can I do for you?'

'I've been studying the notes you gave me on the Wolfman case. Working through most of the night, to be honest. I just couldn't sleep, I was so excited by them. I've made some preliminary observations.'

Rebus touched the bed, feeling its residual warmth. How long since he'd slept with a woman? How long since he'd woken up the following day regretting nothing?

'I see,' he said.

Her laughter was like a clear jet of water. 'Oh, Inspector, I'm sorry, I've wakened you. I'll call back later.'

'No, no. I'm fine, honestly. A bit startled, but fine. Can we meet and talk about what you've found?'

'Of course.'

'But I'm a bit tied up today.' He was trying to sound vulnerable, and thought on the whole that it was probably working. So he played his big card. 'What about dinner?'

'That would be nice. Where?'

He rubbed at a shoulder-blade. 'I don't know. This is your town, not mine. I'm a tourist, remember.'

She laughed. 'I'm not exactly a local myself, but I take your point.

Well in that case, dinner's on me.' She sounded set on this. 'And I think I know just the place. I'll come to your hotel. Seven thirty?'

'I look forward to it.'

What a very pleasant way to start the day, thought Rebus, lying down again and plumping up the pillow. He'd just closed his eyes when the telephone rang again.

'Yes?'

'I'm in reception and you're a lazy git. Come down here so I can put my breakfast on your tab.'

Cli-chick. Brrrr. Rebus slapped the receiver back into its cradle and got out of bed with a growl.

'What kept you?'

'I didn't think they'd appreciate a stark naked guest in the dining-room. You're early.'

Flight shrugged. 'Things to do.' Rebus noticed that Flight didn't look well. The dark rings around his eyes and his pale colouring were not due simply to lack of sleep. His flesh had a saggy quality, as though magnets on the floor were drawing it down. But then he wasn't feeling so great himself. He thought he'd probably picked up a bug on the tube. His throat was a little sore and his head throbbed. Could it be true that cities made you sick? In one of the essays Lisa Frazer had given him someone had made that very claim, stating that most serial killers were products of their environment. Rebus couldn't really comment on that, but he did know that there was more mucus in his nostrils than usual. Had he brought enough handkerchiefs with him?

'Things to do,' Flight repeated.

They sat at a table for two. The dining-room was quiet, and the Spanish waitress took their order briskly, the day not yet having had enough time to wear her down.

'What do you want to do today?' Flight seemed to be asking this only in order to get the conversation rolling, but Rebus had specific plans for the day and told him so.

'First off I'd quite like to see Maria Watkiss's man, Tommy.' Flight smiled at this and looked down at the table. 'Just to satisfy my own curiosity,' Rebus continued. 'And I'd like to talk to the dental pathologist, Dr Morrison.'

'Well, I know where to find both of them,' said Flight. 'Go on.'

'That's about it. I'm seeing Dr Frazer this evening –' Flight looked up at this news, his eyes widening in appreciation '– to go over her findings on the killer's profile.'

'Uh huh.' Flight sounded unconvinced.

'I've been reading those books she lent me. I think there may be something in it, George.' Rebus used the Christian name carefully, but Flight seemed to have no objections.

The coffee had arrived. Flight poured and drank a cup of it, then smacked his lips. 'I don't,' he said.

'Don't what?'

'Don't think there's anything in all this psychology stuff. It's too much like guesswork and not enough like science. I like something tangible. A dental pathologist, now that's tangible. That's something you can get –'

'Your teeth into?' Rebus smiled. 'The pun's bad enough, but I don't agree anyway. When was the last time a pathologist gave you a precise time of death? They always hedge their bets.'

'But they deal in *facts*, in physical evidence, not in mumbo-jumbo.'

Rebus sat back. He was thinking of the character in a Dickens book he'd read a long time ago, a schoolteacher who wanted facts and nothing but. 'Come on, George,' he said, 'this is the twentieth century.'

'That's right,' said Flight. 'And we don't believe in soothsayers any more.' He looked up again. 'Or do we?'

Rebus paused to pour some coffee. He felt his cheeks tingling. Probably, they were turning red. Arguments did that to him; even casual disagreements like this were sometimes enough. He was careful to make his next utterance in a soft, reasonable voice.

'So what are you saying?'

'I'm saying policework is plodding, John.' (Still on first name terms, thought Rebus: that's good.) 'And shortcuts seldom work. I'm saying don't let your Hampton do your thinking for you.' Rebus thought about protesting, but realised he wasn't exactly sure what Flight meant. Flight smiled.

'Rhyming slang,' he explained. 'Hampton Wick, prick. Or maybe it's dick. Anyway, I'm just warning you not to let a good looking woman interfere with your professional judgment.'

Rebus was still about to protest, but saw that there was little point. Having voiced his thoughts, Flight seemed content. What's more, maybe he was right. Did Rebus want to see Lisa Frazer because of the case, or because she was Lisa Frazer? Still, he felt the need to defend her.

'Listen,' he said, 'like I say, I've been reading the books she gave me and there are some good things in them.' Flight looked unconvinced, goading Rebus into ploughing on. And as he fell for it, beginning to speak, he saw that Flight had played the same trick on him as he himself had played on the motorcycle messenger last night. Too late: he had to defend Lisa Frazer, and himself, even though everything he now said sounded stupid and half-baked to his own ears, never mind to Flight's.

'What we're dealing with is a man who hates women.' Flight looked at him in amazement, as though this were too obvious to need saying. '*Or*,' Rebus went on quickly, 'who has to take out his revenge on women because he's too weak, too scared to take it out on a man.' Flight admitted this possibility with a twitch of the head. 'A lot of so-called serial killers,' continued Rebus, his hand unconsciously grasping the butter-knife, 'are very conservative – small c – very ambitious, but thwarted. They feel rejected from the class immediately above them, and they target this group.'

'What? A prostitute, a shop assistant, an office worker? You're saying they're the same social group? You're saying the Wolfman's social group is lower than a tart's? Leave off, John.'

'It's just a general rule,' Rebus persisted, wishing he'd never started this conversation. He twisted the knife in his hand. 'Mind you, one of the earliest serial killers was a French nobleman.' His voice fell away. Flight was looking impatient. 'All I'm saying is what's in those books. Some of it may make sense, it's just that we don't have enough on the Wolfman yet to allow us to see what sense it's all making.'

Flight finished another cup of coffee. 'Go on,' he said, without enthusiasm. 'What else do the books say?'

'Some serial killers crave publicity,' said Rebus. He paused, thinking of the killer who had taunted him five years ago, who had led them all a merry chase. 'If the Wolfman gets in touch with us, we've a better chance of catching him.'

'Perhaps. So what are you saying?'

'I'm saying we should set some snares and dig some pits. Get Inspector Farraday to pass on a few tidbits to the press, all about how we suspect the Wolfman's gay, or a transvestite. It can be anything, so long as it jars his conservatism, and maybe it'll force him into the open.'

Rebus let go of the knife and waited for Flight's response. But Flight wasn't about to be rushed. He ran a finger around the rim of his cup.

'Not a bad idea that,' he said at last. 'But I'm willing to bet you didn't get it from your books.'

Rebus shrugged. 'Maybe not exactly.'

'I thought not. Well, let's see what Cath says to it.' Flight rose from his chair. 'Meantime, on a less lofty plane of existence, I think I can take you straight to Tommy Watkiss. Come on. And by the way, thanks for breakfast.'

'My pleasure,' said Rebus. He could see Flight was unconvinced by his defence, such as it had turned out to be, of psychology. But then was it Flight he was trying to convince, or himself? Was it Flight he was trying to impress, or Dr Lisa Frazer?

They were passing through the foyer now, Rebus carrying his briefcase. Flight turned to him.

'Do you,' he said, 'know why we're called the Old Bill?' Rebus shrugged, offering no answer. 'Some say it's because we're named after a certain London landmark. You can try guessing on the way there.' And with that Flight pushed hard at the rotating door which served as the hotel's entrance.

The Old Bailey was not quite what Rebus had expected. The famous dome was there, atop which blindfolded Justice held her scales, but a large part of the court complex was of much more modern design. Security was the keynote. X-ray machines, cubicle-style doors which allowed only one person at a time into the body of the building and security men everywhere. The windows were coated with adhesive tape so that any explosion would not send lethal shards of glass flying into the concourse. Inside, ushers (all of them women) dressed in flapping black cloaks ran around trying to gather up stray juries.

'Any jurors for court number four?'

'Jurors for court number twelve, please!'

All the time a PA system announced the names of missing single jurors. It was the busy beginning of another judicial day. Witnesses smoked cigarettes, worried-looking barristers, weighed down by documents, held whispered dialogues with dull-eyed clients, and police officers waited nervously to give evidence.

'This is where we win or lose, John,' said Flight. Rebus couldn't be sure whether he was referring to the courtrooms or to the concourse itself. On floors above them were administrative offices, robing rooms, restaurants. But this floor was where cases were held and decided. Through some doors to their left was the older, domed part of the Old

Bailey, a darker, more forbidding place than this bright marbled gallery. The place echoed with the squealing of leather soled shoes, the clack-clack-clacking of heels on the solid floor and the constant murmur of conversation.

'Come on,' said Flight. He was leading them towards one of the courtrooms, where he had a word with the guard and one of the clerks before ushering Rebus into the court itself.

If stone and black leather predominated in the concourse, then the courtroom belonged to wood panelling and green leather. They sat on two chairs just inside the door, joining DC Lamb, already seated there, unsmiling, arms folded. He did not greet them, but leaned across to whisper, 'We're going to nail the cunt', before stiffening into his former position.

On the other side of the room sat the twelve jurors, looking bored already, faces numb and unthinking. To the back of the court stood the defendant, hands resting on the rail in front of him, a man of about forty with short, wiry silver and black hair, his face like something hewn from stone, his open-necked shirt a sign of arrogance. He had the dock to himself, there being no police officer on guard.

Some distance in front of him, the lawyers sorted through their papers, watched by assistants and solicitors. The defence counsel was a thick-set and tired-looking man, his face grey (as was his hair), gnawing on a cheap ballpoint. The prosecutor, however, was much more confident looking, tall (if stout), dressed immaculately and with the glow of the righteous upon him. His pen was an intricate fountain affair and he wrote with a flourish, his mouth set as defiantly as any Churchill impersonator. He reminded Rebus of how television liked to think of QCs, Rumpole aside.

Directly overhead was the public gallery. He could hear the muffled shuffling of feet. It had always worried Rebus that those in the public gallery had a clear view of the jury. Here, the court had been designed in such a way that they stared directly down and onto the jurors, making intimidation and identification that much easier. He'd dealt with several cases of jurors being approached at day's end by some relative of the accused, ready with a wad of notes or a clenched fist.

The judge looked imperious as he pored over some papers in front of him, while just below him the Clerk of Court spoke in hushed tones into a telephone receiver. From the time it was taking to begin proceedings, Rebus realised two things. One was that the case was continuing, not beginning; the other was that some Point of Law had been placed before the judge, which the judge was now considering.

'Here, seen this?' Lamb was offering a tabloid to Flight. The newspaper had been folded to a quarter of its size and Lamb tapped one column as he passed it to his superior. Flight read quickly, glancing up at Rebus once or twice, then handed the paper to Rebus with a hint of a smile.

'Here you go, expert.'

Rebus read through the unattributed piece. Basically, it concerned itself with the progress or lack of it on the Jean Cooper murder inquiry. But the closing paragraph was the killer: 'The team investigating what have come to be known as the "Wolfman Murders" are being assisted by an expert on serial killers, drafted in from another police force.'

Rebus stared at the newsprint without really seeing it. Surely Cath Farraday wouldn't have? But then how else had the newspaper got to know? He kept his eyes on the page, aware that both Flight and Lamb were looking at him. He couldn't believe it: *him*, an *expert*! Whether it was true or not – and it wasn't – didn't really matter now. What mattered was that results would be expected from him, results above the norm. Yet he knew he couldn't deliver and in not delivering he would be made to look a laughing stock. No wonder those two pairs of eyes burned into his head. No hard-working policeman liked to be usurped by 'experts'. Rebus didn't like it himself. He didn't like any of it!

Flight saw the pained expression on Rebus's face and felt sorry for the man. Lamb, however, was smirking, enjoying Rebus's agony. He accepted his newspaper from Rebus and stuffed it into his jacket pocket.

'Thought you'd be interested,' he said.

The judge finally looked up, his attention fixed on the jury. 'Members of the jury,' he began, 'it has been brought to my attention in the case of Crown versus Thomas Watkiss that the evidence of Police Constable Mills contained a passage which may have lodged in your minds, influencing your objectivity.'

So, the man in the dock was Tommy Watkiss, Maria's husband. Rebus studied him again, shaking his mind clear of the news story. Watkiss's face was a curious shape, the top half much wider than the cheekbones and jaw, which fell almost to a point. He had the look of an old boxer who had suffered one dislocated jaw too many. The judge was going on about some cock-up in the police case. The arresting constable had given evidence stating that his first words on reaching the accused had been 'Hello, Tommy, what's going on here?' By giving this in evidence, he had let the jury know that Watkiss was well known to the local constabulary, something which might well influence their judgment. The judge was therefore ordering the jury to be dismissed.

'Good on ya, Tommy!' came a cry from the public gallery, quickly silenced by a glare from the judge. Rebus wondered where he had heard the voice before.

As the court rose, Rebus stepped forward a few paces and turned to look up at the balcony. The spectators had risen, too, and in the front row Rebus could see a young man dressed in bike leathers and carrying a crash-helmet, grinning towards Watkiss. He raised his fist in a gesture of triumph, then turned and began to climb the steps to the gallery's exit. It was Kenny, Samantha's boyfriend. Rebus walked back to where Flight and Lamb were standing, watching him curiously, but Rebus directed his attention towards the dock. The look on Watkiss's face was one of pure relief. DC Lamb, on the other hand, seemed ready to kill.

'Luck of the fucking Irish,' he spat.

'Tommy's no more Irish than you are, Lamb,' Flight said phlegmatically.

'What was the charge?' Rebus asked, his mind still confused by the newspaper story, by Kenny's presence in this place and by his actions. The judge was leaving by a green padded-leather door to the side of the jury box.

'The usual,' said Lamb, calming quickly. 'Rape. When his old woman snuffed it, he needed somebody else on the game. So he tried to "persuade" a girl on his street that she could make a few bob. When that didn't work, he lost his rag and had a go at her. Bastard. We'll get him at the retrial. I still think he did for his old woman.'

'Then find the evidence,' said Flight. 'Meantime, I can think of a certain Police Constable who needs a good kick up the arse.'

'Yeah,' said Lamb. He was grinning evilly at the thought, then took the hint and left the courtroom in search of the unfortunate PC Mills.

'Inspector Flight.' It was the prosecuting counsel, striding briskly towards them with documents and books cradled in his left arm, his right arm outstretched. Flight took the well-groomed hand and shook it.

'Hello, Mr Chambers. This is Inspector Rebus. He's come down from Scotland to help us on the Wolfman investigation.'

Chambers looked interested. 'Ah, yes, the Wolfman. I look forward to prosecuting that particular case.'

'I just hope we can give you the opportunity,' said Rebus.

'Well,' said Chambers, 'meanwhile it's tricky enough landing the little fish like our friend.' He glanced back in the direction of the dock, which now stood empty. 'But we try,' he said with a sigh, 'we try.' Then he paused, and added in an undertone, directed at Flight: 'Get this, George, I don't like being royally shafted by my own team. Okay?'

Flight blushed. Chambers had dressed him down in a way no Superintendent or Chief Constable could ever have done, and he knew it. 'Good day, gentlemen,' he said, moving away, 'and good luck, Inspector Rebus.'

'Thanks,' Rebus called to the retreating figure.

Flight watched as Chambers pushed open the doors of the court, the tail of his wig flicking from side to side, robes flapping behind him. When the doors were closed, Flight chuckled.

'Arrogant prick. But he's the best there is.'

Rebus was beginning to wonder if anyone in London was second-rate. He'd been introduced to the 'top' pathologist, the 'best' prosecuting counsel, the 'crack' forensic team, the 'finest' police divers. Was it part of the city's own arrogance?

'I thought the best lawyers all went in for commercial work these days,' Rebus said.

'Not necessarily. It's only the really greedy bastards who go in for City work. Besides, this sort of stuff is like a drug to Chambers and his ilk. They're actors, bloody good ones at that.'

Yes, Rebus had known a few Oscar-winning advocates in his time, and had lost a few cases more to their technique than to the strength of their defence. They might earn a quarter of the riches earned by their brothers in the commercial sector, might take home a scant £50,000 each year, but they endured for the sake of their public.

Flight was moving towards the doors. 'What's more,' he said, 'Chambers studied for a time in the USA. They train them to be actors over there. They also train them to be hard-nosed bastards. I'm told he came out top of his class. That's why we like having him on our side.' Flight paused. 'Do you still want a word with Tommy?'

Rebus shrugged. 'Why not?'

Out in the concourse, Watkiss was standing by one of the large windows, relishing a cigarette and listening to his solicitor. Then the two men started to walk away.

'Tell you what,' said Rebus, 'I've changed my mind. Let's skip Watkiss for the moment.'

'Okay,' said Flight. 'You're the *expert* after all.' He saw the sour look on Rebus's face and laughed. 'Don't worry about it,' he said. 'I know you're no expert.'

'That's very reassuring, George,' Rebus said without conviction. He stared after Watkiss, thinking: And I'm not the only one leaving court without conviction.

Flight laughed again, but behind his smile he was still more than a little curious about Rebus's action in the courtroom, walking out into the court like that to peer up at the public gallery. But if Rebus didn't want to talk about it, then that was his privilege. Flight could bide his time. 'So what now?' he asked.

Rebus was rubbing his jaw. 'My dental appointment,' he said.

Anthony Morrison, who insisted that they call him Tony, was much younger than Rebus had been anticipating. No more than thirty-five, he had an underdeveloped body, so that his adult head seemed to have outgrown the rest of him. Rebus was aware that he was staring at Morrison with more than common interest. The scrubbed and shiny face, the tufts of bristle on chin and cheekbone where a razor had failed to fulfil its duties, the trimmed hair and keening eyes: in the street, he would have taken Morrison for a sixth-year pupil. Certainly, for a pathologist, albeit a dental pathologist, the man was in stark contrast to Philip Cousins.

On learning that Rebus was Scottish, Morrison had started on about the debt modern-day pathology owed to the Scots, 'men like Glaister and Littlejohn and Sir Sydney Smith' though the latter, Morrison had to admit, had been born in the Antipodes. He then said that his own father had been a Scotsman, a surgeon, and asked if Rebus knew that the earliest British Chair of Forensic Medicine had been founded in Edinburgh. Rebus, swept away by the welter of facts, said that this was news to him.

Morrison showed them into his office with an enthusiastic bounce to his walk. Once inside, however, the dentist's demeanour changed from social to professional.

'He's been busy again,' he said without preamble, leading them to the wall behind his desk, where several ten by eight colour and black and white photographs had been pinned. They showed precise close-ups of the bite marks left on Jean Cooper's stomach. Arrows had been drawn in, leading from particular spots on certain photographs out to where pinned notes gave Morrison's technical summary of his findings.

'I know what to look for now, of course,' he said, 'so it didn't take long to establish that these are probably the same teeth used in the previous attacks. A pattern is also emerging, however, perhaps a disturbing one.' He went to his desk and returned with more photographs. 'These are from victim number one. You'll notice that the indents left by the teeth are less marked. They grow a little more marked by victims two and three. And now –' he pointed to the current crop of pictures.

'They've got even deeper,' Rebus answered. Morrison beamed at him.

'Quite right.'

'So he's becoming more violent.'

'If you can term an attack made on someone who's already dead "violent", then yes, Inspector Rebus, he's getting more violent, or perhaps more unstable would be a better way of phrasing it.' Rebus and Flight exchanged a glance. 'Apart from the change in the relative depth of the bite marks, there's little I can add to my previous findings. The teeth are quite likely to be prosthetic –'

Rebus interrupted. 'You mean false?' Morrison nodded. 'How can you tell?'

Morrison beamed again. The prodigy who liked to show off in front of his teachers. 'How can I best explain this to a layman?' He seemed to consider his own question for a moment. 'Well, one's own teeth – your own, for example, Inspector Rebus – and by the way, you should get them seen to – they get a little ragged over time. The cutting edge gets chipped and worn. The edge on false teeth is more likely to be smoother, more rounded. Less of an edge to the front teeth especially, and less chips and cracks.'

Rebus, lips closed, was running his tongue over his teeth. It was true, they had the serrated feel of a workman's saw. He hadn't visited a dentist in ten years or more, had never felt the need. But now Morrison had commented on them. Did they really look so awful?

'So,' Morrison continued, 'for that reason, as well as for several others, I would say the killer has false teeth. But he also has very curious teeth indeed.'

'Oh?' Rebus tried to speak without showing Morrison any more of his own decaying mouth.

'I've already explained this to Inspector Flight,' Morrison paused so that Flight could nod agreement of this, 'but briefly, the upper set has a greater biting curve than the lower set. From my measurements, I conclude that the person in possession of these teeth must have quite a strangely shaped face. I did draw some sketches, but I've managed to come up with something better. I'm glad you've come this afternoon.' He walked over to a cupboard and opened it. Rebus looked to Flight, who merely shrugged. Morrison was turning towards them again, his right hand supporting a large object covered by an inverted brown-paper bag.

'Behold,' he said, lifting the bag from the object. 'I bring you the head of the Wolfman!'

There was silence in the room, so that the traffic noise from outside became conspicuous. Neither Rebus nor Flight could think of anything immediately to say. Instead, they walked across to meet with the chuckling Morrison, who was regarding his creation with a measure of glee. There was a squeal of suddenly braking tyres outside.

'The Wolfman,' Morrison repeated. He was holding the cast of a human head, constructed so far as Rebus could ascertain from pale pink plaster. 'You can ignore the idea from the nose upwards, if you prefer,' said Morrison. 'It's fairly speculative, based on mean measurements taking into account the jaw. But the jaw itself is, I believe, pretty accurate.'

And a strange jaw it was. The upper teeth jutted out from the mouth, so that the lips over them and the skin below the nose was stretched and bulging. The lower jaw seemed tucked in beneath in what seemed to Rebus a Neanderthal display, to the extent that it almost disappeared. The chin had a narrow, pinched look and the cheekbones were swollen in a line with the nose, but concave as the face extended downwards. It was an extraordinary face, the like of which Rebus could not recall having encountered in the real world. But then this was not the real world, was it? It was a reconstruction, depending upon a measure of averages and guesswork. Flight was staring at it in fascination, as though committing the face to memory. Rebus had the chilling notion that Flight would release a photograph to the papers and charge the first poor soul he came across possessing such a physiognomy.

'Would you call that deformed?' Rebus asked.

'Heavens, no,' said Morrison with a laugh. 'You haven't seen some of the medical cases I've had to deal with. No, this couldn't be termed deformed.'

'Looks like my idea of Mr Hyde,' commented Flight.

Don't mention Hyde to me, Rebus thought to himself.

'Perhaps,' said Morrison, laughing again. 'What about you, Inspector Rebus? What are your thoughts?'

Rebus examined the cast again. 'It looks prehistoric.'

'Ah! said Morrison enthusiastically. 'That was what I thought at first. The jutting upper jaw especially.'

'How do you know that is the upper jaw?' asked Rebus. 'Couldn't it be the other way round?'

'No, I'm pretty sure this is correct. The bites are fairly consistent. Apart from victim three, that is.'

'Oh?'

'Yes, victim three was a strange one. The lower set, that is the smaller set, seemed more extended than the upper set. As you can see from this cast, the killer would have had to make an extraordinary contortion of his face to produce such a bite.'

He mimed the bite for them, opening his mouth wide, lifting his head, and pushing out his lower jaw, then making a biting motion, the lower jaw doing most of the work.

'In the other bites, the killer has bitten more like this.' Again he put on a dumb show, this time drawing his lips back from his upper jaw and biting down sharply so that the upper teeth closed over the lower teeth, the teeth themselves snapping together.

Rebus shook his head. This wasn't making things clearer. If anything, he was growing more confused. He nodded towards the cast. 'You really believe the man we're looking for looks like this?'

'The man or woman, yes. Of course, I may have exaggerated a little with this cast, but I'm more or less convinced.'

Rebus had stopped listening after the first sentence. 'What do you mean, or woman?' he asked.

Morrison shrugged his shoulders theatrically. 'Again, this is something I've discussed with Inspector Flight. It just seemed to me that, purely on the dental evidence you understand, this head could as easily belong to a woman as to a man. The large upper set of teeth seems to me very male, judging from size and what have you, but the lower set, just as equally, seems very female. A man with a woman's chin, or a woman with a masculine upper jaw?' He shrugged again. 'Take your pick.'

Rebus looked to Flight, who was shaking his head slowly. 'No,' Flight said, 'it's a man.'

Rebus had never considered the possibility that a woman might be behind the killings. It had never entered his head. Until now.

A woman? Improbable, but why impossible? Flight was dismissing it out of hand, but on what grounds? Rebus had read last night that a growing number of multiple murderers were women. But could a woman have stabbed like that? Could a woman so completely have overwhelmed victims of similar height, similar strength?

'I'd like to get some photographs of this,' Flight was saying. He had taken the cast from Morrison and was studying it again.

'Of course,' Morrison said, 'but remember, it's only my idea of the look of the killer's head.'

'We appreciate it, Tony. Thanks for all your work.'

Morrison shrugged modestly. He had fished for a compliment and had hooked one.

Rebus could see that Flight was convinced by this whole piece of theatre, the unveiling of the head and so on. To Rebus it was more showmanship than tangible truth, more the stuff of courtroom melodrama. He still felt that to trap the Wolfman they had to get inside his head, not play with plaster mock-ups of it.

His or her head.

'Would the bite marks be enough to identify the killer?'

Morrison considered this. Then nodded. 'I think so, yes. If you can bring me the suspect, I think I can show that he or she is the Wolfman.'

Rebus persisted, 'But would it stand up in court?'

Morrison folded his arms and smiled. 'I could blind the jury with science.' His face became serious again. 'No, on its own I don't think my evidence would ever be enough to convict. But as part of a larger body of such evidence, we might be in with half a chance.'

'Always supposing the bastard makes it to trial,' Flight added grimly. 'Accidents have been known to happen in custody.'

'Always supposing,' Rebus corrected, 'we catch him in the first place.'

'That, gentlemen,' said Morrison, 'I leave entirely in your capable hands. Suffice to say, I look forward to introducing my friend here to the real thing.' And he tipped the plaster head backwards and forwards and backwards again, until it seemed to Rebus that the head was mocking them, laughing and rolling its sightless eyes.

As Morrison showed them out, he rested a hand on Rebus's forearm. 'I'm serious about your teeth,' he said, 'you should get them seen to. I could look at them myself if you like?'

When he returned to headquarters Rebus went straight to the washroom and, in front of a soap-spattered mirror, examined his mouth.

What was Morrison talking about? His teeth looked fine. Okay, one of them had a dark line running down it, a crack perhaps, and a few were badly stained from too many cigarettes and too much tea. But they looked strong enough, didn't they? No need for drills and piercing, grinding implements. No need for a dentist's chair, sharp needles, and a spitting out of blood.

Back at his designated desk he doodled on his notebook. Was Morrison just the nervous type, or was he hyperactive? Was he perhaps mad? Or was he merely dealing with the world in his own idiosyncratic way?

So few serial killers were women. Statistically, it was unlikely. Since when had he believed in statistics? Since he had started to read psychology textbooks, last night in his hotel room after the disastrous visit to Rhona and Samantha. Kenny: what the hell was Kenny doing running around with Tommy Watkiss? His daughter's 'gentleman'. A smiling villain? Forget it, John. You don't control that part of your life any more. He had to smile at this: what part of his life did he control? His work gave his life what meaning it had. He should admit defeat, tell Flight he could be of no help and return to Edinburgh, where he could be sure of his villains and his crimes: drug peddlars, protection racketeers, domestic violence, fraud.

A murder each month, regular as the moon. It was only a saying, wasn't it, regular as the moon? He unhooked a calendar from the wall. Portraits of Italy, donated to the station by Gino's Sandwich Bar. Time of the month. Had there been a full moon around 16th January when Maria Watkiss was found? No, but then they reckoned she might have lain undiscovered for two or three days. Thursday 11th January had been the full moon. The full moon affected the Wolfman in the movies, didn't it? But they had named the killer Wolfman after Wolf Street, not because he, or she, killed by the light of the full moon. Rebus was more confused than ever. And weren't women supposedly affected by the moon, something to do with their time of the month?

May Jessop had died on Monday 5th February, four days *before* another full moon. Shelley Richards had died on Wednesday 28th February, nowhere near a full moon. Morrison had said her case was unusual, the bites had seemed different. And then Jean Cooper had died on the night of Sunday 18th March, two days before the vernal equinox.

He threw the calendar onto the desk. There was no pattern, no neat mathematical solution. Who was he trying to kid? This wasn't the movies. The hero didn't stumble upon the answer. There were no shortcuts. Maybe Flight was right. It was all plodding routine and forensic evidence. Psychology was no shortcut, barking at the moon was no shortcut. He couldn't know when the Wolfman would strike again. He knew so little.

Flight wandered exhaustedly into the room and fell onto a chair, causing it to creak in protest.

'I finally got through to Cath,' he said. 'I put your idea to her, and she's giving it some thought.'

'That's big of her.'

Flight gave him a warning look and Rebus raised his hands in apology. Flight nodded towards the calendar. 'What are you up to?'

'I don't know, nothing much. I thought there might be some pattern to the dates when the Wolfman struck.'

'You mean like the stages of the moon, the equinox, that sort of thing?' Flight was smiling. Rebus nodded slowly. 'Hell, John, I've been through all that and more.' He went to a particular manila folder and tossed it towards Rebus. 'Take a look: I've tried number patterns, distance between murder sites, possible means of transport – the Wolfman's pretty mobile, you know, I think he must have a car. I've tried linking the victims, checking which school they went to, which libraries they used, whether they liked sports or discos or classical bloody music. Know what? They don't have *anything* in common, not a single thing linking the four of them save the fact that they were women.'

Rebus flicked through the file. It was an impressive amount of slogging, all to no end save that of clarification. Flight hadn't climbed the ladder to his present rank by a fluke, or by keeping in with his superiors, or by signifying greatness. He had got there by sheer hard work.

'Point taken,' said Rebus. Then, because this didn't seem quite enough: 'I'm impressed. Have you shown this lot to anyone else?'

Flight shook his head. 'It's guesswork, John. Straw-clutching. That's all. It would just confuse the issue. Besides, do you remember the story of the boy who cried wolf? One day, there really was a wolf there, but by then no one believed him because he'd given them so much crap before.'

Rebus smiled. 'Still, it's a lot of work.'

'What did you expect?' Flight asked. 'A chimpanzee in a whistle? I'm a good copper, John. I may be no *expert*, but I'd never claim to be.'

Rebus was about to remonstrate, then frowned. 'What's a whistle?' he said.

Flight threw back his head and laughed. 'A suit, you plonker. Whistle and flute, suit. Rhyming slang. God sakes, John, we're going to have to educate you. Tell you what, why don't we go out for a meal ourselves tonight? I know a good Greek restaurant in Walthamstow.' Flight paused, a gleam in his eye. 'I know it's good,' he said, "cos I've seen a lot of bubbles coming out of it.' His smile was inviting. Rebus thought quickly. Bubbles? Was the food gassy? Did they serve champagne? Rhyming slang. Bubbles.

'Bubble and squeak,' he said. Then a pause. 'Greeks, right?'

'Right!' said Flight. 'You're catching on fast. So what about it? Or Indian, Thai, Italian, you decide.'

But Rebus was shaking his head. 'Sorry, George, prior engagement.'

Flight pulled his head back. 'No,' he said, 'you're seeing *her*, aren't you? That bloody psychiatrist. I forgot you told me at breakfast. You bloody Jocks, you don't waste any time, do you? Coming down here, stealing our women.' Flight sounded in good humour, but Rebus thought he detected something a little deeper down, a genuine sadness that the two of them couldn't get together for a meal.

'Tomorrow night, eh, George?'

'Yeah,' said Flight. 'Tomorrow night sounds fine. One word of advice though?'

'What?'

'Don't let her get you on the couch.'

'No,' said Dr Lisa Frazer, shaking her head vigorously. 'That's psychiatrists. Psychiatrists have couches, not psychologists. We're like chalk and cheese.'

She looked stunning, yet there was no alchemy involved in the process. She was dressed simply and wore no make-up. Her hair had been brushed straight back and tied with a band. Still, casually, elegantly, simply, she was stunning. She had been dead on time at the hotel and had walked with him, her arm linked in his, along Shaftesbury Avenue, past the scene of his run-in with the patrol car. The early evening was warm, and Rebus felt good walking with her. Men were glancing towards them, okay, be honest, towards *her*. There might even have been a wolf whistle or two. It made Rebus feel good all the same. He was wearing his tweed jacket with an open-necked shirt and had the sudden fear that she would lead him to some fancy restaurant where men were not admitted without ties. That would be just his luck. The city teemed with nightlife, teenagers mostly, drinking from cans and calling to each other across the busy road. The pubs were doing good business and buses chugged grime into the air. Grime which would be falling unseen on Lisa Frazer. Rebus felt valiant. He felt like stopping all the traffic, confiscating all the keys so that she could walk unsullied through the streets.

Since when did he think like that? Where had this tiny unpolished stone of romance come from? What desperate corner of his soul? Self-conscious, John. You're becoming too self-conscious. And if a psychologist didn't spot it, nobody would. Be natural. Be calm. Be yourself.

She brought him into Chinatown, a few streets off Shaftesbury Avenue, where the telephone boxes were shaped like oriental temples, supermarkets sold fifty-year-old eggs, gateways were decorated like relics from Hong Kong and the street names were given in Chinese as well as English. There were a few tourists about, but mainly the pedestrianised walkway was filled with scuttling Chinese, their voices shrill. It was a different world, like something you would expect to find in New York but never dream of finding in England. Yet he could look back along the street and still see the theatres on Shaftesbury Avenue, the red buses chug-chugging, the punks yelling obscenities at the tops of immature voices.

'Here we are,' she said, stopping outside a restaurant on the corner of the street. She pulled open the door, gesturing for him to precede her into the air-conditioned chill. A waiter was upon them at once, showing them to a dimly-lit booth. A waitress smiled with her eyes as she handed them each a menu. The waiter returned with a wine list, which he placed beside Rebus.

'Would you like a drink while you are deciding?'

Rebus looked to Lisa Frazer for guidance. 'Gin and tonic,' she said without hesitation.

'And the same for me,' said Rebus, then regretted it. He wasn't all that keen on gin's chemical smell.

'I'm very excited about this case, Inspector Rebus.'

'Please, call me John. We're not in the station now.'

She nodded. 'I'd like to thank you for giving me the chance to study the files. I think I'm already forming an interesting picture.' She reached into her clutch-purse and produced a collection of a dozen index cards held together with an outsize paper-clip. The cards were covered in lines of tiny, neat handwriting. She seemed ready to start reading them. 'Shouldn't we at least order first?' Rebus asked. She appeared not to understand, then grinned.

'Sorry,' she said. 'It's just that I'm . . .'

'Very excited. Yes, you said.'

'Don't policemen get excited when they find what they think is a clue?'

'Almost never,' said Rebus, appearing to study the menu, 'we're born pessimists. We don't get excited until the guilty party has been sentenced and locked up.'

'That's curious.' She held her own menu still closed. The index cards had been relegated to the table-top. 'I'd have thought to enjoy police work you would need a level of optimism, otherwise you'd *never* think you were going to solve the case.'

Still studying the menu, Rebus decided that he'd let her order for both of them. He glanced up at her. 'I try not to think about solving or not solving,' he said. 'I just get on with the job, step by step.'

The waiter had returned with their drinks.

'You are ready to order?'

'Not really,' said Rebus, 'could we have a couple more minutes?'

Lisa Frazer was staring across the table at him. It wasn't a large table. Her right hand rested on the rim of her glass, barely an inch from his left hand. Rebus could sense the presence of her knees almost touching his own under the table. The other tables in the restaurant all seemed larger than this one, and the booths seemed better lit.

'Frazer's a Scottish name,' he said. It was as good a line as any.

'That's right,' she replied. 'My great grandfather came from a place called Kirkcaldy.'

Rebus smiled. She had pronounced the word the way it looked. He corrected her, then added, 'I was born and brought up not far from there. Five or six miles, to be precise.'

'Really? What a coincidence. I've never been there, but my grandaddy used to tell me it was where Adam Smith was born.'

Rebus nodded. 'But don't hold that against it,' he said. 'It's still not a bad wee town.' He picked up his glass and swirled it, enjoying the sound of the ice chinking on the glass. Lisa was at last studying her menu. Without looking up, she spoke.

'Why are you here?' The question was sudden, catching Rebus off-balance. Did she mean here in the restaurant, here in London, here on this planet?

'I'm here to find answers.' He was pleased with this reply; it seemed to deal with all three possibilities at once. He lifted his glass. 'Here's to psychology.'

She raised her own glass, ice rattling like musical chimes. 'Here's to taking things one step at a time.' They both drank. She studied her menu again. 'Now,' she said, 'what shall we have?'

Rebus knew how to use a pair of chopsticks, but perhaps tonight had just been the wrong time to try. He suddenly found himself unable to pick up a noodle or a sliver of duck without the thing sliding out of his grasp and falling back to the table, splashing sauce across the tablecloth. The more it happened, the more frustrated he became and the more frustrated he became, the more it happened. Finally, he asked for a fork.

'My coordination's all gone,' he explained. She smiled in understanding (or was it sympathy?) and poured more tea into his tiny cup. He could see that she was impatient to tell him what she thought she had discovered about the Wolfman. Over a starter of crabmeat soup the talk had been safe, guarded, had been of pasts and futures, not the present. Rebus stabbed his fork into an unresisting slice of meat. 'So what have you found?'

She looked at him for confirmation that this was her cue. When he nodded, she put down her chopsticks, then pushed aside the paper-clip from her index cards and cleared her throat, not so much reading from the cards, more using them as occasional prompts.

'Well,' she said, 'the first thing I found revealing was the evidence of salt on the bodies of the victims. I know some people think it may be sweat, but I'm of the opinion that these are tear stains. A lot can be learned from any killer's interpersonal relationship with his or her victim.' There it was again: his or her. *Her.* 'To me the tear stains indicate feelings of guilt in the attacker, guilt felt, moreover, not in reflection but at the actual time of the attack. This gives the Wolfman a moral dimension, showing that he is being driven almost against his will. There may well be signs of schizophrenia here, the Wolfman's dark side operating only at certain times.'

She was about to rush on, but already Rebus needed time to catch up. He interrupted. 'You're saying most of the time the Wolfman may seem as normal as you or me?'

She nodded briskly. 'Yes, exactly. In fact, I'm saying that between times the Wolfman doesn't just seem as normal as anyone else, he *is* as normal, which is why he's been hard to catch. He doesn't wander around the streets with the word "Wolfman" tattooed across his forehead.'

Rebus nodded slowly. He realised that by seeming to concentrate on her words, he had an excuse for staring at her face, consuming it with eyes more proficient than any cutlery. 'Go on,' he said.

She flipped one card over and moved to the next, taking a deep breath. 'That the victim is abused *after* death indicates that the Wolfman feels no need to control his victim. In some serial killers, this element of control is important. Killing is the only time when these people feel in any kind of control of their lives. This isn't the case with the Wolfman. The murder itself is relatively quick, occasioning little pain or suffering. Sadism, therefore, is not a feature. Rather, the Wolfman is playing out a scenario upon the corpse.'

Again the rush of words, her energy, her eagerness to share her findings, all swept past Rebus. How could he concentrate when she was so close to him, so close and so beautiful? 'What do you mean?'

'It'll become clearer.' She stopped to take a sip of tea. Her food was barely touched, the mound of rice in the bowl beside her hardly dented. In her own way, Rebus realised, she was every bit as nervous as he was, but not for the same reasons. The restaurant, though hectic, might have been empty. This booth was *their* territory. Rebus took a gulp of the still-scalding tea. Tea! He could kill for a glass of cold white wine.

'I thought it interesting,' she was saying now, 'that the pathologist, Dr Cousins, feels the initial attack comes from behind. This makes the attacks non-confrontational and the Wolfman is likely to be like this in his social and working life. There's also the possibility that he cannot look his victims in the eye, out of fear that their fear would destroy his scenario.'

Rebus shook his head. It was time to own up. 'You've lost me.'

She seemed surprised. 'Simply, he's taking out revenge and to him the victims represent the individual against whom he's taking his revenge. If he confronted them face to face, he'd realise they're not the person he bears the grudge against in the first place.'

Rebus still felt a little bit lost. 'Then these women are stand-ins?'

'Substitutes, yes.'

He nodded. This was getting interesting, interesting enough for him to turn his gaze from Lisa Frazer, the better to concentrate on her words. She was still only halfway through her cards.

'So much for the Wolfman,' she said, flipping to the next card. 'But the chosen location can also say a lot about the inner life of the attacker, as can age, sex, race and class of the victims. You'll have noticed that they are all women, that they are mostly older women, women approaching middle age, and that three out of four have been white. I'll admit that I can't make much out of these facts as they stand. In fact, it was just the failure of pattern that made me think a little harder about location. You see, just when a pattern looks to be emerging, an element arises that destroys the precision: the killer attacks a much younger woman, or strikes earlier in the evening, or chooses a black victim.'

Or, Rebus was thinking, kills outside the pattern of the full moon.

Lisa continued, 'I started to give some consideration to the spatial pattern of the attacks. These can determine where the killer may strike next, or even where he lives.' Rebus raised his eyebrows. 'It's true, John, it's been proved in several cases.'

'I don't doubt it. I was raising my eyebrows at that phrase "spatial pattern".' A phrase he'd heard before, on the loathed management course.

She smiled. 'Jargon, yes. There's a lot of it about. What I mean is the pattern of the murder sites. A canal path, a railway line, the vicinity of a tube station. Three out of four take place near travel systems, but again the fourth case defeats the pattern. All four take place north of the river. At least there's *some* evidence of a pattern there. But – and this is my point – the non-emergence of a pattern seems to me in itself a conscious act. The Wolfman is making sure you have as little as possible to go on. This would indicate a high level of psychological maturity.'

'Yes, he's as mature as a hatter all right.'

She laughed. 'I'm being serious.'

'I know you are.'

'There is one other possibility.'

'What's that?'

'The Wolfman knows how *not* to leave a trail because he is familiar with police work.'

'Familiar with it?'

She nodded. 'Especially the way you go about investigating a series of murders.'

'You're saying he's a copper?'

She laughed again, shaking her head. 'I'm saying he may have prior convictions.'

'Yes, well,' he thought of the file George Flight had shown him a few

470

hours earlier, 'we've checked on over a hundred ex-offenders already. No luck there.'

'But you can't possibly have talked to every man who has ever been convicted of rape, violent assault or the like.'

'Agreed. But there's something you seem to have overlooked – the teeth marks. Those are very palpable clues. If the Wolfman is being so clever, why does he leave us a neat set of bite marks every time?'

She blew on her tea, cooling it. 'Maybe,' she said, 'the teeth are a – what do you call it – a red herring?'

Rebus thought about this. 'It's possible,' he conceded, 'but there's something else. I visited a dental pathologist today. From the marks made by the teeth, he said he couldn't rule out the possibility that the Wolfman is a woman.'

'Really?' Her eyes opened wide. 'That's very interesting. I'd never even considered it.'

'Neither had we.' He scooped more rice into his bowl. 'So tell me, why does he, or she, bite the victims?'

'I've given that a lot of thought.' She flipped to her final card. 'The bite is always on the stomach, the female stomach, carrier of life. Maybe the Wolfman has lost a child, or maybe he was abandoned and consequently adopted and resents the fact. I don't know. A lot of serial killers have fragmented upbringings.'

'Mmm. I read all about it in those books you gave me.'

'Really? You read them?'

'Last night.'

'And what did you think?'

'I thought they were clever, sometimes ingenious.'

'But do you think the theories are valid?'

Rebus shrugged. 'I'll tell you if and when we catch the Wolfman.'

She toyed with her food again, but ate nothing. The meat in her bowl had a cold, gelatinous look. 'What about the anal attacks, John. Do *you* have any theories there?'

Rebus considered this. 'No,' he said finally, 'but I know what a psychiatrist might say.'

'Yes, but you're not with a psychiatrist, remember. I'm a psychologist.'

'How can I forget? You said in your essay that there are thirty *known* serial killers active in the USA. Is that true?'

'I wrote that essay over a year ago. By now, there are probably more. Frightening, isn't it?'

He shrugged, the shrug disguising a shiver. 'How's the food?' he asked.

'What?' She looked at her bowl. 'Oh, I'm not really very hungry. To tell you the truth, I feel a little bit . . . deflated, I suppose. I was so excited at what I thought I'd managed to piece together, but in telling it all to you, I see that really there's not very much there at all.' She was thumbing through the index cards.

'There's plenty there,' said Rebus. 'I'm impressed, honest. Every little bit helps. And you stick to the known facts, I like that. I was expecting more jargon.' He remembered the terms from one of her books, the one by MacNaughtie. 'Latent psychomania, Oedipal urgings, gobbledygook.'

'I could give you plenty of that stuff,' she said, 'but I doubt it would help.'

'Exactly.'

'Besides, that's more in line with psychiatry. Psychologists prefer drive theories, social learning theory, multiphasic personalities.' Rebus had clamped his hands over his ears.

She laughed again. He could make her laugh so easily. Once upon a time he'd made Rhona laugh too, and after Rhona a certain Liaison Officer back in Edinburgh. 'So what about policemen?' he asked, closing off the memory. 'What can psychologists tell about us?'

'Well,' she said, relaxing into her seat, 'you're extrovert, tough-minded, conservative.'

'Conservative?'

'With a small "c".'

'I read last night that serial killers are conservative, too.'

She nodded, still smiling. 'Oh yes,' she said, 'you're alike in a lot of ways. But by conservative I mean specifically that you don't like anything that changes the status quo. That's why you're reticent about the use of psychology. It interferes with the strict guidelines you've set yourselves. Isn't that so?'

'Well, I suppose I could argue, but I won't. So what happens now you've studied the Wolfman?'

'Oh, all I've done so far is scratch the surface.' Her hands were still on the index cards. 'There are other tests to be done, character analyses and so on. It'll take time.' She paused. 'What about you?'

'Well, we'll plod along, checking, examining, taking it –'

'Step by step,' she interrupted.

'That's right, step by step. Whether I'll be on the case much longer or

472

not I can't say. They may send me back to Edinburgh at the end of the week.'

'Why did they bring you to London in the first place?'

The waiter had come to clear away their dishes. Rebus sat back, wiping his lips with the serviette.

'Any coffees or liqueurs, sir?'

Rebus looked to Lisa. 'I think I'll have a Grand Marnier,' she said.

'Just coffee for me,' said Rebus. 'No, hold on, what the hell, I'll have the same.' The waiter bowed and moved off, his arms heavy with crockery.

'You didn't answer my question, John.'

'Oh, it's simple enough. They thought I might be able to help. I worked on a previous serial killing, up in Edinburgh.'

'Really?' She sat forward in her chair, the palms of her hands pressed to the tablecloth. 'Tell me.'

So he told her. It was a long story, and he didn't know exactly why he gave her as many details as he did – more details than she needed to know, and more, perhaps, than he should be telling to a psychologist. What would she make of him? Would she find a trace of psychosis or paranoia in his character? But he had her complete attention, so he spun the tale out in order to enjoy that attention the more.

It took them through two cups of coffee, the paying of the bill, and a balmy night-time walk through Leicester Square, across Charing Cross Road, up St Martin's Lane and along Long Acre towards Covent Garden. They walked around Covent Garden itself, Rebus still doing most of the talking. He stopped by a row of three telephone boxes, curious about the small white stickers covering every available inch of space on the inside of the booths: Stern corrective measures; French lessons; O and A specialist; TV; Trudy, nymphet, Spank me; S/M chamber; Busty blonde – all of them accompanied by telephone numbers.

Lisa studied them, too. 'Every one a psychologist,' she said. Then: 'That's quite a story you've just told, John. Has anyone written it up?'

Rebus shrugged. 'A newspaper reporter wrote a couple of articles.' Jim Stevens. Christ, hadn't he moved to London, too? Rebus thought again of the newspaper story Lamb had shown him, the *unattributed* newspaper story.

'Yes,' Lisa was saying, 'but has anyone looked at it from your point of view?'

'No.' She looked thoughtful at this. 'You want to turn me into a case study?'

'Not necessarily,' she said. 'Ah, here we are.' She stopped. They were standing outside a shoe shop in a narrow, pedestrianised street. Above the rows of shops were two storeys of flats. 'This is where I live,' she said. 'Thank you for this evening. I've enjoyed it.'

'Thank you for the meal. It was great.'

'Not at all.' She fell silent. They were only two or three feet apart. Rebus shuffled his feet. 'Will you be able to find your way back?' she asked. 'Should I point you in the right direction?'

Rebus looked up and down the street. He was lost. He had not been keeping track of their meanderings. 'Oh, I'll be all right.' He smiled and she smiled back but did not speak. 'So this is it then,' he persisted. 'No offer of a coffee?'

She looked at him slyly. 'Do you really want a coffee?'

He returned the look. 'No,' he admitted, 'not really.'

She turned from him and opened the door to the side of the shoe shop. The shop claimed to specialise in handmade and non-leather shoes. Beside the door to the flats was an entryphone boasting six names. One of them read simply 'L Frazer'. No 'Dr', but then he supposed she wouldn't want to be disturbed by people needing a medical doctor, would she? There were times when a qualification was best kept under wraps.

Lisa drew the mortice key out of the lock. The stairwell was brightly lit, its plain stone painted cornflower blue. She turned back towards him.

'Well,' she said, 'since you don't want a coffee, you'd better come on up . . .'

She later explained, running a hand over his chest as they lay together in bed, that she saw no point in the little games people played, the slow edging towards a moment when both would admit that what they really wanted was to make love.

So instead she led Rebus up to her first floor flat, took him into the darkened room, undressed and got into bed, sitting with her knees tucked up in front of her.

'Well?' she said. So he had undressed, too, and joined her. She lay now with her arms reaching behind her to grab at the bedposts, her body dusky in the light cast from a street lamp outside. Rebus ran his tongue back up along the inside of her leg, the inner thigh, her legs supple. She smelt of jasmine, tasted of flowers more pungent still. Rebus was self-conscious at first. His own body had become an embarrassment, while hers was in fine, toned condition. (Squash and swimming, she told him later, and a strict diet.) He ran his fingers over the ripples, the corrugations in her flesh. There was some sagging to the skin above her stomach, some creasing to the sides of her breasts and to her throat. He looked down and saw his own distended chest. There was still some muscle to his stomach, but there was also excessive fleshiness; not supple, tired and ageing. Squash and swimming: he would take up some exercise, join a health club. There were enough of them in Edinburgh.

He was eager to please. Her pleasure became his only goal, and he worked tirelessly. There was sweat in the room now. A lot of sweat. They were working well together, moving fluidly, each seeming to sense what the other was about to do. When he moved slightly too quickly and bumped his nose on her chin, they laughed quietly, rubbing foreheads. And when later he went in search of her fridge and cold liquid, she came too, popping an ice cube into her mouth before kissing him, the kiss extending downwards as she sank to her knees in front of him.

Back in bed, they drank chill white wine from the bottle and kissed some more, then began all over again.

The air between them had lost its nervous charge and they were able to enjoy themselves. She moved on top, rearing above him, her rhythm increasing until all he could do was lie back and watch with his eyes closed, imagining the room in diffuse light, a cold spray of water, a smoothness of skin.

Or a woman. The Wolfman could be a woman. The Wolfman was playing with the police, seemed to know the way they thought and worked. A woman? A woman officer? Cath Farraday came to mind, with her Teutonic face, that wide but angular jaw.

Jesus, here he was with Lisa, thinking of another woman! He felt a sudden pang of guilt, hitting him in the stomach a moment before a very different reaction arched his back and his neck, while her hands pressed down upon his chest, her knees clamped to his hips.

Or a woman. Why the teeth? Leaving not a single clue except those bites. Why? Why not a woman? Why not a policeman? Or . . . or . . .

'Yes, yes.' Her breath escaped with a hiss, the word losing all meaning as she repeated it ten, twenty, thirty times. Yes what?

475

'Yes, John, yes, John, yes . . .'
Yes.

* * *

It had been another busy day for her, a day spent pretending to be what she's not, but now she was out again, prowling. She is beginning to like the way she can move so smoothly through the two worlds. Earlier this evening she was the guest at a dinner party in Blackheath. Mock-Georgian elegance, stripped pine doors, talk of school fees and fax machines, of interest rates and foreign property – and the Wolfman. They asked for her opinion. Her opinion was reasoned, intelligent, liberal. There was chilled Chablis and an exquisite bottle of Chateau Montrose: the '82. She could not choose between the two, so enjoyed a glass of both.

One guest was late arriving, a journalist on one of the better dailies. He apologised. They asked for tidbits from the next day's news, and he supplied them generously. The sister paper to his own was a downmarket tabloid. He told them the next day's front page would have a headline reading SECRET LIFE OF GAY WOLFMAN. Of course, as the journalist knows, this is nothing more than a ruse, to try to bait the killer. And she knows too, naturally. They smile at one another across the table, as she lifts more pasta expertly with her fork. How stupid of them to run a story like that: gay Wolfman indeed! She chuckles into her oversized wine glass. The conversation turns to motorway traffic, wine acquisition, the state of Blackheath Common. Blackheath, of course, is where they buried the plague victims, piling the corpses high. Black Death. Black Heath. One letter separates the two. She smiles at this, too, discreetly.

The meal over, she took a taxi back across the river and got out at the beginning of her street. She intended to go straight home, but walked past her door and kept on walking. She shouldn't be doing this, shouldn't be out here, but it feels right. After all, the toy in the gallery must be lonely. It's always so cold in the gallery. So cold Jack Frost could bite off your nose.

Her mother must have told her that. Her mother. *Long nosehairs, Johnny, are so unbecoming in a gentleman*. Or her father, singing nonsense songs while she hid herself in the garden. 'Fuck art,' she hisses quietly to herself.

She knows where to go, too. Not far. The intersection of one road with a much larger one. There are many like it in London. Traffic lights, and a few women wandering back and forth, sometimes crossing at the lights so that the drivers can see them, can see their legs and their white bodies. If a car window is rolled down, a woman may lean down close to the driver so that they can discuss terms. Professional, but not very discreet. She knows that sometimes the police will make a rudimentary attempt to close down business, knows too that policemen are among the whores' best customers. That's why it's dangerous for her to come here. Dangerous but necessary: she has an itch, and women like these go missing all the time, don't they? No one gets suspicious. No one starts alarm bells ringing. Alarm bells are the last thing you need in this part of the city. Like with her first victim, by the time they got to her she was a meal for rats. Animal feed. She chuckles again, and makes to walk past one of these women, but stops.

'Hello, love,' says the woman. 'Anything you want?'

'How much for the night?'

'For you, love, a hundred.'

'Very well.' She turns and starts back towards her own street, her own house, so much safer there than out here. The woman follows noisily a yard or two behind, seeming to understand. She does not let the woman catch up until she is at the front door and the key is in the lock. The gallery beckons. Only it doesn't look like a gallery any more.

It looks like a butcher's block.

'Nice place you've got, love.'

She puts a finger to her lips. 'No talking.' The woman begins to look suspicious, looks as though she's thinking twice about being here. So she goes to her and grabs at a breast, planting a clumsy, smeared kiss across puffy lips. The prostitute looks startled for a second, then manages a rehearsed smile.

'Well, you're certainly not a gentleman,' she says.

She nods, pleased with this remark. The front door is locked now. And she goes to the door of the gallery, slips the key in, unlocks it.

'In here, love?' The woman is removing her coat as she walks across the threshold. The coat is down past her shoulders by the time she sees the room itself. But by then, of course, it's too late, far too late.

She moves in on her, like a trained worker on a production line. Hand over the mouth, good pressure on the knife and a quick backward arc before the thrust. She has often wondered if they see the knife, or are their eyes closed in terror by then? She imagines them with eyes bulging open, focussing on the knife as, point directed towards them, it swings back and then flies forward towards their face. She can find out, can't she? All she needs is a strategically placed wall-mirror. Must remember that for next time.

Gurgle, gurgle. The gallery is such a marvellous setting, poised between Apollo and Dionysus. The body slips to the floor. Time for the real work now. Her brain is humming – mummydaddymummydaddy mummydaddymummydaddy – as she crouches to her task.

'It's only a game,' she whispers, her voice a mere tremble at the back of her throat. 'Only a game.' She hears the woman's words again: *certainly not a gentleman.* No, certainly not. Her laughter is harsh and abrupt. Suddenly, she feels it again. No! Not already! *Next time.* The knife twitches. She hasn't even finished with this one. She can't possibly do another tonight! It would be madness. Sheer madness. But the craving is there, an absolute and unappeasable hunger. This time with a mirror. She covers her eyes with a bloodstained hand.

'Stop!' she cries. 'Stop it, Daddy! Mummy! Make it stop! Please, make it stop!'

But that's the problem, as she knows only too well. Nobody *can* make it stop, nobody *will* make it stop. On it must go, night after night now. Night after night. No letting up, no pausing for breath.

Night after night after night.

Fibs

'You've got to be kidding!'

Rebus was too tired to be truly angry, but there was enough exasperation in his voice to worry the caller on the other end of the telephone, delegated to order Rebus to Glasgow.

'That case isn't supposed to be heard until the week after next.'

'They moved it,' says the voice.

Rebus groaned. He lay back on his hotel bed with the receiver pressed to his ear and checked his watch. Eight thirty. He'd slept soundly last night, waking at seven, dressed quietly so as not to disturb Lisa and had left her a note before making his exit. His nose had led him to the hotel with only a couple of wrong turnings along the way and now he had walked into this telephone call.

'They brought it forward,' the voice is saying. 'It starts today. They need your testimony, Inspector.'

As if Rebus didn't know. He knows that all he has to do is go into the witness box and say he saw Morris Gerald Cafferty (known in the protection game as 'Big Ger') accept one hundred pounds from the landlord of the City Arms pub in Grangemouth. It's as easy as that, but he needs to be there to say it. The case against Cafferty, boss of a thuggish protection and gaming racket, is not airtight. In fact, it's got more punctures than a blind dressmaker's thumb.

He resigns himself to it. Must it be? Yes, it must be. But there was still the problem of logistics.

'It's all been taken care of,' says the voice. 'We did try phoning you last night, but you were never there. Catch the first available shuttle from Heathrow. We'll have a car meet you and bring you into Glasgow. The prosecution reckons he'll call you about half past three, so there's time enough. With any luck, you can be back in London by tonight.'

'Gee, thanks,' says Rebus, voice so thick with irony the words hardly escape into the air.

'You're welcome,' says the voice.

*

He found that the Piccadilly Line went to Heathrow, and Piccadilly Circus tube was right outside the hotel. So things started well enough, though the tube ride itself was slow and stifling. At Heathrow, he picked up his ticket and had just enough time for a dash into the Skyshop. He picked up a *Glasgow Herald*, then saw the row of tabloids on another shelf: SECRET LIFE OF GAY WOLFMAN; SICK KILLER 'NEEDS HELP' SAY POLICE; CATCH THIS MADMAN.

Cath Farraday had done well. He bought a copy of all three papers as well as the *Herald* and made for the Departure Lounge. Now that his mind was working, he saw all around him people reading the same headlines and the stories below them. But would the Wolfman see the stories? And if so, would he or she make some kind of move? Hell, the whole thing might be about to crack open and here he was heading four hundred miles north. Damn the judicial system, the judges and advocates and solicitors and all. The Cafferty case had probably been brought forward so that it would not interfere with a golf game or a school sports day. Some spoilt child's involvement with an egg-and-spoon race might be behind this whole breathless journey. Rebus tried to calm down, sucking in gulps of air and releasing them slowly. He didn't like flying as it was. Never since his days in the SAS, when they had dropped him from a helicopter. Jesus! That was no way to calm yourself.

'Will passengers for British Airways Super Shuttle flight –'

The voice was cool and precise, triggering a mass movement. People rose to their feet, checked their baggage and made for the gate just mentioned. Which gate? He'd missed the announcement. Was it his flight? Maybe he should phone ahead so they would have the car waiting. He *hated* flying. That was why he had come down by train on Sunday. Sunday? And today was Wednesday. It felt like over a week had passed. In fact, he'd been in London only two full days.

Boarding. Oh, Christ. Where was his ticket? He'd no luggage, nothing to worry about there. The newspapers wriggled beneath his arm, trying to break free and fall in a mess on the floor. He pushed them back together again, squeezing them tightly with his elbow. He had to calm down, had to think about Cafferty, had to get everything straight in his mind, so that the defence could find no chink in his story. Keep to the facts, forget about the Wolfman, forget about Lisa, Rhona, Sammy, Kenny, Tommy Watkiss, George Flight . . . Flight! He hadn't notified Flight. They would wonder where he was. He'd have to phone when he landed. He should phone now, but then he might miss the shuttle.

Forget it. Concentrate on Cafferty. They would have his notes ready for him when he arrived, so he could go through them before he entered the witness box. There were only the two witnesses, weren't there? The frightened publican, whom they had more or less coerced into giving evidence, and Rebus himself. He had to be strong, confident and believable. He caught sight of himself in a full-length mirror as he made for the Departure Gate. He looked like he'd spent a night on the tiles. The memory of the night made him smile. Everything would be all right. He should phone Lisa, too, just to say . . . what? Thank you, he supposed. Up the ramp now, the narrow doorway in front of him, flanked by smiling steward and stewardess.

'Good morning, sir.'

'Good morning.' He saw they were standing by a stack of complimentary newspapers. Christ, he could have saved himself a few bawbees.

The aisle was narrow too. He had to squeeze past businessmen who were stuffing coats, briefcases and bags into the luggage lockers above their seats. He found his own window seat and fell into it, wrestling with the seatbelt and securing it. Outside, the groundcrew were still working. A plane took off smoothly in the distance, the dull roar perceptible even from here. A plump middle-aged woman sat beside him, spread her newspaper out so that half of it fell onto Rebus's right leg, and began to read. She had offered no greeting, no acknowledgement of his existence.

FYT, madam, he thought to himself, still staring out of the window. But then she gave a loud 'tsk', prompting him to turn towards her. She was staring at him through thick-lensed spectacles, staring and at the same time rapping a finger against the newspaper.

'Nobody's safe these days,' she said, as Rebus examined the news story and saw that it was some fanciful piece about the Wolfman. 'Nobody. I won't let my daughter out these nights. A nine o'clock curfew I told her, until they catch him. Even then you can never be sure. I mean, he could be *anybody*.'

Her look told Rebus that he, too, was not beyond suspicion. He smiled reassuringly.

'I wasn't going to go,' she went on, 'but Frank – that's my husband – he said it was all booked so I should.'

'Visiting Glasgow, are you?'

'Not exactly visiting. My son lives there. He's an accountant in the oil industry. He paid for my ticket, so I could see how he's getting on. I worry about him, what with being so far away and everything. I mean, it's a rough place Glasgow, isn't it? You read about it in the papers. Anything could happen up there.'

Yes, thought Rebus, his smile fixed, so unlike London. There was a sound like an electronic doorbell, and the Fasten Seatbelts sign came on, next to where the No Smoking sign was already lit. Jesus, Rebus could kill for a cigarette. Was he in Smoking or No Smoking? He couldn't make out, and couldn't remember which he'd plumped for at the ticket desk. Was smoking allowed on aeroplanes these days anyway? If God had meant man to smoke at 20,000 feet, wouldn't he have given us all longer necks? The woman next to him looked to have no neck at all. Pity the poor serial killer who tried cutting his way through *that* throat.

That was a terrible thing to think, God, please forgive me. As penance, he began to concentrate on the woman's conversation, right up until take-off, when even she was forced to stop talking for a moment or two. Rebus, taking advantage of the situation, tucked his newspapers into the pocket on the back of the seat in front of him, leaned his head against the back of his own seat, and promptly fell asleep.

George Flight tried Rebus's hotel again from the Old Bailey, only to be told that Rebus had 'left in a hurry' earlier in the morning after asking how best to get to Heathrow.

'Looks like he's done a runner,' DC Lamb commented. 'Frightened off by our consummate professionalism, I shouldn't wonder.'

'Leave off, Lamb,' growled Flight. 'Mind you, it is a bit mysterious. Why would he leave without saying anything?'

'Because he's a Jock, with all due respect, sir. He was probably worried you were going to drop a bill into his lap.'

Flight smiled obligingly, but his thoughts were elsewhere. Last night Rebus had been seeing that psychologist, Dr Frazer, and now he was in a hurry to leave London. What had happened? Flight's nose twitched. He liked a good honest mystery.

He was in court to have a quiet word with Malcolm Chambers. Chambers was prosecuting counsel in a case involving one of Flight's snouts. The snout had been incredibly stupid, had been caught red-handed. Flight had told the man there was little he could do, but he would do what he could. The snout had given him a lot of very useful tips in the past year, helping put a few fairly nasty individuals behind bars. Flight guessed he owed the man a helping hand. So he would talk to Chambers, not to influence the prosecutor – that was unthinkable, naturally – but to fill in some details on the snout's useful contribution to police work and to society, a contribution which would come to a sad end should Chambers push for the maximum sentence.

Et cetera.

Dirty job, but someone had to do it and besides, Flight was proud of his network of informers. The idea of that network suddenly splintering was . . . well, best not to consider it. He wasn't looking forward to going to Chambers, begging bowl in hand. Especially not after the farce involving Tommy Watkiss. Watkiss was back out on the street, probably telling the story in pubs up and down the East End to a laughing chorus of hangers-on. All about how the arresting constable had said, 'Hello, Tommy, what's going on here?' Flight doubted Chambers would ever forget it, or let Flight forget it. What the hell, best get the begging over and done with.

'Hello there.' It was a female voice, close behind him. He turned to face the cat-like eyes and bright red lips of Cath Farraday.

'Hello, Cath, what are you doing here?'

She explained that she was at the Old Bailey to meet with the influential crime reporter from one of the more upmarket dailies.

'He's halfway through covering a fraud case,' she explained, 'and never strays too far from the courtroom.'

Flight nodded, feeling awkward in her presence. From the corner of his eye he could see that Lamb was enjoying his discomfort, so he tried to be brave and steeled himself to meet the full force of her gaze.

'I saw the pieces you placed in today's press,' he said.

She folded her arms. 'I can't say I'm optimistic about their chances of success.'

'Do the reporters know we're spinning them a yarn?'

'One or two were a bit suspicious, but they've got a lot of hungry readers out there starving for want of another Wolfman story.' She unfolded her arms and reached into her shoulder-bag. 'Ergo, they've got a lot of hungry editors, too. I think they'll take any tidbit we throw them.' She had brought a pack of cigarettes from her bag, and, without offering them out, lit one, dropped the pack back into her bag and snapped the bag shut.

'Well, let's hope something comes of it.'

'You said this was all Inspector Rebus's idea?'

'That's right.'

'Then I'm doubtful. Having met him, I wouldn't say psychology was his strong point.'

'No?' Flight sounded surprised.

'He doesn't *have* a strong point,' broke in Lamb.

'I wouldn't go that far,' said Flight protectively. But Lamb merely gave that insolent grin of his. Flight was part-embarrassed, part-furious. He knew exactly what Lamb's grin was saying: *don't think we don't know why you're sticking so close to him, why you two are so chummy.*

Cath had smiled at Lamb's interruption, but when she spoke her words were directed at Flight: she did not deign to consort with the lower ranks. 'Is Rebus still around?'

Flight shrugged. 'I wish I knew, Cath. I've heard he was last seen heading off towards Heathrow, but he didn't take any luggage with him.'

'Oh well.' She didn't sound disappointed. Flight suddenly shot a hand into the air, waving. Malcolm Chambers acknowledged the signal and came towards them, walking as though no effort whatsoever was involved.

Flight felt the need for introductions. 'Mr Chambers, this is Inspector Cath Farraday. She's the Press Liaison Officer on Wolfman.'

'Ah,' said Chambers, taking her hand momentarily in his. 'The woman responsible for this morning's lurid headlines?'

'Yes,' said Cath. Her voice had taken on a new, soft, feminine edge, an edge Flight couldn't recall having heard before. 'Sorry if they spoiled your breakfast.'

The impossible happened: Chambers's face cracked into a smile. Flight hadn't seen him smile outside of the courtroom in several years. This really was a morning for surprises. 'They did not spoil my breakfast,' Chambers was saying, 'I found them highly entertaining.' He turned to Flight, indicating by this that Cath was dismissed. 'Inspector Flight, I can give you ten minutes, then I'm due in court. Or would you prefer to meet for lunch?'

'Ten minutes should suffice.'

'Excellent. Then come with me.' He glanced towards Lamb, who was still feeling slightly snubbed by Cath. 'And bring your young man with you if you must.'

Then he was gone, striding on noisy leather soles across the floor of the concourse. Flight winked at Cath, then followed, Lamb silent and furious behind him. Cath grinned, enjoying Lamb's discomfort and the performance Chambers had just put on. She'd heard of him, of course. His courtroom speeches were reckoned to be just about the most persuasive going, and he had even collected what could only be described as 'groupies': people who would attend a trial, no matter how convoluted or boring, just to hear his closing remarks. Her own little coterie of news reporters seemed bland by comparison.

So Rebus had scuttled off home, had he? Good luck to him.

'Excuse me.' A short blurred figure stood before her. She narrowed her eyes until they were the merest slits and peered at a middle-aged woman in a black cloak. The woman was smiling. 'You're not on the jury for court eight by any chance?' Cath Farraday smiled and shook her head. 'Oh well,' sighed the usher, moving off again.

There was such a thing in law as a hung jury, but there were also ushers who would happily see some individual jurors, the rogue jurors, hung. Cath turned on her pointed heels and went off to fulfil her appointment. She wondered if Jim Stevens would remember he was meeting her? He was a good journalist, but his memory was like a sieve at times and seemed especially bad now he was to be a father.

Rebus had time to kill in Glasgow. Time to visit the Horseshoe Bar, or walk through Kelvinside, or even venture down to the Clyde. Time enough to look up an old friend, always supposing he'd had any. Glasgow was changing. Edinburgh had grown corpulent these past few years, during which time Glasgow had been busy getting fit. It had a toned, muscular look to it, a confident swagger rather than the drunken stagger which had been its public perception for so long.

It wasn't all good news. Some of the city's character had seeped away. The shiny new shops and wine bars, the bright new office blocks, all had a homogenous quality to them. Go to any prosperous city in the world and you would find buildings just like them. A golden hue of uniformity. Not that Rebus was grieving; anything was better than the old swampland Glasgow had been in the 50s, 60s and early 70s. And the people were more or less the same: blunt, yet wonderfully dry in their humour. The pubs, too, had not changed very much, though their clientele might come more expensively and fashionably dressed and the menu might include chilli or lasagne along with the more traditional fare.

Rebus ate two pies in one pub, standing at the bar with his left foot resting on the polished brass rail. He was biding his time. The plane had landed on schedule, the car had been waiting, the journey into Glasgow had been fast. He arrived in the city centre at twenty minutes past twelve, and would not be called to give his evidence until around three.

Time to kill.

He left the pub and took what he hoped might be a shortcut (though he had no ready destination in mind) down a cobbled lane towards some railway arches, some crumbling warehouse buildings and a rubble-strewn wasteland. There were a lot of people milling about here, and he realised that what he had thought were piles of rubbish lying around on the damp ground were actually articles for sale. He had stumbled upon a flea market, and by the look of the customers it was where the down and outs did their shopping. Dank unclean clothes lay in bundles, thrown down anywhere. Near them stood the vendors, shuffling their feet, saying nothing, one or two stoking up a makeshift fire around which others clustered for warmth. The atmosphere was muted. People might cough and hack and wheeze, but they seldom spoke. A few punks, their resplendent mohicans as out of place as a handful of parrots in a cage of sparrows, milled around, not really looking like they meant to buy anything. The locals regarded them with suspicion. Tourists, the collective look said, just bloody tourists.

Beneath the arches themselves were narrow aisles lined with stalls and trestle tables. The smell in here was worse, but Rebus was curious. No out-of-town hypermarket could have provided such a range of wares: broken spectacles, old wireless sets (with this or that knob missing), lamps, hats, tarnished cutlery, purses and wallets, incomplete sets of dominoes and playing cards. One stall seemed to sell nothing but pieces of used soap, most of them looking as though they had come from public conveniences. Another sold false teeth. An old man, hands shaking almost uncontrollably, had found a bottom set he liked, but could not find a top set to match. Rebus wrinkled his face and turned away. The mohicans had opened a game of Cluedo.

'Hey, pal,' they called to the stall-holder, 'there's nae weapons here. Where's the dagger an' the gun an' that?'

The man looked at the open box. 'You could improvise,' he suggested.

Rebus smiled and moved on. London was different to all this. It felt more congested, things moved too quickly, there seemed pressure and stress everywhere. Driving a car from A to B, shopping for groceries, going out for the evening, all were turned into immensely tiring activities. Londoners appeared to him to be on very short fuses indeed. Here, the people were stoics. They used their humour as a barrier against everything Londoners had to take on the chin. Different worlds. Different civilisations. Glasgow had been the second city of the Empire. It had been the first city of Scotland all through the twentieth century.

'Got a fag, mister?'

It was one of the punks. Now, up close, Rebus saw she was a girl. He'd assumed the group had been all male. They all looked so similar.

'No, sorry, I'm trying to give up –'

But she had already started to move away, in search of someone, anyone, who could immediately gratify. He looked at his watch. It was gone two, and it might take him half an hour to get from here to the court. The punks were still arguing about the missing Cluedo pieces.

'I mean, how can you play a game when there's bits missing? Know what I mean, pal? Like, where's Colonel Mustard? An' the board's nearly torn in half, by the way. How much d'ye want for it?'

The argumentative punk was tall and immensely thin, his size and shape accentuated by the black he wore from tip to toe. 'Twa ply o' reek,' Rebus's father would have called him. Was the Wolfman fat or thin? tall or short? young or old? did he have a job? a wife? a husband even? Did someone close to him know the truth, and were they keeping quiet? When would he strike next? And where? Lisa had been unable to answer any of these questions. Maybe Flight was right about psychology. So much of it was guesswork, like a game where some of the pieces are missing and nobody knows the rules. Sometimes you ended up playing a game completely different to the original, a game of your own devising.

That was what Rebus needed: a new set of rules in his game against the Wolfman. Rules which would be to his benefit. The newspaper stories were the start of it, but only if the Wolfman made the next move.

Maybe Cafferty would get off this time, but there'd always be another. The board was always prepared for a fresh start.

Rebus gave his evidence and was out of the court by four. He handed the file on the case back to his driver, a balding middle-aged detective sergeant, and settled into the passenger seat.

'Let me know what happens,' he said. The driver nodded.

'Straight back to the airport, Inspector?' Funny how a Glaswegian accent could be made to sound so sarcastic. The sergeant had managed somehow to make Rebus feel his inferior. Then again, there was little love lost between east and west coasts. There might have been a wall dividing the two, such was their own abiding cold war. The driver was repeating his question, a little louder now.

'That's right,' said Rebus, just as loudly. 'It's a jet-setting life in the Lothian and Borders Police.'

His head was fairly thrumming by the time he got back to the hotel in Piccadilly. He needed a quiet night, a night alone. He hadn't managed to contact Flight or Lisa, but they could wait until tomorrow. For now, he wanted nothing.

Nothing but silence and stillness, lying on the bed and staring at the ceiling, his mind nowhere.

It had been one hell of a week, and the week was only halfway through. He took two paracetamol from the bottle he had brought and washed them down with half a glass of tepid tap-water. The water tasted foul. Was it true that London water had passed through seven sets of kidneys before reaching the drinker? It had an oily quality in his mouth, not the sharp clear taste of the water in Edinburgh. Seven sets of kidneys. He looked at his cases, thinking of the amount of stuff he had brought with him, useless stuff, stuff he would never use. Even the bottle of malt sat more or less untouched.

There was a telephone ringing somewhere. His telephone, but he managed to ignore the fact for fully fifteen seconds. He growled and clawed at the wall with his hand, finally finding the receiver and dragging it to his ear.

'This had better be good.'

'Where the fuck have you been?' It was Flight's voice, anxious and angry.

'Good evening to you too, George.'

'There's been another killing.'

Rebus sat up and swung his legs off the bed. 'When?'

'The body was discovered an hour ago. There's something else.' He paused. 'We caught the killer.'

Now Rebus stood up.

'What?'

'We caught him as he was running off.'

Rebus's knees almost failed him, but he locked them. His voice was unnaturally quiet. 'Is it him?'

'Could be.'

'Where are you?'

'I'm at HQ. We've brought him here. The murder took place in a house off Brick Lane. Not too far from Wolf Street.'

'In a house?' That was a surprise. The other murders had all taken place out of doors. But then, as Lisa had said, the pattern kept changing.

'Yes,' said Flight. 'And that's not all. The killer was found with money on him stolen from the house, and some jewellery and a camera.'

Another break in the pattern. Rebus sat down on the bed again. 'I see what you're getting at,' he said. 'But the method – ?'

'Similar, to be sure. Philip Cousins is on his way. He was at a dinner somewhere.'

'I'm going to the scene, George. I'll come to see you afterwards.'

'Fine.' Flight sounded as though he had hoped for this. Rebus was scrabbling for paper and a pen.

'What's the address?'

'110 Copperplate Street.'

Rebus wrote the address on the back of his travel ticket from the trip to Glasgow.

'John?'

'Yes, George?'

'Don't go off again without telling me, okay?'

'Yes, George.' Rebus paused. 'Can I go now?'

'Go on then, bugger off. I'll see you here later.'

Rebus put down the telephone and felt an immense weariness take control of him, weighting his legs and arms and head. He took several deep breaths and rose to his feet, then walked to the sink and splashed water on his face, rubbing a wet hand around his neck and throat. He looked up, hardly recognising himself in the wall-mounted mirror, sighed and spread his hands either side of his face, the way he'd seen Roy Scheider do once in a film.

'It's showtime.'

Rebus's taxi driver was full of tales of the Krays, Richardson and Jack the Ripper. With Brick Lane their destination, he was especially vociferous on the subject of 'Old Jack'.

'Done his first prossie on Brick Lane. Richardson, though, he was evil. Used to torture people in a scrapyard. You knew when he was electrocuting some poor bastard, 'cos the bulb across the scrapyard gates kept flickering.' Then a low chuckle. A sideways flick of the head. 'Krays used to drink in that pub on the corner. My youngest used to drink in there. Got in some terrible punch-ups, so I banned him from going. He works in the City, courier sort of stuff, you know, motorbikes.'

Rebus, who had been slouching in the back seat, now gripped the headrest on the front passenger seat and yanked himself forward.

'Motorbike messenger?'

'Yeah, makes a bleeding packet. Twice what I take home a week, I'll tell you that. He's just bought himself a flat down in Docklands. Only they call them "riverside apartments" these days. That's a laugh. I know some of the guys who built them. Every bloody shortcut in the book. Hammering in screws instead of screwing them. Plasterboard so thin you can almost see your neighbours, never mind hear them.'

'A friend of my daughter works as a courier in the City.'

'Yeah? Maybe I know him. What's his name?'

'Kenny.'

'Kenny?' He shook his head. Rebus stared at where the silvery hairs on the driver's neck disappeared into his shirt collar. 'Nah, I don't know a Kenny. Kev, yes, and a couple of Chrisses, but not Kenny.'

Rebus sat back again. It struck him that he didn't know what Kenny's surname was. 'Are we nearly there?' he asked.

'Two minutes, guv. There's a lovely shortcut coming up should save us some time. Takes us right past where Richardson used to hang out.'

A crowd of reporters had gathered outside in the narrow street. Housefront, pavement, then road, where the crowd stood, held back by uniformed constables. Did nobody in London possess such a thing as a front garden? Rebus had yet to see a house with a garden, apart from the millionaire blocks in Kensington.

'John!' A female voice, escaping from the scrum of newsmen. She pushed her way towards him. He signalled for the line of uniforms to break momentarily, so as to let her through.

'What are you doing here?'

Lisa looked a little shaken. 'Heard a newsflash,' she gasped. 'Thought I'd come over.'

'I'm not sure that's such a good idea, Lisa.' Rebus was thinking of Jean Cooper's body. If this were similar ...

'Any comment to make?' yelled one of the newsmen. Rebus was aware of flashguns, of the bright homing lamps attached to video cameras. Other reporters were shouting now, desperate for a story that would reach the first editions.

'Come on then,' said Rebus, pulling Lisa Frazer towards the door of number 110.

*

Philip Cousins was still dressed in dark suit and tie, suitably funereal. Isobel Penny was in black, too, a full length dress with long, tight sleeves. She did not look funereal. She looked divine. She smiled at Rebus as he entered the cramped living-room, nodding in recognition.

'Inspector Rebus,' said Cousins, 'they said you might drop by.'

'Never one to miss a good corpse,' Rebus replied drily. Cousins, stooping over the body, looked up at him.

'Quite.'

The smell was there, clogging up Rebus's nostrils and lungs. Some people couldn't smell it, but he always could. It was strong and salty, rich, clotting, cloying. It smelt like nothing else on earth. And behind it lurked another smell, more bland, like tallow, candle-wax, cold water. The two contrasting smells of life and death. Rebus was willing to bet that Cousins could smell it, but he doubted Isobel Penny could.

A middle-aged woman lay on the floor, an ungainly twist of legs and arms. Her throat had been cut. There were signs of a struggle, ornaments shattered and knocked from their perches, bloody hand-prints smeared across one wall. Cousins stood up and sighed.

'Very clumsy,' he said. He glanced towards Isobel Penny, who was sketching on her notepad. 'Penny,' he said, 'you look quite delightful this evening. Have I told you?'

She smiled again, blushed, but said nothing. Cousins turned to Rebus, ignoring Lisa Frazer's silent presence. 'It's a copycat,' he said with another sigh, 'but a copycat of little wit or talent. He's obviously read the descriptions in the newspapers, which have been detailed but inaccurate. I'd say it was an interrupted burglary. He panicked, went for his knife, and realised that if he made it look like our friend the Wolfman then he might just get away with it.' He looked down at the corpse again. 'Not terribly clever. I suppose the vultures have gather-ed?'

Rebus nodded. 'When I came in there were about a dozen reporters outside. Probably double that by now. We know what they want to hear, don't we?'

'I fear they are going to be disappointed.' Cousins checked his watch. 'Not worth going back to dinner. We've probably missed the port and cheese. Damned fine table, too. Such a pity.' He waved his hand in the direction of the body. 'Anything you'd like to see? Or shall we wrap this one up, as it were?'

Rebus smiled. The humour was as dark as the suit, but any humour was welcome. The smell in the air had been distilled now to that of raw steak and brown sauce. He shook his head. There was nothing more to be done in here. But outside, outside he was about to create an outrage. Flight would hate him for it, in fact everybody would hate him for it. But hate was fine. Hate was an emotion, and without emotion, what else was left? Lisa had already staggered out into the tiny hallway, where a police officer was trying awkwardly to comfort her. As Rebus came out of the room, she shook her head and straightened up.

'I'm fine,' she said.

'The first one always hits you hard,' said Rebus. 'Come on, I'm going to try out a spot of psychology on the Wolfman.'

The huddle of reporters and cameramen had become a sizeable crowd, now including the interested and the curious amateurs. The line of uniformed policemen had locked arms in a small but unbreakable chain. The questions began: Over here! Can we ask you who you are? You were at the canal, weren't you? A statement – Anything to say – Wolfman – Is it – The Wolfman? Is it – Just a few words if –

Rebus had walked to within a few inches of them, Lisa by his side. One of the reporters had leaned close to Lisa, asking for her name.

'Lisa, Lisa Frazer.'

'Are you working on the case, Lisa?'

'I'm a psychologist.'

Rebus cleared his throat noisily. The reporters were like mongrels in a dogs' home, calming quickly when they realised it was their turn at last for the feeding bowl. He raised his arms, and they fell quiet.

'A short statement, gentlemen,' said Rebus.

'Can we just ask who you are first?'

But Rebus shook his head. It didn't matter, did it? They would know soon enough. How many Scottish coppers were working on Wolfman? Flight would know, Cath Farraday would know and the journalists would find out. That didn't matter. Then one of them, unable to hold back, asked the question.

'Have you caught him?' Rebus tried to catch the man's eye, but every eye was silently asking the same thing. 'Is it the Wolfman?'

And this time Rebus nodded. 'Yes,' he said emphatically. 'It's the Wolfman. We've caught him.' Lisa looked at him in dumb surprise.

More questions, yelled now, screeched, but the chain in front of them would not break and somehow they did not think simply to walk around it. Rebus had turned away and saw Cousins and Isobel Penny standing just outside the door of the house, rigid, unable to believe what they had just heard. He winked at them and walked with Lisa to where his cab still waited. The driver folded his evening paper and stuck it down the side of his seat.

'You fairly got them going, guv. What did you say?'

'Nothing much,' said Rebus, settling back in his seat and smiling towards Lisa Frazer. 'Just a few fibs.'

'Fibs!'

So this was what Flight looked like when he was angry.

'Fibs!'

He seemed unable to believe what he was hearing. 'You call that a few fibs? Cath Farraday's going apeshit trying to calm those bastards down. They're like fucking animals. Half of them are ready to go to print on this! And you call it "fibs"? You're off your trolley, Rebus.'

So it was back to 'Rebus', was it? Well then, so be it. Rebus remembered that they'd promised they'd have dinner together this evening, but somehow he doubted the invitation still stood.

George Flight had been interviewing the murderer. His cheeks were veined with blood, his tie unknotted and hanging loose around his half unbuttoned shirt. He paced what floor there was in the small office. Rebus knew that outside the closed door people were listening in a mixture of fear and amusement: fear at Flight's anger, amusement that Rebus was its sole recipient.

'You're the fucking limit.' Flight's anger had peaked; his voice had dropped by half a decibel. 'What gives you the right –'

Rebus slapped the desk with his hand. He'd had enough of this. 'I'll tell you what gives me the right, George. The mere fact of the Wolfman gives me the right to do anything I think best.'

'Best!' Flight sounded freshly outraged. 'Now I've heard it all. Giving the papers a crock of shit like that is supposed to be "best"? By Christ, I'd hate to see your idea of "worst".'

Rebus's voice was every bit the equal of Flight's now, and rising. 'He's out there somewhere and he's laughing his head off at us. Because he seems to know how we'll play every round, he's knocking hell out of us.' Rebus grew quiet: Flight was listening now, and that was what he wanted. 'We need to get him riled, get him to lift his head over the trench he's hiding in so he can see what the fuck is going on. We need him angry, George. Not angry at the world. Angry at *us*. Because when he raises his head, we'll be ready to bite it off.'

'We've already accused him of being everything from gay to a cannibal from Pluto. Now we're telling everyone he's been caught.'

Rebus was reaching his point, his defence. He lowered his voice still further. 'I don't think he'll be able to take that, George. Really I don't. I think he'll have to make contact. Maybe with the papers, maybe directly with us. Just to let us know.'

'Or kill again,' countered Flight. '*That* would let us know.'

Rebus shook his head. 'If he kills again, we keep it quiet. Total media blackout. He gets no publicity. Everybody still thinks he's been caught. Sooner or later, he'll have to show himself.'

Rebus was completely calm now, and so was Flight. Flight rubbed both hands over his cheeks and down to his jaw. He was staring into space, thinking it over. Rebus did not doubt the plan would work. It might take time, but it would work. Basic SAS training: if you can't locate your enemy, make the enemy come to you. Besides, it was the only plan they had.

'John, what if the publicity doesn't bother him? Publicity *or* the lack of it?'

Rebus shrugged. He had no answer to that. All he had were case histories and his own instincts.

Finally, Flight shook his head. 'Go back to Edinburgh, John,' he said tiredly. 'Just do it.' Rebus stared at him, not blinking, willing him to say something else. But George Flight simply walked to the door, opened it, and closed it behind him.

That was it then. Rebus released his breath in a long hiss. Go back to Edinburgh. Wasn't that what everyone had wanted all along? Laine? Lamb and the rest of them? Flight too, maybe. Even Rebus himself. He'd told himself he could do no good here. Well, he was doing no good, so why not go home?

The answer was simple: the case had grabbed him by the throat. There was no escaping it. The Wolfman, faceless, bodiless, had pressed a blade to Rebus's ear and was holding it there, ready to slice. And besides, there was London itself, full of its own stories. Rhona. Sammy. Sammy and Kenny. Rebus had to remind himself that he was still interested in Kenny.

And Lisa.

Above all there was Lisa. The taxi had dropped her off at her flat. She had been quite pale, but insisted she was all right, insisted he go on without her. He should ring her, check she really was okay. What? And tell her he was leaving? No, he had to confront Flight. He opened the door and went into the Murder Room. Flight was not there. The curious faces looked at him from their desks, their telephones, their wallcharts and photographs. He looked at no one, but especially not at Lamb, who was grinning from behind a manila file, his eyes peering over at Rebus.

Flight was in the hallway outside, deep in discussion with the Duty Sergeant, who nodded and moved off. Rebus saw Flight sag, leaning his back against the wall, rubbing his face again. He approached slowly, giving George Flight an extra moment or two of peace and quiet.

'George,' he said. Flight looked up, smiled weakly.

'You never give up, John, do you?'

'I'm sorry, George. I should have checked with you before I pulled a stunt like that. Block the story if you want.'

Flight gave a short humourless laugh. 'Too late. It's been on the local radio news already. The other stations can't just sit back. It'll be on every local news report by midnight. It's your snowball, John. You started it running down the hill. All we can do now is watch it getting bigger and bigger.' He stabbed a finger into Rebus's chest. 'Cath is going to be after your guts, lad. She's the one they'll blame, the one who'll have to apologise, who'll have the job of gaining their trust all over again.' Flight now wagged the finger backwards and forwards, then grinned. 'And if anyone can do it, Inspector Cath Farraday can.' He checked his watch. 'Right, I've let the bugger stew long enough. Time to get back to the interview room.'

'How's it going?'

Flight shrugged. 'Singing like Gracie Fields. We couldn't stop him if we wanted to. He thinks we're going to pin all the Wolfman killings on him, so he's telling us everything he knows, and some things he's probably making up besides.'

'Cousins said it was a copycat, done to disguise a cocked-up burglary.'

Flight nodded. 'I sometimes think Philip's in the wrong game. This guy's a petty thief, not the bloody Wolfman. But I'll tell you what is interesting. He's told us he sells the stuff on to a mutual friend.'

'Who?'

'Tommy Watkiss.'

'Well, well.'

'Coming?' Flight pointed along the corridor, towards the stairwell. Rebus shook his head.

'I want to make a couple of phone calls. I might catch you up later.'

'Suit yourself.'

Rebus watched Flight go. Sometimes it was only brute stubbornness that kept humans going, long after their limbs and intellect had told them to quit. Flight was like a footballer playing in extra time. Rebus hoped he could see the game out to its end.

They watched him as he walked back through the Murder Room. Lamb in particular seemed to peer at him from behind a report, eyes gleaming with amusement. There was a noise coming from his office, a strange tapping noise. He pushed open the door and saw on his desk a small toy, a grotesque plastic jaw atop two oversized feet. The jaw was bright red, the teeth gleaming white, and the feet walked to a clockwork whirr while the jaws snapped shut, then open, shut then open. Snap, snap, snap. Snap, snap, snap.

Rebus, furious at the joke, walked to the desk, lifted the contraption and pulled at it, his own teeth bright and gritted, until it snapped in two. But the feet kept on moving, stopping only when the spring had run down. Not that Rebus was noticing. He was staring at the two halves, the upper and lower jaws. Sometimes things weren't what they seemed. The punk at the Glasgow flea market had turned out to be a girl. And at the flea market they had been selling teeth, false plastic teeth. Like a supermarket pick'n'mix counter. Any size you liked. Christ, he should have seen it sooner!

Rebus walked quickly back through the Murder Room. Lamb, doubtless responsible for the joke, seemed ready to say something until he saw the look on Rebus's face, an urgent, don't-mess-with-me look. He ran along the corridor and down the stairs, down towards the euphemism known as an Interview Room. 'A man is helping police with their enquiries.' Rebus loved those euphemisms. He knocked and entered. A detective was changing the tape in a recording machine. Flight was leaning across the table to offer a cigarette to a dishevelled young man, a young man with yellow bruising on his face and skinned knuckles.

'George?' Rebus tried to sound composed. 'Could I have a word?'

Flight pushed back his chair noisily, leaving the cigarette packet with the prisoner. Rebus held open the door, indicating for Flight to move outside. Then he thought of something, and caught the prisoner's eye.

'Do you know somebody called Kenny?' he asked.

'Loads.'

'Rides a motorbike?'

The young man shrugged again and reached into the packet for a cigarette. There was no answer forthcoming, and Flight was outside waiting, so Rebus closed the door.

'What was that all about?' asked Flight.

'Maybe nothing,' said Rebus. 'Do you remember when we went to the Old Bailey, how someone shouted out when the case was stopped?'

'Someone in the public gallery.'

'That's right. Well, I recognised the voice. It's a teenager called Kenny. He's one of those motorcycle messengers.'

'So?'

'He's going out with my daughter.'

'Ah. And that bothers you?' Rebus nodded.

'Yes, a bit.'

'And that's what you want to see me about.'

Rebus managed a weak smile. 'No, no, nothing like that.'

'So what's on your mind?'

'I was in Glasgow today, giving evidence. I had a bit of free time and went to a flea market, the sort of place tramps go to do their messages –'

'Messages?'

'Their shopping,' Rebus explained.

'And?'

'And there was a stall selling false teeth. Odds and sods. Top sets and bottom sets, not necessarily matching.' He paused to let those final three words sink home. 'Is there someplace like that in London, George?'

Flight nodded. 'Brick Lane for one. There's a market there every Sunday. The main road sells fruit, veg, clothes. But there are streets off, where they sell anything they've got. Bric-a-brac, old rubbish. It makes for an interesting walk, but you wouldn't buy anything.'

'But you could buy false teeth there?'

'Yes,' said Flight after a moment's thought. 'I don't doubt it.'

'Then he's been cleverer than we thought, hasn't he?'

'You're saying the bite marks aren't real?'

'I'm saying they're not the Wolfman's teeth. The lower set smaller than the upper? You end up with a pretty strange jaw, as Doctor Morrison showed us, remember?'

'How can I forget? I was going to feed the pictures to the press.'

'Which is probably exactly what the Wolfman wanted. He goes to Brick Lane market, or at least to somewhere like it, and buys any upper and lower set. They don't match, but that doesn't matter. And he uses them to make those damned bite marks.'

Flight seemed dismissive, but Rebus knew the man was hooked. 'He can't be that clever.'

'Yes he can,' persisted Rebus. 'He's had everything worked out from the start ... from *before* the start! He's been playing with us like we were clockwork, George.'

'Then we have to wait until Sunday,' Flight said thoughtfully. 'Search every stall at every market, find the ones selling false teeth – there can't be many – and ask.'

'About the person who bought a set of teeth *without trying them for size*!' Rebus burst out laughing. It was ridiculous. It was absolutely mad. But he was sure it was true, and he was sure the stall-holder would remember, and would give a description. Surely most of the customers would try for size. It was the best lead they'd had so far, and it might just be the only one they'd need.

Flight was smiling too, shaking his head at the dark comic reality of it. Rebus held a closed fist in front of him, and Flight brought his open palm to rest beneath it. When Rebus opened his hand, the plastic chattering teeth fell into Flight's palm.

'Just like clockwork,' said Rebus. 'What's more, we've got Lamb to thank.' He thought about this. 'But I'd rather he didn't get to know.'

Flight nodded. 'Anything you say, John. Anything you say.'

Back at his desk, Rebus sat in front of a fresh sheet of paper. The Wolfman had been too clever. Too clever by half. He thought of Lisa, of her notion that the killer might have a criminal record. It was possible. Possible, too, that the Wolfman simply knew how the police worked. So, he might be a policeman. Or work in forensics. Or be a journalist. A civil rights campaigner. Work in the law. Or write bloody scripts for television. He might just have done his reading. There were plenty of case histories in libraries and bookshops, plenty of biographies of murderers, tracing how they were caught. By studying them, you could learn how *not* to get caught. However hard Rebus tried he just couldn't whittle away at the list of possibilities. The teeth might be yet another dead end. That was why they had to make the Wolfman come to *them*.

He threw down his pen and reached for the telephone, trying Lisa's number. But the phone just rang and rang and rang. Maybe she'd taken a couple of sleeping pills, or gone for a walk, or was a heavy sleeper.

'You stupid prick.'

He looked towards the open door. Cath Farraday was standing there, in her favourite position, against the jamb, arms folded. As if to let him know she'd been there for some time.

'You incredibly stupid little man.'

Rebus pinned a smile to his face. 'Good evening, Inspector. How can I help you?'

'Well,' she said, coming into the room, 'you can start by keeping your gob shut and your brain in gear. You never speak to the press. Never!' She was rearing over him now, looking ready to butt him in the face. He tried to avoid her eyes, eyes sharp enough to cut a man open, and found himself staring instead at her hair. It, too, looked dangerous.

'Do you understand me?'

'FYTP,' said Rebus, speaking without thinking.

'What?'

'Loud and clear,' he said. 'Yes, loud and clear.'

She nodded slowly, not seeming completely convinced, then threw a newspaper onto the desk. He hadn't noticed the paper till now, and glanced towards it. There was a photograph on the front, not large but large enough. It showed him talking to the reporters, Lisa standing nervously by his side. The headline was larger: WOLFMAN CAUGHT? Cath Farraday tapped the photograph.

'Who's the bimbo?'

Rebus felt his cheeks growing red. 'She's a psychologist. She's helping on the case.'

Cath Farraday looked at Rebus as though he were something more than merely stupid, then shook her head and turned to leave. 'Keep the paper,' she said. 'There are plenty more where it came from.'

* * *

She sits with the newspaper in front of her. There are several more piled on the floor. She has the scissors in her hand. One of the reports mentions who the policeman is: Inspector John Rebus. The report calls him an 'expert' on serial murders. And another report mentions that standing to his left is a 'police psychologist, Lisa Frazer'. She cuts around the photograph, then cuts another line, splitting Rebus from Frazer. Time and again she does this, until she has two new neat piles, one of John Rebus, one of Lisa Frazer. She takes one of the photographs of the psychologist and snips off her head. Then, smiling, she sits down to write a letter. A very difficult letter, but that doesn't matter. She has all the time in the world.

All the time.

Churchill

Rebus woke to his radio-alarm at seven, sat up in bed and rang Lisa. No reply. Maybe something was wrong.

Over breakfast, he skimmed the newspapers. Two of the quality titles carried bold front page stories recounting the capture of the Wolfman, but they were couched in speculative prose: Police are believed . . . it is thought that . . .; Police may have already captured the evil cut-throat killer. Only the tabloids carried pictures of Rebus at his little press conference. Even they, despite the shouting headlines, were being cagey; probably they didn't believe it themselves. That didn't matter. What mattered was that somewhere the Wolfman might be reading about his capture.

His. There was that word again. Rebus couldn't help but think of the Wolfman as a man, yet part of him was wary of narrowing the possible identity in this way. There was still nothing to indicate that it could not be a woman. He needed to keep an open mind. And did the sex of the beast really matter? Actually yes, probably it did. What was the use of women waiting hours just so that they could travel home from a pub or party in a mini-cab driven by another woman, if the killer they were so afraid of turned out to be a woman? All over London people were taking protective measures. Housing estates were patrolled by neighbourhood vigilantes. One group had already beaten up a completely innocent stranger who'd wandered onto the estate because he was lost and needed directions. His crime? The estate was white, and the stranger was coloured. Flight had told Rebus how prevalent racism was in London, 'especially the south-east corner. Go into some of those estates with a tan and you'll end up being nutted.' Rebus had encountered it already, thanks to Lamb's own particular brand of xenophobia.

Of course, there wasn't nearly so much racism in Scotland. There was no need: the Scots had bigotry instead.

He finished the papers and went to HQ. It was early yet, a little after half past eight. A few of the murder team were busy at their desks, but the smaller offices were empty. The office Rebus had taken over was stuffy, and he opened the windows. The day was mild, a slight breeze wafting in. He could hear the distant sound of a computer printer, of telephones starting to ring. Outside, the traffic flowed in slow motion, a dull rumbling, nothing more. Without realising he was doing it, Rebus rested his head on his arms. This close to the desk, he could smell wood and varnish, mixed with pencil-lead. It reminded him of primary school.

A knock, echoing somewhere, jarred his sleep. Then a cough, not a necessary cough, a diplomatic cough.

'Excuse me, sir.'

Rebus lifted his head sharply from the desk. A WPC was standing, her head around the door, looking in at him. He had been sleeping with his mouth open. There was a trail of saliva on the side of his mouth, and a tiny pool of the stuff on the surface of the desk.

'Yes,' he said, still muzzy. 'What is it?'

A sympathetic smile. They weren't all like Lamb, he had to remember that. On a case like this, you became a team, came to feel as close to the others as you would to your best friend. Closer than that even, sometimes.

'Someone to see you, sir. Well, she wants to speak to someone about the murders, and you're about the only one here.'

Rebus looked at his watch. Eight forty-five. He hadn't been asleep long then. Good. He felt he could confide in this WPC. 'How do I look?' he asked.

'Well,' she said, 'one side of your face is red from where you've been lying on it, but otherwise you'll do.' Then the smile again. A good deed in a naughty world.

'Thanks,' he said. 'Okay, send her in, please.'

'Right you are.' The head disappeared, but only momentarily. 'Can I get you a coffee or something?'

'Coffee would hit the spot,' said Rebus. 'Thanks.'

'Milk? Sugar?'

'Just milk.'

The head disappeared. The door closed. Rebus tried to look busy: it wasn't difficult. There was a mound of fresh paperwork to be gone through. Lab reports and the like. Results (negative) from door-to-door on the Jean Cooper murder from the interviews with everyone who'd been in the pub with her that Sunday night. He picked up the first sheet

501

and held it in front of him. There was a knock on the door, so soft that he only just caught it.

'Come in,' he called.

The door opened slowly. A woman was standing there, looking around her as though her timidity might be about to turn to fright. She was in her late twenties, with closely cropped brown hair, but other than that she defied description. She was more a collection of 'nots' than anything else: not tall, but not exactly short; not slim, but by no means overweight, and her face lacked anything approaching a personality.

'Hello,' Rebus said, half-rising to his feet. He indicated a chair on the other side of the desk, and watched as, with breathtaking slowness, she closed the door, testing it afterwards to make sure it was going to stay shut. Only then did she turn to look at him – or at least towards him, for she had a way of focussing just to the side of his face, so that her eyes never met his.

'Hello,' she said. She seemed ready to stand throughout proceedings. Rebus, who had seated himself again, gestured once more with his hand.

'Please. Sit down.'

At last, she poised herself above the chair and lowered herself into it. Rebus had the feeling that he was the boss at some job interview, and that she wanted the job so much she'd worked herself into a good and proper state about it.

'You wanted to speak to someone,' he said, in what he hoped were soft and sympathetic tones.

'Yes,' she said.

Well, it was a start. 'My name is Inspector Rebus. And yours is . . .?'

'Jan Crawford.'

'Okay, Jan. Now, how can I help you?'

She swallowed, gazing at the window behind Rebus's left ear. 'It's the killings,' she said. 'They call him the Wolfman.'

Rebus was undecided. Maybe she was a crank, but she didn't seem like one. She just seemed jumpy. Perhaps she had good reason.

'That's right,' he cajoled. 'The papers call him that.'

'Yes, they do.' She had become suddenly excitable, the words spilling from her. 'And they said last night on the radio, this morning in the paper . . .' She pulled a newspaper clipping from her bag. It was the photograph of Rebus and Lisa Frazer. 'This is you, isn't it?'

Rebus nodded.

'Then you'll know. I mean, you must. The paper says he's done it again, they're saying you've caught him, or maybe you've caught him, nobody's sure.' She paused, breathing heavily. All the time her eyes were on the window. Rebus kept his mouth shut, letting her calm down. Her eyes were filling, becoming glossy with tears. As she spoke, one droplet squirmed out from the corner of an eye and crept down towards her lips, her chin. 'Nobody's sure whether you've caught him, but I could be sure. At least, I think I can be sure. I didn't get, I mean, I've been scared so long now, and I haven't said anything. I didn't want anybody to know, my mum and dad to know. I just wanted to shut it out, but that's stupid, isn't it, when he could do it again if he's not caught. So I decided to, I mean, maybe I can . . .' She made to stand up, thought better of it, and squeezed her hands together instead.

'Can what, Miss Crawford?'

'Identify him,' she said, her voice almost a whisper now. She searched in the sleeve of her blouse, found a tissue, and blew her nose. The tear dripped onto one knee. 'Identify him,' she repeated, 'if he's here, if you've caught him.'

Rebus was staring hard at her now, and at last his eyes found hers. Her brown eyes, covered with a film of liquid. He'd seen cranks before, plenty of them. Maybe she was, and maybe she wasn't.

'What do you mean, Jan?'

She sniffed again, turned her eyes to the window, swallowed. 'He almost got me,' she said. 'I was the first, before all the others. He almost got me. I was almost the first.'

And then she lifted her head. At first Rebus couldn't understand why. But then he saw. Under her right ear, running in a crescent shape towards her white throat, there was a dark pink scar, no more than an inch long.

The kind of scar you made with a knife.

The first intended kill of the Wolfman.

'What do you think?'

They faced one another across the desk. Four inches of fresh paperwork had appeared in the in-tray, threatening to overbalance the pile and send it slewing down across the floor. Rebus was eating a cheese and onion sandwich from Gino's. Comfort food. One of the nice things about being a bachelor was that you could eat, without fear of regrets, onions, Branston pickle, huge sausage, egg and tomato sauce sandwiches, curried beans on toast and all the other delicacies favoured by the male.

'What do you think then?'

Flight sipped from a can of cola, giving slight closed-mouth burps between times. He had listened to Rebus's story and had met with Jan Crawford. She had now been taken to an interview room to be fed tea and sympathy by a WPC while a detective took her statement. Flight and Rebus both hoped she would not have to deal with Lamb.

'Well?'

Flight rubbed a knuckle against his right eye. 'I don't know, John. This case has gone ga-ga. You're off telling porkies to the press, your picture's all over the front pages, we've got our first – maybe not our last – copycat killing, then you come up with some idea of flea markets and false teeth. And now this.' He opened his arms wide, pleading for help to put his world back into some semblance of order. 'It's all a bit much.'

Rebus bit into the sandwich, chewing slowly. 'But it fits the pattern, doesn't it? From what I've read about serial killers, the first attempt is often botched. They're not quite ready, they haven't planned well enough. Somebody screams, they panic. He didn't have his technique honed. He didn't go for the mouth, so she was able to scream. Then he found that human skin and muscle is tougher than it looks. He'd probably seen too many horror films, thought it was like cutting through butter. So he scraped her, but not enough to do serious damage. Maybe the knife wasn't sharp enough, who knows. The point is, he got scared and he ran.'

Flight merely shrugged. 'And she didn't come forward,' he said. 'That's what bothers me.'

'She's come forward now. Tell me this, George. How many rape victims do we actually *see*? I heard tell somebody reckons it's less than one in three. Jan Crawford is a timid little woman, scared half to death. All she wanted to do was forget about it, but she couldn't. Her conscience wouldn't let her. Her conscience brought her to us.'

'I still don't like it, John. Don't ask me why.'

Rebus finished the sandwich and made a show of wiping his hands together. 'Your copper's instinct?' he suggested, just a little sarcastically.

'Maybe,' said Flight, appearing to miss, or at least to ignore, Rebus's tone. 'There's just something about her.'

'Trust me. I've talked to her. I've been through it all with her. And,

George, I believe her. I think it was him. Twelfth of December last year. That was his first time.'

'Maybe not,' said Flight. 'Maybe there are others who haven't come forward.'

'Maybe. What matters is, one did.'

'I still don't see what good this does us.' Flight picked up a sheet of paper from the desk and read the scribbled details. '"He was about six feet tall, white, and I think he had brown hair. He was running away with his back to me, so I couldn't see his face."' Flight put down the paper. 'That narrows things down nicely, doesn't it?'

Yes, Rebus wanted to say, it does. Because now I think I'm dealing with a man, and before this I wasn't sure. But he kept that particular thought to himself. He'd given George Flight enough grief in the past few days.

'That's still not the point,' he said instead.

'Then what in God's name *is* the point?' Flight had finished the can of cola and now tossed it into a metal wastepaper bin, where it rang against the side, the reverberation lasting for what seemed like an age.

When all was quiet again, Rebus spoke. 'The point is, the Wolfman doesn't know she didn't get a good look at him. We've got to persuade Miss Crawford to go public. Let the TV cameras feast on her. The One Who Got Away. Then we say that she's given us a good description. If that doesn't panic the bastard, nothing will.'

'Panic! Everything you do is designed to panic him. What good does that do? What if it simply frightens him off? What if he just stops killing and we never find him?'

'He's not the type,' Rebus said with authority. 'He'll go on killing because it's taken him over. Haven't you noticed how the murders are coming at shorter and shorter intervals? He may even have killed again since Lea Bridge, we just haven't found the body yet. He's possessed, George.' Flight looked at him as though seeking a joke, but Rebus was in deadly earnest. 'I mean it.'

Flight stood up and walked to the window. 'It might not even have been the Wolfman.'

'Maybe not,' Rebus conceded.

'What if she won't go public?'

'It doesn't matter. We still issue the news story. We still say we've got a good description.'

Flight turned from the window. 'You believe her? You don't think she's a crank?'

'It's possible, but I really don't think so. She's very plausible. She kept the details just vague enough to be convincing. It *was* three months ago. We can check on her if you like.'

'Yes, I'd like that very much.' The emotion had left Flight's voice. This case was draining him of every reserve he had. 'I want to know about her background, her present, her friends, her medical records, her family.'

'I could even get Lisa Frazer to give her some psychological tests?' Rebus suggested, not altogether without tongue in cheek. Flight smiled faintly.

'No, just the checks I've mentioned. Get Lamb onto it. It'll keep him out of our hair.'

'You don't like him then?'

'Whatever gives you that idea?'

'Funny, he says you're like a father to him.'

The moment of tension was over. Rebus felt he had won another small victory. They both laughed, using their dislike of Lamb to strengthen the link between them.

'You're a good policeman, John,' Flight said. Rebus, despite himself, blushed.

'Sod off, you old fart,' he replied.

'That reminds me,' said Flight. 'I told you yesterday to go home. Have you any intention of doing so?'

'None at all,' said Rebus. There was a pause before Flight nodded. 'Good,' he said. 'That's good.' He walked to the door. 'For now.' He turned back towards Rebus. 'Just don't go rogue on me, John. This is my turf. I need to know where you are and what you're up to.' He tapped at his own head. 'I need to know what's going on up here. Okay?'

Rebus nodded. 'Fine, George. No problem.' But the fingers behind his back were crossed. He liked to work alone, and had the feeling Flight wanted to stick close to him for reasons other than traditional Cockney chumminess. Besides, if the Wolfman did turn out to be a policeman, nobody could be discounted, nobody at all.

Rebus tried Lisa again, but without success. At lunchtime, he was wandering around the station when he bumped into Joey Bennett, the constable who had stopped him on Shaftesbury Avenue that first night in London. Bennett was wary at first. Then he recognised Rebus. 'Oh, hello, sir. Was that your picture I saw in the papers?'

Rebus nodded. 'This isn't your patch, is it?' he asked.

'No, not exactly, sir. Just passing through, you might say. Dropping off a prisoner. That woman in the photo with you. She looked a bit of all –'

'Do you have your car with you?'

Bennett was wary again. 'Yes, sir.'

'And you're going back into town now?'

'To the West End, yes, sir.'

'Good. Then you won't mind giving me a lift, will you?'

'Er, no, sir. Of course not, sir.' Bennett broke into the least convincing smile Rebus had seen outside a synchronised swimming event. On their way out to the car, they passed Lamb.

'Teeth stopped chattering yet?' he asked, but Rebus was in no mood to respond. Lamb, undaunted, tried again. 'Going somewhere?' He managed even to make this simple question sound like a threat. Rebus stopped, turned and walked up to him, so that their faces were a couple of inches apart.

'If that's all right with you, Lamb, yes, I'm going somewhere.' Then he turned away again and followed Bennett. Lamb watched them go, half his teeth showing in a parody of a grin.

'Mind how you go!' he called. 'Shall I phone ahead and get the hotel to pack your bags?'

Rebus's reply was a two-fingered salute, a more determined stride, and a whispered 'FYTP'. Bennett heard him.

'Sorry, sir?'

'Nothing,' said Rebus. 'Nothing at all.'

It took them half an hour to reach Bloomsbury. Every second building seemed to sport a blue circular plaque commemorating some writer's having lived there. Rebus recognised few of the names. Finally, he found the building he was looking for, and waved Bennett goodbye. It was the Psychology Department of University College in Gower Street. The secretary, who appeared to be the only living soul around at one o'clock, asked if she could help him.

'I hope so,' he said. 'I'm looking for Lisa Frazer.'

'Lisa?' The secretary seemed unsure. 'Oh, Lisa. Dear me, I don't think I can help. I haven't seen her in over a week. You might try the library. Or Dillon's.'

'Dillon's?'

'It's a bookshop, just around the corner. Lisa seems to spend a lot of her time in there. She loves bookshops. Or there's always the British Library. It's just possible she might be there.'

He left the building with a new puzzle. The secretary had seemed very distant, very fuzzy. Maybe it was just him. He was starting to read things into every situation. He found the bookshop and went inside. 'Shop' was something of an understatement. It was huge. He read on a wall that psychology books were to be found three floors up. So many books. One man could not hope to read them all in a lifetime. He tried to walk through the aisles without focussing. If he focussed, he would become interested, and if he became interested he would buy. He already had over fifty books at home, piled beside his bed, waiting for that elusive weeklong break when he could concentrate on something other than police work. He collected books. It was just about his only hobby. Not that he was precious about it. He did not lust after first editions, signed copies and the like. Mostly, he bought paperbacks. And he was nothing if not catholic in his tastes: any subject matter would do.

So he tried to pretend he was wearing blinkers, pondered the essential difference between catholic and Catholic and finally reached the psychology section. It was a room joined onto other rooms as in a chain, but there was no sign of Lisa in any of the links. He did, however, find where some of her own library of books had no doubt originated. There was a shelf next to the cashier's desk, dedicated to crime and violence. One of the books she had loaned him was there. He picked it up and turned it over to look at the price. Then blinked twice in astonishment. So much money! And it wasn't even a hardback! Still, academic books always did carry steep price tickets. Strange really: weren't students, the intended readership after all, least able to afford these titles? It might take a psychologist to explain that one, or perhaps a shrewd economist.

Next to the criminology section were books on the occult and witchcraft, along with various packs of Tarot cards and the like. Rebus smiled at this curious marriage: police work and hocus-pocus. He picked up a book on rituals and flipped through it. A young, slender woman, in billowing satin dress and with long fiery hair, paused beside him to lift a Tarot set, which she took to the cash desk. Well, it took all sorts, didn't it? She looked serious enough, but then these were serious times.

Ritual. He wondered if there was an element of ritual to the Wolfman's particular spree. So far he had been seeking an explanation from the killer's psyche: what if the whole thing were some kind of rite? Slaughter and defilement of the innocent, that sort of thing. Charlie Manson and his swastika-tattooed forehead. Some said there was a Masonic element to Jack the Ripper's methods. Madness and evil. Sometimes you found a cause, and sometimes you just didn't.

Slash the throat.

Gouge the anus.

Bite the stomach.

The two ends of the human trunk, and something like the mid-point. Could there be a clue in that particular pattern?

There are clues everywhere.

The monster from his past, rearing up out of the dark deep waters of memory. That case had tied him up all right, but not half as much as this. He had thought the Wolfman might be a woman. Now a woman had conveniently appeared to tell him the Wolfman was a man. Very conveniently. George Flight was right to be wary. Perhaps Rebus could learn something from him. Flight did everything by the book, and in scrupulous detail. He didn't go running down the bloody hall with a pair of toy false teeth clutched in his sweaty hand. He was the type to sit down and think things through. That was what made him a good copper, better than Rebus, because he didn't snap at every red herring that came along. Better because he was methodical, and methodical people never let anything escape them.

Rebus left Dillon's Bookshop with his own little thundercloud hanging above his head and a plastic carrier-bag full of newly purchased books swinging from his right hand. He walked down Gower Street and Bloomsbury Street, took a fortuitous left at a set of traffic lights and found himself outside the British Museum, inside which, he knew from memory, was to be found the British Library. Unless, that was, they'd already moved it, as he'd read they were planning to.

But the British Library itself was off-limit to 'non-readers'. Rebus tried to explain that he was a reader, but apparently what this meant was that he had to be in possession of a reader's card. With hindsight, he supposed he could have flashed his ID and said he was on the trail of a maniac, but he didn't. He shook his head, shrugged his shoulders and went instead for a walk around the museum.

The place seemed full almost to bursting with tourists and school parties. He wondered if the children, their imaginations still open, were as thunderstruck as he was by the Ancient Egyptian and Assyrian rooms. Vast stone carvings, huge wooden gates, countless exhibits. But the real throng was around the Rosetta Stone. Rebus had heard of it, of course, but didn't really know what it was. Now he found out. The stone contained writing in three languages and thus helped scholars to work out for the first time what Egyptian hieroglyphics actually meant.

He was willing to bet they hadn't solved it overnight, or even over a weekend. Slow, painstaking graft, just like police work, toil as difficult as anything a bricklayer or miner could endure. And in the end it usually still came down to the Lucky Break. How many times had they interviewed the Yorkshire Ripper and let him go? That sort of thing happened more often than the public would ever be allowed to know.

He walked through more rooms, rooms airy and light and containing Greek vases and figurines, then, pushing open a glass double-door, he found himself confronted by the Sculptures of the Parthenon. (For some reason they had stopped advertising them as the Elgin Marbles.) Rebus walked around this large gallery, feeling almost as though he were in some modern-day place of worship. At one end, a gabble of school-kids squatted before some statues, trying to draw them, while their teacher walked around, trying to keep the grudging artists quiet. It was Rhona. Even at this distance he recognised her. Recognised her walk and the slant of her head and the way she held her hands behind her back whenever she was trying to make a point . . .

Rebus turned away, and found himself face to face with a horse's head. He could see the veins bulging from the marble neck, the open mouth with its teeth worn away to an indeterminate smoothness. No bite. Would Rhona thank him for walking over and interrupting her class, just to make smalltalk? No, she would not. But what if she spotted him? If he were to slink away, it would look like the action of a coward. Hell, he was a coward, wasn't he? Best to face facts and move back towards the doors. She might never spot him, and if she did she was hardly likely to announce the fact. But then he wanted to know about Kenny, didn't he? Who better to ask than Rhona? There was a simple answer: better to ask *anyone*. He'd ask Samantha. Yes, that's what he'd do. He'd ask Samantha.

He crept back to the doors and walked briskly towards the exit. Suddenly all the exquisite vases and statues had become ridiculous. What was the point in burying them behind glass for people to glance at in passing? Wasn't it better to look forward, forget about ancient history? Wouldn't it be better if he just took Lamb's ill-meant advice? There were too many ghosts in London. Way too many. Even the reporter Jim Stevens was down here somewhere. Rebus fairly flew across the museum courtyard only pausing when he reached the gates. The guards stared at him strangely, glancing towards his carrier-bag. They're just books, he wanted to say. But he knew you could hide anything in a book, just about anything. Knew from painful personal experience.

When feeling depressed, be rash. He stuck a hand out into the road and at the first attempt managed to stop an empty black cab. He couldn't remember the name of the street he wanted, but that didn't matter.

'Covent Garden,' he said to the driver. As the cab did what Rebus assumed was a fairly illegal u-turn, he dipped into his bag to claim the first prize.

He wandered around Covent Garden proper for twenty minutes, enjoying an open-air magic act and a nearby fire-eater before moving off in search of Lisa's flat. It wasn't too difficult to find. He surprised himself by recalling a kite shop and another shop which seemed to sell nothing but teapots. Took a left and a right and another right and found himself in her street, standing outside the shoe shop. The shop itself was busy. The clientele, like the serving staff, was very young, probably not yet out of teens. A jazz saxophone played. A tape perhaps, or someone busking in the distance. He looked up at the window to Lisa's flat, with its bright yellow roller blind. How old was she really? It was hard to tell.

And then, only then, he went to the door and pressed her buzzer. There was noise from the intercom, a crackle of movement. 'Hello?'

'It's me, John.'

'Hello? I can't hear you!'

'It's John,' he said loudly into the door frame, looking around him in embarrassment. But no one was interested. People glanced into the shop window as they passed, eating strange-looking snacks, vegetable-looking things.

'John?' As though she had forgotten him already. Then: 'Oh, John.' And the buzzer sounded beside him. 'Door's open. Come on up.'

The door to her flat was open, too, and he closed it behind him. Lisa was tidying the studio, as she called it. In Edinburgh it wouldn't have been called a studio. It would have been called a bedsit. He supposed Covent Garden didn't have such things as bedsits.

'I've been trying to get in touch,' he said.

'Me too.'

'Oh?'

She turned to him, noting the hint of disbelief in his voice. 'Didn't they tell you? I must've left half a dozen messages with, what was his name, Shepherd?'

'Lamb?'

'That's it.'

Rebus's hate for Lamb intensified.

'About an hour ago,' she went on, 'I called and they said you'd gone back to Scotland. I was a bit miffed at that. Thought you'd gone without saying goodbye.'

Bastards, thought Rebus. They really did hate his guts, didn't they? *Our expert from north of the border.*

Lisa had finished making a neat stack from the newspapers lying on the floor and the bed. She had straightened the duvet and the cover on the sofa. And now, a little out of breath, she was standing close to him. He slid his arm around her and pulled her to him.

'Hello,' he murmured, kissing her.

'Hello,' she said, returning the kiss.

She broke away from his hug and walked into the alcove which served as a kitchen. There was the sound of running tap-water, a kettle filling. 'I suppose you've seen the papers?' she called.

'Yes.'

Her head came out of the alcove. 'A friend called me up to tell me. I couldn't believe it. My picture on the front page!'

'Fame at last.'

'Infamy more like: a "police psychologist" indeed! They might have done their research. One paper even called me Liz Frazier!' She plugged the kettle in, switched it on, then came back into the room. Rebus was sitting on the arm of the sofa.

'So,' she asked, 'how goes the investigation?'

'A few interesting developments.'

'Oh?' She sat on the edge of the bed. 'Tell me.'

So he told her about Jan Crawford, and about his false teeth theory. Lisa suggested that Jan Crawford's memory might be helped by hypnosis. 'Lost memory' she called it. But Rebus knew this sort of thing was inadmissible as evidence. Besides, he'd experienced 'lost memory' for himself, and shivered now at the memory.

They drank Lapsang Souchong, which he said reminded him of bacon butties, and she put on some music, something soft and classical, and they ended up somehow sitting next to one another on the Indian carpet, their backs against the sofa, shoulders, arms and legs touching. She stroked his hair, the nape of his neck.

'What happened the other night between us,' she said, 'are you sorry?'

'You mean sorry it happened?'

She nodded.

'Christ, no,' said Rebus. 'Just the opposite.' He paused. 'What about you?'

She thought over her answer. 'It was nice,' she said, her eyebrows almost meeting as she concentrated on each word.

'I thought maybe you were avoiding me,' he said.

'And I thought you were avoiding me.'

'I went looking for you this morning at the university.'

She sat back, the better to study his face. 'Really?'

He nodded.

'What did they say?'

'I spoke to some secretary,' he explained. 'Glasses on a string around her neck, hair in a sort of a bun.'

'Millicent. But what did she tell you?'

'She just said you hadn't been around much.'

'What else?'

'That I might find you in the library, or in Dillon's.' He nodded over towards the door, where the carrier-bag stood propped against a wall. 'She said you liked bookshops. So I went looking there, too.'

She was still studying his face, then she laughed and pecked him on the cheek. 'Millicent's a treasure though, isn't she?'

'If you say so.' Why did her laugh have so much relief in it? Stop looking for puzzles, John. Just stop it right now. She was crawling away from him towards the bag.

'So what did you buy?'

He couldn't honestly remember, with the exception of the book he'd started reading in the taxi. *Hawksmoor*. Instead, he watched her behind and her legs as she moved away from him. Spectacular ankles. Slim with a prominent hemisphere of bone.

'Well!' she said, lifting one of the paperbacks from the bag. 'Eysenck.'

'Do you approve?'

She thought this question over, too. 'Not entirely. Probably not at all, in fact. Genetic inheritance and all that. I'm not sure.' She lifted out another book, and shrieked. 'Skinner! The beast of behaviourism! But what made you −?'

He shrugged. 'I just recognised some names from those books you loaned me, so I thought I'd –'

Another book was lifted high for him to see. *King Ludd*. 'Have you read the first two?' she asked.

'Oh,' he said, disappointed, 'is it part of a trilogy? I just liked the title.'

She turned and gave him a quizzical look, then laughed. Rebus could feel himself going red at the neck. She was making a fool of him. He turned away from her and concentrated on the pattern of the rug, brushing the rough fibres with his hand.

'Oh dear,' she said, starting to crawl back. 'I'm sorry, I didn't mean to. I'm sorry.' And she placed a hand on either of his legs, kneeling in front of him, angling her head until his eyes were forced to meet hers. She was smiling apologetically. 'Sorry,' she mouthed. He managed a smile which said: 'that's okay'. She leaned across him and placed her lips on his, one of her hands sliding up his leg towards the thigh, and then a little higher still.

It was evening before he escaped, though 'escape' was perhaps putting it too harshly. The effort of easing himself from beneath Lisa's sleeping limbs was almost too much. Her body perfume, the sweet smell of her hair, the flawless warmth of her belly, her arms, her behind. She did not waken as he slid from the bed and tugged on his clothes. She did not waken as he wrote her another of his notes, picked up his carrier-bag of books, opened the door, cast a glance back towards the bed and then pulled the door shut after him.

He went to Covent Garden tube station, where he was offered a choice: the queue for the elevator, or the three hundred-odd spiralling stairs. He opted for the stairs. They seemed to go on forever, turning and turning in their gyre. His head became light as he thought of what it must have been like to descend this corkscrew during the war years. White tiled walls like those of public lavatories. Rumble from above. The dull echo of footsteps and voices.

He thought, too, of Edinburgh's Scott Monument, with its own tightly winding stairwell, much more constricted and unnerving than this. And then he was at the bottom, beating the elevator by a matter of seconds. The tube train was as crowded as he had come to expect. Next to a sign proclaiming 'Keep your personal stereo personal', a white youth wearing a green parka with matching teeth shared his musical taste with the rest of the carriage. His eyes had a distant, utterly vacant look and from time to time he swigged from a can of strong lager. Rebus toyed with the notion of saying something, but held back. He was only travelling one stop. If the glowering passengers were content to suffer silently, that was how it should be.

He prised himself out of the train at Holborn, only to squeeze into another compartment, this time on the Central Line. Again, someone was playing a Walkman at some dizzying level, but they were somewhere over towards the far end of the carriage, so all Rebus had to suffer was the Schhch-schch-schch of what he took to be drums. He was becoming a seasoned traveller now, setting his eyes so that they focussed on space rather than on his fellow passengers, letting his mind empty for the duration of the journey.

God alone knew how these people could do it every day of their working lives.

He had already rung the doorbell before it struck him that he did not have a pretext for coming here. Think quickly, John.

The door was pulled open. 'Oh, it's you.' She sounded disappointed.

'Hello, Rhona.'

'To what do we owe the honour?' She was standing her ground, just inside the front door, keeping him on the doorstep. She was wearing a hint of make-up and her clothes were not after-work, relaxing-at-home clothes. She was going out somewhere. She was waiting for a gentleman.

'Nothing special,' he said. 'Just thought I'd pop round. We didn't get much of a chance to talk the other night.' Would he mention that he had seen her in the British Museum? No, he would not.

Besides, she was shaking her head. 'Yes we did, it was just that we had nothing to talk about.' Her voice wasn't bitter; she was simply stating a fact. Rebus looked at the doorstep.

'I've caught you at a bad time,' he said. 'Sorry.'

'No need to apologise.'

'Is Sammy in?'

'She's out with Kenny.'

Rebus nodded. 'Well,' he said, 'enjoy wherever it is you're going.' My God, he actually felt jealous. He couldn't believe it of himself after all these years. It was the make-up that did it. Rhona had seldom worn make-up. He half-turned to leave, then stopped. 'I couldn't use your loo, could I?'

She stared at him, seeking some trick or plan, but he smiled back with his best impersonation of a crippled dog and she relented.

'Go on then,' she said. 'You know where it is.'

He left his carrier at the door, squeezed past her and began to climb the steep stairs. 'Thanks, Rhona,' he said.

She was lingering downstairs, waiting to let him out again. He walked across the landing to the bathroom, opened and closed the door loudly, then opened it again very quietly and crept back across the landing to where the telephone sat on a small and quite grotesque confection of brass, green glass and red hanging tassels. There were London phone books piled beneath this table, but Rebus went straight to the smaller 'Telephone & Addresses' book on the top of the table. Some of the entries were in Rhona's writing. Who, he wondered, were Tony, Tim, Ben and Graeme? But most were in Sammy's grander, more confident script. He flipped to the K section and found what he wanted.

'KENNY', printed in capitals with a seven figure number scribbled below the name, the whole enclosed by a loving ellipse. Rebus took pen and notepad from his pocket and copied down the number, then closed the book and tiptoed back to the bathroom, where he flushed the toilet, gave his hands a quick rinse and boldly started downstairs again. Rhona was looking along the street, no doubt anxious that her beau should not arrive and find him here.

'Bye,' he said, picking up the carrier, walking past her and setting off in the direction of the main road. He was nearly at the end of her street when a white Ford Escort turned off the main drag and moved slowly past him, driven by a canny-looking man with thin face and thick moustache. Rebus stopped at the corner to watch the man pull up outside Rhona's building. She had already locked the door and fairly skipped to the car. Rebus turned away before she could kiss or hug the man called Tony, Tim, Ben or Graeme.

In a large pub near the tube station, a barn of a place with walls painted torrid red, Rebus remembered that he had not tried the local brews since coming south. He'd gone for a drink with George Flight, but had stuck to whisky. He looked at the row of pumps, while the barman watched him, a proprietorial hand resting on one pump. Rebus nodded towards this resting hand.

'Is it any good?'

The man snorted. 'It's bloody Fuller's, mate, of course it's good.'

'A pint of that then, please.'

The stuff turned out to have a watery look, like cold tea, but it tasted smooth and malty. The barman was still watching him, so Rebus nodded approval, then took his glass to a distant corner where the public telephone stood. He dialled HQ and asked for Flight.

'He's left for the day,' he was told.

'Well then, put me through to anyone from CID, anyone who's helpful. I've got a telephone number I want tracing.' There were rules and regulations about this sort of thing, rules at one time ignored but of late enforced. Requests had to be made and were not always granted. Some forces could pull more weight than others when it came to number tracing. He reckoned the Met and the Yard ought to carry more weight than most, but just in case he added: 'It's to do with the Wolfman case. It might be a very good lead.'

He was told to repeat the number he wanted tracing. 'Call back in half an hour,' said the voice.

He sat at a table and drank his beer. It seemed silly, but it appeared to be going to his head already, with only half a pint missing from the glass. Someone had left a folded, smudged copy of the midday *Standard*. Rebus tried to concentrate on the sports pages and even had a stab at the concise crossword. Then he made the call and was put through to someone he didn't know, who passed him on to someone else he didn't know. A boisterous crowd, looking like a team of bricklayers, had entered the bar. One of them made for the jukebox, and suddenly Steppenwolf's *Born to be Wild* was booming from the walls, while the men urged the unwilling barman to 'wick it up a bit'.

'If you'll just hold a minute, Inspector Rebus, I believe Chief Inspector Laine wants a word.'

'But, Christ, I don't want –' Too late, the voice at the other end had gone. Rebus held the receiver away from him and scowled.

Eventually, Howard Laine came on the line. Rebus pushed a finger into one ear, pressing his other ear hard against the earpiece.

'Ah, Inspector Rebus. I wanted a quiet word. You're a hard man to catch. About that business last night.' Laine's was the voice of reasoned sanity. 'You're about a bollockhair's breadth away from an official reprimand, understand? Pull a stunt like that again and I'll personally see to it that you're shipped back to Jockland in the boot of a National Express bus. Got that?'

Rebus was silent, listening closely. He could almost hear Cath Farraday sitting in Laine's office, smirking.

'I said, have you got that?'

'Yes, sir.'

'Good.' A rustling of paper. 'Now, you want an address I believe?'

'Yes, sir.'

'It's a lead, you say?'

'Yes, sir.' Rebus suddenly wondered if this would be worth it. He hoped so. If they found out he was abusing the system like this, they'd have him in the dole office with prospects roughly equivalent to those of a shoeshine boy on a nudist beach.

But Laine gave him the address and, as a bonus, supplied Kenny's surname.

'Watkiss,' said Laine. 'The address is Pedro Tower, Churchill Estate, E5. I think that's Hackney.'

'Thank you, sir,' said Rebus.

'Oh by the way,' said Laine, 'Inspector Rebus?'

'Yes, sir?'

'From what I've been told of Churchill Estate, if you're intending to visit, tell us first. We'll arrange for an SPG escort. All right?'

'Bit rough is it then, sir?'

'Rough doesn't begin to tell the story, son. We train the SAS in there, pretend it's a mock-up of Beirut.'

'Thanks for the advice, sir.' Rebus wanted to add that he'd been in the SAS and he doubted Pedro Tower could throw anything at him that the SAS HQ in Hereford hadn't. All the same, it paid to be cautious. The brickies were playing pool, their accents a mix of Irish and Cockney. *Born to be Wild* had finished. Rebus finished his pint and ordered another.

Kenny Watkiss. So there was a connection and rather a large one at that, between Tommy Watkiss and Samantha's boyfriend. How was it that in a city of ten million souls, Rebus had suddenly begun to feel an overwhelming sense of claustrophobia? He felt like someone had wrapped a muffler around his mouth and pulled a Balaclava down over his head.

'I'd be careful, mate,' said the barman as Rebus took delivery of his second pint. 'That stuff can kill you.'

'Not if I kill it first,' said Rebus, winking as he raised the glass to his lips.

The taxi driver wouldn't take him as far as the Churchill Estate. 'I'll drop you off a couple of streets away and show you where to go, but there's no way I'm going in there.'

'Fair enough,' said Rebus.

So he took the taxi as far as the taxi would take him, then walked the remaining distance. It didn't look so bad. He'd seen worse on the outskirts of Edinburgh. A lot of dull concrete, nuggets of glass underfoot, boarded windows and spray-painted gang names on every wall. Jeez Posse seemed to be the main gang, though there were other names so fantastically contrived that he could not make them out. Young boys skateboarded through an arena constructed from milk-crates, wooden planks and bricks. You couldn't muzzle the creative mind. Rebus stopped to watch for a moment; it only took a moment to appreciate that these boys were masters of their craft.

Rebus came to the entrance of one of the estate's four high-rises. He was busy looking for an identifying mark when something went splat on the pavement beside him. He looked down. It was a sandwich, a salami sandwich by the look of it. He craned his neck to look up at the various levels of the tower block, just in time to catch sight of something large and dark growing larger and darker as it hurtled towards him.

'Jesus Christ!' He leapt into the safety of the block's entrance hall, just as the TV set landed, flattening itself with an explosion of plastic, metal and glass. From their arena, the boys cheered. Rebus moved outside again, but more warily now, and craned his neck. There was no one to be seen. He whistled under his breath. He was impressed, and a little scared. Despite the thunderous sound, nobody seemed curious or interested.

He wondered which television show had so angered the person somewhere above him. 'Everyone's a critic,' he said. And then: 'FYTP.'

He heard a lift opening. A young woman, greasy dyed-blonde hair, gold stud in her nose and three in each ear, spider-web tattoo across her throat. She wheeled a pushchair out onto the concrete. Seconds earlier she would have been beneath the television.

'Excuse me,' said Rebus above the noise of her wailing passenger.

'Yeah?'

'Is this Pedro Tower?'

'Over there,' she said, pointing a sharpened fingernail towards one of the remaining blocks.

'Thank you.'

She glanced towards where the television had landed. 'It's the kids,' she said. 'They break into a flat, and throw a sandwich out of the window. A dog comes to eat it, and they chuck a telly after it. Makes a helluva mess.' She sounded almost amused. Almost.

'Lucky I don't like salami,' Rebus said.

But she was already manoeuvring the pushchair past the fresh debris. 'If you don't shut up I'll fucking kill you!' she yelled at her child. Rebus walked on unsteady legs towards Pedro Tower.

Why was he here?

It had all seemed to make sense, had seemed logical. But now that he stood in the sour-smelling ground-floor hallway of Pedro Tower he found that he had no reason at all to be here. Rhona had said that Sammy was out with Kenny. The chances of them choosing to spend the evening in Pedro Tower must be slim, mustn't they?

Even supposing Kenny were here, how would Rebus locate the flat? The locals would sniff an enquiring copper from fifty paces. Questions would go unanswered, knocked doors would stay unopened. Was this what intellectuals called an impasse? He could always wait, of course. Kenny would be sure to return at some point. But wait where? In here? Too conspicuous, too unappealing. Outside? Too cold, too open, too many armchair critics high above him in the now-dark sky.

Which left him where precisely? Yes, this probably was an impasse. He walked from the block, his eyes on the windows above him, and was about to make off in the direction of the skateboarders when a scream split the air from the other side of Pedro Tower. He walked quickly towards the source of the sound and was in time to see the butt-end of a burning argument. The woman – no more than a girl really, seventeen, eighteen – hit the bedenimed man with a good right hand, sending him spinning. Then she stalked off as he, holding one side of his face, tried to hurl obscenities at her while at the same time feeling in his mouth for damaged teeth.

They did not interest Rebus particularly. He was looking past them to a low-built, dimly illuminated building, a prefabricated construction surrounded by grass and dirt. A weathered board, lit by a single bulb, proclaimed it The Fighting Cock. A pub? Here? That was no place for a policeman, no place for a *Scots* policeman. But what if . . .? No, it couldn't be so simple. Sammy and Kenny couldn't be in there, wouldn't be in there. His daughter deserved better. Deserved the best.

But then she reckoned Kenny Watkiss was the best. And maybe he was. Rebus stopped dead. Just what the hell was he doing? Okay, so he didn't like Kenny. And when he had seen Kenny cheering in the Old Bailey, he had put two and two together and come to the conclusion that Kenny was in deep with Tommy Watkiss. But now it turned out the two were related in some way and that would explain the cheer, wouldn't it?

The psychology books told him that coppers read the worst into every situation. It was true. He didn't like the fact that Kenny Watkiss was dating his daughter. If Kenny had been heir apparent to the throne, Rebus would still have been suspicious. She was his daughter. He'd hardly seen her since she had entered her teens. In his mind she was still a child, a thing to be cosseted, loved, and protected. But she was a big girl now, with ambition, drive, good looks and a grown-up body. She was grown-up, there was no escaping it, and it scared him. Scared him because she was Sammy, his Sammy. Scared him because he hadn't been there all these years to warn her, to tell her how to cope, what to do.

Scared because he was getting old.

There, it was out. He was growing old. He had a sixteen-year-old daughter and she was old enough to leave school and get a job, to have sex, to get married. Not old enough to go into pubs, but that wouldn't stop her. Not old enough for street-wise eighteen-year-olds like Kenny Watkiss. But grown-up all the same; grown-up without him, and now he too was old.

And by God he felt it.

He plunged his left hand deep into his pocket, his right hand still wrapped around the handle of the carrier-bag, and turned from the pub. There was a bus stop near where the taxi had dropped him. He'd go where the bus would take him. The skateboarders were coming along the path in front of him. One of them seemed very proficient, weaving without losing balance. As the boy approached, he suddenly flipped the board up so that it spun in the air in front of him. Both hands neatly grabbed the board by its running-tail and swung the board itself in a backward arc. Too late, Rebus saw the manoeuvre for what it was. He tried to duck but the heavy wooden board hit the side of his head with a sharp crack.

He staggered, dropped to his knees. They were on him immediately, seven or eight of them, hands gouging into his pockets.

'Fuckin' split my board, man. Lookatit. Fuckin' six inch split.'

A training shoe caught Rebus on the chin and sent him flying. He was concentrating on not losing consciousness, so much so that he forgot to fight or to scream or to defend himself. Then a loud voice:

'Oi! What the fuck d'you think you're up to?'

And they ran, rolling their boards until they had gained enough speed, the hard wheels crackling on the tarmac as they fled. Like a posse in an old western, Rebus thought with a smile. Like a posse.

'You all right, mate? Come on, let's get you up.'

The man helped Rebus to his feet. When his eyes regained their powers of focus, he saw blood on the man's lip, smeared across his chin. The man noticed him looking.

'My bird,' he said, his breath rich with alcohol. 'She fuckin' clocked me, didn't she? Got me a good one, too. Couple of loose teeth. Still, they was rotten anyway, probably saved me a fortune at the dentist's.' He laughed. 'Come on, let's get you into the Cock. A couple of brandies'll see you right.'

'Took my money,' Rebus said. He was clutching the carrier-bag to him like a shield.

'Never mind that,' said his Samaritan.

They were kind to him. They sat him down at a table, and every now and again a drink would appear, and someone would say 'That one's from Bill', or 'That one's from Tessa', or 'That one's from Jackie', or 'That one's from . . .'

They were kind to him. They collected a fiver so he could get a taxi back to his hotel. He explained that he was a tourist, down here for a bit of sightseeing. He'd managed to get lost, had jumped off a bus and ended up here. And they, kind souls, believed him.

They didn't bother phoning the police.

'Those bastards,' they spat. 'Waste of time. Wouldn't turn up till tomorrow morning and then they'd do nothing. It's the cops round here that are behind half the crimes, believe me.'

And he did. He did believe them. And another drink arrived, another brandy in a small schooner.

'All the best, eh?'

And they were playing cards and dominoes, a lively crowd, a regular crowd. The TV blared – a musical quiz show – and the jukebox sang and the one-armed bandit bleeped and buzzed and spat out an occasional win. He thanked God Sammy and Kenny weren't here. How would it have looked to them? He dreaded to think.

At one point he excused himself and went to the toilet. There was a jagged triangle of mirror nailed to one wall. The side of his head, jaw and ear, were red and would probably bruise. The jaw would ache for some time. Where the shoe had connected, there was already a red and purple welt. Nothing more. Nothing worse. No knives or razor blades.

No massed assault. It had been a clean, professional hit. The way that kid had flipped the board, caught it and swung it. Professional. An absolute pro. If Rebus ever caught him, he would congratulate him on one of the sweetest moves he had ever seen.

Then he'd kick the little bastard's teeth so far down his throat they'd bite his small intestine.

He reached down the front of his trousers and drew out his wallet. The warning from Laine and the knowledge that he was on uncharted ground, had been enough to persuade Rebus that he should hide his wallet. Not to save him from muggers, no. So that no one would find his ID. It was bad enough being a stranger in this place, but being a copper . . . So he had hidden the wallet, ID and all, down the front of his underpants, tucked into the elasticated waistband. He slipped it back there now. After all, he was not yet clear of Churchill Estate. The night might turn out to be a long one.

He pulled open the door and headed back to his table. The brandy was working. His head was numb, his limbs pleasantly flexible.

'You all right there, Jock?'

He hates that name, absolutely loathes it, but he smiles nevertheless. 'I'm all right. Oh yes, I'm quite all right.'

'Great. By the way, this one's from Harry at the bar.'

* * *

After she has posted the letter, she feels a lot better. She does some work, but soon begins to twitch inside. It's like feeding a habit now. But it's also an art form. Art? Fuck art. So unbecoming in a man. So art unbecoming fuck in a man. So fuck a man in unbecoming art. They used to quarrel, squabble, argue all the time. No, that's not true. She remembers it that way but it wasn't that way. For a while it was, but then they just stopped communicating altogether. Her mother. Her father. Mother, strong, domineering, determined to be a great painter, a great watercolourist. Every day busy at an easel, ignoring her child who needed her, who would creep into the studio and sit quietly in a corner, crouched, trying not to be noticed. If noticed, she would be sent out of the room fiercely, red hot tears streaming down her face.

'I never wanted you!' her mother would screech. 'You were an accident! Why can't you be a *proper* little girl?'

Run, run, run. Out of the studio and down the stairs, through the morning room, and out of the doors. Father, quiet, innocuous, cultured, civilised father. Reading the newspapers in the back garden, one trousered leg crossed over the other as he reclined in his deckchair.

'And how's my little sweet this morning?'

'Mummy shouted at me.'

'Did she? I'm sure she didn't mean anything. She's a bit crochety when she's painting, isn't she? Come and sit here on my lap, you can help me read the news.'

Nobody visited, nobody came. No family, no friends. At first she went to school, but then they kept her at home, educating her themselves. It was all the rage with a certain section of a certain class. Her father had been left money by a great aunt. Enough money for a comfortable life, enough to keep the wolf from the door. He pretended to be a scholar. But then his painstakingly researched essays started to be rejected and he saw himself for what he was. The arguments grew worse. Grew physical.

'Just leave me alone will you? My art's what matters to me, not you.'

'Art? Fuck art!'

'How dare you!'

A dull, solid thump. A blow of some kind. From anywhere in the house she could hear them, anywhere but the attic. But she daren't go to the attic. That was where . . . Well, she just couldn't.

'I'm a boy,' she whispered to herself, hiding beneath her bed. 'I'm a boy, I'm a boy, I'm a boy.'

'Sweetness, where are you?' His voice, all sugar and summery. Like a slide-projector show. Like an afternoon car-ride.

They said the Wolfman was homosexual. It wasn't true. They said they'd caught him. She almost whooped when she read it. Wrote them a letter and posted it. See what they'd make of that! Let them find her, she didn't care. He and she didn't care. But he cared that she was taking over his mind as well as his body.

Sweetness . . . Oranges and lemons say the bells of . . .

So unbecoming in a man. Long nosehairs, her mother had been talking about Daddy's nosehairs. Long nosehairs, Johnny, are so unbecoming in a man. Why did she remember that utterance above all others? Long. Nose. Hairs. So. Unbecoming. In. A. Man. Johnny.

Daddy's name: Johnny.

Her father, who had sworn at her mother. Fuck art. Fuck was the dirtiest word there was. At school it had been whispered, a magic word, a word to conjure up demons and secrets.

And she's on the streets now, although she knows that really she should do something about the Butcher's Gallery. It needs cleaning badly. There are torn canvases everywhere. Torn and spattered. It doesn't matter: nobody visits. No family, no friends.

So she finds another one. This one's stupid. 'As long as you're not the Wolfman,' she says with a laugh. The Wolfman laughs too. He? She? It doesn't matter now. He and she are one and the same. The wound has healed. He feels whole, feels complete. It is not a good feeling. It is a bad feeling. But it can be forgotten for a moment.

Back in his house.

'Some gaff you've got here,' she says. He smiles, takes her coat and hangs it up. 'Bit of a smell though. You haven't got a gas leak, have you?'

No, not a gas leak. But a leak, yes. He slips his hand into his pocket, checks that the teeth are there. Of course they are, they're always there when he needs them. To bite with. The way he was bitten.

'Only a game, sweet.'

Only a game. Bitten in fun. On the stomach. Bitten. Not hard, more like blowing a raspberry. But that didn't stop it hurting. He touches his gut. It still hurts, even now.

'Where do you want me, love?'

'In here will do,' he says, taking out the key and beginning to unlock the door. The mirror was a bad idea. The last one had seen what was happening behind her, had almost screamed. The mirror has been taken down. The door is unlocked.

'Keep it locked, do you? What you got in there, the crown jewels?'

And the Wolfman, showing teeth, smiles.

Know This, Womin

He woke up in his hotel room, which was something in itself, bearing in mind that he had no idea how he'd got there. He was lying on his bed, fully clothed, his hands pressed between his legs. Beside him lay the carrier-bag full of books. It was seven o'clock and by the quality of the light streaming in through the uncurtained window, it was morning rather than evening. So far so good. The bad news was that his head seared with two kinds of pain, bad when he opened his eyes, unbearable when he closed them. With eyes closed, the world spun at an awkward tilt. With eyes opened, it merely floated on a different plane.

He groaned, attempted to unglue his furred tongue from the roof of his mouth. Staggered to the sink and ran the cold tap for some moments, then splashed his face and cupped his hand, lapping water from it the way a mongrel might. The water was sweet, chlorinated. He tried not to think of kidneys . . . seven sets of kidneys. Knelt by the toilet-pan and retched. The big white telephone receiver to God. What was the score? Seven brandies, six dark rums – he'd lost count after that. He squeezed an inch-long strip of toothpaste onto his brush and scrubbed at his teeth and gums. Then, only then, did he have the courage to examine himself in the wall-mirror.

There were two kinds of pain. One from the hangover, the other from the mugging. He'd lost twenty quid, maybe thirty. But the loss to his pride was above price. He held in his head a good description of a couple of the gang and especially the leader. This morning, he would give what he knew to the local station. His message would be clear: seek out and destroy. Who was he kidding? They'd rather protect their own villains than help an intruder from north of the border. *Our man from north of the border. Jockland. Jock.* But to let the gang get away with it was worse. What the hell.

He rubbed his jaw. It felt worse than it looked. There was a pale mustard bruise down one cheek and a graze on his chin. Good thing training shoes were all the rage. In the early 70s it would have been a steel-capped Airwear boot and he would not have been so chipper.

He was running out of clean clothes. Today, he would have either to buy some new bits and pieces or else find himself a laundrette. He had come to London intending to stay no more than two or three days. He'd thought that after that the Met would come to see that he could add nothing to the case. But instead here he was, coming up with possible leads, making himself useful, getting beaten up, turning into an over-protective father, having a holiday romance with a psychology lecturer.

He thought about Lisa, about the way the secretary at University College had acted. Something jarred about the whole incident. Lisa, who slept so soundly, the sleep of a clear conscience. What was that smell? That smell creeping into his room? The smell of cooking fat mingled with toast and coffee. The smell of breakfast. Somewhere downstairs they were busy perspiring over the griddles, breaking eggs to sizzle beside thick sausages and grey-pink bacon. The thought sent Rebus's stomach on a tiny rollercoaster ride. He was hungry, but the thought of fried food repelled him. He felt his just-cleaned mouth turning sour.

When had he last eaten? A sandwich on the way to Lisa's. Two packets of crisps in the Fighting Cock. Christ, yes, he was hungry. He dressed quickly, making a mental note of what needed buying – shirt, pants, socks – and headed down to the dining-room clutching three paracetamol tablets in his hand. A fistful of dullers.

They weren't quite ready to start serving, but when he announced that he needed only cereal and fruit juice, the waitress (a different face each day) relented and showed him to a table set for one.

He ate two small packets of cereal. A cereal killer. Smiled grimly and went to the trestle table to help himself to more juice. Lots more juice. It had a funny artificial smell to it, and a taste best described as 'wersh'. But it was cold and wet and the vitamin C would help his head. The waitress brought him two daily papers. Neither contained anything of interest. Flight had not yet used Rebus's idea of the detailed description. Maybe Flight had passed it on to Cath Farraday. Would she sit on it out of spite? After all, she hadn't been too happy about his last little stunt, had she? Maybe she was holding back on this one, just to show him that she could. Well, sod them. He didn't see anyone coming up with better ideas, with any ideas at all, come to that. Nobody wanted to make a mistake; they'd all rather sit on their hands than be seen to get it wrong. Jesus Christ.

When the first customer proper of the morning ordered bacon, eggs and tomatoes, Rebus finished his orange juice and left the restaurant.

In the Murder Room, he sat at one of the typewriters and prepared detailed descriptions of the gang members. His typing had never been proficient at the best of times, but today's hangover was compounded by an electronic typewriter of infernal complexity. He couldn't get the thing to set a reasonable line length, the tabs appeared not to work and every time he pressed a wrong key the thing bleeped at him.

'Bleep yourself,' he said, trying again to set it for single space typing.

Eventually, he had a typed description. It looked like the work of a ten-year-old, but it would have to do. He took the sheets of paper through to his office. There was a note from Flight on his desk.

'John, I wish you wouldn't keep disappearing. I've run a check on missing persons. Five women have been reported missing north of the river in the past forty-eight hours. Two of these could be explicable, but the other three look more serious. Maybe you're right, the Wolfman's getting hungrier. No feedback from the press stories yet though. See you when you've finished shagging the Prof.'

It was signed simply 'GF'. How did Flight know where he'd been yesterday afternoon? An inspired guess, or something more cunning and devious? It didn't really matter. What mattered were the missing women. If Rebus's hunch were true, then the Wolfman was losing some of his previous control and that meant that sometime soon he was bound to make a mistake. They need only goad him a little more. The Jan Crawford story might just do that particular trick. Rebus had to sell the idea to Flight – and to Farraday. They had to be made to see that it was the right move at the right time. Three missing women. That would bring the count to seven. Seven murders. There was no telling where it would stop. He rubbed at his head again. The hangover was returning with a steel-tipped vengeance.

'John?'

She was standing in the doorway, trembling, her eyes wide.

'Lisa?' He rose slowly to his feet. 'Lisa, what is it? What's wrong?'

She stumbled towards him. There were tears in her eyes and her hair was slick with sweat. 'Thank God,' she said, clinging to him. 'I thought I'd never ... I didn't know what to do, where to go. Your hotel said you'd already left. The Sergeant on the desk downstairs let me come up. He recognised me from the photo in the papers. My photo.' And then the tears came: hot, scalding, and loud. Rebus patted her on the back, trying to calm her, wanting to know just what the hell had happened.

'Lisa,' he said quietly, 'just tell me about it.' He manoeuvred her onto a chair, with his hand rubbing soothingly at her neck. Every bit of her seemed damp with perspiration.

She pulled her bag onto her lap, opened it, and drew from one of the three compartments a small envelope, which she handed silently to Rebus.

'What is it?' he asked.

'I got it this morning,' she said, 'addressed to me by name and sent to my home.'

Rebus examined the typed name and address, the first class stamp, and the postmark: London EC4. The frank stated that the letter had been posted the previous morning.

'He knows where I live, John. When I opened it this morning, I nearly died on the spot. I had to get out of the flat, but all the time I knew that maybe he was watching me.' Her eyes filled with water again, but she threw back her head so that the tears would not escape. She fished in her bag and came out with some paper tissues, peeling off one so that she could blow her nose. Rebus said nothing.

'It's a death threat,' she explained.

'A *death threat?*'

She nodded.

'Who from? Does it say?'

'Oh yes, it says all right. It's from the Wolfman, John. He says I'm going to be next.'

It was a rush job, but the lab, when they heard the circumstances, were happy to cooperate. Rebus stood with hands in pockets watching them at work. There was the crackle of paper in his pocket. He had folded the description of the gang members and tucked it away, perhaps for future use: for now, there were more important matters to attend to.

The story was straightforward enough. Lisa had been scared out of her wits by the letter, and more so by the fact that the Wolfman knew where she lived. She had tried contacting Rebus and when that failed had panicked, fleeing from her flat, aware that *he* might be watching her, might be about to pounce at any moment. The pity was, as the lab had already explained, she'd messed up the letter, gripping it in her hand as she fled, destroying any fingerprints or other evidence that there might have been on the envelope itself. Still, they'd do their best.

If the letter was from the Wolfman and not from some new and twisted crank, then there might well be clues to be had from the envelope and its contents: saliva (used to stick down both flap and stamp), fibres, fingerprints. These were the physical possibilities. Then there were more arcane elements: the typewriter itself might be traceable. Were there oddities of speech or misspellings which might yield a clue? And what about that postmark? The Wolfman had outwitted them in the past, so was the postal address another red herring?

The various processes involved would take time. The lab was efficient, but the chemical analyses could not be hurried. Lisa had come to the lab, too, as had George Flight. They were off in another part of the building drinking tea and going over the details for the fourth or fifth time, but Rebus liked to watch the lab boys at work. This was his idea of sleuthing. It also helped calm him to watch someone working in such painstaking detail. And he certainly needed calming.

His plan had worked. He had prodded and teased the Wolfman into action. He should, though, have realised the danger Lisa might be in. After all, her photo had been in the papers, as had her name. They had even mistakenly termed her a police psychologist – the very people who, according to the earlier planted story, had come to the conclusion that the Wolfman might be gay, or transsexual, or any of the other barbs they had used. Lisa Frazer had become the Wolfman's enemy, and he, John Rebus, had led her into it by the nose. Stupid, John, oh so very stupid. What if the Wolfman had actually tracked her to her flat and . . .? No, no, no: he couldn't bear to think of it.

But though Lisa's name had appeared in the newspapers, her address had not. So how had the Wolfman found out her address? That was much more problematic.

And much more chilling.

She was ex-directory, for a start. But as he knew only too well, this was no barrier to someone in authority, someone like a police officer. Jesus: was he *really* talking about another police officer? There had to be other candidates: staff and students at University College, other psychologists – they would know Lisa. Then there were those groups who could have linked an address to a name: civil servants, the local council, taxmen, gas and electricity boards, the postman, the guy next door, numerous computers and mailshot programmes, her local public library. Where could he start?

'Here you are, Inspector.'

One of the assistants handed him a photocopy of the typed letter.
'Thanks,' said Rebus.

'We're testing the original at the moment, scanning for traces of anything interesting. We'll let you know.'

'Right. What about the envelope?'

'The saliva tests will take a little longer. We should have something for you in the next couple of hours. There was also the photograph, of course, but it won't photocopy too well. We know which paper it was from, and that it was cut out with a pair of fairly sharp scissors, perhaps as small as manicure scissors judging from the length of each cut.'

Rebus nodded, staring at the photostat. 'Thanks again,' he said.

'No problem.'

No problem? That wasn't right; there were plenty of problems. He read through the letter. The typing seemed nice and even, as though the typewriter used was a new one, or a good quality model, something like the electronic machine he'd been using this morning. As for the content, well, that was something else again.

GET THIS, I'M NOT HOMOSEXUL, O.K.? WOLFMAN IS WHAT WOLFMAN DOES. WHAT WOLFMAN DOES NEXT IS THIS: HE KILLS YOU. DON'T WORRY, IT WON'T HURT. WOLFMAN DOES NOT HURT; JUST DOES WHAT WOLFMAN IS. KNOW THIS, WOMIN, WOLFMAN KNOWS YOU, WHERE YOU LIVE, WHAT YOU LOOK LIKE. JUST TELL THE TRUTH AND NO HARM CAN CUM TO YOU.

On a piece of plain A4-sized paper, folded in four to get it into the small white envelope. The Wolfman had cut a picture of Lisa from one of the newspapers. Then he had cut her head off and drawn a dark pencilled circle on her stomach. And this photograph of her trunk had accompanied the letter.

'Bastard,' Rebus hissed. 'Jesus, you bastard.'

He took the letter along the corridor and up the stairs to the room where Flight was sitting, rubbing at his face again.

'Where's Lisa?'

'Ladies' room.'

'Does she seem . . .?'

'She's upset, but she's coping. The doctor's given her some tranqs. What have you got there?' Rebus handed over the copy. Flight read through it quickly, intently. 'What the hell do you make of it?' he asked. Rebus sat himself down on a hard chair still warm from Lisa's presence. He reached out a hand and took the paper from Flight, then angled his chair so that both men could inspect the letter together.

'Well,' he said. 'I'm not sure. At first sight, it looks like the work of a near-illiterate.'

'Agreed.'

'But then again, there's something artful about it. Look at the punctuation, George. Absolutely correct, right down to every comma. And he uses colons and semi-colons. What sort of person could spell "woman" as "womin", yet know how to use a semi-colon?'

Flight studied the note intently, nodding. 'Go on.'

'Well, Rhona, my ex-wife, she's a teacher. I remember she used to tell me how frustrating it was that nowadays no one in schools bothered to teach basic grammar and punctuation. She said that kids were growing up now with no need for things like colons and semi-colons and no idea at all of how to use them. So I'd say we're dealing either with someone who has been well educated, or with someone in middle age, educated at a time when punctuation was still taught in every school.'

Flight gave a half-smile. 'Been reading your psychology books again I see, John.'

'It's not all black magic, George. Mostly it's just to do with common sense and how you interpret things. Do you want me to go on?'

'I'm all ears.'

'Well,' Rebus was running a finger down the letter again. 'There's something else here, something that tells me this letter is genuinely from the killer, and not the work of some nutter somewhere.'

'Oh?'

'Go on, George, where's the clue?'

He held the paper out towards Flight. Flight grinned for a moment, then took it.

'I suppose,' he said, 'you're talking about the way the writer refers to the Wolfman in the third person?'

'You've just named the tune in one, George. That's exactly what I mean.'

Flight looked up. 'Incidentally, John, what the hell happened to you? Did you get in a fight or something? I thought the Scots gave up wearing woad a couple of years back?'

Rebus touched his bruised jaw. 'I'll tell you the story sometime. But look, in the first sentence, the writer refers to himself in the first person. He's taken our homosexual jibe personally. But in the rest of the letter, he speaks of the Wolfman in the third person. Standard practice with serial murderers.'

'What about the misspelling of homosexual?'

'Could be genuine, or it could be to throw us off the scent. "U" and "a" are at different ends of the keyboard. A two-fingered typist could miss the "a" if he was writing fast, if he was angry.' Rebus paused, remembering the list in his pocket. 'I speak from recent experience.'

'Fair enough.'

'Now look at what he actually says: "Wolfman is what Wolfman does". What the books say is that killers find their identity through killing. That's exactly what this sentence means.'

Flight exhaled noisily. 'Yes, but none of this gets us any closer, does it?' He offered a cigarette to Rebus. 'I mean, we can build up as clear a picture as we like of the bastard's personality, but it won't give us a name and address.'

Rebus sat forward in his chair. 'But all the time we're narrowing down the possible types, George. And eventually we'll narrow it down to a field of one. Look at this final sentence.'

'"Just tell the truth and no harm can cum to you,"' Flight recited.

'Skipping the pun, which is intriguing in itself, don't you think there's something very, I don't know, official sounding about that construction? Something very formal?'

'I don't see what you're getting at.'

'What I'm getting at is that it seems to me the sort of thing someone like you or me would say.'

'A copper?' Flight sat back in his chair. 'Oh, come on, John, what kind of crap is that?'

Rebus's voice grew quiet and persuasive. 'Someone who knows where Lisa Frazer lives, George. Think about it. Someone who knows that kind of information, or knows how to get it. We can't afford to rule out –'

Flight stood up. 'I'm sorry, John, but no. I simply can't entertain the notion that . . . that someone, some copper, could be behind all this. No, it's just not on.'

Rebus shrugged. 'Okay, George, whatever you say.' But Rebus knew that he had planted a seed now in George Flight's head, and that the seed would surely sprout.

Flight sat down again, confident that this time he had won a point from Rebus. 'Anything else?'

Rebus read the letter through yet again, sucking on his cigarette. He remembered how at school, in his English class, he had loved writing summaries and close interpretations of texts. 'Yes,' he said eventually. 'Actually there is. This letter seems to me more of a warning, a shot across the bows. He starts off by saying that he's going to kill her, but by the end of the letter he's tempered that line. He says nothing will happen if she tells the truth. I think he's looking for a retraction. I think he wants us to put out another story saying he's not gay.'

Flight checked his watch. 'He's in for another fright.'

'How do you mean?'

'The lunchtime edition will be hitting the streets. I believe Cath Farraday's put out the Jan Crawford story.'

'Really?' Rebus revised his idea of Farraday. Maybe she wasn't a vindictive old bat after all. 'So now we're saying we've got a living witness, and he must realise it's a fact. I think it might just be enough to blow what final fuses he's got up here.' Rebus tapped his head. 'To send him barking mad, as Lamb would put it.'

'You reckon?'

'I reckon, George. We need everybody at their most alert. He could try anything.'

'I dread to think.'

Rebus was staring at the letter. 'Something else, George. EC4: where's that exactly?'

Flight thought it over. 'The City, part of it anyway. Farringdon Street, Blackfriars Bridge, all around there. Ludgate, St Paul's.'

'Hmm. He's tricked us before, making us see patterns where none exist. The teeth for example, I'm sure I'm right about them. But now that we've got him rattled —'

'You think he lives in the City?'

'Lives there, works there, maybe just drives through there on his way to work.' Rebus shook his head. He didn't yet want to share with Flight the image which had just passed through his mind, the image of a motorcycle courier based in the City, a motorcyclist with easy access to every part of London. Like the man in leathers he'd seen on the bridge that first night down by the canal.

A man like Kenny Watkiss.

'Well,' he said instead, 'whatever, it's another piece of the jigsaw.'

'If you ask me,' said Flight, 'there are too many pieces. They won't all fit.'

'Agreed.' Rebus stubbed out the cigarette. Flight had already finished his own, and was about to light another. 'But as the picture emerges, we'll know better which bits we can discard, won't we?' He was still studying the letter. There was something else. What was it? Something at the back of his mind, lurking somewhere in memory . . . Something stirred momentarily by the letter, but what? If he stopped thinking about it, maybe it would come to him, the way the names of forgotten actors in films did.

The door opened.

'Lisa, how are you?' Both men rose to offer her a seat, but she lifted a hand to show she preferred to stand. All three of them stood, a stiff triangle in the tiny box of a room.

'Just been sick again,' she said. Then she smiled. 'Can't be much more to bring up. I think I'm back to yesterday's breakfast already.' They smiled with her. She looked tired to Rebus, exhausted. Lucky she had slept so soundly yesterday. He doubted she'd get much sleep for the next night or ten, tranqs or not.

Flight spoke first. 'I've arranged for temporary accommodation, Dr Frazer. The less people who know where, the better. Don't worry, you'll be quite safe. We'll have a guard on you.'

'What about her flat?' asked Rebus.

Flight nodded. 'I've got two men there keeping an eye on the place. One inside the flat itself, the other outside, both of them hidden. If the Wolfman turns up, they'll cope with him, believe me.'

'Stop talking as though I'm not here,' Lisa snapped. 'This affects me too.'

There was a cold silence in the room.

'Sorry,' she said. She covered her eyes with her ringless left hand. 'I just can't believe I was so *scared* back there. I feel –'

She tipped her head back again. The tears were too precious to be released. Flight placed a hand softly on her shoulder.

'It's all right, Dr Frazer. Really it is.' She gave a wry smile at this.

Flight kept on talking, feeding her with comforting words. But she wasn't listening. She was staring at Rebus, and he was staring back at her. Rebus knew what her eyes were telling him. They were telling him something of the utmost importance.

Catch the Wolfman, catch him quickly and destroy him utterly. Do it for me, John. But just do it.

She blinked, breaking the contact. Rebus nodded slowly, almost imperceptibly, but it was enough. She smiled at him, and suddenly her eyes were dry sparkling stones. Flight felt the change and lifted his hand away from her arm. He looked to Rebus for some explanation, but

Rebus was studying the letter, concentrating on its opening sentence. What was it? There was something there, something just beyond his line of vision. Something he didn't get.

Yet.

Two detectives, one of them extraordinarily burly, like the prop-forward from a rugby team, the other tall and thin and silent, came to the labs to take Lisa away with them, away to a place of safety. Despite vigorous protests, Rebus wasn't allowed to know the destination. Flight was taking all of this very seriously indeed. But before Lisa could go, the lab people needed her fingerprints and to take samples of fibres from her clothes, all for the purpose of elimination. The two bodyguards went with her.

Rebus and Flight, exhausted, stood together at the drinks machine in the long, brightly-lit hallway, feeding in coins for cups of powdery coffee and powdery tea.

'Are you married, George?'

Flight seemed surprised by the question, surprised perhaps that it should come only now. 'Yes,' he said. 'Have been the past twelve years. Marion. She's the second. The first was a disaster – my fault, not hers.'

Rebus nodded, taking hold of the hot plastic beaker by its rim.

'You said you'd been married, too,' Flight remarked. Rebus nodded again.

'That's right.'

'So what happened?'

'I'm not really sure any more. Rhona used to say it was like the continental drift: so slow we didn't notice until it was too late. Her on one island, me on another, and a great big bloody sea between us.'

Flight smiled. 'Well, you did say she was a teacher.'

'Yes, she still is actually. Lives in Mile End with my daughter.'

'Mile End? Bloody hell. Gentrified gangland, no place for any copper's daughter.'

Rebus smiled at the irony. It was time to confess. 'Actually, George, I've found out she's going out with someone called Kenny Watkiss.'

'Oh dear. Who is? Your missus or your daughter?'

'My daughter. Her name's Samantha.'

'And she's going out with Kenny Watkiss? How old is he?'

'Older than her. Eighteen, nineteen, something like that. He's a bike messenger in the City.'

Flight nodded, understanding now. 'He was the one who shouted from the public gallery?' Flight thought for a moment. 'Well, from what I know of the Watkiss family history, I'd say Kenny must be Tommy's nephew. Tommy's got a brother, Lenny, he's doing time just now. Lenny's a big softie, not like Tommy. He's in for fraud, tax evasion, clocking cars, naughty kites, I mean bad cheques. It's all fourth division stuff, but it mounts up, and when there's enough of it against you at any one sitting of the bench, well, it's odds on you'll go inside, isn't it?'

'It's no different in Scotland.'

'No, I don't suppose it is. So, do you want me to find out what I can about this bike messenger?'

'I already know where he stays. Churchill Estate, it's a housing estate in –'

Flight was chuckling. 'You don't have to tell any copper in Greater London where Churchill Estate is, John. They use that place to train the SAS.'

'Yes,' said Rebus, 'so Laine said.'

'Laine? What's he got to do with it?'

In for a penny, thought Rebus. 'I had Kenny's telephone number. I needed an address.'

'And Laine got it for you? What did you tell him it was for?'

'The Wolfman case.'

Flight flinched, his face creasing. 'You keep forgetting, John, you're our *guest* down here. You don't go pulling stunts like that. When Laine finds out –'

'If he finds out.'

But Flight was shaking his head. '*When* he finds out. There's no "if" about it, believe me. When he finds out, he won't bother with you. He won't even bother with who's directly above you. He'll go to your Chief Super back in Edinburgh and give him the most incredible verbals. I've seen him do it.'

Do a good job, John. Remember, you're representing our force down there.

Rebus blew on the coffee. The notion of anyone giving 'verbals' to Farmer Watson was almost amusing. 'I always did fancy getting back into uniform,' he said.

Flight stared at him. The fun was over. 'There are some rules, John. We can get away with breaking a few, but some are sacrosanct, carved into stone by God Almighty. And one of them states that you don't muck around with someone like Laine just to satisfy your own personal curiosity.' Flight was angry, and trying to make a point, but he was also whispering, not wanting anyone to hear.

Rebus, not really caring any more, was half-smiling as he whispered back. 'So what do I do? Tell him the truth? Oh hello there, Chief Inspector, my daughter's winching with someone I don't like. Can I have the young man's address, please, so I can go and belt him? Is that how I do it?'

Flight paused, then frowned. 'Winching?'

Now he too was smiling, though trying hard not to show it. Rebus laughed aloud.

'It means dating,' he said. 'Next you'll be telling me you don't know what hoolit means.'

'Try me,' said Flight, laughing too.

'Drunk,' explained Rebus.

They sipped their drinks in silence for a moment. Rebus thanked God for the linguistic barrier between them, for without it there would be no easy jokes, jokes which broke the tension. There were two ways to defuse tension: one was to laugh it away, the other was to resort to physical action. It was laugh or lash out. Once or twice now they had come near to trading punches, but had ended up trading grins instead.

Praise be for the gift of laughter.

'Anyway, I went to Hackney last night looking for Kenny Watkiss.'

'And you got those for your pains?' Flight was nodding towards the bruises. Rebus shrugged. 'Serves you right. Someone once told me hackney's French for a nag. Doesn't sound French, does it? But I suppose it would explain the hackney carriage.'

Hackney. Nag. That horse in the British Museum, no bite. Rebus had to talk to Morrison about the bite marks.

Flight finished his drink first, draining the cup and tossing it into a bin beside the machine. He checked his watch.

'I better find a phone,' he said. 'See what's happening back at base. Maybe Lamb will have found something on that Crawford woman.'

'"That Crawford woman" is a victim, George. Stop making her sound like a criminal.'

'*Maybe* she's a victim,' said Flight. 'Let's get our facts straight before we go for the tea and sympathy routine. Besides, when did you join this little victim support group of yours? You know the way we have to play this sort of thing. It isn't nice necessarily, but it means we don't get it wrong.'

'That's quite a speech.'

Flight sighed and examined the tips of his shoes. 'Look, John, has it ever occurred to you that there might be another way?'

538

'The way of Zen perhaps?'

'I mean, a way other than your own. Or are the rest of us just thick, and you're the only policeman on the planet who knows how to solve a crime? I'd be interested to know.'

Rebus desperately did not want to blush, which is probably precisely why he did blush. He tried to think of a smart answer, but none came to mind right that second, so he kept silent. Flight nodded approval.

'Let's go find that phone,' he said. Now Rebus found the courage he needed.

'George,' he said. 'I need to know: who brought me here?'

Flight stared at him, wondering whether or not to answer. He pursed his lips as he thought about it, and came up with an answer: what the hell.

'I did,' he said. 'It was my idea.'

'You?' Rebus seemed puzzled. Flight nodded confirmation.

'Yes, me. I suggested you to Laine and Pearson. A new head, fresh blood, that sort of thing.'

'But how in God's name did you know about me?'

'Well,' Flight was beginning to look sheepish. He made a play of examining the tips of his shoes again. 'Remember I showed you that file, the one with all the guesswork in it? On top of that I did some background reading on multiple murderers. Research, you could call it. And I came across that case of yours in some newspaper clippings from Scotland Yard. I was impressed.'

Rebus pointed a disbelieving finger. 'You were reading up on serial killers?'

Flight nodded.

'On the *psychology* of serial killers?'

Flight shrugged. 'And other aspects, yes.' Rebus's eyes had widened.

'And all this time you've been having a dig at *me* for going along with Lisa Frazer's – no, I don't believe it!'

Flight was laughing again. The apparently arch anti-psychologist revealed in his true light. 'I had to examine every angle,' he said, watching as Rebus, having finished his coffee, tossed the cup into a waste-bin. 'Now come on, we really should make that phone call.'

Rebus was still shaking his head as he followed Flight down the hall. But though he appeared to be in good humour, his brain was more active than ever. Flight had pulled the wool over his eyes with consummate ease. How far did the pretence actually stretch? Was he now seeing the real Flight, or yet another mask? Flight whistled as he walked and kicked at an imaginary football. No, not George Flight, Rebus decided in an instant: never George Flight.

There was a telephone in the admin offices. There was also, seated at a desk having a conversation with one of the senior staff, Philip Cousins, immaculate in grey suit and burgundy tie.

'Philip!'

'Hello there, George. How are things?' Cousins spotted Rebus. 'And Inspector Rebus, too. Still lending a Caledonian hand?'

'Trying,' said Rebus.

'Yes, very,' rejoined Flight. 'So what brings you here, Philip? Where's Isobel?'

'Penny's rather tied up, I'm afraid. She'll be sorry to have missed you, George. As for my presence here, I just wanted to double-check some facts on a murder case from last December. You might remember it, the man in the bathtub.'

'The one that looked like suicide?'

'That's right.' Philip Cousins's voice was as rich and slow as double cream. Rebus reckoned that the word 'urbane' had been invented with him in mind. 'I'm in court later today,' Cousins was saying. 'Trying to help Malcolm Chambers pin the deceased's wife for manslaughter at the very least.'

'Chambers?' Flight shook his head. 'I don't envy you that.'

'But surely,' Rebus interrupted, 'you'll be on the same side?'

'Ah yes, Inspector Rebus,' said Cousins, 'you are quite correct. But Chambers is such a scrupulous man. He'll want my evidence to be water-tight, and if it isn't, then he's as likely to undo me as is the defence counsel. More likely, in fact. Malcolm Chambers is interested in the truth, not in verdicts.'

'Yes,' said Flight, 'I remember him having a right go at me once in the witness box, all because I couldn't recall offhand what kind of clock had been in the living-room. The case nearly crumbled there and then.' Flight and Cousins shared a comradely smile.

'I've just been hearing,' said Cousins, 'that there's fresh evidence on the Wolfman case. Do tell.'

'It's beginning to come together, Philip,' said Flight. 'It's definitely beginning to come together, due in no small part to my associate here.' Flight laid a momentary hand on Rebus's shoulder.

'I'm impressed,' said Cousins, sounding neither impressed nor unimpressed.

'It was luck,' said Rebus, as he felt he ought. Not that he believed what he was saying. Cousins's eyes on him were like packs of ice, so that the room temperature seemed to drop with every glance.

'So what do we have?'

'Well,' said Flight, 'we've got someone who claims she was attacked by the Wolfman but escaped from him.'

'Fortunate creature,' said Cousins.

'And,' continued Flight, 'one of the . . . people helping us on the case this morning received a letter claiming to be from the Wolfman.'

'Good God.'

'We think it's kosher,' Flight concluded.

'Well,' said Cousins, 'this *is* something. Wait till I tell Penny. She'll be thrilled.'

'Philip, we don't want it getting out –'

'Not a word, George, not a word. You know it's all one-way traffic with me. But Penny should be told.'

'Oh, tell Isobel by all means,' said Flight, 'only warn her it's not to go any further.'

'Total secrecy,' said Cousins. 'I quite understand. Mum's the word. Who was it, by the way?' Flight appeared not to understand. 'To whom was this threatening letter addressed?'

Flight was about to speak, but Rebus beat him to it. 'Just someone on the case, as Inspector Flight says.' He smiled, trying to alleviate the brusqueness of his response. Oh yes, his mind was working now, working in a fever: nobody had told Cousins the letter was threatening, so how did he know it was? Okay, it was simple enough to work out that it wouldn't exactly have been fan mail, but all the same.

'Well then,' said Cousins, choosing not to press for details. 'And now, gentlemen,' he scooped up two manila files from the desk and tucked them under his arm, then stood, the joints of his knees cracking with the effort, 'if you'll excuse me, Court Eight awaits. Inspector Rebus,' Cousins held out his free hand, 'it sounds as though the case may be drawing towards its conclusion. Should we fail to meet again, give my regards to your delightful city.' He turned to Flight. 'See you soon, George. Bring Marion round for supper some evening. Give Penny a tinkle and we'll try to find one night in the calendar when all four of us are free. Goodbye.'

'Bye, Philip.'

'Goodbye.'

'Goodbye.'

'Oh.' Cousins had stopped in the doorway. 'There is just one thing.' He turned pleading eyes on Flight. 'You don't have a spare driver, do you, George? It's going to be hell getting a taxi at this time of day.'

'Well,' Flight thought hard, then had an idea, 'if you can hang on for a couple of minutes, Philip, I've got a couple of men here in the building.' He turned to Rebus, whose eyes had widened. 'Lisa won't mind, will she, John? I mean, if her car drops Philip off at the Old Bailey?'

Rebus could do little but shrug.

'Excellent!' said Cousins, clasping his hands together. 'Thank you so much.'

'I'll take you to them,' Flight said. 'But first I need to make a phone call.'

Cousins nodded towards the corridor. 'And I must visit the WC. Be back in a tick.'

They watched him leave. Flight was grinning, shaking his head in wonderment. 'Do you know,' he said, 'he's been like that ever since I met him? I mean, the sort of ambassadorial air, the aged aristocrat. Ever since I've known him.'

'He's a gentleman all right,' said Rebus.

'But that's just the thing,' said Flight. 'His background is every bit as ordinary as yours or mine.' He turned to the lab man. 'All right if I use your phone?'

He did not wait for an answer, but started dialling straight away. 'Hello?' he said into the receiver when he was finally connected. 'Who's that? Oh, hello, Deakin, is Lamb there? Yes, put him on, will you? Thanks.' While he was waiting, Flight picked invisible threads from his trousers. The trousers were shiny from too many wearings. Everything about Flight, Rebus noticed, seemed worn: his shirt collar had an edge of grime to it and the collar itself was too tight, constricting the loose flesh of the neck, pinching it into vertical folds. Rebus found himself transfixed by that neck, by the tufts of grey sprouting hair where the razor had failed in its duty. Signs of mortality, as final as a hand around a throat. When Flight got off the phone, Rebus would protest about sending Cousins off with Lisa. *Ambassadorial. Aristocrat.* One of the earlier mass killers had been an aristocrat, too.

'Hello, Lamb? What have you found on Miss Crawford?' Flight listened, his eyes on Rebus, ready to communicate anything of interest. 'Uh-huh, okay. Mm, I see. Yes. Right.' All the time his eyes told Rebus that everything was checking out, that Jan Crawford was reliable, that she was telling the truth. Then Flight's eyes widened a little. 'What's that again?' And he listened more intently, moving his eyes from Rebus to study the telephone apparatus itself. 'Now that is interesting.'

Rebus shifted. What? What was interesting? But Flight had again resorted to monosyllables.

'Uh-hu. Mmm. Well, never mind. I know. Yes, I'm sure.' His voice sounded resigned to something. 'Okay. Thanks for letting me know. Yes. No, we'll be back in about, I don't know, maybe another hour. Right, catch you then.'

Flight held the receiver above the telephone, but did not immediately drop it back into its cradle. Instead, he let it hang there.

Rebus could contain his curiosity no longer. 'What?' he said. 'What is it? What's wrong?'

Flight seemed to come out of his daydream, and put down the receiver. 'Oh,' he said, 'it's Tommy Watkiss.'

'What about him?'

'Lamb has just heard that there isn't going to be a retrial. We don't know why yet. Maybe the judge didn't think the charges were worth all the aggro and told the CPS so.'

'Assault on a woman not worth the *aggro*?' All thought of Philip Cousins vanished from Rebus's mind.

Flight shrugged. 'Retrials are expensive. *Any* trial is expensive. We cocked it up first time round, so we lose a second chance. It happens, John, you know that.'

'Of course it happens. But the idea of a snake like Watkiss getting away with something like that –'

'Don't worry, he can't keep his nose clean for long. Breaking the law's in his blood. When he does something naughty, we'll have him, and I'll see to it there are no balls-ups, mark my words.'

Rebus sighed. Yes, it happened, you lost a few. More than a few. Incompetence or a soft judge, an unsympathetic jury or a rock-solid witness for the defence. And sometimes maybe the Procurator Fiscal thought a retrial not worth the money. You lost a few. They were like toothache.

'I bet Chambers is fuming,' Rebus said.

'Oh yes,' said Flight, smiling at the thought, 'I bet he's got steam coming out of his bloody shirt-cuffs.'

But one person would be happy at least, Rebus was thinking: Kenny Watkiss. He'd be over the moon.

'So,' said Rebus, 'what about Jan Crawford?'

Flight shrugged again. 'She seems straight as a die. No previous, no record of mental illness, lives quietly, but the neighbours seem to like her well enough. Like Lamb said, she's so clean it's frightening.'

Yes, the squeaky clean ones often were. Frightening to a policeman the way an unknown species might be to a jungle explorer: fear of the new, the different. You got to suspect that everyone had something to hide: the schoolteachers smuggled in porn videos from their holiday in Amsterdam; the solicitors took cocaine on their weekend parties; the happily married MP was sleeping with his secretary; the magistrate had a predeliction for underage boys; the librarian kept a real skeleton hidden in the closet; the angelic looking children had set fire to a neighbour's cat.

And sometimes your suspicions were correct.

And other times they weren't. Cousins was standing at the door now, ready to leave. Flight laid a hand softly on his arm. Rebus recalled that he'd meant to say something to Flight, but how to phrase it? Would it do to say that Philip Cousins seemed almost too clean, with his surgeon's cold, manicured hands and his ambassadorial air? Rebus was wondering now, *seriously* wondering.

Since Flight had gone off with Philip Cousins to find Lisa and her protectors, Rebus went back to the lab to hear the result of the first saliva test.

'Sorry,' said the white-coated scientist. He looked not yet to be out of his teens. Beneath his lab coat, there lurked a black T-shirt decorated with the name of a heavy metal band. 'I don't think we're going to have much luck. All we're finding so far is H_2O, tap-water. Whoever stuck the envelope down must have used a wet sponge or a pad or one of those old-fashioned roller things. No traces of saliva at all.'

The breath left Rebus's lungs. 'What about fingerprints?'

'Negative so far. All we've found are two sets which look like they're going to match Dr Frazer's. And we're not having any better luck with fibres or grease stains. I'd say the writer wore gloves. Nobody here has seen such a clean, speck-free job.'

He knows, Rebus was thinking. He knows everything we might try. So damned smart.

'Well, thanks anyway,' he said. The young man raised his eyebrows and spread his palms.

'I wish we could do more.'

You could start by getting a haircut, son, he thought to himself. You look too much like Kenny Watkiss. He sighed instead. 'Just do what you can,' he said. 'Just do what you can.'

Turning to walk away, Rebus felt a mixture of fresh rage and impotence, sudden savage frustration. The Wolfman was too good. He would stop killing before they could catch him; or he would simply go on killing again and again and again. No one would be safe. And most of all, it seemed, Lisa would not be safe.

Lisa.

She was being blamed by the Wolfman for the story Rebus had invented. It had nothing to do with Lisa. And if the Wolfman should somehow get to her it would be Rebus's fault, wouldn't it? Where was Lisa going? Rebus didn't know. Flight thought it was safer that way. But Rebus couldn't shake off the idea that the Wolfman might well be a policeman. Might well be *any* policeman. Might be the brawny detective or the thin and silent detective. Lisa had gone off with them thinking them her protection. What if she had walked straight into the clutches of . . .? What if the Wolfman knew exactly . . .? What if Philip Cousins . . .?

A loudspeaker sounded from its recess in the ceiling.

'Telephone call for Inspector Rebus at reception. Telephone call for Inspector Rebus.'

Rebus walked quickly down the rest of the corridor and through the swing-door at the end. He didn't know if Flight was still in the building, didn't care. His mind was filling with horrors: Wolfman, Lisa, Rhona, Sammy. Little Sammy, his daughter. She'd seen enough terror in her life. He'd been responsible before. He didn't want her to be hurt ever again.

The receptionist lifted the receiver as he approached, holding it out to him. As he grabbed it, she pressed a button on the dial, connecting him to the caller.

'Hello?' he said, breathlessly.

'Daddy?' Oh Christ, it *was* Sammy.

'Sammy?' Nearly yelling now. 'What is it? What's wrong?'

'Oh, Daddy.' She was crying. The memory flashed in front of him, scalding his vision. Phone calls. Screams.

'What is it, Sammy? Tell me!'

'It's,' a sniff, 'it's Kenny.'

'Kenny?' He furrowed his brow. 'What's wrong with him? Has he been in a crash?'

'Oh no, Daddy. He's just . . . just *disappeared*.'

'Where are you, Sammy?'

'I'm in a call-box.'

'Okay, I'm going to give you the address of a police station. Meet me there. If you have to get a taxi, that's fine. I'll pay for it when you arrive. Understand?'

'Daddy.' She sniffed back tears. 'You've got to find him. I'm worried. Please find him, Daddy. Please. *Please!*'

By the time George Flight reached reception, Rebus had already left. The receptionist explained as best she could, while Flight rubbed his jaw, encountering stubble. He had argued with Lisa Frazer, but by Christ she'd been stubborn. Attractively stubborn, he had to admit. She'd told him she didn't mind bodyguards but that the idea of a 'safe location' was out of the question. She had, she said, an appointment at the Old Bailey, a couple of appointments actually, interviews she was doing in connection with some research.

'It's taken me weeks to set them up,' she said, 'there's no way I'm going to blow them out now!'

'But my dear,' Philip Cousins had drawled, 'that's just where we're headed.' He was, Flight knew, keen for a close to proceedings, glancing at his watch impatiently. And it seemed that Lisa and Cousins knew one another from the murder at Copperplate Street, that they had things in common, things they wanted to talk about. That they were keen to be going.

So Flight made a decision. What did it matter after all if she did visit the Bailey? There were few better protected spots in the whole city. It was several hours yet until the first of her interviews, but that didn't really bother her. She did not, she said, mind hanging around in the 'courthouse'. In fact, she rather enjoyed the idea. The two officers could accompany her, wait for her, then drive her on to whatever safe location Flight had in mind. This, at any rate, was Lisa Frazer's argument, an argument defended by Philip Cousins who could see 'no flaw in the reasoning, m'lud'. So, to smiles on their part and a shrug on Flight's, the course of action was decided. Flight watched the Ford Granada roll away from him – the two officers in the front, Philip and Lisa Frazer in the back. Safe as houses, he was thinking. Safe as bloody houses.

And now Rebus had buggered off. Oh well, he'd catch up with him no doubt. He didn't regret bringing Rebus down here, not a bit. But he knew it had been *his* decision, not one entirely endorsed by the upper echelons. Any balls-ups and it would be Flight's pension on the block. He knew that only too well, as did everyone else. Which was why he'd stuck so close to Rebus in the first few days, just to be sure of the man.

Was he sure of the man? It was a question he would rather not answer, even now, even to himself. Rebus was like the spring in a trap, likely to jump no matter what landed on the bait. He was also a Scot, and Flight had never trusted the Scots, not since the day they'd voted to stay part of the Union . . .

'Daddy!'

And she runs into his arms. He hugs her to him, aware that he does not have to bend too far to accomplish this. Yes, she's grown, and yet she seems more childlike than ever. He kisses the top of her head, smells her clean hair. She is trembling. He can feel the vibrations darting through her chest and arms.

'Sshh,' he says. 'Ssshhh, pet, ssshhh.'

She pulls back and almost smiles, sniffs, then says, 'You always used to call me that. Your pet. Mum never called me pet. Only you.'

He smiles back and strokes her hair. 'Yes,' he says, 'your mum told me off for that. She said a pet was a possession and that you weren't a possession.' He is remembering now. 'She had some funny ideas, your mum.'

'She still does.' Then she remembers why she is here. The tears well up anew in her eyes.

'I know you don't like him,' she says.

'Nonsense, whatever gives you that —'

'But I love him, Daddy.' His heart spins once in his chest. 'And I don't want anything to happen to him.'

'What makes you think something's going to happen to him?'

'The way he's been acting lately, like he's keeping secrets from me. Mum's noticed it, too. I'm not just dreaming. But she said she thought maybe he was planning an engagement.' She sees his eyes widen, and shakes her head. 'I didn't believe it. I knew it was something else. I thought, I don't know, I just . . .'

He notices for the first time that they have an audience. Until now they might have been in a sealed box for all the notice he has taken of their surroundings. Now, though, he sees a bemused desk sergeant, two WPCs clutching paperwork to their bosoms and watching the scene with a kind of maternal glow, two unshaven men slumped in seats against the wall, just waiting.

'Come on, Sammy,' he says. 'Let's go up to my office.'

They were halfway to the Murder Room before he remembered that it was not, perhaps, the most wholesome environment for a teenage girl. The photos on the walls were only the start of it. A sense of humour was needed on a case like the Wolfman, and that sense of humour had begun to manifest itself in cartoons, jokes and mock-ups of newspaper stories either pinned to the noticeboards or taped onto the sides of computer screens. The language could be choice, too, or someone might be overheard in conversation with someone from forensics.

'. . . torn . . . ripped her right . . . kitchen knife, they reckon . . . slit from ear . . . gouged . . . anus . . . nasty bastard . . . makes some of them seem almost human.' Stories were swapped of serial killers past, of suicides scraped from railway lines, of police dogs playing ball with a severed head.

No, definitely not the place for his daughter. Besides, there was always the possibility that Lamb might be there.

Instead, he found a vacant interview room. It had been turned into a temporary cupboard while the investigation continued, filled with empty cardboard boxes, unneeded chairs, broken desk-lamps and computer keyboards, a heavy-looking manual typewriter. Eventually, the computers in the Murder Room would be packed back into the cardboard boxes, the files would be tidied away into dusty stacks somewhere.

For now, the room had a musty, barren feel, but it still boasted a lightbulb hanging from the ceiling, a table and two chairs. On the table sat a glass ashtray full of stubs and two plastic coffee cups containing a layer of green and black mould. On the floor lay a crushed cigarette packet. Rebus kicked the packet beneath some of the stacked chairs.

'It's not much,' he said, 'but it's home. Sit down. Do you want anything?'

She seemed not to understand the question. 'Like what?'

'I don't know, coffee, tea?'

'Diet Coke?'

Rebus shook his head.

'What about Irn-Bru?'

Now he laughed: she was joking with him. He couldn't bear to see her upset, especially over someone as undeserving as Kenny Watkiss.

'Sammy,' he asked, 'does Kenny have an uncle?'

'Uncle Tommy?'

Rebus nodded. 'That's the one.'

'What about him?'

'Well,' said Rebus, crossing his legs, 'what do you know about him?'

'About Kenny's Uncle Tommy? Not a lot.'

'What does he do for a living?'

'I think Kenny said he's got a stall somewhere, you know, in a market.'

Like Brick Lane market? Did he sell false teeth?

'Or maybe he just delivers to market stalls, I can't really remember.'

Delivers stolen goods? Goods given to him by thieves like the one they'd picked up, the one who had pretended to be the Wolfman?

'Anyway, he's got a few bob.'

'How do you know that?'

'Kenny told me. At least, I think he did. Otherwise how would I know?'

'Where does Kenny work, Sammy?'

'In the City.'

'Yes, but for which firm?'

'Firm?'

'He's a courier, isn't he? He must work for a company?'

But she shook her head. 'He went freelance when he had enough regular clients. I remember he said that his boss at the old place was pissed off –' She broke off suddenly and looked up at him, her face going red. She'd forgotten for a moment that she was talking to her father, and not just to some copper. 'Sorry, Dad,' she apologised. 'His boss was angry with him for taking away so much of the trade. Kenny was good, see, he knows all the shortcuts, knows which buildings are which. Some drivers get confused when they can't find some tiny alleyway, or when the numbers on a street don't seem to make sense.' Yes. Rebus had noticed that; how sometimes the street numbers seemed illogical, as though numbers had been skipped. 'But not Kenny. He knows London like the back of his hand.'

Knows London well, the roads, the shortcuts. On a motorbike, you could cut across London in a flash. Tow-paths, alleys – in a flash.

'What kind of bike does he have, Sammy?'

'I don't know. A Kawasaki something-or-other. He's got one that he uses for work, because it's not too heavy, and another he keeps for weekends, a really big bike.'

'Where does he keep them? There can't be too many safe places around the Churchill Estate?'

'There are some garages nearby. They get vandalised, but Kenny's put a reinforced door on. It's like Fort Knox. I keep kidding him about it. It's better guarded than his –' Her voice falls flat. 'How did you know he lives on Churchill?'

'What?'

Her voice is stronger now, curious. 'How did you know Kenny lives on Churchill?'

Rebus shrugged. 'I suppose he told me, that night I met him round at your place.'

She's thinking back, trying to recall the conversation. But there's nothing there, nothing she can latch onto. Rebus is thinking, too.

Like Fort Knox. A handy place to store stolen gear. Or a corpse.

'So,' he says, pulling his chair a little further in to the table. 'Tell me what *you* think has happened. What do you think he's been keeping from you?'

She stared at the table-top, shaking her head slowly, staring, shaking, until finally: 'I don't know.'

'Well, had you fallen out over anything? Maybe you'd been arguing?'

'No.'

'Maybe he was jealous?'

She gave a desperate laugh. 'No.'

'Maybe he had other girlfriends?'

'No!'

When her eyes caught his, Rebus felt a stirring of shame inside him. He couldn't forget that she was his daughter; nor could he forget that he needed to ask her these questions. Somehow he kept swerving between the two, careering into her.

'No,' she repeated softly. 'I'd have known if there was someone else.'

'Friends, then: did he have any close friends?'

'A few. Not many. I mean, he talked about them, but he never introduced me.'

'Have you tried calling them? Maybe one of them knows something.'

'I only know their first names. A couple of guys Kenny grew up with, Billy and Jim. Then there was someone called Arnold. He used to mention him. And one of the other bike messengers, I think his name was Roland or Ronald, something posh like that.'

'Hold on, let me jot these down.' Rebus took notebook and pen from his pocket. 'Right,' he said, 'so that was Billy, Jim. What was the other one?'

'Roland or Ronald or something.' She watched him writing. 'And Arnold.'

Rebus sat back in his chair. 'Arnold?'

'Yes.'

'Did you ever meet Arnold?'

'I don't think so.'

'What did Kenny say about him?'

She shrugged. 'He was just someone Kenny used to bump into. I think he worked the stalls, too. They went for a drink sometimes.'

It couldn't be the same Arnold, could it? Flight's bald sex-offender snitch? What were the chances? Going for a drink? They seemed unlikely supping companions, always supposing it was the same Arnold.

'All right,' Rebus said, closing the notebook. 'Do you have a recent photo of Kenny? A good one, one that's nice and sharp.'

'I can get one. I've got some back at the house.'

'Okay, I'll get someone to drive you home. Give them the picture and they'll bring it back to me. Let's circulate Kenny's description, that's the first thing to do. Meanwhile I'll do some snooping, see what I can come up with.'

She smiled. 'It's not really your patch, is it?'

'No, it's not my patch at all. But sometimes if you look at something, or some place, for too long, you stop seeing what's there. Sometimes it takes a fresh pair of eyes to see what's staring you in the face.' He was thinking of Flight, of the reason Flight had brought him down here. He was thinking, too, of whether he, Rebus, could muster enough clout to organise a search for Kenny Watkiss. Maybe not without Flight to back him up. No, what was he thinking of? This was a missing person, for Christ's sake. It had to be investigated. Yes, but there were ways and ways of investigating, and he could count on no preferential treatment, no favours, when it came to the crunch. 'I don't suppose,' he asked now, 'you know whether or not his bikes are still in the garage?'

'I took a look. They're both still there. That was when I started to get worried.'

'Was there anything else in the garage?' But she wasn't listening to him.

'He hardly ever goes anywhere without a bike. He hates buses and stuff. He said he was going to name his big bike after . . . after me.'

The tears came again. This time he let her cry, though it hurt him more than he could say. Better out than in, wasn't that how the cliché went? She was blowing her nose when the door opened. Flight looked into the small room. His eyes said it all: *you might have taken her somewhere better than this.*

'Yes, George? What can I do for you?'

'After you left the lab,' the pause showed displeasure at not having been informed or left a message, 'they gave me a bit more gen on the letter itself.'

'I'll be with you in a minute.'

Flight nodded but directed his attention to Samantha. 'Are you okay, love?'

She sniffed. 'Fine, thanks.'

'Well,' he said archly, 'if you *do* want to register a complaint against Inspector Rebus, see the desk sergeant.'

'Ach, get away, George,' said Rebus.

Sammy was trying to giggle and blow her nose at the same time, and making a bit of a mess of both. Rebus winked towards Flight who, having done as much as he could (and for which Rebus was grateful), was now retreating.

'You're not all bad, are you?' said Samantha when Flight had gone.

'What do you mean?'

'Policemen. You're not all as bad as they say.'

'You're a copper's daughter, Sammy. Remember that. And you're a *straight* copper's daughter. Be sure to stick up for your old dad. Okay?'

She smiled again. 'You're not old, Dad.'

He smiled, too, but did not reply. In truth, he was basking in the compliment, whether it was mere flattery or no. What mattered was that Sammy, his daughter Sammy, had said it.

'Right,' he said at last, 'let's get you into a car. And don't worry, pet, we'll track down your missing beau.'

'You called me pet again.'

'Did I? Don't tell your mother.'

'I won't. And, Dad?'

'What?' He half-turned towards her just in time to receive her peck on the cheek.

'Thanks,' she said. 'Whatever happens, thanks.'

Flight was in the small office of the Murder Room. After the close confines of the interview cupboard, this space had suddenly taken on a new, much larger dimension. Rebus sat himself down and swung one leg over the other.

'So what's this about the Wolfman letter?' he said.

'So,' replied Flight, 'what's this about Kenny Watkiss disappearing?'

'You tell me yours and I'll tell you mine.'

Flight picked up a folder, opened it, took out three or four closely typed sheets of paper, and began to read.

'Typeface used is Helvetica. Unusual for personal correspondence, though used by newspapers and magazines.' Flight looked up meaning-fully.

'A reporter?' Rebus said doubtfully.

'Well, think about it,' said Flight. 'Every crime reporter in England knows about Lisa Frazer by now. They could probably find out where she lives, too.'

Rebus considered this. 'Okay,' he said at last, 'go on.'

'Helvetica can be found on some electronic typewriters and electric golfball machines, but is more commonly found on computers and word processors.' Flight glanced up. 'This would correlate with density of type. The type itself is of very even quality . . . blah, blah, blah. Also, the letters line up neatly, suggesting that a good quality printer has been used, probably a daisywheel, suggesting in turn the use of a high quality word processor or word-processing package. However,' Flight went on, 'the letter K becomes faint towards the tips of its stem.' Flight paused to turn the page. Rebus wasn't really paying a great deal of attention as yet, and neither was George Flight. Labs always came up with more information than was useful. So far, all Rebus had really been hearing was the chaff.

'This is more interesting,' Flight went on. 'Inside the envelope particles were found which appear to be flecks of paint, yellow, green and orange predominating. Perhaps an oil-based paint: tests are still continuing.'

'So we've got a crime reporter who fancies himself as Van Gogh?'

Flight wasn't rising to the bait. He read through the rest of the report quickly to himself. 'That's pretty much it,' he said. 'What's left is more to do with what they failed to find: no prints, no stains, no hair or fibres.'

'No personalised watermark?' Rebus asked. In detective novels, the personalised watermark would lead to a small family business run by an eccentric old man, who would recall selling the paper to someone called . . . And that would be it: crime solved. Neat, ingenious, but it seldom happened like that. He thought of Lisa again; of Cousins. No, not Cousins: it couldn't be Cousins. And besides, he wouldn't try anything with those two gorillas in attendance.

'No personalised watermark,' Flight was saying. 'Sorry.'

'Oh well,' Rebus offered, with a loud sigh, 'we're no further forward, are we?'

Flight was looking at the report, as though willing something, some clue, to grab his attention. Then: 'So what's all this about Kenny Watkiss?'

'He's scarpered under mysterious circumstances. Good riddance, I'd say, but it's left Sammy in a bit of a state. I said we'd do what we could.'

'You can't get involved, John. Leave it to us.'

'I don't want to get involved, George. This one's all yours.' The voice seemed ingenuous enough, but Flight was long past being fooled by John Rebus. He grinned and shook his head.

'What do you want?' he asked.

'Well,' said Rebus, leaning forward in his chair, 'Sammy did mention one of Kenny's associates. Someone called Arnold who worked on a market stall, at least she thinks he works in or around a market.'

'You think it's my Arnold?' Flight thought it over. 'It's possible.'

'Too much of a coincidence, you think?'

'Not in a city as small as this.' Flight saw the look on Rebus's face. 'I'm being serious, actually. The small-time crooks, they're like a little family. If this was Sicily, you could cram every small-timer in London into a village. Everybody knows everybody else. It's the big-timers we can't pin. They keep themselves too much to themselves, never go down the pub shooting their mouths off after a couple of Navy Rums.'

'Can we talk to Arnold?'

'What for?'

'Maybe he knows something about Kenny.'

'Even supposing he does, why should he tell us?'

'Because we're police officers, George. And he's a member of the public. We're here to uphold law and order, and it's his duty to help us in that onerous task.' Rebus was reflective. 'Plus I'll slip him twenty quid.'

Flight sounded incredulous. 'This is London, John. A score can hardly get a round of drinks. Arnold gives good gen, but he'll be looking for a pony at least.' Now he was playing with Rebus, and Rebus, realising it, smiled.

'If Arnold wants a pony,' he said, 'tell him I'll buy him one for Christmas. And a little girl to sit on it. Just so long as he tells me what he knows.'

'Fair enough,' said Flight. 'Come on then, let's go find ourselves a street market.'

The Gallery

Flight was struggling with half a dozen large brown-paper bags, the fruits – literally – of asking for Arnold at three or four market stalls so far. Rebus had refused the offers of free bananas, oranges, pears and grapes, though Flight had prodded him to accept.

'It's a local custom,' Flight said. 'They get annoyed if you don't accept. Like a Glaswegian offering you a drink. Would you turn it down? No, because then you'd offend him. Same with these guys.'

'What would I do with three pounds of bananas?'

'Eat them,' said Flight blandly. Then, cryptically: 'Unless you were Arnold, of course.'

He refused to explain the meaning of this, and Rebus refused to consider the various possibilities. They moved from stall to stall, passing most, stopping at only a few. In their way, they were like the women who crushed in all around them, feeling this or that mango or aubergine, checking prices at the various stalls, pausing only at a few to make their final purchases.

''Allo, George.'

'Blimey, George, where you been hiding yourself?'

'All right there, George? How's your love life?'

It seemed to Rebus that half the stall-holders and most of their box- and tray-carrying assistants knew Flight. At one point, Flight nodded behind one of the stalls, where a young man was disappearing rapidly along the street.

'Jim Jessop,' he said. 'He skipped bail a couple of weeks back.'

'Shouldn't we . . .?'

But Flight shook his head. 'Another time, eh, John? The little bugger was three-A's standard in the thousand metres. I don't feel like a run today, what about you?'

'Fair enough,' said Rebus, aware that here, in this place, on this 'patch', he was very much the bystander, the tourist. This was Flight's territory. The man moved confidently through the throng, spoke easily with the various vendors, was in every way quite at home. Eventually, after a chat with the man behind the fresh fish counter, Flight returned with a bag of mussels, another of scallops and information on where Arnold might be found. He led Rebus behind the market stalls onto the pavement and then into a narrow alleyway.

'Moules marinière,' he said, holding up one of the white polythene bags. 'Beautiful. Easy to cook, too. It's the preparation that takes up all the time.'

Rebus shook his head. 'You're full of surprises, George. I'd never have taken you for a cordon bleu.'

Flight just smiled, musing. 'And scallops,' he said, 'Marion loves those. I make a sauce with them and serve it with fresh trout. Again, it's all preparation. The cooking's the easy part.'

He enjoyed showing Rebus this other side of his personality, though he couldn't say why. Nor could he exactly say why he hadn't told John Rebus that Lisa had gone to the Old Bailey; had instead mumbled something about seeing her safely on her way. He thought probably his reasoning had to do with Rebus's spring-loaded emotions: if the Scotsman thought Lisa Frazer was *not* in Flight's place of safety, he'd probably go haring off after her, making a fool of himself 'neath blindfolded Justice herself. And Rebus was still Flight's responsibility, still the liability he always had been, if not more so.

They had come out of the alley onto a small-scale housing estate. The houses looked fairly new, but already the paint was flaking from the window sills. There were cries and squeals from just ahead. A kiddies' playground, concrete surrounded by concrete. A huge section of pipe had become a tunnel, a den, a hiding place. There were swings, too, and a see-saw. And a sand-pit which had become second home to the area's cats and dogs.

The children's imaginations knew few bounds: Pretend you're in hospital, and I'm the doctor; And then the spaceman's ship crashed on the planet; Cowboys don't *have* girlfriends; No, you're chasing *me*, because I'm the soldier and you're the guard; Pretend there isn't a pipe.

Pretend. There was no pretend about the energy they were expending. They couldn't stand still, couldn't pause for breath. They had to yell and jump and get involved. It made Rebus tired just to look at them.

'There he is,' said Flight. He was pointing towards a bench on the edge of the playground. Arnold was sitting there, his back very straight, hands clasping his knees. He had an intent look on his face, neither happy nor unhappy. The kind of look you sometimes saw at the zoo, when someone was peering into a particular cage or enclosure. It was best described as an interested look. Oh yes, Arnold was interested. It made Rebus's stomach queasy just to watch him. Flight seemed to take it all quite casually. He walked across to the bench and sat down beside Arnold, who turned, his eyes suddenly taking on a hunted, frightened look, his mouth creasing into an O. Then he exhaled noisily.

'It's you, Mister Flight. I didn't recognise you.' He gestured towards the bags. 'Been shopping? That's nice.'

The voice was flat, lacking emotion. Rebus had heard addicts talk like that. Five per cent of their brain was fixed on dealing with the external world, the remaining ninety-five concentrating on other things. Well, he supposed Arnold was a kind of addict too.

'Yes,' said Flight, 'just buying a few bits. You remember Inspector Rebus?'

Arnold followed Flight's eyes, staring up from his bench to where Rebus stood, his body purposely shielding Arnold from the children.

'Oh yes,' Arnold said blandly, 'he was in the car with you the other day, Mr Flight.'

'Well done, Arnold. Yes, that's right. You've got a good memory, haven't you?'

'It pays to have, Mr Flight. That's how I remember all the things I tell you.'

'Actually, Arnold,' Flight slid along the bench until his thigh was almost touching that of the other man. Arnold angled his own legs away from the policeman, his eyes intent on Flight's proximity to him. 'Speaking of memory, maybe you can help me. Maybe you can help Inspector Rebus, too.'

'Yes?' The word was stretched almost to breaking point.

'We were just wondering,' said Flight, 'whether you've seen Kenny lately. Only, he doesn't seem to have been around much, does he? I wondered whether he'd maybe gone on holiday?'

Arnold gazed up with milky, childlike eyes. 'Kenny who?'

Flight laughed. 'Kenny Watkiss, Arnold. Your mate Kenny.'

For a moment, Rebus held his breath. What if it was another Arnold? What if Sammy had got the name wrong? Then Arnold nodded slowly.

'Oh, that Kenny. He's not really a mate, Mr Flight. I mean, I see him now and again.' Arnold stopped, but Flight was nodding, saying nothing, expecting more. 'We have a drink together sometimes.'

'What do you talk about?'

The question was unexpected. 'What do you mean?'

'It's a simple enough question,' said Flight with a smile. 'What do you talk about? I wouldn't have thought the two of you would have much in common.'

'We just, we talk. I don't know.'

'Yes, but what do you talk about? Football?'

'Sometimes, yes.'

'What team does he support?'

'I don't know, Mr Flight.'

'You talk about football with him and yet you don't know what team he supports?'

'Maybe he told me and I forgot.'

Flight looked dubious. 'Maybe,' he agreed. Rebus knew his part in the drama now. Let Flight do the talking. Just keep quiet but look ominous, standing over Arnold like a thundercloud, staring down like an avenger onto that gleaming bald dome of a head. Flight knew exactly what he was doing. Arnold was growing nervous, his body jerking, unable to keep his head still, his right knee bobbing up and down.

'So what else do you talk about? He likes motorbikes, doesn't he?'

'Yes,' Arnold answered, guardedly now, for he knew what was happening to him.

'So do you talk about bikes?'

'I don't like bikes. Too noisy.'

'Too noisy? Yes, you've got a point there.' Flight nodded towards the play area. 'But this place is noisy, too, Arnold, isn't it? Yet you don't seem to mind the noise here. Why's that?'

Arnold turned on him, eyes burning. But Flight was ready with a smile, a smile more serious than any grimace. 'What I mean is,' he went on, 'you like some noises but not others. That's fair, isn't it? But you don't like motorbikes. So what else do you talk about with Kenny?'

'We just *talk*,' said Arnold, his face creased with anguish. 'Gossip, how the city's changing, the East End. This used to be all rows of cottages. There was a field and allotments. The families all used to have picnics on the field. They'd bring tomatoes or potatoes or a cabbage to your mum, saying they grew too much, and the kids would all play in the street. There weren't any Bangladeshis or what have you. Just proper East Enders. Kenny's mum and dad didn't live far from here. Two streets away from where I lived. Course, I was older than him. We never played together or anything.'

'And where did Uncle Tommy live?'

'He was over that way.' Arnold pointed with a finger. He had grown a little more confident now. Reminiscences couldn't do any harm, could they? And to talk freely came as such a relief after the careful duel he'd just gone through. So he opened up to them. The good old days. But between his words, Rebus could see a truer picture, a picture of how the other kids used to beat him up, play tricks on him, of how his father used to lock him in his room, starve him. The family breaking apart. Drifting into petty crime. Painfully shy, unable to form relationships.

'Do you ever see Tommy around?' Flight asked suddenly.

'Tommy Watkiss? Yes, I see him.' Arnold was still basking in the past.

'Does Kenny see him?'

'Of course he does. He works for him sometimes.'

'What? Deliveries, that sort of thing?'

'Deliveries, pick-ups –' Arnold halted, aware of what he was saying. This wasn't the past they were talking about any longer. This wasn't safe.

Flight leaned across so that his nose was almost touching Arnold's. All Arnold could do was lean back against the bench, its hard spars stopping him from escaping.

'Where is he, Arnold?'

'Who? Tommy?'

'You know bloody well who I mean! Kenny! Tell me where he is!'

Rebus half-turned, to see that the children had stopped playing and were watching this grown-up game.

'You going to fight, mister?' one of them called. Rebus shook his head and called back, 'Just pretending.'

Flight still had Arnold pinned to the bench. 'Arnold,' he hissed, 'you know me. I've always played fair by you.'

'I know that, Mr Flight.'

'But I'm *not* pretending. What I'm doing is losing my rag. Everything's going to hell in this city, Arnold, and I'm inclined to just shrug my shoulders and join in. Understand me? Why should I play fair when nobody else does, eh? So I'll tell you what I'm going to do, Arnold. I'm going to have to pull you in.'

'What for?' Arnold was terrified now. He didn't think Flight was playing a game. Rebus had the same feeling; either that or Flight was in line for an Oscar.

'For indecent exposure. You were going to expose yourself to those kids. I saw you getting ready. I saw your dick hanging out of your fly.'

'No, no.' Arnold was shaking his head. 'That's a lie.'

'Previous convictions don't lie, Arnold. Inspector Rebus saw you, too. He saw your prick waving in the air like a cocktail sausage. We both saw you, and that's what we'll tell the judge. Now who's he going to believe, eh? Think about that for a moment. Think about solitary. They'll have to hold you in solitary so the other prisoners don't kick the shit out of you. But that won't stop them pissing in your tea and gobbing in your food. You know the score, Arnold. You've been there. And then one night, you'll hear your door being unlocked, and in they'll come. Maybe the screws, maybe the prisoners. They'll come in and they'll hold you down. One of them'll have a brush-handle, and one'll have a rusty old razor blade, won't they, Arnold? Won't they Arnold?'

But Arnold was trembling too violently to speak, trembling and babbling, bubbles of saliva bursting at either side of his mouth. Flight slid back along the bench away from him, then looked up at Rebus with sad eyes. Rebus nodded solemnly. This wasn't a nice business that they were in, not nice at all. Flight lit a cigarette. Rebus refused one. Two words were bouncing around the inside of John Rebus's skull.

Needs must.

And then Arnold started to talk. And when he had finished, Flight dug into a trouser pocket and drew out a pound coin, which he slapped down on the bench beside his shattered victim.

'There you go, Arnold. Get yourself a cup of tea or something. And stay away from playgrounds, all right?' Flight picked up his carrier-bags, picked out an apple from one, and tossed it into Arnold's lap, causing the man to flinch. Then he picked out another one and began to crunch on it, starting off back towards the market.

Needs must.

Back at HQ Rebus thought about Lisa. He felt the need for some human contact, for something clean and warm and separate from this other world he chose to inhabit, something to wash out his badly soiled mind.

Flight had warned him on the way back – 'no messing about this time, John. Leave it to us. You've got to stay out of it. It would look bad in court, copper with a grudge, that sort of line.'

'But,' Rebus had replied, 'I do have a grudge, George. This guy Kenny might have been shagging my daughter!'

Flight had glanced from the windscreen into Rebus's face, then had looked away.

'I said leave it to us, John. If you can't play it that way, I'll personally see that you go bouncing back down the ranks like a ball down a fucking stairwell. Got that?'

'Loud and clear.'

'It's not a threat, John. It's a promise.'

'And you always keep your promises, George, don't you? You seem to be forgetting something. It's your fault that I'm down here in the first place. You sent for me.'

Flight had nodded. 'And I can send you back just as quick. Is that what you want?'

Rebus had stayed silent, though he knew the answer. Flight knew it too, and smiled at this small triumph. They drove in silence after that, both men tainted by the memory of a playground and of a silent man, hands clasping his knees, staring ahead of him, his thoughts sweet with corruption.

Now Rebus was thinking of Lisa, thinking of how it would feel to take a shower with her, to scrub away a layer of London from them both. Maybe he would ask George again for the secret address. Maybe he could visit her. He remembered a conversation they'd had in bed. He'd asked if he could see her office in University College sometime.

'Sometime,' she'd said. 'Mind you, it's not a very nice room, nothing like those huge antique Oxbridge rooms you see in television dramas. It's a pokey little hole, to be honest. I hate it.'

'I'd still like you to show me around.'

'And I said okay.' She sounded on edge. Why was that? Why had she been so nervous of letting him see her room? Why had the secretary – Millicent, Lisa had called her – been so vague the day Rebus had visited? No, not just vague. Uncooperative. *Downright* uncooperative, now that he thought of it. What the hell was it they were keeping from him? He knew one way he could find out the answer, one sure and certain way. What the hell: Lisa was safe, and he'd been told to stay out of the Watkiss case, so what was stopping him from following up this latest mystery? He got to his feet. The answer was: nothing was stopping him, nothing at all.

'Where are you going?'

It was Flight, yelling at him from an open door as Rebus stalked down the hall.

'It's personal,' Rebus called back.

'I warned you, John! Don't get involved!'

'It's not what you think!' He stopped, turning to face George Flight.
'Well, what is it then?'

'Like I said, George, it's personal, okay?'

'No.'

'Look,' said Rebus, his emotions suddenly getting the better of him,
all those thoughts he'd been keeping on a tight rein – Sammy, Kenny
Watkiss, the Wolfman, the threat against Lisa – all boiling up. He
swallowed, breathing hard. 'Look, George, you've got plenty to keep
you busy, okay?' His finger stabbed at Flight's chest. 'Remember what I
said: it could be a copper. Why don't you do some of your careful,
precious, nit-picking investigation on *that*. The Wolfman could be here
in this building. He could be working on the bloody case, hunting
himself!' Rebus heard his voice growing hysterical and calmed quickly,
regaining control over his vocal chords if nothing else.

'A sort of wolf in the fold, you mean?'

'I'm serious.' Rebus paused. 'He might even know where you've sent
Lisa.'

'For Christ's sake, John, only three people know where Lisa's going.
Me, and the two men I sent with her. Now you don't know those guys,
but I do. We go back all the way to training college. I'd trust them with
my life.' Flight paused. 'Will you trust me?'

Rebus said nothing. Flight's eyes narrowed disbelievingly, and he
whistled. 'Well,' he said, 'that certainly answers my question.' He shook
his head slowly. 'This case, John. I've been in the force God knows how
many years, but this case, it's the worst. It's like every victim was
somebody close to me.' He paused again, gathering strength. Now his
finger jabbed at Rebus. 'So don't you *dare* think what I know you're
thinking! It's the ultimate fucking insult!'

There was a long silence in the corridor. Typewriters chattered
somewhere. Male voices were raised in laughter. A hummed tune
floated down the hall towards and past them. It was as though the
whole world were indifferent to this quarrel. And there they stood, not
quite friends, not quite enemies, and not quite sure what to do any
more.

Rebus studied the scuff marks on the linoleum. Then: 'Lecture over?'

Flight seemed pained by this response. 'It wasn't a lecture, it was just
. . . I want you to see my side of things.'

'But I do, George, I do.' Rebus patted Flight's arm and turned away
from him again. He started to walk.

'I want you to stay here, John!' Walking. 'Do you hear me? I'm *ordering* you not to go.'

Rebus kept walking.

Flight shook his head. He'd had enough, absolutely up to his eyes, so that they stung now, stung as though he were in a smoky room. 'You're out on your ear, Rebus,' he called, knowing this to be the final warning. If Rebus kept walking now, Flight would be compelled to keep his word or else lose face, and he was damned if he'd lose face for a hard-headed Jock copper. 'Just keep walking!' he yelled. 'Keep walking and you're finished!'

Rebus walked. He didn't know exactly why, perhaps more out of pride than anything else. Stupid pride, pride he couldn't explain, but pride all the same. The same emotion that made grown men cry at football matches when *Flower of Scotland* was played as the Scots national anthem. All he knew was that he had something to do, and he would do it, like the Scots knew their job was to be footballers with more ambition than ability. Yes, that was him all right: more ambition than ability. They'd put it on his gravestone.

At the end of the corridor, he shoved open the swing doors. He didn't look back. Flight's voice followed him, trailing off as it grew in anger.

'Damn you, you stupid Jock bastard! You've bitten off more than you can chew this time, do you hear me? More than you can bloody well chew.'

FYTP.

Rebus was moving through the entrance hall when he came face to face with Lamb. He made to move past him, but Lamb placed a hand on Rebus's chest.

'Where's the fire?' he said. Rebus was trying to ignore him, was trying to make Lamb invisible. The last thing he needed now was this. His knuckles tingled with anticipation. Lamb was still talking, apparently oblivious to the danger he was in.

'She found you then, your daughter?'

'What?'

Lamb was smiling. 'She phoned here first, and they put her on to me. She sounded a bit upset, so I gave her the lab's number.'

'Oh.' Rebus could feel himself deflating. He managed a grudged 'thanks' and this time succeeded in moving around Lamb. But then Lamb spoke again.

'She sounded a bit tasty though. I like them young. How old is she again?'

Rebus's elbow shot back into Lamb's unprotected stomach, cutting off breath, doubling him over. Rebus studied his work; not bad for an old man. Not bad at all.

He walked.

Because he's on personal business, he stands outside the station and looks for a cab. One of the uniformed officers, who knows him from the scene of Sunday's murder, offers a lift in a patrol car, but Rebus shakes his head. The officer looks at him as if an insult has just been traded.

'Thanks anyway,' says Rebus, trying to sound conciliatory. But all he sounds is mad. Mad with Lamb, with himself, mad with the Wolfman case, mad with Kenny bloody Watkiss, mad with Flight, with Lisa (why did she have to be in Copperplate Street in the first place?) and, most of all, mad with London. Where are all the cabs, all the greedy black cabs, beetling like insects as they try to pick up fares? He's seen thousands of them this past week, but now that he needs one, they're all avoiding him. He waits anyway, eyes slightly unfocussed. And as he waits, he thinks, and as he thinks he calms a little.

What the hell is he doing anyway? He's asking for trouble doing this. He's *begging* for it, like a black-clothed Calvinist pleading to be beaten for his sins. A lash across the back. Rebus had seen them all, all the available religions. He had tasted them and each one tasted bitter in its own particular way. Where was the religion for those who did not feel guilty, did not feel shame, did not regret getting angry or getting even, or, better yet, getting more than even? Where was the religion for a man who believed that good and bad must coexist, even within the individual? Where was the religion for a man who believed in God but not in God's religion?

And where were all the bloody taxis?

'Sod it then.' He walked up to the first patrol car he saw and tapped on the window, flashing his ID.

'Inspector Rebus,' he announced. 'Can you give me a lift to Gower Street?'

The building seemed as deserted as ever and Rebus feared that on this occasion perhaps even the secretary might have scarpered for an early start to the weekend. But no, she was there, like the retainer of some dusty mansion. He cleared his throat, and she looked up from her crochet.

'Yes?' she said. 'Can I help you?' She appeared not to remember him. Rebus brought out his ID and pushed it towards her.

'Detective Inspector Rebus,' he said, his voice stiff with authority. 'Scotland Yard. I want to ask you a few questions about Dr Frazer.'

The woman looked frightened. Rebus feared he had overdone the menace. He tried a don't-worry-it's-not-you-we're-interested-in sort of smile, a peaceable smile. But the woman looked no less afraid, and her fear flustered her.

'Oh, gracious,' she stammered. 'Oh my, oh my.' She looked up at him. 'Who did you say? Dr Frazer? But there's no Dr Frazer in the Department.'

Rebus described Lisa Frazer. The woman suddenly raised her head, recognising the description.

'Oh, Lisa? You mean Lisa? But there's some mistake. Lisa Frazer isn't a member of staff here. Gracious me, no. Though I believe she *may* have taken a tutorial or two, just filling in. Oh dear, Scotland Yard. What, I mean, surely she hasn't . . . What has she done?'

'She doesn't work here?' Rebus needed to be certain. 'Then who is she?'

'Lisa? She's one of our research students.'

'A *student*? But she's –' He was about to say 'old'.

'A mature student,' the secretary explained. 'Oh dear, is she in trouble?'

'I came here before,' Rebus said. 'You didn't tell me any of this then. Why?'

'Came here before?' She studied his face. 'Yes, I remember. Well, Lisa made me promise not to tell anyone.'

'Why?'

'Her project, she said. She's doing a project on, now, what is it exactly?' She opened a drawer of her desk and pulled out a sheet of paper. 'Ah yes, "The Psychology of the Investigation of Serious Crime". She explained it to me. How she needed access to a police investigation. How she needed to gain trust. The courts, police and so on. She told me she was going to pretend to be a lecturer. I told her not to, I warned her, but she said it was the only way. The police wouldn't waste time with a mere student, would they?'

Rebus was stuck for an answer. The answer was no, they wouldn't. Why should they?

'So she got you to cover for her?'

The woman shrugged. 'Lisa is quite a persuasive young woman. She said probably I wouldn't have to tell lies. I could just say things like she's not here, she's not teaching today, that sort of thing. Always supposing anyone bothered to check up on her.'

'And has anybody checked up on her?'

'Oh yes. Why, only today I had a telephone call from someone she had arranged to interview. He wanted to be sure that she really was part of University College, and not just a journalist or a Nosey Parker.'

Today? An interview today. Well, that was one appointment she wouldn't be keeping.

'Who was this person?' Rebus asked. 'Do you remember?'

'I think I wrote it down,' she said. She lifted the thick notepad beside her telephone and flipped through it. 'He did say who he was, but I can't remember. It was at the Old Bailey. Yes, that's right. She'd arranged to meet him at the Old Bailey. I usually write these things down as soon as someone mentions their name, just in case I forget later. No, there's no sign of it. That's funny.'

'Perhaps in the bin?' Rebus suggested.

'Well, perhaps.' But she sounded doubtful. Rebus lifted the small wicker paper-basket onto her desk and sifted through it. Pencil shavings and sweet-wrappers, an empty polystyrene coffee cup and crumpled bits of paper. Lots of bits of paper.

'Too big,' she would say as he started to uncrumple one, or: 'too small.' Until finally, he pulled out a sheet and spread it out on the desk. It was like some bizarre work of art, filled with doodles and hieroglyphs and little notes, phone numbers, names, addresses.

'Ah,' she said, sliding a finger over to one corner where something had been written in very faint, wavering pencil. 'Is that it?'

Rebus looked closer. Yes, that was it. That was most definitely it. 'Thank you,' he said.

'Oh dear,' said the secretary. 'Have I got her into trouble? Is Lisa in trouble? What has she done, Inspector?'

'She lied to us,' said Rebus. 'And because of that, she's ended up having to go into hiding.'

'Hiding? Gracious, she didn't mention anything about that.'

Rebus was beginning to suspect that the secretary was a couple of keys short of a typewriter. 'Well,' he said, 'she didn't know she was in trouble until today.'

The secretary was nodding. 'Yes, but she only phoned a little over an hour ago.'

Rebus's face creased into an all-over frown. 'What?'

'Yes, she said she was calling from the Old Bailey. She wanted to know if there were any messages for her. She told me she had time to kill before her second appointment.'

Rebus didn't bother to ask. He dialled quickly, the receiver gripped in his hand like a weapon. 'I want to talk to George Flight.'

'Just a minute, please.' The ch-ch-ch-ch of a re-routing. Then: 'Murder Room, Detective Sergeant Walsh speaking.'

'It's Inspector Rebus here.'

'Oh yes?' The voice had become as rudimentary as a chisel.

'I need to speak to Flight. It's urgent.'

'He's in a meeting.'

'Then get him out! I told you, this is urgent.'

There was doubt, cynicism in the Sergeant's voice. Everyone knew that the Scotsman's 'urgent' wasn't worth its weight in breath. 'I can leave a message —'

'Don't fuck me around, Walsh! Either get him, or put me on to someone with a spare brain they're not sitting on!'

Ca-click. Brrrrr. The ultimate put-down. The secretary was staring at Rebus in horror. Perhaps psychologists never got angry. Rebus attempted a reassuring smile, but it came out like a clown's drunken greasepaint. He made a bowing motion before turning to leave, and was watched all the way out to the stairwell by a woman mortified almost to the core of her being.

Rebus's face was tingling with a newly stoked anger. Lisa Frazer had tricked him, played him like a fool. Christ, the things he'd told her. Thinking she wanted to help with the Wolfman case. Not realising he was merely part of her project. Christ, the things he had said. What had he said? Too much to recall. Had she been taping everything? Or simply jotting things down after he'd left? It didn't matter. What mattered was that he had seen in her something solid and believable amidst a sea of chaos. And she had been Janus. Using him. Jesus Christ, she had even slept with him. Was that, too, part of the project, part of her little experiment? How could he ever be sure it wasn't? It had seemed genuine enough, but . . . He had opened his mind to her, as she had opened her body to him. It was not a fair exchange.

'The bitch!' he exploded, stopping dead. 'The lying little bitch!'

Why hadn't she told him? Why hadn't she just explained everything? He would have helped her, he would have found time for her. No, he wouldn't. It was a lie. A research student? A project? He would have shown her the door. Instead he had listened to her, had believed her, had learned from her. Yes, it was true. He had learned a lot from her. About psychology, about the mind of the killer. Had learned from her books. Yes, but that wasn't the point. The point was that it had all become crass and diluted, now that he knew her for what she was.

'Bitch.' But his voice was softer, his throat tightening, as though a hand had slid around it and was slowly applying pressure. He swallowed hard, and began to take deep breaths. Calm down, John. What did it matter? What did any of it matter? It mattered, he answered himself, because he felt something for her. Or had felt something for her. No, still did feel something. Something he thought might have been returned.

'Who are you trying to kid?' Look at him, overweight and in his forties. Stuck at Inspector level and going nowhere except, if Flight carried out his promise, down. Divorced. A daughter distraught and mixing with darkness. Someone in London with a kitchen knife and a secret and a knowledge of Lisa. It was all wrong. He'd been clutching at Lisa the way drowning men reached out for a thin snap of straw. Stupid old man.

He stood at the main door to the building, not really sure now. Should he confront her, or let it go, never see her again? Usually he relished confrontation, found it nourishing and exciting. But today, maybe not.

She was at the Old Bailey to interview Malcolm Chambers. He, too, was at this moment being tricked by her mock credentials, by that falsely prefixed 'Doctor'. Everyone admired Malcolm Chambers. He was smart, he was on the side of the law, and he made pots of money. Rebus had known coppers who were none of these; most could score only one out of three, a few managed two. Chambers would sweep Lisa Frazer off her feet. She would loathe him, until that loathing mingled with awe, and then she'd probably think that she loved him. Well, good luck to her.

He'd head back to the station, say his farewells, pack his bags, and head north. They could get along without him very well. The case was heading nowhere until the Wolfman bit again. Yet they had so much now, knew so much about him, had come so close to opening him up like a soft fat peach. Maybe he'd bite Lisa Frazer. What the hell was she doing at the Old Bailey when she should be in hiding? He needed to speak to Flight. What the hell was Flight up to anyway?

'Ach, to hell with the lot of you,' he muttered, plunging his hands into his pockets.

Two students, their voices loudly American, were heading towards him. They seemed excited, the way students always did, discussing this or that concept, ready to change the way the world thought. They wanted to get past, wanted to go into the building. He moved aside for them, but they didn't so much move past him as *through* him, as though he were insubstantial as exhaust fumes.

'Like, y'know, I think she likes me, but I'm not sure I'm ready for something like –'

So much for difficult concepts, thought Rebus. Why should students be different from anyone else in the population? Why should they be thinking (and talking), about something other than sex?

'Yeah,' said the other one. Rebus wondered how comfortable he felt in his thick white T-shirt and thicker checked lumberjack shirt. The day was sticky. 'Yeah,' the American repeated. His accent reminded Rebus of Lisa's softer Canadian tones.

'But get this,' continued his companion, their voices fading as they moved deeper into the building, 'she *says* her mother hates Americans because one of them near raped her in the war.'

Get this. Where had Rebus heard that expression before? He fumbled in his jacket pocket and found a folded piece of paper. Unfolded it and began to read.

'GET THIS, I'M NOT HOMOSEXUL, O.K.?' It was the photocopy of the Wolfman's letter to Lisa.

Get this. It did have a transatlantic ring to it, didn't it? A curious way altogether of starting a letter. Get this. Be warned, watch out. There were several ways of starting a letter so that the reader knew he was to pay particular attention to it. But *get this*?

What did they know, or what did they suspect, about the Wolfman? He knew about police procedure (past offender, copper, both were possible). He was a he, if Jan Crawford were to be believed. He was quite tall, she thought. In the restaurant, Lisa Frazer had added her own ideas: he was conservative; most of the time he not only seemed normal, he was normal; he was, in her phrase, 'psychologically mature'. And he had posted a letter to Lisa from EC4. EC4, wasn't that where the Old Bailey was? He recalled his first and only visit to the building. The courtroom, and seeing Kenny Watkiss there. Then meeting Malcolm Chambers. What was it Chambers had said to George Flight?

Royally shafted. Own team. I don't like. Flight, I don't like being royally shafted . . . own team . . . get this. Get this, George.

Jesus Christ! Every ball on the table suddenly fell into a pocket until only the cue ball and the black were left. Every single ball.

'Get this, George, I don't like being royally shafted by my own team.'

Malcolm Chambers had studied in the USA for a while. Flight had told Rebus that. You tended to pick up mannerisms when you wanted to fit into a new and strange place. *Get this.* Rebus had tried to avoid the temptation in London, but it was strong. Studied in the USA. And now he was with Lisa Frazer. Lisa the student, Lisa the psychologist, Lisa with her photo in the newspapers. *Get this.* Oh, how the Wolfman must hate her. She was a psychologist after all and the psychologists had pronounced him gay, they had insights into what was wrong with him. He didn't think anything was wrong with him. But something was. Something that was slowly taking him over.

Old Bailey was in EC4. The Wolfman, rattled, had slipped up and posted his letter from EC4.

It was Malcolm Chambers, Malcolm Chambers was the Wolfman. Rebus couldn't explain it, couldn't exactly justify it, but he knew it all the same. It was like a dark polluted wave rolling over him, anointing him. Malcolm Chambers. Someone who knew about police procedure, someone above suspicion, someone so clean you had to scratch beneath the skin to find the filth.

Rebus was running. He was running along Gower Street in what he hoped was the right direction for the City. He was running and he was craning his neck to seek out a taxi. There was one ahead of him, at the corner beside the British Museum, but it was picking up a fare. Students or tourists. Japanese. Grins and cameras. Four of them, two men, two young women. Rebus stuck his head into the back of the cab, where two of them were already seated.

'Out!' he yelled, jerking a thumb towards the pavement.

'Oi, mate, what's your game?' The driver was so fat he could barely turn in his seat.

'I said out!' Rebus grabbed an arm and pulled. Either the young man was surprisingly light, or else Rebus had found hidden strength, for the body fairly flew from its seat, uttering a string of high-pitched comment as it went.

'And you.'

The girl followed obligingly and Rebus hurled himself into the cab, slamming shut the door.

'Drive!' he yelled.

'I'm not moving till I —'

Rebus shoved his ID against the window separating the back seats of the taxi from the front.

'Inspector Rebus!' he called. 'This is an emergency. I need to get to the Old Bailey. Break every traffic law you like, I'll sort it out later. But get your fucking skates on!'

The driver responded by switching his headlights on full beam before setting out into the traffic.

'Use your horn!' Rebus called. The driver did so. A surprising number of cars eased out of his way. Rebus was on the edge of his seat, gripping it with both hands to stop himself being thrown about. 'How long will it take?'

'This time of day? Ten or fifteen minutes. What's the matter, guv? Can't they start without you?'

Rebus smiled sourly. That was just the problem. Without him, the Wolfman could start whenever he liked. 'I need to use your radio,' he said. The driver slid his window further open.

'Be my guest,' he said, pulling the small microphone up towards Rebus. He'd worked on the cabs for twenty-odd years, but he'd never had a fare like this.

In fact, he was so excited, they were halfway there before he remembered to switch on the meter.

Rebus had told Flight as much as he could, trying not to sound hysterical. Flight sounded dubious about the whole thing, but agreed to send men to the Old Bailey. Rebus didn't blame George Flight for being wary. Hard to justify arresting a pillar of society on the strength of a gut feeling. Rebus remembered what else Lisa Frazer had said about serial killers: that they were products of their environments; that their ambitions had been thwarted, leading them to kill members of the social group above them. Well, that certainly wasn't true in Malcolm Chambers's case, was it? And what had she said about the Wolfman? His attacks were 'non-confrontational', so perhaps he was like that in his working life. Hah! So much for theory. But now Rebus began to doubt his own instincts. Jesus, what if he *was* wrong? What if the theory was right? He was going to look more than a little psychologically disturbed himself.

Then he recalled something George Flight had said. You could build up as neat a picture as you liked of the killer, but it wouldn't give you a name and address. Psychology was all well and good, but you couldn't beat a good old-fashioned hunch.

'Nearly there, guv.'

Rebus tried to keep his breathing regular. Be calm, John, be calm. However, there were no police cars waiting by the entrance to the Old Bailey. No sirens and armed officers, just people milling around, people finishing work for the day, people sharing a joke. Rebus left the cab driver unpaid and untipped – 'I'll settle later' – and pushed open the heavy glass door. Behind more bulletproof glass stood two security personnel. Rebus stuck his ID in front of their noses. One of them pointed towards the two vertical glass cylinders by which people were admitted to the building one at a time. Rebus went to one cylinder and waited. Nothing happened. Then he remembered, pushed the heel of his hand against the button and the cylinder door opened. He walked in, and waited for what seemed an eternity while the door slid shut behind him, before the door in front slid just as slowly open.

Another guard stood beside the metal detection equipment. Rebus, still holding open his ID, walked quickly past until he found himself behind the bulletproof glass of the reception area.

'Can I help?' said one of the security men.

'Malcolm Chambers,' said Rebus. 'He's a barrister. I need to see him urgently.'

'Mr Chambers? Hold on, I'll just check.'

'I don't want him to know I'm here,' Rebus warned. 'I just want to know where I can find him.'

'Just one moment.' The guard moved off, consulting with one of his companions, then slowly going through a sheet of paper attached to a clipboard. Rebus's heart was pounding. He felt like he was about to explode. He couldn't just stand here. He had to *do* something. Patience, John. Less haste, more speed, as his father had always said. But what the hell did that mean anyway? Surely haste was a kind of speed?

The guard was coming back.

'Yes, Inspector. Mr Chambers has a young lady with him at present. I'm told they're sitting together upstairs.'

Upstairs meant the concourse outside the courtrooms. Rebus flew up the imposing flight of steps two at a time. Marble. There was a lot of marble around him. And wood. And glass. The windows seemed huge. Bewigged counsels came down a spiral staircase, deep in conversation. A frayed-looking woman smoked a cheap cigarette as she waited for someone. It was a quiet pandemonium. People were moving past Rebus, moving in the opposite direction from him. Juries, finished for the day. Solicitors and guilty-looking clients. The woman rose to greet her son. The son's solicitor had a bored, drawn look. The concourse was emptying rapidly, the stairs taking people down to more glass cylinders and to the outside world.

About thirty yards from where Rebus stood, the two men were sitting, legs crossed, enjoying a cigarette. The two men Flight had sent with Lisa. Her bodyguards. Rebus ran to them.

'Where is she?'

They recognised him, seemed to realise immediately that something was wrong, and rose to their feet.

'She's interviewing some barrister –'

'Yes, but *where*?'

The man nodded towards one of the courtrooms. Court Eight! Of course: hadn't Cousins been due to give evidence in Court Eight? And wasn't Malcolm Chambers the prosecuting counsel?

Rebus pushed through the doors into the courtroom, but, cleaners apart, it was completely empty. There had to be another exit. Of course there was: the green padded door to the side of the jury-box. The door leading to the judges' rooms. He ran across the court and up the steps to the door, pulling it open, finding himself in a bright carpeted corridor. A window, flowers in a pot on a table. A narrow corridor, doors only on one side, the other wall a blank. Judges' names above the doors. The doors themselves locked. There was a tiny kitchenette, but it too was empty. One door eventually gave, and he peered into a jury room. Empty. Back into the corridor again, hissing now with frustration. A court usher, cradling a mug of tea, was coming towards him.

'No one's allowed –'

'Inspector Rebus,' he said. 'I'm looking for an advocate . . . I mean, a barrister. Malcolm Chambers. He was here with a young woman.'

'They've just left.'

'Left?'

She gestured along towards the far end of the corridor. 'It leads to the underground car park. That's where they were headed.' Rebus made to squeeze past her. 'You won't catch them now,' she said. 'Not unless they're having trouble with the car.'

Rebus thought about it, gnawing at his bottom lip. There wasn't time. His first decision had to be the right one. Decision made, he turned from the usher and ran back towards the court, back across the court itself and out into the concourse.

'They've gone!' he yelled to the bodyguards. 'Tell Flight! Tell him they're in Chambers's car!' And then he was off again, down the steps towards the exit, pausing only to grab at a security man's sleeve. 'The car park exit, where is it?'

'Round the other side of the building.'

Rebus stuck a finger in the guard's face. 'Buzz down to the car park. Don't let Malcolm Chambers leave.' The guard stood there dumbly, staring at the finger. *Do it!'*

And then he was off again, running, taking the stairs down three at a time, great leaps which almost sent him flying. He pushed his way to the front of the crowd waiting to leave.

'Police,' he said, 'emergency.' Nobody said anything. They were like cows, patiently waiting to be milked. Even so, it took a silent scream of an age for the cylinder to empty its cargo, close its doors, then open them again for Rebus.

'Come on, come on.' And then the door sucked itself open and he was out, out in the foyer, bursting through the main doors. He ran up to the corner, took a right, and ran again along the face of the building. Another right. He was on the other side of the building now. Where the car park exit was. A slope of road down into darkness. The car screeched as it came to the surface, hardly slowing as it climbed the hill to Newgate Street. It was a long gloss-black BMW. And in the passenger seat sat Lisa Frazer, looking relaxed, smiling, talking to the driver, not realising.

'Lisa!' But he was too far away, the traffic around him too loud. 'Lisa!' Before he could reach it, the car had turned into a flow of traffic and disappeared. Rebus cursed under his breath. Then looked around him for the first time and saw that he was standing next to a parked Jaguar, in the front of which sat a liveried chauffeur, staring out of the window at him. Rebus yanked at the doorhandle and threw open the door, reaching in with one hand to pull out the bemused driver. He was getting to be a dab hand at this: relieving people of their vehicles.

'Hoi! What the bleedin' 'ell —'

The man's cap rolled along the ground, given force by a gust of wind. For a moment, he knelt on the pavement, undecided whether to rescue the cap or the car. The moment was enough. Rebus gunned the engine and pulled away from the kerb, horns sounding behind him as he did so. At the top of the slight incline, he pressed his hand hard on the horn and careered left into the main road. A squeal of brakes. More horns. The pedestrians looking at him as though he were mad.

'Need lights,' he said to himself, glancing at the dashboard. Eventually, he found the headlamp switch and flipped them to full beam. Then took a hard right to bring himself into the middle of the road, passing the traffic, scraping the passenger side against an oncoming red bus, clipping a central bollard, uprooting the flimsy plastic construction and sending it flying into the path of the oncoming traffic.

They couldn't be too far ahead of him. Yes! He caught a glimpse of the BMW's tail-lights as it braked to turn a corner. He'd be damned if they'd lose him.

'Excuse me?'

Rebus flinched, startled, and nearly pulled the car onto the pavement. He looked in the rear-view mirror and saw an elderly gentleman sitting in the back seat, arms spread so as to keep himself upright. He appeared calm as he leaned forward towards Rebus.

'Would you kindly mind telling me what's going on? Am I being kidnapped?'

Rebus recognised the voice before he remembered the face. It was the judge from the Watkiss case. Jesus Christ, he'd run off with a judge!

'Only, if you are kidnapping me,' the judge went on, 'perhaps you'd allow me to call my wife. She'll burn the chops otherwise.'

Call! Rebus looked down again. Below the dashboard, between the driver's and front passenger seats, there was a neat black car-phone.

'Do you mind if I use your phone?' he asked, grinning with a face full of adrenalin.

'Be my guest.'

Rebus grabbed at the contraption and fiddled as he drove, his steering becoming more erratic than ever.

'Press the button marked TRS,' the judge suggested.

'Thank you, your honour.'

'You know who I am? I thought I recognised the face. Have I had you before me recently?'

But Rebus had dialled and was now waiting for the call to be answered. It seemed to take forever. And meantime, the BMW had nipped across an amber traffic light.

'Hold tight,' Rebus said, baring his teeth. The horn was a banshee wail as they pushed past the waiting traffic and flew across the intersection, traffic from left and right braking hard. One car dented the back of another. A motorcycle slewed on the greasy road. But they were across. The BMW was still in sight, less than half a dozen cars ahead now, yet still apparently unaware of the pursuing demon.

Finally, the call was answered.

'It's Rebus here.' Then, for his passenger's sake: 'Detective Inspector Rebus. I need to speak to Flight. Is he there?' There was a long pause. The connection crackled wildly, as though about to short out altogether. Rebus gripped the handset between hunched shoulder and angled cheek, driving with both hands to take first one bend and then another.

'John? Where are you?' Flight's voice sounded metallic and distant.

'I'm in a car,' said Rebus, 'a car I commandeered. I'm following Chambers. He's got Lisa Frazer with him. I don't think she knows he's the Wolfman.'

'But for Christ's sake, John, *is* he the Wolfman?'

'I'll ask him when I catch him. Did you send any cars to the Old Bailey?'

'I sent one, yes.'

'That was generous.' Rebus saw what was ahead. 'Oh shit!' He braked hard, but not hard enough. The old lady was shuffling slowly across the zebra crossing, her shopping trolley a step behind her like a pet poodle. Rebus swerved but couldn't avoid winging the trolley. It flew into the air as though fired from a cannon, dispensing groceries as it went: eggs, butter, flour, cornflakes raining down on the road. Rebus heard the woman screaming. At worst she'd have a broken arm. No, at worst the shock would kill her.

'Oh shit,' he said again.

The judge was staring out of the rear window. 'I think she's all right,' he said.

'John?' It was Flight's tin-can voice on the line. 'Who was that speaking?'

'Oh,' said Rebus. 'That was the judge. It's his Jaguar I've commandeered.' He had found the windscreen wiper switch and was letting them deal with the pancake mixture on the windscreen.

'You *what*?' So that was what a roar sounded like. The BMW was still in sight. But it had slowed a little, perhaps aware of the incident behind it.

'Never mind,' said Rebus. 'Look, just get some patrol cars up here.

We're on . . .' He glanced out of windscreen and side window, but could see no street signs.

'High Holborn,' said the judge.

'Thanks,' said Rebus. 'We're on High Holborn, George.'

'Wait a second,' said Flight. There was a muffled exchange at his end of the line. Then he came back on again. He sounded tired. 'Please, John, tell me it isn't you behind these reports we're getting. The switchboards are lighting up like Christmas trees.'

'That's probably us, George. We took a bollard out a little way back, caused a couple of accidents and now we've just sent an old woman's messages flying everywhere. Yes, that's us.'

If Flight groaned, he did so quietly. Then: 'What if it's not him, John? What if you're wrong?'

'Then it's all a bit of a balls-up, George, and I'll probably get to see what the inside of a dole office looks like, if not a prison cell. Meanwhile, get those coppers down here!' Rebus looked at the handset. 'Judge, help me. How do I –'

'Just press Power.' Rebus did, and the illuminated digits faded. 'Thanks,' he said.

The traffic was slowing, a jam of lights up ahead. 'And,' the judge was saying, 'if you intend using the apparatus again, I should probably inform you that it can be used in hands-free mode. Just dial and leave it in its little compartment there. You'll be able to hear the caller and they'll be able to hear you.' Rebus nodded his thanks. The judge's head was close to Rebus's ear, peering over his shoulder at the road ahead.

'So,' he said excitedly, 'you think Malcolm Chambers is behind all these killings?'

'That's right.'

'And what evidence do you have, Inspector?'

Rebus laughed, and tapped his head. 'Just this, your lordship, just this.'

'Remarkable,' said the judge. He seemed to be considering something. 'I always thought Malcolm was rather an odd young man. Fine in court, of course, very much the star prosecutor, playing to the gallery and what have you. But outside the courtroom, he seemed very different. Oh, very different indeed. Almost sullen, as though his mind were wandering.'

His mind had wandered all right, thought Rebus, wandered all the way over the edge.

577

'Would you like to speak to him?'

'You think I'm chasing him for a bet?'

The judge chuckled, pointing to the car-phone. 'I meant talk to him right now.'

Rebus went rigid. 'You mean you've got his number?'

'Oh yes.'

Rebus thought it over, but shook his head. 'No,' he said. 'He's got someone with him. An innocent woman. I don't want to panic him.'

'I see,' said the judge, settling back again. 'Yes, I suppose you're right. I hadn't thought of that.'

And then there was an electric purring inside the car. It was the phone, its display illuminated now and flashing. Rebus handed the set to the judge.

'Probably for you,' he said drily.

'No,' said the judge, 'just put it back and press Receive.' Rebus did so. Only then did the judge speak. 'Hello?'

The voice was clear, the reception signal strong. 'Edward? Is that you following me?'

It was Chambers's voice, sounding amused about something. The judge stared at Rebus, who could offer no suggestion for an answer.

'Malcolm?' said the judge, his composure intact. 'Is that you?'

'You should know. You're only about twenty yards behind me.'

'Am I? Which road are you on?'

The voice altered, taking on an edge of sudden viciousness. 'Don't fuck with me, Ted! Who's driving the fucking car? Can't be you, you haven't even got a licence. Who is it?'

The judge looked to Rebus again, seeking guidance. They listened together in silence and heard Lisa's faint voice.

'What's going on?' she was saying. 'What's happening?'

Then Chambers's voice. 'Shut up, bitch! You'll get yours.' The voice rose a chilling octave, sounding like a bad female impersonator, making the hairs on Rebus's neck bristle. 'You'll get yours.' Then it dropped again, speaking into the handset. 'Hello? Who's that? Who's there? I can hear you breathing, you little shit.' Rebus bit his lip. Was it better to let Chambers know, or to stay silent? He stayed silent.

'Oh well,' said Chambers with a sigh, as though resigned to this stalemate. 'Out she goes.'

Ahead, Rebus saw the BMW's passenger door swing open as the car veered onto the pavement.

'What are you doing!' screamed Lisa. 'No! No! Let me go!'

'Chambers!' Rebus yelled towards the handset. 'Leave her!' The BMW swerved back into the road, the door drifting shut. There was a pause.

'Hello,' said Chambers's voice. 'To whom am I speaking?'

'My name's Rebus. We met at –'

'John!' It was Lisa's voice, very afraid now, almost hysterical. The sound of the slap was a static crack in Rebus's ear.

'I said leave her!' Rebus yelled.

'I know you did,' said Chambers, 'but then you're hardly in a position to give orders. Anyway, now that I know you two know each other, that makes things interesting, doesn't it, Inspector?'

'You remember me?'

'I have an intimate knowledge of everyone on the Wolfman case. I've taken an interest in it from the start – for obvious reasons. There was always someone around willing to tell what they knew.'

'So you could keep one step ahead?'

'*One* step?' Chambers laughed. 'You flatter yourself. So tell me, Inspector, what do we do now? Do you stop your car – Edward's car, I should say – or do I kill your friend here? Do you know, she wanted to ask *me* about the psychology of court trials. She couldn't have picked better, could she, the little bitch?' Lisa was sobbing. Rebus could hear her, and every sound cut him a little deeper. 'Picture in the paper,' Chambers was cooing. 'Picture in the paper with the big tough detective.'

Rebus knew he had to keep Chambers talking. By keeping him talking, he was keeping Lisa alive. But the traffic had stalled. Red lights ahead. The BMW only a few cars in front, prevented from jumping the lights by another car directly in front of it. Could he . . .? Should he even be thinking of it? The judge was still gripping Rebus's headrest, staring out towards the gleaming black car, the car that was so close to them. So close . . . and so stationary.

'Well?' It was Chambers's voice. 'Do you pull over, Inspector, or do I kill her?'

Rebus was staring hard at Chambers's car. He could see that Lisa was leaning away from Chambers, as though making to escape. But Chambers was gripping her with his left arm, his right presumably resting on the steering-wheel. So the man's attention would be focussed on the passenger side of the car, leaving the driver's side unguarded.

Rebus made up his mind and quietly opened his door, slipping out onto the reassuringly solid surface of the road. Horns were sounding around him. He paid them no heed. The lights were still at red. He began to move forward, crouching, but moving quickly. Chambers's driver's-side mirror! If Chambers looked into it, he'd have a clear view of Rebus's approach. Make it fast, John, make it.

Amber.

Shit!

Green.

He had reached the BMW, had gripped the doorhandle. Chambers looked out at him, a stunned expression on his face. And then the car in front moved off, and Chambers gunned the engine, the car accelerating forwards, tearing itself free of Rebus.

Shit! Car horns all around. Angry. Angry drivers rolling down their windows and yelling at him as he ran back to the Jaguar. Started the car, moved off. The judge's hand patted his shoulder.

'Good try, my boy. Good try.'

And Chambers's laughter on the car-phone. 'Hope I didn't hurt you, Inspector.' Rebus examined his hand, flexed it painfully. The fingers had nearly been pulled out of their joints. His little finger was swelling already. A break? Perhaps.

'So,' said Chambers, 'for the last time I make you an offer you can hardly refuse. Stop the car, or I kill Dr Frazer.'

'She's not a doctor, Chambers. She's just a student.' He swallowed: now Lisa knew that he knew. Not that it mattered one way or the other, not now. He took a deep breath. 'Kill her,' he said. Behind him, the judge gasped, but Rebus shook his head, reassuring him.

'What did you say?' asked Chambers.

'I said kill her. I'm not really bothered. She's led me a merry little dance this past week. It's her own fault she's in this deep. And after you've killed her, I'll take great pleasure in killing you, Mr Chambers.'

He heard Lisa's faint voice again. 'God, John, please no!' And then Chambers, seeming to grow calmer as Rebus grew more excited: 'As you wish, Inspector. As you wish.' The voice was as cold as a mortuary floor, any vestige of humanity gone. Perhaps partly it was Rebus's fault, taunting him with newspaper stories, with fabrications. But Chambers hadn't picked on Rebus: he had picked on Lisa. Had Rebus arrived a minute later at the Old Bailey, she would be on her way to certain death. As it was, nothing was certain.

Nothing but the fact of Malcolm Chambers's madness.

'He's turning onto Monmouth Street,' said the judge, his voice level. He had grasped the fact of Chambers's guilt, the horror of what had happened and what might still happen.

Rebus heard a flapping sound overhead, and glanced up towards where a helicopter was shadowing the chase. A police helicopter. He could hear sirens, too. So, it seemed, could Chambers. The BMW spurted ahead, slashing the side of another car as it squeezed into a space. The injured car stopped dead. Rebus braked, pulled on the steering-wheel, but still clipped it with his driver's-side bumper, the headlamp shattering.

'Sorry about that.'

'Never mind the car,' said the judge. 'Just don't let him get away.'

'He won't get away,' said Rebus, with sudden confidence. Now where the hell had that come from? The moment he thought about it, it disappeared again, leaving behind a quivering vapour.

They were on St Martin's Lane now. People mingling, pre-theatre or after work. The busy West End. Yet the traffic ahead had thinned for no apparent reason and the crowds gawped as first the BMW, then the Jaguar sped past.

As they approached Trafalgar Square Rebus saw, to right and left, police officers in luminous yellow jackets holding up the traffic in the side-streets. Now why would they do that? Unless . . .

Road block! One entrance to the Square left open, all exits blocked, the Square itself kept empty for their arrival. In a moment they'd have him. God bless you, George Flight.

Rebus picked up the handset, his voice a snarl, specks of saliva dotting the windscreen as he spoke.

'Stop the car, Chambers. There's no place to go.'

Silence. They were skidding into Trafalgar Square now, traffic blaring in queues all around them, held back by the gloved, raised hand of authority. Rebus was buzzing again. The whole West End of London, brought to a standstill so that he might race a Jaguar against a BMW. He could think of friends who'd give whole limbs to be in his place. Yet he had a job to do. That was the bottom line. It was just another job to be cleared up. He might as well have been following teenage Cortina thieves through the streets of some Edinburgh housing-scheme.

But he wasn't.

They'd done one full circuit around Nelson's Column. Canada House, South Africa House and the National Gallery were just blurs. The judge was being thrown against the door behind Rebus.

'Hang on,' Rebus called.

'To what, pray?'

And Rebus laughed. He roared with laughter. Then he realised the line was still open to Chambers's BMW. He laughed even harder, picking up the handset, his knuckles white against the steering-wheel, left arm aching.

'Having fun, Chambers?' he yelled. 'Like the TV programme used to say, there's no hiding place!'

And then the BMW gave a jolt, and Rebus heard Chambers gasp.

'You bitch!' Another jolt, and sounds of a struggle. Lisa was retaliating, now that Chambers was intent on this speeding circuit without end.

'No!'

'Get off!'

'I'll —'

And a piercing scream, two piercing screams, both high-pitched, feminine in their intensity, and the black car didn't take the next bend, flew straight for the pavement, mounted it and bounced into a bus shelter, crumpling the metal structure and driving on into the walls of the National Gallery itself.

'Lisa!' Rebus cried. He brought the Jaguar to a sudden, pivoting stop. The driver's door of the BMW creaked open and Chambers stumbled out, slouching off in a half-run, clutching something in his right hand, one leg damaged. Rebus struggled with his own door, finally finding the handle. He ran to the BMW and peered in. Lisa was slumped in the passenger seat, a seatbelt passing in a diagonal across her body. She was groaning, but there were no signs of blood. Whiplash. Nothing more serious than whiplash. She opened her eyes.

'John?'

'You're going to be all right, Lisa. Just hang on. Somebody will be here.' Indeed, the police cars were closing in, uniforms running into the Square. Rebus looked up from the car, seeking Chambers.

'There!' The judge was out of the Jaguar and pointing with a rigid arm, pointing upwards. Rebus followed the line to the steps of the National Gallery. Chambers had reached the top step.

'Chambers!' Rebus yelled. 'Chambers!'

But the body disappeared from view. Rebus started towards the steps, finding his own legs to be less than solid. As though rubber instead of bone and cartilage were keeping him upright. He climbed the steps and entered the building by its nearest door – the exit door.

A woman in a staff uniform was lying on the ground in the foyer, a man standing over her. The man gestured towards the gallery's interior.

'He ran inside!'

And where Malcolm Chambers went, Rebus would surely follow.

* * *

He ran and he ran and he ran.

The way he used to run from his father, running and climbing the steps to the attic, hoping to hide. But always caught in the end. Even if he hid all day and half of the night, eventually the hunger, the thirst, would force him back downstairs, to where they were waiting.

His leg hurts. And he's cut. His face is stinging. The warm blood is trickling down his chin, down his neck. And he's running.

It wasn't all bad, his childhood. He remembers his mother delicately snipping away at his father's nosehairs. 'Long nosehairs are so unbecoming in a man.' It wasn't his fault, was it, any of it? It was theirs. They'd wanted a daughter; they'd never wanted a son. His mother had dressed him in pink, in girls' colours and girls' clothes. Then had painted him, painted him with long blonde curls, imagining him into her paintings, into her landscapes. A little girl running by a riverbank. Running with bows in her hair. Running.

Past one guard, past two. Lunging at them. The alarm is ringing somewhere. Maybe it's just his imagination. All these paintings. Where have all these paintings come from? Through one door, turn right, through another.

They kept him at home. The schools couldn't teach him the way they could. Home taught. Home made. His father, some nights, drunk, would knock over his mother's canvases and dance on them. 'Art! Fuck art!' He'd do his little dance with a chuckle in his throat and all the time his mother would sit with her face in her hands and cry, then run to her room and bolt shut the door. Those were the nights when his father would stumble through to *his* bedroom. Just for a cuddle. Sweet alcoholic breath. Just for a cuddle. And then more than a cuddle, so very much more. 'Open wide, just like the dentist tells you.' Christ, it hurt so much. A probing finger . . . tongue . . . the wrenching open . . . And even worse was the noise, the dull grunting, the loud nasal breathing. And then the sham, pretending it had been just a game, that was all. And to prove it, his father would bend down and take a big soft bite out of his stomach, growling like a bear. Blowing a raspberry on the bare flesh. And then a laugh. 'You see, it was only a game, wasn't it?'

No, never a game. Never. Running. To the attic. To the garden, to squeeze behind the shed, where the stinging nettles were. Even their bite was not so bad as his father's. Had his mother known? Of course she had known. Once, when he had tried to tell her in a whispered moment, she had refused to listen. 'No, not your father, you're making it up, Malcolm.' But her paintings had grown more violent: the fields now were purple and black, the water blood-red. The figures on the riverbank had grown skeletal, painted stark white like ghosts.

He'd hidden it all so well for so long. But then she'd come back to him. And now he was mostly 'she', consumed by her, and by her need for ... Not revenge, it couldn't really be called revenge. Something deeper than revenge, some huge and hungry need without a name, without a form. Only a function. Oh yes, a function.

This way and that. The people in the gallery make way for him. The alarm is ringing still. There's a hissing in his head like a child's rattle. Sss-sss-sss. Sss-sss-sss. These paintings he is running past, they're laughable. *Long nosehairs Johnny.* None mimicked real life, and less so the life beneath. None could ape the grim caveman thoughts of every human being on the planet. But then he pushes open another door and it's all so very different. A room of darkness and shadowplay, of skulls and frowning bloodless faces. Yes, this is how it is. Velasquez, El Greco, the Spanish painters. Skull and shadow. Ah, Velasquez.

Why couldn't his mother have painted like this? When they died. *(Together, in bed. A gas leak. The police said the child was lucky to be alive. Lucky his own bedroom window had been open a couple of inches.)* When they had died, all he'd taken with him from the house had been her paintings, every single one of them.

'Only a game.'

'Long nosehairs, Johnny.' Snipping with the scissors, his father asleep. He'd pleaded with his eyes, pleaded with her to stick the point of the scissors into his father's fleshy noiseless throat. She'd been so gentle. Snip. So kind and gentle. Snip. *The child was lucky.*

What could they know?

* * *

Rebus walked up the stairs and through the bookshop. Other officers were close behind him. He motioned for them to spread out. There would be no escape. But he also warned them to keep their distance.

Malcolm Chambers was *his*.

The first gallery was large, with red walls. A guard pointed through the doorway on the right and Rebus strode towards it. By the side of the doorway, a painting showed a headless corpse, spouting blood. The painting mirrored Rebus's thoughts so well that he smiled grimly. There were spots of rust-coloured blood on the orange carpet. But even without these, he would have had no difficulty following Chambers's trail. The tourists and attendants stood back from him, pointing, showing him the way. The alarm bell was bright and sharp, focussing his mind. His legs had become solid once again and his heart pumped blood so loudly he wondered if others could hear it.

He took a right, from a small corner room into another large gallery, at the far end of which stood a set of hefty wooden and glass doors. Near them another attendant stood nursing a wounded arm. There was a bloody handprint on one door. Rebus stopped and looked through into the room itself.

In the furthest corner, slouched on the floor, sat the Wolfman. Directly above him on the wall was a painting of a monastic figure, the face cowled and in shadow. The figure looked to be praying to heaven. The figure was holding a skull. A smear of blood ran down and past the skull.

Rebus pushed open the door and walked into the room. Next to this painting was another, of the Virgin Mary with stars around what was left of her head. A large hole had been punched through her face. The figure beneath the paintings was still and silent. Rebus took a few paces forward. He glanced to his left and saw that on the opposite wall were portraits of unhappy looking noblemen. They had every right to be unhappy. Slashes in each canvas almost ripped their heads from their bodies. He was close now. Close enough to see that the painting next to Malcolm Chambers was a Velasquez, 'The Immaculate Conception'. Rebus smiled again. Immaculate indeed.

And then Malcolm Chambers's head jerked up. The eyes were cold, the face stippled with glass from the BMW's windscreen. The voice when it spoke was dull and tired.

'Inspector Rebus.'

Rebus nodded, though it had not been a question.

'I wonder,' Chambers said, 'why my mother never brought me here. I don't remember being taken anywhere, except perhaps

Madame Tussaud's. Have you ever been to Madame Tussaud's, Inspector? I like the Chamber of Horrors. My mother wouldn't even come in with me.' He laughed, and leaned against the foot-rail behind him, ready to push himself to his feet. 'I shouldn't have torn those paintings, should I?' he was saying. 'They were probably priceless. Silly really. They're only paintings, after all. Why should paintings be priceless?'

Rebus had reached out a hand to help him up. At the same time, he saw the portraits again. Slashed. Not torn, *slashed*. Like the attendant's arm. Not by human hand, but with an instrument.

Too late. The small kitchen-knife in Chambers's hand was already pushing through Rebus's shirt. Chambers had leapt to his feet and was propelling Rebus backwards, back towards the portraits on the far wall. Chambers was infused with the strength of madness. Rebus felt his feet catch on the foot-rail behind him, his head fell back against one painting, thudding into the wall. He had his own right hand clasped around Chambers's knife-hand now, so that the tip of the knife was still gouging at his stomach but could go no deeper. He jerked a knee into Chambers's groin, at the same time jamming the heel of his left hand into Chambers's nose. There was a squeal as the pressure lessened on the knife. Rebus twisted Chambers's wrist, trying to shake free the knife, but Chambers's grip held fast.

Upright again, away from the wall now, they wrestled for control of the knife. Chambers was crying, howling. The sound chilled Rebus, even as he grappled with the man. It was like fighting with darkness itself. Unwanted thoughts sped through his mind: crammed tube trains, child molesters, beggars, blank faces, punks and pimps, as everything he'd seen and experienced in London washed over him in a final rolling wave. He dare not look into Chambers's face for fear that he would freeze. The paintings all around were blurs of blue, black and grey as he danced this macabre dance, feeling Chambers growing stronger and himself growing more tired. Tired and dizzy, the room spinning, a dullness coursing through his stomach towards the hole made by the knife.

The knife which is moving now, moving with new-found power, a power Rebus feels unable to counter with anything more than a grimace. He dares himself to look at Chambers. Does so, and sees the eyes staring at him like a bull's, the mouth set defiantly, the chin jutting. There is more than defiance there, more than madness, there is a resolution. Rebus feels it as the knife-hand turns. Turns one hundred and eighty degrees. And then he is being pushed backwards again. Chambers is rearing up, driving him on, powerful as an engine, until Rebus slams into another wall, followed by Chambers himself. It is almost an embrace. The bodies seemingly intimate in their contact. Chambers is heavy, a dead weight. His cheek rests against Rebus's. Until Rebus, recovering his breath, pushes the body away. Chambers staggers backwards into the room, the knife buried in his chest all the way up to the hilt. He angles his head to look down, dark blood dribbling from the corners of his mouth. He touches at the handle of the knife. Then looks up at Rebus and smiles, almost apologetically.

'So unbecoming . . . in a man.' Then falls to his knees. Trunk falls forward. Head hits carpet. And stays like that. Rebus is breathing hard. He pushes himself up from the wall, walks to the centre of the room, and pushes at the body with the toe of his shoe, tipping Chambers sideways. The face looks peaceful, despite the welts of blood. Rebus touches two fingers to the front of his own shirt. They come away moist with blood. That didn't matter. What mattered was that the Wolfman had turned out to be human after all, human and mortal, mortal and dead. If he wanted to, Rebus knew he could take the credit. He didn't want the credit. He'd get them to take away the knife and check it for fingerprints. They would find only Chambers's. That didn't mean much, of course. The likes of Flight would still think Rebus had killed him. But Rebus hadn't killed the Wolfman, and he couldn't be sure exactly what had: cowardice? guilt? or something deeper, something never to be explained?

So unbecoming . . . in a man. What kind of obituary was that?

'John?'

It was Flight's voice. Behind him stood two officers armed with pistols.

'No need for silver bullets, George,' said Rebus. He stood there, surrounded by what he supposed would be millions of pounds' worth of damaged works of art, alarm bells ringing, while outside the traffic in central London would be backed up for miles until Trafalgar Square could be opened again.

'I told you it'd be easy,' he said.

Lisa Frazer was fine. Shock, a few bruises, whiplash. The hospital wanted to keep her in overnight, just to be sure. They wanted to keep Rebus in, too, but he refused. They gave him painkillers instead, and three stitches in his stomach. The cut, they said, was fairly superficial, but it was best to be safe. The thread they used was thick and black.

By the time he arrived at Chambers's huge two-storey flat in Islington, the place was crawling with police, forensics, photographers and the usual retinue. The reporters outside were desperate for a quote, some recognising him from the impromptu conference he had given outside the house on Copperplate Street. But he pushed past them and into the Wolfman's lair.

'John, how are you?' It was George Flight, looking bemused by the day's proceedings. He had placed a hand on Rebus's shoulder. Rebus smiled.

'I'm fine, George. What have you found?'

They were standing in the main hall. Flight glanced back into one of the rooms off this hall. 'You won't believe it,' he said. 'I'm still not sure I do.' There was a tang of whisky on Flight's breath. The celebrations had begun already.

Rebus walked to the door and into the room. This was where the photographers and forensics people were busiest. A tall man rose to his feet from behind a sofa and looked across to Rebus. It was Philip Cousins. He smiled and nodded. Near him stood Isobel Penny, sketchbook in hand. But Rebus noticed that she wasn't drawing, and her face had lost all traces of liveliness. Even she, it seemed, could still be shocked.

The scene was certainly shocking. But worst of all was the smell, the smell and the buzzing of flies. One wall was covered in what had been paintings – very crudely done paintings, as even Rebus could tell. But now they had been slashed into tatters, some of which lay across the floor. And on the opposite wall was as much graffiti as would befit any tower block in Churchill Estate. Venomous stuff: FUCK ART. FEEL THE POOR. KILL PIGS. The stuff of madness.

There were two bodies thrown casually behind the sofa, and a third lying under a table, as though some rudimentary effort had been made to tidy them out of sight. Carpet and walls were stained with fine sprays of blood and the cloying smell told Rebus that at least one of the bodies had been here for several days. Easy to confront this now, now that it was at an end. Not so easy to work out the 'why?'. That was what worried Flight.

'I just can't find a motive, John. I mean, Chambers had everything. Why the hell did he need to . . .? I mean, why would he just . . .?' They were in the flat's living-room. No clues were being offered up.

Chambers's private life seemed as tidy and innocuous as the rest of his home. Just that one room, that one secret corner. That apart, they might have been in any successful barrister's apartment, poring over his books, his desk, his correspondence, his computer files.

It didn't really bother Rebus. It wouldn't bother him supposing they never found out why. He shrugged.

'Wait till the biography's published, George,' said Rebus, 'maybe then you'll get your answer.' Or ask a psychologist, he thought to himself. He didn't doubt there would be plenty of theories.

But Flight was shaking his head, rubbing at his head, his face, his neck. He still couldn't believe it had come to an end. Rebus touched a hand to his arm. Their eyes met. Rebus nodded slowly, then winked.

'You should have been in that Jag, George. It was magic.'

Flight managed to pull a smile out of the air. 'Tell that to the judge,' he said. 'Tell that to the judge.'

Rebus ate that night at George Flight's home, a meal cooked by Marion. So at last they were having the promised dinner together, but it was a fairly sombre occasion, enlivened only by an interview with some art historian on the late-night news. He was talking about the damage to the paintings in the National Gallery's Spanish Room.

'Such pointless waste . . . vandalism . . . sheer, wanton . . . priceless . . . perhaps irreparable . . . thousands of pounds . . . heritage.'

'Blah, blah, blah,' said Flight sneeringly. 'At least you can patch up a bloody painting. These people talk half the time out of their arses.'

'George!'

'Sorry, Marion,' said Flight sheepishly. He glanced towards Rebus, who winked back at him.

Later, after she had gone to bed, the two men sat together drinking a final brandy.

'I've decided to retire,' said Flight. 'Marion's been nagging me for ages. My health's not what it was.'

'Not serious, I hope?'

Flight shook his head. 'No, nothing like that. But there's a security firm, they've offered to take me on. More money, nine till five. You know how it is.'

Rebus nodded. He'd seen some of the best of his elders drawn like moths to a lightbulb when security firms and the like came to call. He drained his glass.

'When will you be leaving?' Flight asked.

'I thought I'd go back tomorrow. I can come back down again when they need me to give evidence.'

Flight nodded. 'Next time you come, we've got a spare bedroom here.'

'Thanks, George.' Rebus rose to his feet.

'I'll drive you back,' said Flight. But Rebus shook his head.

'Call me a cab,' he insisted. 'I don't want you done for D and D. Think what it would do to your pension.'

Flight stared into his brandy glass. 'You've got a point,' he said. 'Okay then, a cab it is.' He slipped a hand into his pocket. 'By the way, I've got you a little present.'

He held the clenched fist out to Rebus, who placed his own open palm beneath it. A slip of paper dropped from Flight's hand into his. Rebus unfolded the note. It was an address. Rebus looked up at Flight and nodded his understanding.

'Thanks, George,' he said.

'No rough stuff, eh, John?'

'No rough stuff,' agreed Rebus.

Family

He slept deeply that night, but woke at six the next morning and sat up in bed immediately. His stomach hurt, a burning sensation as though he had just swallowed a measure of spirits. The doctors had told him not to drink alcohol. Last night he had drunk just the one glass of wine and two glasses of brandy. He rubbed the area around the wound, willing the ache to go away, then took two more painkillers with a glass of tap-water before dressing and putting on his shoes.

His taxi driver, though sleepy, was full of tales of yesterday's action.

'I was on Whitehall, wasn't I? An hour and a quarter in the cab before the traffic got moving again. Hour and a bleedin' quarter. Didn't see the chase either, but I heard the smash.'

Rebus sat back in silence, all the way to the block of flats in Bethnal Green. He paid the driver and looked again at the slip of paper Flight had given him. Number 46, fourth floor, flat six. The elevator smelled of vinegar. A crumpled paper package in one corner was oozing under-cooked chips and a tail-end of batter. Flight was right: it made all the difference having a good network of informers. It made for quick information. But what a good copper's network could get, so too could a good villain's. Rebus hoped he'd be in time.

He walked quickly across the small landing from the open lift to the door of one of the flats where two empty milk bottles stood to attention in a plastic holder. He picked up one bottle and hurried back to the lift just as its doors were shuddering to a close to place the milk bottle in the remaining gap. The doors stayed where they were. So did the lift.

You never knew when a quick getaway would be needed.

Then he walked along the narrow corridor to flat six, braced himself against the wall and kicked at the door-handle with the heel of his shoe. The door flew open and he walked into a stuffy hall. Another door, another kick and he was face to face with Kenny Watkiss.

Watkiss had been asleep on a mattress on the floor. He was standing now, clad only in underpants and shivering, against the furthest wall from the door. He pushed his hair back when he saw who it was.

'Jee-Jesus,' he stammered. 'What are you doing here?'

'Hello, Kenny,' said Rebus, stepping into the room. 'I thought we'd have a little chat.'

'What about?' You didn't get as frightened as Kenny Watkiss was by having your door kicked in at half past six in the morning. You only got that frightened by the idea of *who* was doing it and *why*.

'About Uncle Tommy.'

'Uncle Tommy?' Kenny Watkiss smiled unconvincingly. He moved back to the mattress and started pulling on a pair of torn denims. 'What about him?'

'What are you so scared of, Kenny? Why are you hiding?'

'Hiding?' That smile again. 'Who said I was hiding?'

Rebus shook his head, his own smile one of apparent sympathy. 'I feel sorry for you, Kenny, really I do. I see your kind a hundred times a week. All ambition and no brain. All talk but no guts. I've only been in London a week, and already I know how to find you when I want you. Do you think Tommy *can't*? You think maybe he'll lay off? No, he's going to nail your head to the wall.'

'Don't talk daft.' Now that he was dressed, having pulled on a black T-shirt, Kenny's voice had lost some of its trembling. But he couldn't hide the look in his eyes, the haunted, hunted look. Rebus decided to make it easy for him. He reached into a pocket and brought out a packet of cigarettes, offered one to Kenny and lit it for him before taking one himself. He rubbed at his stomach. Jesus, it was hurting. He hoped the stitches were holding.

'You've been ripping him off,' Rebus said casually. 'He handled stolen goods, you were his courier, passing it down the chain. But you've been skimming a little off the top, haven't you? And with each job you'd take a little more than he knew about. Why? Saving for that Docklands flat? So you could start your own business? Maybe you got greedy, I don't know. But Tommy got suspicious. You were in court that day because you wanted to see him go down. It was the only thing that could have saved you. When he didn't, you still tried putting one over on him, yelling out from the public gallery. But by then it was only a matter of time. And when you heard that the case had been dropped altogether, well, you knew he'd come straight after you. So you ran. You didn't run far enough, Kenny.'

'What's it to you?' The words were angry. But it was the anger that came of fear. It wasn't directed at Rebus. He was merely the messenger.

'Just this,' Rebus said calmly: 'keep away from Sammy. Don't ever go near her again, don't even try to talk to her. In fact, your best bet right now is to get on a train or a bus or whatever and get the hell out of London. Don't worry, we'll pin Tommy for something sooner or later. Then maybe you can come back.' He had slipped a hand into his pocket again. It came out holding a fold of ten pound notes, four of which he peeled off and threw onto the mattress. 'I'm offering you a one-way ticket, and I'm suggesting you take it right now, this morning.'

The eyes and voice were wary. 'You're not going to take me in?'

'Why should I?'

The smile this time was more confident still. He looked at the money. 'It's just family, Rebus. That's all. I can take care of myself.'

'Can you?' Rebus nodded, taking in the room with its peeling wallpaper and boarded-up window, the mattress with its single rumpled sheet. 'Fair enough.' He turned to go.

'It wasn't just me, you know.'

Rebus stopped but didn't turn. 'What?' He tried not to sound interested.

'There was a copper, too. He was on a cut from the robberies.'

Rebus sucked in air. Did he need to know? Did he *want* to know? Kenny Watkiss didn't give him the choice.

'A detective called Lamb,' he said. Rebus exhaled silently, but, saying nothing, showing nothing, walked back out of the flat and, pulling open the lift doors, kicking away the milk bottle, pressed the button for the ground floor and waited for the slow descent.

Outside the block, he paused to stub out his cigarette. He rubbed at his stomach again. Stupid not to have brought the painkillers with him. From the corner of his eye, he could see the unmarked transit van in the car park. Six forty-five. There could be a perfectly rational explanation for it, for the fact that two men sat stonily in its front seats. They might be about to go to work, mightn't they?

In fact, Rebus knew damned fine that's what they were doing. And he had another choice now. He could let them go to work, or he could stop them. It took him another second or two to decide, but finally, with a picture of Samantha's face in his head, he walked across nonchalantly to the van and, the men still ignoring his existence, thumped hard on the passenger-side window. The passenger looked at him with undisguised enmity, but, seeing that Rebus was undeterred, rolled down the window.

'Yeah?'

Rebus stuck his ID so far into the man's face that the plastic coating brushed against his nose.

'Police,' he snapped. 'Now get the fuck out of here. And tell Tommy Watkiss we've got his nephew under twenty-four hour watch. Anything happens, we'll know where to come and who to charge.' Rebus stood back and looked carefully at the man. 'Think you can remember all that, or do you want me to write it down?'

The passenger was growling audibly as he rolled the window back up. The driver was already starting the van. As it began to move off, Rebus gave its side a farewell kick. Maybe Kenny would leave and maybe he'd stay. It was up to him. Rebus had given him a chance. Whether the young man took it or not was out of Rebus's hands.

'Like Pontius Pilate,' he mumbled to himself as he made for the main road. Standing by a lamppost, waiting and praying for a black cab to come along, he saw Kenny Watkiss emerge from the flats, a duffel-bag slung across his shoulder, and, looking around him, start to jog towards the far end of the estate. Rebus nodded to himself. 'That's my boy,' he said, as, with protesting brakes, a cab slowed to a halt beside him.

'You're in luck, mate,' said the driver. 'I'm just starting my shift.' Rebus clambered in and gave the name of his hotel, then settled back, enjoying the city at this quiet hour. The driver, though, was in practice for the day ahead.

'Here,' he said, 'did you hear about that rumpus yesterday at Trafalgar Square? I was in a queue for an hour and a half. I mean, I'm all for law and order, but there must've been another way of going about it, mustn't there?'

John Rebus shook his head and laughed.

His suitcase sat closed on the bed beside the little-used briefcase and the bag of books. He was squeezing the last few items into his sports bag when there was a soft tapping at his door.

'Come in.'

She did. She was wearing a solid-foam neck-brace, but grinned it away.

'Isn't it stupid? They want me to wear it for the next few days, but I –' She saw the cases on the bed. 'You're not leaving already?'

Rebus nodded. 'I came here to help with the Wolfman case. The Wolfman case is finished.'

'But what about –'

He turned to her. 'What about us?' he guessed. She lowered her eyes. 'That's a good question, Lisa. You lied to me. You weren't trying to help. You were trying to get your bloody Ph.D.'

'I'm sorry,' she said.

'Me too. I mean, I can understand why you did it, why you think you *had* to do it. Really I can. But that doesn't make it any better.'

She straightened her back and nodded. 'Fair enough then,' she said. 'So, Inspector Rebus, if all I was doing was using you, why did I come here straight from the hospital?'

He zipped shut the bag. It was a good question. 'Because you got found out,' he said.

'No,' she said. 'That was bound to happen eventually. Try again.' He shrugged his shoulders. 'Oh,' she said, sounding disappointed. 'I was hoping you could tell me. I'm not really sure myself.'

He turned towards her again and saw that she was smiling. She looked so stupid in the neck-brace that he had to return the smile eventually. And when she came towards him he returned her hug, too.

'Ouch!' she said. 'Not too hard, John.'

So he relaxed his muscles a little, and they kept on hugging. He was actually feeling mellow; the painkillers had seen to that.

'Anyway,' he said at last, 'you weren't much help.'

She pulled away from him. He was still smiling, but archly. 'What do you mean?'

'I mean all that stuff we talked about in the restaurant. All those index cards.' Rebus recited the list. 'Thwarted ambition. Victims from a social class above the killer. No confrontation . . .' He scratched his chin. 'None of it fits Malcolm Chambers.'

'I wouldn't say that. We've still got to look at his home life, his background.' She sounded defiant rather than merely defensive. 'And I was right about the schizophrenia.'

'So you'll still do your project?'

She tried to nod; it wasn't easy. 'Of course,' she said. 'There's plenty of work to be done on Chambers, believe me. There must be clues there somewhere in his past. He must have left something.'

'Well, let me know what you find out.'

'John. Before he died, did he say anything?'

Rebus smiled. 'Nothing important,' he said. 'Nothing important.'

*

595

After she'd gone, after the promises of return trips and of weekends in Edinburgh, promises of postcards and phone calls, he took his luggage down to reception. George Flight was at the desk. Rebus put his key down next to where Flight was signing his name to several forms.

'Do you realise how much this hotel costs?' Flight said, not looking up. 'Next time you visit, you really will have to bunk at my place.' Then he glanced towards Rebus. 'But I suppose you were worth it.' He finished with the forms and handed them to the receptionist, who checked them before nodding that everything was in order. 'You know the address to send them to,' Flight called back as the two men started towards the hotel's swing-doors.

'I really must get the lock on the boot fixed,' Flight said, shutting the car's back door on Rebus's luggage. Then: 'Where to? King's Cross?'

Rebus nodded. 'With one slight detour,' he said.

The detour, in Flight's words, turned out to be more than slight. They parked across from Rhona's flat in Gideon Park and Flight pulled on the handbrake.

'Going in?' he said. Rebus had been thinking about it, but shook his head. What could he tell Sammy? Nothing that would help. If he said he'd seen Kenny, she'd only accuse him of scaring him off. No, best leave it.

'George,' he said, 'could you maybe have someone drop in and tell her Kenny's left London. But stress that he's okay, that he's not in trouble. I don't want him lingering too long in her memory.'

Flight was nodding. 'I'll do it myself,' he said. 'Have you seen him yet?'

'I went this morning.'

'And?'

'And I was just in time. But I reckon he'll be all right.'

Flight studied the face next to him. 'I *think* I believe you,' he said.

'Just one thing.'

'Yes?'

'Kenny told me one of your men is involved. The baby-faced redneck.'

'Lamb?'

'That's the one. He's on Tommy Watkiss's payroll, according to Kenny.'

Flight pursed his lips and was silent for a moment. 'I think I believe that, too,' he said at last, very quietly. 'Don't worry, John. I'll deal with it.'

Rebus said nothing. He was still staring out at the windows of Rhona's flat, willing Sammy to come to one of them and see him. No, not see him, just so that *he* might see *her*. But there was no one at home. The ladies were out for the day with Tim or Tony or Graeme or Ben.

And it was none of Rebus's business anyway.

'Let's go,' he said.

So Flight drove him to King's Cross. Drove him through streets paved with nothing so very different from any other city. Streets ancient and modern, breathing with envy and excitement. And with evil. Not much evil, perhaps. But enough. Evil, after all, was pretty well a constant. He thanked God that it touched so few lives. He thanked God that his friends and family were safe. And he thanked God he was going home.

'What are you thinking about?' Flight asked as they idled at yet another set of traffic lights.

'Nothing,' said Rebus.

He was still thinking about nothing when he boarded the busy Inter City 125, and sat down with his newspapers and his magazines. As the train was about to move off, someone squeezed into the seat opposite him and deposited four large cans of strong lager on the table. The youth was tall and hard-looking with shorn hair. He glared at Rebus and turned up his personal cassette player. Tscchh-tscchh-tscchh it went, so loud Rebus could almost make out the words. The youth was grasping a ticket denoting Edinburgh as his destination. He put the ticket down and pulled on a ring-pull. Rebus shook his head wearily and smiled. His own personal hell. As the train pulled away, he caught its rhythm and beat that rhythm out silently in his head.

FYTP

FYTP

FYTP

FYTP

FYTP

FYTP

All the way home.

Acknowledgements

Thanks for help with facts, figures, psychopaths and garden paths (*viz* leading the reader up the . . .) go to the following:

In London: Dr S. Adams, Ms Fiona Campbell, Chris Thomas,
  Mr Andrew Walker, the officers of Tottenham Police Station
In Newmarket: L. Rodgers
In Edinburgh: Professor J. Curt, Ms Alison Girdwood
In Fife: Mr & Mrs Colin Stevenson
In Glasgow: Alex Blair
In Canada: Mr Tiree Macgregor, Dr D. W. Nichol
In the USA: Dr David Martin, Ms Rebecca Hughes

Suggested further reading:

Elliott Leyton, *Hunting Humans* (Penguin)
Clive R. Hollin, *Psychology and Crime* (Routledge)
Professor Keith Simpson, *Forty Years of Murder* (Grafton)
Martin Fido, *Murder Guide to London* (Weidenfeld)
R. M. Holmes & J. DeBurger, *Serial Murder* (Sage)
R. H. C. Bull *et al.*, *Psychology for Police Officers* (Wiley)
David Canter, 'To Catch a Rapist', *New Society*, 4 March 1988
David Canter, 'Offender Profiles', *The Psychologist*, Vol 2, No 1, January 1989